Not Wisely, but Too Well

by

Rhoda Broughton

edited with an introduction and notes
by Tamar Heller

Victorian Secrets 2013

Published by

Victorian Secrets Limited
32 Hanover Terrace
Brighton BN2 9SN

www.victoriansecrets.co.uk

Not Wisely, but Too Well by Rhoda Broughton
First published in 1867
This Victorian Secrets edition 2013

Composition and design by Catherine Pope
Cover image: American actress Adah Isaacs Menken (1835-1868)

A catalogue record for this book is available from the British Library.

ISBN 978-1-906469-45-0

CONTENTS

INTRODUCTION

As this introduction, particularly the latter part, contains plot spoilers, first-time readers might wish to return to it after they have finished the book.

> Awfully exciting Book. Sorry it's finished. — Pencilled marginalia, ca. 1872, in an 1871 edition of *Not Wisely, but Too Well*

Geraldine Jewsbury, a reader for the London publishing house of Bentley and Son, was outraged by a manuscript she reviewed in July 1866. "The most thoroughly sensual tale I have read in English for a long time," she complained in her report, concluding "It is a bad style of book altogether & not fit to be published."[1] The work Jewsbury found so objectionable was *Not Wisely, but Too Well*, the first novel by Rhoda Broughton, the twenty-six year old daughter of a Staffordshire clergyman.[2] Initially serialized in *The Dublin University Magazine*, *Not Wisely* was brought to the attention of the senior Bentley by that journal's editor, J. S. Le Fanu, Broughton's uncle and a noted writer of Gothic fiction. In addition to not sharing Le Fanu's opinion of the "great promise & power" of his niece's work,[3] Jewsbury was irked that, in a departure from standard procedure, Richard Bentley had agreed to publish the book before asking her opinion. "I am sorry you have accepted it[.] I shd have recommended you to decline it," she scolded, and the following day sent an urgent postscript: "[P]eople will wonder at a house like yours bringing out a work so *ill* calculated for the reading of decent people . . . I entreat you if you have made any bargain to break it." [4]

Jewsbury's disapproval of *Not Wisely*—which she deemed "as bad as any French novel"[5]—might seem odd given her own cosmopolitan tastes. A free-thinker and feminist fond of smoking, swearing, and donning

---

1 Appendix A, p. 379.

2 Scholars and critics frequently refer to the novel as *Not Wisely but Too Well.* In this edition, however, I give the title as *Not Wisely, but Too Well*, as this is the way it appears in both serial and volume formats.

3 Appendix A, p. 377.

4 Appendix A, p. 379.

5 Appendix A, p. 379.

male dress in imitation of George Sand, she had herself authored some twenty years earlier a provocative novel, *Zoë*, featuring risqué scenes between a married woman and a Catholic priest. Yet, both as reader for Bentley and prolific reviewer of fiction for the conservative journal *The Athenaeum*, Jewsbury took seriously her cultural role as—in Monica Fryckstedt's words—"guardian of moral conventions."[6] Assuming this persona, Jewsbury declared that if Broughton's novel were published she would "carefully keep it out of the hands of all the young people of my acquaintance."[7] Her hostility, though it did not prevent the publication of *Not Wisely*, did delay it. Placed in an awkward position by his reader's scathing report, Bentley, with Le Fanu's help, persuaded Broughton to void the contract for *Not Wisely* and sign one instead for an expanded version of her second novel *Cometh Up as a Flower*, which, like its predecessor, had originally been serialized in *The Dublin University Magazine*.

Though she submitted to this arrangement, Broughton still sought to bring out *Not Wisely* with Bentley, promising, in a letter to the publisher, to revise the work "to a very considerable extent" and "expunge it of coarseness & slanginess."[8] As it turned out, however, Broughton rejected the financial terms Richard Bentley offered for the new version, publishing it instead with Tinsley in fall 1867, around six months after the appearance of *Cometh Up*. Ironically, then, Jewsbury's attempt to block the publication of Broughton's fiction ensured that the aspiring writer published not just one but two bestsellers in the same year. For both novels were wildly successful despite, or more likely because, of their controversial depiction of young women only narrowly escaping the temptation of adulterous liaisons. (As it turned out, *Cometh Up* was scarcely less scandalous than *Not Wisely*.) Although a number of critics, following Jewsbury's lead, lambasted her early work for coarseness and immorality, Broughton was definitively launched in 1867 on a career as one of late nineteenth-century England's most popular writers, producing a total of twenty-six novels, as well as some fine supernatural fiction, in the fifty-three years between the appearance of her first two books and the posthumous publication of her last in the year of her death, 1920. Joining such "Queens of the Circulating Libraries" as Mary Elizabeth Braddon and Ouida, Broughton counted among her many

6 Monica Fryckstedt, *Geraldine Jewsbury's* Athenaeum *Reviews: A Mirror of Mid-Victorian Attitudes to Fiction* (Stockholm: Uppsala UP, 1986), 37.

7 Appendix A, p. 379.

8 Appendix A, p. 381.

fans the politician Gladstone, who was spotted in his club engrossed in one of her novels, and naval officers who, devouring her stories on an Arctic expedition, named a mountain in Canada for her.

This republication of *Not Wisely, but Too Well*—the novel's first scholarly edition—contributes to the ongoing reevaluation of Broughton's work after a long period of critical neglect. *Not Wisely* is a particularly important text to make available again because of its pioneering portrayal of female sexuality. In this regard Broughton's first novel is even more noteworthy than her second, *Cometh Up as a Flower*, which, though its protagonist teeters on the brink of adultery, does not include the wealth of detail about the heroine's physical response to the male lead that Jewsbury found so unacceptable in *Not Wisely*. Indeed, in its representation of "highly coloured & hot blooded passion," as Jewsbury called it,[9] *Not Wisely* is a standout even for sensation fiction, a controversial genre popular in the 1860s with which both of Broughton's first two novels were associated.[10] Notorious for plots structured by such sexual transgressions as bigamy and adultery, as in Mary Elizabeth Braddon's *Lady Audley's Secret* (1861) and Mrs. Henry Wood's *East Lynne* (1862), sensation fiction nonetheless tends not to depict female desire in convincing depth: *East Lynne*'s adulterous wife Isabel Vane wallows far more in guilt than she does in lust, and that quintessential *femme fatale*, Lady Audley, is motivated more by economic than sexual drive. There can be no doubt, though, that the vibrant heroine of *Not Wisely* is magnetically drawn to the "deep-chested" and "thin-flanked" body of her muscular lover (p. 66) by what Jewsbury disgustedly calls "animal magnetism."[11]

Broughton's frank portrayal of female eroticism predates by some fifty years Virginia Woolf's vision of a time when women might finally be able to "tell[] the truth" about their "experiences as a body."[12] For all that *Not Wisely* anticipates the daring of modernist women writers, however, the novel's rocky journey from serial to triple-decker highlights the considerable

9 Appendix A, p. 378.

10 For more on controversies surrounding Victorian sensation, see Lyn Pykett, *The 'Improper' Feminine: The Women's Sensation Novel and the New Woman Writing* (London: Routledge, 1992), and *Sensationalism and the Sensation Debate*, ed. Andrew Maunder , Vol. I of *Varieties of Women's Sensation Fiction: 1855-90* (London: Pickering and Chatto, 2004).

11 Appendix A, p. 378.

12 Virginia Woolf, "Professions for Women," in *Women and Writing*, by Virginia Woolf, ed. Michèle Barrett (New York: Harcourt Brace Jovanovich, 1979), 62.

barriers a Victorian woman encountered in writing about sexuality. In order to publish the triple-decker form of the novel, Broughton had to bowdlerize portions in the serialized version deemed improper, as well as replace the original, more violent ending with a less sensational one. Yet it would be simplistic to assume that every one of Broughton's revisions weakened the novel aesthetically or blunted its critique of convention. In fact, as I shall argue below, some of Broughton's changes to *Not Wisely* could be said to enhance the radical elements of her portrayal of marriage.

Reproducing the text of its first appearance in volume form, the present edition of *Not Wisely* illuminates the novel's ideological and aesthetic complexity through appendices related to its publication history, revision, and reception. These appendices include a section which contains Jewsbury's reader's report and Broughton and Le Fanu's correspondence with the Bentleys, a list of variants between serial and volume formats of the novel, and a selection of contemporary reviews of *Not Wisely*. Together these materials provide a fascinating case study of the coming to print, and reception, of a controversial Victorian text, while also attesting to the challenges Broughton faced in representing female desire in her inaugural fiction.

Rhoda Broughton: Life, Career, Historical Context

The third daughter of Reverend Delves Broughton, a clergyman of aristocratic descent, and Jane Bennett (sister of J. S. Le Fanu's wife Susanna), Rhoda Broughton was born and partly brought up in Denbigh, Wales. (Her familiarity with this area is reflected in the Welsh setting of several of her novels, including the first part of *Not Wisely*.) Following her father's appointment to the living at Broughton in Staffordshire when Rhoda was still young, the Broughtons moved to the family seat, seventeenth-century Broughton Hall, where she penned the earliest drafts of *Not Wisely, but Too Well* and *Cometh Up as a Flower* in 1862-63; purportedly *Not Wisely*, the first manuscript, was produced in only six weeks. By the time Broughton became a published author for the first time in 1865, when her uncle J. S. Le Fanu began to serialize *Not Wisely* in *The Dublin University Magazine*, both her parents had died, her father in 1860 and her mother in 1863. For thirty years, between 1864 and 1894, Broughton (who never married herself) lived with her married sister Eleanor Newcome, first in Upper Eyarth, Denbyshire, and then, after her sister was widowed, in Oxford (1878-90) and London (1890-94). Moving back to Oxford from London six years after her sister's death, in 1900, Broughton died there, aged eighty, in 1920. Despite the popularity of her books, she died in poverty, her custom of selling her copyrights at the time of publication rather than continuing to receive royalties limiting her income in old age.

In personal life Broughton was a memorably witty conversationalist with a wide literary acquaintance, including Thomas Hardy, Matthew Arnold, Walter Pater, Richard Monkton Milnes, Robert Browning, Mary Cholmondeley, and Henry James—the last a warm friend despite his harsh review of her 1876 novel *Joan.* Loyal as she was to her friends, though, Broughton could prove a formidable opponent; when the Oxford classicist Mark Pattison offended her, she retaliated by caricaturing him in *Belinda* (1883) as the desiccated Professor Forth, who marries the heroine with disastrous results. Forthright as she was, Broughton struck some contemporaries as unfeminine and abrasive; one acquaintance called her "a little hard and masculine,"[13] while another, describing her in 1874, reported "[s]he walked about in such a 'strong-minded' manner, stared at people and talked loud, and showed by every look and action that she knew perfectly well that she was the most important person there."[14]

Yet however "strong-minded" she appeared in person, in her professional life Broughton shared the paradoxical situation—at once powerful and contested—common to Victorian women writers.. On one hand, women writers commanded a certain cultural authority by sheer force of numbers; as Monica Fryckstedt points out, the journal *Temple Bar,* which was to serialize many of Broughton's novels, estimated in 1862 that around two-thirds of all novels were by women.[15] On the other hand, the taint of the marketplace—the public sphere supposed to be the province of men in Victorian gender ideology—clung to authorship, especially given the increased association of popular literature with pandering to the less refined tastes of the proletariat. Reflecting a common reluctance among female authors to advertise their participation in the economic sphere, Broughton published her first three novels anonymously, starting to sign her name only when others laid claim to her work. It is notable too that, despite her own success, Broughton depicts female authorship farcically: the heroines who attempt to become writers in the metafictional novels

13 Michael Sadleir, *Things Past* (London: Constable, 1944), 116.

14 Sadleir, 91.

15 Fryckstedt, 11.

A Beginner (1894) and *A Fool in Her Folly* (1920) fail miserably. In the latter novel Charlotte Hankey's aborted career is the more striking because in many ways her character—a Victorian clergyman's daughter who writes risqué fiction—is autobiographical. In her foreword to *A Fool in Her Folly* —Broughton's last, posthumously published book—her friend Marie Belloc Lowndes sees in this plot a reflection of the "Victorian tradition" of "consider[ing] professional authorship as not at all suitable for ladies."[16] According to Lowndes, Broughton was "curiously humble" about her work, as if merely "content to regard her literary gift as a kind of elegant accomplishment."[17] Indeed, when Helen C. Black interviewed her in the 1890s for a book on "Notable Women Authors of the Day," she found no copies of Broughton's novels on her own shelves: "She says that she sells them out and out at once, and then has 'done with them.'"[18]

Underlying such apparent diffidence, however, was a tough professionalism. As the selections in Appendix A from her correspondence with the Bentleys demonstrate, Broughton was not shy either about demanding the best possible payment for her books or rejecting offers she deemed inadequate. In addition, her frequent allusions in her novels to other literary works—a topic to which I shall return later—shows how seriously she took herself as a writer in dialogue with other writers. Among the writers whom Broughton references in her work are some of the more notable female authors of the century—authors who, though they also struggled with the difficulties facing women writers, achieved fame and critical attention: Madame de Staël, Jane Austen, the Brontë sisters, and George Eliot. Not only did the fiction of these women influence Broughton's—*Not Wisely*'s plot has parallels with *Jane Eyre*'s—but, like them, she daringly addressed issues of women's disadvantaged social status. Indeed, a review of Broughton's first two novels in the *Spectator*, reproduced here in Appendix C, perceptively noticed this resemblance, likening *Not Wisely*'s Kate Chester to such passionate and thwarted heroines as Lucy Snowe of *Villette* and Maggie Tulliver of *The Mill on the Floss*.[19] Labelling Broughton a "novelist

16 Marie Belloc Lowndes, "Foreword," to *A Fool in Her Folly*, by Rhoda Broughton (London: Odhams, 1920), 6.

17 Lowndes, 6.

18 Helen C. Black, "Rhoda Broughton," in *Notable Women Authors of the Day* (1893; Rpt. Brighton: Victorian Secrets, 2011), 58.

19 Appendix C, p. 438.

of revolt" in her portrayal of female discontent,[20] the *Spectator* review situates her, along with Brontë and Eliot, in the context of the nineteenth-century debates about women's role and nature called the "Woman Question."

Like the *Spectator* reviewer, other commentators noted the way Broughton's work engaged contemporary controversies about gender. In 1917, Walter Sichel summed up her depiction of the changing status of women during her career by claiming that her novels span "the distance between the 'Girl of the Period' and the 'New Woman.'"[21] Predating the emergence of the fin-de-siècle feminist or New Woman, "The Girl of the Period," a stereotype of the modern young woman popularized in an essay of that title by Eliza Lynn Linton, is particularly relevant to Broughton's early career. Published in *The Saturday Review* in 1868, the year after Broughton's literary debut, Linton's antifeminist diatribe attacks the "slang, bold talk, and fastness" of girls of her day[22]—all habits attributed to Broughton's heroines by her critics. Even in an 1874 essay defending Broughton against charges of vulgarity and immorality—an essay excerpted in Appendix C of this edition—Alfred Austin admits that her heroines are, like Linton's "GOP" stereotype, "unruly, rebellious, 'fast,' and at times even what is called 'slangy.'"[23] In obviously qualified praise, Austin characterizes Broughton's protagonists as "very outrageous young ladies indeed; young ladies we would rather not have for our sisters, sweethearts, wives, or sisters-in-law, but with whom, nevertheless, we could imagine ourselves spending a not unpleasant quarter of an hour."[24] Like both Linton and the reviewer for the *Spectator*, Austin saw Broughton's unruly heroines as evidence of a historical trend, claiming that, in "an age of women's rights and the emancipation of a sex supposed to have been long-enthralled," it is not surprising that increasingly young women will, like Broughton's heroines, "not be too particular in drawing the line between being made love to and making it."[25]

In an otherwise sympathetic assessment of her early work, Anthony

20 Appendix C, p. 436.

21 Marilyn Wood, *Rhoda Broughton: Profile of a Novelist 1840-1920* (Stamford: Paul Watkins, 1993), 116.

22 Eliza Lynn Linton, "The Girl of the Period," in *Criminals, Idiots, Women, and Minors: Victorian Writing by Women on Women*, ed. Susan Hamilton (Peterborough: Broadview, 1995), 173.

23 Appendix C, p. 441.

24 Appendix C, p. 442.

25 Appendix C, p. 442.

Trollope also disapproved of how Broughton's heroines, rather than waiting for men to initiate courtship, "throw themselves at men's heads, and when they are not accepted only think how they may throw themselves again."[26] Such sexual forwardness was particularly alarming to Broughton's more hostile critics. No respectable young woman was supposed to arrange clandestine, unchaperoned meetings with a lover, as do both Kate Chester in *Not Wisely* and Nell Lestrange in *Cometh Up*. Even when the heroines of Broughton's early novels do not, in a major transgression of female modesty, take the initiative in declaring their desire to men, their soliloquies about their love, in which the reader voyeuristically participates, reveal the depth and desperation of their sexual passion, as when Kate in *Not Wisely* bemoans God's refusal to let her have what she wants, declaring she would do "anything wicked, anything insane" to win the love of the man whose "grand eyes . . . scorch and shrivel up my soul" (p. 90).

Indeed, in an influential diatribe against female sensationalism published in *Blackwood's* in September 1867—after the publication of *Cometh Up* but before the release of *Not Wisely*—the redoubtable Margaret Oliphant, like Geraldine Jewsbury a self-appointed guardian of female propriety, singled out Broughton's work as a prime example of the "abomination in the midst of us": women writers who, portraying their heroines' "sensuous raptures," represent "this intense appreciation of flesh and blood, this eagerness of physical sensation" as the "natural sentiment of English girls."[27] According to Oliphant, even apparently "innocent indecency," in which a female character "makes uncleanly suggestions in the calm of her ordinary talk," acts as a poisonous influence on impressionable female readers; she is especially critical of a passage in *Cometh Up* in which the "free-spoken" heroine hopes she and her lover will not be "sexless, passionless essences" after their death, a wish that, like Dante Gabriel Rossetti's poem "The Blessed Damozel," conjures up fantasies of sex in heaven.[28] "It is a shame to women so to write," proclaims Oliphant, "and it is a shame to the women who read and accept as a true representation of themselves and their ways the equivocal talk and fleshly inclinations here attributed to them."[29] For Oliphant and those who shared her opinions, fiction like

26 Wood, 42.

27 Margaret Oliphant, "Novels," *Blackwood's Edinburgh Magazine* (Sept. 1867), 268, 259.

28 Oliphant, 274, 268, 267.

29 Oliphant, 275.

Broughton's threatened nothing less than the fall of the British empire, undermining the female chastity that is "of invaluable importance to [a woman's] country and her race ... There is perhaps nothing of such vital consequence to a nation."[30]

Understandably, Broughton found it demoralizing to be accused of undermining western civilization. She defied her detractors; Bentley had to dissuade her from dedicating *Red as a Rose Is She* (1870), the novel that followed *Not Wisely* and *Cometh Up*, "TO MY ENEMIES, ALL AND SUNDRY."[31] Yet she continued to be frustrated by negative reviews, lamenting in a letter to Bentley in 1873 that "I cannot get used to the coarse & indiscriminate abuse with which I am belaboured" and declaring she had "half a mind never to put pen to paper again."[32] Significantly, in the two novels that followed *Not Wisely* and *Cometh Up*—*Red as a Rose Is She* (1870) and *Good-bye, Sweetheart!* (1872)—Broughton steered away from the topic of adultery that had proved so unsettling in her first two works. Though sexual propriety is still an issue, the heroines are not adulterous but rather overly flirtatious (or at least their disapproving fiancés think so). When Broughton raised the spectre of adultery again in *Nancy* (1873), she did so in order to exorcise it. Married to an older man for whom she has no romantic feelings, the nineteen-year old heroine nonetheless resists the advances of a young neighbor who mistakes her naïveté for willingness to be seduced.

In representing sexuality, then, Broughton trod a fine line between caution and daring. Authors of the period had strong financial, as well as critical, incentives for censoring themselves: the circulating libraries that purveyed novels to the public—readers rented books rather than paying exorbitant prices for triple-deckers—filtered the sexual content of fiction, which was not considered appropriate family fare if it could not be read by the typical teenage girl (or, as this prototypical reader was called, the Young Person). Yet if outraging propriety could damage a writer's career, so could dullness: the transgressive frissons of Broughton's fiction, after all, were their major attraction. When her relatively tame seventh novel,

30 Oliphant, 275.

31 Rhoda Broughton, Letter to George Bentley, 20 Jan. 1870, in *Archives of Richard Bentley and Son 1829-1898*, Pt. 2, Reel 22 (Cambridge: Chadwyck-Healey; Teaneck, NJ: Somerset House, 1976).

32 Letter to George Bentley, 28 Nov. 1873, *Archives of Richard Bentley and Son 1829-1898*, Pt. 2, Reel 22.

Second Thoughts (1880), sold poorly, she wrote to Bentley that "since the public like it hot & strong, I am not the person to disoblige them … to a public accustomed to absinthe, ginger beer is naturally not palatable."[33] She returned, then, to an idea she had originally thought too racy, and which became *Belinda* (1883), a more transgressive version of *Nancy* (not to mention Eliot's *Middlemarch*), with its heroine who marries an elderly pedant while still in love with a younger man.

Still, by the late 1880s and 1890s Broughton no longer needed to fret much about the unconventionality of her novels. So seismically were sexual mores and gender roles shifting in the *fin de siècle* that the middle-aged Broughton seemed stodgy compared to such iconoclastic New Woman writers as George Egerton and Mona Caird, who assailed marriage and the sexual double standard with an explicit feminist agenda. Now it was the former rebel's turn to sound the tocsin of moral disapproval; following the lead of Eliza Lynn Linton's *The Rebel of the Family* (1880) and Henry James's *The Bostonians* (1886), in *Dear Faustina* (1897) Broughton caricatured the New Woman as a lesbian vamp out to corrupt the naïve protagonist. Even after resisting the sinister feminist, however, the heroine postpones marriage to do settlement work—a conclusion that could end a New Woman novel.[34]

In the last few decades of her career, in fact, Broughton experimented in particularly fascinating ways with the romance conventions which had become her trademark, placing herself, as Pamela Gilbert says, in the paradoxical position of being classified as a writer of love stories "long after love had ceased to be even arguably the primary theme of her novels."[35] One reason that Broughton could engage in greater narrative innovation during this period was the demise of the triple-decker system, which, in addition to lessening censorship of the content of fiction, freed authors from the bulky multi-volume format at which Broughton had chafed.

33 Letter to George Bentley, 22 June 1880, *Archives of Richard Bentley and Son 1829-1898,* Pt. 2, Reel 22.

34 Two readings of the gender politics of *Dear Faustina* are Patricia Murphy, "Disdained and Disempowered: The 'Inverted' New Woman in Rhoda Broughton's *Dear Faustina*," *Tulsa Studies in Women's Literature* 19.1 (Spring 2000): 57-79, and Lisa Hager, "Slumming with the New Woman: *Fin-de-Siècle* Sexual Inversion, Reform Work and Sisterhood in Rhoda Broughton's *Dear Faustina*," *Women's Writing* 14 (2007): 460-75.

35 Pamela K. Gilbert, *Disease, Desire and the Body in Victorian Women's Popular Novels* (Cambridge: Cambridge UP, 1997), 113.

Including such notable examples after 1890 as *Mrs. Bligh* (1892), *The Game and the Candle* (1898), *A Waif's Progress* (1905), and *Between Two Stools* (1912), Broughton's structurally elegant and deftly ironic single-volume works defer, undercut, and even outright derail romance conventions. Such revisions of the typical happily-ever-after telos of the courtship narrative highlight the high psychic costs inherent for both men and women in traditional gender roles. Indeed, in "Girls Past and Present," an essay Broughton wrote for *Ladies Home Journal* in 1920, the year of her death, she concluded that the flapper was happier than her convention-bound Victorian precursors because marriage—which she calls "the nuptial yoke"—"is to many of the girls of to-day an unessential accident, which may or may not happen to them, but which in any case cannot materially affect the serious business of their lives, their professional or political activities."[36]

In the same essay Broughton wryly remarked on how tame her once shocking novels seemed to a younger generation; hoping to gratify her, a visitor told her "that in Italy mine was the only English fiction thought innocent enough to be given as pabulum to schoolgirls."[37] Elsewhere Broughton said she began her career as Zola (the controversial French naturalist) and ended it as Charlotte Yonge (prim High Church author of didactic fiction). "[I]t's not I that have changed," Broughton is supposed to have claimed, "it's my fellow countrymen."[38] And yet, by disseminating popular fiction insistently reminding her audience that, as Everett F. Bleiler says, women have "bodies, desires, and passions,"[39] Broughton herself helped to bring about this change in British attitudes toward gender and sexuality.

Not Wisely, but Too Well: From Serial to Triple-Decker[40]

Having surveyed Broughton's career to its close, I would now like to return to its beginning, specifically the complicated transition of her daring

36 Rhoda Broughton, "Girls Past and Present," *Ladies Home Journal* (Sept. 1920), 38.

37 "Girls Past and Present," 141.

38 Wood, *Rhoda Broughton*, 122.

39 Everett F. Bleiler, Headnote to Rhoda Broughton, "The Man with the Nose," *A Treasury of Victorian Ghost Stories*, ed. Everett F. Bleiler (New York: Charles Scribner, 1981), 127.

40 Again, first-time readers should be warned that from this point the introduction contains plot spoilers.

first novel from serial to triple-decker. In tracing this history, I draw on documents reproduced together for the first time in Appendix A of this edition: correspondence relating to the book in the archives of Richard Bentley and Son which includes, in addition to Jewsbury's negative report, letters from Broughton and Le Fanu. As I have already discussed Jewsbury's report, my focus here will be on Le Fanu's and Broughton's correspondence with the publishers, and what it reveals about the circumstances of the novel's publication in volume form—as well as, in Broughton's case, her feelings about the novel after it was published. I will then provide an overview of the types of changes Broughton made in the *DUM* version, and conclude with some thoughts on the way these revisions affect the novel's representation of sexuality.

It is immediately apparent from the Bentley correspondence what a significant role J. S. Le Fanu played in the publication of *Not Wisely*. Not only, of course, had he originally serialized the novel, but he recommended it to Bentley and acted as a go-between in his niece's initial dealings with the publisher. Obviously, Broughton benefitted greatly from her connection to this well-established male author in gaining an entrée into the world of London publishing. While her uncle believed the serial version required some revision,[41] he highly praised the "great promise and power" of the tale and predicted "It strikes me as a story that might quite possibly make a hit."[42] In a letter to Richard Bentley written several weeks before Jewsbury's report, Le Fanu confidently assumes he could receive proofs for the novel in as little as a week's time to give to his niece.[43] When Richard Bentley sent word instead of Jewsbury's scathing critique, it was Le Fanu who relayed the news to Broughton and "strongly urged the expediency of withdrawing the book."[44]

In her biography of Broughton, Marilyn Wood criticizes Le Fanu for not standing up more strongly for the novel he had initially recommended. "[F]ar from being a strength in time of trouble," Wood claims, Le Fanu "placed himself, artistically speaking, at a safe distance from the source of such adverse criticism" and "watered down" his enthusiasm about the novel[45] in letters to Bentley such as the one in which he ascribes the

41 Appendix A, p. 377.

42 Appendix A, p. 377.

43 Appendix A, p. 378.

44 Appendix A, p. 380.

45 Wood, *Rhoda Broughton*, 12.

work's "boldness of style" to an "unfortunate ignorance of the actual force of some of what is set down."[46] It is true that Le Fanu suddenly seemed to have discovered flaws in a work he had only recently described as "carefully revised,"[47] assuring Bentley that even before hearing about Jewsbury's report he had become convinced that the novel's "last scene" needed "remodelling" as it "[would] not do."[48] Still, Le Fanu's response to Jewsbury's report may have been not so much cowardly as pragmatic. In his history of *The Dublin University Magazine*, Wayne Hall argues that, in advising his niece to compromise and negotiate with the publisher rather than to defend her work, Le Fanu advocated tactics similar to those he employed with publishers in regards to the more controversial aspects of his own fiction.[49] Moreover, rather than losing enthusiasm for *Not Wisely*, as Wood claims, Le Fanu continued in his letters to Bentley to praise the novel for its "cleverness & power," slyly inserting a dissenting view to Jewsbury's in the form of comments by his friend Percy Fitzgerald, who claimed to have "expressed strong regret" at the decision to "postpone" the novel's appearance as he remained convinced it would be "a success—& might be a great one."[50] In urging his niece to withdraw the novel, Le Fanu claims to be motivated by a fear that Jewsbury's report would be "a foreshadowing of what some of the reviewers might say," and his desire to spare his niece such a "peculiarly painful" experience.[51]

Whether or not Le Fanu could have done more to defend *Not Wisely* in the wake of Jewsbury's report, his anxiety about reviewers echoing her opinion—an anxiety that was in fact borne out by the novel's mixed reviews—suggests a concern that criticism of the work's morality would be especially traumatic for a young female author. At the same time, Broughton's response to the precipitate change in the fortunes of her first novel shows that, rather than needing to rely on a male patron such as Le Fanu to negotiate with publishers, she was both able and willing to do so herself.

Writing directly to the Bentleys for the first time in December 1866

46 Appendix A, p. 379.
47 Appendix A, p. 378.
48 Appendix A, p. 379.
49 Wayne Hall, *Dialogues in the Margin: A Study of the Dublin University Magazine* (Washington, D. C.: The Catholic U of America P, 1999), 197.
50 Appendix A, p. 380.
51 Appendix A, p. 380.

in regards to *Cometh Up as a Flower*, Broughton makes it clear that, while she acquiesces to the arrangement to substitute that work for *Not Wisely*, she was not pleased by what had happened. Arranging a date to submit the expanded *Cometh Up*, she tartly hopes "there will be no miscarriage of this work."[52] and when she sends the manuscript ends her letter with the barbed comment, "Hoping that this tale avoids offending your reader's delicate sense of propriety."[53] Still, despite these defiant notes, Broughton agreed with Bentley, at least on paper, as to *Not Wisely*'s "unfitness for publication in its present state."[54] In a letter written in summer 1867 in which she first professed that she was "anxious to know whether you could ever be induced to bring out 'Not Wisely' if modified to a very considerable extent," Broughton promised that "I could if you gave me any encouragement to attempt such a thing with ease omit all the slang & coarseness of expression, and soften the violence of the situations & rewrite altogether the end, which is melodramatic and savours of a Surrey theatre."[55] Even as she deferred to the standards of propriety against which she had offended, however, the young author reminded Bentley of a risqué novel's potential profitability:

> My friends agree in telling me that tho' an improper book, it is cleverer far than "Cometh Up" & I myself confess to thinking that there is infinitely more verve & strength in it … I am almost sure it would be read which after all is the great thing, dullness being the one unpardonable fault in a writer.[56]

Reiterating her pledge to "expunge [the novel] of coarseness & slanginess," Broughton vowed to "rewrite those passages which cannot be toned down," philosophically adding "If I fail in altering it sufficiently to meet with your approbation you can but refuse it again."[57] On August 22, 1867 Broughton reported to Bentley that she was "very busy altering and rewriting parts of 'Not Wisely'" so that "it will be quite ready to appear in your autumn lists."[58] Though she claimed that she understood the novel's previous appearance in *The Dublin University Magazine* would affect the price

52 Appendix A, p. 380.
53 Appendix A, p. 381.
54 Appendix A, p. 381.
55 Appendix A, p. 381.
56 Appendix A, p. 381.
57 Appendix A, p. 381.
58 Appendix A, p. 382.

Bentley would pay for it, she still wished to know the sum he was willing to give her, warning that she would not think it worth her while to publish *Not Wisely* unless she was "certain of sufficient remuneration."[59] At this point, negotiations quickly broke down: only three days later, on August 25, Broughton tersely rejected Bentley's offer of £250 for the novel, declaring that she was "not by any means inclined to let 'Not Wisely' go for the very small sum you mention; add to which I have not the slightest interest of spoiling the story by padding it out to three volumes."[60] Writing to his niece several times to urge her not to decline Bentley's offer, Le Fanu also received a curt missive, a "short & rude letter," as he ruefully described it to George Bentley, which seemed to imply "that she considered my interference impertinent."[61] Stung, he resolved to "trouble her with no more advice on literary matters."[62]

Broughton's refusal to "pad[]" *Not Wisely* "out to three volumes" might seem disingenuous given that, unlike *Cometh Up*—to which Broughton had added ten chapters in submission to Bentley's wishes—*Not Wisely* was not significantly lengthened during the transition to volume form. Still, as the publisher seems to have wished her to make the novel even longer, Broughton evidently sought to exert some control over the form the revised *Not Wisely* would take, as well as to obtain the best financial outcome possible. This determination—striking in a fledgling writer who might be expected to jump at any chance to publish her work—informs a letter Broughton wrote in September 1867 to George Bentley explaining why "your father & I have been utterly unable to come to an agreement about 'Not Wisely.'"[63] Bluntly stating her disinclination "to spoil my tale for the sake of a little additional profit to your father," she added "If Mr Bentley is inclined to give me a good price for some future work perhaps we may be able to come to terms"[64]—a pointed reminder that Broughton would come back to Bentley from his rival Tinsley only if she were well paid for doing so. George Bentley may have called Broughton "wilful" in his diary,[65] but once her work proved popular he was apparently willing to

59 Appendix A, p. 382.
60 Appendix A, p. 382.
61 Appendix A, p. 383.
62 Appendix A, p. 383.
63 Appendix A, p. 382.
64 Appendix A, p. 382.
65 Hall, 198.

offer her terms she would accept.

Even after revising *Not Wisely*, however, Broughton remained dissatisfied with it. Indeed, one of the more poignant revelations of the Bentley correspondence is the degree of detestation with which she regarded the book, at least in the years immediately following its publication, referring to it as "that vile 'Not Wisely'"[66] and proclaiming "I hate it as it stands & so does every body else."[67] Professing herself "unwilling that anyone should know I wrote it,"[68] Broughton urged Bentley to buy back the rights from Tinsley so that she could revise the story yet further. Though George Bentley seemed simply to have ignored her pleas, in no fewer than five letters between 1870 and 1871 Broughton expressed herself anxious to "begin whitewashing 'Not Wisely'":[69] "I am very anxious to write a different story with different characters with less violence, diffuseness & vulgarity, on the same or a nearly similar plot."[70] While she apparently remained interested in the storyline of a young woman falling in love with a married man (Broughton called the plot of *Not Wisely* "the best I ever had"), she dismisses the rest of the novel as "crude vulgar & in parts *canting*, all in the highest degree."[71]

Broughton's references to *Not Wisely* as "crude" and "vulgar" show that, at least to some extent, she agreed with critics' assessment of the novel's impropriety.[72] At the same time, Broughton's description of the book as "*canting*," or overly preachy, also suggests that she regretted the moralistic tone she had included to dilute the story's more shocking features. Significantly, when indicating her desire to start with a "quite fresh" version of *Not Wisely*, Broughton offers to "leave out," among other supporting characters, the novel's resident super-ego, the clergyman James Stanley, to whom she refers as "the wishy washy good parson."[73] Apparently, then,

---

66 Rhoda Broughton, Letter to George Bentley, 21 May 1871, in *Archives of Richard Bentley and Son 1829-1898*, Pt. 2, Reel 22.

67 Appendix A, p. 383.

68 Appendix A, p. 384.

69 Appendix A, p. 384.

70 Appendix A, p. 384.

71 Appendix A, p. 384.

72 In her memories of Rhoda Broughton, Ethel Arnold recalls Broughton describing *Not Wisely* as "crude and vulgar and marred by that impropriety which is so often the fault of very young writers" ("Rhoda Broughton As I Knew Her," *Fortnightly Review* [Aug. 1920], 275).

73 Appendix A, p. 383.

even as she wished to prune further "anything ... that could give offence" in the novel,[74] she nonetheless desired to liberate the narrative from a too-intense didacticism. Moreover, in a letter to George Bentley in 1876, she explicitly regretted one of her major revisions intended to tone down the *DUM* version. Rereading the end of the novel as it originally appeared in serialization, she professes herself "struck with its much greater power than the later published version": "tho crude & coarse it seems to me rather fine."[75] Broughton concludes with a *cri de coeur* that eloquently identifies the aesthetic price she felt she had paid in making her work more respectable: "Oh! I have bought my increased refinement of a great wealth of power."[76]

The changes that Broughton made to the *DUM* version of *Not Wisely* in order to attain "increased refinement" include, in some instances, additions to the text, such as the narrator's defensive disclaimer in Volume I as Kate pursues Dare with unladylike aplomb:

> Let no one think I am defending this girl, or holding her sentiments up as the pattern of what a young woman's should be; nor let anyone, however incapable of separating the historian's own ideas from those of the people whose history he is telling, imagine that I am describing Dare as being in anywise a hero or fine fellow. I think him as great and unmitigated a scoundrel as any strictest censor of morals can do ... To describe bad actions is not, as I would meekly submit to indignant virtue, to be an accomplice in them; otherwise he who relates a murder is equal in iniquity to him who commits it[.] (p. 147).

When she has her narrator "meekly submit to indignant virtue," it is hard to imagine that Broughton did not have in mind Jewsbury's self-righteous report.

In general, however, Broughton's revisions to the serialized *Not Wisely* do not involve defensive additions so much as deletions and substitutions. The most obvious of these substitutions involve what Broughton called "slanginess" in her letters to Bentley; hence "hooked it" becomes "eloped" (p. 57), "spooning" becomes "flirting" (p. 93), and "Hookey Walker!"

74 Appendix A, p. 383.
75 Appendix A, p. 384.
76 Appendix A, p. 384.

becomes "Ahem!" (p. 78).[77] While such changes might seem superficial, that Broughton had coupled the term "slanginess" with "coarseness" in her correspondence with Bentley underscores the ideological weight of informal speech. As I mentioned earlier, conservative Victorians saw slang not only as lacking in genteel gravitas but, when used by a woman, as a sign of potential, if not actual, immorality; Eliza Lynn Linton accused "the Girl of the Period"—a being she likened to a whore—of "talking slang as glibly as a man, and by preference leading the conversation to doubtful subjects."[78] Although the charge of "slanginess" clung to her work into the 1870s, in the revised version of *Not Wisely* Broughton attempts to lessen her association, and that of her heroines, with informal and racy speech. One intriguing example of the link between sexuality and slang occurs early in the novel, when Broughton not only edits out of one of Kate's internal monologues such terms as "twaddle" and "bosh," but revises her heroine's comment upon surveying the windswept skirts of a woman on the beach. Changing "What an exhibition of legs!" to "What an exhibition of Magenta stockings!"—and moreover removing a line about the unattractive thickness of the body parts in question—Broughton downplays her heroine's assumption of a voyeurism traditionally associated with men (p. 52).[79]

Other deletions in the serial text involve particularly outrageous sentiments voiced by the heroine; from a speech in which her heroine laments her hitherto unrequited love. For example, Broughton cuts several lines in which Kate defies religious strictures: "Oh, Dare, if I had you, what should I care for heaven, or hell either? I would defy heaven to make me more utterly happy; I would defy hell to make me miserable."[80] Broughton also rewrites several scenes in which Kate is especially irreverent of male authority, such as one in Volume I in which she is disrespectful of her guardian Rev. Piggott, and another at the end of Volume II in which she resists her cousin George Chester's attempts to chaperone her.[81] A striking instance of a passage in which Broughton plays down Kate's unconventionality occurs at the end of Volume I, when, shortly before he reveals he is already married, Dare urges Kate to swear she will elope with

77 See Appendix B, p. 387, p. 392, p. 390.
78 Linton, "The Girl of the Period," 175.
79 See Appendix B, p. 386.
80 Appendix B, p. 391.
81 Appendix B, p. 392 and p. 411.

him: "The devil's fire was in his eyes again—the fire she had been wont to shrink under" (p. 152). In the triple-decker version, the next line is "She winced now under it," emphasizing Kate's timidity. In the serial version, however, Kate not only refuses to wince but vies with her tempter for daring: "She had grown worse of late, bolder; she did not shrink now; she fronted those eyes undaunted, reckless."[82]

The most controversial scenes in the serialized *Not Wisely* were those depicting sexual passion. Targeting the physicality of this representation, in her report Jewsbury had described the narrative as "a series of love scenes (if love it can be called)" in which a "'big Titan' … 'crushes' & 'kisses' & 'devours' & 'holds in [his] iron grasp'" the "'little,'" "'round,'" and "'soft'" heroine.[83] Unsurprisingly, in the revised version Broughton deleted some of the more vivid evocations of Kate and Dare's bodily sensations. Several instances where each lover imagines embracing the other are edited out, as when Dare reflects "what a singularly delightful sensation it would be to have those warm white arms flung round his neck."[84] In one scene in which Dare actually embraces Kate, Broughton, as Sally Mitchell notes, deletes a line from the *DUM* version that evokes orgasm; "the strain that fulfilled the wild longing, the burning dreams of weeks, was quite painful."[85] As a result of such revisions there are fewer instances in which the reader vicariously indulges along with the characters in erotic fantasies, as when Kate's brother, waxing lyrical about Dare's magnificent physique, encourages the reader to imagine him unclothed: "'If you could but see the muscle on his back,' he said, rapturously, turning to his sisters."[86]

Yet Broughton's expurgations are incomplete. Though Broughton cut the line in which Kate asks "Oh, Dare, if I had you, what should I care for heaven, or hell either?," the declaration several lines later that one of his smiles "would overpay centuries in hell!" (p. 89) remains untouched. Similarly, though Broughton removes the line about Kate's orgasmic response while embracing Dare ("the strain … was quite painful"), she retains a passage in the same scene in which, exclaiming over hothouse flowers that figuratively mirror her own lush form, Kate expresses a delight

82 Appendix B, p. 399.
83 Appendix A, p. 378.
84 Appendix B, p. 389.
85 Appendix B, p. 397; Sally Mitchell, *The Fallen Angel: Chastity, Class and Women's Reading* (Bowling Green: Bowling Green State U Popular P, 1981), 89.
86 Appendix B, p. 388.

very like climax: "The wealth of enjoyment there was in that last 'Oh!' beggars description" (p. 134). Given its narrative of illicit love, after all, *Not Wisely*'s erotic energies are impossible fully to contain.

Broughton's radical revision of the original ending, however, might seem one of her more thorough bowdlerizations. True to her promise to Bentley to "soften the violence of the situations and rewrite altogether the end, which is melodramatic and savours of a Surrey theatre,"[87] Broughton replaced the conclusion in which the jealous Dare shoots to death first Kate, and then himself, with one in which he is fatally injured in a carriage accident and the bereaved girl enters an Anglican sisterhood. As I have mentioned, Broughton apparently regretted this change in the letter to George Bentley in 1876 in which she claimed that the original ending possessed "much greater power than the later published version."[88] Certainly the *DUM* ending is better suited to Broughton's Shakespearean title "Not Wisely, but Too Well," a phrase taken from the speech in which Othello describes his love for Desdemona after killing her and before killing himself, actions mirrored in the murder-suicide that climaxes the serialized *Not Wisely*. Following as it does ominous hints earlier in the serial text that the jealous Dare will eventually kill Kate if she refuses to become his mistress, this violent conclusion provides the novel with an undeniable structural cohesion, not to mention shock value.

Yet the triple-decker's supposedly tamer ending arguably represents a more subversive attack on sexual convention than the original conclusion. This is not to deny the power of Broughton's portrait in the serial of a violently possessive male—a type who, unfortunately, exists all too often in real life as well as in fiction. Still, the murderous Dare of the *DUM* conclusion—a villain complete with eyes that are "wells of burning hell-fire" and a laugh "hollow and malignant like a fiend's"[89]—is almost laughably cartoonish. Broughton's changes in her representation of Dare—which include pruning passages earlier in the serial in which, foreshadowing its climax, he threatens to rape or kill Kate if she does not obey him—cannot completely whitewash his character: he remains a Byronic bad boy with problematically controlling attitudes toward women. Yet the softened characterization of Dare at the end of the triple-decker not only makes him more sympathetic, but, significantly, more sympathetically represents

87 Appendix A, p. 381.

88 Appendix A, p. 384.

89 Appendix B, p. 425.

Kate's transgressive desire. The original ending has highly moralistic overtones, implying, in a Victorian version of *Waiting for Mr. Goodbar*, that "fast" girls who flirt with sexual danger court untimely death. In contrast the triple-decker, by depicting the dying Dare as a man in whom "passion was dead, and love reigned immortal among the ruins of mortality" (p. 368), downplays this didacticism to emphasize instead the oppressive role played by convention in separating the star-crossed couple. Underscoring this message, in the revised version the narrator describes Kate's arrival at the wounded Dare's side in these terms: "In moments of profound mastering emotion we shake ourselves free from the artificial restraints of society and education, as some strong runner, ere setting forth on a long hard race, casts away the heavy garments that would hinder his flight, and returns to the instinct and impulses of Nature" (p. 367).

More than the serial ending, then, the conclusion of the revised version underscores the novel's implicit critique of marriage laws and the constraints they place on sexuality. True, the plight that dramatizes lack of access to divorce is a man's, as it is Dare who pays for the "boyish folly," as he puts it (p. 277), of marrying at eighteen a woman he later finds incompatible. At the same time, however, Dare's predicament, which inhibits not only his but Kate's sexual self-expression, suggests that social rules governing desire are, in the words of the passage above, "artificial" rather than "the instinct and impulses of Nature." This implicit critique of sexual mores is consistent with Broughton's depiction in other novels, such as *Cometh Up as a Flower* and *Belinda*, of the emotional and erotic frustration experienced by women trapped in uncongenial marriages.

The Plot of a Woman's Life: Broughton and the Representation of Femininity

Not Wisely's implicit critique of marriage laws links it with other female sensation fictions of the 1860s which, in their portrayal of such issues as bigamy, adultery, incompatibility, and domestic abuse, similarly represent the negative effects of marriage on women's social and sexual identities. Still, it would be misleading to suggest that *Not Wisely*, any more than such sensation novels as *Lady Audley's Secret*, constitutes a thorough-going rejection of sexual convention and misogynist stereotypes. *Not Wisely* has conservative elements that cannot be wholly explained away as a nod to potentially disapproving readers; it would, indeed, be unrealistic to assume that Broughton could escape the beliefs and values of her day. Embedded in the text at the level of imagery and structure—and thus predating Broughton's attempts to "tone[] down" the novel's controversial elements—are numerous references to contemporary anxieties about female sexuality and rebellion. Imagery linking the modern young woman to dirt, disease, and decay are particularly rife in that part of the novel in which Kate, flirting outrageously with her cousin George, does unchaperoned social work in the slums. As both Pamela Gilbert and Laurence Talairach-Vielmas note, Broughton's descriptions of Kate's transitions between bourgeois space and fever-infested slums threaten to dissolve the boundaries of respectability (Gilbert calls Kate a "typhoid Mary" of sexual contagion).[90] Similarly, Kate's acceding to Dare's demand to become his mistress in the Crystal Palace—a site purportedly celebrating British achievement and industry—evokes, like many other texts of the period, a narrative of social and imperial decline (the frequent descriptions of Kate as a "southern-souled" girl (p. 151) recall the fear of "going native" in many late-Victorian texts).[91]

Even the conservative elements of *Not Wisely*, however, are complicated by Broughton's sophisticated awareness of the ways in which prior texts and conventions shape the representation of women. One way in which Broughton evinces this awareness is through her unreliable narrator; an elite male unrequitedly in love with Kate ("She was everything to me, and I was less than nothing to her"[p. 45]), he delights in comparing the woman who preferred Dare to himself to such legendary *femmes fatales* as Helen of Troy, Cleopatra, and Venus. In general, Broughton's numerous references to, and quotations from, prior literary works constitute a self-conscious dialogue with traditions, often male-authored, of representing

90 Pamela Gilbert, *Disease, Desire and the Body in Victorian Women's Popular Novels* (Cambridge: Cambridge UP, 1997), 121. Like Gilbert, Talairach-Vielmas explores Kate's problematic boundary-crossing in *Moulding the Female Body in Victorian Fairy Tales and Sensation Fiction* (Aldershot: Ashgate, 2007), 89-112. For more on the conservative as well as subversive messages in *Not Wisely*, see Tamar Heller, "'That Muddy, Polluted Flood of Earthly Love': Ambivalence about the Body in Rhoda Broughton's *Not Wisely but Too Well*," in *Victorian Sensations: Essays on a Scandalous Genre*, ed. Kimberly Harrison and Richard Fantina (Columbus: The Ohio State UP, 2006), 87-101.

91 A useful discussion of the late-Victorian fear of "going native" can be found in Patrick Brantlinger's chapter on "imperial Gothic" in *Rule of Darkness: British Literature and Imperialism, 1830-1914* (Ithaca: Cornell UP, 1988), 227-53.

gender and sexuality. Reading *Not Wisely* through the lens of Bakhtinian theory, Helen Debenham sees Broughton's dense network of literary allusion as a "carnivalesque heteroglossia" of "discourses and genres" that record her need to "negotiat[e] her right of entry to and her difference from the literary establishment" and its often stereotyped definitions of women as either temptresses or objects of male desire.[92] According to Debenham, Broughton's frequent invocations of high-culture authors and artworks in deliberately quotidian settings, as well as her mingling of poetry with slang, results in a "persistent destabilising" or even parody of conventional notions of femininity.[93]

Certainly, some of the satiric passages Debenham cites—for example the narrator's jaded line "I'm tired of writing about love-making" (p. 138)—anticipate the cynical attitude toward romance that would increasingly mark Broughton's fiction in her later career. Even as she sends up traditional representations of women, however, Broughton shows to what extent they still limit the narrative options available to heroines. In a particularly revealing passage that Broughton inserted in the triple-decker, the narrator says:

> Since this time yesterday [Kate] had made the pleasing discovery that she was fast falling in love violently, and as it now appeared unrequitedly, with a man her superior in station, and in every respect unlikely to prove a satisfactory object for that passion which forms the main plot of a woman's life, and is only a small secondary byplay in a man's. Yes, the play of her life had begun, and whether it was to be a tragedy or a comedy who could tell? (p. 83)

The cynicism about romance that Debenham sees as key to *Not Wisely* informs the observation that the love so central to a woman "is only a small secondary byplay" for a man. Yet the narrator's use of literary terms to define Kate's story—"play," "tragedy, "comedy"—reflects the way that cultural discourses about femininity, as filtered through literary conventions such as the courtship plot, shape and limit women's perceptions of the choices available to them. Indeed, we see this process exemplified by

92 Helen Debenham, "*Not Wisely but Too Well* and the Art of Sensation," in *Victorian Identities: Social and Cultural Formations in Nineteenth-Century Literature*, ed. Ruth Robbins and Julian Wolfreys (Hampshire: Macmillan's/New York: St. Martin's, 1996, 15, 10.

93 Debenham, 19.

Kate, who, in the first scene in which we see her, is defined as a reader. Sitting on the beach with the book she has just finished, Whyte Melville's *The Interpreter*, Kate ponders whether love can be, as represented in the novel, "such an irresistible power, such an all-conquering influence," but then decides that books give an "absurdly false pictures of love": "They represent it as the one main interest of life, instead of being, as it mostly is, a short unimportant little episode" (p. 52). While Kate wishes to be like men who, in the passage quoted above, consider love "a small secondary byplay," however, she changes her mind when she recalls romantic texts that have enthralled her:

> Do Juliet, and Imogene, and Francesca of Rimini, and Fatima talk nonsense? If they do, I would rather have their nonsense than any other people's sense. Yes, yes, after all I do believe they are pretty nearly right. Love must be the one great bliss of this world[.] (p. 52)

Thus, though the narrator's query whether Kate's story will be "a tragedy or a comedy" seems open-ended, Kate's acceptance of the message conveyed in her reading—that romance is in fact the "main plot" of a woman's life—limits her fate to only a few narrative possibilities. "Comedy" would, in the original sense derived from Greek drama, be the usual telos of the courtship plot exemplified in Jane Austen's novels, in which young women choose between two suitors, as Kate does here between Dare and George Chester. Unlike Austen's Elizabeth Bennett or Marianne Dashwood, however, Kate does not choose the man who offers financial and social stability. Nor does she find the happy closure to her Gothic romance that Charlotte Brontë somewhat implausibly appended to *Jane Eyre*, a novel whose bigamy plot presumably influenced *Not Wisely*'s, and whose rakish male undergoes religious conversion even as his unwanted first wife is conveniently killed off.[94] If Broughton refuses to transform Kate's story into this sort of "comedy," then, it must end in tragedy, and indeed both versions of the ending of *Not Wisely* dramatize typical fates suffered by heroines of unhappy love stories: death or retirement to a convent.

Though it recycles the stereotype of the convent as refuge for the damsel disappointed in love, however, Kate's fate in the triple-decker gestures towards an innovative option in which the heroine escapes the

94 See Debenham (15) for more on the how *Not Wisely* evades *Jane Eyre*'s "providential framework."

marriage plot altogether. In this regard, the comments of Kate's sister upon hearing of her plan to enter an Anglican religious order are revealing, as is Kate's response:

> "Kate, I always hated these sisterhoods; they have been a curse to numberless families, I am certain; a number of women huddled together, cut off from their lives, and their friends, and all their prospects in life. Why cannot women keep to their right functions of marrying and being happy?"
>
> "'Be happy if they can, by all means; people's ideas about happiness differ'" (p. 351).

As Susan Mumm shows in her history of emergent Anglican women's orders in the Victorian period, such sisterhoods were controversial not only because they smacked of "Papistry," but, arguably even more subversively, they provided an alternative to domesticity that enabled women to work outside the home (by 1900 almost ninety Anglican sisterhoods existed in England, most devoted, like the fictional one Kate enters, to working among the poor).[95] In this sense, the Anglican nun prefigures the *fin-de-siècle* New Woman and her flapper successor.[96]

In the late 1860s, however, Broughton could not imagine a fiction in which the romance plot is downplayed in favor of female professional identity. As the would-be author, Charlotte Hankey, says wistfully in Broughton's last novel, *A Fool in Her Folly,* the notion taken for granted in the post-World War I era, that "a couple of girls should find an affinity in each other … and, 'forsaking all other,' betake themselves to a joint flat, to maintain which their own industries should furnish the means" would, in the mid-Victorian period "have consigned the holder of it to Bedlam."[97] Yearning to find "some work in the world to do" (p. 374), Sister Kate

95 Susan Mumm, *Stolen Daughters, Virgin Mothers: Anglican Sisterhoods in Victorian Britain* (London: Leicester UP, 1999). The whole of Mumm's study bears out her point that Anglican sisterhoods enabled women to "carve out for themselves satisfying careers outside of the normal sphere for Victorian women" (210), but for public perceptions of the sisters' subversion of domesticity in particular, see 166-206.

96 Martha Vicinus includes Anglican sisterhoods as one group paving the way for late-Victorian feminists in *Independent Women: Work & Community for Single Women 1850-1920* (Chicago: U of Chicago P, 1985), 46-84.

97 Rhoda Broughton, *A Fool in Her Folly* (London: Odhams, 1920), 9.

soldiers away at social work along with her female companions, but she only does so because the "main plot" of her life—her romance with Dare—is no longer possible. For all this, however, Broughton's self-conscious meditation in *Not Wisely* on literary texts and their (in Nancy Miller's words) "plots and plausibilities for women,"[98] opens the door for options other than the "comedy" or "tragedy" of the traditional heterosexual narrative.

Broughton's innovations in depicting female desire provide ample grounds for her reevaluation. Yet there is another, no less significant, reason for readers today to pick up one of her novels: she is a superb story-teller. On the last page of an early edition of *Not Wisely* that I own, the same faded handwriting that scrawled the date "1872" on the flyleaf declares: "Awfully exciting Book. Sorry it's finished." If you feel the same, I encourage you to seek out other Broughton novels and stories, and so speed the well-deserved rediscovery of her work.

98 Nancy Miller, "Emphasis Added: Plots and Plausibilities in Women's Fiction," *PMLA* 96 (Jan. 1981): 36-48.

CHRONOLOGY OF RHODA BROUGHTON

1840	29 November: Broughton born in Denbigh, Wales, the third daughter of Reverend Delves Broughton and his wife Jane.
1855	The Broughton family moves to 17th-century Broughton Hall, in Staffordshire, where Reverend Broughton is offered a living, or parish ministry.
1860	Death of Broughton's mother.
ca 1862-63	Broughton writes *Not Wisely, but Too Well* and *Cometh Up as a Flower.*
1863	Death of Broughton's father.
1864	Broughton's sister Eleanor marries William Charles Newcome; Broughton makes her home with them at Upper Eyarth in Denbyshire. She shows her uncle by marriage, J. S. Le Fanu, the manuscript of *Not Wisely, but Too Well.*
1865-66	Both *Not Wisely, but Too Well* and *Cometh Up as a Flower* serialized in *The Dublin University Magazine*, which Le Fanu edits. Le Fanu recommends *Not Wisely* to the publisher Bentley and Son. Broughton signs a contract for the novel, but her uncle persuades her to void it following Geraldine Jewsbury's unfavorable reader's report. Bentley agrees to publish an expanded *Cometh Up* in place of *Not Wisely.*
1867	March: Bentley publishes *Cometh Up as a Flower.* In the fall, Broughton publishes a revised *Not Wisely, but Too Well* with Tinsley after rejecting an offer from Bentley.
1870	Broughton's third novel, *Red as a Rose is She*, published by Bentley, who will remain her publisher until 1898. The novel was initially serialized in the Bentley-run journal *Temple Bar*, in which a number of Broughton's other fictions would be serialized.
1872	*Good-bye, Sweetheart!.* Broughton, who has hitherto published anonymously, releases this novel under her own name.

1873	*Nancy*. Broughton also publishes *Tales for Christmas Eve*, a collection of supernatural stories reissued under the title *Twilight Stories* in 1879.
1876	*Joan.*
1878	Following the death of her brother-in-law, Broughton moves with her widowed sister to Oxford, where she will live until 1890 and to which she will return in later life.
1880	*Second Thoughts.*
1883	*Belinda.*
1886	Publication of two novellas in the volume *Betty's Visions and Mrs. Smith of Longmains.* The novel *Doctor Cupid* is published this year as well.
1890	*Alas!* (Broughton's last triple-decker novel). In the fall she moves with her sister to Richmond in London.
1891	*A Widower Indeed* (co-authored with the American writer Elizabeth Bisland).
1892	*Mrs. Bligh.*
1894	*A Beginner.* Death of Broughton's sister Eleanor Newcome.
1895	*Scylla or Charybdis.*
1897	*Dear Faustina.*
1898	*The Game or the Candle*, published by Macmillan, who will remain Broughton's publisher until 1910.
1900	*Foes-in-Law.* Broughton moves back to Oxford, where she will live until her death.
1902	*Lavinia.*
1905	*A Waif's Progress.*
1908	*Mamma.*
1910	*The Devil and the Deep Sea.*
1912	*Between Two Stools* (published by Stanley, Paul, and Co.).
1914	*Concerning a Vow.*
1917	*A Thorn in the Flesh.*
1920	5 June: Broughton dies. Her last novel, *A Fool in Her Folly*, is published posthumously by Odham's. Publication too in September of Broughton's essay "Girls Past and Present" in *Ladies Home Journal.*

SELECT BIBLIOGRAPHY

Those wishing to learn more about Broughton should consult the sole biography of her to date, Marilyn Wood's *Rhoda Broughton: Profile of a Novelist* (Stamford: Paul Watkins, 1993). Other biographical material may be found in Michael Sadleir, *Things Past* (London: Constable, 1944), 84-116, and Ethel Arnold, "Rhoda Broughton as I Knew Her," *Fortnightly Review* CVIII (Aug. 1920): 262-78. Helen Black includes her account of meeting Broughton in *Notable Women Authors of the Day* (1893; Rpt. Brighton: Victorian Secrets, 2011), 51-58. Articles and book chapters from the past several decades that reevaluate Broughton's fiction and legacy are listed below; these include introductions to the Pickering and Chatto (2004) and Broadview (2007) editions of *Cometh Up as a Flower*, the only one of her novels, other than *Not Wisely, but Too Well*, in print at the time of this writing (her short story collection *Twilight Stories*, originally *Tales for Christmas Eve*, has been reprinted as well, edited and with an introduction by Emma Liggins [London: Victorian Secrets, 2009]).

Debenham, Helen. "*Not Wisely but Too Well* and the Art of Sensation." In *Victorian Identities: Social and Cultural Formations in Nineteenth-Century Literature*. Ruth Robbins and Julian Wolfreys, eds. Hampshire: Macmillan/ New York: St. Martins, 1996. 9-24.

Despotopoulou, Anna. "Trains of Thought: Challenges of Mobility in the Work of Rhoda Broughton." *Critical Survey* 23.1 (2011): 90-106.

Faber, Lindsey. "One Sister's Surrender: Rivalry and Resistance in Rhoda Broughton's *Cometh Up as a Flower*." In *Victorian Sensations: Essays on a Scandalous Genre*. Ed. Kimberly Harrison and Richard Fantina. Columbus: The Ohio State UP, 2006. 149-59.

Gilbert, Pamela K. "Rhoda Broughton: Anything but Love." Ch. 4 of *Disease, Desire and the Body in Victorian Women's Popular Novels*. Cambridge: Cambridge UP, 1997. 113-39.

----. Introduction. *Cometh Up as a Flower*, by Rhoda Broughton. Peterborough: Broadview Press, 2010. 9-31.

Hager, Lisa. "Slumming with the New Woman: *Fin-de-Siècle* Sexual Inversion, Reform Work and Sisterhood in Rhoda Broughton's *Dear Faustina*." *Women's Writing* 14 (2007): 460-75.

Heller, Tamar. "Disposing of the Body: Literary Authority, Female Desire and the Reverse Künstlerroman of Rhoda Broughton's *A Fool in Her Folly*." In *New Woman Writers, Authority and the Body*. Ed. Melissa Purdue and Stacey Floyd. Cambridge: Cambridge Scholars Publishing, 2009. 139-58.

----. Introduction. *Cometh Up as a Flower*, by Rhoda Broughton. Ed. Tamar Heller. *Varieties of Women's Sensation Fiction*. Gen. ed. Andrew Maunder. Vol. 4b. London: Pickering and Chatto, 2004. xxxiii-1.

----. "'That Muddy, Polluted Flood of Earthly Love': Ambivalence about the Body in Rhoda Broughton's *Not Wisely but Too Well*." In *Victorian Sensations: Essays on a Scandalous Genre*. Ed. Kimberly Harrison and Richard Fantina. Columbus: The Ohio State UP, 2006. 87-101.

----. "Rewriting *Corinne*: Sensation and the Tragedy of the Exceptional Woman in Rhoda Broughton's *Good-bye, Sweetheart!*" *Critical Survey* 23.1 (2011): 58-74.

----. "Rhoda Broughton." In *A Companion to Sensation Fiction*. Ed. Pamela K. Gilbert. Chichester: Wiley-Blackwell, 2011. 281-92.

Jones, Shirley. "`LOVE': Rhoda Broughton, writing and re-writing romance." In *Popular Victorian Women Writers*. Ed. Kay Boardman and Shirley Jones. Manchester: Manchester UP, 2004. 208-36.

Murphy, Patricia. "Disdained and Disempowered: The `Inverted' New Woman in Rhoda Broughton's *Dear Faustina*." *Tulsa Studies in Women's Literature* 19.1 (Spring 2000): 57-79.

Talairach-Vielmas, Laurence. "A Journey through the Crystal Palace: Rhoda Broughton's Politics of Plate-Glass in *Not Wisely But Too Well*." Ch. 5 of *Moulding the Female Body in Victorian Fairy Tales and Sensation Fiction*. Aldershot: Ashgate, 2007. 89-112.

Terry, R. C. "Delightful Wickedness: Some Novels of Rhoda Broughton." Ch. 5 of *Victorian Popular Fiction, 1860-80*. London: Macmillan, 1983. 102-32.

NOTE ON THE TEXT

Not Wisely, but Too Well was originally serialized in twelve parts in *The Dublin University Magazine*, Vols. 66-68, from August 1865 to July 1866 (for details see below), and then printed in a revised three-volume version by Tinsley Brothers in fall 1867. This text follows the first edition of the triple-decker, with obvious errors silently corrected. To compare, by page, the differences between the triple-decker and original *Dublin University Magazine* (*DUM*) version, see Appendix B, "Textual Variants." These variants include the novel's original ending, which Broughton completely rewrote for volume publication.

Despite her many revisions of *Not Wisely*, however, Broughton did not, as she did with her other novel serialized in the *DUM*, *Cometh Up as a Flower*, add new chapters when she prepared the story for volume publication. Hence, the chapter divisions in the *DUM* text of *Not Wisely* largely correspond to those in the triple-decker, except for several instances where chapters in the triple-decker either run together or break up chapters in the serialization. These changes, as well as the demarcation of volumes in the triple-decker, are indicated overleaf.

Readers should be aware that, in this edition, footnotes identifying the sources of quotations to which Broughton alludes will sometimes begin with the word "inexact." A prodigious reader, Broughton knew a vast fund of literature by heart. She could, however, be inaccurate in reciting from memory, either getting words wrong or merely misremembering punctuation. "Inexact" covers any of these bases; readers are encouraged to look up the original version if they wish to compare it to Broughton's.

All citations from the Bible in footnotes are to the King James version.

Serialization of *Not Wisely, but Too Well* in *The Dublin University Magazine*:

Part	Date	Chapters	Pages
1	Aug. 1865	1-6	123-45[1]
2	Sept. 1865	7-10	258-77
3	Oct. 1865	11-16[2]	406-22
4	Nov. 1865	17-18	502-16
5	Dec. 1865	19-20	619-31
6	Jan. 1866	20(cont.)-23	44-63
7	Feb. 1866	24-25	140-51
8	Mar. 1866	26[3]	260-73
9	Apr. 1866	27	373-84
10	May 1866	28	497-505
11	June 1866	29-31	681-96
12	July 1866	32-35[4]	58-75

1. The page on which the novel starts is 121 in the *DUM*, but this is misnumbered.
2. In the 1867 triple-decker edition, Vol. I ends here. Vol. II begins with ch. 17 in the *DUM* serialization.
3. In the 1867 edition, Vol. II ends on p. 263 of ch. 26 in the serial edition; Vol III, ch.1, picks up thereafter.
4. The original ending begins partway through ch. 34 and continues through ch. 35.

ACKNOWLEDGEMENTS

I would like to thank both the Taft Research Center and the Department of English and Comparative Literature at the University of Cincinnati for their support in granting me leaves that enabled me to work on this edition. The Taft Research Center also provided international conference funding that allowed me to travel to London in 2009 and present a paper on Broughton's revisions of *Not Wisely, but Too Well* at the Victorian Popular Fiction Association meeting, where I received useful feedback from many colleagues, especially Jane Jordan, Greta Depledge, Pamela Gilbert, Anna Despotopoulou, Carolyn Oulton, and Janice Allan. I thank Broughton's biographer Marilyn Wood for taking the time to respond to my questions. In preparing the notes, I benefitted from the help of members of the VICTORIA listserv who generously fielded arcane queries. Evanthia Speliotis patiently helped me translate and transcribe Broughton's Greek. Thanks to Jay Jenkins for his help, and for sharing an 1890s edition of the novel. Catherine Pope at Victorian Secrets Press is doing a wonderful job reprinting unjustly neglected nineteenth-century texts; I am deeply grateful to her for publishing this edition. Finally, I would like to thank my husband and fellow Victorianist, Charles Hatten, for copious support, feedback, encouragement, and help trying to decipher Broughton's notoriously illegible handwriting.

ABOUT THE EDITOR

Tamar Heller teaches Victorian literature at the University of Cincinnati, with an emphasis on gender issues and on the genres of Gothic and sensation fiction. The author of *Dead Secrets: Wilkie Collins and the Female Gothic* (1992), she has co-edited two essay collections: *Approaches to Teaching Gothic Fiction: The British and American Traditions* (MLA, 2003) and *Scenes of the Apple: Food and the Female Body in Nineteenth- and Twentieth-Century Women's Writing* (SUNY, 2003). The editor of Rhoda Broughton's 1867 sensation novel *Cometh Up as a Flower* for Pickering and Chatto's *Varieties of Women's Sensation Fiction* series (2004), she is currently working on a book-length study of Broughton's fiction entitled *A Plot of Her Own: Rhoda Broughton and English Fiction.*

NOT WISELY, BUT TOO WELL.[1]

A Novel.

BY THE AUTHOR OF
"COMETH UP AS A FLOWER."

IN THREE VOLUMES.
VOL. I.

LONDON:
TINSLEY BROTHERS, 18 CATHERINE ST. STRAND.
1867

1 See Shakespeare, *Othello* (first printed 1622), V.ii.344. About to kill himself after slaying Desdemona, Othello asks to be remembered as "one who lov'd not wisely but too well."

NOT WISELY, BUT TOO WELL.

GLOBE LIBRARY. Vol. I, No. 241.
April 27, 1896. Bi-Weekly. Year, $7.00.
Entered at Chicago Post Office as second-class matter.

RAND, McNALLY & CO., PUBLISHERS,
Chicago and New York.

Cover from the 1896 paperback edition

CHAPTER I.

"A THING of beauty is a joy for ever."[2] That is my text for this chapter, and my service is going to be an amplification and enlarging upon that idea. Keats meant it in a purely material sense, for his intense perception of the beautiful was confined to material objects; but I, having adopted it for my motto, intend it to be taken in a nobler, wider, more spiritual sense. The subject I am going to write about is to my mind "a thing of beauty;" for what is more preëminently so than a tender, "loving, passionate, human soul, made more tender, more loving, by many a sore grief,"[3] by many a gnawing sorrow, till towards the hour of its setting, whether calm or whelmed to the last in storm-clouds, it shines with a chaste mellow radiance such as our earth lamps do not afford us here, borrowed (oh, priceless loan!) from the fountains of light above? Love in such a soul, growing purified from the drossy, worthless part of earthly passion which oftentimes forms the largest share of it, is raised higher and higher above this world's low level, above its dull swampy flats, till it merges in that better, boundless love which is the essence of the Deity, a love free from the sharp sting of disappointment, free from the mortal taint of satiety, and which decay is powerless to soil with its foul, polluting fingers.

Even taking it in its narrow material sense, I agree very fully and heartily with the sentiment of Keats' suggestive line, and thank him most humbly and sincerely for saying for me, so pithily and concisely, what I should never have been able to say so well for myself. Yes! I subscribe to the opinion of that born Greek, whom some anachronism isolated from his kin and his country, and set amongst uncongenial money-making Britons, full twenty centuries too late. I subscribe to it; but yet I know, on the other hand, that we all learned, on no less authority than the copy-books, which exercised our powers of handwriting in the days of our hard-worked, highly educated youth, that "Beauty is a fading flower;"[4] and, applied particularly to woman's loveliness, there is none more favourite among that bundle of dull platitudes, of insipid, trite commonplaces which enrol themselves under

2 First line of John Keats's *Endymion* (1818).

3 Unidentified quotation.

4 See 4 Isaiah 28: 1.

the head of moral maxims. Of course it is true—tiresomely, provokingly, heart-breakingly true; so true as to be almost a self-evident proposition. Which of you, O daughters of Eve! has not made this interesting discovery in natural history for yourself, by one or other of the following pleasant processes? Either, standing after the manner of your kind, considering your *tout ensemble*,[5] in that teller of such gall-bitter, such treacle-sweet truths, your looking-glass, you make the discovery, some fine day, that you have lost your most effective, aggressive weapon against mankind. Your little sword is dinted; your pretty arrows have lost their points; your power is gone from you. Disarmed you stand there; like "brave Kempenfelt," your "victories are o'er,"[6] and very ruefully you have to own to yourself that your soft, much prized fascinations, which, perchance, made your small world so cheery a place, have gone away from you, never to come back again any more. "Eheu fugaces!"[7] They have slipped away, treacherous ones, out of your reluctant clasp, "most cunningly did steal away,"[8] as is the wont of the brief good things of this troublesome world of ours, leaving us very heart bare, and sore, and grumbling; none the worse, perhaps, for that at last. Or else you have this truth exemplified in a manner some degrees less painful to your own feelings; seeing old Time, that busy artificer, performing on the countenance of an intimate friend. Curiously you watch him, as, with his graver's tool, he draws horizontal, parallel lines along the smooth brow; designs skilfully a simple yet ingenious pattern of crow's feet at the corner of each haggard eye, pares down the rounded contours, and cuts them into sharp points and angles, and paints out with his dull grays and drabs the rosy flush of colour from the once love-bright cheek. Ay, me! Ay, me! indeed. What so frail, so butterfly lived as beauty in the individual? Hardly are we consoled by the reflection that at least in the species it seems perennial. But though the visible presence of this fairest of earth's visitants—this living witness that Eden once existed—is so sadly short, yet in memory it outlives all the other powers that sway our destinies. Great kingdoms grew into being in the old times, at least we suppose so, we having now nothing of them but their dark old tombs. Big men did big things, and might as well never have done them for all we

5 All together (French); the total impression created by details.

6 William Cowper, "On the Loss of the Royal George" (1782), ll. 14, 34.

7 From Horace: "Eheu! Fugaces labuntur anni" (Latin): "Alas! Our fleeting years pass away."

8 George Herbert, "Life" (1633), l. 5.

know about them, seeing that they rot now in such unrescued, irrecoverable oblivion. Even the most learned of our pundits in the historical and antiquarian line have but the most shadowy impression of what brave deeds were done, of what wise thoughts were thought, of how men lived and loved, and believed and hoped that dim far dawning. As for the bulk of us ignoramuses or *ignorami* (as I suppose would be the correct plural), it is a great chance if we know the names of the four great empires that people talk so much about nowadays.

But when shall we cease to hear the trailing garments of Helen the well-robed, the goddess of women, sweeping down the shadowy echoing corridors of Priam's cool, wide palace?[9] And when, oh when, save at the hour when recollection's self perishes, shall we forget "the serpent of old Nile;"[10] made up of delicious contradictions, enchanting termagent! the tempest of whose anger blew sweeter than the breath of the west wind come straight from a garden of roses; whose scolding angry words seemed more caressing, more utterly bewitching than other women's love-whispers! Frail, vain, variable, heartless coquette! who could yet love so exceeding well "her curled Antony,"[11] her mailed Roman darling, as to choose the aspick's cold kisses on her soft flesh, rather than existence without him—who could lay aside life, with so queenly rare a grace, as to make us "half in love with dreamful death!"[12] still, yes still, though dead, you snare us "in your strong toil of grace."[13] That was a lovely conception of the mightiest and sweetest of all singers that have sung for many a day, embodied in the "Dream of Fair Women." Those "far renowned brides of ancient song"[14] were worthy denizens for the fragrant chambers of a great poet's soul. He who has been able to set before us—

---

9 In Greek mythology the Trojan War started when the famously beautiful Helen, wife of King Menelaus of Sparta, was abducted by the Trojan prince Paris and brought to the palace of his father, King Priam.

10 Shakespeare, *Antony and Cleopatra* (first printed 1623), I.v.25.

11 *Antony and Cleopatra* V.ii.304. Legend has it that Cleopatra killed herself by placing a poisonous asp ("aspick") on her breast.

12 Inexact; Keats's "Ode to a Nightingale" (1820), l. 52.

13 *Antony and Cleopatra*, V.ii.348.

14 L. 17 of "A Dream of Fair Women" (1832), by Alfred, Lord Tennyson (the "mightiest and sweetest of all singers," and, based on the number of times she quotes from his work, apparently one of Broughton's favorites).

"Idalian Aphrodite, beautiful,
Fresh as the foam, new-bathed in Paphian wells,"[15]

who has called her back from her old Cyprian home, with her own rosy cloud of love and maddening witchery round her, taking the senses by storm, who can, even now, make men's veins throb and their pulses beat with ecstasy, leading them into the presence of her divine ambrosial loveliness, he, I say, is one of the few great artists—the one great artist indeed, in these barren days, that is equal to the task of limning those "imperial moulded forms"[16] that haunt his dim wood. How great a treat, how rich a banquet for the half-starved fancy to wander with the great enchanter among the shadowy aisles, the faintly seen archets of those great dew-drenched ancient trees, to see him conquer the unconquerable one, foil the prime victor over human kind, touching the dry dust, and making it re-assume the forms of those "Daughters of the Gods,"[17] making us reach across the centuries, and awaking them out of their nameless graves, with the sleep of many ages still heavy on their long-closed eyelids, making us behold them, shining in the noonday rays of his strong imagination, more perfectly, flawlessly fair, more absolutely free from mortal stain or blemish, than when first they ravished the eyes of their demigod lovers! I could babble on, on this theme, for ever: it opens out such long lines of thought. I am not Tennyson, as I need hardly inform anyone who has got thus far. I am also pretty sure that I am not possessed of that greatest of gifts, a poetic soul,—in its creative power coming next (though at an immeasurable distance) to God Himself. But, for all that, I too have, this night, had a "Dream of Fair Women." My fair women were not celebrated ones, though. The world never heard, never will hear of them. Indeed, there is nothing for it to hear. Their voices were too low and gentle to be audible above its dull roar. But none the less for that are they pleasant visitants. Nor are they only dream-faces bending over me, in their evanescent intangible bloom, as I lie on my bed, and, when morning dawns, leaving only a vague unreal impression of something far pleasanter than the work-a-day world of realities affords. No, they are real flesh-and-blood faces; the faces of the women who, at different times, in different relations of

15 Tennyson, "Œnone" (1832), ll. 70-71.

16 Tennyson, *Guenevere*, in *Idylls of the King* (1859), l. 545.

17 In "A Dream of Fair Women" (1832), Tennyson describes Helen of Troy as "A daughter of the gods, divinely tall,/ And most divinely fair" (ll. 87-88).

life, have influenced and moulded my destiny. Rather should I say that, in an inner chamber of my spirit, I have a secret picture-gallery. None enters there but myself;[18] small beauty would a stranger see, perchance, in some of those woman portraits. Some of my pictures were painted many years ago; some have been slightly, poorly sketched, and their colours are getting *wishy washy* and blurred. Others glow with more vivid, liquid, melting hues, every time I look upon them. But the gem of the collection has been hung there but a short time. The paint is hardly dry yet. Often I stand before that girl image, and gaze and gaze till my eyes ache and burn, in the intensity of my longing that those lips should unclose but *once* again, for one little minute; should just say *one* word, whether cross or kind, or cruel or tender, would make but small difference, so as it were conveyed by that obstinately silent voice. But they never do. They never will again, though I should gaze till my eyes shrank up in their sockets—till their light were quenched for aye. O dead woman! you have caught his speechlessness from your grim bridegroom, Death. My case is not an uncommon one, I think, if that could console me. She was everything to me, and I was less than nothing to her; and now she is dead, and I *must* talk about her to some one. I will tell the simple story of her short life. I do not want her to be forgotten, though now there has been for twelve months past a small white tablet, with a marble lily drooping broken upon it, among the knightly brasses, the cold "Hic jacets"[19] of the gray old church where so many Chesters are sleeping. But let no one be afraid that I shall make an elegy of this life. Let no one dread a long threnody, breathing despair, with tears in every line. I do not despair. I know so *surely*, I am so utterly persuaded, that it is *well.*

CHAPTER II

O, THE sea, the sea! The unpalling, the opal-coloured, the divine! What a thing a sea-place is in the summer weather! What does it matter if it is the most frightful collection of unsightly houses that ever disgraced a low coast—if dreary flats, than which nor pancakes nor flounders could be

---

18 Broughton may be echoing the Duke in Robert Browning's "My Last Duchess" (1842), who says of the jealously guarded portrait of his last wife "none puts by/ The curtain I have drawn for you, but I" (ll. 9-10).

19 Here lies (Latin); common epitaph on tombstones.

flatter, stretch away behind it, flank it on either side; if not the most abortive attempt at a tree is to be had, for love or money, within a circle of ten miles round it? What matter if it is crammed to overflowing with shopkeepers garmented in the brightest of their own wares (no great drawback to my mind), for why should not the poor souls disport themselves as well as we, though *we* are vessels made of the finest porcelain clay, while they are nothing but common red delft? But anyhow, have not we got the dear, dear sea, and what can we want beside? What more do our eyes desire to light on, except perhaps the unfailing row of white bathing-machines,[20] standing unsteadily on ricketty red wheels in various stages of paralysis, waiting to jolt down with us into the cool waters that look so caressing in their greenness? I appeal to everybody—which of our short joys since can, for a moment, be compared to the utter bliss, in one's child-days, of that arrival towards the end of some long June day, together with one's brethren, at one's poky seaside lodgings, where the six weeks of midsummer holidays went by like a morning dream? In spirit I see myself again, my small body clothed in a paletot[21] of railway dust, my nurses groaning under a forest of wooden spades, laden with dozens of holland[22] frocks warranted to resist the combined action of sand and salt water. How much, how deceptively sweeter the bread and butter tasted than in the despised nursery at home! What delicacy at any aldermanic banquet since has equalled the flavour of those goggle-eyed shrimps? And then to go to bed with a smell of seaweed in one's button-nose, and the boom of the sea in one's sleepy ears, and have beatific visions of such cockle-shells as the real world does not dream of.

Of the few people who know Pen Dyllas, most have an ill word for that small, dull, North-Wales watering-place. Innocent of band is it. Neither parade nor pier can it show, and its one pleasure-boat is generally looked upon with a suspicious eye as being liable to the imputation of unseaworthiness. It seems to me to be like a modest young person, totally eclipsed, annihilated by its exceedingly full-blown elder sister, ugly Ryvel—all lodging-houses and dust and glare. Poor little place! It is only a child of two years old, and not a well-grown, well-thriven child either. A few clumsy strokes will make a very sufficient drawing of it. Two rows of

20 Roofed wooden carts in which swimmers changed into their bathing suits, and which could be rolled into the water to allow their occupants to wade in discreetly.
21 Overcoat.
22 Linen fabric, originally from Holland, used in children's clothing.

narrow slight houses gaze at each other placidly across a street, which has only lately been metamorphosed into a street from a little-traveled country road. There the portraits of groups of hatted Welshwomen[23] on the letter-paper in the window of the librarian, stationer, and toy-merchant, stare calmly all day long at the one drab crinoline[24] swinging sportively in the breeze outside the door of the mercer, grocer, and ironmonger opposite. Walk on but a few steps further and you come to that set of first-class residences (as the advertising placard thinks them) which rejoice in the martial name of Inkerman-terrace.[25] Pin for pin alike are those bow-windowed houses; lucky are they in that they have no *vis-à-vis*[26] across the road to overlook them. If they were not so entirely shadeless they would be perfect, at least so say the widowed ladies who own them. There Breadalbane House and its titled neighbours look with dignified repose into a green field, where feeble cricket tries to get itself played, sometimes by two efficient elevens of one long young man and three small boys.[27] Then comes the rail-way, where luggage-trains drag their weary length, and where expresses flash by at night like some dark fabulous beast, with vague shape and far-seen glowing eyes, rushing roughly into the sleeper's dreams. And last, come the wind-blown broad sand-flats, where the tide goes out so absurdly far as to give one the idea of hiding itself somewhere round the corner out of sight.

Grand days, as to weather, come to despised Pen Dyllas as well as to finer places, and one had come on the 16th of June 186-. The sun blazed away in his rare glory,—rare in these rainy isles,—and held out unconcealed threats of sunstroke to any who ventured too impudently into his kingly presence. But in his very fierceness there was benevolence, and nobody was afraid of him. Every ray of light which turned the shabby lodging-house carpets into cloth of gold, every mignonette-sweetened little breeze which stirred the scanty lodging-house curtains, said as plain as could be, "Come out, come out, and be happy." The birds said the same;

---

23 Rural Welsh women traditionally wore hats with a flat brim and tall crown.

24 The 1860s was the heyday of the crinoline, a wide, circular steel cage over which women draped their skirts.

25 In the Crimean War, British and French forces defeated the Russians at the Battle of Inkerman (1854).

26 Opposite (French).

27 Each of the two teams in a game of cricket is supposed to have eleven players. Evidently these teams are undersupplied.

at least they turned it into an anthem, and sang it with a full choir. But it certainly was meltingly hot. The woody hills behind quiet Aber Fynach town were so drowsy that now, at mid-day, they were sleeping soundly, hazy, purple-hollowed, and the road trailed itself along like a dusty white snake.

The same course of reasoning brought everybody to the same conclusion. "It is too bakingly hot for a long walk. Let us go to the shore." And so on the shore, towards half past twelve o'clock, you might have seen all the élite of Pen Dyllas drinking in the faint ocean wind, thirstily, thriftily, as if afraid of wasting any, and saying in their hearts that God was good. There young men threw stones by thousands and never hit anything; did not intend to, they would have averred, if you had asked them. There muslin-clad damsels paddled daintily with their fingers in little sea-pools and miniature lagoons, and fished out infinitesimal bits of seaweed, and small green crabs, actively unwilling, or filled little fancy baskets with ugly, worthless, dingy stone, changed in the crucible of the imagination into agates, and onyxes, and amethysts. There old people tottered, and basked, and the great sun-god warmed even their froggy old blood for a bit. And they looked out rheumy-eyed, over the sea, and pondered, perhaps, on its everlastingness—in its perpetual change, defying change—in contrast to their own short tether. Pondered much, more probably, on their gout, and their port wine, and their knitting, and their grandchildren. And those grandchildren dug, and squabbled, and got coated with dirt, and bored their adoring relatives, after the manner of such small deer.

One group did not precisely come under any of these heads, but, I think, it was enjoying itself as much as any. It was a very small group, consisting of only two persons. Lovers, of course? Well, no. Not exactly. The first person was a white Pomeranian dog, with the face of a fox, with an excitable temperament, a great deal of fluffy hair, and a tail rather resembling a prolonged rabbit's scut.[28] This said hound was smelling, with scientific enjoyment, at a delicious heap, composed of sea-tangle, rotten wood, and dead starfish. The other person was a young woman, sitting very comfortably on the shingle, all alone. She was not in any peculiarly graceful attitude; in fact, ease seemed to have been more in her thoughts than elegance, when she chose her position. Her hat was pulled down à la highwayman, very low over her eyes, to balk the sun's inquisitiveness

28 Stubby tail.

(it rather whetted other people's curiosity, by the by, which she might or might not have been aware of, I would not say which); and her hands were holding each other tight round her knees. N.B.[29] Being innocent of gloves, they were in process of being dyed a good rich oak colour.

Not a beauty, this young woman. She would cut but a sorry figure amongst a set of straight-featured, lily and rose fair ones. A face that there would be about a thousand different opinions of, and perhaps not one altogether commendatory or approbative. Yet, for some reason or other, Kate Chester was a girl that men were apt to look twice at: whom some looked at once too often for their peace of mind. Now for an inventory of her few charms; which, somehow, did the work of other people's many. Olivia's description of herself in Shakespeare's *Twelfth Night*,—"Two gray eyes, item, two lips indifferent red,"[30] &c., will not serve here. A great deal, though no miraculous quantity, of bright hair; bright, without a speck of gold near it. Neither wholly red nor wholly brown, were those well-plaited locks. Brown was, of the two, their predominant hue, with just a dash of red to keep them warm and a-glow. They could have been easily matched out of the dead leafy treasures that autumn scatters in a dank wood. Very, very low down, faultily low, some good judges said, they grew on a fairly white brow, and thence went off, crisply, fuzzily, in a most unaffected wave. Big green eyes, rather deeply put in; not peculiarly luminous or eloquent, on ordinary occasions; rather soft, not very; but which when the torch of passion should light up their green depths, would (you felt sure) have power to look through and through you; would follow you about, perhaps, as the eyes of some well-limned pictures do. A small turn-up nose, much animadverted on by contemporary girls (what a handle that inquisitive little feature did give to Kate's adversaries!) Well, it did defy all rules, certainly, but then it never got red. Cheeks pale, not very apt at blushing prettily; mouth came under the head of the wide, full-lipped, smiling, but with a good deal of lurking gravity, and an immensity of latent, undeveloped passion in some of the curves it fell into. Laughing innocent lips that seemed to expect life to be one long pleasant jest. Such as this face was, it was nicely set on a warm, round throat, like a pillar (only that a pillar is cold), as unlike a swan's as one thing could be unlike another.

Now for Kate's figure. I do not think it was exactly of the cut of

29 Nota bene: note well, take note (Latin).

30 Inexact, *Twelfth Night* (first printed 1623), I.v.247.

the Venus de Medici,[31] but, for all that, it always seemed to me rather ensnaring to the fancy, in its partridge-like plumpness, soft undulating contours, and pretty roundnesses; so removed from scragginess, and free from angles. Many *women* affirmed that it was too full, too developed for a girl of twenty. The Misses M'Scrag, whose admirers might have sat with comfort in the shade cast by their collar-bones, were particularly stiff on this point; but no *man* was ever yet heard to give in his adhesion to this feminine fiat. Anyhow the light did seem to fall lovingly, as in the case of the "Gardener's Daughter," on "the bounteous wave of such a breast as never pencil drew,"[32] and on the waist—no marvel of waspish tenuity, but naturally healthily firm and shapely.[33] Her common little blue and white cotton gown draped the pretty shoulders and bust, and expressed them as well as a grander garment would have done. She and it were on good terms, did each other good service, and became one another very satisfactorily. There she sat, lazy, happy, passive; a pretty patch of blue on the gray stones.

Lamb[34] says that he has tried reading out of doors in a sunny garden, and has found it only a pretence, a thing impossible of accomplishment; and such seemed to have been Kate's case, for her book was tossed down by her side, and an inquisitive little gust was turning over the leaves, as if it too was interested in the story, and wanted to see what the end was. But it was only appearances that were against Kate. She had read every word of it without skipping; had come to "Finis" about five minutes ago, and had very barely escaped the degradation of crying over the last page. Her book was one that, I think, few people were willing to put down when once they had taken hold of it. It grasped the attention, and held it prisoned in a sweet detention, and its name was Whyte Melville's *Interpreter*.[35] Kate had just been reading with rather a lump in her throat, how, when the sacristan opened the door of the De Rohans' vault, the gentle breeze went in with him, into that grim charnel-house, and "stirred the heavy silver fringe on the pall of Victor's coffin." Those few words had a sort of fascination for

31 Famous Greek statue of a nude Aphrodite (the Roman Venus), goddess of love.

32 Tennyson, "The Gardener's Daughter" (1842), ll. 138-39.

33 Unlike most Victorian women, Kate is apparently not wearing a corset.

34 Charles Lamb (1775-1834), famous essayist.

35 1858 novel about the Crimean War by Scottish writer George Whyte-Melville (1821-78).

Kate. Her brain was passively recipient of the idea they conveyed, and her deep eyes looked out over the water, full of a girl's speculations.

"Poor Victor! poor Victor!" she thought; and then she tried mentally to project herself into the situation of the wretched, remorseful Frenchwoman, the coquette whose penitence came too late; the frail wife, whose heart was lying by the cold heart of the gallant young Hungarian noble. "I would not have treated him so; at least I do not think so, and yet who knows what I might do, if I were a great beauty and a princess like her? Some say that virtue is only absence of temptation. Bah! That is a hateful, godless maxim, worthy of Rochefoucauld.[36] I suppose that he got his idea of woman's character from studying Madame de Longueville's excellences.[37] But I wonder, now, is love such an irresistible power, such an all-conquering influence (the greatest of human influences), as they make out in books like this, or is it an odd sort of pleasant dangerous drunkenness that one is well rid of? Well, it is evident that I do not know much about it practically, or I could not analyze it so coolly. Could I, Tip? Now, where is that misguided dog gone? Tip, Tip, Tip!" And she broke off the thread of her reflections short, to throw a very small stone, weakly, at Tip, who appeared to be coming to a decided difference of opinion with another *dog errant*,[38] whose taste for dead starfish, &c., clashed with his own. "I cannot but think that there are plenty of other enjoyments that would fill one's life quite as well, and sufficiently, and a good deal more peaceably, without any of those dreadful hot and cold fits that one is subject to in typhus fever and love. Why, there are so many things in this world that are positively delicious, that have no more to say to love than I have to that Bluecoat boy[39] over there. The very fact of being alive and well and breathing this sea-breeze ought to satisfy any rational creature. Look at me now. I have done very well without love, at least love in that technical sense, without this fine passion, for twenty years, and I do not see why I should not do it for twenty years more. That is rather a pretty girl, and the man is not unlike a gentleman. They were the people that sat before us in church last Sunday. They are bride and bridegroom, I'm sure; for they

36 François, Duc de la Rochefoucauld (1613-80), author of a collection of aphorisms entitled *Maximes*.
37 The unhappily married Anne de Longueville (1619-79) fell in love with the Duc de la Rochefoucauld (see previous note) who eventually abandoned her.
38 A play on "knight errant," or questing knight found in chivalric romance.
39 Students at English charity schools wore long blue coats.

had only one prayer-book between them, and it had an ivory back. What absurdly false pictures novels do give one of love, the drawings they make of it are so out of perspective! They represent it as the one main interest of life, instead of being, as it mostly is, a short unimportant little episode. I declare it is enough to give one a disgust for the whole concern. I do believe it is one great imposture, one of those old well-established lies that the world will go on believing. Ah, yes; mine is the right view. What a pity that I cannot get anybody to agree with me! *Juste ciel!*[40] what an exhibition of Magenta stockings!

'Oh, wad some power the giftie gi'e us,
To see oursels as others see us!'[41]

Well, if it did, there would be a great many more suicides in the world than there are at present. Yes, I am wiser than the rest of the world. Wiser than Dante and Shakespeare, and Tennyson perhaps? Ah, by the by, that is the rub! Do Juliet, and Imogene, and Francesca of Rimini, and Fatima talk nonsense?[42] If they do, I would rather have their nonsense than any other people's sense. Yes, yes, after all I do believe they are pretty nearly right. Love must be the one great bliss of this world, though I know nothing about it. I wonder what it feels like? Perhaps that great bliss will never come to me; most likely not. I never yet saw the man who could arouse it. Did not I, though? I am not so sure of that. I may as well keep to truth, now I am alone. I wonder was Victor anything like Colonel Stamer? Oh, no—not a bit. Victor was light, and about six times as good-looking. Dear me, how silly! And how disgracefully hungry the sea makes one. Why, it is one o'clock, and shall not I get a homily from old Piggy for being late?"

Up she jumped on this reflection and took off herself, her cotton gown, and her Pomeranian dog, at a pretty quick rate, with her thoughts divided between love in the abstract and luncheon in the concrete, and followed at her departing by the admiring eyes, the utterly-approving gaze, of a retired grocer and a brace of attorney's clerks.

40 Good Heavens! (French).

41 Robert Burns, "To a Louse" (1786), ll. 43-44.

42 An assortment of romantic heroines. Shakespeare's Juliet from *Romeo and Juliet* (first printed 1597) is joined here by his Imogene from *Cymbeline* (first printed 1623); Francesca da Rimini, who whirls endlessly in hell with her lover in Dante's *Inferno* (first printed 1314), is the subject of a poem by Byron (1820) which Kate reads later; Fatima, the speaker of a Tennyson poem (1833), details her erotic response to her lover.

Poor little Kate! she looked cheery and light-hearted enough now, one would say; and yet, but two years ago, she had vehemently protested, and firmly believed, that she never, *never* could feel happy again in this world; it was nonsense to suppose that she could. That was in one of those brain-rending moments which one wonders afterwards, curiously, how one could live through,—which one never could live through and be sane if a blessed numbness were not sent us to wrap our senses in,—when she had pressed her warm quivering lips, half shrinking from the clayey contact, but resolute in despairing, detaining affection, on her mother's dead brow, whose cold would but feebly be compared to polar ice or statued marble. She had taken it as an insult, and spoken out angrily in answer, when some pitying friend had hinted to her that part-agonising part-soothing truth, that time would dull her anguish, would bring her comfort. "Comfort!" she said, scornfully; "comfort must be the result of forgetfulness," and she did not want to forget. She would rather be miserable for ever than that. And then, too, she had prayed more ardently than she had ever supplicated any boon before that she might die also. Selfish, cruel mortal! She would have dragged that lost one back out of those welcoming skyey gates if she had had the power. But God was more merciful. He took the poor patient mother, very suffering, very world-weary, to Himself, and gave her rest, and left the little daughter to toil and moil and weep for yet a little space—*but* a little one, before His messenger came to fetch her too. And the sun shone, and the birds sang, and the mignonette on Mrs. Chester's grave sent up a sweet message from earth to heaven, from the resting-place of the dead woman's tired body to the resting-place of the living woman's satisfied soul; and before the crape on her dress had grown shabby, Kate had begun to laugh again very heartily, had begun to care whether her black gown fitted well or not, and would have shuddered and trembled sorely if she had seen near her the mower with his scythe whom she had invoked in the madness of her grief.

CHAPTER III

EVERYBODY at Pen Dyllas dined at one. That was one of the manners and customs of the place. Such an idea as a late dinner had never entered their primitive heads. Everybody was dining now, and what was more, almost everybody was dining on mutton; for does not the sheep seem to be, *par excellence*, the beast of Wales? In almost every house down Inkerman-terrace some self-sacrificing mother was *sawing* away at a neck, or a saddle, or a leg, trying to make it go satisfactorily the round of the ten children, and feasting on the cat's bit herself. In Breadalbane House there was mutton too, and to judge by the smell, it seemed to have been walking up and down the stairs all the morning, and paying a good long visit to each of the bedrooms in turn. Whatever it had been doing with itself all morning, however, there is no doubt that at the particular moment I allude to, it had just been set down on the parlour-table by a damsel, preëminent among women for the dirtiness of her fingers, the dilapidation of her wardrobe, and the exceeding Welshness of her tongue. Very slovenly and unappetising did the banquet look, after the manner of lodging-houses, and the family were gathering round the table languidly, ungreedily, for really the weather was too broiling for any viands less etherial than ambrosia and claret-cup;[43] and the flies were a great deal hungrier, and ate a great deal more than the Christians. There were places and nasty dull pewter forks for five, but only four were at present in possession. At the bottom of this social board, with his back to the cut-paper-adorned fireplace, anatomising the late so-active Welsh leg, sat the Reverend Josiah Piggott, black-coated, clerical, flabby-faced. He was not a handsome man, certainly. I have seldom seen one less so; but two or three very handsome men might have been made out of him, for there was fleshy material enough in the vast acreage of his mild pendulous cheeks, in the bone-work of his portentous hooked nose, for several very good-looking countenances, if they could but be made up differently. Those who believed in the uncomfortable Pythagorean theory of the transmigration of souls[44] were much impressed with the idea that the spirit of the Reverend Piggott had but recently evacuated the body of a well-fattened south-down.[45] Even those who were sceptical as to this notion could not fail to remark that in the sound of Mr. P.'s speech there was an undeniable kinship to a *baa*. Opposite to him, employed in the distribution of the fly-haunted salad, sat Mrs. Josiah Piggott, the partner of his joys, who, report said, had once been a fair enough woman to look upon. She was rather haggard and mahogany-

43 Claret-cup was a punch made with red wine, lemon, sugar, and carbonated water; ambrosia (in Greek mythology the food of the gods) is a fruit salad.

44 Pythagoras, Greek mathematician and philosopher (ca. 569-490 BCE), purportedly believed in the migration of souls from one body to another.

45 Breed of sheep raised for mutton.

coloured now, and in a chronic state of weariness from the requirements of her exacting old incubus, who had put himself on the sick-list exactly twenty years ago, and resolutely refused to get off it again. And yet, even though his best friends could not deny that he was unto them a very grievous bore, let it be clearly understood that he was in the main as worthy and benevolent and harmless an old south-down as ever waddled along in fleecy unwieldiness. Now for the sides of the table. On one side, then, ruling over the potatoes, sat Margaret Chester, Kate's elder by three or four years. An elegant-looking young woman, people called her,—a vague term of approbation, I always think,—very fragile, and more ladylike than three-fourths of the well-bred women one might see in a county ball-room, with a figure whose exaggerated slenderness, and the tenuity of the 17-inch wasp-waist, was not ungraceful in morning-dress, but which displayed very unmistakably that want of development which is so grievous and common a fault among English girls. However, everyone to his taste. The Americans, attenuated by hot rooms and incessant dancing and sweetmeat-eating, condemn our British beauty as being too much of the coarse and dairy-maid type. I have heard people say that Margaret's figure was more refined than Kate's. If that be the case, a skeleton's was more refined still. To continue: Miss Chester was gifted with that sort of nice-lookingness, arising principally from a passable nose, inoffensive eyes, and a rather clear unmixed complexion, which approaches very near the boundary-line of prettiness, and sometimes passes over it. After all, it is difficult to be very ugly when one is young. *Vis-à-vis* to her, with his soul absorbed in helping himself to cauliflower, sat Blount Chester,—a long-legged, loose-jointed, thoroughbred-looking hobbledehoy, ridiculously like Kate, only with an expression of even more utter bliss and jubilation in the very fact of animal existence than hers on his jolly wide mouth, which seemed to have made itself yet wider by chronic laughter.

"Dear ma," bleated the Reverend Piggott,—Mrs. Piggott was not his mother, but his wife; but he called her "dear ma" by reason of their joint right of proprietorship in a precocious young gentleman of fourteen, at present honouring one of England's public schools with his company,—"Dear ma, shall I give you a little bit of this mutton? I'm afraid it does not look very nice, though I bought it myself. Now, my dear love, I'll tell you what I did: I went down to the market, and I made the man cut if off before me himself; and I told him my name, and I told him to send it up to Breadalbane House; but I'm sure, dear ma, that this is not the same one that I chose—it is not nearly so fat. These tradespeople are so dishonest. Which day was it that I walked all the way down to the market? Don't you remember, my love? It was that day that I was so terribly giddy going up to bed."

Whether it was the leg of his choice or another, Mrs. Piggott signified her intention of partaking of it. The other two did the same; so that for some little time his slow plump hands had to continue their cannibal occupation of dissecting a brother's limb.

"My love," he began again, when his duties were ended, "do you think I could eat a little bit of mutton? I am afraid I am not very hungry; my head is not very well." And he patted the sandy-brown hair that scantily covered his eminently respectable pate compassionately. "I have been a good deal worried all morning, writing business-letters; and I wanted you very much, dear ma, to consult you about Mrs. Barton's business. I called for you all over the house, but I could not find you anywhere. It tired me a good deal; but of course that did not matter much," he said with flabby plaintiveness.

"Indeed, love, I'm very sorry," said Mrs. Piggott, penitent yet cheery; "but I assure you I was only away ten minutes on the shore, with Maggie, looking for onyxes; that was all, indeed, pappy."

"It was not ten minutes," said Maggie indignantly; "it was only eight and a half, for I looked at the clock as we came in; and we ran all the way from the post-office. Have you been to bathe to-day, Blount?" she continued rapidly, with great presence of mind, bent on stemming the current of Mr. Piggott's laments, across the table to her brother, who was grinning covertly at his revered relative.

"I should think so," said he expressively. "My good girl, you really should reflect before you ask such silly questions. What other way of improving the shining hours in this gay Babylon is there except dabbling them away in the water? Why, I swam right round in front of the ladies' bathing-place. I thought you'd be sure to see me; and I kicked up my heels, and made a tremendous splashing in hopes you'd think I was drowning."

"Promising, amiable youth!" Maggie said, with an affectionate smile (I'm sure I don't know why, or for what remarkable virtues his sisters adored that young scamp so); "but you might have saved yourself the trouble, for really I was so hot and cross that I don't think I should have cared much if you had been."

"Should you not? Well, that's the sensiblest speech I've heard you make for many a day. I say, what a set of idiots they are about here! They cannot swim a stroke, one of them. What's become of Kitty, the flower of Dunblane? By the bye, now I come to think of it, her name was not Kitty; it was Jessie."[46]

"I don't know," said Miss Chester indifferently. (They were not a family that made much fuss about one another; never called one another "dear," and only kissed, as a great ceremony, when setting off or on returning from a journey.) "She went out after breakfast with a book, and Tip went with her; so I don't suppose she can have come to any harm."

"Perhaps she has eloped with that red-headed youth that she admired so much yesterday—I always tell that girl that her levity will bring her to some fearful end—or perhaps the tide has washed her away," said Blount, without emotion at the idea of either catastrophe. "Well, if she prefers the sad sea waves to her dinner, it's her business, not mine, however much I may deplore her infatuation."

A few more bleats, a few more words, a few more mouthfuls of mutton, and then a running upstairs was heard, and a young person in a blue-cotton gown came quickly in, rather hot, rather flushed, and a little bit cross in consequence.

"My love," was Mr. Piggott's meekly hortatory greeting, "I wish you could manage to be in proper time of a day; you know, love, how much I like punctuality and order, and that I don't allow any irregularity in my house. Do you hear, my love? Don't let it occur again."

"Early dinner is an institution that ought to have been abolished at the Christian era," replied his dutiful niece, throwing off her hat, and sinking exhausted into her chair.

"Hear, hear!" said Blount, rubbing his hands approvingly.

"It's a remnant of paganism," continued Kate, half-laughing, but cross still; "a disgrace to a civilised country. I wish someone would set up a Society for the Suppression of Early Dinners; I would be chairman or secretary with all the pleasure imaginable."

"I'd be bottle-holder," cried Blount with excitement, "By the bye, that's a mixture of metaphors."

Poor Mr. Piggott collapsed, silenced by the anathemas obliquely launched at him. Well he knew that it was for his "stomach's sake, and his

46 "Jessie, the Flower of Dunblane" is a famous Scottish folk song with words by Robert Tannahill (1774-1810).

often infirmities," like St. Timothy's of old,[47] that the daily banquet was so prematurely spread. Never from his partner's meek lips did he hear such rough language.

And then, having discharged the little darts of her ill-humour, Kate relapsed into amiability; tried fruitlessly with warm white fingers to pat into tidiness and smoothness the hopelessly erratic locks of her dead-leaf hair, and telegraphed across the table to the sympathetic and responsive Blount a *moue*[48] intended to be very ugly, and witheringly derisive of her unconscious adversary.

And then the father of the flock lifted up his voice, and baaed as follows:

"My dear loves, is not this the day that our kind friends, Sir Guy and Lady Stamer, invited us to dine with them? I hope, dear mamsey, that you kept the note, that there may be no mistake?"

"Yes, love," responded the female Piggott, "it is the day. By the bye, girls, which of you two is coming with us?"

"Maggie," said Kate.

"Kate," said Maggie. Both very promptly.

"Of course you will go," said Maggie.

She was looked upon by her friends and the public in general as a passing, lively, light-hearted individual; for after all what do one's friends or the public either know about one? But in private she was much given to fits of despondency when reflecting on Kate's dealings with her; and, indeed, heretofore she had not been very lucky.

"Of course you will go; you are one of those people whom fortune always favours. You always get everything you want."

"Get everything I want!" said Kate, in a high key of surprise and indignation. "I don't know what you mean. Why, if I got everything I wanted, do you suppose I should be sitting here now, eating cold mutton, and have this horrid old blue garment on? Not exactly!"

"Well, there are degrees of unluckiness," said Maggie in a despondent tone; "you may not be particularly fortunate in the abstract, but, compared to me, you are a prodigy of good luck."

"I'll tell you what you shall do, my children," suggested Blount, with a parental air; "you shall draw lots, and I'll hold them for you. I'll hold them quite fair, without fear or favour; I promise I will. You know, so exactly

47 See 1 Timothy 5:23.

48 Pout (French).

are my affections balanced, that I don't care a straw which of you comes; and, in fact, it won't kill me if neither of you do."

"No, no," cried Kate, clasping her little dimpled hands quite tragically on his shoulder, "indeed you sha'n't; I always draw the shortest lot, and I'm sure you'd cheat me."

"My good Kitty," he said, "cast one more slur upon my probity, and I shall be compelled to box your ears. Well, if you persist in distrusting the best of brothers, let uncle Piggott hold them; you cannot suspect him."

But Kate would not consent. She longed with such surprising intensity—surprising even to herself—for this trifling pleasure, that she could not bear to risk it on such a dangerous chance. And yet dinner-parties generally were a decided *gêne*[49] to her. Low within her soul she marvelled why Margaret could not yield to her without saying any more about it. What could it be to her? and she felt almost spiteful towards the sister who would thus stand in her light. Somehow she could not eat any more of her fast-cooling mutton after that question was mooted, and her heart beat foolishly against its blue-cotton covering.

O dear, O dear! what should she do, if she should be left at home to-night in these close dull lodgings, with nothing to do but to picture to herself Margaret sitting listening—pleased, animated, flattered—to a certain deep man's voice, in whose tones she, poor fool, was beginning to find an odd sort of magic, of power to chase away all pain, and to evoke such great, such utter bliss as she had not begun to taste till now—such as she began now thirstily to long to take deep satisfying draughts of? How suprisingly bitter it was to imagine Maggie, by her jokes and little piquant fast speeches, calling up laughter and amusement into a certain dark strong face, which had begun of late to look into the still, private places of her soul as never man's face had looked before! Even if Margaret did not snare the fancy of the owner of that face (as it was sadly possible she might), yet at all events she would have the privilege of being near him, of hearing him talk to other people—would have her fortunate fingers prisoned for one sweet second in his broad hand. O dear, O dear! it made her hot and cold in a minute to think of it; and she pushed away her plate, and drummed a dreary little tune on the table with her fingers to get rid of some small portion of her unpleasant, silly excitement. Certainly it is possible to love one's sister very dearly, and yet at times to wish honestly

49 Annoyance (French).

that Providence had awarded her a cast in the eye or a crooked nose.

Then came comfort in a most unwonted, unlooked-for form: the voice of Mr. Piggott, who spoke slowly (for his utterance was always rather impeded by the fact of his tongue being a size or so too large for his mouth) as follows:

"Do you know, my love, I have been thinking that, if you could make an excuse for me to our kind friends, perhaps it really would be better for me to stay at home. You know, dear ma, I'm not very fond of the night air, and I think the jolting of the carriage would not do my head any good. So, if you please, my love, I think you shall go without me; and if I feel well enough, you know, I can take a little stroll along the shore this evening, if I take my time, and don't hurry myself too much. Don't you think so, my dear love?"

"Yes, love, I daresay you could."

Maggie jumped up, and clapped her hands impulsively.

"My dear Kate," she said, laughing, "let us embrace; we were on the very verge of hating each other, but uncle Piggott's most judicious suggestion has restored peace to our souls, has not it? There's no need for drawing lots now, Blount, dear boy, because we can both go."

"So much the worse," said Blount unfeelingly; "so much less room for me in the carriage."

"I daresay it will be so much the worse for me, too," replied Margaret, as a recollection of how Fate usually behaved to her came over her; "the chances are a thousand to one that, as usual, nobody will take the slightest notice of me. Of course I shall enact my usual *rôle* of foil to you all evening, Kate—Leah and Rachel over again.[50] I wonder has anybody any idea how tired I am of being Leah. I suppose if I were amiable, I should enjoy it; but as it is, I certainly don't."

"Absurd!" said Kate, with brevity.

But for all that, she was as much relieved as if she had been reprieved from hanging; and, in the satisfaction of her soul, could not help smiling broadly—showing the dear little dimples in her white cheeks—foolish as it was to be so glad about such a trifle.

"I suppose Colonel Stamer will be there?" remarked Blount

50 See Genesis 29: 15-31. Although Jacob serves his uncle Laban for seven years to earn the hand of his beautiful daughter Rachel, at the wedding Laban substitutes his plain elder daughter Leah for the promised bride. Jacob must work another seven years in order to marry Rachel.

meditatively.

"Probably," said Maggie; "I saw him driving through Aber Fynach this morning, with one of his sisters, looking as cross and bored—I wonder why men's sisters' society always has such a depressing effect upon them."

"It has not on me," said Blount, crossing his arms on the back of his chair, and reposing his smooth young chin on them; "at least, I struggle against it, because I know they are a necessary evil. Stamer's sisters are particularly aggravated cases; at least, they look so in church. I hate a person who never looks up from his book, and makes all the responses louder than the clerk."

"You certainly cannot make that complaint of him," said Maggie, laughing.

"No, I cannot. Do you know, my dear loves," he said, with a faint but perceptible mimicking of his uncle's voice, "that your little brother would give a good deal to be as strong as that fellow is? Why, he is about as broad as this room, and as hard as iron," he ended rapturously, turning to his sisters.

"What is the use of physical strength nowadays?" Maggie said contemptuously. "Jack-the-Giant-killer's day is over!"

"Well, there's something in that," replied the boy; "and yet it would be pleasant to think that you could knock down a fellow as soon as look at him, even if you don't mean to try."

"He has got an ugly face enough," said Maggie disparagingly.

"Hem!" answered Blount, "neither one thing nor the other, I should say. I've seen a good many better, and a great many worse; and besides, what does a man's *face* matter? I'd as soon have the face of an ourang-outang as any other, so as I had a good figure under it."

"Well, he is not much like an ourang-outang, whatever else he is like; in fact, I never saw any monkey look half so ill-tempered—they generally have a bland expression of countenance."

"I suppose he will be there," Blount said again. "I hope so, for I want to talk to him about that army tutor Phillips, you know, at Woolwich. Somebody told me he had been there."

"I *think* he will be there," Kate said in a very small demure voice, entering into the conversation for the first time since it had fallen upon Colonel Stamer, and sedulously turning away her head.

"And might I ask, my young friend, how *you* know?" said her brother, all but overbalancing his chair in his laudable endeavour to get a good view of her averted face; "are you the depository of that gallant officer's plans?"

"No—o," said Kitty, in confusion, "of course not; what stupid things you do say! But I happened to hear—"

"O!" interrupted the boy, jumping up in a sort of ecstasy, as a new and invaluable light dawned on him, "I see now. Well, I *was* slow of understanding. Of course, *now* I know why you were so unaccountably anxious to go to-night; it never struck me before—it actually never did! O Catherine, Catherine, why did not you confide in your brother?"

"That's the *last* confidant we should choose," said Margaret gaily; "isn't it, Kate?"

"My daughter, will you be so good as to turn your face this way?" resumed the unfeeling youth; and then, without saying anything, he called Margaret's attention to the fact very evident, though she was sitting with her back to the light, that Kate had suddenly undergone an unbecoming metamorphosis—being transformed from an unpainted garden lily into the gaudiest of gaudy peonies. She was made to look almost plain by the too generally diffused, too intense flush. It was one of the small family cruelties practised by the Chesters scrupulously to take notice of and point out each other's foolish, causeless blushes.

"I'm not blushing, Blount," asseverated the poor peony unwisely; it is to be hoped, for the sake of her veracity, that she believed what she said.

"Blushing!" said that young inquisitor, with an air of surprise and interest; "O, dear no! What made you think so? Who said you were?"

Then Kate rose up in her redness, and, half ashamed, half vexed, and yet half diverted (if there can be three halves in any whole), she ran round the table, and sprang upon him, soft-handed, boxed his ears, then fled out of the room quicker than the mild avuncular reproof could follow her.

And how did this most foolish of foolish virgins[51] spend most of the glorious June afternoon? Why, in trying which amongst her poor little assortment of head-gears and bracelets and brooches made her by their aid seem most comely. This would be a happy evening, she felt sure. She did not know why she thought so, but she knew it would; and so she would do her best to foil nature, and, in spite of all defects, would shine lovely

51 See Matthew 25: 1-13 for the parable of the five wise virgins who, unlike their five foolish compeers, are prepared for the unexpected arrival of the bridegroom, who symbolizes the second coming.

to-night, in one pair of eyes, that ought to have terrified her by the way in which, absent or present, they now pursued and persistently looked away her girl's soul. Of course she did not care much about the owner of those eyes, she remarked parenthetically to herself—they were nothing to her; but still he to whom they appertained was a person whom one might naturally and harmlessly desire to please. And so she figured before the glass; looked at herself frontways, sideways, backways; rubbed her cheeks to see whether she looked better red or white; and finally came down adorned as a flower-filleted victim, to be offered to one of the coarse bloody rulers of Olympus in the old pagan times.[52]

"My dear loves," was the substance of Mr. P.'s last *baa*, as they prepared to pack themselves into the fly,[53] "be sure you put on your cloaks, all of you, and fasten them well round your throats. You young people do not know how dangerous the night air is. As for you, dear ma, you must positively promise me to put your hood over your head when you come out of those hot rooms into the cold night air. Indeed, dear love, I cannot let you go unless you promise me this faithfully. And be sure you come back in good time, or I shall be getting very uneasy about you all. And I hope you will all enjoy yourselves, my dear loves; and be sure and make proper excuses to our kind friends for me; and good-bye, my dear loves."

CHAPTER IV

HOW I hate shams! And consequently, by correct logical deductions from my premises to my conclusions, how I hate Llyn Castle! For is not it a sham of shams? And it is the more to blame, because it ought to be, and might be, such a delectable place; nestling on the woody hill-side, looking over the leafy crown of its own spreading sycamores and beeches, out on the wide dark sea. Instead of which, it is a positive eye-sore; at least, to my fancy. A pseudo-castle, with mock towers[54] rising one above another on the well-timbered, crag-adorned slope. Ivy—that kind garment which

52 In Greek mythology Olympus is the home of the gods.

53 Light-covered carriage drawn by a single horse.

54 In the *DUM* the castle's towers are "mock Brummagem towers" (see Appendix B, p. 389); a corruption of "Birmingham," the name of a northern industrial city, "Brummagem" signified a gaudy affectation of gentility (the castle is a "sham of shams"). Although the Stamers are an old aristocratic family, they are associated nonetheless with the Industrial Revolution's *nouveaux riches*.

beautifies the ugliest wearer—had done its best for the wretched little pinchbeck[55] imitation of feudal grandeur, wrapping round it a wide, thick mantle of dark-green leaves, which grew wider and thicker every year. Inside, the house is not nearly so objectionable as one would have supposed, in one's just indignation at its deceptive exterior; and on this June evening, one would have said that there was not much fault to be found with the dining-room in particular towards half-seven o'clock. It looked comfort and luxury's self. Windows wide open; air flowing through them, coolly and revivingly, from the "flowering squares"[56] of the garden outside. The effigies of many dead Stamers—some who did evil in their day, some who did well—looked down, smiling graciously most of them, in their immovable serenity, from the well-covered walls. Ladies clad in such easy flowing loose robes that one wonders by what matchless ingenuity they got them to stick on at all; gifted all of them with those snowy, taper, impossible hands and arms which Sir Peter Lely bestows so lavishly on all the subjects of his pencil.[57] Those calm picture eyes were looking down now on such a scene as they once, no doubt, often took part in; a cheery scene enough, though common as common could be: a party of Englishmen and Englishwomen dining together, sociable, and hungry—refreshing themselves with pleasant food and pleasant drinks and pleasant chat, after the fatigues of the long hot day. How nice and inviting the table did look, to be sure, draped with snowy, well-bleached linen, shining with much well-polished plate, and with plenty of bright-hued, delicate china, beautiful to the eye, with great piled-up clusters of bloomy purple grapes, with pyramids of peaches and nectarines, and having at intervals, all down its length, big silver vases rough with sculptured figures, perfuming all the air with their heavenly load of roses, some crimson glowing, some passion-pale, of slender, feathery, hot-house ferns, and cool damp moss! How delightfully different from the dinner-table at Breadalbane House, whose sole adornment was the tumbledown cruet-stand, that never had anything in it! And then the servants—so numerous, so velvet-footed, so attentive—how different from Jane of the dirty fingers!

The Stamers were one of the hundred thousand British families who habitually live in clover, and make no more account of it than if it was mouldy hay; are not conscious, indeed, that it is clover, having been born

55 Cheap imitation.

56 See Tennyson, *In Memoriam* (1850), 115.3.

57 Dutch-born artist (1618-80) known for his portraits of English aristocrats.

and brought up in it. There, at half-past seven, this June evening, was sitting Sir Guy Stamer, bald-headed, *beaky*,[58] ill-natured; and there, too, was Lady Stamer, bald-headed, beaky, ill-natured; and there were the two Misses Stamer, beaky too, neither ill-natured nor good-natured—not bad sort of young women in the main, but, being London girls themselves, rather apt to look down with supercilious pity and oppressive condescension on those dark ones who led a benighted cabbage existence in the country all the year round. And there, too, was Guy Stamer, Esq., Sir Guy's hopeful son and heir, beaky also—for when beaks get into a family they generally run pretty nearly through it—good-natured, foolish, and horsey; and by him was sitting Kate Chester, with the expression of a small female martyr, and rather a sulky female martyr, on her highly discontented little features. Not a bit was she enjoying the luxurious room or the well-served dainty meats, so decidedly superior to the comfortless style in which she had been living lately,—so utterly displeased with her position as to be incapable of enjoying anything. Everybody else appeared so well satisfied, so calmly appreciatory of their dinner, each one so perfectly undesirous of changing places with anyone else. All but her. As for Blount, he was evidently quite in his element. That was a comfort, at all events, dear old fellow! He had got for his share of the spoil the second Miss Stamer, and had actually succeeded in warming that young lady up into a poor imitation of animation. In the intervals of the general hum of voices, she caught sometimes his jolly, cheery, young tones, talking pleasant, foolish nonsense, and Miss Augusta's faint, high-bred laugh approving him. And then, O cruel Fate! just over the way, as opposite as opposite could be, was sitting Colonel Dare Stamer, Sir Guy's troublesome younger son, an individual as unlike the rest of his family as could possibly be. To his share the lucky Margaret had fallen, by some mistake as to ages; and there he was, talking away to her, with that appearance of deep devotion and attention which he always made a habit of displaying towards his next-door neighbour, however little he might care about her; talking away rapidly and easily, not exactly in a whisper, but what fulfilled all the purposes of a whisper, in that nobody could catch a syllable of his remarks save the person to whom they were addressed. How different from Kate's neighbour! Everyone at table (had they thought it worth while to listen) could have heard every word of his speeches; and such stupid things as he said

58 Having an aquiline nose.

too! Such uninteresting subjects!—and nothing new about them either. How wrapped up Colonel Stamer did seem, in making himself agreeable to Margaret! "What can have come to him? Why, he has positively not looked across at me once, though he is only just opposite." And then, while trying to persuade herself that the hotness of her soup was the reason why she found such difficulty in swallowing it, Kate made an interesting discovery, and this discovery was, how intensely, how acutely pleasant it had become to her to be looked at by this stranger, whose name, heard three weeks before, would have awakened no ideas whatever in her mind. And then, while the servants were handing round the side-dishes, and she was constrained to say "No, thank you," every minute, there was revealed to her, within her soul, a bottomless depth, a wild, mad, reckless fervour of passion, which bid fair to blast all the life that lay before her, which had begun its blasting roar already, withering up all her little innocent joys with the furnace-breath of its fiery flame, taking the sap out of her girl's pleasures, and making them like the dry twigs on a tree whose principle of life is extinct. That muddy, polluted flood of earthly love (for is not all earthly love, even that of the purest woman, polluted with the taint of mortality?) had, with its bitter waters, swallowed up and choked the spring of higher, better love, which might have refreshed and watered her soul for the garden of God. O, idiot!—to make so losing a bargain with this dull, passing world.

And what sort of man was he who this day had been so lavishly gifted with a great dower of new-born, uncalculating passion? Did he deserve the rich present, or was Kate casting her soul's costly pearls before swine?[59] This is he. A man with just such a face as one often sees among human creatures, endowed with an ordinary degree of intellectual powers,—of the two, perhaps, leaning to the side of superior intelligence,—and with a big powerful figure; a figure deep-chested, clean-limbed, thin-flanked, that promised strength,—and strength he had—not such, indeed, as Samson's, whose giant gripe dragged down the solid stone pillars and the shrieking Philistine lords about his head, nor such as Guy Livingstone's, who, dying, could crush a massive silver cup between his moribund fingers;[60] but as

59 See Matthew 7:6: "Give not that which is holy unto the dogs, neither cast ye your pearls before swine, lest they trample them under their feet, and turn again and rend you."

60 Broughton compares Dare not only with Samson, legendary Biblical strongman (Judges 13-16), but with the protagonist of George Lawrence's highly popu-

much as—not being a prize-fighter by profession—he would be likely to require in his walk through life; arms long and sinewy, with the muscle—much developed in many a boxing-match, or many a cricket-field—rising in knotted cords upon them; and a great columnar throat. An ugly man, everybody said; those who had an eye for form added with enthusiasm, a magnificent-looking one. Children thought him hideous. A splendid physical conformation certainly. I do not know why it is, but one seldom finds a very lofty, very noble, or very holy mind inhabiting such a dark-haired head, rich in thick-growing, deep-brown locks, regulation cut; a head rather apt at towering stately over the heads of other men; penthouse brows that had been seen to scowl; dwelling under them, in their shadow, luminous dark eyes—eyes that could look very angry or very tender, but which ordinarily only looked rather lazily amused at things in general, seen through the eyeglass stuck into one of them; harsh, swart features, with the marks of the world's wear and tear upon them, brightened by no light reflected from a happier region, and a great, soft, black-brown moustache, drooping silkily. So much for what all men could see and judge of about him for his outside. Now for the stuff that he was made of inside, which it required more intimate knowledge to give an opinion of. Not a good man at all. A bad man, if tried by a high standard—that standard we shall all be tried by at last; measured and weighed by the world's weights and measures, a good fellow enough. O, the immeasurable distance between a good man and a good fellow! A dissipated, self-indulgent man, like all the other men in his set. One who walked along life's pathway with his eyes glued to the crumbling dust-heaps of the earth, instead of raised in glad expectancy and awed contemplation to those skyey chambers, built all of pure, untarnished gold, which are waiting for us above the sun and the moon and the stars. He might hug himself with the satisfactory reflection that, during the six lustres[61] of his existence, he had not done one atom of good to any human being, but, on the contrary, had done a good deal of harm: had broken one or two extra brittle woman-hearts; had dangerously cracked several others; all without much compunction. "Women," he used to say in his club (where he was listened to with the respect due to much experimental knowledge)—"women were fair game;" "and game very easily winged too," he sometimes subjoined. And yet in his soul he kept

lar *Guy Livingstone* (1857)—a moody, muscular sort who, even when dying from a hunting accident, crushes a silver cup with his bare hands.

61 A lustre is a period of five years; Dare is thirty.

a higher standard by which he measured just three or four of his female acquaintance, and found them of not deficient stature; but he was utterly unable rightly to estimate the worth of that best of God's creatures, a good woman, as a mole would be to descant on the radiance of the sun. That line might be well applied to him—

"Bid the hoarse chough becroak the moon."[62]

He had enjoyed, more than he would have cared to confess, making "*les yeux doux*"[63] at this little stranger maiden, whom fortune had sent to lessen the intense bore of vegetating in this dullest of dull holes, and for six weeks, as his affairs made it otherwise highly convenient that he should. By her aid he had begun to think that he might scramble on to the end, without cutting his valuable throat. The soft luxuriance of Kate's irregular style of beauty—for, after all, beauty of some kind or other she must have had—enthralled his senses a little. She pleased his sated taste more than he could have believed possible. And then she used to say such pleasant, fresh, diverting things, that she quite stimulated his jaded fancy. The point of view from which she looked at things was so different to his, that it really made her rather an interesting study.

Dare Stamer was not very much more conceited than men generally are. He knew he was tolerably successful, certainly. High-bred guardsman that he was, that ugly face of his did more execution than that of an Apollo Belvedere,[64] if country-bred, would have done. He had that thin coat of veneering, that much-prized polish, only to be acquired by habitually breathing the air of the upper ten thousand,[65] and which holds its own and carries the day with women, old and young, experienced and inexperienced, against more solid qualities.

I have said that Colonel Stamer was not more conceited than the generality of men; but notwithstanding, he had a moral conviction—and in this case a correct one—that a very few more tender speeches, a very few more ardent gazes on his part, would make Kate Chester desperately in

62 Owen Meredith (pseudonym of E.R.B. Lytton), *Tannhäuser* (1861), l. 849.

63 Amorous looks (French, literally "sweet eyes").

64 Famous Roman copy of a bronze Greek statue of the god of the sun, truth, and poetry.

65 Social elite; a term used by N. P. Willis to describe the upper crust of New York society.

love with him. It would be excessively pleasant, certainly, to have her desperately in love with him. Dear little thing! He had more than half a mind to say the two or three more tender speeches, to gaze the two or three more ardent gazes, that would have the effect of making her so. It would be well worth the expenditure of a good deal of time and trouble to have those great unusual-looking eyes droop under their white lids guiltily for him, and him only.

But then, on the other hand, Dare somehow felt mistily that this girl was not exactly like other girls. If this girl did love, it would be no trifle with her. There were wells of undeveloped passion in that young soul, whose depths his plumb-line could not fathom. She, he felt sure, was one of those who would think the world well lost for love.[66]

And so a good fit came over him, and he resolved to spare her. It was not his way, but he would do it this once,—"if he could," a man more diffident of himself would have added; but his own ability to do anything or forbear anything was what Dare Stamer never doubted. He would let her quite alone—leave her growing on her stalk, dear little fresh lily, till some lucky man should come by and gather her, and wear her with joy and pride, esteeming her the fairest flower that ever grew in the world's wide garden. As for him, he was too poor to indulge in such a sweet luxury, besides other reasons.

And so, with his good fit hot upon him, this self-denying hero tried to content himself with doing his best to make a fool of Margaret, nor looked once across at the little fresh lily he had renounced. And yet, though he did not look once, he knew and felt, with an odd sort of thrill which he had not indulged in for over ten years, exactly what aspect she wore as she sat there.

"Gowned in pure white, that fitted to the shape,"[67] soft-fleshed, soft-eyed, a doleful-feeling unconscious little siren, with one "heavy-folded rose"[68] stuck in by the artist-hand of love amongst the burnished twists of her rich hair,—he knew that the reason why it nestled there solitary was because he had one day uttered a chance condemnation of wreaths. Kate was painfully conscious also, in her guilty little soul, of having been actuated by this reason, and felt now intensely angry with and ashamed

66 Reference to Dryden's version of the Antony and Cleopatra story, the play *All for Love; or the World Well Lost* (1678).

67 Tennyson, "The Gardener's Daughter" (1842), l. 125.

68 Tennyson, *In Memoriam* (1850), 95.59.

of herself for having let a thought of what this fickle, indifferent, fine gentleman's opinion would be influence her in what regarded her toilet or anything else about her. She felt mightily inclined to tug the great yellowy-white creamy rose, the innocent offender, by main force out of her head, tear it to pieces viciously, and scatter its petals to the four winds of heaven, or else to lay down her head on the tablecloth and burst out crying, or perhaps combine all advantages and do both.

And so the swift minutes flew by, and added their little quota to the great whole of that gigantic ever-growing monster, the past; and Dare Stamer ate his dinner, and enjoyed it pretty well—not quite so much as usual, perhaps; and Kate ate nothing, and kept up her dreary stealthy watch on her *vis-à-vis*.

"How pleased and flattered Maggie does look, to be sure!" thought the sore-hearted one enviously. "O, if she could but know how unbecoming it is to her to laugh, she would look grave immediately. I wonder what excellent joke that was? Not worth hearing, no doubt. O, if Maggie could but see how flushed and hot her face is! She is not looking at bit well. That is a comfort, at all events. O dear, O dear, how spiteful I am growing! What has made me so odious? What has poor Maggie done to me? I wonder, though, if I am looking as red as that?"

And she took a covert peep at herself in the back of a big spoon. Her face looked very long, certainly, drawn out on the convex surface; but it was as pale as "the naïad-like lily of the vale,"[69] to whom Dare in his thoughts had likened her.

And then Guy Stamer asked her suddenly whether she was fond of horses—a sort of test or shibboleth which he applied to all the young ladies of his acquaintance; and she had made answer tartly, that she knew little and cared less about them.

Before Guy, the slow-witted, had had time to be very much astonished, Kate had grown suddenly penitent and terrified to find what a thorough vixen she was growing, and did her best to pay a decent amount of attention to his well-meant *bald* utterances.

Many desirable young ladies would have thought but meanly of her understanding for finding it a labour so to do—would have paid her gladly something considerable for the chance of listening sprightly and attent to the equine anecdotes of a good-natured few-brained jockey, heir to a rent-

69 Percy Bysshe Shelley, "The Sensitive Plant" (1820), l. 21.

roll of a clear 15,000*l.* per annum; but Kate was never, all through her few and evil days, a good hand at this sort of world's arithmetic.

CHAPTER V

IT seems a stupid hackneyed sort of thing to say—a thing whose point by much wear is worn out, a thing which everybody says, and consequently which it is below my dignity to say—that the half-hour after dinner, when ladies, according to English manners, are left to themselves, is not an enjoyable period; but though it is hackneyed, it is true—at least I fancy so, from what I can gather.

To see the evil in its worst shape, read Corinne's account of the after-dinner female *séances* at Lord Edgermont's castle of dulness.[70] It is certainly a true saying when the members of the society are very few and know each other very slightly, and, moreover, have not the smallest desire to know each other any better.

Such was the case in the drawing-room at Llyn Castle this aforementioned evening, and the result was stagnation. As for Lady Stamer, she could not keep awake after dinner for anything under a prince of the blood. Self-indulgent, as worldly old women so often are, she cast her fat old person into an arm-chair, and straightway fell asleep, like a rude old porpoise as she was. The Misses Stamer did not go to sleep. They sat and fanned themselves, and made low-voiced remarks, and asked their girl-visitors a catechism of low-voiced condescending questions. Did they like croquet? Did they like lawn billiards? Many people liked lawn billiards better than croquet. Were they fond of bathing? Could they swim? Did they like Pen Dyllas? It was a pleasant change for them, no doubt.

Dialogues *de haut en bas*[71] are difficult things to carry on for both interlocutors, particularly when one side feels indignantly that there is no reason why it should be *de haut en bas*.

As for Kate, it was not much use condescending to her. She was so absent and self-absorbed as to be perfectly unaware whether she were be-

70 In Bk. 14 of Madame de Stäel's *Corinne* (1807)—the premier nineteenth-century saga of the female artist—the heroine recalls how the boredom of genteel female existence at her stepmother's house in Scotland inspired her to seek an independent life in Italy.

71 From top to bottom (French); here a reference to the class superiority of the Stamers to the Chesters.

ing condescended to or not. It was a matter of the most utter indifference to her whether these aristocratic lean young ladies were civil to her or not. Oppressed with the heat, bitterly disappointed, and heartsore about nothing, she leant one white elbow on the table, and dropped scant "*yeses*" and "*noes*" at haphazard among the Misses Stamer's questions, and was as dull a companion as any little woman need be. It was a pity, for it looked underbred not to be able to talk to ladies; and at any other time, in any other person, Kate would have animadverted upon it pretty severely with her sharp little tongue.

Margaret was much better behaved. Nature had presented her with a set of manners as nicely made as if they had been fashioned in Mayfair;[72] and she used them every day of her life—at least almost every day. She was mostly disposed to be polite and friendly to every man, woman, and child that came in her way. And so now she did her best to fill up the outlines of the Misses Stamer's sketchy ideas, to practise that hardest of all manufactures, making talk; but it was rather too heavy a burden for one slender pair of shoulders.

There really got at last to be nothing more to say on the subject of croquet, or of bathing either, and poor Miss Chester began to cast reproachful glances at her lazy sister. And then, at last, at last, after two or three false alarms, as of tea and coffee coming in, the few gentlemen did make their welcome appearance—welcome "as flowers in May."[73]

Now there happened to be close to Kate a vacant chair,—a roomy, comfortable chair, made for a person to sit and chat confidentially in,—and it was rather turned towards her. She kept her eyes cast down resolutely, for she knew that there would be such dumb invitation in them if they were to be raised. But though not seeing, she could feel that a two-legged black thing had noticed the desirability of the situation, and was hastening to it. Kate might have known by that haste that it was not Dare. He would not have hurried himself to save his own or his best friend's life.

Not till the two-legged thing was fairly seated, and close to her, did she lift up her eyes with a delicious new-born shyness in them, and raised them to the beaky countenance (the "eagle face" his admirers called it) of her late neighbour, Guy Stamer.

"Do you sing, Miss Chester?" asked at the same moment Dare, in that deep voice which made even silly things sound fine.

72 Fashionable district in London.

73 Popular phrase derived from James Howell's *Epistolæ Ho-Elianæ* (1645-50).

And he leaned broad-shouldered against the mantelpiece with a cup in his hand, and drank his tea—at least tried to do so as much as his moustache would let him—and looked down full-eyed at Margaret, and indulged himself in one surreptitious glance at Kate.

A little," said Margaret. (Women always say "a little." I believe, if Jenny Lind were asked whether she could sing, she would say "a little.")[74] "Only to amuse myself, though; never in public."

"O, but we are not public," said Dare, with polite sophistry; "and, 'pon my honour, we are none of us good judges of music—what you call critical judges—so you need not be shy."

"Thank you," said Margaret, laughing. "You need not be uneasy; I do not feel at all shy; but I have not sung in any society but my own for six or seven years, and I am not going to begin now."

"How unkind of you!" said Colonel Stamer languidly, looking at himself in a pier-glass opposite; "and I am so awfully fond of music too." (He thought he knew "God save the Queen" when he heard it, but was not sure).

"Why, you told me at dinner you did not care two straws about it," said Margaret, having detected him in a falsehood.

"Did I?" said he, glancing a second time at the pier-glass, and reflecting that his hair wanted cutting. "O, I did not mean it. You should never believe a word I say. I always mean exactly the reverse of what I say; I find it such a good plan."

Then he moved slowly to the table, put down his cup, and hesitated—

"Sighed and looked, sighed and looked, sighed and
looked, and sighed again"—[75]

but finally took the trouble of wheeling the smallest lowest chair he could find close to Margaret,—on the same principle, I suppose, which induced Beau Brummel[76] to drive through the streets of Brighton in the tiniest carriage he could procure,—reposed himself thereon in lazy strength, and kept up, for the best part of an hour, one of those low-voiced conversations in which foolish, trivial, mawkish things sound so much less foolish, less trivial, more sentimental than they would do if

74 Jenny Lind (1820-87), renowned Swedish opera singer.
75 Inexact, John Dryden, "Alexander's Feast" (1697), ll. 112-13.
76 George Bryan "Beau" Brummel (1778-1840), famous Regency-era dandy.

spoken out in an honest loud voice in the ears of the world. And all the time he felt nothing but Kate, Kate, Kate, all through his throbbing veins. As for the rest of the company, Sir Guy followed his wife's example. After sitting very upright for five minutes, nodding and bobbing, and recovering himself with a little start every time, he fell fast asleep, and his dreams were of mangel-wurzels and swedes.[77]

As for Blount, he industriously pursued his project of insinuating himself further into the good graces of the fair Augusta, and succeeded so well that at night he carried off with him the prize of a rather damaged rose-bud which that young lady had worn all evening on her virgin breast.

And lastly, as for Kate. After receiving Guy at his first coming with positive ferocity, she was now trying to dissuade her brows from curving into a frown every time he addressed her. He, good soul, was perhaps a little dazzled with the light of the green eyes, and not being, at the best of times, quick at observation, was unconscious of her aversion; so she had just had a second attack of remorse, melted by his forbearance and desire to be pleasant. He had sharpness enough to perceive that his *horsey* talk would not succeed with her; so he exercised self-denial and laid it aside, and they began to understand each other better. They looked at the photographic albums of all the family, with their heads close together over them; and Kate tried very hard to be interested in hearing the names of countless people, standing, sitting, and lounging in various attitudes of studied ugliness, not one of whom she had ever seen or heard of before.

What a relief it was when the folding-doors at length opened slowly, and a stately form appeared in the aperture, whose utterance was such as one can fancy that Pythian voice which came forth from Delphi was.[78] Only there was nothing ambiguous in this oracle. These were the words which the *vates*[79] uttered loudly, solemnly: "Mrs. Piggott's carriage!" O, blessed sound! not likely to be disobeyed: signal to put off constraint and put on ease; signal for Margaret to go home and look in the glass, and marvel, with that unaffected self-distrust and modesty which made her so lovable, why Fate had been so amiable to-night; signal for Blount to go home and put his damaged rose-bud in water, and take out his best studs,

77 Mangel-wurzels are a root vegetable of the beet family used for feeding livestock, swedes a vegetable related to turnips.

78 "Pythian" refers to the Greek city of Delphi, where in ancient times a priestess at the oracle relayed messages supposedly sent by the god Apollo.

79 Roman soothsayers who foretold the future using augury.

and lie down to such slumbers as only greyhound hobbledehoys know of; signal for Kate to go home and take off her unsuccessful little gauds, and lie awake, and see, all through the quiet hours, that face, as *she* thought,

"Dark, splendid, speaking wondrous things,"[80]

drawn accurately on the sable canvas of night—to ponder on those rugged, swart features, on those deep-set, maddening, averted eyes—to cry comfortably and privately, and long for the brief summer night to be half as short again. Truly, Colonel Stamer's prudent maxim of "Prevention better than cure" had come too late.

"Well, that's a relief," said Miss Stamer, getting up and yawning as soon as the door had closed behind their guests—almost before it had closed.

"I thought they were never going. It *is* terribly difficult and fatiguing, my dear, to entertain those kind of people," said Lady Stamer, having just awoke. "I never know what to say to them. One seems to have no subjects in common."

Just then Dare came back from putting the Misses Chester into their shabby fly, having been unable to resist the temptation of squeezing Kate's little passive hand, and being just in the act of thinking that he hoped she had perceived it. His sister Augusta came to meet him, and made a sort of little mock bow to him.

"I congratulate you, Dare," she said, with a slight laugh.

"What about?" said he shortly; "on having spent the dullest evening of my life, and consequently not having it yet to spend?"

"No, not on that," she answered; "but on having managed so nicely to keep clear of that stupid little pale rustic. I caught the green eyes wandering lackadaisically after you once or twice."

"They are not bad-looking girls, either of them," said Miss Stamer; "only they have no style."

"That is what women always say of other women, when they cannot discover any other fault to find with them," said Dare sardonically.

"The little one is certainly not bad-looking," said Augusta condescendingly; "at least she would not be, if it was not for that dreadful *re-*

80 Inexact reference to Tennyson's "Lancelot and Elaine" from his *Idylls of the King* (1859), ll. 336-37: "Dark-splendid, speaking in the silence, full/ Of noble things."

troussé[81] nose; that quite spoils her."

"Dreadful!" said Guy, with good-natured indignation. "Why, I think that dear little nose is the jolliest thing about her, and she is a very jolly little thing altogether."

"She seemed so when she was talking to you, Guy," said his sister with a sneer.

"Do not you know," said Dare politely, and the black eyes flashed wickedly, "that Augusta always makes of a point of depreciating any girl who is younger and better-looking than herself."

"You need not get into a rage, and be rude as usual," said his sister rather good-humouredly. "I was not aware that you would think it necessary to take up the cudgels for the young lady; but, come now," she added teasingly, "you must own that she is a 'green-eyed monster.'[82] Confess that at least;" and Miss Augusta appeared pleased with her own wit.

"I do not know anything about her," said Dare with a scowl, "except that she is extremely pretty and *piquante*, and consequently a mark for the envy and ill-nature of all other women, who do not enjoy the same advantages, to aim at."

"Envious of poor little Kate Chester!" cried Miss Stamer, laughing. "Mamma, do you hear what we are accused of? My dear Dare, what *has* become of the fastidiousness you used to pique yourself upon?"

"Not a good feature in her face," said Miss Augusta with animation.

"Insignificant!"

"The sort of face one would never give a second look at," chorused Lady Stamer and her eldest daughter, as Colonel Stamer stalked out of the room, in a vile temper his sisters said; disgusted with himself, and infinitely more disgusted with his family. And he did not get into a much better temper even when he had endued himself with a gorgeous dressing-gown, and had established himself pretty comfortably in the balcony, with a cigar between his lips.

"How peculiarly unfortunate I am in my sisters!" he mused. "Well, I suppose they only act after their kind in declaring war à la *outrance*[83] against every pretty woman they meet. But what harm has that poor little girl done to them? What an idiot I was to imagine she was so ready to jump

81 Turned-up (French).

82 Term for jealousy derived from Shakespeare's *Othello* (first printed 1622), III. iii.166.

83 To the death (French).

down my throat that I must, for conscience' sake, keep from saying half a syllable to her! Conscience indeed! *I* do anything for conscience' sake! That is something new. What an utter fool I was to debar myself from the pleasure of a little quiet, harmless flirtation with her, when she is the only creature fit to speak to in this abominable hole! By the bye, that sister of hers is not a bad sort of girl, and not bad-looking either; but she is not to be compared to little Kate;" and his veins throbbed as he thought about her, and a most sweet thrill passed lightly through his captive senses.

"Kate, Kate! what a pretty little name it is! Darling little witch! I wonder what bedevilment there is about the child that I feel so besotted about her. I believe that little white country chit could do anything she pleased with me. How soft and downy she is, like a kitten! only I am morally certain that she would never scratch." (A pause. Puff, puff, puff; smoking away vigorously.) "I hope I am not getting in love with little Kate; that would not exactly do; but there is no chance of that. I leave that sort of thing to boys and old men. Well, one thing is certain, I will not be such a fool again in a hurry, or throw away the good things Providence puts in my way. If pretty women will fall in love with me, why, I cannot help it; it is my misfortune, not my fault. She was hurt at my never going near her to-night—I could see that. Dear little thing!—I will not gratify those venomous old maids again in the same way. I will take good care of that!"

And then he fell a-thinking that Kate was too pale, and how, when next he should see her, he would do his best to bring the warm colour into those pure cheeks, as he had succeeded in doing once or twice before, and been pleased with the result. But when should he see her again? Well, if opportunities did not come of themselves, he would make them. About this time his cigar came to an end, so he finished it and his reflections together.

CHAPTER VI

"WELL, my dear loves," said the benevolent *ovine*[84] voice of the Rev. Piggott next morning, as he came into the breakfast-room slowly and carefully, after his manner, holding out a fat hand to each of his nieces, and presenting a vast expanse of barren cheek to each in turn to kiss, he being meanwhile perfectly passive under the operation,—"well, my dear loves,

84 Sheep-like.

and how did you enjoy yourselves last night? Very much, I hope. I was very glad to hear you come back in such good time. I had gone to bed, but I was not asleep. Was I, dear Ma? I thought at first that I would try and sit up till you came back; but then, my loves, I thought I had really better not, or I should be so terribly tired and poorly to-day; and I am very glad that I did not now, as I am not nearly so giddy to-day; am I, Mamsey?"

"No, love, I do not think you are," said "Mamsey" cheerfully.

How she knew heaven knows, for I do not.

"I missed you very much, my old queen," continued Mr. Piggott lamentably; "but you must stay with me all to-day; indeed you must, my dear love. I do not think I shall ever be able to spare you for so long again. But you have not told me, my dear loves, how you enjoyed yourselves. How did you enjoy yourself, my little maid?" he asked, turning to Kate, for whom, despite her impudence, he had rather a kindness, and who was sitting with her empty plate before her, wan and listless, with a neglected ruffled sort of look, such as birds get in very cold weather.

"Not at all, uncle Piggott," she said emphatically. "It was horribly dull; and I do not care if I never see one of those people again."

"Ahem!" remarked Blount briefly.

It was all the refutation he attempted, and it was ample.

"Well, of course, you need not believe me if you do not like, Blount. I cannot help that, but it is perfectly true," asseverated silly Kate eagerly. "I do not care; and, indeed, I would much rather not see one of them again."

"Ahem!" again remarked Blount slowly and impressively.

"Well, indeed, I thought it was rather pleasant," interposed Margaret, between the intervals of eating her bread and butter; hungry, fresh-cheeked, and wholesomely pleasing to the eye.

"Of course *you* did," said Blount; "we all know that;" and he gave a knowing, highly diverted grin, which grin cut one insane passionate heart, like as a knife would have done, making it ache and heave in bitter pain.

"Why?" asked Margaret, affecting ignorance, but at the same time looking a little conscious, a little pleased, and smiling to herself at one or two nice things that her thoughts said to her at the same time.

"Margaretta, Margaretta, don't affect ignorance of what you know better than anyone else in the room," cried Blount, the tormentor in ordinary[85] to his sisters; "don't you know that it is as wicked to act a lie as

85 To hold a position "in ordinary" means to fill it constantly.

to tell one? I should think," he added, descending from the general to the particular, "that our large friend would come and call on you to-day, should not you, Kate?"

"O, of course," said Kate, with a smile that was so sickly it was positively at death's door.

"And bring a gift in his hand," continued Blount, warming with his theme.

"In that case he'll be trebly welcome," said Margaret, laughing; "it may be more blessed to give than to receive, but it is very blessed to receive too."

"And ask uncle Piggott's blessing, and *mine*," pursued her brother, following out his own train of ideas.

"I hope you'll give yours."

"I'm not at all sure I will," said Blount, shaking his fair-haired young head. "I never will give my sanction to poaching, and Stamer was Kate's property."

"Poor man!" said Maggie, with an amused smile; "he would be rather surprised at hearing that he was the property of either of us, would not he, Kate? I don't think he has the least intention of being anybody's property except his own."

"I'm sure I don't know," said Kate crossly, "and don't care."

"In the whole course of a long and eventful life," said Blount, with good-tempered irony, "I never saw complete indifference more successfully expressed; I think I should advise my Catherine to go on the stage; she is such an adept at concealing her emotions." And he patted Kate's shoulder in a benevolent brotherly way. She pulled her shoulder away sharply from his hand, but could not say a word, good or bad. "Does even *my* delicate sympathy grate upon you?—then you must be in evil case. Kitty, if he was not so big I'd call out the villain that has destroyed my family's peace, and made them quarrel with their bread-and-butter."

"Don't tease her, there's a good boy!" said Margaret, observing the heaving breast and the sudden flushed cheeks of her sister, and guessing pretty correctly the cause of these phenomena.

"Tease her!" replied Blount, with affected surprise. "What do you mean? I was only giving her a piece of advice."

His bump of sympathy for love woes[86] was as yet very imperfectly

86 The early nineteenth-century pseudo-science of phrenology held that bumps and hollows on the scalp revealed a person's talents and temperament.

developed, and he went on in a tone of consolation and soothing, such as one would use to a child who had broken its doll.

"Well, she shall not be teased, poor little Kitty. She shall have a nice new lover, that she shall; and he is a great ugly black fellow, not worth crying about."

Here he made a second effort to smooth her down, thereby manifesting a more malignant cruelty than ever Master Thomas Torment was guilty of in his dealings with the flies.[87]

"Do leave her alone, Blount," said Margaret again.

She was sorry for the poor little girl, though she was a little fool to imagine that that gay ugly Lothario[88] had ever cared a straw about her.

And then Kate surreptitiously dragged out a small pocket-handkerchief, and dried her wet eyes stealthily therewith, and then thrust it back swiftly into her pocket, and trusted that nobody had seen the manœuvre.

And then Daddy Piggott, as he was familiarly styled, spoke up opportunely; for Master and the Misses Chester's conversation had come through Kate's weeping to a rather untimely end.

"And now, my dear loves, I'll tell you what I did after you were all gone last night. Well, dear ma, I must tell you that I took quite a long walk. I went down to the shore and I sat on some stones by the sea for a very long time, and then I was afraid it was getting rather damp, so I went home again, and Mrs. Price sent me up my tea; but to tell you the truth, my love, I'm afraid I did not fancy it very much; and indeed now, while I think of it, I must remind you, dear ma, to try and get us some different tea, for I almost fancy that what we have had lately had disagreed with me. Will you try and remember, my dear love?"

"Yes, love," responded Mrs. Piggott promptly. She always said "Yes, love." I believe if he had said, "And now, my dear love, I think, if you please, that we will cut off your head," she would have said "Yes, love," as glibly as possible.

What a grand day it was that day! I remember it as if it had been yesterday. I do not know why, but I always fancy that the last day that will ever

87 See the Victorian children's book *The Fate of Tom Torment, Wherein You are Told, How the Boy Who'd Been Cruel Was Bought and Sold* (1860). Apparently the book was dedicated to the "Animals' Friends Society," and concerns a protagonist who, though he later reforms, enjoys pulling the wings off flies.

88 Lady's man or seducer, from a character in Nicholas Rowe's play *The Fair Penitent* (1703).

dawn upon this world—the day so emphatically called "The Day of Judgment"—will be, as to the aspect of outward things, just such a day. The sun poured out his radiance in full measure, flooding every object, sightly and unsightly alike; not beaming capriciously on one spot, and leaving another cold in the absence of his smile, as his sunship does sometimes, but shining away on all impartially, as if he wished to show what he could do in the way of shining, when he tried. And the sea sent in at the windows the sweetest of all her sweet messages, sweeter than the song of her daughters, the Sirens, which even many-counselled home-sick Odysseus dare not listen to,[89] and this message was nothing but the plashing sound of many little restless waves,

"Giving a gentle kiss to every stone."[90]

And all things on the face of the green earth seemed to be forestalling the appearance they shall wear,

> "When the old world passeth away, and the new world taketh its place."[91]

How is it that on such a day, dressed in the brave attire of its high noon,

"The bridal of the earth and sky,"[92]

there falls on the spirit of the happiest among us (the least sad among us, I should say) a tender melancholy, which we would not willingly have away? Is it because we know

---

89 In Homer's *Odyssey* Odysseus is warned not to listen to the sirens, whose beautiful singing lures sailors to their doom. Broughton is incorrect is implying that Odysseus does not hear the sirens' song, but he does first instruct his crew to bind him firmly to the mast and stop their own ears as they pass the treacherous rocks on which the sirens are perched.
90 Inexact, Shakespeare, *Two Gentlemen of Verona* (first printed 1623), II.vii.29.
91 Unidentified reference, but presumably drawing on such Bible verses as Revelation 21:1: "And I saw a new heaven and a new earth; for the first heaven and the first earth passed away"; see also 2 Corinthians 5:17.
92 George Herbert, "Virtue" (1633), l. 2.

"That there has passed away a glory from the earth"?[93]

Is it some slight reminiscence, some torn shred of our original whole garment of innocence, when—O, thought hardly to be compassed now!—when we had done no evil? Is it some shadowy remembrance, some faint recollection, not quite lost in its transit through all the generations of articulate men, of that time in the earth's rose-hued prime, when, perfect souls in perfect bodies, we dwelt in the garden of God's own planting, in a state of utter (soon forfeited) bliss, before there had been any need of

"The sound about us dropping coldly, purely, of spirits' tears"?[94]

A bliss, too, unrent by the struggles and rack of that most sweet torture, earthly passion. Perhaps it is that on such a day we feel more strongly those dim intimations, those vague conceptions, which even natural religion affords us, of a far country of whose geography we know nothing; where, if it can but attain to it, the soul shall regain her pristine freedom, and more than her pristine beauty; divorced, at last, from her unequal marriage with this present clayey, corrupting body, so soon to become

"A heap, to make men tremble who never weep,"[95]

over whose threshold Sin and Death, that foul mother and foul child, are powerless to set their grim feet.[96] Perhaps our melancholy arises from the feeling of how indistinct and distant those shores loom, rising, in hazy majesty, out of the great sea of eternity; of how thick is the curtain of invisibility drawn between us and them; so thick that no hand of one born of woman can draw it aside; of how heavy the world's cloying kisses

93 Inexact, William Wordsworth, *Ode: Intimations of Immortality from Recollections of Early Childhood* (1807, 1815). The language of this paragraph is infused with echoes of the *Ode* and its Platonic theory of an originary innocence pre-existing birth, and only remembered fleetingly in adulthood. See, for example, not only Broughton's reference to "dim intimations," which echoes the *Ode*'s title, but the image of "some shadowy remembrance, some faint recollection" which evokes Wordsworth's "shadowy recollections" (l. 149).

94 Inexact, Elizabeth Barrett Browning, "A Drama of Exile" (1844), ll. 249-50.

95 Shelley, "The Sensitive Plant" (1820), part 3, ll. 20-21.

96 In Book II of Milton's *Paradise Lost* (1667), Death is born of an incestuous union between Satan and his daughter Sin.

weigh on our eyelids, making it so hard for us to lift up our heavy eyes to those Delectable Mountains,[97] whose tops, if we look steadily, we can discern.

There is something high and ennobling, I think, in these aspirations of ours, weak and often intermitted as they are, after something loftier, purer, happier, than is to be found, after much searching, in this tear-soaked earth,

> "Where but to think is to be full of sorrow and
> leaden-eyed despair."[98]

There is, I think, in the glimpses we get, broken and fragmentary though they are, of that far-away good land, something exalting, sublime; particularly if we take as ours Hartley Coleridge's grand definition of the sublime, as

> "The Eternal struggling out of Time."[99]

This tender melancholy was not, however, the melancholy that was oppressing Kate Chester. All the sweet influences of earth and air and sky were utterly thrown away on her. It was not the sense of her own mortality nor of anybody else's that had made her out of temper with life, and incapable of eating her breakfast. Since this time yesterday she had made the pleasing discovery that she was fast falling in love violently, and as it now appeared unrequitedly, with a man her superior in station, and in every respect unlikely to prove a satisfactory object for that passion which forms the main plot of a woman's life, and is only a small secondary byplay in a man's. Yes, the play of her life had begun, and whether it was to be a tragedy or a comedy who could tell?[100] Probably, neither; most people's are neither the one nor the other,—too prosaically free from any great emotions or grand situations for tragedy, too *triste*[101] and serious for comedy. To me most people's lives seem like melodramas without a *dénoue-*

97 In John Bunyan's *Pilgrim's Progress* (1678), the Delectable Mountains are a haven where pilgrims rest while journeying to the Celestial City.
98 Inexact, John Keats, "Ode to a Nightingale" (1820), ll. 27-28.
99 Hartley Coleridge, posthumously published Sonnet 12 (1851), l. 5.
100 Broughton is using comedy in its original sense of a play ending in marriage.
101 Sad (French).

ment. The first three or four acts are played, and while we are waiting for the fifth, which is to be the key to all the others, which is to explain all that is unaccountable, and reconcile all incongruities, lo, the curtain drops! The fifth is played in some other world, and we must suspend our curiosity till we get there.

A woman's soul is such a small room that it has only space for one idea at a time; consequently, if a passion, a desire, an impulse lays hold of her, it possesses her with infinitely more force and concentration than it would a man in like case. A woman in love thinks of nothing but her love; a man in love thinks of his love parenthetically, episodically; it shares his thoughts with his horses, trade, his books, his dinner. Yes; it must be a very exceptional passion that can rival that dearest object of his thoughts, his dinner. Women have decidedly less of the brute, less of the "ape and tiger," as Tennyson hath it,[102] than men; but *en revanche*,[103] they have also infinitely less of the god. What a digression!

Now, and for many days henceforth, Kate saw all things through the medium of one feeling, so strong that it seemed to have driven all other feelings out of their places in her soul; to have exiled them out of her being, as having no room for them. In what hues this mad, uncurbed passion painted all things below the sky, in those hues she saw them. And now, in all the sun's genial, living beams, she could see (through the glamour that was upon her sight)[104] nothing but the lurid devil's light of two flashing wicked eyes, that had seen much evil and had smiled upon it; eyes that from their deep dwelling-places under shaggy brows had sent forth poisoned arrows of lambent splendour, and had smitten her so sorely that hope of healing seemed gone for ever. In all the cadenced murmurs of the salt sea waves, her dazed ears heard but one name. They said to her nothing but "Dare, Dare, Dare!"

"Will you come and bathe to-day, Kate?" asked Margaret kindly, with a woman's instinct of compassion for a sorrow she either had felt or might feel.

"No," said Kate apathetically.

There was a neglected, disconsolate limp sort of look about the blue-cotton frock, which usually sat so trim and coquettish, about the billowy,

---

102 See *In Memoriam* (1850), 118.28.

103 In return (French).

104 A glamour is a spell that makes someone appear more attractive than he or she really is.

red-brown hair. What did it matter how ugly and untidy she was? Who would take the trouble of looking at her?

"O, come," persisted Margaret. "You had much better. It would do you all the good in the world."

"No," replied Kate tartly, and cross this time. "*No; I won't.*"

"Kate, you might infuse a little more courtesy into your refusal," said Margaret, irritated; "people seem to think they may keep all their little rudenesses for their family circle, and, after all, civility costs nothing."

It *is* infuriating to be taken up short, and snubbed when you meant to be kind. Anger, in such a case, seems a kind of virtue, and puts on the aspect of justice.

"Don't squabble, girls," said Blount. "'Your little hands,'&c.[105] Well, I don't know what anyone else is going to do, but I know I must be off to bathe before the tide goes out much farther. It is so awfully shallow at the best of times in this hole, that one has to walk out half a mile before one can get it over one's ankles."

And he rose up, light haired, light coated, light hearted, and stretched himself, as a dog does, first head and neck, then fore legs, then hind legs. In no dog's stretches have I seen that order departed from.

"Now, do take care, and not get drowned, dear boy," implored Kate, roused out of her apathy by this fear, which was an event of every-day recurrence. Regularly every day she tormented herself, picturing how Blount's dear, jolly face would look, seen

"Under the whelming tide."[106]

"Can't promise," answered Blount, nonchalantly, holding a bit of bread just out of the reach of poor Tip's most frantically excited jumps, after the manner of teasing young men.

"I *may* get cramp in the water, you know. There's no reason why I should not. There was a fellow drowned that way down at Surly last year," said this condensed essence of Job's comforters.[107]

---

105 See Isaac Watts, "Against Quarrelling and Fighting," in *The Divine and Moral Songs for the Use of Children* (1715), ll. 5-8: "But, children, you should never let/ Such angry passions rise;/ Your little hands were never made/ To tear each other's eyes."

106 John Milton, *Lycidas* (1638), l. 157.

107 False comforters, from the bungling attempts at consolation of Job's friends

"Now, my dear boy," interposed his uncle, "there's one thing I must beg of you, and that is that you will go out of the room a little more quietly than you generally do. I declare the last time that you went out of the room you banged the door so that it went quite through my head."

"What? The door did?"

"My dear boy, you know very well what I mean."

"All right! I'm very sorry, but it really is difficult to know what will damage your head and what won't!"

So Blount made his exit, whistling a valse,[108] which was never long absent from his lips, and by which his anxious relatives could discern his coming at the distance of several miles.

CHAPTER VII

FOUR o'clock, P.M. About the hottest hour in all the hot twenty-four. Somewhere near that hour, this day, the fairy who, in that pretty tale which seems pretty even to grown-up children, sent off the fair sixteen-year-old princess and all her attendants in the midst of their drinking, love-making, cooking, &c., into their comfortable century sleep,[109] seemed, for want of better occupation, to have been laying a light finger on Pen Dyllas. Everything there was slumbering—shops, houses, bathing-machines, "men, animals, quadrupeds, horses, donkeys, and ponies."[110] Even the little hired carriages, which usually kept up a dreary procession in front of Inkerman-terrace all day, in faint hopes of a job, were resting from their wanderings, and vehicles, beasts, and drivers were all asleep together. In Breadalbane House peace and silence held their sway; Mrs. Piggott was retired out of sight to some distant chamber, where she was ministering to the requirements of the old woman who was to her in the place of a husband, listening, in all probability, to a catalogue of his diseases. So the young Chesters had the general sitting-room to themselves. Blount lay on the sofa, taking an open, unconcealed nap, with his limbs relaxed in gentle slumber, and an ill-used novel standing on its head on the floor be-

---

in the Book of Job.

108 Waltz.

109 Reference to the fairy tale of Sleeping Beauty, where an enchanted princess and her court sleep for a hundred years.

110 Unidentified reference.

side him. Margaret reposed in one arm-chair with her feet upon another, and pretended hypocritically to be performing some intricate evolutions with a crochet-needle and a ball of cotton; and Kate knelt by the open window, and rubbed her fingers up and down upon the sill, and made them very dusty and dirty, and did not mind a bit. She had a restless fit upon her, and could not settle to anything. As for going to sleep, that was a thing that would never occur to her again now. She was always so intensely, painfully wide awake. There was nothing to be seen in the road below, but still she looked out. At last an idea dawned upon her. She took a resolution, and her face brightened by just one small shade the less. She rose up hastily, waking Blount very unfeelingly, and passed out of the room. Upstairs she ran lightly, into the upper chamber where, on the two little narrow hard beds, Margaret and she reposed nightly; where they had their small quarrels, and their confidential talks, and their mild abuse of that old bore, Daddy Piggott, &c. Kate dived into a wardrobe, snatched up a hat, tossed it on, without one look in the looking-glass, ran down stairs again lightly, opened the house-door as quietly as might be, and stood out in the glaring street. Truly she must indeed have had some very determinate purpose in her mind to make her brave such a broiling when she might have had the shelter of a good thick roof over her head; and a purpose she had, though, like most of her purposes nowadays, it was a silly one. Up the quiet road to Aber Fynach she went, and through that little dead town, where Lady Godiva might have ridden up and down with impunity every day of the week except market-day.[111] Not a creature did she see about except three depressed curs and one old woman. Then on, on, still on, along the dusty, baking, shadeless high-road, towards the soft, swelling hills. Very few people met her as she went, for most people about Pen Dyllas were sane and of sound mind, but those few (hot as they were) could not help looking with interest at the little white, firm-set face, that looked so business-like; at the little figure trudging along so fast and resolutely, evidently to some clearly proposed end. And then, at length (it was lucky it fell out so when it did), for even she, although impelled and kept up by her strong will, and goaded on by distracting thoughts, could not have trudged on much farther without tumbling down in a faint,—at length, I say, her tired feet brought her to a place where two roads met. To

111 The 11th-century Lady Godiva supposedly rode naked through the streets of Coventry on market day so that her miserly husband would reduce taxes on the inhabitants.

the left stretched a lane that she knew well, where she had often strolled with Blount, laughing mostly, both of them, as they went. A lane where trees twined their lissome arms together, and kissed each other lovingly over the way; a lane where there was twilight even in a summer noon, shady, and dusk, and little travelled. On one side of this lone byroad a thick wood clothed the rising slope. Up a little forest path, into the heart of this wood, with its timely protecting shelter, fled poor Kate, with a last spurt of energy—fled like a hunted stag to the leafy covert—a little stricken deer, with the demon of despair close upon her flying heels. There she fell down weary, and lay all along in the warm long grass, starred with wild flowers. She buried her head with impatient misery among the moss and the short fern, and all the delicious, profuse, weedy treasures of a June wood, where Nature had been throwing

"All her quaint enamelled eyes."[112]

They made a very soft pillow for the little glossy head; and the tall grasses, and the catchfly,[113] and the harebells whispered together pityingly, sighingly, as they looked down upon her; while she found some little relief in pouring out the full flood of tears she had come here, thorough all the hot afternoon, to weep. Yes, this was the purpose—the very silly purpose—which had given her strength to brave the sun, and the long bare road, and the fatigue. Nothing could spy upon her or disturb her here. Neither beast nor man was near; and though a few birds saw her and were sorry for her, yet they were too sleepy to take much notice or say much about her. How she did weep and wail and moan, to be sure, stirred up to these exercises by that passion which was surely

"No vernal motion of the vital blood,"[114]

but rather that

"Fiery gloom that glares within the spirit's living tomb"![115]

She had come here now to have a good cry all to herself, and then to hug her idol for the very last time to her stormy heart; to consider its

112 Inexact, Milton, *Lycidas* (1638), l. 139.

113 Flowering plant with pink blossoms.

114 Inexact, Hartley Coleridge, Sonnet 31 (1833), l. 3.

115 Inexact, Hartley Coleridge, Sonnet 31 (1833), ll. 13-14.

face—a dead face now; to bury it in this dark wood, under one of these branching trees; to put it away from her wholly for evermore; and then to rise up and go away, widowed, desolate, but mad no more.[116] Yes, she would cry her heart out to-day—if it gave her a splitting headache, that was her own look-out—would think of *him* (the one *him*) for just one half-hour more; would ponder once again over every line of those rugged world-marked features, over every outline of that iron-thewed, gladiator form; would run over lingeringly once again in her soul all the words that false tongue had ever uttered to her; and then she would say good-bye to him, and go home calm and composed, and never let one thought stray again that way—would go home and begin a new life, a sensible, joyless, sorrowless life; for what could cause her sorrow or joy any more now?—would be a good old maid-aunt to Margaret's children—would save up all her money for Blount; and then at last, she supposed, after a great many dreary years marked by no happy landmarks, she should die and be buried, and there would be an end of her:—a pleasant probable programme for a bewitching little person of twenty, with an insnaring little figure and wonderful green eyes, to map out for herself.

"O, why will not God let us have what we like and be happy in this world in our own way," she groaned, "instead of making us always be lifting up our eyes strainingly to a country we cannot see, and which we shall most likely never get to at last? O, Dare, I'd do anything wicked, anything insane for you, and you'd not walk across the room to save my life! To think that I could ever have been happy before I knew you! Would I have that time back again when I had never seen your dark cruel face? No: I'd rather be as I am—utterly wretched—than never have heard your voice, never seen you smile upon me as you did that day by the shore. O, such a minute as that would overpay centuries in hell! If I could make a bargain this minute that I should have Dare all to myself for just one month—to be with him always—that he should love me as I love him (ah, no, he never could do that!)—but that he should love me just a little, as I have so

116 Helen Debenham hears an echo of the scene in ch. 36 of Charlotte Brontë's *Villette* (1855) in which the heroine Lucy Snowe buries her letters from John Bretton in a secluded wood, symbolically entombing her hopes that he will requite her love,; see "Not Wisely but Too Well and the Art of Sensation," in *Victorian Identities: Social and Cultural Formations in Nineteenth-Century Literature*, ed. Ruth Robbins and Julian Wolfreys (Hampshire: Macmillan/New York: St. Martin's, 1996), 24 n.8.

often fancied he did—that I might be everything to him, as he is everything to me, for just one month, only a month, and then to die and live in tortures for all the countless ages of eternity,—why, I'd do it this second, that I would, without a moment's hesitation. O, if I had the chance of being tried! But God will not let us make such bargains, I know. If He did, life would be starved and death-glutted within six weeks."

Frantic passion, utterly uncurbed, made this girl blasphemous—this girl who, if she could have had her own wild will, would have been altogether wrecked for time and for eternity. I think we have as much reason to thank God for the prayers He is deaf to as for those He hears.

"O, Dare, Dare," moaned the soft woman-voice again, "what grand eyes you have! How they seem to scorch and shrivel up my soul, looking always, always through it! O, I wish those eyes would look away from me for a little bit, that I might have a little peace! As it is, I cannot eat or sleep or take any rest. They have withered up all the pleasantness of my life. A pretty fool I must be!—I know that. Such a fool never existed before, I should think. O, if Blount could but see me now!—would he ever stop laughing? Well, there's one comfort—if I do not eat or sleep, I cannot live much longer. O, shall not I, though—a great strong thing like me? It would take a great deal to kill me. I'm not one of those fortunate little ethereal creatures that a breath will knock down. Ugly great fat thing," she said, pinching her own round firm arm quite spitefully, "it would take something to make you crumble back again into the dust I wish you had never come out of."

And so the dreary soliloquy went on, rather the dreary dialogue of self with self—the ravings of an utterly ungoverned soul. One thing I must say in her behalf. She was not a woman to give love uncalled for—to go mad, or die for one who had never wasted a thought on her. In this last fortnight Dare had done his very best to make her go wild about him; and his *very best* was a good deal, as many ladies could have testified. Sometimes she would start up in petulant agony,

"Plucking the harmless wild flower on the hill,"[117]

and would curse the day on which she was born, and then fling herself back on her grassy couch, and whisper an eager, panting prayer to

117 Inexact, Tennyson, *Maud* (1855), 2.3.

mother Earth, to take her back to her calm breast,

"Till days go out, which now go on."[118]

And all the while the great heart of Time went beating on evenly, as it always does, however much poor humanity may agonise to accelerate or retard its still pulsations. And Kate, with her dulled ears, never once listened to the great comforting truth to which all the flowers and the grasses and the insects gave by their beauty a quiet testimony, that truth which the sky spake of through all its blue fields of ether—

"That far beyond this gulf of woes
There is a region of repose
For them that pass away."[119]

In her present state of mind it could bring her no comfort. It was null and void—a dead letter to her. No one, however much in love, can spend his or her whole life, or even a whole day, on the ground in a lone wood; so at last Kate raised herself out of the dry, warm grass, and stood for a moment looking down on her fragrant lair, where the outline of her form was clearly marked out by the crushed herbage.

"Good-bye, darling Dare," she said aloud, bidding him farewell as if he had been present—only in that case she would have said, "Good-bye, Colonel Stamer;" and the sound of her tremulous voice fell softly on the silent wood. "I have done with you for ever now."

And then she turned and went away mechanically. She took out her watch and looked at it. Half-past eight! Impossible! Had she been all those hours making these adieux? Well, Daddy Piggott would be in a rage at her coming in so late; but what did that matter? She certainly should not hurry herself for him. And so, with slow reluctant feet she paced down into the lane; for was not unconstraint much better than constraint—was not solitude much more endurable than society? On and on, between the straggling hedges, sauntered the little wanderer, taking her time in a very leisurely manner, and behind her came the sound of a carriage, and the trot-trot of a horse's hoofs, sometimes very distinct and clear, sometimes deadened by some twisting of the road, but getting perceptibly nearer

118 Inexact, Elizabeth Barrett Browning, "De Profundis" (1862), l. 59.
119 Hartley Coleridge, "Sense, if You Can Find It" (1833), ll. 18-20.

and nearer. Well, what of that? a very common sound. Parties went out so often picnicing from Pen Dyllas on fine days, and came back in the evening. No doubt this was one. Kate felt no curiosity on the subject, not even enough to make her turn round and ascertain the nature of the approaching vehicle. Trot, trot, trot, on it came; quite close now and then. With an odd thrill of fear, Kate discovered that it was stopping beside her. Such a start she gave, and looked up really frightened. Though death in the abstract a good way off might be sweet, yet robbers and murderers and tramps close by were anything but pleasant. She raised her eyes quickly, and, lo, they encountered the pleasantest sight the earth could have showed them—the rugged world-marked features she knew so well—the herculean shoulders, whose breadth she had just been measuring with her mind's eye. Yes, it was Colonel Stamer, and none other; no wraith or tantalising apparition taking his shape, but himself in substantial bodily flesh and blood. He had been out on a fishing expedition all day, and had been now bowling along towards home and dinner, quite by himself, without even a groom, and with his fishing-basket and tackle sitting up on the seat beside him, in the place of a companion. And then suddenly ahead of him, flitting along under the dark green trees, he had caught sight of a little figure that enchained his eyes by its resemblance to a little figure he had been seeing a good deal of lately. He never stirred his eyes from that girl form, and as the distance between them diminished, he ascertained, with a bounding heart, that it had not a resemblance to, but an identity with, that figure he knew of. Well, his star was in the ascendant. Fortune *was* kind, although one wretched little quarter-of-a-pound trout was reposing, as the sole product of the long hot day's sport, in the basket beside him. What good luck to light upon her in this solitary place, all alone, and with no tiresome old duenna[120] to look after her! He might make ever such a fool of her, and himself too, now, and no soul be one atom the wiser. And so, as he came alongside the unconscious Kate, he pulled his horse up sharply, so sharply as to bring it almost upon its haunches, and an ill light flashed over his face as he turned towards her—a light bred of earthly exhalations—a will-o'-the-wisp, potent to lead astray—a light that came, not from heaven, and which brought no blessing to the woman on whom it fell.

"How are you?" said he. "How fortunate it is meeting you here! I half

120 Chaperone (Spanish).

thought of going round by the other road, as it is rather the shorter; but I am uncommonly glad I did not now. Is not it rather late for a small person like you to be sauntering about these roads all by yourself?" he added, with an assumption of the paternal which was amusingly absurd.

Kate came up to the side of the dog-cart,[121] and stretched out a very ready little hand to him as he bent down towards her, and her face caught a reflection of the will-o'-the-wisp light.

"It *is* rather late; but I have been wandering about, and lost my way," said she, not in the least knowing what she said. "No—how stupid I am!—I do not mean that," she added, correcting herself, with a little shake of the head, and a slight confused laugh at her own incoherence. "I have been sitting in the wood all the afternoon, and I had no idea that the time went so fast,"—and she lifted upturned eyes to his hairy countenance. How well upturned eyes do look! Guido[122] thought so, I am sure. His women, saints, Magdalenes, virgins, all have their eyes raised to the sky, and uncommonly becoming it is.

"Were you by yourself in the wood?" asked Dare quickly, with a pang of jealousy; and that scowl, which his sisters knew so well, and which his papa and mama were not unacquainted with, seemed inclined to visit his heavy brows.

"Yes, of course," answered wondering Kate. "I left Margaret and Blount very sleepy at home. Who should be with me?"

"No one, of course," said Dare, relieved. "It was a stupid question to ask. What an idiot I was to suspect her of flirting with any other fellow!" he added mentally.

It was a pretty sight. Overhead the broad green leaves, rustling, shimmering, sighing; and the evening sun, flickering down through their interstices, filtered through their green and gold. Below the dusk winding lane, flower-sprinkled, woodbine-scented, and standing in the lane the handsome well-appointed dog-cart that had but lately ceased to breathe the air of its native Long Acre; the flea-bitten gray mare, with her thoughts full of oats, impatient to be off again. And the big gentlemanlike-looking man in light clothes bending down to the small girl, who made such a fair contrast to him. Her face looked so bright, and speaking as she stood there,

121 A dog-cart is a light, often two-wheeled, horse-drawn carriage.

122 The Italian Baroque painter Guido Reni (1575-1642) produced a slew of sensuously remorseful Magdalenes with unbound hair, for instance "The Penitent Magdalene" (1635).

with one hand laid on the side of the carriage,

> "Half light, half shade: a sight to make an old man young."[123]

"What a dull evening we had last night!" pursued Dare, anxious to repair past errors, and take time by the forelock;[124] "had not we?"

"Yes," answered Kate, with more ingenuousness than politeness. "I thought it was rather dull; though, indeed," she added, remorsefully reproaching herself, "I ought not to say so, for your brother was very good-natured, trying to amuse me."

"O, if you come to a question of gratitude," said Dare the conceited, "I suppose I ought not to say anything about its being dull either, because your sister was very good-natured, trying to amuse me." And his teeth gleamed white under his thick moustache, in a broad laugh.

Intimation on the part of the gray mare that she is ready to move on.

Counter-intimation on Colonel Stamer's part that he is not ready.

"But, seriously," said Dare sentimentally, "I did not have half a minute's talk with you last night. You were flirting with Guy so outrageously, that I felt inclined to knock him down. 'Pon my honour I did; only he is my elder brother, you know, and it would not have been respectful; so I did not."

It was an odd way of stating the case; but it certainly was rather pleasant to have it put that way, and Kate thought so decidedly.

"Well, it was not my fault," she answered. "You know I could not well drag a chair across the room, and sit down by you, on purpose to have a chat, because you would not come to me. Why, it would have been Mahomet and the mountain[125] over again." And she laughed with soft glee.

"Do you know," said Dare, changing the subject, not being able to say much upon it, "I really do not half like your walking home at this time of night by yourself. Suppose," said he,—and he tossed down the basket

123 Inexact, Tennyson, "The Gardener's Daughter" (1842), ll. 139-40.

124 The allegorical figure of Time was traditionally represented as bald save for a lock on his forehead, implying that one can only seize hold of the present moment.

125 Reference to the proverb "If the mountain will not come to Mahomet, Mahomet must go to the mountain"; if something one wants does not happen, one must make it happen. The proverb is based on a story told by Francis Bacon in his Essays about the prophet Muhammad (Mahomet is an archaic form of the name).

and fishing-gear off the seat to the bottom of the vehicle,—"suppose you come up here, and let me drive you home? You had much better; and I will give you my word to take great care of you, and not break your neck."

Kate's heart leaped up at the prospect, but her lips said:

"O, no. Indeed, I dare not; I should be frightened."

Such a faint negation! An honest, downright "Yes" could not have been more really acquiescent, and a troubled joy streamed over her small up-looking visage.

"Frightened! With me?" said he, in tender scorn. "Impossible! I will not believe that."

"O, Mr. Piggott would not like it, I don't think," demurred Kate still, liking to prolong the pleasure of being persuaded.

Poor old scapegoat of a Daddy Piggott! Much she cared about his displeasure.

"Mr. Piggott be— Please don't drive me to the incivility of using strong language about your revered uncle," answered Dare irreverently. "Why need he ever know anything about it? Who is going to tell the old gentleman? I won't, I promise you." ("Little witch," thought he, "does she know how tantalised I am? She had better make haste, or I will pick her up and carry her off, and not let her go again in a hurry.")

Kate put one small foot on the step, but hesitated still.

"It is market-day at Ryvel, and there are scores of drunken men about," urged Dare, mendaciously working upon her fears.

She looked up to see whether he was telling truth.

"*Do* come, there's a good little child," besought the rich voice—besought more plainly still the flashing eyes.

She obeyed those eyes. She thought she could not help. She would have obeyed them whatever they had enjoined upon her, even if it had been her own utter destruction. So this good little child gave him her "flower-soft"[126] hand, and jumped in pretty agilely; tearing, however, a vast rent in the cotton frock.

"That's all right," said Dare then, with considerable satisfaction at his own powers of rhetoric. "And now, Miss Firefly, if you please, I do not think we will go quite straight home. We will take a little drive instead, if you do not mind. You know it is the best time of day for driving," he added, to the bird he had snared; and so he turned round Firefly's unwill-

126 See Shakespeare, *Antony and Cleopatra* (first printed 1623), II.ii.210.

ing head, away from oats, away from stable, and set her off trotting along the road back again in the direction he had just come.

"What a shame!" cried Kate, at this manœuvre, with a feeling of delightful excitement and wonder at what strange blessed portent would happen next. "I see you are bent on getting a scolding for me." And that was all the remonstrance she attempted.

How supremely pleasant it was being borne swiftly along through the balmy summer evening; the breeze they met, gently kissing away the distressful redness out of cheeks that much crying had made burning hot! All alone with him! Not more than three inches distant from his great shoulder. She did not want him to speak, or anything to happen, only that there should be a continuance of this happy trance. She lived entirely in the present, which is a thing one does not do more than four times in one's life at the most. Hope was merged in fruition. To be quite near him, and to be able sometimes to steal up a glance at his face to assure herself she was not asleep; and she asked for no better boon.

"You've been crying," remarked he at last, after staring at her for a long time with a deliberate intentness, which he would as soon have thought of cutting his own throat as indulging in, in a London drawing-room, to a London beauty.

"Yes," owned Kate reluctantly; "I have—a little. I suppose my eyes look dreadfully red and ugly?" she added, looking up inquiringly at him.

"Dreadfully," replied he. But there was such open fierce admiration in his own that she shrank away under them, thrilled and passive.

"Who's been bullying you?" asked Dare further; "your brother, or your sister, or your uncle?"

"None of them," faltered Kate, still perusing the splash-board, downcast-eyed.

"I should just like to know now," continued Dare, with meditative vague wrath (it did not take much to rouse his wrath), "who's been bullying you, and I'd try whether I could not teach him better manners."

"Nobody has been bullying me, I assure you," replied Kate rapidly, as red as any damask rose. "I have been bullying myself. I very often do. It's a way I have; and besides it's very wholesome to cry a little sometimes, you know. One cannot always be cheerful, or one would be rather oppressive to one's relatives."

And she tried to make a little joke feebly; for it was impossible to joke, and very hard to speak at all, under the searching flame of his gaze, that had no restraint imposed upon it now in this lonely place.

"What were you crying about? won't you tell me?" he asked very gently, after they had been rolling along a few minutes without speaking.

"O, nothing," she answered, turning away her head in confusion.

"Merely *pour passer le temps*,[127] in fact?" he said ironically. "Well, it *is* tolerably difficult to make him *passer* at all here; but I should not think your method made him go any quicker."

"I was weeping over my sins, of course," she said lightly.

"I should not have thought you the sort of person to retire to desert places to deplore your iniquities. Do you often do it?"

"No, not often; it is not good for the eyes; and I know, however soon I wear mine out, that I never can get a new pair."

"There are few sins that ever were committed under this sun that are worth spoiling such a pair for," he said emphatically.

Kate blushed furiously.

"I did not mean to fish for compliments," she said, half indignantly.

He did not pay much attention to her little protest.

"Poor sweet eyes!" said the deep bell-like tones, passion-shaken; "they should never shed a tear again, if I could help it."

He was getting rather mad; he felt that; and it would not do. He must not go much further; so he prudently looked away. Kate knew that it was very wrong, foolish, improper of her to have trusted herself at this time of day, or rather night, to the tender mercies of this man, whom, through all her blind infatuation, she somehow felt instinctively not to be a good man; who, as I and all his friends knew, was a man who never had any higher guide than his own giant passions, his own curbless will. And then there was silence—a silence that said far more than the voice of a great multitude would have done; a silence when the very air seemed redolent of love; when all nature seemed listening breathless, with curious attentive ears, to catch what the next soft-falling syllables would be. On and on, on and on; by the scented hayfields, whence the warm gusts came slow and heavy, "oppressed with perfume;"[128] by the blossoming crofts;

127 To pass the time (French).

128 Possibly an inexact rendering of Byron, "The Bride of Abydos" (1813), 1. i. 7 ("oppress'd with perfume"), or, as Helen Debenham argues, a conflation of Tennyson's "The Gardener's Daughter," l. 110 ("one warm gust full-fed with perfume") and Richard Monckton Milnes's "The Northern Knight in Italy," ll. 302-03 ("the air/ Oppressed with odours"); see "Not Wisely but Too Well and the

by the lichen-painted gray stone walls; by the furzy heathery hills. No doubt it was shockingly improper; but what of that? thought Kate. It was utter unimagined bliss. More murmured, whispered speeches; whispered, though they were out all alone on the quiet road, and not an ear could hear them; whispered, merely because whispers sound so infinitely sweeter. A few more draughts of poison; two pairs of lips sipping out of one cup; more of

"The delight of happy laughter; the delight of low replies."[129]

A few more intoxicating silences; when, according to Monckton Milnes' rather pretty conceit,

"The beating of their own hearts was all the sound they heard."[130]

Kate knew the road they were going; knew that it would take them a round of good eight miles; but what of that? Why should she try to shorten the period of her great joy? Did ever eight miles seem so magically short? Already they are drawing very near a close. It is ten o'clock. Evening has sunk into the arms of night, and the air beats their faces refreshingly with its dusk glad wings, telling of ocean caves and mermaid-haunted sea-bowers. They have rattled through dead Aber Fynach, where the drowsy Welsh are most of them gone to bed, and are rolling noiselessly now down the sheltered road to Pen Dyllas, where the ivy hangs in great leafy bunches over the wall. They have pulled up at last at the corner, where they must part.

"Already!" said Dare, with a deep sigh, half of strong pleasure, half of pain. "I never knew an hour to fly half so quick before. I suppose I must let you go now?" he whispered lingeringly.

"Yes," said Kate, jumping up quick, and preparing to take a good bold jump down.

"Stop a minute," said Dare, laying a detaining hand upon her, whose

Art of Sensation," in *Victorian Identities: Social and Cultural Formations in Nineteenth-Century Literature*, ed. Ruth Robbins and Julian Wolfreys (Hampshire: Macmillan/ New York: St. Martin's, 1996), 24 n. 12.

129 Tennyson, *Maud* (1855), 2.169-70.

130 Inexact, Richard Monckton Milnes, "The Brook-side" (1840), ll. 31-32: "For the beating of our own hearts/ Was all the sound we heard."

touch made her quiver and tremble. "I have not said a tithe of what I wanted to say to you. You *must* come out with me again to-morrow; do you hear?"

And he caught her hand, and held it unreproved, with familiar fondness. And his eyes glittered on her in the holy moonlight.

"O, no, indeed," said Kate, in a troubled whisper, dallying with the prospect of her own happiness. "Indeed I don't think I can. I'm sure Mr. Piggott would not let me," she said, bringing in the unfortunate old scapegoat again.

"Why, good heavens, child!—you would not think of asking him!" exclaimed Dare, startled by her innocence. "Why should he ever hear a word about it? He is not your father. You don't owe him any obedience, you know," urged the sophist, holding her still.

"But what shall I say if he asks me where I have been, when I come back?" inquired this apt scholar in the school of deception, rather ashamed of her own meanness.

"Say!" repeated the tempter. "Why, say that you have not been out all afternoon; that you have been lying down with a bad headache."

He knew his part pretty well. He had played it once or twice before.

"What a good innocent little thing you must be," he said, "that I'm obliged to give you lessons in story-telling, and in all kinds of wickedness!" and he gave a short deep laugh.

"I shall never be a good hand at telling stories," said Kate meditatively, quite content to stand there and be detained by him. "I cannot do it a bit naturally; I blush so, and look guilty."

"Why, have you ever tried it before?" asked Dare, with quick suspicion, more anxiously than he would have cared to own.

"Never!" answered Kate emphatically; and her fair large eyes spoke unmistakable truth. "There never has been anyone that I cared a straw to go out with before."

"Then you must begin now, and do it for me. What harm could there be in taking a little quiet country walk? I won't listen to any more silly doubts. You'll do it for me; won't you, Kate?" he asked; and his voice fell to a very soft key as he spoke her name.

It was the first time he had ever called her Kate, and it was a stroke of profound policy. She could not resist that; she succumbed at once.

"Well, I'll try," she said brightly. "I don't know what time will be best, I'm sure," she added, passing her hand over her brow reflectively. "After dinner, I think; because Mr. Piggott generally goes to sleep then."

"Well, then," said Dare decisively, "listen to me. I will be here at this identical place at four o'clock to-morrow afternoon, waiting for you, and you'll be here to meet me. Yes, you will. You need not shake your head. Are you afraid of trusting yourself with *me*, child? Don't you know you would be safer with me than anywhere else under the sun?" and he gazed earnestly, longingly under the shady hat to see what answer the moonlit eyes gave.

"I'll try," again whispered Kate.

"*Try!*" said Dare impatiently, not much used to being thwarted. "You must *do* it. I tell you, you must; and what's more, you sha'n't go until you promise. No, you sha'n't—not an inch, if you stay here all night," he added, with the same short laugh he had given before.

"Well, then, I promise," said Kate, loving him too intensely to fear him; "and now let go my hand. Have not I done just what you told me? Please, let me go. *Please.*" (Very imploringly the last "please.")

So he loosed her arm. He let her go, as a cat lets a small mouse go a little way, still keeping it, in reality, between her paws, and she jumped down agilely.

"Good-night, Kate. Remember!" were Dare's last words, bending down for a last look.

"Good-night, and thank you for the drive," said Kate gaily; and off she ran swiftly, down the still road.

CHAPTER VIII

POOR erring Kate! She had no father to look after her. What a claim for commiseration for any poor young thing to be possessed of; what a plea for treating errors, and shortcomings, and indiscretion, with a lenient tongue! Her father, before God took him, had been a good man, and a just, but she had never known him, except by hearsay. He had been a hard-working barrister; likely to make a name in the world, men said; but God said differently. His sun went down while it was yet noon; sank below this earth's horizon into the great flood of Eternity:

> "So sinks the day star, in the ocean's bed."[131]

131 Inexact, Milton, "Lycidas" (1638), l. 168.

Sore sickness and gnawing pain sapped the slight walls of the bodily house, till they tottered and fell; and the house was laid even with the earth; and no earthly builder could ever build it up again; but a heavenly builder shall. He departed this life, but he did not leave his infant children penniless to the cold wild world, or, worse fate still, to the tender mercies (sometimes tender enough too—sometimes niggardly doled out) of relatives and friends. Poor, they certainly were: witness the shabby cotton frock (the faded sheath of a fresh flower); but, for all that, they were independent. They need not be governesses, or schoolmistresses, or spend themselves in any such sad woman-trade. Their obligations to Mr. and Mrs. Piggott were not of a pecuniary description, else they might have been induced to treat the old south-down with less disrespectful levity and more gratitude. However, now there was nothing much to be grateful for: it was a mere case of mutual accommodation. And then, a month or two ago, it had occurred to the two Chesters (both being fully agreed this time), that old Daddy Piggott certainly was an old bore, and that it would be a decidedly more agreeable state of things if they were to have a little house of their own (even if ever such a little one) to rule over, and be as untidy as they pleased, instead of being for ever pinned on to the clerical skirts of the Piggott establishment. Consequently, after much deliberation as to the place where for this new domicile, after listening attentively to much good advice from generous friends, and carefully avoiding taking any of it, they had acted for the first time in their lives for themselves, and had picked out a small nutshell to deposit their pretty selves in; and it was now (this 17th of June) exactly a month till they were to take possession of it—exactly a month longer for them to tarry in the sheepfold. Kate had been telling Dare of this fact to-day, and he had said with three parts of serious and one part of joking in his speech, that he would take upon himself to escort them to their new home when the day should come. Blount should take care of Margaret, and he himself would look after Kate; and he had asked whether it would not be nice, and she had said, "Yes, very, very nice," like an utter little fool as she was. Meanwhile, Miss Kate's truant feet had brought her to the hospitable portals of Breadalbane House, and she gave a bold knock, and rang a bold peal, though her heart did quake a little, for it *was* so late; but luck was her portion this day at least. Along the passage came, with a long-wicked tallow candle, Mrs. Price, the once nurse, now maid (a metamorphosis almost as regular in some families as chrysalis into butterfly).

"Why, my darling child," she said, opening the door, and the tallow candle flared with surprise too, "where upon earth have you been all this while?" and her good-natured face looked excessively wondering. "I have been in such a fright. I did not know what upon earth to do about you. Do you know what time of night it is?"

"O, yes, I know all about it," said Kate; "but, my dear old woman," she cried, enfolding Mrs. Price in a close embrace that owed its birth more to fear than affection, "your fright *can* be nothing to mine. Just picture to yourself the scolding I shall get: prison-diet, solitary confinement, and a lecture that would reach from here to Ryvel. I anticipate nothing less."

"O, as to that," responded Mrs. Price, shutting the door, "they're none of them at home. They went out driving in one of them ould carriages after tea, and they haven't come back yet. I wonder they are not back; Mr. Piggott so fidgety about himself, and so fearful of the night air too."

"Praise Allah!" said Kate, drawing a long breath. "Then they need never know anything about it; and you won't turn informer, will you, you dear old lady?" she said, laying an anxious little hand on each of Mrs. Price's shoulders.

"No, darling, I sha'n't say nothing about it," responded the accommodating Mrs. Price; "but where have you been?—for it certainly is oudaciously late for you to be out all by yourself."

"O, I don't know; I have been sitting in the wood," said Kate lightly; "but where's Blount?"

"He went out with one of them nasty guns just now, and I wish he'd come back again. I am always so frightened of his shooting himself with one of them horrid things."

"O, nonsense," said Kate; "there's no fear of that;" and upstairs she ran, relieved in mind, having snatched the tallow candle out of Mrs. Price's grasp. Broad awake all through the rolling hours, she

"Failed to draw the quiet of the night into her blood,"[132]

and then sank into a short light morning slumber, and was waked by the light flowing in under her eyelids from the scant-curtained window. Before full consciousness returned, she had a feeling of some weight of blessedness belonging to her, something delightful that had happened,

132 Inexact, Tennyson, "The Marriage of Geraint" in *Idylls of the King* (1859), ll. 531-32 .

something more delightful still that was going to happen, some rich jewel in the treasure-house of the future waiting for her to wear. And then she sat up, and jumped out of bed, and ran barefooted to the window, pulled aside the blind, and peeped out. The newborn day, climbing swiftly up out of the eastern chambers that had seen his birth, was a mighty infant, worthy of his glorious predecessors, smiling broadly, not weeping—as mortal infants, prescient of fate, do—at his first glimpse of the awakened earth. According to the ancients' lovely fable, Aurora had just risen out of the saffron couch of Tithonus,[133] and was floating rosy-fingered through the kindling sky. And then Kate peeped into the looking-glass; rounded cheeks, slumber-flushed; tangled disorderly hair; eyes of the colour of sea water, lying unsunned in an ocean cave; smiles, dimples,—this was what she saw.

"What are you making such a noise about?" grumbled Margaret, with sleepy indistinctness. "Do go to bed again."

To bed again! No, indeed. On the contrary, Kate dressed quickly, ran down stairs, and went abroad to meet the morning, under the high clear sky. Through the green fields, where the grass, dew-drenched, was shedding myriad pearly tears of joy at the departure of darkness and the coming back of light; where the daisies and the buttercups were half unclosing their coy lips, under the kisses of their kingly lover. Through them all she went, and then passed down to the shore of the great sea whose breast was heaving gently for the love of Hyperion, the mighty sun god,[134] who was smiling welcomingly, coquettishly, under his burning eyes, through all her countless waves. Kate strolled along, her whole being saturated with pleasure, ran for very light-heartedness races with Tip, and got once or twice nearly tripped up by that excited animal getting under her feet; and she threw stones, splash into the water, and stood and watched how the small ripples stole ever noiselessly, insidiously, further and further up on the tawny sands. She made acquaintance, too, with the seagulls, both those which flapped heavily, white-winged over head, and those which sat gravely in vast conclaves—a sort of gull parliament—on the ever-

133 In classical mythology Aurora, goddess of the dawn, asks Zeus to grant her mortal lover Tithonus immortality, but forgets to ask for eternal youth; eventually she turns the withered Tithonus into a grasshopper. The legend is retold in Tennyson's "Tithonus" (1842).

134 One of the twelve Titans in ancient Greek mythology, Hyperion was father of Helios, the sun, with whom he is sometimes confused.

diminishing beach. And so she came back, looking more like a dog-rose than any lily, to breakfast, and fancied she was ravenous for coffee and bread-and-butter; but, lo, when the coffee and bread-and-butter came, she could not touch them; the inward excitement would not let her.

The morning, certainly, was rather hard to live through: there are so many hours; such a great number of minutes in a whole morning, from breakfast to dinner! O, if one could unpick some patches of time from one part of one's life and tack them on to another! If one could take from the superfluity of some dreary days, to add to the scant measure of some beatific moments! But we are not allowed to practise these ingenious sums of subtraction and addition. And so Kate first took up a little red stocking she was knitting, and after knitting three rows, dropped a stitch by reason of the absence of her mind, and threw it aside disgusted. Next she tried to read some of Lamb's *Essays*,[135] which, in better times, had been very dear to her; a dish whose delicate flavour her mental taste had highly relished, but now their tone was too healthy and wholesome to tempt a diseased palate; and the book was soon shut up. Then she read Byron's *Francesca of Rimini*, and found that answer better. That exquisite tale of hopeless, boundless passion spoke to her soul a language that it loved, and she never thought of taking to herself the warning—

"How many sweet thoughts, what strong ecstasies,
Led these their evil fortune to fulfil?"

"He who from me shall be divided ne'er"[136]

was the line that she took to herself; and she said it over softly, with a confident smile, and then the volume fell back into her lap, and she tried how doing nothing answered, and found that it answered best of all.

One o'clock at last: only three hours—180 minutes, until the gates of Paradise should be thrown open. Ah, but then dinner had to intervene, and dinner is rather an ordeal. It lasts so long, and people talk so much at it, and introduce so many subjects, and one cannot get up and rush away, when one feels that the room is getting too hot to hold one. But, however, it must be gone through, there is no avoiding it, and here it is, being borne

135 The collected essays of Charles Lamb (see p. 50 n. 34) were published in 1823 under the title *Essays of Elia*.

136 These passages from Byron's *Francesca da Rimini* (1820) come, respectively, from ll. 17-18 and 39.

up the narrow stairs by Jane of the dishevelled locks; and here, moreover, comes Blount too, carrying a dead gull, whose sudden death he had just succeeded in effecting.

"Ah, Blount, you horrid boy!—do take the dreadful thing away!" cried Margaret in an agonised voice, hiding her face with her hands, while Blount stood at the door—sunburnt, knickerbockered, deriding her terrors.

Then Kate danced out of the room after him—her feet positively refused to walk to-day; they *would* dance to a little song that the heart had written for them, and the senses set to music; and she executed various gymnastic feats around him,and pulled his hair severely, and pinched him, knowing that having his hands full he could not avenge himself on her. No more he could; he stood there helpless.

"You idiot!" he said politely; grinning and diverted, but contemptuous, "What's made you so uncommonly jolly to-day, all of a sudden?"

Kate was rather a phenomenon to her brother and sister today, by reason of her transformation from Il Penseroso to L'Allegro[137]—from the rapidity of her rising out of yesterday's blues into the seventh heaven of to-day. They both, being sharp young people, had their suspicions concerning her.

"Could she have met that man out walking yesterday?" pondered Miss Chester; a little vexed, and only a little, at the thought.

People who know each other very well, near relatives, intimate friends, and the like, understand the dumb language which we all involuntarily make use of, full as well as that other spoken language of which the tongue is the vehicle. The Chesters could both speak and read this language fluently, and so they both smelt a rat, and made internal resolutions to set traps for that obnoxious little beast. And so, and so (as one used to say in the tales one used to spin out of one's empty, infant brain, to one's compeers, all listening with rapt attention); and so they went to dinner, and Daddy Piggott baaed a grace, and they all ate and drank; at least such of them as could. And the meat passed away, and the pudding passed away, and all went smooth as satin—as cream, and none but the most perfectly innocuous themes were even hinted at.

Two o'clock and the danger over. Well, not quite; although Blount did get up and walk to the window, saying recitatively—

137 "Il Penseroso" and "L'Allegro" ("the thoughtful one" and "the cheerful one" in Italian) are two short poems by Milton (1645).

"Fate cannot harm me: I have dined to-day."[138]

"Mr. Piggott," began Margaret, "don't you think we'd better have another drive to-day; it was so pleasant yesterday, and you know it is so much wholesomer, driving than walking this hot weather, and you see it has not done you a bit of harm, being out a little late?"

Miss Chester was generally not too partial to taking carriage-exercise with her uncle, but she made this remark with an object.

"Well, indeed, my dear love," replied Mr. Piggott slowly (for how could he talk fast with the plum Nature had put into his mouth?), "I am almost inclined to think that it would be a good plan to take a little drive—not a very long one, you know, my love. I was a little nervous last night at being out so much in the night air; but I'm really in hopes that it has not done me much harm. My head feels really very tolerable to-day. But what does dear ma say? Do you think I might venture, my old queen?"

Need I say that Mrs. Piggott made answer:

"Yes, love."

It was her formula. She said it as regularly as the clerk says "Amen" to the parson.

"And you'll come too; won't you, Kate?" pursued Margaret tentatively, observing her sister narrowly, with a rather meaning look on her face. "I know you are so fond of driving; you said so only the other day."

"No, thank you; I think not," stammered luckless Kate, pretending that she had dropped her pocket-handkerchief and diving under the table for it. "I—I've got rather a headache."

"A headache!" exclaimed Blount, coming back from the window, with broad incredulity. "O, come now; that *is* a fine idea, after the way you were rushing about before dinner, making my life a burden to me. A very funny sort of headache it must be, I should think."

"O, indeed, my dear little maid," interposed Mr. Piggott, "if you've got a headache, I really should not advise you to go out of doors at all. If you take my advice you will go and lie down on your bed, and keep very quiet, and try to take a little nap, dear love, and get Mrs. Price to bring you up a cup of good warm tea; or else, perhaps, Maggie will kindly bathe your forehead with eau-de-Cologne, as dear ma does mine, when I have one of my bad headaches."

138 Sydney Smith, "Recipe for a Salad" (1839), l. 20.

"O, it's not so bad as all that," said Kate, unable to help laughing, despite her vexation, at all this paraphernalia of remedies for a disorder that was purely imaginary; "it's only rather uncomfortable."

"She has not got a headache at all," said Blount—indignant champion in the cause of veracity—to his uncle; "she's only pretending. She has no more a headache than I have."

"Did not I hear you say, my dear love," inquired Mr. Piggott,—rather confused by these opposite statements, appealing to Kate—"did not I hear you say that you had got a headache?"

"Well, it isn't exactly a headache," explained Kate, shifting her ground, and sinking deeper at every step into the slough of lies; "it's only that I don't feel very well. It's a sort of indescribable feeling," she said, delighted to have hit upon so vague a complaint.

"O, then," said Margaret, with a malicious smile, "a drive will be the very best thing in the world for you—much better than wandering about the roads all by yourself, which must be dreadfully dull, too;" and she laid a slight accent on the words, "all by yourself," and gazed steadily at her sister, encouraged by an approving look from Blount.

Kate could not return that gaze; she lost her temper instead.

"I don't know what business it is of yours, Maggie," she cried, with uncomfortably hot cheeks and blazing eyes—a small wild beast at bay; "or yours either, Blount. I wish to goodness you would go off and shoot some more ugly sea-gulls, instead of staying and teasing here."

"Indeed, my little maid," interposed Daddy Piggott blandly, "I must say I think that Maggie is quite right in what she says about your wandering about the roads, all by yourself." (He was an old fellow who paid a good deal of attention to the *bienséances*[139] of life.) "Indeed, my love, I do not like it at all. You know you were not in at tea-time last night; and I do not think it is at all fit that you should be strolling about by yourself so late in the evening. You know the night air is very injurious; and besides, my love, one does not know what kind of people you might fall in with; so I hope, my dear love, you'll take dear Maggie's advice, and come out for a nice quiet little drive with dear ma and me!"

At Mr. Piggott's alarms at the sort of people she might meet, Kate blushed furiously. Even the soft round throat caught some of the crimson flush, as the moon on a summer evening sometimes reddens under the

139 Proprieties (French).

gaze of the dying sun.

"Well, then, you *will* come, Kate?" reiterated Margaret cruelly, amused at the success of her Machiavellian policy.

"Yes, dear love," Mr. Piggott answered for her gravely. "I shall expect you to be ready to come out for a nice little drive with dear ma and me this afternoon, unless you have any very particular reason to the contrary," he added, roused to something like suspicion. "Do you hear, my dear love?"

"Good-bye, sweet Kitty," cried Blount, from the door, in mischievous exultation, firing off a parting shot; "I do hope you'll enjoy your drive."

And Kitty succumbed.

CHAPTER IX

"WHAT is truth?" quoth jesting Pilate;[140] only, begging Bacon's pardon, jesting Pilate was never more in earnest in his life, and with good reason. What is right, and what is wrong? Where does one end, and the other begin? Where does the boundary-line come? It seems to me, sometimes, so thin and faint a thread, that it requires careful, diligent, honest search to trace its course exactly, even in the high noon of this nineteenth century of ours. I marvel much, pondering upon those lamps that the past has hung out for us to gape and stare and wonder at—those grand old Greek heathens. Groping, as they did, in such utter darkness—rather, perhaps, I should say, such a dusk twilight—owning no light at all, save faint emanations from within, from their own clear spirits, helped on and kindled into broad sunlight, by no aiding light from without them, from some higher sphere. The great world-concerning truths we know for certainties that we possess as heritages, through no merit, by no labour of our own, they felt after with blind hands, vaguely grasping after something, they knew not what; they strove to work them out for themselves, and could gain but blurred, indistinct outlines of them. Whence did they get their conception of the καλον καγαθον?[141] What could they know of the beautiful, or the good, save the materially beautiful, and the materially good, with which

140 Francis Bacon opens his essay "On Truth" (1601) with the line "'What is truth?' quoth jesting Pilate, and would not stay for an answer," a reference to John 18:38, where Pilate, Roman governor of Judaea, questions Jesus's claim that he is witness to the truth.

141 Beautiful and good (Greek); reference to the classical Greek ideal of noble conduct.

their own fair Hellas[142] was so lavishly dowered? Whence, save from some instinct planted in their own subtle minds, did they borrow their lofty ideas of honour and fortitude and purity? Not from their religion, certainly; a religion totally unallied with, divorced from, morality. By precept it did not teach them these good things, for by precept it taught them nothing, being in no degree a doctrinal religion, but merely and entirely a sacrificial one; and by example it assuredly taught them the contrary of all these high qualities. A religion of the earth, earthy;[143] bearing so plainly on its features the stamp of its parentage that one wonders how any intelligent being who thought at all could ever ascribe to it any other birth, so self-evidently was it a daughter of the brain of men, and of sensual, impure men, too. A lovely, voluptuous mythology, with its gods and goddesses sitting

"Distinct in dissolute beauty,"[144]

perennial, amaranthine bloom, by their nectar, on the heights of cloudy Olympus. Men and women in everything but their freedom from the dominion of death; men and women with stronger passions and greater power of gratifying them. Persecuting human creatures with their irresistible loves; wreaking their petty spites and jealousies and feuds upon them; making men only conscious of their divinity by the curses it brought upon them. Gods, indeed! Foul demons rather, set up in high places to be the scourge of the dwellers on earth. With such examples before them how did the great men of old manage to perform such high deeds of virtue, and endurance, and self-sacrifice as they did? Even we, as I said before, rich as we are in a glorious illumination from above, find it (through the film that is ever on these mortal eyes) hard sometimes to say positively what is good and what is evil. The excess of virtue becomes vice sometimes. At what point does it cease to be virtue and begin to be vice? To come down to what I have been tending to all along, when does love cease to be the most ennobling and highest of our purely natural impulses? When does it begin to be a crime, an idol set up in the heart?

All these sage reflections arising from the fact that Breadalbane House had a back door! Not that I mean to say that Kate's love passed

---

142 Greece.

143 See I Corinthians 15:47: "The first man is of the earth, earthy; the second man is from heaven."

144 Inexact, Owen Meredith (E. R. Bulwer-Lytton), *Tannhäuser* (1861), l. 207.

from the realms of virtue into those of crime at the very moment when she first began to let her thoughts dwell significantly on that back door. It had ceased to wear the garb of a virtue some time before it excited her to think of surreptitious exits and entries; it had become to her a master, a god—an exacting master, a tyrannical god. But there is nothing easier than to walk out by a back door, nor, in some cases, more convenient. Kate's fuming spirit turned to it, and resolved that it should not stand there, leading into the cindery lane behind, in vain. It was positively unendurable, the thought of keeping Dare walking up and down there, waiting for her, so offended most likely at her faithlessness that he would never ask her to come out with him again. Earth, too, has such a few utterly bright moments that it is only a reckless spendthrift that would throw any aside. Dare would be frowning, his great dark brows would be coming together, as she had seen them do once or twice. How stern, how grandly thunder black he looked when he frowned! Would not anything in the world be better than rousing that strong lion to wrath? Merely to gratify a ridiculous whim of old Daddy Piggott's, too, of all people in the world! And she owed no obedience to him either; Dare had said she did not. Thus mused the bird, fluttering nearer and nearer to the cat outside its safe cage. Consequently on these reflections, at about ten minutes to 4, P.M., a young person stole very, very quietly out of the parlour at Breadalbane House, and ran up-stairs, silently as night, to the narrow-bedded little upper chamber to get her hat, and to make herself look fair in the eyes of him she loved. In she burst, hasty, unsuspecting, and came face to face with Margaret. Poor Kate! One big start she gave, after which she did her best to recover herself, turned aside to hide her guilty cheeks to a chest of drawers that stood kindly near, and pretended she had come up to hunt for a ball of cotton, or a pair of scissors, or some such feminine valuable.

"Where are you going, Kate?" asked Margaret coolly, in a voice in which amusement and irritation were mixed in equal parts.

"I'm not going," began Kate, with great fluency; but the lie died on her lips half spoken.

"You're going to meet Colonel Stamer somewhere," replied Margaret, with great distinctness of utterance. "Come, now, don't tell stories. You know you are as well as I do;" and she came round to watch the effect of her words on her sister's face, which had quarrelled with her tongue, and refused to lie in consort with it.

"No, I'm not," lied Kate. "Yes, I am," she cried in a breath, taking a sudden resolution, and she faced round and braved the cruel light. "He only asked me to go and take a quiet little walk with him, when I met him yesterday, and I said I would; and what harm is there in that?" She said thus much with downcast eyes, and then got excited with her theme, and appealed imploringly to her sister. "O, Margaret, don't try and stop me! I shall only do something utterly idiotic if you do. I know I shall! O, *do* let me go—*do*, dear, sweet Maggie, and I'll do you a good turn some day when I have the chance! O, Maggie, please don't stop me!"

Now Margaret Chester was a young woman who would as soon have thought of flying in the air as of moving a finger to nip any love-affair in the bud. Her sole object this day had been that of giving Kate a little fright, and proving to her how utterly futile her weak little endeavours at concealment had been. And so now she spoke with a slight tincture of good-natured scorn in her voice.

"Stop you, my good child! How could I, if I wanted ever so much? and I'm sure I sha'n't try. It's no business of mine. I only wanted to show you that you could not steal off to meet your lovers without my finding out. I'm sure I wish some of your admirers would carry you off. I *am* so tired of these never-ending flirtations."

"This is not a flirtation," answered Kate, drawing herself up, and feeling remarkably dignified. "Da—Colonel Stamer never flirts with me." (O, Kate!) "O, Margaret, you do not know what he is to me!" she went on, lifting up her eyes, with a rapturous light in them. "I don't know what is come to me, I'm sure, but of late I have felt, when I have been with him, that nothing in this world, or any other world, could make me very unhappy, ever again. You need not tell me I'm a fool, as I see you are going to, because I know it already."

"He is a dreadful *roué*,"[145] remarked Margaret consolingly. "Blount has just been telling me about him. Young Wilson told him to-day, that he was about the fastest[146] man in the Coldstreams, and I'm sure he looks it."

"I don't care," answered Kate, walking up and down the room, with fingers twisted together, and the rapt look in her eyes still. "I don't care how wicked he is. I should not love him a bit the less if I were to know that he was as wicked as sin itself. He is more to me than all the good men that ever were born."

145 Rake (French).

146 To be "fast" is to flirt and form romantic attachments to the point of, if not actually crossing into, impropriety.

"I'm afraid he is making a very great fool of you," observed Margaret, regarding her as one regards a "lusus naturæ,"[147] a three-legged hare, or a two-headed chicken.

"I don't care what he's making of me," returned Kate, hopelessly insane. "O, dear, O dear, how late it is getting! He'll be waiting. Let me go; there's a dear good Maggie."

"But what shall I say to Daddy Piggott?" inquired Maggie, puzzled.

"O, say that my headache got worse, and that I really had to lie down after all," said Kate quickly; as fertile in inventions as Ithaca's subtle king.[148]

"Then he'll be sure to send up aunt Harriet to see you, with some potion of his concocting," objected Maggie, further.

"O, say I'm asleep—say I'm dead—say anything;" and Kate dashed about the room, collecting the various articles of her toilette in a frenzy of haste; totally regardless of the falsehoods she had been scattering with so lavish a hand.

"Here, I'll get your hat," cried Margaret, good-natured and helpful, having got over her small attack of the spleen, "and go down-stairs very gently, because old Piggy is in his room; and don't let that bad man make too great a fool of you."

And at last Kate did get off in good earnest.

CHAPTER X

THE corner of a shady road; gray stone walls, ivy-draped; donkeys standing in a row, saddled, drooping-headed, waiting to be ridden and belaboured and generally ill-used; boys, appertaining to the said company of asses, playing marbles on the *trottoir*,[149] chattering harsh Welsh—the ugliest of all ugly tongues; and, lastly, a big gentlemanlike man in light clothes, with a cigar between his lips, puffing away, and walking up and down rather impatiently.

"Why the deuce does not she come? What's keeping her? I'm sure she'd come if she could. Has that old woman of an uncle stopped her? What a blessing it would be, to be sure, if girls had no uncles and fathers!"

Five minutes more; several turns up and down; much puffing.

147 Freak of nature (Latin).

148 Odysseus.

149 Sidewalk or footpath (French).

"Curse that old noodle!"

Take back that curse, O Dare Stamer! Rightly (to my thinking) called bad—O, fine body and starved soul!—for behold there comes now on the stage a small woman running very quickly, who, when she catches sight of you, drops into a decorous walk.

"O, here she is at last! Hurrah! I wish to heavens I was not quite so glad to see her!" and Dare threw away the end of his cigar, and advanced with less stately languor than he usually practised to meet her.

He took her hand, and holding it, looked down from his six-feet-two to her five-feet-three with glad possession.

"Good little thing," said he approvingly; "here you are at last."

"Yes," panted Kate, "here I am. I have got off at last. I really began to think at one time that I never should. I ran all the way, and I had to tell Margaret, because she found out."

Here breath failed, and she stopped.

"I'm sorry for that," answered Dare, in an annoyed voice, and his brows, always ready and willing for a frown, lowered slightly, after the fashion Kate admired so much. "I don't see what concern it was of your sister's. I wish you could have managed not to have told anyone; but, come, let's get out of this glaring road as quick as we can. I have no desire that your uncle should find us here together."

So off they went, away from the garish eyes of Welshmen and Welshwomen, away from all eyes but each other's, on a *quiet country walk*, down deep Welsh lanes, whose long tresses that ogre, high-farming, had not reduced to the dreary shortness of a convict's locks;[150] where wild roses stretched out their long sweet arms to detain them as they passed; where vetches and little pansies and ragged robin,[151] so fair in its pink tatters, were sprinkled so thickly that it seemed as if Nature, passing quickly by, had tossed them out of her basket, as too common to be kept for her dearer haunts. There foxgloves stood up tall above the other flowers, like the church does above the low roofs of the village, all of them doing what they were intended to do—calmly, unfailingly performing their easy mis-

150 In the mid nineteenth century new agricultural practices, known as "high farming," introduced such scientific innovations as selective breeding and the use of steam-powered implements. While many hailed these changes as progress, the narrator's reference suggests that some, at least, questioned their environmental and aesthetic cost.

151 A wildflower of the pink family.

sion of being lovely. And they passed (this pair) through green cornfields that the sun had not yet put into his crucible and transmuted into gold; and the spirit of the summer, unperceived, unheeded, went with them, and heightened their joy—added her quota to their great bliss, though they took no notice of her, or of any of her presents to them, nor were a bit grateful. And the rosy hours whirled round in their mazy dance, with their hands linked in those of the Graces;[152] and Dare and Kate strolled along, along (a goodly pair to look upon), through the smiling land, talking the sweet sentimental nonsense which forms the conversation of undeclared lovers; and sometimes they did not talk at all, but I don't think that the silence was irksome. At last Kate pulled off her hat, and pushed the hair away from her low forehead.

"I'm tired," she said, looking up at him in whose company she never could feel weariness of the soul.

"Tired! Are you? Poor dear little thing!" Dare answered, and compassion made the deep voice as soft and low as a summer wind at evening tide—dreadfully soft that voice could be when it chose. "I'd better carry you a bit, hadn't I?" he asked, with a caressing little laugh. "What a featherweight you would be!" he said, gazing at the white rule-defying profile beside him. He felt strongly inclined to do as he said, and take her up there and then. He would have given up his pay and his allowance for the next two years, and all his studs and pins, for a good deep bridgeless brook, or anything else that would have afforded him a decent pretext for so doing; and truly she would have been as a baby in his arms.

"No need for that, I think," said Kate, swinging her hat to and fro for something to do; and the idea of being carried by Dare brought a *soupçon*[153] of shell-pink into her cheeks.

"Let's sit down and rest," said Dare. "It's awfully nice on the grass in this bit of shade."

It *was* "awfully nice;" but was it "awfully" wholesome? I think not.

"I do not know what has made me so tired to-day," said Kate, and she closed her eyes, giving Dare scope for gloating over those fringed wonders, the thick white curtains that fell over them so softly. "I suppose it is because I did not sleep last night," she added, withdrawing the fringed

152 In Greek mythology the three Graces Aglaia, Euphrosyne, and Thalia (respectively embodiments of splendor, mirth, and good cheer) brought goodwill and charm to humankind.

153 Bit (French).

curtains again.

"And what kept you awake?" asked Dare, with tender interest, coming a little bit nearer.

"I don't know, I'm sure," replied Kate briefly, not feeling equal to a catechism on that theme.

"Was it the scolding you got last night for going out driving with me that hindered you?" he continued. "I'm afraid I always bring disagreeables on anybody I love or like," he ended despondingly.

"I did not get any scolding," said Kate, looking down. "I have no doubt I should have done if anybody had known about it, but they did not. You know you told me not to tell them, and of course I did not," she said simply, with the most absolute confidence that what he told her must be right.

"And do you always do and leave undone exactly what you are told?" asked Dare incredulously, thinking how delightful such docility would be.

"O, no!" said Kate, with her pretty dimpling laugh; "please don't get such a meek idea of me; I only do what I'm told when it happens to coincide with what I wish. Were your people very much surprised at your coming home so late?" she continued, a little hurriedly, rather embarrassed by the persistency with which his eyes dwelt upon her face.

"If they were," he said, with a rather grim smile, "they kept it to themselves. They know that I won't stand any catechism upon my goings and comings: it has cost me years of labour, but I have at length, I flatter myself, succeeded in empressing upon them the beauty and advisability of minding their own business."

"I wish you could give me your recipe," Kate said playfully; "I should like to apply it to uncle Piggott; though indeed," she added, a little compunctiously, "I suppose he is right in thinking that minding my business is minding his own, as I am his ward."

"Well, he does not seem to exercise any very oppressive supervision over you," Dare said, leaning his elbow lazily down on the grass, and pulling the brim of his hat down over his great dark eyes.

"No," said Kate, and a rather distressed expression flitted over her tell-tale little face, "because he trusts me; and though he certainly is a very tiresome old person," she continued naïvely, "yet I'm sure he means well, and that's why I don't like the idea of doing anything double-faced or deceitful to him."

"Double-faced or deceitful!" repeated Dare impatiently; "that is straining at a gnat. Why, surely he does not expect you to account for every half-hour of your life to him! Why, a galley-slave's existence would be liberty itself compared to that!"

"Of course it would," she answered dubiously. "And yet," she went on, looking up with sudden, earnest, innocent eyes at his face, and clasping her pretty hands impulsively,—"and yet—please don't be angry with me, nor think my notions of duty very overstrained,—but if you would let me just mention this walk to them—"

"Nonsense!" said Dare roughly; "*of course* I won't!" and then seeing her face cloud with a look of surprised fear, he added more gently, but frowning heavily still, "my dear child, cannot you see that the truth is not always the best to be spoken? There are many things perfectly harmless to do, and yet better not to talk about. Kate, you are not willing, are you, to give up my society for the sake of a hypochondriacal old simpleton's prudish, antiquated code of propriety—for the obsolete prejudices of thirty years ago?"

Kate was silent.

"Speak to me," he said, his anger merging into anxious tenderness,—"conventionality or me? Which is it to be, Kate?"

"You," she said, looking up quickly, and her eyes seemed to have caught some of the passion of his. And then she rose up, notwithstanding her alleged tiredness, and braving prosecution, went in amongst the standing corn, and took the trouble of plucking several wheat-ears and a whole handful of poppies. Laden with these, she came back, and sat down again. Then some girlish caprice prompted her to put a selection from the bunch of poppies and wheat-ears in amongst the plaits of her hair.

"Are not they lovely?" she asked, with a coquettish lowering of the eye-lids.

He did not answer her.

"I suppose you don't care for flowers," she said, pouting. "Men never do."

"Kate, I *do* care for them. Give me one," he said, and his voice sounded harsh, as it always did when any strong emotion had got possession of its owner.

"Are you sure you'll behave well to it?" said Kate, half laughing, and making a feint of withholding it; "because if not—"

"Give it me," he said again, almost in a whisper. "Not one of those others; one of the very ones you have got in your hair; I *must* have it. No flower will ever be the same to me again. I'll keep it as long as I live—I swear I will; and it shall be buried in my grave with me, for the love of little Kate."

And he came nearer still, and put forth his hand, and took one of the coveted poppies out of its resting-place in her deep hair, and having got possession of it, kissed it madly, passionately—a piece of sentimentality that he would have been the first to sneer at in any other man. Kate sat passive, thrilled through every nerve, and a very little alarmed at the storm she and her poppies had raised.

"You need not have taken it," she said, rather reproachfully, shrinking away a little from him; "I'd have given it you with pleasure. I like you to have it if it reminds you of me."

"Reminds me of you, indeed!" he said harshly, his eyes drinking deep at the fountain-head of intoxicating witchery contained for him in her simple eloquent face. "Much need to remind me of a person whose image keeps tormenting me day and night, sleeping and waking. If you would give me something to make me forget you for five minutes, it would be more to the purpose."

Kate looked down, and twisted a wheat-stalk round her small pink fingers.

"Why do you want to forget me?" she said shyly. "If anything pleasant has ever happened to me, I always wished to remember it."

"Because," he said gloomily, looking away from her over the gently-waving corn,—"because if I did what was right, I should never look in your face nor hear your sweet little voice again. Well, I have not been much in the habit of doing what was right from my youth up, and I don't see why I should begin now: there's a certain beauty in consistency, isn't there?" he ended, laughing ironically.

Kate left this question unanswered. Something in these reckless caverned eyes kept her dumb in a sort of tremulous expectancy, and they sat silent for a space; but it was as the hush of the elements before a storm; and as they sat, a light sound travelled to their ears, borne by the warning breeze, the evident undeniable sound of some people, a good way off still, but coming nearer every moment, talking in the next field—a small inoffensive sort of sound, not much louder than the buzzing of a summer gnat; but for all that it made Dare and Kate start asunder, quite as effectually as if it had been a cannon-shot. Kate rose up swiftly, crimson as the heart of a many-folded rose, bathed in a flood of confusion.

"There's some one coming," she said, in a horrified whisper; visions of an incensed Daddy Piggott and a derisive Blount flashed before her guilty little soul.

"It's my sisters!" replied Dare, after a rapid glance at the disturbers of this harmless *tête-à-tête*, whispering unconsciously too. By no means pleased did he seem at the rencontre; in bitter wrath and vexation, on the contrary.

"Your sisters, is it?" said Kate, drawing a long breath of relief. "O I'm so glad. I thought it was uncle Piggott!"

"What on earth brings them here, of all places in the world?" he ground out between his teeth. "Curse them!" And then he turned to Kate, and said rapidly, "Good-bye, Kate. You must go home by yourself now. I shall have to walk home with *these women!*" And again he ground his teeth at the thought of them. "It seems abominable to ask you to do such a thing," he went on, while a dark flush of anger and shame crossed his face; "but *for my sake*, Kate, my own darling, get over the stile now, this minute, and run down the lane as quick as you can. It's for your own good, Kate. I would not have their prying eyes find you here with me now for any consideration. Good-be, my darling—my own little Kate!" he added; "and remember what I asked you."

Kate involuntarily held up her head rather higher than usual.

"I am neither ashamed nor afraid to meet your sisters," she said proudly; "what business is it of theirs what I do or where I go? But of course," she added, her soft voice falling to a lower key, "if *you* think I had better go, I will."

"I *do* think so," he said earnestly, and glancing uneasily over his shoulder; "they are an ill-natured gossiping pair, though they are my sisters; and I don't want them to have the chance of tattling about you."

"Perhaps you are right," she said gravely; and having so said, she was not slow in obeying his injunctions. She sprang over the stile with remarkable agility. "Good-bye," she said, smiling, and nodding her graceful little head at him; "a pleasant walk to you;" and then she disappeared, and was out of sight in a moment.

Then Dare drew a deep breath, put his hands into his pockets, and lounged, lazy and *blasé*, to meet the advancing young ladies, as if nothing had or ever could have power to draw him out of his state of thorough indifference as regarded things in general. Was it fancy, or did the high-bred Annette and the polished Augusta look decidedly odd as he came up?

"Well, Dare, what have you been doing with yourself all the afternoon?" asked Annette, with a rather constrained attempt at easiness of manner. "One does not often meet you ruralising."

"How can you ask what I have been doing?" said Dare, with reproachful languor; "as if there was anything on earth or under the earth to do here. I have not been doing anything that I know of. I have been suffering a good deal. I have been conjugating the verb *s'ennuyer*[154] in all its moods and tenses, as I do every afternoon, and indeed forenoon too, in this hole."

"I suppose you have been picking buttercups or making daisy chains now, have not you?" asked Augusta, with a sneer.

"Well, I have not yet, but I am fast coming to that stage. I feel I am," and he sighed deeply. "I'll give you the first I make, Gussy, I promise you, to wear in your hair. It'll look so charmingly girlish, you know."

Having paid Miss Augusta off with that gentle blow aimed at her age, he felt better. Miss Augusta was a little exasperated. Exasperation and inquisitiveness together made her bolder than usual; for in ordinary cases, both she and Annette had a wholesome dread of their second brother, and had learned to abstain from questioning him as to his goings out and comings in. Augusta was naturally more valiant than her sister, so these combined causes made her spokeswoman now.

"I thought," she said, "that there was some one with you, some *woman*, when first we caught sight of you, Dare."

Not a trace of confusion on Dare's face as he took off his hat and passed his hand across his forehead, with an expression of utter boredness.

"Extremely probable," he said, without hesitation. "I met that little Williams's girl,—the red-faced one, you know,—and she kept on chattering to me till I really thought I never should get away from her. I had to say at last that I saw my sisters coming, and I must go and meet them, or I should not have got rid of her by now."

Well lied, Dare, boldly and ingeniously. His sisters were staggered.

"Which way did she go?" asked Augusta, suspicious still.

"'Pon my honour, I don't know," drawled Dare, with a triumph of perplexity on his troubled features. "O, it must have been this way, I fancy, over the fields; but 'pon my honour I could not swear."

"Over the fields?" said Annette, interrogatively, with one foot on the

154 To be bored (French).

stile in that direction.

"Ye-e-s, I think so," said Dare, doubtful still, and yawning. "O, you're going to rush off after her, are you? O, all right; but I don't think you'll overtake her, because she said she was in a devil of a hurry; no, I don't mean that, but she said she was in a tremendous hurry about something or other, and should run home the whole way. I believe she intended me to run with her," he subjoined, with well-affected lazy conceit.

That remark was so much in Dare's style that his sisters were more staggered than ever. That one lie did more towards convincing or unconvincing them than all the former ones.

"What! Is she a victim too?" asked Annette, laughing pleasantly.

"O, heaven forbid! I hope not!" said Dare fervently; "I cannot help it if she is," he added resignedly. They were walking very fast to overtake Miss Williams. "It's extremely hot work, posting along in the broiling sun at this rate," remarked Dare crossly; "I'm sure I wish to goodness you could get up to the girl, for I suppose your suspicions would be allayed then, and we might walk at a less heathenish rate. Yes," he went on, and he could not resist the temptation of dealing an ireful glare apiece to them—"I know you think I have been telling lies to *you*;" and he put vast scorn into the "*you*."

"I'm sure I didn't suspect you," stammered Annette, convicted and repentant. "Did you, Augusta?"

"No-o," said Augusta reluctantly. "At least, I don't now."

So they gave over their chase, fairly burnt out by the baking sun, which made the delicately-nurtured Misses Stamer feel quite faint; and Dare subsided into a sulky silence, having lied with great success.

CHAPTER XI

DARE went to London next day; got into a carriage all by himself; and smoked and pondered, pondered and smoked, all the way from Pen Dyllas to Euston. He had told Kate he was going, must go, on business, and I do believe he spoke the truth for once; that he would have stayed if he could have managed it. Going away! A death-knell; but then only going away for a few days. Kate could live without him for a few days; at least she must try. On the whole she was not very disconsolate, for he had said something to her of his intended absence which kept her spirits from flagging much.

"Only three days," said Kate next morning, standing before the glass, smiling at herself; plaiting away with deft white fingers at the hair on one side of her head, while at the other side it fell unattacked as yet; billowy, like the hair of one of Guido's ravishing Magdalenes[155] over her white dressing-gown. "Dear me! How late I am! The result of my headache, of course." Then Kate looked out of the window, and reflected that, after all, perhaps Dare's going away was rather a good thing of the two. It was a pouring wet day, and they could not well have strolled out together under an umbrella, and moreover she could not, for very shame, have got up another headache again so soon, after never having had one in her life before. She smiled at herself again then. "Well, I don't look much like one with a headache to-day, certainly," she said half aloud. O no, no, she should never have anything more to say to headache, or heartache either, after what passed yesterday. A warm blush which only herself and the glass had the benefit of. "We'll always have a bed of poppies in our garden, Dare and I will. I never cared much about them before, because they had no smell; but now, I don't think there's any flower in the world to be compared to them." Ready at last; and Kate ran down to breakfast, singing as she went, about the most thoroughly contented individual then breathing in Pen Dyllas. "Good-morning, everybody!" said she, giving a glad little nod to the company generally; "and I beg everybody's pardon for being so late; but it really was not my fault. I could not help it; everything went crooked with me to-day. I hope it is not a bad sign."

"Well, my little maid," inquired Mr. Piggott, with very unnecessary solicitude, "and how is your head this morning?—pretty well, I hope, my love. I got dear Ma to mix you one of those nice saline draughts that I take sometimes, when I have one of my bad headaches, and I was just going to send her up with it to your room, my dear love, when Maggie told us you were taking a little nap; so I told dear Ma that I thought we had better leave you quite quiet for a little bit, instead."

"O, it's all right now, thank you, Mr. Piggott," said Kate, a little ashamed, and resolving she would never tell the headache lie again.

"I don't remember that you ever used to complain of headache until lately, my dear love," continued Mr. Piggott, musing. "I think you must be taking after your old uncle, must not she, dear Ma?"

---

155 See p. 93, n. 122.

"Holy Saint Bridget, I hope not," said Kate devoutly, startled at this new resemblance; "at least," she said, perceiving her own incivility, "I mean about headaches, of course."

But Mr. Piggott was revelling in the vision of his own many and great ailments, and her caution was unnecessary. How the rain did patter down outside, to be sure!—not coming down in slant intermittent bursts, wind driven, but falling steadily straight down from heaven to earth, as if bent on fulfilling its mission, and soaking the ground as quickly and thoroughly as possible. It washed every one of the broad leaves on the sombre dust-whitened trees; so that they shone polished, making them "reassume the forms of their earlier"[156] leafhood. It washed the faces of the houses too; but they did not like it; they looked very gloomy and sulky under the operation. As for the sea, she had a coy fit, and had put on her very thickest veil, so that it was impossible to get a glimpse of her features through it, even when you stood quite close to her. Splash, splash, splash, went a few people, umbrella'd and clogged, along the sloppy pavement. The chickens puffed out their feathers as much as ever they could, turned up their coat-collars as it were, and stood morose and shivering in acrobatic attitudes, supporting themselves on one leg, under such shelter as they could obtain. The ducks, on the contrary, thought it good sport, and found even more delicious tid-bits than usual in the gutter. What a deplorable thing a wet day at the sea-side is, to be sure! Kate thought so, as she stood, after breakfast, drumming with her fingers on the dim window, and watching the progress of a drop down the pane with as much interest as ever Bruce watched his spider with.[157] Then Margaret spoke. "I would not say so before *them*," she began, in rather a low voice, shaking her head in the direction of the room where Daddy Piggott had retired, with the "one lone spirit"[158] that was his minister, ostensibly to write business letters, but in reality to have a good comfortable "bleat" about giddiness and vertigo and general debility—"I would not say so before them, of course, but I have had what I consider uncommonly good news to-day. I think you'll think so too, Blount. I don't think you will, Kate."

"Well, what is it?" asked Blount, from the easy-chair where he sat

156 Unidentified reference.

157 According to legend, Bruce I of Scotland, hiding in a cave after being defeated in battle, was inspired to overcome adversity after seeing a spider succeed in weaving a web despite numerous difficulties.

158 Unidentified reference.

with his legs dangling over the arm. "Make haste and tell us; don't keep us on the rack of expectation—it's worse than St. Lawrence's gridiron;[159] it is, indeed. I would not mind betting that it is some ridiculous nonsense I shall not care a straw about; *nascitur ridiculus mus*,[160]—if you know what that means."

Kate turned from the window to hear.

"Why," pursued Margaret, "it's just this: that I have had a letter from that man about our new house, and he says his present tenants are leaving sooner than he expected, and that we can have it any day we like now—the earlier the better."

"Hallelujah! Hallelujee!" said Blount, jumping up, and upsetting the chair. "That is something better worth hearing than I expected. Let's leave to-morrow by the first train, by all means."

"No, that's absurd, of course," answered Maggie meditatively, biting the top of her crochet-needle; "but I don't see why we should not get away next Monday. I am so sick of this place. It was only this morning I was reflecting how awful it was to think that we should have three more Sundays here yet."

"How provoking!" exclaimed Kate, with irrepressible vexation, biting her lips hard. "I cannot understand why you hate this place so. I don't know what you want, I'm sure."

"Want!" repeated Blount, taking on himself the office of explainer; "why, we want a place where there's something to do or something to see. Why, what is there here? There's no boating, no billiards, no nothing."

"You see," resumed Margaret, taking up the thread where Blount's eloquence had come to an end. "It may be all very pleasant for you, Kate, but it's not particularly lively for Blount and me looking on. You know you need not come if you don't like, nobody wants you; but, indeed, my poor child," she went on with compassionate significancy, "even if you stay I'm afraid it will be useless. I am indeed."

"Do you mean to say," exclaimed Blount, with surprised contemptuous amusement, "that the reason why she wants to stay so much is to try and get that big, conceited, black fellow to smile upon her again? O, ye

159 Legend has it that the third-century martyr St. Lawrence was roasted to death on a gridiron.

160 From the Latin of Horace, "Parturient montes, nascitur ridiculus mus" (the mountains will labor, a ridiculous mouse will be born); the trivial result of a great deal of effort.

gods and little fishes! that I should live to see this day!"

Blount's withering scorn had the effect of silencing Kate's objections and Kate altogether. Bitterly antagonistic to this plan as she was, yet she could not face ridicule on that theme. It made her wince so absurdly. And intensely annoyed and resistant as she was, she turned back to the contemplation of the streaming pane, and listened impotently, angry, and grieved, to Margaret and Blount laying their plans with much mutual satisfaction and accord; while her younger sister's portion of being slaughtered Juggernaut-wise[161] under her elder's chariot-wheels tasted in her mouth as unsavoury as dust and ashes. The weather outside looked more drab and dirt-coloured than ever now; the houses more damp and lachrymose; the chickens more humped up; even the ducks quacked and waddled less jubilantly. Poor Kate! there were several people in Pen Dyllas more contented than you now. She had not the consolation of resolving to tell Dare her troubles and have them vanish under his sympathy, his deep-voiced "Poor little child,"—for was not Dare gone steaming up to London, every minute further and further away from her? One thought still had power to comfort—the thought of that something which Dare had said to her, and thereby made her feel his absence a trivial grievance. This "something" was merely this. Colonel Stamer had told her that his sisters intended giving a school-feast—"a tea-fight[162] or some such violent form of dissipation," Dare phrased it,—a few days hence—the very day of his intended return, in fact—and that he had heard them say that they intended asking the Chesters to this mild entertainment.

"*Do* come; you must, for my sake," Dare had urged. "It's horribly dull I know, and I know too that you hate my sisters—and I'm sure I don't wonder at it; in fact, I'm not at all certain that I don't agree with you; but we'll try and entertain one another, won't we, Kate, and not trouble them much? Promise you'll come, now; just promise for my sake, Kate, for my sake!"

So Kate's mental eyes were fixed now on this tea-fight as earnestly (I don't suppose they could have been more so) as any of the Welsh urchins who purposed within their gluttonous little souls to lay in, on that auspicious occasion, such a stock of buns and weak tea as would serve them for the ensuing blank twelvemonth. Who knew what might happen

161 A juggernaut (from the Hindu name for the god of the world) crushes everything in its path.

162 Slang for tea-party.

on that day? What delicious continuation of the field scene? Something might by possibility occur which would make it indifferent to her whether she went from Pen Dyllas or stayed there.

CHAPTER XII

SO the slow days went lagging by, only two whole ones, and they were as two years. When one thinks one is most utterly miserable and forlorn, one is, I think, often not in one's worst estate. There are tears that are better than much laughing. There is a joy that is worse than many tears. At several subsequent periods of her short history, Kate thought herself immeasurably worse off than at this epoch; but, to my thinking, never was she in more completely evil case than under the blaze of these long-tarrying June noons. She had made her selection for ever it seemed—had chosen her home in this great lazar-house of ours—

"Here, where men sit and hear each other groan"—[163]

had taken for her bosom friends those plague-stricken and earth-spotted ones like herself. All the good that had ever been in her, all the pith and marrow of her soul's being, seemed to have been scorched away, to have been shrivelled up "like a parched scroll."[164] How impossible it was to her now to lift up her sick heavy soul from below to above, from the low, smoky, toiling valleys near at hand, to the calm, blue, distant hills! It would not be dragged up; it did not want to be. Like a log it fell back to earth again, and lay all along among the smoke and the dirt, and the weary din, and revelled in them. "The world's accursed trinity," as Leighton grandly calls them,[165] pinned it to earth and tied down its wings. Kate knelt down, indeed, as usual at exactly the same time every morning and

163 Keats, "Ode to a Nightingale" (1820), l. 24.

164 From "That Day of Wrath, That Dreadful Day," words by Thomas of Celano, 13th century; music by John Dykes, 1861, a hymn that vividly evokes the Judgment Day "when, shriveling like a parched scroll,/ The flaming heavens together roll" (ll. 5-6).

165 Robert Leighton (1611-84), author of the posthumously published "A Practical Commentary upon the First Epistle of Peter" (1693); the "accursed trinity" are "the lust of the flesh, and the lust of the eyes, and the pride of life" condemned in 1 John 2:16.

evening, and mumbled a few words to God with her lips, and a good many to Dare with her heart. She knelt down because she had always so knelt down from a child, because it was as invariable a part of her toilet as brushing her hair or putting on her dress. But how could she practise such flagrant, foul hypocrisy as to pretend to ask for those heavenly gifts which seemed to her so savourless and insipid, so little worth the having when won? Savourless and insipid indeed! O, unreckoning fool! She guessed not that those gifts were of so delicate and rare a flavour that to those who have once tasted of them, all the heaped up high-seasoned dainties of earth seem rank and nauseous in comparison. How could she blaspheme God by craving from Him that one earthly boon which was the sole thing, under the sky or above it either, that seemed to her worth the taking? One face and one form which (wait but a few years at the most) would be resolved into its primal dust; would have to trust to its coffin-plate for the poor satisfaction of being distinguished from the other dust around it; this one face and form, evanescent as the cloud-faces one sees in dreams, filled up so completely the gazing space of her soul's eyes, as to leave no room for the smallest glimpse, the faintest vision of the adamant walls and towers and joy-giving gates of "Jerusalem the golden."[166] One voice, whose tones (let but a few summers roll by) would be as unalterably dumb as the sand-whelmed Sphinx; as forgotten as the sound of last year's showers; this one voice surged and rung in her ears so that not to them could come the weakest echo of

"The shout of them that triumph; the song of them that feast."[167]

She could never think of her dead mother now. When her thoughts wandered off to that happy woman, she called them back again, shuddering; they dare not pursue her into the inner courts of

"Zion David, urbs tranquilla."[168]

Formerly, how often, how very often she had gone to her in thought;

166 "Jerusalem the Golden," hymn by Bernard de Morlas, 12th century; trans. John M. Neale, 1849.
167 "Jerusalem the Golden," stanza 3, ll. 3-4.
168 "Zion, peaceful city of David" (Latin); from the 12th-century hymn "Syon Cœlestis," by Hildebert of Lavardin, l. 2.

had talked to her, with the drear one-sided conversation one can hold with the dead! How she used to cry at her prayers! tears that, with all their bitter softness, had a dash of uncloying sweetness too; knowing keenly, with bare chilling certainty, that this little darling mother had gone beyond the province of the eye, or the ear, or the touch, to join that great host that every minute swells of the departed ones. They had been as the two women grinding at the mill: the one had been taken, the other had been left.[169] How many times, in the past days, Kate had pictured to herself after what fashion they would meet!—with what greeting, not of earth's framing, when the King's messenger should have come across the flood to fetch her too, as he came to fetch Christian, and Hopeful, and Mercy, and Much Afraid.[170] Yes, she should see her again; not pale, indeed, and thin, and pain-racked, and patient any longer (for patience implies the existence of suffering); but, for all that, the very same mother, and not another, who had taught her her letters, and scolded her, and talked to her, and taken such an interest in her as no one had ever done since; that same mother whom she had nursed and been often disrespectful to, and loved utterly, and lost! These last weeks seemed to have borne Kate many, many miles farther away from that pure saint. Her image, when it visited her now, had a mute reproach in its spirit eyes. It did not come often; Kate would not let it, it tortured her. She had exchanged her dead mother for living Dare it seemed, and she clasped her bargain to her heart, and repented not of it. As for Dare, he had taken a resolution, and was in such an amiable humour as he had not been seen in for exactly a year and a half.

CHAPTER XIII

HOWEVER much the days lag, they do go by; they are not stationary, they are ever on the move; so now they had brought round the day of the Misses Stamers' school-feast, "their nonsensical tea-fight," as their admir-

169 See Luke 17:35.

170 Characters from John Bunyan's allegorical *The Pilgrim's Progress* (1678). Christian, the protagonist, is an Everyman figure, Hopeful one of Christian's companions on his pilgrimage, Mercy the neighbor of Christian's wife Christiana, and Much Afraid the daughter of Mr Despondency, a prisoner rescued from the Doubting Castle. In the second part of *Pilgrim's Progress*, the messenger of the King (Christ) informs pilgrims of their imminent death and safe passage to the Celestial City (heaven).

ing brother had styled it. And the clocks had ticked round all through the morning and the noon, and had ticked on into the lazy, do-nothing afternoon. The earth had recovered her temper, and after her peevish tears was laughing again broadly, and the sea had taken off her veil, and thrown it away, and was coquetting with the sky as boldly and openly as ever.

"Good-bye, Daddy Piggott," said Kate, coming armed *cap-à-pie*,[171] for the day's encounter, into the room where her uncle was leaning back in an elbow-chair, flabby, amiable, and suffering as usual. "I hope your head will be pretty comfortable when we come back." She was so running over with general benevolence and *bonhomie*,[172] that she must vent it on some one, and old Daddy Piggott was the nearest at hand.

"Thank you, my love," he said slowly, with the smile of a fat martyr, "but I am afraid there is not much chance of that."

"O, I hope so," replied Kate, unfeelingly cheerful, in a fever to be off. "Had not we better be going now, Maggie?"

"Now, my dear loves," interposed Mr. Piggott, rising up in his chair, in the interest of the moment, "there's one thing I must beg of you, and that is that you will be very careful not to be sitting in wet feet. I hope you have all got strong boots on, my loves. Now, my little maid," he cried, detecting Kate in a natty little pair, which certainly did not come under the head of hobnails, "I see that yours are not at all fit for walking; indeed, my love, I must insist on your putting on a pair of galoches; if you have not got a pair dear Ma will lend you hers with pleasure, I'm sure; will you not, dear Ma?"

"O, thank you, Mr. Piggott, I'm very much obliged," said Kate, turning up her small nose behind his back even more than nature had done it for her, at the idea of incasing her dainty little feet in aunt Harriet's coalboxes.

"Ask him to lend you his," said Blount, *sotto voce*.[173] "I know he has got some," and he exploded in untimely mirth.

"Wait one moment, my dear loves," said Mr. Piggott's voice again, lifted up in mild detention. "There's one other thing I want to warn you all against, and that is against sitting down on the damp grass. You know, my dear loves, that it must be so very wet after all the rain we have had, and indeed it is always very dangerous sitting out on the grass. Do you

171 From Old French (literally, from head to foot), meaning armed for battle.
172 Good will (French).
173 In a low voice (Italian).

remember what a terrible cold I got, dear Ma, after I had been sitting out on the grass one day, many years ago now?"

"O, I'll promise not to sit down anywhere at all, nor let the others either," cried Kate impatiently; and having made this rash vow she went.

How pleasant after the dusty Aber Fynach road looked the dappled lawns, spreading out, carpet-wise, at the feet of that before-mentioned pinchbeck[174] structure, Llyn Castle—that prince of shams! How cool the grass looked, shivering, rippling, shimmering in the little gentle breeze; bright light green in the sun, dark green under the sombre, shady trees, that spread their shelter so wide. They sheltered unwonted objects this afternoon—objects which the cows surveyed suspiciously from afar, and imagined first to be placed there with some reference to themselves. These objects were long tables and benches laid out after the usual fashion of tea-fights. Down their centre went, with a certain monotony which fatigued the fancy, piled-up dishes of buns, currant-bread, bread-and-butter—buns, currant-bread, bread-and-butter—buns. But amply equal to compensate this monotony was the infinite variety of the army of mugs which flanked this social board; a heterogeneous assembly, of which not one was like his brother; presents and tokens and keepsakes from every place under the sun, at least the sun of Wales. On these benches, in fruition of this banquet, were deposited in erect postures the bodies of the owners of these mugs, a company of small Welsh Christians, male and female, realising the last week's dream, eating acres of bread and scrape,[175] and cuneiform portions of cake—

"Greasing their fistisses
Up to their wristisses."[176]

Twice blessed were these young people, for what they ate they ate twice—once with their round eyes, once with their unintelligent Welsh mouths. And reversing the order of society, ministering to the wants of these beatified little boors, keeping up the supply of acres of bread-and-butter, and cuneiform portions of cake, moved several young ladies, glid-

174 See p. 64 , n. 55.

175 Thin coating of butter or meat dripping.

176 From a nursery rhyme: "Three little ghostesses/ Sitting on postesses,/ Eating buttered toastesses/ Three little ghostesses/ Greasing their fistesses/ Up to their wristesses."

ing and flitting about, all grace and white muslin and activity, reminding one of the houris that will bring good Moslems their sherbet and light their chibouques for them in their high-souled, intellectual paradise.[177] *There* were the Misses Stamer, condescending, shady-hatted *passées*,[178] *there* were also two dear friends they had staying with them; and there were Margaret and Kate Chester, neither condescending nor *passées*, fresh and active and good-natured, running about with decoctions of the feeblest of feeble tea out of the big urns, and asking *gorged* little boys whether they did not think they could manage one bit more. But there is a limit to even school-children's capacity. Wait but patiently enough and you'll bring them to acknowledge it in time. The Aber Fynach children were no exception to this rule, they had to cry "Hold, enough!"[179] at last; and then, urged on and incited thereto by a crinolined[180] government schoolmistress, and a lank-haired government schoolmaster, they stood up, laid their dirty little hands together, and, after the fashion of school-children, burst forthwith, uncomfortably soon after tea as it was, into song. They set up (not quite simultaneously) what was, I must say, if I pay any regard to truth, a dreadful hymn. By which I don't mean to say anything against the hymn itself, which was, I daresay, a very pretty well-composed hymn; but what I allude to was the manner in which it was conveyed by about fifty squeaky little voices, nobly regardless of time and tune. Six staves[181] it had; six several times it rose and fell, but the tortured air had peace at last, and it died away for good. And all this while Dare Stamer lay on the grass, a little way off, doing nothing, in lazy luxuriance, watching the active, summer-robed maidens; watching *one* rather from under the eaves of his hat—the youngest and smallest of all the maidens, as she passed hither and thither, freighted with buns and steaming mugs, taking, sometimes, cautious arrow-swift peeps in his direction.

Much as Dare looked down upon his sisters, and thoroughly good order as he kept them in, he was in reality profoundly afraid of them now—afraid of Augusta's sharp eyes; so he gave them no occasion against him,

---

177 Houris are the beautiful virgins said to reward believers in the Koranic paradise. A chibouque is a Turkish tobacco pipe.

178 Past ones (French); in this case a reference to the Misses Stamers' being over marriageable age.

179 See Shakespeare, *Macbeth* (first printed 1623), V.viii.34.

180 See p. 47, n. 24.

181 Stanzas.

as he lay there, paying no attention to any woman under the sun, having given no sign that he was aware of Kate's presence beyond a formal shake of the hand and a brace of languid remarks about the weather. But this neglect did not pain her, as the former one had done, for his eyes were upon her, and his eyes were to her as the sun is to the earth. Their warmth stirred her up to be so busy and laudably benevolent; perhaps if he had been away she might have been idle and slack-handed; but I do not know. I may do her injustice in that. Her thick white-muslin frock was as common and plain as a frock could be, and had been washed ever so many times; but, for all that, how close it sat, without a crease, to that well-sculptured form, how clearly it defined the outline of that fairy bust! And the sun kissed her hair, and her soft throat, and her hands—kissed away as if he never could be sated, and made Dare quite jealous. He would be a lucky Moslem that should have his sherbet brought him by such a houri.[182] The hymn came to an end, I have said; the last nasal hallelujah became the property of the past, and it was intimated to Cambria's[183] sons and daughters by the crinolined government schoolmistress and the lank-haired government schoolmaster that they were at liberty to disport themselves as seemed good in their eyes. So now they were scattered all over the pleasant lawns and meadows, playing with a business-like vigour, which excited the marvel of those elders who had seen them feed, and roused envy of their digestive powers.

"I should think we had done our duty now," said Miss Stamer to the company generally. "I suppose we may leave the little wretches to their own devices. I'm sure another of those verses would have killed me outright."

"Let's walk down to the fernery," suggested Augusta; "I want to show Florence my new bit of cristata:[184] it will make her so envious. Will you come, Miss Chester?"

So they sauntered away, sweeping, trailing-robed, over the grass and the buttercups. They went down the hill; but Kate did not accompany them,—*dis aliter visum*,[185]—and the choice morsel of cristata remained unseen by her till the day of its death, or hers, for I don't know which *came first*. She had risen reluctantly from the bench, where she sat fanning her-

182 See p. 130, n. 177 above.

183 "Cambria" is an ancient term for Wales.

184 Plant known as cockscomb because its blooms resemble a rooster's comb.

185 The gods decreed otherwise (Latin).

self with an improvised fan of horse-chestnut leaves after her exertions, and prepared, with a very ill grace, to follow—for what shred of an excuse had she for staying behind? But that was not Dare's intention; his turn had come now. He leapt up from his comfortable lounging-place, came quickly towards her, and said, in an eager whisper:

"Stop here; don't go off with those women. I want you to come to the conservatory with me instead. Only wait till they're round the corner out of sight. You'll come, Kate, won't you?"

Kate nodded her head.

"Yes, I'll come," she said; and she sat down contentedly again, and fanned herself with fresh vigour.

"There, they're gone now," said Dare, drawing a long breath of pleasure as the last petticoat disappeared round a bend in the drive. "And now let's have a look at you after all these days."

And he did take one of those long, unshackled looks he loved; his eyes, after their three days' fast, were ravenous, and feasted now royally. Kate stood before him, as good and docile a little creature as could be seen, with her hands folded, and her eyelashes caressing her cheek—on approval, like a Circassian slave at the market of Constantinople.[186]

"Will that do?" she said at last, looking up inquiringly, with a laugh.

And it would have been insulting to those features then to say that that erring, *retroussé* nose, and that briefest of brief upper lips were piquant—they were piquancy's self.

"Not near," replied Dare's low voice, with strong emphasis.

"Well, then, it must," rejoined Kate, laughing again, provokingly and provocatively. "You are unreasonable;" and a devil of coquetry entered into her, and she half covered her face with the broad horse-chestnut fan. "I thought we were going to the conservatory," said she, peeping between the leaves at her companion.

"All in good time," said Dare coolly, becoming master of the fan, and tossing it to the winds of heaven. "But before we go you'll be kind enough to put on your hat, won't you? or you'll be burnt all manner of colours," he added, affecting airs of ownership which felt uncommonly pleasant.

His Circassian must not have her white skin tanned.

"I shall do nothing of the kind," said Kate rebelliously. "I don't care

186 Inspired by tales of their living in the sultan's harem during the time of the Ottoman empire, Circassian women of the northern Caucausus symbolized enslaved and objectified female beauty in nineteenth-century Orientalist discourses.

if I'm burnt as black as a coal."

"I should like to see you then," said Dare; and his lips curved into one of his gleaming laughs. "What a dear little negro you would make! But come," said he, not accustomed to have his will run counter to, fully intending to be obeyed this time, "put on your hat, there's a good child;" and he picked it up off the grass.

"*No, I will not,*" replied Kate, with great distinctness of utterance, setting her small teeth firmly, impelled thereto still by the demon of coquetry; and she smiled, defiant and saucy, and pushed away her ill-used head-gear.

"You wicked little thing!" said Dare, vexed and bewitched. "I do believe the very fact of asking a woman to do a thing makes her resolute against it."

"If I may not tan my own complexion, whose may I?" she said gaily, and so saying, she lifted up her happy, beautiful eyes to his, and he, looking down into them, lost himself in their light, as we "lose the lark in heaven."[187]

CHAPTER XIV

OFF they strolled then, as slowly as two people with the right complement of legs apiece could stroll, in the direction of the conservatory; and as it was not much more than a hundred paces off, even they got there before long. And how marvelously pleasant it was when they were fairly inside that "box where sweets compacted lie;"[188] how almost oppressive, overpowering, the fragrance of the warm damp atmosphere, where a thousand sweet smells strove perpetually for mastery! There, side by side, gathered from the far east and the far west, blossomed and reigned Nature's most regal flower-daughters. Gorgeous, stately flowers, that had hitherto revealed their passionate hearts, fold after fold, to the fainting air of some cloudless, rainless, brazen tropic sky, now poured forth all their sweets, put on all their brilliant apparel, under our watery, sickly sunbeams. There great dark leaves, moss-green, rose-veined, drooped heavy with their own weight; there crimsons and scarlets burned and flamed, imperial, with a depth and intensity of colour which our dear, pale-faced northern flowers never dreamed of putting on. What of man's devising

187 Tennyson, "Lancelot and Elaine," in *Idylls of the King* (1859), l. 655.
188 George Herbert, "Virtue" (1633), l. 10.

can be more intoxicating than one of these temples dedicated to rich odours and brave tints? And when there stands in this temple, among those gorgeous flowers, a lovely woman—lovely, with the ripe womanly development of one of Titian's Venuses,[189] not with the emaciated prettiness of modern young ladies—the subjugation of the senses may be supposed to be complete. Kate was in ecstasies. She ran hither and thither, smelling first one, and then another.

"Delicious!" she cried, "wonderful! I wish I was gardener here. Flowers are one of the very few weak points in my character. O, O!"

The wealth of enjoyment there was in that last "O!" beggars description.

"Well, you certainly are an adept at smelling," called out Dare at last, from the comfortable position he had taken up on a rustic seat with wooden legs, very ingeniously contorted in a sort of elephantiasis.[190] "There, you've gone the round of them all now about seven times. Do come and sit down here; I want to talk to you."

Kate worshipped at the shrine of one more gardenia, and then came and filled the situation indicated.

Dare rested his arm on the much-twisted wooden back behind her, and prepared for a comfortable chat.

"You have not told me yet," he began, sinking his voice to that low soft key which made tender things sound so infinitely more tender,—"you have not told me yet how much you have missed me these last few days."

Kate, very rudely, took no notice of this question. She was much interested in drawing an ingenious design on the pavement, with the point of the afore-mentioned natty little boots. Let us hope she did not hear it. At last the silence became rather a weight to her, so she raised herself up, and asked with great irrelevancy:

"Where's the rose you said you wanted to show me?"

"O, hang the rose!" replied Dare, laughing; "there is not one that I know of; but come, Kate, you have not answered my question yet. How much did you miss me? Very badly, or rather badly, or only a little? I know you did miss me a little," he added confidently, smoothing down, with big, leisurely fingers, the great silky-brown moustache which was the one

189 Fond of painting fleshy women with red hair, the sixteenth-century Italian painter Titian (1488/90-1576) produced several famous images of the goddess of love, including Venus of Urbino (1538) and Venus Anadyomene (circa 1555).
190 Disease that thickens the skin.

beauty of his ugly face. "So come, confess it, there's a good child. You know it is horribly wicked to tell stories. You'll go to some awfully bad place if you do."

"Well, it *was* rather dull," owned Kate reluctantly, dropping the words out very slowly, one after another, as if they were forced out of her; "but O," she went on, more quickly, looking up, as a remembrance of her woes flashed back upon her, "I've got such bad news to tell you—something that happened since you went away."

"I suppose that valuable dog of yours has broken his leg or tumbled into a fit," suggested Dare, with the same condescending sort of petting pity one might express towards a child whose doll had begun to bleed sawdust.

"No; worse than that," replied Kate, shaking a sage Lord-Burleigh head.[191] "O, you'd never guess; it is that we are going away on Monday next, instead of when I told you;" and she added another stroke or two to the device on the pavement.

"Going away!" said Dare, without a grain of the anticipated dismay in his tones, in a voice *so* cool—the eldest son of indifference—that Kate looked up, astonished and staggered, to see whether his face did not give the lie to his ice-cold words. But no; he did not look a bit vexed; he was smiling; a smile not only executed by the lips, but consented to and shared in by all the harsh dark features.

"And I'm sure we shall never come back again," pursued Kate, bitterly disappointed, but still nourishing a faint hope that he had not taken in the meaning of her words. ("He must be strangely altered, if that does not move him," she thought.)

"*Indeed!*" answered Dare, with polite interest; calmly as he might have heard of the going away of Daddy Piggott; and the smile still hovered over the swart face and brightened it.

Kate could not dissimulate what she felt, even to save her life.

"I'm sure I don't know why I told it you as bad news to you, or to anyone else either. I told stories; it is not bad news;" and she turned her face away pettishly; leaving only for Colonel Stamer's consideration a very neat parting down the back of her head, and much furzy hair.

191 During the play-within-a-play about the Spanish Armada in Richard Brinsley Sheridan's *The Critic* (1779), the character of Lord Burleigh, Elizabeth I's chief advisor, enters shaking his head over affairs of state, giving rise to the phrase "Burleigh's nod."

"And you don't know any of the people we know, and you never go up to town," said Dare, with a fund of unrestrained amusement, and a much greater fund of restrained something else in his voice; "so I don't suppose we shall ever meet again."

"Certainly not, I should say," answered Kate with tragic solemnity; very firm and distinct at the "certainly;" very shaky and weak at the "say."

"Well, then, Kate," said Dare, liking to prolong his pleasure, and watching her as a cat does a mouse, "I suppose we may consider our acquaintance as come to an end, mayn't we?" and the bad, bold eyes read off her poor tell-tale face like a book.

Where were all the short-lived little coquetries now?

"I suppose so," answered Kate, and she lifted the green eyes to his cruel face, and they shone through two big tears, clear and pellucid as ocean water over yellow sand on a shining day.

Kate did not look pretty when she cried, any more than any other woman under the sun; her nose got red and her eyelids swelled like any other young lady's; but she was not crying now. Those tears were never shed, and had no successors.

Dare set his teeth hard for a minute, and drew in his breath determinately, keeping shut the sluice-gates of the great flood that was surging, boiling, raging within him, which he would have to give into soon. Not yet, not yet! One moment more.

"No more walks, Kate," said the mellow voice, when at length its owner could persuade it to speak at all; and it sounded to Kate as utterly sad as the knell that goes toll, toll, from the church close by, when the funeral is winding slow and black up the hill.

"No more," replied Kate, choked; and it seemed impossible but that those two tears must have many successors.

"I shall have to stroll about with my sisters, sha'n't I, Kate? Won't it be dull? And who'll you walk with?" asked Dare tormentingly, feeling that he could not go on in this strain much longer.

"Nobody!" answered Kate, nearly broken-hearted at the turn things had taken; so different from what she had pictured them.

"Nobody!" repeated Dare: "poor little lonely Kate!"

It was no use talking, she could not bear it any longer; the compassion of that rich falling cadenced voice stabbed her; he was *pitying* her for loving him so much. She got up hastily, intending to rush off blindly somewhere; it did not matter where; what did she care if she did meet all those women, and they knew all about her?

"Stop, Kate," said Dare, then catching hold of her by the hand, and the change in his tones made her cease her agonising pleadings.

"Let me go; let me go."

The flood was rising up now in him higher, higher; taking giant steps; fiercer than ever it surged and boiled; he *could* not stand against it any longer. It was stronger than he. Devils are mightier than men. What good wasting one's strength wrestling with them? He gave in.

"Don't you think, Kate," he said, and the mounting flood made his voice very husky, "that as we are going to part so soon we had better say good-bye now?"

"Yes," answered Kate, standing there captive, dazed, and not knowing exactly what she said.

"And how do friends bid each other good-bye, Kate?" asked Dare again.

He could not speak above a deep whisper now, and the light he had been keeping out of his eyes with such difficulty blazed full in them; lurid, like a watchfire on a dark night.

"I don't know," said Kate mistily, with the shade of something that was coming dim on her soul.

"Is it this way, Kate?" came the low whisper, shaken and hurried; and off went the last rag of restraint, and he wrapped his arms around her as she stood before him, tighter, tighter, and bent down his head from its stately height to her small uplifted face, nearer, nearer, till their lips met, and were joined in a wedlock so fast, so long enduring, so firm, that it seemed as if they never could be divorced again. Such a kiss as the one that Fatima spake of—

"Once he drew
In one long kiss my whole soul through
My lips, as sunlight drinketh dew."[192]

Silence, except that the flowers rustled their leaves, and waved their bright heads sympathetically. They had seen something of that kind before, when they lived in the tropics. At last Dare spoke, husky-voiced yet, holding his prize still in her iron bondage, as if he never intended to loose her out of that strong prison again.

192 Tennyson, "Fatima" (1833), ll. 19-21.

"Kate, do you love me? I don't know why I ask; I know you do; but I like to hear you say so."

"Yes," replied Kate, almost inaudibly, drunk with a sense of her own bliss.

"Say, yes, Dare," urged he again; for having now succumbed for good, he felt as if he never could have enough of clasping her there to himself.

"Yes, Dare," replied she obediently; more inaudibly than ever.

"Much or little, Kate?" asked he again, with hoarse-toned, exacting fervour.

"Much," said Kate briefly.

"How much?" asked he, thirsting to have her own voice make her altogether his for ever and ever.

Kate being thus catechised, took courage.

"O, why do you ask me?" she said, and she gazed right up in those wells of liquid fire, his eyes, and was not a bit terrified of them now. "Why, I love you better than anything or anybody in this or any other world: better, O, much better, than my own soul; so well that I am quite frightened at myself sometimes;" and a shadow fell on the rapt green eyes.

"Darling!" whispered Dare, satisfied at last; and indeed it would have been very odd if he had not been. "And how much do you suppose I love you, Kate?"

"I don't know," said Kate, having subsided into shyness, after making her declaration.

"So much," said he, with condensed passion, and the heavy brows drew together in the intensity of his emotion, "that I'd cut your dear little soft throat here, this very minute, if I thought any other man would ever kiss you again as I have done to-day."

I've done. I'm tired of writing about love-making. When two people have climbed up to the extremest pinnacle of insane bliss, it is best to leave them alone there. They come tumbling down quick enough, without any one's help; and so there I leave Dare and Kate.

CHAPTER XV

SUNDAY morning, in June, by the sea-side. Rest for the bathing-machines; rest for the abominably overworked rickety-legged riding horses; rest for the numberless donkeys; rest for the wooden spades; rest for everything and everybody. Sunday morning, with that peculiar peacefulness, that freedom from bustle and turmoil which our fancy is apt to impute to every object in earth and sea and sky on that one day. A peacefulness which is merely and entirely the daughter of our own imaginations; prone to project their feelings and sensations on all inanimate objects around them, which has no foundation in reality. It is a very pardonable freak of the imagination, I think, on such a Sunday as the one I am going to talk about. The sky seemed to rise higher, clearer, bluer than its wont; making one vast cathedral of the one universal catholic faith[193] for men to fall down and worship their God in; that great dome which those mighty forefathers of ours, the Normans, with a noble spirit of imitation, tried to copy in those round arches of theirs, which still stand, in their solid stateliness, monuments of their veneration and their zeal.[194] The sea, too, had put on its Sunday garb of quiet; it had laid aside all its smiles, its dimples, and its sparkles, all the weapons of its coquetry, and exchanged them for a most sweet gravity. There it lay, smooth and waveless, as a stagnant inland pool. But there was nothing of stagnation in this gravity. Rather it seemed as if the ocean was looking up in solemn contemplation to the heavens,

"Held in holy quiet, still."[195]

She had fallen into a nun-like, St.-Agnes[196] sort of humour, which suited her marvelously well. It is near church-time, and the bells are giving out their voices—those bell-tones which seemed so passing merry and jocund to some, so unutterably sad to others; the church's full chimes, and the Wesleyan's[197] one shrill tinkle mingling amicably together. And the road up to Aber Fynach,—that road which is always so cool and refreshing in summer, so shady and windless on winter days; that road where the ivy hangs great dark-green nosegays over the wall to the passers-by,—how much more thronged than usual it is! Along it all Pen Dyllas is streaming saunteringly in their Sunday best. Comfortable fathers and mothers

193 "Catholic" refers here not to Roman Catholicism but to a universally held belief.

194 When they invaded England in 1066, the French Normans brought with them their style of architecture, one of whose distinctive features were rounded, so-called "Romanesque" arches.

195 Unidentified reference.

196 An early Christian martyr who died aged 12 or 13, St. Agnes symbolized virginal innocence.

197 Methodist chapel, after John Wesley (1703-91), founder of the denomination.

of families, broad-backed, well-to-do, who have been getting fat in each other's society for the last twenty or thirty years; young men in lavender gloves and infinitesimal prayer-books; young women in crisp well-starched Sunday dresses, and parasols that rival the hues of the prism; each group chattering away about the trifles which were of such interest to it, and such caviare to all the others. And all the chatting and laughing went on, unconsciously, in a more subdued key than on other days; for is not it Sunday, and are not we going to church?

> "On to God's house the people press'd,
> Passing the place where all must rest;
> Each enter'd like a welcome guest."[198]

The bells have ceased their calling and inviting now; for the feast is ready, and the guests are set; the dissenting tinkle has the field all to itself. The stream of people has flowed inside the gray weather-beaten walls, and made a many-coloured pool there, all but a few hopelessly belated ones who come in, puffing and panting, towards the second lesson. And the chants rise and fall in mellow cadences; the voices of the choir distinct and separate each from the other, but well blended,—for a wonder, it is a good choir,—resting on, as it were, and supported by the organ's "monotonous undertone."[199] And the psalms, the sweet singer's glad verses,[200] swell out jubilant; and now we have got to the litany, and everybody has gone down on their knees, and is burying their head in their pocket-handkerchief, or their coat-sleeve, according to the sex, and finding it very hot and exceedingly uncomfortable. The grand simple words go up to heaven reverently as they do every Sunday—"In the hour of death, and in the day of judgment, good Lord, deliver us."[201] Solemnest of all the solemn petitions the Church offers to her Spouse![202] I wonder to how many those words are as husk and chaff, to how many the very pith and marrow

198 Tennyson, "The Two Voices" (1842), ll. 409-11.
199 Possibly from Henry Wadsworth Longfellow's "The Inn at Genoa" in "The Golden Legend" (1851), l. 63.
200 David, traditionally considered author of the Psalms.
201 Litany from the Anglican Book of Common Prayer: "In all time of our tribulation; in all time of our prosperity; in the hour of death, and in the day of judgment, Good Lord, deliver us."
202 See Ephesians 5: 22-23, where the Church is described as the bride of Christ.

of their soul's being. The parson has put on his black gown now, and is gone up into his pulpit, and all the congregation try to settle themselves in positions as little torturing as the over-full pews and the hard seats and the June sun will let them. Kate Chester's green eyes are fixed upon the ceiling as if in rapt attention, as she sits there close to the door, on a humble bench between Margaret, pink-bonneted, wakeful, on the one side, and Blount, tawny-haired, drowsy, on the other. The good man, after St. Paul's pattern, "reproves, rebukes, exhorts; reasons of righteousness, temperance, and judgment to come;"[203] tells loathingly of the dross, and the filth, and the weary hollowness of this earth's joys, of that death into whose jaws we fall, hundreds of us, every hour that beats; points lovingly upward; beseeches all with eager zeal to set their feet on the lowest rung of that steep ladder that scales the sky.

"A beautiful sermon," everybody said; and Kate sat entranced, with rapt green eyes, and did not hear one word of it. She was saying over again all that wonderful dialogue that was spoken yesterday among the flowers, when lips did more and better than speak; was inventing a yet more entrancing dialogue for to-night; was wondering whether that was Dare's or Guy's coat-sleeve which she saw up the vista of the long aisle, resting easefully on the door of the Stamers' big pew. Only twenty, and all her troubles over already. What a lie to say that the course of true love never ran smooth![204] A whole lifetime with Dare before her, sixty years perhaps, or at all events fifty; and what an immense time fifty years was! Why, old Daddy Piggott was only fifty. And they'd be buried together, when they died, in the Stamer vault, so close that in a few years people could not distinguish the dust of one from the dust of the other. And one monument should be put up to them both, somewhere amongst those frightful cenotaphs and hatchments that are looking down now, grim, on the party of live Stamers below. The inscription should be in English, that everybody might know how Dare Stamer and his wife Catherine Stamer departed this life on the same day, and now lie buried underneath this chancel. Kate had not quite satisfied herself with the wording of this inscription, when she was conscious that the sermon had come to an end, by everybody rising. And the benediction has fallen soft on the ear, and all are flowing out again into the cool churchyard. Kate lingers in God's

203 See 2 Tim. 4:2.

204 Aphorism inspired by Shakespeare's *A Midsummer's Night Dream* (first printed 1600), I.i.34: "The course of true love never did run smooth."

Acre, as the Germans call it, where the grasses are waving and swaying as joyfully in the June breeze as they could in a less serious place, where each green mound and small inequality in the smooth turf marks the spot where someone is waiting, waiting; where

> "Each in his narrow cell for ever laid,
> The rude forefathers of the hamlet sleep."[205]

Kate strays from tomb to tomb, willing to delay her going; marks the neglected rose and the choked wallflower, that tell of a love that has waned; reads the uncouth verses; the consoling words of promise; reads the dates when John Hughes and Robert Jones, and Hugh Owens said good-bye to earth with eyes that did not see them. Her patience is rewarded at last. A big man comes out of the low porch in a tall hat, and a faultless Sunday coat that sits like wax to his magnificent figure; comes out quickly, and strides over the graves to her side,—a big man, who has been pushing and hurrying through the issuing crowd, with dark-browed impatience, towering like King Agamemnon among the Achæans,[206] a full head and shoulders over most of them.

"Here you are, darling!" he says hurriedly, when he gets up to her. "I could not get out before, and I cannot stay a second now, for Augusta is hurrying out to spy after me as quick as she can;" and he cast a black look, half of dread, half of bitter anger, at the door behind him; "but I was bent on seeing you, Kate, to tell you you must meet me to-night at eight o'clock on the shore by the bridge across the railway. Now don't fail on any account; remember, eight o'clock exactly."

She says "Yes," and puts out a small gray glove for him to shake. He just touches it, and then turns away quickly, and strides back leisurely, in time to receive Miss Augusta coming in haste out of the porch, with a scowl, which shows that young lady she has again been found out. And Kate strolls home, demure and decorous, perfectly satisfied with the manner in which morning service is conducted at Aber Fynach church.

---

205 Thomas Gray, "Elegy Written in a Country Churchyard" (1751), ll. 15-16.

206 Agamemnon was commander of the Greek (Achaean) forces during the Trojan War.

CHAPTER XVI

SUNDAY evening now; evening service over, and all the church-goers trying to cool their hot cheeks, after the close, stuffy pews, in the breeze that comes so freshly from somewhere over the waves. Everybody is on the shore; all the élite and the all the non-élite; those who on week-days are divided between drives in little hired carriages, mountain rambles, and railway excursions are all poured out on the beach. Maid-servants are conducting boisterous flirtations with loutish, slouching youths, in a sort of mongrel, quasi-nautical attire. Uncouth hobble-de-hoys and shrill "gamins"[207] are parading about in noisy, loud-laughing parties, luring any unwary dog they may meet into the water with far-thrown splashing stones. The sun was preparing for his daily death; but dying with slow majesty, as a king should die. Even though he was "*in extremis*,"[208] his face kept so much of its own brightness that you could not look at it yet with steady, undazzled eyes; all his fire-rays were round him still, going down to meet extinction with him in the baths of ocean. And from him a tremulous fluctuating path of rose and flame led over the waters, as if all seas and floods wanted still to commemorate the blessed feet that once walked Galilee's dark waves so many ebbing years ago.[209] The sea still kept her sweet Sunday gravity; all her innumerous smiles laid aside till to-morrow—not one curving her cheek. Lovingly she stretched out her arms to embrace the slow-descending sun (his strength so nigh spent now), and invited him to sleep, quiet and cool, all night on her breast. The moon climbed shy and silent meanwhile up the dusk summer sky, over the shoulder of a low hill, at the head of the quiet valley, and blushed red and warm under the sun's regal eyes, though it was but an expiring gaze he could give to "that orbed maiden"[210] now. The great level sand-plains stretched away, yellow and brown-streaked, so smooth and ridgeless that one could fancy that elves and fairies would be whirling round in airy cir-

---

207 Street urchins (French).

208 At the point of death (Latin).

209 Gospel accounts of Jesus walking on water may be found in Matthew 14: 22-33, Mark 6: 45-52, and John 6: 16-21.

210 Percy Bysshe Shelley, "The Cloud" (1820), ll. 45-46.

cles on their shining surface, when everybody else was in bed and asleep. I have said that all Pen Dyllas was out on the beach, and so they were; that part of the beach which was just opposite the place itself, and for about a quarter of a mile on each side of it, in both directions. But further on there were stillness and untrodden flats—unpeopled as Sahara itself. The gulls had it all to themselves here, at least, to speak exactly, nearly all to themselves; for there were just two people besides, whom it seems hardly worth while mentioning. A big, dark gentleman, and a small fair lady sauntering along, as if most decidedly not engaged in a walking wager.

"Come away from here, Kate," Dare had said, when Kate had first joined him, obedient to his injunctions, exactly on the stroke of eight; and the dark face had a preoccupied, angered look upon it, as if its possessor had just been crossed in something he desired. "There's no possibility of having any peace or privacy in this abominable hole. There's not a spot where one can have the smallest chance of being left alone. These snobs," he said, raising his voice a little, so that the aforesaid snobs might hear, "seem as if they had never seen a lady or gentleman either before!"

This was not all Dare's conceit. There was some slight foundation in fact for his wrath, as he glared irefully at a couple of innocuous young haberdashers, who were turning their heads back to look, with admiring interest, at two figures which were made after a cut not common in Pen Dyllas. So he had hurried her away from among the honest, fat burghers, and the comfortable Sunday-clothed tradespeople, beyond the last group of gossiping women and befurbelowed children; on and on, further still, round the base of a little rugged hill that in spring tides stands ankle deep in salt-water, out of sight of the little cottage by the railway—out of sight of Pen Dyllas itself; saying hardly anything, either of them, as they passed along; for Dare seemed to have got a silent fit upon him, and Kate, chameleon-like, took her colour from him. Her love was not exacting; with Elaine, she could have said,

"Nay, but near thee, dear lord, I am at rest."[211]

Nothing but sea-gulls now round the sheltering corner of this little hill—ubiquitous sea-gulls,—and Dare stops short, and heaves a deep sigh out of his great chest, and says,

---

211 Inexact, Tennyson, "Lancelot and Elaine," in *Idylls of the King* (1859), l. 828.

"There! we're safe from inquisitive snobs now, I think, Kate. Let's sit down here and rest."

So they sat down on a heap of stones, and Dare took off his hat and threw it beside him, and pushed off the dark rings of hair, not allowed to be long enough to amount to curls, from off his wide deep-lined brow; and for a space they both sat silent, looking out over the broad blue desert before them, with gravity in their eyes. But their gravity was not of the same sort in its inward workings, through it was alike in its outward manifestations. Kate's rose out of her deep gladness; the weight of which was so heavy that it crushed out all desire for light laughter and little jokes and pretty playfulnesses.

One does not laugh when one is most blessed. She was holding communion and talk with this great bliss within her now, trying to take its measure and its weight, trying to feel how wide it spread, trying to fathom the depth of the sea of passion that lay calm and untempest-shaken now in her breast, and failing utterly.

Dare's gravity was not so simple in its origin; it was of a more compound character; it had two parents. One was the strongest, wildest joy he had ever felt, or ever could feel, and the other the bitterest annoyance he had ever experienced in all his thirty years of evil doing. He had to-day been thwarted and bored and badgered; roused, in fact, into one of his worst rages by a combined attack on the part of his relatives. "D—n them all," he was saying now, with gentlemanlike pious affection. Moreover, he was registering an inward vow—an oath, not loud, but deep as his being's self—that let him be worried and bullied and set upon by his father, by his mother, by his brother, by his sisters, by his uncles, by his aunts, by his cousins, and by anyone else who chose to try, together or severally, that no human power should avail to take little Kate out of his fast-enclosing arms again. It would have been all very well to talk of giving her up a fortnight ago; but *now* all the men upon earth and all the devils in hell should not snatch her away out of his grasp.

He was better now, and turned round to Kate.

"I'm a dull fellow to take a walk with; aren't I, Kitty?" he asked; and his stern ill-tempered mouth relaxed into a smile that was quite gentle. "Here I have been sitting for the last half hour, never uttering to you a word. It was a great mistake your not taking Guy instead of me. Why, he'd have rattled away by the hour to you."

"You could never be a dull fellow to me," said Kate, very openly, with sweet flattery, which was yet bare truth. "I should not be a bit dull if you were to sit here all night till the sun comes up again over there;" and she pointed to the east. She did not see why she should keep that irksome cloak over her love any longer now; there was no need for it.

"So you like to be with me, little Kate, do you?" asked Dare, who never could hear this formula repeated too often; and he picked up a stone and aimed it at an inoffensive gull that had come unwarily close; however, he did not hit it.

"Of course I do," replied Kate, with a ridiculous imitation of one of Dare's frowns; "and you know that as well as I do, only you like to hear me make a fool of myself."

Another gull came quite close with impunity now, for Dare's eyes had found their favourite resting-place.

"So you like me, do you?" he asked.

"Yes, yes, yes," cried Kate, quasi impatient. "How many times must I tell you so?"

"You're rather singular in your opinion, Kate," he went on; "most people do not like me," he said, with haughty indifference as to what anybody thought of him; "they say I'm a sulky, ill-conditioned sort of beggar."

"I don't care how sulky you are," replied Kate stanchly. "I'm sure you can get into dreadful rages; nobody that had seen you frown could doubt that. But I don't mind that at all. I would not have you altered if I could."

"You've the bad taste to like me, sulks and all, eh, Kate?" said Dare, with a deep pleased laugh; and then it occurred to him that she was absurdly and disagreeably far off; and he stretched out an arm, and pulled her gently to him. "Are you contented now, you small person?" he asked, with tender possessiveness; "or are you very anxious to get away? not that I should let you, if you were."

"Perfectly contented," said Kate, with great candour, and then silence reigned yet a little while again. The sea creeps up a few yards nearer, with stealthy ripples; the sun is almost gone; there is hardly anything remaining of him, but the bright memory he has left in the western sky. And the moon steals up higher and higher, looks down on the lovers, and dashes some of her white light on that full recumbent form, and under those green eyes. Then Kate withdrew herself from Dare's arms, and said suddenly to him, looking quite excited at some thought that had just visited her. "Dare, do you remember that day you met me in the road?"

"Of course I do," answered Dare. "What a wicked, tantalising little sinner you were that day, Kate!"

"Was I?" said Kate, smiling a satisfied little smile. "Well, you know just before I met you, I had been in the wood, O, for ever so long. O, Dare, you don't know how wonderfully miserable I was that day, such a fuss I made, all by myself, because I thought you did not care about me!" and the thought of her past woes interrupted the thread of her narrative.

"Poor little soft kitten!" he said, "but what was the nice little anecdote you were going to tell me? do let's have it."

"Why," said Kate; "when I was there, all by myself, I said such wicked things. I said that I wished to goodness I could make a bargain with God, that I might have you all to myself, for just one month, to be always with you; and then afterwards I said I should be quite content to be lost and miserable and ruined for all ages afterwards. And since yesterday, I have been thinking, Dare, that perhaps God has taken me at my word, and that I'm going to get my bargain. It seems like it, doesn't it?" she asked, and the green eyes looked rather awed and sobered. "Well," she said, shaking off that feeling, "even if it is so, I don't repent of my bargain. I'd do it again."

"Superstitious little goose!" said Dare, laying his dark hairy face caressingly against her smooth pale one. "You shall have me, since you think me such a prize, and heaven too, if there is such a place. But what have you go to do with heaven now? Plenty of time for that yet awhile. I could not spare you now," and his voice sank to one of the deepest of its rich bell tones.

"I'm glad of it," said Kate, not caring much whether what she said was very impious or not; "I'm sure I don't want to go there. You are not going there, I don't believe; and it would be very dreary without you."[212]

Wicked Kate has been running down hill very fast this week; she would have shuddered to say that ten days ago. Let no one think I am defending this girl, or holding her sentiments up as the pattern of what a young woman's should be; nor let anyone, however incapable of separating the historian's own ideas from those of the people whose history he is telling, imagine that I am describing Dare as being in anywise a hero or fine fellow. I think him as great and unmitigated a scoundrel as any strict-

212 Compare the scene in Volume I, chapter 9, of Emily Brontë's *Wuthering Heights* (1847), where Catherine, declaring she is far more similar to the outcast Heathcliff than to the conventional Edgar Linton, tells Nelly Dean that were she to go to heaven "I should be extremely miserable."

est censor of morals can do. For my part, I shall not pity him in the least when Nemesis overtakes him (if that grewsome lady ever does).[213] To describe bad actions is not, as I would meekly submit to indignant virtue, to be an accomplice in them; otherwise he who relates a murder is equal in iniquity to him who commits it, and the police-reporters are deeper dyed in guilt than any other members of the community. But to return.

That word "dreary" recalled Dare to a sense of his own afflictions; of the worries lying couchant,[214] ready to spring upon him so soon as he should reënter the hospitable portals of Llyn Castle. He brooded over them for a little bit, and then spoke, harsh-voiced and stern (for his spirit was in the gall of bitterness just then), harsh-voiced even to the small woman whose utter surrender would have made him merciful.

"You talk a great deal about your love for me, Kate. You have none of the pretty little mock coynesses that most women affect. You speak out more openly than many would be willing to do. I wonder is it all talk, all froth, and surface-bubbles, or would it be of force enough to make a sacrifice, even a great one, that should be asked of it?" and doubt and distrust reigned over the rugged features as he spoke.

"Try me!" said Kate briefly, with a calmness that was born of a deep consciousness of inward strength to do anything and dare anything he bid her.

"Are you like other women, I wonder—feeble and puny-spirited—whom a breath will blow away, lightly won and lightly lost?" said Dare again, thinking suspiciously of the many frail ones whom he had seen as darts running into that hand that leaned on them; "or are you made of sterner stuff, that would not stop at a trifle for the man you loved? Let me look at you, Kate." And he took her small white face between his two hands, and read it intently with soul-reaching steadfast gaze.

"I don't know what stuff I'm made of, I'm sure," said Kate, softly rubbing her cheek coaxingly against one of the hands that picture-wise framed it; "but I know I'd keep to you through thick and thin."

"So you say, Kate—so you say," replied Dare, distrustful still; "but you are a woman, and women are born to tell lies and drive men mad. Could you stand a great test, Kate—a test that other women would wince

213 Nemesis is the Greek goddess of retribution.

214 In heraldry a lion couchant (from the French verb "coucher," to lie down) lies down with its head raised. Dare's worries are like beasts ready to spring upon their prey.

and shrink away from?"

"Try me," again repeated Kate; and in the soft voice there was strong determination, as she lay there restful in all the wealth of her dead-leaf hair washed in moonlight on his breast.

"Perhaps, if I did, you'd fail me; perhaps, if I asked any sacrifice as a gift at your hands, you'd answer me, like other women, with puling objections of right and wrong, paltry cut-and-dried maxims about sin and folly," said Dare with fierce gloom.

"You are my right and wrong, Dare, now," returned the soft voice, resolute still.

A great light of joy rushed into Dare's eyes as he heard.

"Do you know what you are saying?" he said very eagerly. "Am I really your right and wrong? Do I stand in the place of Providence to you? If I were to tell you to do anything, however startling and terrifying it might be to you, would you do it simply, unquestioningly, *because* I told you?"

"*If—if*," answers Kate evasively, taking up a few grains of sand in her small hand and shaking them out to the wind again; "I hate *if*; it is an ugly word. Why should we speculate on impossible possibilities?"

"They are not impossible, Kate; they are eminently probable. Suppose, child, that I ask of you something that will make society sweep away its Pharisaical[215] garments and turn up its sanctified eyes at you?"

"O, society!" said Kate, with a light-hearted little laugh; "society, in the sense you mean, and I have only a bowing acquaintance. Every cloud has a silver lining; and that is one advantage of being completely insignificant, that you are not in much terror of Mrs. Grundy."[216]

"Why *will* you evade my question, child?" Dare said impatiently. "Let me put it so that there may be no mistake. If *here*, on this very spot, to-night, I ask you, with no other inducement but my love, to do something that will run counter to the whole course of your education, to every idea of right that has ever been instilled into you,—something indisputably wicked, according to the narrow bigots who lay down the law of what is wicked and is good,—would you do it, or would you not?"

Kate's smooth brow contracts into a frown of pain, and there is deep pain in her voice.

---

215 Hypocritical; from the sect of Pharisees in the New Testament, seen as rigid adherents to the letter, rather than the spirit, of the law.

216 Character in Thomas Morton's *Speed the Plough* (1798) who came to symbolize prudery and censorship.

"If you were to ask me to do anything very wicked you would not be *you*; at least you would not be the *you* you are to me."

"If you have been unwise enough to set me up on an *good-boy* pedestal," cries Dare fiercely, "for Heaven's sake pull me down again. God knows I have never lent you a finger to help myself up there. Kate" (emphasising every word), "once for all, never fancy that I shall not do anything because it is too wicked. If I have an end in view, get to it I must, even if the way lay through hell."

"But what opposition is there between love and goodness?" cries Kate passionately. "If it is wicked of us to love one another, why did God put it into our hearts?"

"*Why! why!*" repeats Dare scornfully; "if you stop to answer all the *whys* that meet you at every turn in this world you'll have to wait some time. But answer me, Kate, you *must* answer. Yes or no is the point that my life, and yours too, hangs upon."

"O, Dare, I don't want to answer," turning her head from side to side uneasily; "I hate suppositions."

"Answer, Kate!" with displeased command in the deep voice.

"Why do you drive me to such horrible alternatives?" she asked plaintively. "O God, I'm very wicked! I'd do anything almost sooner than lose you; and yet—"

"There must be no 'and yets' between you and me. If you give yourself to me—into my hands—it must be for ever. There must be no taking back the present again, as a child takes back a toy it has given to another child. The gift must be absolute, or in my eyes it is worthless. O, Kate, Kate, if I find I have tried you by too hard a test, harder than even you can stand,—find it out when it's too late, when I have lost you,—what should I do then, Kate? O God, what should I do?" and the hard deep-hued face looked quite white and drawn at the agony of the bare thought of that bereavement, that destitution.

"You'll never lose me unless you throw me away," returned Kate, with gentle tender firmness. "I should like to be asked to do some hard thing, that you might see how easily I'd do it. Nothing could be hard to me now—nothing, at least, that you'd ask."

"Put your arms round my neck, Kate," Dare bid her now, imperatively fond. "Let me feel them warm about me. Look up in my face and call me 'Dare,' as you did yesterday in the conservatory. Perhaps it is the last time you'll ever do it," he said, with bitter anticipation, fearing so much because he loved so much. "Perhaps to-morrow you'll call me Colonel Stamer, and bow to me," he added, gnawed with sharp pain. "Perhaps, after I've told you what I have got to tell you, you will not even bow to me."

Kate was very obedient. She threw her round firm white arms about his neck. She feigned no shyness, no aversion to so doing; she was past the stage for such hypocrisy here to-night on this lone beach.

"Dare," she said, steady and distinct; "my own Dare! The Dare for whom I'd have my head cut off, and not mind the axe coming down on it, hardly a bit."

"Darling little witch!" he said at last, under his breath, but she heard him. "O, Kate, you must keep to me indeed," he went on, with the wrecked pathos of a storm-shaken rudderless soul. "What would become of me if you did not? What should I do if I was to lose my little Kate, now when I've felt what it is to have her?"

"Hush, hush, hush! you're talking nonsense," said Kate, stroking his hairy countenance very soothingly. "Is not your little Kate close to you? Is not she disgracefully, shamefully willing to give up everything and everybody for you? What more can she say?"

Dare hardly seemed to hear her. He was looking out over the sea, that the moon had nearly clothed in her ghostly shimmering amice[217]—looking out with luminous eyes that had the anguish of the fallen archangel written in their bold shadowy depths. The stakes were the highest he had ever played for. If he lost, he should be a bankrupt for life, and the odds were against him. Strong to do and to dare as that southern-souled girl was for him, he knew she would shrink back from the precipice he was going to lead her to. Well, shrink as she might, she must take that dread leap with him to-night. He'd force her into the chasm if she would not go there of her own accord. There was no help for it now; she should not go back. So the fiends that ruled this man's soul with a continual wearing tyranny whispered to him, and he said:

"Yes," to them. "What should I do without the great green eyes that have looked away all my heart as never woman-eyes did before?" he went on; and the rich organ-tones fell shaken, and as it were jangled by the inward rack. "What devilries have you been practising on me, you little sorceress?" he inquired almost fiercely of her. "You're not beautiful, Kate; I doubt your being even pretty. My sisters laugh at the idea of your be-

217 Liturgical vestment.

ing good-looking. You've no fine, straight, regular features; your face has more faults than I can count; and yet you seem to me the loveliest woman that ever drove a man out of his senses."

"That's because you are blind," said Kate, smiling; "and I hope you'll continue so. You know it is to my advantage you should." And she tried to lure him back to cheerfulness by a little feeble attempt at a joke.

But Dare would not be so lured back. It would take a good deal to pull him out of the abyss he had got into. There was no joking with him to-night.

"Will you vow, Kate?" he asked, taking hold of both her hands, and bending down eagerly over her; "will you swear by everything you hold most sacred that nothing I can tell you, nothing that you can hear from anybody else about me, nothing that can by possibility happen, shall have power to make you give me up? Will you swear to do anything I bid you—*anything*, however wrong and abandoned it may seem in the eyes of the prudish world? Will you, Kate, will you?"

The devil's fire was in his eyes again—the fire she had been wont to shrink under. She winced now under it.

"Oaths were made for people who break their promises," she said restlessly. "I don't break mine. What makes you think I should?"

"It may be a caprice of mine—a fancy—what you will; but one likes to humour even the caprices of those one loves. I want to hear you yourself bind yourself to me; it will seem to me then a knot that neither man nor God can untie."

"It's that already, I think," she said firmly; "but since you will have it, I swear by everything I hold most sacred that nothing that can happen shall make me turn away voluntarily, of my own accord, from Dare Stamer. There!" she said, "see my perfect trust in you. I put my soul in your hand."

Dare was intensely relieved.

"Brave little child!" he said admiringly. "You are made of the right stuff, Kate—staunch to the backbone. And now let me tell you what has been weighing on my mind all this time; let me tell you the sacrifice I am going to ask of you. I tell you beforehand it is a great one—the greatest you could make. I wish I had done the job, I'm sure. I wish to God it was over!" and he looked as if the pill was a very bitter one to swallow. "But come nearer to me, Kate, while I talk to you. Let me hold you fast, and feel that you're not slipping out of my arms, little witch as you are!"

Kate laid down her head on his shoulder, as if its natural home was there, and a very dear home too.

"There," said she with a sigh, "that'll do, I suppose. Now go on."

END OF VOL. I.

VOLUME II

CHAPTER I

"WELL, you see," began Dare's narrative, "it seems that yesterday there was some prying, meddlesome fool of a gardener hanging about when you and I were in the conservatory together. He appears to have been watching us, in fact; pleasant thought, is it not? I wish to goodness I'd caught him! I'd have broken every bone in his body. Well, however, of course he immediately went and told Annette's maid, and of course she told Annette, and of course my sisters, with their usual good-nature, went and told my father. D—n them!" he said, forgetting his manners, as he thought of the trick they had played him, grinding his teeth, and feeling much disposed for woman-slaughter. "I'll punish them some day. Well, of course the governor and I had the most tremendous quarrel this morning. I never saw an old gentleman in such a rage in my life. Odd, was not it, on a Sunday morning, when he makes such a fuss, too, about the due observance of the Sabbath?" said Dare, with a pungent sneer. "Well, of course I got into a rage too, and no wonder; and we called each other some very ugly names, I can assure you, though it was Sunday. I flatter myself I made some remarks to the old gentleman that rather made him open his eyes," he went on, with a gleam of malignant pleasure. "I left him at last foaming at the mouth. I really thought he'd have gone into a fit, and that was the last thing I have seen of him."

"How unlucky!" said Kate, sympathetically, not much disturbed as yet.

"He vowed," continued Dare, "that he'll go to-morrow to your uncle and expose the whole thing. He was determined, he said, to save that misguided, ill-conducted young woman—that was you, Kate; those were the flattering terms he alluded to you in," Dare said, with sardonic, grim mirth. "Old fool! why cannot he mind his own business?"

"How cruel of him!" chimed in Kate. "Why are people's fathers so often their worst enemies? I wonder what would mine have been if he had lived. But, Dare, why need you mind him so much?"

"Why, you see," said Dare slowly (the words as if wrenched out of him, and with that dark flush which was his equivalent for blushing), "the fact of the matter is, that he's got rather a handle against me. There's one particular threat he can always hold over me, which gives him completely the whip-hand of me."

How galling that slight yoke was, Dare's face told pretty plainly. Kate did not ask what the one threat was. She was not inquisitive—willing to know just what he chose to tell her, and no more.

"So you see, Kate," said Dare, bringing his narration to a close, "that if we cannot manage to get the start of them to-morrow, those two old men will lay their wise heads together, and will take you away from me so effectually that I don't suppose you'll ever hear my name again; or, if you do, it'll only be with opprobrious epithets and maledictions attached to it."

I would not have been one of those two old men for something, if Dare could have got him in some retired spot—just then. Kate sprang up with positive terror in her whitened cheeks and quivering lips.

"Take me from you! O, Dare, don't let them do that; anything but that."

And she clung to him. Dare was the calm one now; her emotion stilled him.

"The only thing left to do now, Kate," he said, with low emphasis, "is to take some irrevocable step, some step that there can be never any going back from. We have got a few hours before us yet; the night is ours. It will be a good while before it begins to get red over there," he said, pointing to the dusk east. "It is for you to decide, Kate, whether the next sun that gets up there shall see us two parted, never to meet again anywhere, or joined so close and firm that there'll be no unjoining us again, that they may find their sage precautions have come a little too late."

"What step?" asked Kate, startled, but with a glimmering hope; and her eyes melted, big and loving and tearful, on his face.

"Can you take a leap with me to-night, Kate?" he asked, in answer, looking down into those dewy, green wells; "can you bear to be called bold and unmaidenly—though quite innocent? can you bear to do a thing that has come to be considered out of fashion, and vulgar? can you bear to have that bugbear, the world, turn a cold shoulder to you? can you bear to leave your sister, and your dear Blount, and your old uncle? can you bear to run away with the man you say you love so much *to-night?* Answer me, Kate, quick; answer me. I can't bear to be kept in suspense now. Yes or no."

And the second that elapsed till she spoke seemed two hours to him.

This, then, was the sacrifice to which, through the cloak of all his emphatic eager questioning, he had been pointing! He wanted to steal her for his wife, instead of asking her as a costly gift from those who had the keeping of her; wanted her to pass away with him stealthily through the darkness, like a thief or an assassin, as if he was ashamed of her. To a proud woman, like Kate, it *was* a sacrifice.

"To-night!" she said, with a startled shrinking look in her innocent passionate eyes,—"without telling *them*, when they have been so good to me these many, many years! at your bidding too, whom six weeks ago I had never seen; and they'd be so glad to hear of the great good luck that has happened to me! O, Dare, must it be *to-night?*"

"To-night, or never; choose, Kate, which. You must choose between them who, as you say, love you so much, and have been so kind to you all these years, and me, who have known you but a month, and love you—not at all perhaps."

"I choose," she said impulsively, her resolution coming back strong and firm, "whatever happens, I choose you!"

"You'll never repent of your bargain, child," answered Dare eagerly. He could breathe again now. "Not anybody or anything will dare to come and worry my little soft kitten as long as she is here," he said, dropping a light kiss on the dim moon-flooded hair that lay in such utter abandonment now on his breast. "At least, I don't think you'll repent, Kate," he repeated confidently.

"No, I'm sure I sha'n't," said Kate, strong-willed, though great sobbing sighs would come uninvited; and then she closed her eyes, and tried to realise the great plunge she was going to take. Still the thought would recur, the puzzling unanswerable doubt,—what was there in a union with her so impracticable and undesirable that it should have to be accomplished under the cover of night and secrecy, like a crime? Well, he was giving up position and parents' love for her: she must not be behindhand in generosity, nor hesitate about giving up something for him too. Why count the cost, when the gain was so immeasurably greater? What were the *bienséances*[1] of an artificial state of society? what were even Blount's boyish reproaches and Maggie's wounded feelings to her in comparison with him?

Then Dare spoke:

"Are you gone to sleep, Kitty, that you are so quiet?" and he tried to

1 See p. 107, n. 139.

get a good look under the heavy drooping lids—heavy with unshed tears, caused by the thought of Margaret and Blount's grieved surprise at her want of sisterly confidence in them. "Rouse up, darling!" he said tenderly. "Poor little child! she'll have to travel fast and far to-night. I'm afraid she'll be dreadfully tired."

"Where are you going?" asked Kate, half sick with excitement.

"To town to-night, and to Portsmouth to-morrow," said Dare with decision. He was not morose or gloomy now; mightily exultant rather, and his deep chest heaved with proud joy at the thought of getting utterly rid of all his home worries and vexations and galling chains; of balking and angering sorely all his kindred; of speeding away victorious, with his prey in his grasp. "My yacht is at Portsmouth; by the greatest luck in the world I had her brought round there only the other day."

"Your yacht!" exclaimed Kate, decidedly aghast. "Then we are going by sea!"

"Yes, by sea!" replied Dare, with strong rejoicing, mimicking her tones. "But you need not look so horror-struck, my little coward. You could not be frightened with me; you know you could not! And we'll float up and down all the summer months on the Mediterranean. Such a sea, Kate! Not a great gray blanket as this usually is, but as blue—as blue as the sky was to-day; and we'll sail in and out among those wonderful Greek islands I have told you about so often. How lovely my little white lily will look among those black-eyed Greek girls! And your old uncle and my old father may hunt in couples after us—pursue us over the high seas, if it amuses them. Will you come, Kate, now—will you come?"

"Yes," said Kate, almost inaudibly.

"We have not much time to lose," went on Dare, looking at his watch; "it's ten o'clock now. You see, Kate, after I had had that quarrel with my father this morning, I determined upon one last desperate effort. I made up my mind to try and persuade you to this plan,—which, by the bye, I composed principally in church this morning. And see what a conceited fellow I was, darling! how confident in my own powers of rhetoric, and what a teachable good little thing I expected to find you! I was right there, you see; for I told Johnson (that is my man) to have the dog-cart standing ready in the Llan Dyllas road, by Pen-y-Bryn, at half-past ten to-night. I daresay he'll be there soon now. There is a train for Ryvel at 11.30, for I looked, and we shall just be able to catch that, if we go at a good pace. I think we had better be going. Come, Kate!"

How near his prey was to his grasp!—quite within his reach! What can save her now? Kate began mistily to wonder why she could not have Dare, and yet avoid this equivocal step. Why could not she in the direct and open way become his wife, seeing that he loved her so much?

"But, Dare," she said, rising up and looking him straight in the face, "why is your father so very angry with you for loving me? Why cannot you take me openly, nobody hindering you, since you do like me, although I am so far inferior in every way to you?"

"There is a very excellent reason why I cannot, Kate," said Dare—and his face grew black as a winter's night—"because," and he positively writhed (strong young man as he was) in the agony of that moment—"because—O, Kate, the tug is coming now! Can you stand it, I wonder? Kiss me once more before I tell you. O, again, again! I would never tell you, only that I know you would find it out through some of my kind friends—because—I'm married already."

Silence—such a silence! How many years of anguish condensed into those few pulse-beats!

"Married!" said Kate at last, in a voice like an old man's. Where had her sweet little low tones gone to?

"Yes, married!" said Dare distinctly, feeling as if a great knife were running into his heart. "But don't speak in that voice, for heaven's sake, Kate; I cannot stand it. I had sometimes hoped you would have guessed it. Let me tell you all about it," he went on rapidly, determined, now he had begun, to go through the wormwood-flavoured[2] recital quickly, and have done with it for ever. "It was twelve years ago now. You were a little thing in the nursery then, Kate, and I was reading with an army-tutor at Bournemouth. Well, it was just such a dead-alive sort of place as this is; nothing on earth for a young fellow to do but get into mischief. Well, for want of anything better to do, just to kill time, in fact, I scraped acquaintance one day with the daughter of a retired skipper, who lived there. For ever accursed be the day when first I saw her red-and-white dairy-maid face! She was a very fine woman, people said—I believe they say so still.[3] As for me, you may imagine it is some time since I have seen Mrs. Stamer's beauties," he went on, with a grim merriment, which was more painful than any tears; with

2 Wormwood or artemisia, a plant used in making the dangerously toxic drink absinthe as well as herbal remedies, is known for its bitter taste.

3 During this period "fine" meant voluptuous. Dare complains elsewhere of his wife's corpulence.

an intensity of hate in his sneer, which friends might have admired and tried, at a respectable distance, to imitate. "Well, I used to wander about for hours with her—she with her great meaningless black eyes drawing me on as much as she could, and I—infatuated idiot that I was!—fancying myself every day more desperately in love with her; till at last one day I put the finishing stroke to my insanity, cutting my own throat irremediably, blasting my whole life to come, by walking into a church, and getting married to her.[4] There, that's all, and enough too, I think. I have made a full confession now, haven't I?"

After a moment Kate spoke, in that same unnatural old-man's sort of voice:

"Is she fond of you, Dare?"

"Yes, I suppose she is," replied Dare reluctantly; "unpleasantly fond, I should say. With my usual ill-luck, she has heard some false, trumped-up stories about you and me, Kate, and she has been sending me in consequence a series of the most lamentable effusions you ever read, all about her love, and her sufferings, and agony—all that sort of absurdity—till at last I had in self-defence to take to burning unopened any letters I saw addressed in my beloved consort's dear, lady-like handwriting."

Those gall-bitter sneers seemed to be the only things that saved him from choking.

"Pah! it kills me to think of her!"

"Have you seen her lately?" asked Kate calmly, so calmly that Dare was deceived. He began to believe that Kate had taken the news more coolly than he could have believed possible.

"Indeed I have," said he, with a countenance expressive of the most intense disgust. "Why, that was the business I had to go up to London about. I had to go up to pacify that woman, or I really believe she would have thrown herself over Waterloo Bridge, as she was always threatening to

---

4 Compare Dare's account of his marriage with Rochester's narrative of his disastrous union with Bertha Mason in chapter 27 of Charlotte Brontë's *Jane Eyre* (1847), a novel whose bigamy plot presumably influenced *Not Wisely*. Like Mrs. Stamer, Bertha is described as a "fine," or buxom, beauty whose charms temporarily dazzle a naïve youth. While the adulterous and insane Bertha, however, is linked to unruly colonial natives through her West Indian background, the Otherness of Dare's sane and faithful wife apparently consists of her inferior class origins (Dare's sneering comments indicate she is not a lady). Although the couple seems generally incompatible, it is presumably Mrs. Stamer's embarrassing class status above all which causes Dare and his snobbish family to conceal his marriage.

do. I'm sure I wish to God that I had let her now. But then I thought that it would make such an éclat[5] and fuss that it had better be avoided," remarked the would-be widower, with great *sang-froid.*[6]

"Was she glad to see you?" inquired Kate calmly, still bent on sparing herself no pang.

"*That* she certainly was," answered Dare emphatically, getting more and more easy in his mind. "Such a scene we had, Kate! I should have died laughing if I had been spectator instead of sufferer. I thought she would never have ended the enacting of the Prodigal Son over me.[7] Six fatted calves would not have been too many to slay in honour of my return. Such a giantess as she is, too, Kitty! She would make ten of you. Faugh! She is not my wife at all; she is a horrible nightmare."

"Good-bye, Dare," Kate said shakily. "You said right. Your test *was* too strong for me. I'm going."

Dare let her go a few unsteady paces in sheer astonishment; then he sprang up, made one step after her, laid his iron hand on her arm, and said in a low hissing whisper:

"*Going*, Kate! Are you mad, or is it a very bad joke that you are trying to play off on me? It is an execrable joke, if it is one, and very unseasonable."

She turned and faced him in the moon-light, all the youth gone out of her face.

"What have I done that you should think me so vile?" she groaned, smiting her hands together in her despair.

"Vile!" he repeated excitedly. "I thought you were made of nobler clay than other women—clay that could stand a stronger test. But I find you are all alike. As long as it is smooth sailing in a pleasure-boat on a summer sea with a man it is all right; but let there be any question of breasting a storm together, and we soon hear a different tale."

Kate hardly seemed to hear him.

"O, God!" she said, with a great laboured sigh, as if heaving up, with infinite strain and difficulty, some mighty weight from the depths of her soul, "what *have* I done? And *this* is your love—*this!* O, why were not you more merciful? Why did not you kill me, and let me die in my delusion?"

"Delusion!" he said fiercely. "If there has been any delusion it has been

5 Scandal (French).

6 Composure (French).

7 See Luke 15: 11-32 for the story of the Prodigal Son whose father feasts him when he returns home repentant.

of your own making. I never tried to deceive you. I told you plainly I was going to ask a sacrifice of you—a sacrifice too great, apparently, for your puny love and your pious scruples."

"Yes," she said, recovering her firmness with a mighty effort, and looking full and calm at him, with scornful, level fronting eyes; "immeasurably too great. There's no death so bitter I would not have—O, Dare" (her voice breaking down into a wail), "is it true, *really*? Are you *really* not my Dare, but another woman's? O, not really—not really!"

Dare sank on the ground, and covered his face with his hands.

"Yes," he said with sullen desperation, "where's the use of denying it now? Why cannot you believe me? I have told you once."

Kate wrung her hands. That cup was unbearably bitter to drink. Without another word she turned to go. What further business could she have with that other woman's husband? Dare sprang to his feet.

"Where is your vow, Kate?" he asked hoarsely, great drops of perspiration standing on his brow; "that oath you swore so solemnly?"

"I throw my vow to the winds," she said, braving him. She was quite past fear now. "God will forgive that perjury, I'm sure. It is a virtue, not a crime. *You* to talk of oaths broken!" she went on, summoning boundless scorn into her voice. "How many hundred vows have you made to your wife, and how have you kept them?"

Her taunts stung him to the quick.

"I have made one vow at all events that I won't break," he said determinedly, mastered by his fury. "You shall see that I *can* keep an oath. That oath shall be fulfilled, as I stand here."

"No, it won't," replied Kate, standing there in the moonlight, helpless, powerless, but dauntless; and the soft white face that had grown so haggard looked more resolute than anyone could have believed possible. Not a bit pretty now; not a bit bewitching; only very pale, and very brave, and very despairing.

"It is too late to go back now," said Dare, with a great effort mastering himself enough to speak tolerably collectedly. "You have gone over the stream and cut away the bridge behind you. O, child, I know I'm a villain. Don't look at me with those reproachful eyes. I know it better than you can tell me. But you grew into my very heart and soul, Kate, before I knew it. I *cannot* tear you out again. I *cannot*, I tell you, I *cannot*."

"You *must*," said Kate, with not a tremor in her resolute voice. "We have been terribly mistaken in one another all along; but at last we are undeceived, and in time. I, in my idiotcy, have been thinking you the truest, worthiest lover ever woman had; and you—O God!" she cried clasping her hands together in bitter indignation; "what *have* you been thinking of me?"

He tried to speak, but could not, overwhelmed under the weight of her contempt.

"Was it," she went on, in her clear low voice, "because I showed you so plainly my love, because I did not cover it up under hollow affectations of indifference, as you told me just now other women would, that you thought me capable of this unspeakable vileness? You jump to conclusions too rapidly, Colonel Stamer," she ended with concentrated bitterness.

He could answer nothing, struck dumb by that calmness of hers that feared nothing. Then she changed her tone—she could not keep that one to him for long for the life of her.[8]

"O, Dare!" she said, and tears came to her relief—tears that watered the drought of her parched soul—and her eyes looked up to him big and loving as ever,—"O, Dare! you won't do this, I know you won't. You would repent it more bitterly than you ever did anything in your life. O Dare!" she went on with pitiful urgency, because she felt so weak within, crying bitterly now; "you sometimes said you were fond of me, and I believe you are, because you are so sorry to lose me. If you are, O, for pity's sake, show me the greatest proof you could ever give of it. O, Dare! put me out of my tortures, and let me go away in peace."

Dare spoke roughly to her; he could not help it, with those vultures gnawing at his heart.

"I cannot do it, Kate. It's no use talking,—I cannot. Ask me anything but that, and I'll do it; but not that—not that."

But Kate would not be baffled so. With tender importunity she began again, and the tears seemed to have given back more than its former sweet bewitchment to her low woman's voice.

"O, do, Dare, my darling, *do* let me go; don't try to keep me. It *is* bitter to part, I know. Don't you suppose I feel that? It is a terrible wrench; but O, Dare, do—*do* it, for *my* sake! What can I say to persuade you?" she said in her sore trouble. "O, my darling—my own Dare—let me go, let me go!

8 In the *DUM* version Dare's response to Kate's refusal to become his mistress is considerably more violent; he first threatens to kill her and then to abduct her. While Kate claims not to care if he kills her, she is defiant and scornful of his threat to carry her off. See Appendix B, pp. 399-402 for more details of the extensive reworking of this chapter.

If this goes on much longer it will kill me!"

And the agony of that night reached its highest pitch then. Dare was mightily moved, shaken, vanquished. By her love she overcame. Who would withstand her when she asked, as she had asked him, for that deadly boon?

"There," said he, with a groan that came from the depths of his soul, "I'll let you go, as you are so anxious to get away from me." And he loosed her wrists. "You'd better go quick, if you *are* going, or I may alter my mind, and take you back again!" She turned to leave him. "Stop a moment," he said, quite broken-voiced; and he clasped her once more in his despairing arms—strained her, his own little Kate, to his desolate heart once again, whilst

"In that last kiss, that never was the last,
Farewell, like endless welcome, lived and died."[9]

"Good-bye, little cruel darling!" he said, while tears, the first he had shed for twenty years, tempered the blaze of his dark agonised eyes. "Good-bye, since you *will* go away and leave me. It's no use making you promise, for your oaths are as brittle as glass. But, Kate, I charge you, and it is the last charge I shall ever have the chance of giving you here—I charge you, now that I've sealed these lips of yours, never to let any other man touch them again as long as you live. We shall never see each other's faces again in this world, Kate, I don't suppose; but when we meet in the other world—if there is another world—let me find these kisses there still. There, go now!" And he almost pushed her away.

She said not a word to him. She could not have spoken to save her life; but she went away, over the yellow sands, and left him to wrestle with his despair alone. Kate got over the ground somehow—she never exactly knew how—she supposed afterwards that she must have been rather giddy and dazed. But as she nears Pen Dyllas, she sees three gentlemen coming to meet her, with enormously long black shadows running before them; she remembers that: three gentlemen—an old one, and a middle-aged one, and a very young one—Sir Guy Stamer, and Mr. Piggott, and Blount Chester. For Sir Guy has improved upon his first idea, has been afraid of his son being too quick for him, and has ridden down to Inkerman-terrace, and laid his little statement before Mr. Piggott to-night.

9 Tennyson, "Love and Duty" (1842), ll. 65-66.

"Here she is!" cries one of the three gentlemen (I don't exactly know which), as the small figure comes in sight. "And all by herself, too, after all. What a comfort!"

"Well, my little maid," says another of the gentlemen—a gentleman rather in the habit of bleating, extremely relieved, but very injured and cross, "and what are you doing out, all by yourself, at this time of night? You seem to have quite forgotten, my love, how particularly I desired you not to be wandering about at these improper hours all alone; and I declare, my dear love," he goes on peevishly, "it seems as if it really was not the slightest use my desiring you young people to do anything—it really does not. And now I have been so very much alarmed by what Sir Guy Stamer has been so very kind as to come down and tell me about you, that I determined to come out in all this terrible damp and dew to see myself what had become of you. I am afraid I shall be sadly poorly to-morrow in consequence," he winds up reproachfully.

"I was afraid you had been with my son, my dear," says old Sir Guy kindly; "and I'm very thankful to find you're not."

Kate looks up, haggard-eyed, in his face; in her utter recklessness she positively smiles such a heart-breaking smile.

"I *have* been with your son, Sir Guy," she says, speaking quite plainly and openly. "I've only just left him. I was very near running away with him—very near. If I had, you'd have come rather too late. But you see I didn't. And now," she went on with rapid excitement, "you may scold me just as much as you like, any of you. You may do whatever you choose with me. It's all one to me now. You cannot do me any harm now; and I don't care what becomes of me one bit! O, Dare, Dare!"

The forced wretched smile vanishes utterly at that exceeding bitter cry; and Kate, mad, not knowing what she does, flings herself down violently, clean Sunday frock and all, on the hard sand, and covers her face with her hands, and desires to die. There we'll leave her, lying prone, the little fool, at the feet of the two astonished old gentlemen. And now I have come to the end of the first division of Kate Chester's history. She has passed the turning-point—only just passed it; she is saved. We will see afterwards how the world wags with her from this time forwards, and whether fortune and her own idiotcy have got any more blows in store for her yet.

CHAPTER II

"TIME put his sickle in among the days." [10] He reaped a good many of them and bound them into his sheaves, and laid them by with the other sheaves he has been binding ever since the world was. Sundays and Mondays, and all the other days, went racing by, and no king could stop them.

"The rose burnt out; red autumn lit the woods;"[11]

then nipping winter put out the warm flame, and put on them his white cloak; then spring came, with marsh marigolds and cuckoos and east winds; then summer again, imperial, rose-filleted, and now late autumn again, hovering on the borders of winter—November, with its fogs and its slushy streets, and its "hounds and horn," that

"Cheerly rouse the slumbering morn."[12]

A year and a half has gone by, positively—not a day less—quick as it has passed. People have been born and married, and loved and hated, and gossipped and slandered, and feasted and starved, and cried and laughed. Good men have gone joyful to their home with God, and evil men have gone hopeless to their dark home, about whose exceeding horrors we can but speculate—the home they have chosen and been furnishing for themselves for so long. And all the three Chesters are still alive, and breathing the breath of life; walking erect above ground, instead of lying flat under it. And old Daddy Piggott is alive still and kicking, except that he never was known to indulge in such violent exercise as that implies—alive, despite head-aches and vertigo. Neither the one nor the other had carried him off as yet, though they still swayed his large sandy head as completely as ever; but, however, there he was, baaing away as meekly as in his best days, and earth had the gift of his presence left her still. Kate Chester is alive, as I have said. She has been given yet a little space—a little space to do evil or to do good in—a little space to run smoothly down the broad road, or

10 Owen Meredith (E. R. Bulwer-Lytton), *Tannhäuser* (1861), l. 226.

11 Inexact, *Tannhäuser*, l. 331.

12 Inexact, John Milton, "L'Allegro" (1645), ll. 53-54.

agonise, scratched and bleeding, along the narrow one.[13] That fair tree is given yet a few more days to bring forth flowers and good fruit in, before the axe comes to cut her down.

It is a very cold day; nobody can deny that. The sky such a pale clear blue overhead, not a cloud upon it. The ground hard—O, so hard! it rings under the horses' hoofs as they trot smartly along, shaved and shivering. The birds are next door to famished; how can they get at the grubs and worms, nestling so safe and secure under the iron crust? Boys are sailing down the streets on slides, one after another, with balanced arms extended finger-post fashion, gloriously happy; and ill-fated passengers, tripped up by the said slides, and proving experimentally the hardness of the frosty ground, are hailing maledictions on their ragged heads. Hunters are eating their heads off in warm stables; red coats are lying, folded up, in drawers, and their owners are endeavouring to kill time, and avert despair, by much skating and much love-making[14]—both carried to a decidedly dangerous pitch. Everybody is looking red and blue and purple, and passing ugly as they bustle along; a white nose could not be procured this day for love or money between the three seas. Inside the houses things look decidedly better. Very big fires, and lots of beef and mutton, and plenty of pheasants hanging up in the larders, and not a few pretty girls beginning to think seriously of balls and partners. Let us look into one of these houses, in one of London's pretty fast-growing children. A small unpretending house, standing rather back from the road, with the Thames flowing on calmly before its gate, and heavy-laden barges being tugged laboriously up stream by a good big team of horses, and the rope breaking very often, and falling in a splashy, *sprayey* line into the water. Let us figuratively take off the roof of this house, and just glance into the snug little drawing-room. Warm green curtains, drooping in heavy folds; a thick-piled carpet, with a pattern of big lilies and ferns and red twirls; one or two tables covered with a pretty untidy litter; lots of books—poetry and novels and periodicals; a small stocking in course of knitting, with the needles sticking out in all directions, inviting the knitter to resume her task; a half-finished drawing,

13 See Matthew 7: 13-14: "Enter ye in at the strait gate: for wide is the gate, and broad is the way, that leadeth to destruction, and many there be which go in thereat: Because strait is the gate, and narrow is the way, which leadeth unto life, and few there be that find it."

14 Not as risqué in the Victorian period as it now sounds; flirting and courting.

not particularly well done; a piano open, with "Santa Lucia"[15] standing up, waiting to be sung upon it. A strong smell of violets all about. You could swear that women lived in this room, and women with nice ladylike tastes too. And on the fluffy, woolly, long-haired white rug before the fire sits a fluffy, woolly, long-haired dog, that looks as if he was a piece of the rug which had been made up into the shape of a dog, sits there blinking; and there—there sits also a young woman,—Kate Chester, in fact,—a young woman aged twenty-one and a half. She has got a multitude of tracts and small good books scattered all about and around her, all to be covered with paper covers, but as yet they are one and all naked, and unclothed with their brown-paper robes. There she sits, dressed in a thick dark winter gown, that fits quite tight, and quite plain, without fringes or trimmings or furbelows, to the full bust and the firm round waist. Kate was fond of having her garments made after that simple fashion; perhaps she was conscious that that figure, with its soft undulations and rich contours, could afford to dispense with the frillings and paddings that a less perfect form would avail itself of. Kate cared still about her appearance then—despite all her woes, despite that grovelling on the yellow sand at Sir Guy Stamer's feet? Apparently, quite as much as ever—took quite as much pains about it, at least. The furzy hair is swept off behind the round ears in just as elaborate burnished plaits as ever; none of the small adornments are wanting. It is only in books that pretty women neglect their toilette because they have been crossed in love. Love and grief have dealt kindly with Kate in one respect. They have not taken one iota from those puzzling charms of hers, which can be classed under no head of Greek or Roman. They have not worn her down to a skeleton, nor made the bones of her neck start out prominent and unsightly, neither have they made her look haggard or old. Not all her many tears have washed one bit of colour out of those rare green eyes. No one would say that she was wearing the willow,[16] she kept it so well out of sight. Kate could be merry, and smile almost as well as ever; better than almost anyone else still. She could make a good or a bad joke as the case might be, and laugh at one still, and that without forcing or constraining herself at all. Because Dare was married was no reason why ridiculous things were not ridiculous still. But though Kate was not outwardly altered for the worse—not *gone off*, as the phrase is; though men seemed to find that soft white face more oddly, tiresomely bewitching than

15 Traditional Neapolitan song transcribed by Teodoro Cottrau (1827-79).

16 A maiden mourning a lover lost before marriage.

ever; though it would persist in intruding itself unasked into the nightly visions of those rash unlucky ones who had been studying it in the daytime, beaming cloudy upon them in its utter paleness, and fading and vanishing quite, quite away,—yet, for all that, Kate was changed, very much changed too. There had come a look into the green eyes—a look that used not to be there before, a look that would never go away again now. I don't think it was quite confined to the eyes either; the rest of the face had something of it, particularly the full, curved lips, which had always been so inconveniently ingenuous and open in what they said, even when the tongue was silent, which had been always so extremely unlike a rosebud (the stereotyped pattern, I suppose, for heroines' mouths). That look was of one who had been mentally in a burning fiery furnace—who had been dragged through very deep waters, where there was no resting-place for the feet; of one who had known what it was to be very, very sad, and could never again quite forget that lesson. Things did not, somehow, look the same as they once had done in those eyes, so shadowy, so very soft in their green depths, so intensely, hopelessly sorrowful sometimes, when they were left to themselves, when nobody was trying to amuse or divert their possessor,—as if, gazing on the past, there could not possibly be any joy for them in the present, any scrap of hope in the future. I do not know how many times I have said that Kate was sitting before the fire, but anyhow, so she was, burning one cheek like the sunny side of a peach, giving her countenance a one-sided kind of look. She was doing nothing at all, notwithstanding all the coatless tracts before her, honestly as she had intended to work at them with might and main when first she had taken up her position, in order to have a regular good roast with blinking Tip.

"Little torments," she is saying inwardly to the harmless little good books, "how many of there are you, I wonder? Twenty or thirty, I dare-say—not a single one less: I won't count them, or I shall be so discouraged and out of heart. And all to be done to-day, too, everyone; and that abominable district-visitors'[17] meeting hanging over my devoted head too.

---

17 District visitors were volunteer charity workers, largely from the ranks of middle- and upper-class women, who sought to instil bourgeois values of cleanliness, piety, and thrift in the poor. As Seth Koven points out, however, this was by definition a contradictory project: "Elite women's willingness to 'go dirty' . . . made it possible for them to flout bourgeois class and gender expectations even as they acted as missionaries bringing bourgeois values and culture to the working poor" (Slumming: Sexual and Social Politics in *Victorian London* [Princeton, Princeton

Such nonsense as you all are, too, I don't doubt," she says, and she opens a title-page and looks. "*Crumbs for the Pantry*, I suppose, and *Buttons for little Sinners' Breeches*. Well, not exactly, but very near. I wonder what earthly good they'd do to any human soul—not a morsel; at least, I'm sure they would not to me. Fine district-visitor I am, to be sure!—never anyone mistook their vocation so completely, I should think. What a moment of temporary insanity it must have been when I lifted such an old man of the sea[18] upon my shoulders! Well, after all, one may almost as well do that as anything else. There is not much taste in anything that I can find out—it's all pretty much the same. Was there ever such a good comparison as Macbeth's of life to 'a tale told by an idiot, full of sound and fury, signifying nothing'?[19] Well, I suppose we must go on with the tale till we come to the end. Come, *Little Sinners' Breeches*, I'm going to put a coat upon your sinful little backs. There, I've got no needle now! I shall have to get up and hunt for one. I'll stay till the clock gets to the quarter—just five minutes' reprieve.

'O, what shall I be at fifty,
  If I am then alive,
I find the world so bitter,
  When I am but twenty-five?'[20]

Only that I am not twenty-five, nor anywhere near it, thank goodness! I wonder what sort of a thing I shall be when I am an old woman? A dreary old hag, I expect, and hideously ugly certainly. Those turn-up faces are only bearable as long as people are young. I hope luncheon will be punctual to-day, for I'm desperately hungry, despite all my woes: one must eat, blighted being as one is. O dear, how can I joke even to myself about that?"

A heavy sigh.

A knock at the house door comes, rat-tat-tat-tat.

"Who on earth can that be calling at this unearthly hour of the morning? O, I know; James Stanley, to be sure. Shall not I get well scolded for

---

University Press, 2004], p. 198). The nervous comments made by Kate's acquaintances about her excursions into the slums betray anxiety about the ambiguous nature of the district-visitor's role.

18 In the tale of Sinbad the Sailor from *The Arabian Nights*, the old man of the sea makes travelers carry him on their backs until they die of exhaustion.

19 Shakespeare, *Macbeth* (first printed 1623), V.v.26-27.

20 Tennyson, *Maud* (1855), 1.219-22.

not having begun these horrid things yet? Well, it all comes in the day's work! Poor little fellow! I wish I had done them, though."

It is to be presumed that somebody else heard the knock and went to open the door, for within about the expected amount of time a maid-servant entered (one of a somewhat neater, less blowsy type than Pen-Dyllas Jane), and announced—

"Mr. Stanley."

Then in walked Mr. Stanley; not much of a person to look at when he did walk in—a small, pale, delicate-looking man—a scion who, by his appearance, did no credit to the great old house he came of. A parson too; not a muscular Christian at all[21]—not of the sledge-hammer type of divine, who could floor an ox with his fist, or pummel his refractory flock into submission; a small ugly man, with a big forehead, one whose soul seemed to be eating up its dwelling-place. Two things you could predicate of him at the first glance—a gentleman and a good man, one of those blessed ones

"With whom the melodies abide
Of the everlasting chime."[22]

A little poor-looking man, who, as I thought very often, and as his landlady thought too, knew pretty well what it was to feel hungry; for though "passing rich on eighty pounds a year,"[23] but a small portion of that noble sum went to the provisioning and clothing of that slight frail body, that only the brave spirit that inhabited it seemed to keep from fading away altogether. Not a pet-parson at all. No young ladies had ever made him a pair of slippers in all his life—it would not have been a paying concern; and I don't think he had ever owned an embroidered pocket-handkerchief from the time he was born. His coat was very tidy indeed, and clerical and well brushed—but O, how shiny at the seams!—and his gloves looked as if they had been mended a good many times; not so well mended though

---

21 Inspired by the work of such authors of boys' fiction as Thomas Hughes (*Tom Brown's Schooldays*) and Charles Kingsley (*Westward Ho!*), muscular Christianity was a late nineteenth-century movement that celebrated the athletic development of the healthy male body as a prerequisite for spiritual growth.

22 Inexact, John Keble, "St Matthew," in *The Christian Year* (1827), ll. 27-28.

23 See the description of the exemplary parson in Oliver Goldsmith's "The Deserted Village" (1770): "A man he was to all the country dear,/ And passing rich with forty pounds a year" (ll. 141-42).

as they used to be when his little sister lived, and toiled, and laboured with him, sorrowing when he grieved, and laughing when he was joyful. The little sister's deft hands have been crossed quietly over each other under the dark thick yew in the populous church-yard for six months past; they will not have to work any more now; they have done their task. While dark yew's fibres

"Net the dreamless head,"[24]

the little sister has entered upon her rest. He has a rather longer, harder road to travel than she had; more miry and stony; it takes longer getting home; but he goes on cheerfully, with a good courage, for he knows that when he gets to the end she'll be there, expecting him, waiting for him. She told him she would when she lay a-dying on her little white bed, and he believes her. Such as this man was, he came in now shivering, for a great-coat was not among his worldly goods. A greatcoat would have cost five pounds, and he would as soon have thought of cutting off his head as of spending five pounds on himself all at once.

"How are you, James?" says Kate, smiling up at him, covered with tracts from her lowly resting-place. "I'm so glad you're come!" and she stretched out a very friendly hand with frank heartiness to him. She *was* glad; she spoke truth there, and indeed she had given up telling lies of late. James and she had known each other since they were both in petticoats together,[25] and somehow she had of late got into a habit of relying on him with a greater sense of rest and comfort than on anybody else. She had some vague hope that he might, perhaps, make her good, get her to be moderately contented and useful, and rather religious, sometime hence—a good many months or years off. She generally did feel less dully apathetic and bored after a good talk with him. She got good out of his visits, somehow; not so much from hearing him talk, because talk is cheap, but seeing how hard and how ceaselessly he strove to live up to his talk.

"You're come just in time,"she says, turning her semi-burnt face towards him. "I deserve the most tremendous scolding you can invent. You don't know what a dreadful temper I've been in all morning. I've been so savage that nobody dare come within half a mile of me. You see I have

24 Tennyson, *In Memoriam* (1850), 2.3.

25 During this period boys and girls wore dresses until boys were "breeched" at anywhere from around 4-8 years old.

cleared the room of everybody but Tip! Such a fit of the blues!" she said, lifting up hands and eyes theatrically.

"Blues!" he said, laughing at her; "in here with all these violets! I won't hear a word about them. Now, if you'd been out of doors, I might have listened to your woes; but, with this grand fire, and all these books, you and Tip ought to be as happy as a king and a queen;" and he warmed himself at the grand fire; it was the first he had seen that day, except through a window.

"Look here," went on Kate, exposing her own shortcomings, confessing her sins; "all these nasty good books to do, and not one of them done! What do you say to that?"

"Never mind," he said leniently. "You're out of sorts, I suppose, to-day; so am I, very often. I don't want to make a toil of a pleasure. I'll take them home, and do them myself this evening. I shall be quite glad of something to do," he went on, to make her mind easy, good little man as he was.

"No, you sha'n't," cried Kate, ashamed of herself. "You make me blush, though you cannot see it, because I always blush inside; but come," she said, jumping off the fluffy rug, and wheeling an arm-chair very politely close to the fire for him, "do sit down, and warm yourself. You look as blue as the sky!"

"O, Kate, please don't! You don't know how conceited you'll make me. I'm not accustomed to be waited on at all, I can assure you, much less by a young lady! Old Mrs. Lewis mostly lets my fire go out by the time I come in of a night. You don't know how I have to blow her up about it."[26]

"I daresay," said Kate incredulously; "but come, I want to have a talk with you to-day;" and she sank down again on the rug beside him; "and first tell me how those few tiresome old 'women' of mine are getting on."

"They are wanting very much to know how you are getting on," he answered, looking down on her rather gravely. "They cannot make it out at all, poor old things. They seem to think me answerable for your keeping away. I believe they are beginning to suspect me of making away with you, somehow."

"I have not been near the old things—O, I don't know when," says Kate, telling the very worst. "O, I know as well as you that I ought; but it makes me so sick when they tell me all their unpleasant ailments, as they

---

26 To "blow up" is slang for "scold."

are always doing."

"I hate to be always lecturing you, Kate, and doing parson to you," he says reluctantly, for he likes doing kind things himself, much better than scolding his neighbours for not doing them; "and it seems absurd to say, that telling their ailments can be any pleasure to them, poor old things; but we cannot, somehow, measure them by our own rule, and they all enjoy talking about them, odd taste as it is. They've so few pleasures," he says, half to himself, very softly. "Don't you think, Kate, you could give them this one a little bit oftener? You'd be glad, afterwards, I know."

Kate's feelings are worked upon: strong-willed woman as she is, in great things, it is not difficult to do that. She feels compunction, sitting there, warm clad, so well and so prosperous, on the long-haired white rug.

"I'm sorry," she says, brightly looking up at him and nodding; "and I'll go to-day. One can't say more than that, can one?"

"It's what I knew you'd say," he answers her, looking very pleased.

"By the by, I can't, though," says Kate then, a sadder recollection striking her, clasping her pretty plump hands together; "for I have got to do what is, if possible, even more disagreeable, and that is, spend the afternoon with my dear sweet cousins, the Chesters. Don't you pity me?" she asks pathetically; "having to spend ever so many hours, talking and hearing of nothing but lovers and dress—other people's, too; it would not be so hard if it was one's own. What would you do if you were in my unfortunate situation?"

"Goodness knows," says he, laughing. "I'm afraid I should not have much to say upon either of them. I should hold my tongue altogether, for fear of exposing my gross ignorance." He has never played the *rôle* of lover in his life, and never will. No woman could care for him, he thinks—ugly, sickly, poor. It's all right; he knows earth's small sweetness to him; her frown, always cold upon him, makes him turn for smiles and sweetness to another place—a better one by a good deal. He would fain, very fain, be away when the good time shall come, but he tries hard not to be impatient.

"You don't pity me a bit, I see," says Kate, with sweet mock ferocity. A pretty woman pretending to be ferocious is a very insnaring thing; a pretty woman being ferocious is not quite so much so. "I begin to think you are not a bit of a sympathetic disposition. You don't sympathise with me a bit, and you'd expect me to be, O, ever so sympathetic to you if you had not quite so many soup-tickets and blankets as you wanted for those beloved coalheavers and bargees[27] of yours."

"Ah," he says, passing his hand in a careworn sort of fashion over his forehead, and a look of heavy anxiety visits his pale thin features, "I'm sadly afraid there'll be more need for soup-tickets and blankets in the town this year than ever there was before. I am, indeed. The weather has set in cold so soon, and there's so much fever and sickness about. I shall come begging here, almost every day, I warn you," he goes on, smiling a little bit. "I expect you'll get so tired of me, at last, that you'll tell your servant always to say 'not at home' when the parson calls."

"No, I sha'n't," says Kate. "I sha'n't have any scruple in saying 'no' to you every time you come. I won't give you a farthing's worth for them; they are daughters of the horseleech.[28] Yes—you need not shake your benevolent head—they are. I'll tell you what I'll do, though." She goes on, fiddling with a little coquettish locket, with *aie*, in Greek letters,[29] and a true love-knot upon it, which she wears round her pillar throat night and day—a strong amulet to keep her from loving man ever again, containing as it does the rich treasure of a short lock of Dare's beautiful vine-tendril hair. "I'll have an elegant collation laid out for you yourself, when you arrive; it shall be the object of my life to get a little flesh upon your bones. You might, if all trades failed, make an honest livelihood as "'living skeleton,'[30] as you are now."

"I'm an unkind beast, I think," he answers, laughing—and he could laugh very heartily, which is what not everybody is able to do. "Nothing would fatten me; but, O, Kate," he goes on, the anxious look coming back quick again, "you'd pity them I know, though you pretend not to. Just think how patient they are," he says (he is very pitiful). "I can't make it out at all how they bear up as they do—it is an enigma to me—except that a dull apathy seems to numb their poor souls. They take up their crushing burden so naturally, as if they knew they were born to it. They toil and moil, and suffer and grieve so much, as a matter of course—as much a matter of

27 Employee on, or person in charge of, a barge.

28 See Proverbs 30:15: "The horseleech hath two daughters, crying Give, give." Horseleeches were used into the nineteenth century by doctors to let blood; Kate compares James Stanley's impoverished parishioners to parasites who suck him dry.

29 In Greek letters αει; always or eternally.

30 Like Kafka's Hunger Artist, a performer who made a living by appearing to starve himself into a state of extreme emaciation.

course as we think it to eat and drink and amuse ourselves."

"Patient!" exclaims Kate, with much scorn. "I've no patience with them. They are always sponging on you, greedy things!"

They did sponge on him pretty often, I think. He was cheated almost every day of his life; there was no world's cuteness[31] about him. But he did not much mind; he did not expect interest for his money or his hard work here; he know he should be overpaid—principal and interest and compound interest—when the hot long day should be over, and the Master come to pay the labourers their wages. Taken in very often; and those who took him in laughed at him behind his back for his exceeding simplicity. But, on the whole, I am inclined to think his simpleness answered better than their guile.

"What's made you so hard-hearted to-day?" he asks, rather vexed (for he is human after all), and he determines to say something that he knows will rouse her. "Go down to Liver-lane, Kate, and see that woman dying there of cancer; that'll do you more good than sixty talks with me. See how it is possible to bear sorrows that dwarf your fancied griefs into perfect insignificance."

Kate's eyes flashed green fire upon him when he said that; those full soft lips trembled visibly.

"How dare you try," she asks passionately, "to exalt their wretched griefs at the expense of mine? It's measuring a giant with pigmies. Why, according to your own showing, their sorrows are halved by that brutish apathy you spoke of; they are of a kind too that death must end before long; but does any blessed numbness ever dull mine?—tell me that. Does it get any better?—you who seem to know about it so much better than I do. Or is there any chance of my dying, and getting quit of it so? Not the slightest. O God, how I wish there was!" and she clasped her hands hard, and rocked herself backwards and forwards, and thirsted for one glimpse of that dark forbidden face she loved so.

James was very sorry for what he had done; he had hoped her better of that madness. She had said nothing about it for a good time now.

"It was a stupid thing of me to say," he pleads remorsefully; "I'm always saying those kind of things. No human creature can judge of another's troubles, or measure them in any way. Forgive me, Kate—won't you?—and don't lose heart. You'll find comfort and peace at last, I do trust, after

31 Acuteness, common sense.

all your sore spirit-tossings, if you do but try and beg hard enough for it. What can we, any of us, do but beg, destitute as we are? We are all God's poor patients, you know," he says reverently, "and He gives us very bitter physic sometimes; but His physic is not like earthly doctors'; it always cures if we take it right."

"O, don't talk of me," she says, recovering herself, with a dreary sigh. "I'm an incurable job, I think; but go on about your dear coalheavers, if it amuses you, and I'll try and feel as sorry for them as I do for myself. And, first, please to tell me what earthly good the few miserable pennies I can spare from my gowns and bonnets could do to the poor hungry wretches?"

"Our pennies are terribly few,—I feel that," he says regretfully, going back to his pet theme at this gracious permission; "but just think, Kate," he goes on, with glad thankfulness, "what a comfort it is to be able to tell them of a good country that they can all get to if they try,—that you'll get to, I trust, poor Kate!—where they'll not have to toil or moil, or be sick or sorry, any more at all."

Let me here testify James Stanley was not a man to pull in religion by the head and shoulders on every possible occasion, to lard his talk with inapt, ill-fitting texts; his intellect was too wide, his taste too correct for that. Cant was a thing he shunned like the plague; only that's a bad comparison, for he would not have shunned the plague. Only when one thinks a great deal about a thing, one must speak about it sometimes. If one has some pleasant thought warm at one's heart, it will drop out in one's talk. And when he did speak of this assured hope of his, or heard others speak of it, a quiet joy would shine over the pale insignificant face, transforming material ugliness into spiritual beauty.

"Ah, it's all very fine your talking," says Kate discontentedly. "Of course you can talk good to them, because you live good; but how could I have the face to? Why, the words would stick in my throat! What do I know about that country?—less, if possible, than any of them do."

"Have you read the book I gave you?" he asks then, the quiet light shining still clear and holy upon his face. "I had hoped it would have been a guide-book to you, to show you the way there a little bit."

"I read a few pages," answers Kate, more discontentedly than ever, "but I did not like it; it made me very uncomfortable; it seemed all beside the mark—to have nothing whatever to do with me. But don't begin to talk solemn now, for goodness' sake; I can't bear it to-day; it'll make me in even a worse temper than I was before."

"You are a sad naughty child to-day," he says, smiling down rather sorrowfully upon her; "but I have hopes of you yet."

And that is all he says, for he is dreadfully afraid of giving her an overdose of that which to him is most palatable food, but which to her sickly palate tastes like unsavoury physic.

"I've a good mind to say something that'll shock you awfully," proceeds Kate. "It will be some amusement to me to watch your reverence's clerical countenance lengthening rapidly, and I'm horribly in want of amusement. I could say most truly with Mrs. Barrett Browning—

'We are so tired, my heart and I.'"[32]

And the white lids Dare had hungered so to kiss dropped very wearily over the eyes that had got so fixed an expression of utter sadness in them of late.

"Speak on," says he cheerily, "if it'll do you any good. You sha'n't be scolded much to-day."

"Well, then," says Kate, looking up at him, "I could not help thinking just now how gladly I'd change lots with Tip. I would, if I could, be like him—a bundle of fluffiness lying on the rug. I'd snooze away my life in peace, with intervals of gnawing mutton-bones and barking; and then, when my little day was over, I'd come to an end altogether, and have no reckoning to shudder at. O James, just think of being utterly freed from all responsibility—no remorse for what is gone, no fear of what is to come. I'd be annihilated this minute if I could."

She ends emphatically, getting quite excited. James did not look very shocked, as many a parson would have thought it his duty to do. He knew compassionately that rawness of heart which prompted the desire for complete extinction. A grand thought came like a friend to him, and dignified his poor paltry form and countenance—made it look quite noble, with a nobility not of earth's framing.

"No, you wouldn't, Kate," he says, looking up quite inspired. "You did not feel that when you stood by your mother and saw her die. It would have killed you if you had. You could not have borne so unbearable a smart. O Kate, Kate, what but the putting altogether out of one's head the dust and the corruption and the feasting worms—what but dwelling altogether on

32 Inexact, Elizabeth Barrett Browning, "My Heart and I" (1862), l. 42.

the meeting soon, very soon, again could make endurable, almost joyful, those partings our dear Lord calls upon us to make for His sake?"

His voice trembled, he was so moved, and the tears came into his eyes. Kate knew he was thinking of the little dead sister whom he missed so sorely when he came back of a night to his poor dreary lodgings. It is provoking and enraging, but she feels disposed to cry herself, too; she does not know why; and very heartily glad she is when a diversion is effected by Margaret's opening the door and coming in. In came that young lady, looking very flourishing and exceedingly cheerful; as unlike Kate as one pretty young woman could be unlike another pretty young woman. No odd shadow, puzzling and fascinating her acquaintance, has fallen upon her light-gray eyes; she has not been made to look poetic and haunting at the expense of her peace of mind. She comes in shivering, like everybody else to-day.

"You here?" she says. "I did not know that, and I'm glad of it now I do know it;" and she smiles in a pleasant, hearty, welcoming fashion. "Isn't it cold?" she goes on (a very unnecessary question which everybody asks to-day). "Just look at my hands;" and she holds up a pair of those members. "I hope you have been giving Kate a good scolding," Maggie says further, kneeling down with her hands held over the blaze, rubbing away with a will at them. "She has been so awfully cross and disagreeable all the morning, there's been no bearing her;" and she glances rather hostilely across at her sister, with whom she had rather a smart engagement not very long ago.

"I was just going to begin, I think, when you came in," says James; "but I think she is going to be good without it now;" and he looks with loving pity (from which any approach to scolding was miles distant) at the soft profile beside him.

"No, I'm not good," says Kate doggedly, looking very hard at the fire, and winking away the tears, "nor ever shall be. Leave me alone, do."

"Have you been here long?" inquires Margaret of James, complying with Kate's desire, but inwardly resolving to have it out with her afterwards.

"Yes, indeed, I have," he answers; "and that reminds me that I must be going; I must indeed;" and he picks himself up out of the deep arm-chair, and walks to the window and looks out through the frozen pane on the white-topped bushes, like so many Christmas-cakes; on the dark-hued river stealing swift-currented by; on the scarlet-cloaked girls and sober-coated men passing briskly along to and fro.

"O, nonsense!" says Margaret, "you must stay for luncheon; it is very rude of you to be going away just the moment I come in."

She likes him. She has a woman's tender-hearted compassion for him; so poor, so sickly, so alone in the world now, with that deep crape on his rubbishy old hat; and he is a gentleman too; and she enjoys such pleasant security that he will not inflict upon her grave clerical lectures or mild clerical love.

"Can't possibly; thank you, Maggie," he answers, shaking his head. "I've been idling too long already. I can't afford many more such pleasant lazy half-hours."

This is not exactly one of those parsons who, somehow, always drops in accidentally as the luncheon-bell rings; who prefer tending their flocks at the feeding-troughs than anywhere else.

"O, just stay ten minutes more, then; there's a good creature. What can be the hurry?" urges Margaret's kind voice; and Kate looks up and seconds the invitation with still moist, mournful eyes, that try to smile upon him.

He hesitates; it seems wonderfully delicious to him, like a fairy tale, in that warm, scented room, with those low, caressing woman voices speaking to him—those kind, sweet woman faces looking friendship and sympathy at him; but suddenly it strikes him that he is growing self-indulgent; one of those shepherds that the immortal blind man uttered his strong testimony against.

"Of other care they little reckoning make,
Than how to scramble at the shearer's feast."[33]

What business had he to rest thus in the lap of luxury (as he considered it), while those poor rough sheep of his were sinning and toiling and shivering in their cold joyless garrets and alleys? That decided him. He saw his course, and no earthly power could turn him from it now. "Absurd, overstrained notions!" folk will say. Perhaps so; I do not know; it is rather misty to me. He would have made a grand Jesuit, of the old original Ignatius Loyola type,[34] this man would; at least as regarded that magnificent abnegation of self, which makes men able to do and to dare everything,

33 John Milton, "Lycidas," (1638), ll. 116-17. Milton is called the "immortal blind man" because he had lost his vision by the time he wrote his great epic *Paradise Lost* (1667).

34 St. Ignatius Loyola (1491-1556), founder of the Society of Jesus, practiced severe mortifications.

anything, even apparent impossibilities. It is the object of most men, I think, to pamper up their bodies, to deal kindly and fondly with them, treat them well and coax them into staying a good while, to forget their essential materiality. This was not James Stanley's way at all. His poor fragile body might be sick, and sorry, and weary, and full of aches and pains. No matter; it must perform all the task the brave stout spirit laid upon it, without flinching; the time for resting was not come yet. What matter to him how tarnished and broken the setting is, so as the jewel shines bright and luminous?

"No, no," he says gently, but quite firm. "I must not; indeed, I must not. You are very good, kind girls to me, both of you, and this room is the sweetest, warmest spot my heart has yet to turn to now in the world; but," he went on, looking very earnest and serious, "there's so much work for me to do, and such a little day to do it in. We cannot, any of us, tell how soon the night may come, you know, and I sometimes fancy my night is getting very near. Perhaps it isn't! Perhaps it is only a superstitious fancy; but still I'd like to be getting on quick with my work against it does come."

And he bids them good-bye, picks up the little scattered, coverless, good books, while Kate looks on ashamed and remorseful, tucks them tidily under his arm, and goes his way.

CHAPTER III

THERE were other houses in Queenstown besides the Chesters', naturally, or it would have been but a small place. I intend to go and take a peep now into one of these other houses—a much finer one than the two girls' little nutshell—a grand, staring, square white house, with plenty of stucco, and a portico, and a good many green blinds. Grove House it was called, on the *lucus a non lucendo*[35] principle, I suppose, seeing there was not a tree near it. Let us look into the drawing-room here, too; unseen as a spirit, it is my intention to see what is going on there. A much finer room than the Chesters' little snuggery—six times as large at least—two drawing-rooms, indeed, opening into one another with imposing folding-doors, town fashion, and an aviary at the end full of shrill-voiced canaries, that sang fit to stun, fit to deafen one, whenever the sun shone. Not so trim-looking and fresh in its garniture was this fine room as the smaller one we have visited; it looked

35 A dark grove of no light (Latin); a far-fetched, and presumably erroneous, theory.

as if a large family had been living, and sitting, and romping in this room for a good many years—at least, if one judged by the rather faded aspect of the big cabbage-roses, and convolvuluses that straggled and bloomed luxuriantly on the chintz chair-covers; by the knocked-off corners of divers once gaily gilt tables, now of a rather shabby genteel appearance. However, there was a great warm fire and a lot of arm-chairs; it felt very hot and cosy; there was a pleasant smell of sandal-wood work-boxes, and attar of roses, and that sort of subtle vague odours that women delight in. At the first glance you would have said that there were a great many ladies in the room, but on looking closer and counting, you would have found that there were only four, and those not very large-sized ones; the four Miss Chesters, Jane and Fanny, and Louisa and Emily, as like one another as four peas, having rather a resemblance in shape to four peas too, their adversaries said sometimes; four short, squat, pale-faced girls, with hair and eyes and tinting all exactly the same hue; not one good feature to be discovered after much searching in all their four round faces; undeniably plain girls, who yet managed, by some means best known to themselves, to attract and draw to their fat selves an amount of attention, and what seemed like admiration, which was wont to rouse the ireful wonder of their fairer, more neglected compeers; always as neat as a new pin—that was one of their strongest points—always managing, somehow, to have a smart, natty, spruce look. If those girls had been condemned to wear sackcloth and ashes, it is my belief that they would have made their sackcloth take the form of a fashionable garment; would have twined their ashes into becoming wreaths; always up to anything that was proposed to them to do; always possessed of some little piece of high-seasoned news or racy gossip, to divert their acquaintance withal; girls that had a sea of small talk ever flowing through their lips—a sea that knew no ebb; always ready to flirt; always ready to laugh at any joke, however verging on the broad it might be; always ready to do a good-natured thing; always ready to be helpful and handy; commonplace housewifely girls, that would furbish up a shabby-coated, empty-pursed husband very gallantly, and breast poverty and adversity with a cheerful, jolly sort of courage. Great successes that rather ill-favoured quartette were, and so their proud mother said to herself when she used to watch them whirling ceaselessly round with partner after partner at the county balls, while other less lucky mothers had their lambs safely benched beside them. Besides these young persons there was yet one other tenant of the room, a male creature, their brother, lounging about, and stretching and yawning, as lamentably short of a job[36] as any other *un*-literary young man, in a hard frost; doomed to a house that possessed not a billiard-table, and having not yet been driven by despair to amateur photography; a comely, personable man enough, as men go, with a good, strong, useful figure, and solid-looking, square-cut, regular features, rather disposed to be fat; which last circumstance was the one great grief of George Chester's young life; a good-looking fellow despite this tendency, you would say, always supposing you had not heard before hand his sisters' description of him, in which case your first emotion would certainly have been disappointment, having been led to expect the figure of Hercules and the face of Antinous;[37] an ordinary, light-hearted sort of young man; not very clever or very stupid; not very good or very bad; nothing very striking or startling about him, mind or body; not a character that could be drawn in black and white, neatly and accurately described in opposites, like heroes in novels, but made up of a great many grays, and drabs, and neutral tints, as the characters of all living men are; not a bad-hearted fellow, on the whole; did not run up very long bills for his papa; brought his sisters presents occasionally; and submitted with a tolerably good grace when his mama kissed him; one who was a passably good brother and son now, and who, one felt sure, would make in the course of time a passably good husband and father. The whole room gave one, at first, the idea of being filled to overflowing with a vast expanse of muslins and laces, and fiddle-faddles,[38] which wandered billowy over the floor and the chairs and the tables. Jane and Fanny were sitting with their feet upon the fender, stitching away for the bare life against time. Most people have some one talent given them, poorly endowed as they may be on the whole. The Chesters' talent was amateur dressmaking, and they had it in a high degree; all their brains seemed to have gone into their fingers. Louisa sat on the sofa, half-buried in manifold gauzes and airy fabrics, stitching away too with busy, ugly fingers. Emily was singing at the piano, not exactly in tune—I cannot say, but with a very fine air, and altogether to the satisfaction of herself and family. And this was the sort of improving, edifying conversation that was going on, not much more interesting to an averagely intelligent hearer than that of Lady Edgermond's circle in *Corinne*.[39]

36 To be short of a job means to be unemployed or have nothing better to do.
37 A lover of the Roman emperor Hadrian, Antinous exemplified male beauty.
38 Nonsense, fripperies.
39 See p. 71, n. 70

"Look here, Jane," says Fanny, pausing for a brief instant from her labours, with grave, serious deliberation in her tone. "Do you think I'd better put a third ruche[40] on here? I've put two on already, and I almost think a third, another pink one, perhaps, would not look amiss; but what do you say? I'll abide by your advice. How've you done your own?"

"I don't think I'd put another," responds Jane slowly, biting the top of her thimble in profound consideration. "I've only got two; I think three would perhaps look heavy. But, then, I've put mine further apart than yours. I think it looks lighter, don't you know."

"Ah!" says Fanny, dubious still on this knotty point.

"Let's look at yours, Loo," proceeds Jane, raising her voice, and withdrawing her lips from the thimble, which began to taste metallic and not palatable.

Now Louisa was the genius of the family; she had in times past effected wonders in the way of devising new garments and furbishing up old ones. Family tradition pointed to her as an oracle. Now and again she had inspirations on the subjects of trimmings and ornamentations. This talented being now raised her round, sandy, sleek-haired head at this appeal, and, with modest pride, held up what an approving conscience told her to be a triumph of art.

"Vandykes!"[41] exclaimed both her sisters under their breath, with awed admiration. "How lovely! What on earth put that into your head?" and they gazed at her as their respective family circles may have gazed at the inventors of gunpowder, of printing, and of steam-engines.

"I'll unpick mine, and do it like it," said Fanny with laudable emulation, with a Briton's determination not to be beaten; and the needles click, and the clock ticks, and the four commonplace little tongues go wagging on after the manner of such tongues.

Meanwhile, George stands by, silent, with his whole soul occupied in the endeavour to dissect one of his sister's pair of scissors, and metamorphose it into a couple of knives. Jane happens to catch sight of him thus employed, and sets up a shout of horror.

"You wretched boy! you are spoiling my only scissors. Give them to me back this moment."

"I'm sure I wish to goodness I could," responds George very gravely, having now got the handle of the scissors, apparently irrecoverably, far

40 Ruffle or pleat.

41 Decorative edging for a dress.

over his big thumb, and struggling futilely to free himself from them.

Jane jumps up, and comes to the rescue.

"Come here, you mischievous wretch. I'm sure Satan finds some mischief still for your idle hands to do.[42] Let me try and get them off your clumsy old thumb."

She succeeds in drawing them off, gradually, with nimble, persevering fingers, hurting him a good deal, it must be confessed, and making his flesh look very red and injured.

"The Chester girls are coming here this afternoon, George," said Louisa, raising a mealy potato countenance from among her pink vandykes—to which it formed a happy contrast—and looking up to see what effect her words produced.

"So you told me before," answers George sedately.

"Aren't you delighted to hear it?" continues his sister. "I'm sure you are, and don't attempt to deny it."

"I'm rather glad," owns George. "It is rather a comfort to see some other girls besides one's own sisters sometimes."

"Ungrateful boy!" sighs Fanny, a little injured; "you've always got a snub for your poor sisters."

"Do you call that a snub?" asks George, laughing; "because I don't" (and, to say truth, no more do I either).

"You'll be quite vanquished by Kate, my poor fellow," says Jane; "you always are rather an easy victory; and with her it is generally a case of 'I came, I saw (or rather have seen), I conquered.'"

"She did not strike me in that light when we met her the other day in the road," answers George nonchalantly. "A little white-faced thing. I hate turn-up-noses."

"Ah, that's only because you did not get a good look at her that you think that," says Jane. (These young persons are always ready to give other girls their full meed of praise, and to own that they are pretty when they are—that is another good point about them.) "We shall hear another tune to-night; sha'n't we, girls?"

"Talk of the devil, etcetera," remarks George, coolly looking out of the window. "Here she is, this man-trap; at least, I suppose so. I see two red-legged partridges, or girls, or something,—it's difficult to tell what ex-

42 See Isaac Watts, "Against Idleness and Mischief," in *The Divine and Moral Songs for the Use of Children* (1715), ll. 11-12: "For Satan finds some mischief still/ For idle hands to do."

actly, in this light,—vainly struggling to get in at the gate."

The red-legged partridges did prove to be none other than Maggie and Kate, in all the wintry glory of their scarlet hosen. In a few minutes they came in, and brought a gust of cold frosty air in with them, with cheeks freshened into bright bloom, even Kate's snowdrop white ones, by the cutting bitter north-easter. And now, O Muse! give me strength to tell of all the feminine osculations that ensued—everybody kissing everybody else; all, except Kate, who was passive, not active, who had some difficulty in undergoing her share with moderate complacency; for these promiscuous female embraces were very distasteful to her. And George stood by, meanwhile, the only excluded one, and not enjoying his exclusion.

"So glad to see you! What on earth has kept you so long? How late you are! We have been expecting you for two hours. O, what a nice hat! Never saw it before. Where did you get it? Not in Queenstown, I'm sure." And then, when the subject of the hats was exhausted, when everything was said about them that could be said, they all turned back to the consideration of the gowns, of the rose-clouds of gauze and tulle[43] which obtruded themselves on their notice. Fully and thoroughly they went into the question—the vexed question—of ruches and vandykes—all of them, without exception, none with more genuine zest than poor broken-hearted Kate, despite her high-souled contempt for dress—despite the vanity and emptiness of all earthly things—picked up, in fact, some slight hints for the decoration of that fair person which, in all human probability, black-browed Dare Stamer would never see again. It was very dull for George, being so completely put on one side; and so he thought. He kicked against his fate. In an indifferent, accidental way, with his hands in his pockets, he sauntered round to despised, turn-up-nosed Kate, leant his arms on the back of the pre-dieu chair[44] she was sitting upon, and prepared to do the agreeable. He always did; it was a habit of his. One science he did know thoroughly, both theoretically and practically, and that was the science of love-making. If fate had placed his lot in the Gallic land,[45] and during the reign of the Grand Monarque, he might have materially assisted Mademoiselle de Scudéry in her map of the kingdom of Tenderness.[46] In the art of

43 Lightweight gauzy material.

44 Chair with low seat and high straight back.

45 France.

46 The first volume of Madeleine de Scudéry's *Clélie* (1654-60) contains an allegorical map of the human heart. The "Grand Monarque" is Louis XIV of France.

flirting he as far distanced his sisters as he did in beauty; they knew it, they acknowledged it, and at a distance they followed his bright example.

"You don't care a straw about all this rubbish," he begins, spurning his sisters' gauzy treasures with scornful foot, "do you, Kate?"

He had never called her "Kate" before, and he found some satisfaction in doing it now. Cousinship is such a truly delightful relationship! It is so pleasant to be able to call a pretty young woman, the very first time you see her, by her Christian name, without the smallest chance of being rebuked and snubbed for your impudence!

"Yes, I do, George," answers Kate promptly, blushing a very little at this first essay in Christian-naming this new-found cousin. Soft, downy, kittenish, she sits there, and glances obliquely at him as she speaks, "takes a side glance, and looks down,"[47] after a way she has.

Kate could flirt still, then? Most decidedly, and practised the accomplishment more; was a far greater proficient in it than ever she had used to be in former happy days, before things had turned to dust and ashes on her palate. She could even feel a mild faint pleasure in seeing man after man play needle to her magnet. She would wreak the wrongs done her by one on the sex in general; and then, when they waxed tender and loving, how she turned to hate them! bullied them, and punctured their manly hearts without a grain of pity—little tyrant! more miserable so many degrees than the most miserable of her captives.

"Why, I thought you were quite a blue,"[48] remarks George, wishing he could get her to look up again. "I always heard so—much above this sort of thing, you know."

"O, so I am," answers Kate, with another very brief glance, which yet, short as it was, managed to contain a good deal of impudence in it. "I always talk Greek as a regular thing in my family circle, and I frequently joke in Hebrew." Not a very good piece of wit, but it served to amuse the easily-pleased George.

"She'll do," he says inwardly; "she's worth cultivating; not ugly either, when you see her close;" and he laughs (which is kind of him) at Kate's rather lame waggery; and prepares, at short notice, to merge the facetious into the sentimental, in which he was more at home. But then, after a while, his roving faithless eyes chanced to light upon Maggie.

By Jove, she is not bad-looking either; more colour than Kate; higher

47 Inexact, Henry Wadsworth Longfellow, "Beware" (1847), l. 9.

48 Blue-stocking, a stereotype of the intellectual woman.

forehead. There's no one to talk to her except those chattering girls. What a shame! She really must not be so completely neglected; he must go and talk to her a little bit now; she looks as if there was some fun in her. These are Lieutenant George Chester's fragmentary reflections; and acting upon them in a little pause of their sprightly talk, he takes away his resting arms, lifts up himself, and saunters across to Maggie. Kate, it must be confessed, felt a little atom surprised, and a very little atom vexed (though she would have denied vehemently had any one accused her of either of those sensations), that her small wiles, usually not unblessed with success, had been unable to chain this fat young man to her side. Meanwhile George leans over Maggie, as he had formerly leant over Kate, softens his voice to the proper insinuating pitch and says, "I've come to rescue you, Maggie." He calls *her* by her name too, and finds just the same amount and kind of gratification as he had before done, in giving utterance to Kate's monosyllabic cognomen.

"These girls have been teasing you awfully, I see that!"

"You're quite wrong, there!" replies Maggie, likewise glancing up and smiling, very nicely and sweetly and archly, no doubt, but not quite like Kate; for indeed I think Kate's ways were all her own, peculiar to herself, that no other woman I knew ever shared in, and that died with herself when she died. Lucky, perhaps, for men that they did. Maggie is not at all bad-looking either, thinks George complacently; some points better than Kate; livelier colouring, straighter nose. Many people at first sight gave the elder sister the palm of fairness over the younger; but I hardly ever knew the delusion last longer than two days. 'Pon his honour, they're both very nice girls; he does not know which he likes best; 'pon his honour he does not.

"Been into your district lately?" inquires one of the girls, it does not much matter which, of neglected, deserted Kate.

"Don't mention it," responds Kate, wringing a pair of soft, plump hands rather prettily. "I might as well never have had such a thing by the way I behave to it. I'm daily expecting to be drummed out of the delightful society of district-visitors for all my delinquencies; but I *am* going to mend, really," she continues, nodding her head resolvingly. "I'm going to make a tour of all the diseases in Queenstown to-morrow. I should have gone to-day, only that I had this delightful preëngagement here."

"I'm sure I would not go near it, if I were you," advises the philanthropic Jane. "You'll only be catching some of those horrid nasty diseases that those kind of people are always having."

"If I do, I'll come instantly and impart them to you, Miss Jane, so prepare yourself."[49]

"You'll be getting something dreadful said to you," chimes in Fanny croakingly, "I expect. Pa says it is not at all right for such a pretty girl as you to be walking about, all by yourself; and that if you were his daughter, he'd as soon think of cutting your throat, as letting you go about those back streets all alone."

"Yes, such a pretty girl," says Louisa emphatically, confirming her sister's speech; "those were the very words he said." She thought Kate must be pleased at this testimony to her charms; it was so very pleasant she knew to hear that anyone had said, behind one's back, how pretty one was—a pleasure she did not herself very often indulge in.

"Very kind of uncle George to be so flattering," answers Kate, laughing; "but I have not found my beauty very inconvenient at present. If he thinks it necessary, I'll wear two or three extra-thick veils every time I put my lovely nose out of doors."

"You're joking now," says Louisa; who, being passing matter-of-fact herself, thought that this was a discovery she had made.

"Will you come with me on my errand of mercy, as they say in tracts?" asks Kate, rather scornful in her merriment. "Do, that's a good girl; come to-morrow, in a big turned-down hat, with strings tied under your chin, and an umbrella and galoches. I'll engage that you sha'n't come to any harm through your charms. We should be almost sure to meet some one of your many admirers, and you know you've never tried the charitable philanthropic plan yet; it might answer beyond your wildest expectations;" and she laughed with rather grim mirth.

Louisa laughed too. She had a laudable slowness to take offence, a dense armour of good-humour, proof against ridicule. Sensitiveness was a

49 To readers today Kate and Jane's conversation might suggest a knowledge of the germ theory, but this is unlikely. Although by the 1860s pioneers such as John Snow, Louis Pasteur, and Joseph Lister were discovering the role of pathogens in the spread of disease, many still held to the belief that a "miasma," or effusion of noxious air (especially the emissions of decaying organic matter), carried infection. Thus, even as hygiene-conscious Victorians were increasingly aware of the link between dirt and disease, the miasmatic theory, by misunderstanding the nature of that link, tended to reinforce class prejudices. In particular, the implication that the living spaces and bodies of the poor were imbrued with poisonous exhalations stoked bourgeois anxieties about the contaminating influence of the lower orders.

quality altogether unknown to her.

"Perhaps it might indeed," she answered; "but I don't think I'll run the risk of small-pox and typhus even for that."[50]

"It would be quite a different matter if you were a clergyman's daughter and lived in the country, Ma says," remarks Jane, with solemnity.

"Pa" and "Ma" Chester when absent figure as conspicuously and authoritatively in their offsprings' conversation as the mystic Harris in Mrs. Gamp's;[51] when present,

"Flat contradiction do they bear,"[52]

now and then, as doubtless the Delphic oracle would have done, had he allowed himself to be seen and cross-examined by his votaries.

"O, yes, of course," remarks Louisa decisively; "if one lived in the country one would go to the Sunday-school every Sunday and teach Watts's Catechism;"[53] and she looks as if she thought rural joys were pretty nearly contained within the modest limits she has mentioned.

"Exactly what Kate and I underwent for a whole summer down at Daddy Piggott's," cried Maggie, laughing. "Do you recollect, Kate? What was Abraham? who was Job? who was Huz? who was Buz? who was everybody you can think of?"

"Recollect! I should think so," says Kate laughing. "O, the Herculean labour of getting Abraham firmly established in the infant agricultural mind as 'the pattern of believers and the friend of God.' He was so fond of shifting into 'a better man than Cain, and therefore Cain hated him;' or into 'the most patient man under pains and losses.' I have even known him, in aggravated cases, figure as 'the first woman that God made, and she was the mother of us all.'"[54]

---

50 The rest of this chapter is heavily changed from the *DUM* version; see Appendix B, pp. 404-407.

51 In Charles Dickens's *Martin Chuzzlewit* (1844), the midwife Sairey Gamp repeatedly refers to her friend Mrs. Harris who, it turns out, is fictitious.

52 Unidentified reference.

53 Isaac Watts (1647-1748), writer of religious works and hymns (see p. 184, n. 42) published a catechism "for children and youth" in 1730.

54 Quoting from the beginning of the section of Watts's catechism which concerns "scripture names for little children," Kate claims that the children she taught confused Abraham with Abel ("a better man than Cain"), Job ("the most patient man under pains and losses"), and even Eve ("the first woman God made").

"Dear me, Kate! what an irreverent way of talking!" exclaimed Fanny, whose little ideas rolled always with convenient smoothness along their conventional grooves, and could not have been shaken out of them without a dislocation of the whole small machine of her mind.

Kate shrugged her shoulders slightly.

"I confess," she said indifferently, "that I have no very profound reverence for the Gospel according to St. Watts."

"But, Kate," said Fanny, returning resolutely to her *moutons*,[55] "I cannot see what need take you down to those dreadful places, where one may see and hear all sorts of dreadful things. Pa says it's not as if there was nobody to look after the people. But there's that little sickly curate; I have forgotten his name; O, yes, Stanley, to be sure. Why, I know he is always with them when they are ill, praying, you know, and—and talking about their souls, and—and—where they are going to, and that sort of thing."

"There we certainly shall not clash," says Kate decisively;"I have not the slightest desire to mention their souls to them; I know too little about those appendages. I intend to confine myself entirely to their bodies."

"I cannot see what concern you have with either; it is not your business; in fact, business very unfit for any young person," says Miss Jane modestly; "and it *is* his. Why, he is paid for it."

"*Que voulez-vous?*"[56] replied Kate, yawning; "one must do something. There are twenty-four long hours in every day, and sixty immense long minutes in every hour; and one cannot spend them all in eating and sleeping, which are at present my only two definitive employments."

"Dear me, how odd!" said Emily, opening two perfectly round eyes. "We always find the day too short; don't we, girls? particularly now, when the evenings close in so soon. What with skirts to run up and bonnets to make and hats to trim, one never has a minute to spare.—By the bye, George dear, ring the bell for the lamp; I must finish these two gores to-night."

"You see Providence has not vouchsafed me the gift of stitching," said Kate; "my fingers are harmless idiots. Everyone's genius goes out in a different character; and I am still searching for the *habitat* of mine."

"Searching for anything, are you, Kate?" cries George, from the other side of the room, catching the one word; "let me look for it. Where did

---

55 Sheep (French); the phrase "revenons à nos moutons" (let's go back to our sheep) means to return to the topic.

56 What can you expect? (French).

you drop it? Wait till the light comes;" and he prepares to fall on his knees, and seek under the table and among the legs of the chairs for Kate's genius.

Kate laughs a gay little laugh, and looks up at him from under her long lashes, not exactly as she would have looked at her grandmother, had that admirable matron still been blooming in wig and spectacles here below.

"How kind you are! But I have not lost anything, thanks very much all the same. I was speaking figuratively, telling your sisters that I had not yet discovered in what direction my genius lay, but was still searching for it."

"That is one comfort of having none," says George philosophically; "one need never be at the trouble of looking for it."

"I don't think I care for geniuses in every-day life," says Kate obligingly; "they are generally poor puny little sickly things, that cannot do anything manly; I like a manly man, that can shoot and ride. I'm not ethereal enough to have much sympathy with people who are all soul and no body."

"Nice sensible little thing!" thinks the manly man beside her, feeling himself exactly described, as it was intended that he should.—"Are the three chairs you are at present occupying absolutely indispensable to you, Kate?" he asks, looking down on her with the bland beneficence of a superior being, "or can you spare me one, or a bit of one?"

Kate sweeps away the ample folds of her warm gray drapery very readily, and makes room for him beside her.

"O, how rude I am!" she says, with low-voiced penitence; "mannerly people, like poets, are born, not made, I'm afraid; to think of my keeping you standing there all this time! and it's so much pleasanter for myself too, now you are sitting down, and on a level with me; it gives one such a pain in one's neck looking up at you tall people; I don't think I'm fond of looking up to people in any sense."

"You like looking *down* on them better, you mean to say," replies Chester plaintively, disposing his head comfortably between two sofa-cushions, whence he has a commanding view of a very clean-cut small profile—Nature has tried rather "her prentice hand"[57] on the few female profiles usually submitted to his gaze. "How cruel of you to begin our acquaintance with a snub! Many acquaintances *end* that way, but to begin one—!"

"How you mistranslate me!" says Kate, casting her large mendacious eyes down to the carpet. "What I meant was, that in a case of either looking up or looking down there can be no equality; consequently no sym-

57 Robert Burns, "Green Grow the Rushes" (1783), l. 23.

pathy; consequently no friendship: friends must be on a level; two people cannot stand hand in hand one on a mountain, one in a valley."

"You and Mr. Stanley are on a dead level then, I suppose, Kate," says Emily *quasi* wittily; "for there is a very *prononcé*[58] friendship between you, isn't there?"

"Very," says Kate laconically.

"Ma says that in her younger days such a thing as a friendship between a young man and a young woman was never heard of," remarks Louisa, looking up from a conquered box-plait,[59] with which she has been for the last ten minutes wrestling in silence.

"No more were such things as steam-engines heard of, nor croquet, nor circulating libraries,[60] nor any of the modern assuagements of the annoyance of being alive; I'm afraid the author of your being does not make sufficient allowance for the march of civilisation; that is the worst of one's elders and betters, they never do," replies Kate, with mild irritation.

"Do you like Platonics?"[61] asks George ingeniously, trying to unravel one of the tassels of his cushion, and speculating as to whether the huge chignon that crowns the top of Kate's little head is her own, or the property of some other pretty woman.

"I don't like the *word*," says Kate; "it is soiled by all ignoble use. I like the *thing*."

"You really believe in them?"

"Between *some* people, yes." (Strong emphasis on the *some*.)

"What sort of some people?" asks Bellona's son[62] inquisitively.

"Well, I cannot define exactly what sort; but I think it is rather hard that two souls should not be allowed to speak friendly to each other, because one has the good fortune to be in a masculine cage, and the other the ill fortune to be in a feminine one, don't you?" appealing with docile eye and voice to the superior male intelligence.

"Uncommonly hard," assents George, with indignation, arranging his soul's substantial cage yet more luxuriously upon the ruffled chintz of the

---

58 Pronounced (French).

59 Double pleat where material is folded down on each side.

60 Due to the exorbitant expense of three-volume novels, a system of circulating libraries (Mudie's being the most famous) rented books to readers.

61 Non-romantic relationships between men and women.

62 George is called the son of Bellona, Roman goddess of war, because he is in the army.

sofa, and feeling not unlike Sardanapalus with his Myrrha beside him.[63]

"I'm so glad you agree with me," says Myrrha, *sotto voce*, "I thought you would;" and she launches at him one little arrow out of the ample store contained under the blue-veined curtain of her lids, but it was such a little one and flew so fast that it left him in his original state of uncertainty as to whether her eyes were blue or green or purple.

"You may pooh-pooh what Ma says, because she is old," remarks Miss Jane, who likes to have a monopoly of bullying her parent; "but for all that, I fancy that people's hearts and feelings and ways of going on are made on much the same pattern in one generation as another."

"Kate's friendship," strikes in Margaret, with what may be called a pleasant acid in her voice, "always reminds me of a little poem I used to learn in my youth—

'Will you walk into my parlour? said the spider to the fly;
'Tis the prettiest little parlour that ever you did spy!'"[64]

I'm not so sure that they do always find it such a pretty little parlour, do they, Kate?"

It is sweet, saith Lucretius, to sit on a bank, and see a good ship battered to pieces by the waves under your very eyes;[65] but it is not sweet to sit in a comfortable arm-chair and watch your younger sister putting her hook in the nose and her bridle in the jaws of any man you come in contact with.

"I deny the justness of the metaphor altogether," replies Kate, with a shadow of irritation in her clear young voice; "and anyhow, the parallel is very incomplete; for if any fly does not like my parlour, he is more than welcome to leave it with his full complement of legs and wings; you see what a character they give me" (sorrowfully to George). "'Give a dog a bad name,'[66] you know; and such an innocent-minded dog, too!"

She looks innocence itself, as she turns her great eyes wide open in a

63 In Byron's Sardanapalus (1821), Myrrha is concubine of the debauched king of Assyria.

64 Mary Howitt, "The Spider and the Fly" (1829), ll. 1-2.

65 In *De Rerum Natura*, the first-century Roman writer Lucretius uses this example to illustrate the point "Quibus ipse malis careas quia carnere suave est" (you view with pleasure that which does not affect you), claiming that witnesses of a shipwreck would derive satisfaction from their own safety.

66 Reference to the aphorism "Give a dog a bad name and hang him": once one acquires a bad name, it is hard to lose it.

sort of aggrieved surprise, limpid as wells of water in a limestone country, upon him. Flirting is ingrained in the blood and bone and fibre of some women. One can no more blame them for it than for having a cast in the eye or a stammer. Kate would flirt with the undertaker who came to measure her for her coffin.

When the Chester family were retiring to bed that night, Jane went up to George, put a hand on each shoulder, and asked smiling:

"Well, George, did I say right? Is she Venus Victrix,[67] or no?"

"Don't be absurd," replies George, hastily shaking her off. "She seemed a nice sensible little thing, with no nonsense or flirting about her, and grateful to anybody who took any notice of her. I hate your bread-and-butter misses."

If George could have taken a look into Kate's past, he would perhaps have been less surprised at the absence of the bread-and-butter element in her.

CHAPTER IV

THE next day to this, the morrow of George Chester's meeting with his cousins, was, as far as I remember (and I remember even small circumstances that concerned these years and these days with great distinctness), even colder, brighter, more hopeless for the hunting world than its predecessors. The bushes looked more than ever like thick-sugared Christmas cakes; the slides were more treacherously dangerous, and betrayed greater numbers of tottering old gentlemen, unsteady on their legs, to their destruction. The ground rang with a more obstinately frosty ring, and the birds' hearts died within them; despair took them, and one or two lay down and died, and were found by compassionate housemaids with their little feathers puffed out, and their little legs straight up in the air, on divers icy window-sills. A sort of day when Nature revolts at the dread fiat that it is eight o'clock; when, if one shrinking feature ventures forth from the drowsy bed-clothes, a great shudder passes through the whole chilled frame; a day when one could provide ices for all one's neighbors round out of one's own water-jug. And then, when, blue-fingered, one has at last passed through the ordeal of the toilette, has fumbled at buttons, and scrambled through the enduing of the manifold male or female garments, one comes down shiv-

67 Venus, goddess of love, in her victorious incarnation.

ering to the sitting-room, and finds the fire blazing cheerfully indeed, but with a hollow deceptive brightness which has no heat in it, which has not attempted to warm one inch of the raw morning atmosphere. O, Hercules! it requires a more eloquent pen than mine to speak the feelings of the sufferer on such a morning. The only course to pursue to make life bearable on such a day, at least for women (I speak not of men, considering their case hopeless, unless they skate), is, immediately after breakfast to draw a chair as close to the fire as a chair will go, without tumbling in, and to seat yourself upon it, with a book. By all means let the book be a shabby one as to outside, else your pleasure will be marred by alarms as to the warping of its fine back by the action of the fire. A shabby book then, either an old friend, whose worth you know well, having gauged it and measured its value on many a happy day before,—an old friend with turned down leaves, and dashes and pencil-marks, and, if you are sentimental, a sprig of some flower, so long dead as to be unrecognisable, between two pet pages,—or else, a stranger with a pleasant new face, whose acquaintance you are glad to make, and let agreeable, fresh ideas filter through your passively recipient mind from its open pages. Vary the recipe if you are young—not else. Do not have a book at all. Sit before the fire, and spread your hands over the flickering flame till they get burnt to a dull ugly red, and indulge in the most gorgeous and cheapest of all styles of architecture, the erection of many-towered, massive-buttressed air castles, such as most folks build many of in their first five lustres.[68]

The first of these occupations Kate Chester loved. Give her a book, and she could be happy still. It was one of the few pleasures that remained to her quite intact, quite unmarred by all that had come and gone. Allow her to sit on the rug, and burn her face; allow her to bury herself in some essay, some life, some account of how better men and women than she had comported themselves, had borne sorrow, had borne joy, and done great things, and thought them little, and how, at last, they had departed this life, as she should have to depart it soon or late; and she seemed once more to be the free-hearted, joyous Kate Chester of two years ago, to whom life was a continual feast. These books did her ever so much good; they took her out of herself, took away, quite, for the time, her morbid self-pity and continued introvision, substituted for them wider sympathies, broader fields of compassion; effaced for a while her own narrow circle of

68 See p. 67, n. 61

interests, replaced them with higher, nobler interests—interests that are the eternal heritage of us men, not in our paltry subdivisions of families and tribes and nations, but as men, as *man*—*man* as he has ever been since the days of Adam, as he will be to the end of time. But for castle-building Kate had no toleration; she never practised it herself now. How could she? She had no stuff to build stately castles in Spain with; and there needs some slight material to erect even such airy, unsubstantial fabrics with. Without a moment's hesitation she jumped up this morning as soon as the dread fiat of past eight o'clock sounded in her drowsy ears, despite the cold, despite the inclination that always came strong over those sad green eyes, to close and go to sleep again for ever, whenever they opened to full consciousness, to full remembrance on any morning, whether of hoary winter, with his icicles and holly berries, or summer, rose-crowned, ushered in by ministering south winds.

This was to be a day of self-abnegation, the beginning of a life of self-abnegation, like James Stanley's, only not quite so rigorous—not quite so excluding of good clothes, and parties, and world's pleasures generally. She would live for other people henceforth, throw herself into their concerns, and try to become identified with them. Her own *rôle* in life had become very dull, very stupid, and there was no possibility of its mending. She would leave it altogether, and enjoy life vicariously; laugh with the cheerful, and cry with the sad.

O dear, O dear! if it was not quite so hard to do that! The Chesters' breakfast-room was but a little dot of a place; but it looked very snug, with its bright fire, the glow of which shone, reflected in the urn and the spoons; its white tablecloth; its coffee-pot; its bread-and-butter and eggs, and pretty cups and saucers, with hawthorn on them, for two people. But Kate, in her new austerity, looked upon hot coffee and eggs and bread-and-butter as a temptation, keeping her from her work. She swallowed her share of breakfast in a way that might have excited the envy of Yankees. And then she spoke up:

"Don't laugh at me, Maggie, please; but I'm going out *Dorcasing*[69] this morning. Don't wait luncheon for me, for I don't know when I shall be back, or how long my old women and their aches may keep me. If I'm not back by dinner-time, send a few policemen down Liver-lane, and have the river dragged; that's all. Good-bye."

---

69 To do charity work; after Dorcas, a charitable woman of Joppa in Acts 9:36-42.

And off she ran, leaving Maggie in a state of amazement at the freaks that entered into the heads of blighted young ladies, to whom life was a vain show. Five minutes spent in rushing upstairs, in pulling out drawers and pushing them back again, in fishing out various articles of apparel, and in rushing downstairs again, and then Kate emerged from the hall-door on the steps, in process of washing, wrapped up warm in wintry raiment, that looked too well chosen and eye-pleasing for a young anchorite[70] like this. However, she had a big philanthropic-looking basket on her arm, which rather took away from the fashionableness of her appearance along the little sheltered approach where the laurustinus was unsuccessfully trying to come out into the broad public way.

"What a figure I have made of myself, with this horrid old basket!" thinks Kate. "There wants nothing but the wolf to make Red Ridinghood complete.

'One day with basket on her arm,'"[71]

she hums. "I doubt if anyone would say it was goodly fare I'm provided with."

A quick hurried look up and down, to see that nobody that *was* anybody saw her. She was mortally afraid of meeting any of her acquaintance. How they would laugh at her, dragging along that great unwieldy basket! Considering how dead she was to the world, she was singularly susceptible to the world's opinion of her.

Nobody was near that she knew. A few government clerks, hurrying, black-bagged, to the station to catch their daily train up to town, a few nursery-maids, and a postman or two,—that was all.

Quickly she passed along, down the road, by the side of which the river swept, spanned further down by the old bridge with the many arches, that the morning sun was lighting up so clear, swept along with its barges, and its myriad diamonds—calm, and smiling, and cold. Then on and on,

70 Hermit.

71 Reference to the fairy tale of Red Ridinghood, familiar to Victorians in versions by Charles Perrault (17th century) and the Brothers Grimm (early 19th century). See chapter 5 of Laurence Talairach-Vielmas's *Moulding the Female Body in Victorian Fairy Tales and Sensation Fiction* (Ashgate, 2007) for a reading of Kate's reenactment of the Ridinghood story (complete with red cloak) as a "moralizing vignette" about the dangers awaiting bourgeois women who stray into city slums (106).

into Queenstown; along its frost-bound streets; past the Swan, where the county-ball was going to be, a good time hence—two months off, quite; past the draper's shop, where the furs and muffs and cuffs made one almost warm to look at; past the grocer's, where the raisins and currants looked prophetically forward to Christmas; past the butcher's, where the pigs hung up, grunting no longer, squabbling no longer over the pig-trough, amicably cheek-by-jowl; across the market-place, where stood, iron-railed, the Sebastopol cannon;[72] its loud voice silent now; its bellowings come to an end. Then down a street not so broad or so well-paved, or so well endowed with gas, as the one we have left—a street that leads off, away from the market-place, down into the back undesirable parts of the town. You do not often meet any of the *beau monde*[73] of Queenstown there; and indeed they show their good taste in keeping out of it, at least as far as their bodily comfort is concerned, for there are very often very nasty smells there—nondescript compound sort of smells, that defy description or analysis; a street much frequented by coalheavers—black-faced, white-stockinged in their hours of leisure—where you may hear the choice language employed by bargees in the bosom of their families, over the puppy-pies,[74] which report affirms them to partake of with such relish. Tall narrow houses, standing thick together, that have stood there for a great many years now, some with gables and dormer windows, some without, most with funny red roofs, that remind one of an old Flemish town; windows put in crooked, with such small panes that but very little of the blessed light can get through them on the brightest day; poor little shops, whose whole stock-in-trade does not look as if it were worth five shillings. Not a very aristocratic quarter. But Kate's district is not here; she wishes it was: nothing so respectable has fallen to her lot.

Down a narrow bricked passage, with old placards stuck all over it, she passes—down into the region of back slums and alleys, where the sun has far too good taste to show his grand kingly face.

72 The year-long siege of Sebastopol, or Sevastopol, by Britain and its allies (1854-55) was one of the most notable conflicts of the Crimean War.

73 High society (French).

74 According to Peter Ackroyd in *Thames: The Biography* (New York: Random House, 2008), the question "Who ate the puppy pie under Marlow Bridge?" was a "famous" one (140), and concerned an urban legend about a landlord who, upon hearing that bargees were about to raid his kitchen, made a pie out of drowned puppies and left it in the larder for them to find. Supposedly they consumed it under Marlow Bridge.

At the entrance to a court, a shade more dingy than the others, the pretty, willing feet stop and stand irresolute a moment. Kate rather thinks her province begins here; but she is not sure, there is such a sameness of squalor about all these slums. There are some parts in Queenstown terribly bad and wicked, she knows, where no respectable woman dare put her nose. Perhaps she is on the point of falling into one of these lion's dens. That requires consideration. Robbed and murdered, perhaps! That might be the next event in her history. Paragraph in the police-reports: Found, the body of a young woman, apparently about twenty-one years of age, genteelly dressed, fair, plump, red-haired. (She was not red-haired, only she called herself so.) Well, if they did rob her, they would not get much out of her; that was a comfort: a ring, value about five shillings, and a small locket, value more than all the world to the owner, and about fivepence to anyone else. Well, courage! There have not been many cases of garotting in Queenstown this winter—at least not very many. "Faint heart," &c.[75]; though it's rather doubtful there being any fair lady to be won in these reeking alleys.

There cannot be much harm in knocking at one of these rickety closed doors, and seeing what sort of people the in-dwellers look. If they look very alarmingly sinister or ticket-of-leavish,[76] why one can take to a pair of sufficiently nimble heels, and leave them the basket of tracts, to make the most they can of. Such a court! Such a place for articulate men to live out all their days in! Think of

"Man, the great heir of eternity, dragging the conquests of time,"[77]

having fallen so low as to drag out a swinish embruted existence among these pestilential gutters, whose power the kind frost had weakened for a little space! Dreary houses, with big cracks across them; thin walls, propped up, in some cases, by helping beams; apologies for windows, with great hiatuses in them, filled up by filthy, bulging clouts; a clothes-line, with a great many singular-shaped garments, flapping in the slight cold wind, on

75 "Faint heart never won fair lady," an aphorism found in Camden's *Remains Concerning Britain* (1614).

76 A ticket of leave was given to a convict whose sentence was not yet completed, but who was released on the understanding that his liberty could be revoked for bad behavior.

77 Owen Meredith (E. R. Bulwer-Lytton), "Last Words of a Sensitive Second-Rate Poet" (1868), l. 80.

it—having just undergone their biennial washing; a pavement of uneven stones—some round, some sharp-edged—interspersed with puddles of dirty water, hardened now by the benevolent disinfecting ice. A few fowls, which art, not nature, had made blacker than the raven's wing, moved about objectlessly, creaking out the lugubrious tale of their woes to each other. A small dog with painfully distinct ribs—a dog which, if fate had placed him in a higher sphere of life, would have been white, which looked now as if it spent its whole life in being kicked and feeling hungry, was squatting down in a corner, with the marvellous and unaccountable treasure-trove of a perfectly bare bone between its poor little paws, which it was gnawing away at with such gusto as only a little cur dog in Bootle-court, who dined once a month, could experience.

Looking at this court for a year and a day would not mend it, would only make one feel all the more disgusted with it; and so Red Ridinghood, having explored it, searching-eyed, felt. She made up her mind then, and put her resolution into action without further delay. Up to the first dingy door she walked, and knocked rap-a-tap-tap with three small knuckles, dog-skin clothed. She had not long to wait in suspense as to the result of her appeal. In about two seconds a woman opened the door a little, and looked out. A woman—at least one had to call her so by courtesy, though certainly, at first sight, one felt disposed to suspect her of being a walking hoax, a bundle of rags made up into a faint resemblance of the female shape—a lady who, if a fancy ball had been given in her neighborhood, might assuredly have gone, without change of costume, as a scarecrow, or *mawkin*, as we expressively call it in the breezy north country. Poor thing! it is not good-natured to laugh at her, or very witty either, forlorn, draggled creature as she is. How impossible it seemed to believe that she was of the very same genus and species as the gracious being with the melting eyes and the coiled chestnut hair that confronted her now so unexpectedly, and smiled up in her battered, untidy face! She had come to see her; might she come in, just for a minute, Kate asked, in that low wooing voice that, to my thinking, was sweeter than the monotonous cooing of half-a-dozen ringdoves in a summer wood; a voice such as other women don't seem to have nowadays; a voice like that with which martyred Cordelia soothed her poor brain-sick old father at his mazed waking.[78] The grim woman looked rather askance at

78 See Shakespeare's *King Lear* (first printed 1608), IV.vii.43-69; Cordelia, whom Lear had exiled but who, in fact, is the loyalest of his three daughters, reunites with him when they both are imprisoned by the traitorous Edmund. Cordelia, whose

her, not that she had any particular animosity to Kate, but being tired, and being hungry, and being up late and early for these many years past, and having not much hope in this world or knowledge of another, had made her look with a soured spirit at even kind faces, had made her in a manner colour-blind, so that nothing could look rose-coloured to her now. No very good excuse for keeping out her visitor, however, occurring to her, and a faint hope of getting something out of her, passing dimly through the twilight of dull cunning in her poor mind, she opened the door a little wider, in a sulky, resigned sort of way, and let her pass into the interior. And now that poor Kate had penetrated into this hospitable mansion, how much the better off was she? What was the next step? Ask them whether they went regularly to church; read them a good lecture if they did not, and sweep out again in all the glory of her crinoline and her feathers? Not exactly. Nobody offered her a seat, so she pulled forward a thing which had once been a straw-bottomed chair, as two or three remarkably-adhesive straws still testified, but which was now, to all intents and purposes, a no-bottomed chair, displaying a *vacuum quod inane vocamus*,[79] on which it required a good deal of agility and presence of mind to balance oneself without falling through. Trying to look at ease and keep in a sitting posture on this desirable resting-place, Kate remarked, in an amicable friendly tone, that it was very cold to-day. "Yes, it was," the woman asserted, and then scratched her elbow meditatively, and did not enlarge upon the idea. O, me! O, me! visiting the poor in a town is a different thing to visiting the tenants on your father's estate in the country. It is no great hardship certainly to walk up between neat little gay borders of gillyflowers and sweetwilliams into a tidy little kitchen, to have the apron applied to the best chair before it is considered worthy of your reception; to have your remarks about the potatoes and the crops in general, your inquiries after the boy who is 'prentice[80] to somebody, and the girl who is in service with somebody else, received with the respectful gratitude, the willing civility that such great condescension merits. What shall she say next, thinks Kate, feeling very uncomfortable. There's a background of another grim woman, with flying gray hair that had nothing venerable about it, and a horde of little old men and women in

voice is remembered by Lear as being "ever soft, gentle and low, an excellent thing in woman" (V.iii.275), is called "martyred" here because she is unjustly executed at the play's end.

79 A wide expanse (Latin); from Lucretius, *De Rerum Natura* (see p. 193, n. 65).

80 Apprentice.

child-shapes, dwindle-limbed, cunning-faced—a small promising academy of thieves and pickpockets. Kate's anxious eyes roving round, trying to draw food for talk from the wall, fell by chance on one child more goblin-faced than the others, who was peering inquisitively at the big basket.

Blessed thought! that child must have a name and an age.

"How old is he?" she asks aloud.

"Turned seven years ould," answers the woman briefly.

He might be any age, from one to one hundred, judging by his countenance.

"And what's his name?" further inquires Kate, with another smile, which George Chester would have said "thank you" for, which would have made Dare feel as if he did not exactly know whether he was on his head or his heels, but which was quite thrown away here.

"Jeames," replies his mamma, not looking very graciously at these useless queries; and she fetches "Jeames" a motherly cuff for some delinquency which just then caught the maternal eye, or else as a providing against future delinquencies. Very interesting and satisfactory, but not a suggestive subject. Ah, yes! at all events there are six or seven more pinched-looking little goblins; consequently six or seven more names and ages. It will spin out the time well to inquire all these. In two minutes she is in possession of all, and neither of the grim women looks a bit relenting, or makes any effort to continue the conversation. She cannot stand it any longer, and the air feels so stuffy and foul too; so she gets up gingerly off the sketchy, anatomical chair, says she is afraid she must be going, and lifts up the big basket, which begins to weigh very heavy, on the soft arm again. That basket is full to the brim of good books, that have got into their covers at last, thanks to James Stanley. Kate had intended to sow them broadcast; to give one at least, or perhaps two, at each house; but now she had not the heart to offer one. How absurd it seemed to offer food for the mind, as a substitute for that bodily food which was evidently so sorely wanted! What a mockery to present warnings against drunkenness and gluttony to one who had not the means of getting drunk, if she had wanted ever so, whose only scope for the manifestation of gluttony was over a crust of bread and an onion! As long as flesh is flesh, the material must so dominate the immaterial, that the soul can receive but small nourishment till its master and its slave, the body, have its cravings satisfied, or at least dulled. Soft-hearted Kate fumbled in her pocket, and pulled out a small purse, not very well furnished.

"Here's a shilling for you," she said, blushing very unnecessarily, and holding it out between her thumb and forefinger.

The woman seized it eagerly, giving Kate space to remark that even that stolid apathetic face could light up into some sort of interest and expression; and then she passed quickly out, had the door closed upon her, and stood once more under the frosty sky, in the dead-alive court, where the poor little dog was still gnawing his bone, having completed her first philanthropic visit—having got through it somehow. When she was quite sure that no eyes but the absorbed cur dog's and the plaintive fowls could see, she indulged herself in a little ebullition of feeling. She stamped indignantly on the jagged pavement; she did more, she set down the big basket, and kicked it.

"Stupid old thing!" she said, apostrophising it acidly. "I wonder what you and all your canting load are, except to break my arm. O dear, O dear, how it aches!" and she rubbed hard. "it would have been much more to the purpose if you had been filled with beef and mutton bones. What an imposition it all is! I don't care who says it isn't. I've a good mind to go home as fast as my legs can carry me, and give up the whole thing for ever and a day. I wonder how much good I have done—finding out that one brat's name is Jeames, and his brother's Chawls. What business had that nasty cross old woman to be so rude to me? I'm sure I was civil enough to her. I bet something that shilling of mine goes to the gin-shop, and that they are laughing at my verdancy[81] now." A slight pang of regret shot through this ministering angel that her shilling had not fulfilled its original mission of buying the last number of *Macmillan*,[82] with the new story, that looked so inviting, glimmering through its uncut pages at the railway station. "Well, I suppose the more disagreeable it is, the more of a duty it is; the usefulness of anything is generally in an inverse ratio to its pleasantness. I shall get a good word from poor little Jemmy, that's one comfort. I know exactly how his good little ugly face will brighten when I narrate the story of my conversion and my good works. Here I go, then. Off again on this cheerful mission. Better luck next time." And the dog-skin knuckles go rap-a-tap-tap at the door that came next, and at many successive doors. Great sameness in the character of the *visitées*.[83] More grim women, with wild gray, or

81 Greenness, inexperience.

82 Reputable magazine whose founders were themselves concerned with the lot of the London poor.

83 Ones visited (French).

red, or rusty-black hair straggling about haggard faces; more elf-children, with legs of the tenuity of knitting-pins. Conversation not very rife either. Kate had to have recourse to the name-and-age plan. Within an hour she had gained a knowledge of the statistics of Bootle-court, which, had she been able to remember them, would have rendered her invaluable to the census.

How disgusted Kate grew with herself, and with the mothers and children! her sole gleam of comfort arising from the fact that a few old women had complained, with feeble senility, of the length of time that had passed since she had been seen by their arm-chairs; had remarked, incidentally, that they had not had a pinch of snuff they did not know when. At about the twenty-first door, a little variety—something that promised a slight difference—a small opening for being benevolent and helpful. When the knuckles gave their customary rap, a grim man came this time to the door; a man in a dirty slop, with hair cut suspiciously short,[84] and a face which seemed from constant companionship to have become assimilated in expression to the countenance of the bulldog which peeped between his legs, frowning with all the wrinkled might of its tawny forehead at the intruder. There was a grim woman belonging to this house too; but she was not trudging about any longer on tired, slatternly feet, in the dreary round of heartless, unrewarded daily work, or the still more dreary soulless pleasures. She was lying prone instead, close to the door, on what in Bootle-court they were in the habit of calling, with unconscious irony, a bed. Such a thing, so filthy, so thin-clothed, it seemed a mockery to suppose that weary, aching limbs could get any rest thereon. But she who lay on it was past caring, knowing whether it were filthy or clean, whether it were straw or down—past almost everything; one look told one that, struck down with so sore a sickness, off that bed would she get up never more at all—never more off it, save to go, feet foremost, in her narrow, thin-walled, deal house over the threshold to the corner of the dank town churchyard, where paupers lay rotting so thick together.

"May I come in?" asked Kate, very softly, almost under her breath; for she caught a glimpse beyond the man in the slop and his bulldog, into the inside of the poor house.

"I suppose so," returned the man indifferently; and then he turned his back upon her, and left her.

84 A slop is a smock-like garment; the man's hair is "suspiciously" short because it recalls the cropped heads of convicts.

Kate stepped in very reverently over the door-sill; for she felt there was a visitor there before whom we must all needs bow our heads and hold our breaths. Why was it; from what subtle connection of thought with thought, of the ideas suggested by the present scene with some other idea or memory latent in the brain—that when Kate stood by that low bed, looking down earnestly on its occupant—that occupant that was now a person, and soon would be—O, fearful metamorphosis!—but a thing,—why was it that the recollection of her own mother flashed so arrow-swift, so lightning-bright, across her? What possible resemblance could there be found between this poor plebeian, with the swollen, debased features, with the coarse, weather-stained, care-wrinkled skin, and her mother, with her patient, saintly face and spirit eyes? What resemblance indeed! Why this, just this one, which struck Kate through and through: she had seen on both the stamp of the valley of the shadow of death.[85] There is that much resemblance between us all. We acknowledge it in words; but we do not often feel it to our heart's core; do not realise how near of kin that ineradicable stain of mortality makes us all.

The wind blew in coldly through a good many chinks—in, over, at the sides of, and under the bottom of the ill-fitting door; blew in, as a winter wind does, and swayed and flapped the coverlet of rags and tatters. But what matter? The woman felt nothing of it, did not shiver or stir at all—she was so occupied with that great business that comes, thank God, but once to us all; that business we shall all have to transact, shudder and kick at it as we may—the business of dying. For forty lagging summers and forty hoar winters she had toiled and laboured; had been kicked and cuffed and sworn at; had borne children, and lost them, and felt too lifeless to cry; had dwelt and fed and slept amongst the scum of the people, and had grown scum too; had done evil, because no one had shown her much how to do good; and now she had come to the end,—yes, the very end,—the end of the world to her. The few last grains of sand were dribbling out slowly, one by one; the man on the pale horse[86] was drawing very, very near, though no eye could see him—coming to take away this woman with him to her account. Poor, poor, darkened, desolate creature! surely she shall be beaten with few stripes.

Kate did not care a straw about this sick woman; of course she had

85 See Psalm 23: 4: "Yea, though I walk through the valley of the shadow of death, I will fear no evil: for thou art with me[.]"

86 Death; an image taken from Revelation 6:8.

never seen her before. There was no grief in her heart; but she felt inexpressibly awed and grave. Young people always do; they seem to be so many miles away, at such a safe distance from the great precipice, that they come and peer over the edge of the abyss with curious inquisitive eyes. Elder people either will not look at all, because it makes them dizzy and sick, or else, in better case, gaze down into its depths with eyes that faith has made very clear and fearless.

If Kate felt awed, she was the only person in the room that did. None of the men who were present—and there were two or three besides the one who had admitted her—seemed to have a scrap of that feeling; they were drinking gin-and-water, and talking in voices not much lowered from their usual rough pitch. They did not see anything to be awed at, and would have been surprised if they had known it was expected of them. They had seen heaps of people die before now. Human lives very often went out, like the snuff of a candle, in Bootle-court. They did not see anything out of the way in it; there was nothing very odd or awful in a person "going off the hooks." Everybody did it; they should do it themselves some day; they did not care how soon.

Kate looked round once or twice at them very indignantly when their voices rose to a pitch she thought most unseemly in that chamber; but they were perfectly unaware of her disapprobation. They did not take the smallest notice of her; she would have been very much alarmed if they had. At last, to her great relief, having finished their gin, they got up and clumped and stumped out, banging the door behind them.

Kate seemed to breathe freer when she was alone. She sat down on the bed and touched one of the hands lying there so useless, nerveless—so utterly, eternally idle. She could do no good there, that was certain; not the least tittle. This sick woman was totally unconscious of her presence, wanted nothing at her hands. No sound could reach those dull ears; no sight could affront those glazing eyes, that were closed, and yet not closed. But still Kate sat on there, and the idea of going away never entered her head; sat, with her cloak falling round her, in its warm scarlet folds, the only bit of colour in that room, where neutral tints held their dingy sway. It seemed so cruel, so heartless, to leave this poor unknown creature to die all by herself here. It would not be cruel really; but she could not divest herself of the notion that it was.

Folks have an odd idea that it is somehow more sociable to die in company, with a fit complement of tear-stained faces round you, than to give your last sigh as a present to solitude. So the odd deep eyes gleamed softly from under their bright lashes, very solemn and speculative, upon the dying face. The passionate southern lips parted one from the other and trembled, as a great many moving thoughts stirred the brain they were the mouth-piece of; and Kate fell into a long pondering. If she was able to do no good to this expiring woman, the woman did some good to her. She furnished a text from which Kate preached herself a very wholesome sermon. What Yorick's skull said to Hamlet,[87] this woman said to Kate. So she should be just like that some day, lying back like a log; only a log would not pant and heave, and breathe so loud and stertorously. Pant like that! how dreadful! It made her out of breath now to think of it. She would have those awful co-lours on her face—green and yellow and ashy. Who would care to kiss her then? And all this would happen, must happen; not possibly, not perhaps, but certainly, undoubtedly. There's one single combat we must all engage in, though we know for a surety that we shall be beaten; we cannot shirk it, and give Death the game; he will wrestle it out with us. She, too, should some day have the clammy sweat of that appalling duel on her brow. She passed her hand over the low smooth forehead as she mused on this, and pitied herself very much, and the poor pretty face that would have to grow so unsightly. But it must come; it *must*, it *must*. O, the desolation of that thought! What if God should not send her the gift of the dense cloak of insensibility He had sent this woman? What if she should be able to watch her own dissolution, to see the steps of the divorce between the clinging body and the terrified soul? What if she should be able to gaze with horri-fied despairing eyes down into the gulf she was being forced into so utterly, so fearfully against her will? Life certainly was not so jocund a thing to her as to most young women. She had had one or two very hard blows—blows that had knocked her down so much that she could not hope ever to stand up again quite so upright and firm as she had done before; and though no one was giving her blows now, yet the days somehow lagged, and she did not seem to care much whether it were even or morning, noon or night. But still, however chill and drear life might be, was it not immeasurably better than this last dread tussle? How coming into the presence of this tremendous personage, this "spectre with the bony head,"[88] did render in-

87 See Shakespeare, *Hamlet* (first printed 1603), V.i.184-95, where Hamlet uses the skull of the dead jester Yorick as a lesson on mortality.

88 Inexact, Hartley Coleridge, "Think Upon Death, 'Tis Good to Think Upon Death" (1851), l. 3.

significant all other personages and things whatever! She was not having an interview with him herself either. She was only in the ante-room, hearing him hold converse with another; and yet all the sorrows and the interests that had seemed giants exceeding the stature of Goliath of Gath[89] when she entered that door had changed all of a sudden into pigmies. O God! what did it matter whether one cried or laughed, whether one had fair weather or foul? What mattered any aggregation of evils that could be possibly crowded into one's narrow space? What did anything matter? Of what consequence (she could even say) was it that, on a certain moon-dowered June night, while the waves were plashing their caressing lullaby, that dark man with the rough-hewn strong features and the lurid agonised eyes had kissed her heart-brokenly, and bid her go away quickly from him out of his sight? Of what consequence was it that she had lain all along on the yellow sand, and stretched out desolate white arms, and called upon Death to come and take her from a world where there could never be any joy for her any more? It was all grasping at shadows she saw now, neglecting the substance. Looked back on from the high mountain-tops of eternity, all life in its length and breadth would seem but a speck, a pin's point.

How was it that the tiny bagatelles of time present, from being held so close to the eye, obscured and shut out the huge bulk of things future? Why could not one always feel like this? Why could not one always stay in that state of mind? It was the only right state, the only wholesome state, the only sane state. All other states of mind were nothing but disease and madness. Why was one always like the dog in the fable—dropping the good solid piece of meat into the water to snatch greedily at the reflection?[90] Why would not things always look the same as they did on a Sunday evening, when one is reading Jeremy Taylor[91] or some other good book? Why is it so hard to distinguish between what will grow bigger and bigger every day, and will last for ever, and what will each day wax smaller and smaller, and in a few to-morrows will be gone as if it had never been? Why do things not keep their shapes, but are always mazing and puzzling one by their shiftings and windings? Why, why, why? All those questions that people ask them-

89 See 1 Samuel 17:4: the gigantic Philistine champion killed by David.

90 In one of Aesop's fables, a dog carrying a piece of meat sees its reflection in a brook and, mistaking it for another dog, opens its jaws to lunge for the meat in its mouth. The moral of the story—the dog loses his original meal in trying to seize its reflection—is not to mistake shadows for substance.

91 Puritan writer and clergyman (1613-67).

selves and ask other people so often, and so seldom get answers to them.

Kate went on, sitting there at the foot of the low bed, not shrinking from the contact with the poor chilling rags motionless; and the only sound in the room was the heavy stertorous breathing that was going to stop so soon. There she sat, and fell a pondering on life and immortality, or the wonderfulness and inexplicability of the very fact of existence—pondering on a great many deep things, that no pondering on can make very clear to men and women's dim eyes.

She might have gone on sitting there to this day, for aught I know, in her complete absorption; but after a long while she was roused by the door being unlatched and opened by a rough uncareful hand; and the man who had first received her—the man with hair dressed à la hulks,[92] with the countenance that made one think of the ring, to man to whom this "*domus et placens uxor*"[93] appertained—came in and stamped across the bricked floor, heavy-footed, not much caring whether he made a noise or not. He did not look particularly pleased at finding Kate there still; and the bulldog apparently also considered her *de trop*,[94] for he growled in a not very conciliatory manner, and appeared to have his thoughts filled with *pinning*[95] in general.

Kate rose up with great dignity off her low seat as brave as a lion, and faced both dog and man. She felt boiling with indignation against the latter.

"I'm going," she said, fronting him. "I see you think I have been here quite long enough; but I had not the heart to leave your poor wife all by herself here. Are not you ashamed of yourself, letting her die all alone here, and not caring a bit about it? I wonder how you'll like to be served so yourself."

There she stopped short, and wondered much and trembled a little at her own boldness.

The man shifted uneasily from one leg to the other, knocked one dirty hobnail against the other, and looked uncommonly sheepish. He was not any great monster of iniquity—only an ignorant, big, hulking fellow, who had lived with bad men and heard bad words and done bad things from his earliest youth; and there did not seem to be much natural affection or any other good thing left in him now. He did look very sheepish now, however,

92 Derelict transport ships used as prisons.

93 Home and a good wife (Latin); phrase coined by the Roman poet Horace.

94 Too much (French); superfluous.

95 The verb "pin" is used here in the sense of seizing or holding on to.

and rather ashamed of himself.

So Kate thought, and with her usual impetuosity repented of having given him such a large piece of her mind. She fumbled again for the small lean purse, took out the very last shilling, and said hurriedly,

"Here; I'm afraid nothing will do her any good now, poor thing! I wish to goodness I had come here before; but I'll come again to-morrow, and—and—here, take this." And she pushes the shilling into his dirty hand, and goes quickly out.

CHAPTER V

"HELL is paved with good intentions," said someone once, says everybody now; but I suppose that means intentions that never come to be anything but intentions, that remain fruitless to their last days.

Kate certainly did not intend that hers should serve the purpose of macadamising Hades. And what good resolutions she did make that winter's day in that little squalid court! She would spend a great deal of her time with these poor wretched people—would go among them five days a week at least; and they would have to get more civil to her before long—there could be no doubt of that. She would do such an immense deal of good; people always did when they put their shoulder really with a will to the wheel. It was evidently the course chalked out for her now in life, and she would follow it. After all, it was less "flat, stale, and unprofitable"[96] than any other course. She would practise such self-denials. That copy of Cowper's *Letters*[97] that she had coveted for the last month, lying there in the bookseller's window in its green-cloth covering, might lie there for the next ten years, and get sun-faded and fly-flecked, for all she would do to rescue it. How valiant she felt too! Being in the presence of the great king and lord of all terrors had made any minor fear or alarm utterly despicable. She did not think anything could frighten her to-day. She would confront all the ticket-of-leave men[98] in London, and not flinch. And then it occurred to her that, at all events, for to-day she had done her duty; she was getting very tired and cold; she might go home and enjoy luncheon with a clear conscience, and that arm-chair by the fire which she knew would woo her

96 See Shakespeare, *Hamlet* (first printed 1603), I.ii.133.

97 William Cowper (1731-1800), English poet.

98 See p. 199, n. 76.

open-armed, and the old small-printed Shakespeare that opened so easily at a good many places.

So she turned about, and set her face in the direction of home. She thought she knew her way perfectly, and remembered every twist and turning of the way she had come; so she took small heed to her steps, but let her feet lead her pretty much where they would, feeling confident they would guide her all right. So she passed along, wrapped up in her own thoughts, in the serious thoughts her day's unwonted labours had suggested. But then, after a while, she caught her foot on a sharp stone and hurt herself, with difficulty saving herself from falling on her face; and that brought her out of her meditations very effectually. She looked round her, and began to reflect that she seemed to have come through more courts and streets and back places than she had done before; this place she was in now looked unfamiliar. She had never seen before, she was sure, that dingy red-brick building, with J. E. Frickner, Timber Merchant, in big black letters, stuck upon it. She was perfectly sure she had never seen that before, or she should have remarked that the E was turned the wrong way.

How stupid of her to have lost her way! got into the dangerous bad parts of Queenstown, perhaps. Heaven forbid! Another look round; rather an uneasy look, despite the newborn valour. O, thank goodness, that is a comfort! She must be right after all; for there, at the bottom of that lane, runs the street she first diverged from in the morning. So she goes on with a good courage down the lane and into the street; but when she gets there she is rather discomfited by the discovery that it is not the same street after all. It runs parallel to it, and has the same variety of gabled and ungabled, tall and short houses—but it is not the same; it is narrower, darker, dirtier; altogether rather a villanous-looking street. Shall she go up or down—which?

A few moments' consideration, and then she sets off down. That direction must bring one to the river, and the river must bring one home in time. She is not frightened, for what harm can happen to her, for it is still broad day? but she is glad that there seem so few people about, and she has no inclination to fall back into her musings. She looks about, indeed, with very wide-awake, anxious eyes. Some way on, down the street, there is a low public-house, standing a little forwards from the other buildings, displaying an effigy which a person of lively imagination and great ingenuity might discover to be intended to represent a pair of keys hanging up across one another; a public-house, with a dingy bow-window, and a barmaid with a great many flowers about her head, standing, arms akimbo, at the door. A good many men of a very low class—coalheavers, bargees, &c.—were loafing about, hands in breeches-pockets, pipes in mouths, and on their heads those singular coiffures appropriated to their profession, and which are distinguished by the care with which they shade and protect the napes of their delicate necks.

Kate had a mortal fear of men of the lower orders generally—it was a standing joke against her; perhaps her great and exaggerated timidity on this score arose from the fact that a year or two ago a drunken sailor had met her in a lone country road, had stopped her, and made some not over polished joke at her expense, which combined actions had frightened her almost out of her wits. Being stared at she did not mind a bit—she was quite used to it; every man who met her, from a king to a tinker, would be sure to look twice at her; she did not dislike that; perhaps she would have missed it if they had not; but of tramps, beggars, common men generally, she had an absurd and unreasonable horror and fear. She crossed the street now, that she might get further from this idle loafing knot, and marched along with rather a quaking heart, very firm and solemn, looking neither to the right nor the left, trusting then to escape notice. But some star unfavourable to Kate was in the ascendant to-day.

As I have said, there were but few people in the street, consequently, those men had, unfortunately, not much to look at besides Kate: add to which, that a person of her appearance was a sight not very often beheld in this part of the town. She was sadly noticeable in her enveloping scarlet cloak and little neat-shod tripping feet. Before she gets opposite the Cross Keys they stop talking, they stare unpleasantly at her; one bargee, a youngish one, takes his pipe out of his mouth, and prepares to speak. Kate does not look, but somehow knows it, and her heart begins to beat very fast. And then this delicately facetious remark comes in a great strong loud voice across the road, distinct on the frosty air, to her ears:

"I'll gi'e you a ha'penny for your crinoline, miss." She pretends not to hear; she takes no notice, and tries to walk faster, without seeming to run. Then there comes a coarse approving *guffaw* from the other men, and the barmaid with the bad brazen face applauds, shrill-voiced also. The young bargee's head is turned by the success of his wit, he had not calculated on such approbation; he does not see now why he should not pursue it further. So he strides across the road, and quick as the terrified little feet go, he is almost too quick for them. O horror! she sees that in a second he will be before her, will be standing in front of her, barring the road. In that one terrified moment she had time for a flash of intense longing for Dare by her side, to knock him down; but as no Dare was there, Kate did the best she could for herself. Ridiculous little coward! on the instant all her fortitude and dignity fled: she thought, for a certainty, that all the dreadful things she had ever heard or read of in books were going to happen to her. Now the bargee was not a particularly bad sort of fellow in his way: foul-mouthed, certainly, after his kind, and perhaps a shade tipsy; but for all that, his sole object and intention in the present case was to be funny. But people's ideas of wit are so exceedingly different, it is a thing that nobody has yet been able to define, any more than anybody has yet been able to see the wind. Kate's notions of wit were so totally different from his, that she did not even believe that his end and aim was to be witty, and nothing more nor less. Down went the basket of tracts: *Little Sinners' Breeches* grovelled on its face in the gutter; *Crumbs for the Pantry* was borne on a light breeze to the shrill-voiced barmaid's feet. Kate gave one short small species of shriek, took to her heels, and fled for the bare life, as if ten thousand devils were behind her, goaded on by the nightmare idea of the big, grimy bargee following hard upon her tracks. Down one street, up another, along a dark alley, across a court, round a corner, bang up against a woman with a baby in her arms, down another street, between two startled policemen, whom she did not see—on and on and on, till she was brought up at last, stopped in her Mazeppan course[99] by very nearly tumbling right over a harmless little gentleman in black clothes, walking orderly along, looking at a book in his hand, and who consequently had not seen the imminent danger that threatened him, and who, by the impetus of her rush, had been sent spinning into the middle of the road.

"Hullo!" exclaims the little gentleman, picking himself up, and a good deal surprised, naturally, at the vicissitudes of this life. "Hullo, *Kate!*" he adds, in accents of vast astonishment, as he discovers the individual who

---

99 Byron's "Mazeppa" (1819) is about a Ukrainian page at the Polish court who, discovered having an affair with a count's wife, is tied naked to a runaway horse by the irate husband. In comparing her unconventional heroine to Mazeppa, Broughton may have had in mind an 1860s dramatization of the poem starring, in a cross-dressing role, the controversial American actress Adah Isaacs Menken (shown on the front cover). Wildly popular on both sides of the Atlantic, this production climaxed with Menken, strapped to a real horse, wearing flesh-colored tights which made her appear nude.

has made him describe this parabolic curve.

"James!" exclaims Kate in equal surprise, but quite under her breath; for she is completely spent now with her violent exertions, and she leans against a lamp-post, and pants, and the rich carmine that that mad wild run had brought into her cheeks ebbed away quicker than it came, leaving her pale even to the lips—a fair marble image of fear.

"What on earth has come to you, Kate? What's frightened you? Has anything happened?" asks James rapidly, in an anxious concerned voice; and he goes up to the lamp-post and takes a small hand that is trembling and shaking like a leaf.

"*Happened!*" repeats Kate in almost a whisper, still panting hard;"I should think so indeed! I have been running away for my life from a dreadful man. O dear, O dear! I thought he was close behind me. He's somewhere near now, I'm sure;" and she shuddered and cast a frightened look around her.

James looked up the street and down the street, gazed in search of this man, this bogie, but could see nothing but an old orange-woman at her stall, haggling with a very little boy, and two or three highly respectable personages, evidently occupied entirely and wholly in their own concerns. Then he brings back his eyes to Kate's face.

"Dreadful man!" he says in a surprised tone; "what do you mean, Kate? There's no dreadful man in sight that I can find out, unless I am one myself. Are you quite sure you have not been dreaming?"

"Dreaming!" repeats Kate with indignation, and she stops, leaning against the lamp-post, and speaks out of breath still, decidedly, but rapid and excited. "Do you mean to say that I dreamt that the great big brute tried to stop me in the road, and said something to me—O, I do not know what—something horrible? Dreaming, indeed! I don't admire such dreams."

James listens attentively, and is convinced. Then Kate comes quite to herself again; picks up her courage now that there is nothing to test it, and the ludicrous side of the adventure striking her, she begins to laugh.

"Well, I've left them one token of affection; they've got the tract-basket to amuse themselves with—all those little good books you covered so nicely. I forgot all about the basket and it slipped, of course, off my arm, and tumbled down—O, dear, what fun!—with such a noise on the ground. I should have died laughing, I'm sure, if I had not been in such an awful fright."

"I'm exceedingly vexed that you should have met with such a disagreeable adventure. I should not have thought it the least likely in broad daylight; it is most annoying—*most*," says James.

And it seems to be so to him; for his pale white face looks graver and sterner than she had ever seen it before; graver and sterner than one could have imagined such a face could look; but even the great Jewish lawgiver's brows curved into a frown sometimes—the brows of him who was the meekest man upon earth.

"O, what does it matter now?" answers Kate lightly; "something to put in my journal, that's all. You see I'm very well able to take care of myself, by the swiftness of my movements; and I daresay the man only meant to be facetious; only bargee's wit is of the most cumbrous. I was not afraid of anything the moment I saw you;" and she smooths her fuzzy hair, and laughs again at the thought of the scattered tracts.

James felt such a thrill of pleasure when she said that, and immediately felt excessively angry with himself for what he called his puerile vanity; the cause was so much disproportioned to the effect. He must stop this girl from poisoning him with her sweet unconscious flattery. He speaks sternly to her, unpleasantly the reverse as he feels.

"Your flattery is too broad, Kate; even I cannot swallow it. Much protection I should have been to you, should not I? Much chance I should have against any bargee that ever was born. You must know that it would be more than ridiculous for anyone to come to me for physical help;" and he feels for a moment a sharp smarting scorn and loathing for his own *punyness* of outward make.

"Is it part of your code of religion," asks Kate gaily, "to snub everybody who is so impertinent as to have a good opinion of you? because if so, I shall do my best to frustrate your intentions by paying you a series of the prettiest of pretty speeches."

"Don't talk nonsense, Kate," goes on James, not able quite to resist the incense of that pleasant voice; "but tell me what on earth brought you into this bad part of the town; you have been in amongst all these roughs?"

"What brought me?" says Kate, drawing herself up with much assumed dignity; "why duty, of course; what else? I've been ministering to my sheep, as the Evangelicals[100] would say. There—respect and admire me as much as you please."

100 Begun in the 17th century, the Protestant Evangelical movement stressed Biblical authority and a personal conversion experience.

"Have you, indeed?" asks James; and he allows himself to feel very pleased now. It is a legitimate subject for clerical rejoicing, he thinks. "And how did you get on with them?" he asks with eager interest.

"O, very well," answers Kate, without thinking; "at least pretty well; at least middling; they did not seem particularly rejoiced to see me; your people are not very polished. I cannot say they are of the most boorish; I must say that for them. I don't think they can have any of them paid the extra twopence for manners."[101]

"They've not been rude to you, any of them?" asks James hastily, feeling a momentary movement of most unchristian rage and hatred vaguely against someone of his remarkably rough flock; showing that, after all, he was a man with blood in his veins, and not a god, with cool, passionless ichor.[102]

"O, dear no," answers Kate; "nothing but their innate incivility; nothing peculiar to me. I was only joking when I said they had not paid the twopence."

"O, but I know they haven't," says James; "not paid the twopence as you express it; I know it to my cost;" and then he goes on speaking almost to himself as it were.

"After all, I'm sure that doing things that go against the grain is wholesome diet for our sluggish, self-indulgent souls—for men, I know it is; but for all that, I'm half sorry I put you upon this plan, Kate. I'm beginning to be afraid that you are too young and delicate and beautiful to come into contact with such a set of boors and ruffians." He has the immense reverence and veneration for woman in the abstract of a man who has never had much to say to them; he looks upon them as infinitely tender and brittle; he does not know what tough things they are.

Kate covered him with confusion now by bursting out laughing in his face.

"Well done!" she says; "thank you a thousand times. I'd take off my hat, only it would not look well in the street. That's the very first compliment you ever paid me, James, and it is fit that it should be a good big one." And then she repents of having made him blush so, and goes on quickly, "But I assure you you're quite mistaken in thinking me delicate. I am as strong as six horses; self-indulgent I am, I know; but what I have been

101 In Ireland teachers were supposedly paid two pennies extra to teach their charges manners; rude students were said not to have made the payment.

102 Fluid supposed to run in the veins of the gods.

seeing to-day has made me feel as if I never could be so again. O, James," she says, her thoughts going back to that late scene—"O, you know I've been sitting by a woman, watching her die. Just think of that! I cannot say how awed and grave and solemn it made me feel. I declare it seemed as if I never could be frivolous and flirting and silly again, as long as I lived. It made me think—O, I don't know what it made me think;" and she broke off, ashamed of showing so much of her inner self.

"It made you think, Kate," says James, with the high glad look ennobling his face as it sometimes did, "that since death is the end and crown of all life, it would be but prudent and wise so to walk that that dark crown may not press down your brows with an intolerable weight when you come to wear it at last."

"Yes, that's pretty much what I meant, I suppose," says Kate, looking down; "I should not have put it so poetically. But really," she went on, "you have no notion how good and steady and practical I'm going to turn. I intend to set up a serge gown, with a rope round the waist, and a poke bonnet,[103] through which my friends may catch transient glimpses of my face as through a tunnel. Won't it be becoming?"

"I'll tell you when I see," responds James, laughing, "not before. My imagination is not lively enough to conceive such a metamorphosis."

"Seriously," says Kate, "I have got half a hundred plans in my head, that I want to unfold to you; but I don't see why we should stand here, catching our deaths of cold. I'm sure my nose'll drop off soon. Come and walk home with me, and we can talk as we go along. Come."

He would like intensely to walk home with her, and there's no reason why he should not; he is not particularly busy to-day; but that over-strained notion of duty will not let him.

"No indeed, Kate, I cannot," he says reluctantly; "it is very bad manners to refuse to escort a young lady—I'm aware of that; but I'll engage that you shall come to no harm between this and your own door."

"Well, it's very uncivil of you, I must say," answers Kate, rather vexed, biting her lips; not accustomed to have anything she asked of men denied her. "O come, there's a dear fellow," she adds softly, laying a small, beseeching hand on his arm. He feels what he never felt before to-day, that those eyes and those tones are making him drunk.

He shakes her off, and speaks very harshly again to her. "Kate, Kate,

103 Bonnet with broad brim that shades the face.

why will you always be a hindrance to me instead of a help? Have not you learned to-day what a lot of work there is to do, and how little time to do it in?"

"Don't come then," says Kate, vexed still; "you're a tiresome, disagreeable old thing. I'll do you that justice; good-bye:" and she shakes hands, nods her small head, and walks off down the street with her light springy step, pondering on the marvellous circumstance of James having spoken crossly to her twice in ten minutes.

And poor James walked off in the other direction, out of the broad streets with the shops and the frequent gas-lamps, down into the dreary slums out of which Kate had just emerged; past the Cross Keys, where the brazen-faced barmaid was still standing, arms akimbo, where the men were yet laughing, coarse-voiced, at the excellent joke they had played upon the young 'ooman in the red cloak; passed on and on, with his head bent, abased in his own eyes. He was finding out fast that he loved this girl—this girl who had sent him spinning off the *trottoir*, loved, not in a pastoral, brotherly way, for he would not keep that flimsy veil before his eyes; loved her with infinite purity and reverence indeed, as it was his way to love, but for all that, as man loves woman. He who had said to himself rejoicingly a hundred times, that his bride was the Church, and none other, now found himself hankering after an earthly bride. He who had been dowered with high ecstasies, with lofty communings with the skies—he who had over and over again longed to be rid of the shackles of the body, that he might feel the airs of heaven blowing at last freshly on a free brow—was now being bound tighter and tighter by the manacles and fetters of the flesh. That heart which had been wont to throb with a oneness of longing for the service of his Lord, now beat as quickly and tumultuously as any other man's at seeing a little coquettish figure coming tripping along to meet him; at seeing rare green eyes smiling frankly upon him under the black shadow of a little hat. He to think of loving any woman—the utter ludicrousness of the idea!—he whose face and figure could provoke nothing but either laughter or pity in any woman's breast. Only very great genius could counteract the effect of such an outward man, he told himself scornfully; and if he possessed great genius, it had been all these years hid under a bushel, and remained latent still to all appearance. The admirable presumption, too, of loving Kate Chester!—a girl before whom men went down like ninepins; a girl, moreover, whose eyes glanced and melted so only yesterday with untamed, boundless passion for another man—"a great brutal butcher of a fellow," he felt inclined to call him to his own soul, but he checked the impulse; a man certainly as much his superior in all external gifts as in all probability he was in all mental ones. Of this girl, whom he had so foolishly, rashly hoped to be of use to, to make good and happy,—of this girl Satan was making a gin[104] and a trap to snare his own soul. It was the bitterest, sharpest temptation he had ever had to go through; but he should be enabled to pull through yet; he knew that confidently. He would work harder than ever—ceaselessly, and eat less—starve out this earthly demon. He should kill himself most likely. Kate had said so; there, *Kate* again! Well, what matter? it would only be opening the prison-door, and letting the captive out; for what after all is life but a prison-house? So he toiled on that day with a will, going in and out at many a low door, praying, comforting, exhorting, spending, and being spent; and when he came home late at night, toil-worn and faint, he rejected the mutton-bone his landlady offered to his notice, supped off a crust of bread, and went to bed, and dreamed all night that he was engaged to Kate Chester, and that she was looking up into his face, with her hand resting light and warm on his arm, as she had done under the lamp-post in the frosty street to-day.

CHAPTER VI

WHAT a nice thing cousinhood is! After over twenty years' experience I say still, what a nice thing! I said that before once; but, after all, there's no great harm in saying a thing just twice. Dreary reiterations and self-repeatings are, as a general rule, only permissible to the old and toothless (by the bye, nobody is toothless nowadays); but I think that even a person who is some way off thirty may be allowed to state a fact twice when they wish to impress that fact on their hearers. Cousinhood then, let it be affirmed, for "positively the last time," is a nice thing; nice, both in what it presents, and in what it does away with. Half one's life is taken up in breaking the ice; in thawing new acquaintances into warmth and good-fellowship. Perhaps after all, when one has succeeded at last in hammering a little hole in the ice, one finds nothing but an unsavoury puddle underneath. It is so nice to be able to skip altogether over the long twilight of formality, to jump at once into the broad daylight of intimacy. Add to which, the chances are that cousins will have something of the same sort of tastes—will amalgamate

104 A device for catching game.

well, having the same quality of blood running in their veins. The prologue is over; now for the play.

The four Chester girls' ideas of this delicate relationship were much what I have been writing down. All their lives they had been in the habit of being kissed *ad lib.*[105] by about half a hundred male cousins—soldiers, sailors, lawyers, parsons; of telling home truths, too, and generally fraternising with about the same number of female ditto; and they had now no wish to exclude new-found Kate and Maggie from the menagerie, or Happy Family. Enlarged views those four virgins held on this theme, certes—they went beyond me. The claims, indeed, of friendship and kinship seemed to be verged into one, and each augmented the other in this case. To be running continually in and out of each other's houses like tame cats—to have no privacy as regarded each other—to borrow each other's gowns, and copy each other's head-gears—to tell each other everything that could be brought under the head of a love-affair, not forgetting, indeed, minor passages of arms—to stand up and battle boldly for each behind the other's back when attacked—to quarrel a little now and then—to keep the river of their loves from stagnating into a currentless pool,—these were in full their ideas and notions of the whole duty of cousins to each other; and these ideas and notions they honestly tried to put into action—not letting them rest in theory. Anyone very short of a job may listen a little, and hear a few words of talk at Grove House after breakfast.

One cold frosty morning, Jane comes bustling into the room, neat, dapper, sleek-haired, with an armful of garments to mend for the family in her fat arms.

"Any of you girls going down to Cadogan-place to-day?" she asks; "I suppose, of course, somebody is."

Now Cadogan-place was the blest spot which harboured the prettiest girls in Queenstown; at least so Queenstown said, having only tantalising glimpses of them as they passed along the road in speckled black veils that foiled curiosity—Margaret and Kate Chester.

"I think most likely I shall run down there some time after twelve," replies Emily, in the intervals of reading a long, crossed, young-lady-friend-ish-looking letter. "Ma teases so about one's complexion if one does not take a walk in the morning, and it's as well to go there as anywhere else."

"I never take any notice of Ma's lectures about complexion," answered

105 Abbreviation of the Latin "ab libitum," at one's pleasure.

the calm Jane dutifully. "What's the good? Walking in the morning or at dead of night either will not change tallow into roses and lilies; but do go all the same, and get Kate to show you how she does her hair—rolled, you know—and stay luncheon; and get the recipe of that pudding they had the other day—Pa liked it so much; perhaps they will not give it to you. Some people won't, I know; but you can but try; and I'll come and join you there afterwards if I can possibly make time, for I have hundreds of things to do."

"I wonder you girls aren't ashamed of yourselves, the way you have taken to living upon these unfortunate creatures at Cadogan-place; you're always wearing their clothes, or eating their dinners, or sponging upon them somehow."

All this George growls, looking up from the *Field*,[106] which he is perusing; apparently the fights and other instructive things he finds there are not very interesting or enchaining to the attention.

"I don't know what you mean by sponging," replies Jane, rather nettled (and it is an obnoxious word).

"If we wear their clothes and eat their dinners, they wear our clothes and eat our dinners. You might have seen my black tiara on Maggie's head at the concert the other night, if you had had any eyes for anything but her face. It is quite a case of mutual accommodation; is it not, girls?"

"Well, anyhow," resumes George, with more ingenuousness than politeness, "you know there can be no doubt that they must get thoroughly tired of you; popping in and out, as you are doing every hour of the day and night. It must be a deuce of a bore never to have two seconds that you can call your own; that you can feel free from an invasion of Goths and Vandals,[107] or women, which is worse. They don't tell you so, of course—they are too civil to do that; but take my word for it they are wishing you away a good deal oftener than you think."

"George, did it ever occur to you to mind your own business?" answered his sister, with reddened cheeks and an angry irritation. "It is not the least consequence to anybody what you think; but allow me to say that I am certain, perfectly certain, as certain as you're sitting there, that it is a great charity going to see those poor girls, and that they think so; it must be dreadfully dull for them, not knowing a soul to speak to in all the place

106 Victorian journal devoted to country gentlemen's interests such as field sports and agriculture.

107 Germanic tribes credited with the destruction of the Roman empire.

except us."

"It's their own fault, and nobody else's, that they don't know a soul," replies George, rustling his newspaper, and looking up and down the columns vaguely: "they might know anyone there is to know, such as they are," he interposed, with slight contempt for the Queenstown aborigines, "if they chose. It was only yesterday that young Gresham was asking me to introduce him to my cousin—the tall one, he said. I suppose he meant Maggie. I think he is rather a victim to her; poor little fellow." None of George's womankind are convinced by all this cogent reasoning—not even silenced.

"I don't see why you should suspect them of telling lies," begins his second sister's pertinacious voice, "just because you would not care to see us yourself. Margaret always tells us she is charmed to see us; and I'm sure she looks it; so I don't know what else you would have."

"Margaret, perhaps," answers the warrior dubiously, putting down the *Field*; "but how about Kate?"

"O, poor Kate," replies the young lady lightly, "she sits on the rug and gazes out of the window with those great melancholy green eyes of hers, and does not say much one way or the other, except when you are there."

"She looks awfully stupid sometimes," puts in Mary[108] from the other end of the room, where she is doing up accounts,—"six and five, eleven, and seven, eighteen,—as if she had been crying her eyes out,—and four, twenty-two."

"I should not think your chatter would be likely to make her much better," mumbles George crossly, standing with his back to the fire: "rather worse; at least if she is anything like me, it would."

Let us now see in what light the same subject was regarded in the much-talked-of Cadogan-place.

"Dear, dear," exclaims Maggie, on the very same morning, at the very same hour, looking in a bored way out of the window, whence there was nothing to be seen but the river flowing broadly on, fatiguing the senses with the thought of how many centuries it had been rolling along there in its monotonous brownness between its low banks, "how awfully dull it is to be sure! It's the dullest place I ever was in, without any exception. I declare I wish I was back in the sheepfold with old Daddy Piggott; it was a shade less stagnant. I wish to goodness Blount would come home to enliven one a bit. I wish almost anything would happen to me; except, of course, break-

108 Apparently Broughton forgot that she previously gave the sisters' names as Jane, Emily, Louisa, and Fanny.

ing my legs, or dying. It is such a bore not knowing a soul to speak to except the Chesters. I declare I don't know what we should do without them."

Kate shrugged her shoulders after the French fashion De Quincy inveighs against so bitterly.[109] "I'm beginning to come to the conclusion," she said, turning down the corners of that undulating mouth of hers in a rather disgusted way, "that it is quite possible to have too much of a good thing. I sometimes have the incivility to fancy that I should not at all mind trying to live without them a bit, for a change. They're *too* kind, don't you know?"

"Not for me," says sociable Maggie stoutly. "I agree with Alexander Selkirk:

'O Solitude, where are thy charms?'"[110]

"Now, yesterday," pursues Kate, trying meanwhile cruelly to induce Tip to growl by pulling his elementary tail, "I could have cursed them circumstantially with pleasure, if it had not been wicked. When I had just established myself so comfortably by the fire, with my book, and then to hear that unfailing rat-a-tat-tat, that comes as regularly as the baker's and the butcher's ring, I knew that peace had fled to the realms above then."

"Ah," said Maggie, with the shadow of a mild sneer, "I'm not such a superior creature as you, you know. I like to see my fellow-creatures now and then. I confess, indeed, I can hardly see too much of them to please my own taste."

"Well, tastes differ," replies Kate. "That's all very lucky and right, you know. I'd rather never see a human face all the year round, except my own, of course. It's always pleasant to see that, looking in the glass—always except when one's nose gets red."

Young ladies are proverbial for not meaning exactly what they say in any case. I don't think Kate exactly hated the "human face divine,"[111] as she protested she did. Habit is second nature too, as everybody knows. One gets almost always rather to like what comes into one's day's work every day for a good long time together. I think even Kate (little as she thought

109 Thomas De Quincy (1785-1859), known for his essays and *Confessions of an English Opium Eater* (1821).
110 A Scottish sailor marooned on an island for four years, Alexander Selkirk was the inspiration for Defoe's *Robinson Crusoe*. Maggie quotes William Cowper's poem "The Solitude of Selkirk" (1782), l. 5.
111 John Milton, *Paradise Lost* (1667), III.44.

it) would have missed her snub-faced cousins if they had ceased to come bustling in, cheery and laughing, with their vast animal spirits and their four black hats, with their frequent black feathers, to provide which many a Gallinacean fowl[112] must have gone tailless. Anyhow, like them or not, Kate had to swallow a good dose of them in these sharp winter-days. As their remonstrating brother had said, they were always dropping in, either together or severally, to learn a new stitch, to borrow the last number of somebody's new novel, or with some other such Lilliputian[113] excuse.

Now the Chesters, as I have before stated, were wonderful hands at scraps of news—quite wonderful. I never knew their equal. One girl used to come rather near them, but not up to them, and she died young. They had a knack of retailing a small thing so as to make it seem good-sized, by dint of pleasant little well-salted additions and comments.

Now, however high-souled and fine and above sublunary matters we may be, or fancy ourselves, I think myself that there are few of us, whether old or young, man or maid, who do not care a little bit to hear whether Mr. Smith is going to marry Miss Brown, or whether Mr. Robinson does really bully that poor starved-looking wife of his, as they say, or whether (best of all this) that odd story about young Snooks and the Irish girl can have any truth in it, or whether it is only slander.

Man is so entirely dependent on man—so much a part, so little a whole—that I do not believe he is intended to be so self-sufficing and self-contained, so like a snail in his portable house, as some folks say. I think he is intended to take a little interest in his neighbours' concerns: not a spiteful Paul-Pry interest,[114] but a genuine, well-wishing, hearty one.

Maggie was honest, at least on this score. She owned that news in the abstract, news as news, was dear to her. It was a pleasant sauce to the every-day solids of household and sensible business-talk. She did not see why a slight appetite for gossip need, of necessity, abase the female mind, which was made for small things, which had to be uncomfortably stretched to take in big ones; why it need unfit one to enjoy the high and the good and the beautiful that one meets with in books. They need not clash these two things—this iron and this pottery vessel.[115] But then Maggie was a be-

112 Large ground-feeding domestic or game birds.

113 Little or insignificant; from the nation of Lilliput inhabited by miniature people in Book I of Jonathan Swift's *Gulliver's Travels* (1726).

114 Title character of a comedy by John Poole (1826); a meddling type.

115 See the apocryphal book of Sirach 13:2: "Burden not thyself above thy power

nighted creature, who did not set up to be anything but a fairly intelligent woman, who thought the world not at all a bad sort of place, and liked to suck as much pleasure out of it as her innocent woman-lips could get.

Kate, I am ashamed to say—for I liked Kate a great deal the best in most things—was in this a small humbug. She affected to be lifted up many miles in air above her cousins' matrimonial and erotic (not erratic) talk. She would get a book, and pretend to read it, finding the conversation below her intellect; but before long the book would drop out of the white fingers, the eyes would shine with very unfeigned interest, and the lips would frame some question that showed she had been listening all the time, despite the book and the high-souled contempt for "such rubbish." Young women are such unconscious hypocrites.

George Chester, though he rebuked his sisters pretty smartly for their proneness to frequent the little house standing back from the road, with the laurestine bushes before it, was not by any means free from the same weakness himself; he somehow found himself turning in at that white gate very often, in the gloaming of those short December days. He would drop in to afternoon tea; that was mostly the excuse. Now George had been wont to turn up his massive square nose in a manner not intended by nature at the mere mention of this illegitimate interloper between luncheon and dinner, had given it as his opinion, and that of the –th[116] generally, that any man must be a muff[117] who, as a habit, indulged in it; but I suppose George had altered his mind now, or else was content to be a muff, which, by the bye, is a thing that no man that ever yet lived thought himself to be. Yes, George sauntered down that little sheltered drive very often. The maid got to know his face, with the tawny moustache, and the wide mouth that was mostly laughing under it, almost as well as she did her own. Up the little narrow stairs, into the warm scented room, almost every day of his life; and, moreover, did not get a cold shoulder turned to him by any means when he got there; got, on the contrary, a very frank, hearty welcome, though he did come so often. A chair by the fire, in which nobody else ever sat when he was present, and which was fast getting the pleasant home-sounding name of "George's chair;" Tip wagging and fawning and

---

while thou livest; and have no fellowship with one that is mightier and richer than thyself: for how agree the kettle and the earthen pot together? for if one be smitten against the other, it shall be broken."

116 Reference to the number of George's regiment.

117 Incompetent or useless person.

wriggling his body into the shape of a comma about his feet, as soon as his face shows itself inside the door. Maggie looks up from her work, and smiles, and says, "How d'ye do, George?" and looks down again—blushes mostly. She's not exactly in love with this young man; I'll tell anyone who is curious upon this point that much. He is such a flirt that she fears it would be rather a losing bargain to think of loving him; so she holds her heart back with two small strings of prudence and caution, which may go snap any moment. It is just a chance whether she fall head over ears into this dangerous pond, or wisely skirt the edge, and walk away. She may do one; she may do the other. Time will show. Kate does not care a straw about this man—not half, nor a quarter of a straw; of course not. She does not care, never again will care for anybody in such a shape, but that big dark person in the Coldstreams, with the rings of brown hair, and the teeth that gleam so white in the wicked curving smile; the big person, who has unfortunately got a wife already, and would like so much to ignore her. But for all that, Kate also blushes when George comes up and shakes hands with her, and asks how she is getting on—stupid, meaningless blushes, that signify just nothing, that there is no accounting for; blushes that inspire their perpetrator with a desire to tear off her lying cheeks, and lead George and his sisters to false conclusions. She blushes, and sparkles too, up at him. The blushes are involuntary; the sparkles are not. Runs down, sometimes very unnecessarily, and opens the hall-door for him, when she sees him coming; stands talking a few minutes in the passage, her gray draperies hanging ghostly round her in the dim, uncertain light; does not seem in any hurry to return to the warm peopled drawing-room. She practises several other little wiles; I forget now exactly what they were. Wiles they were, however, indubitably—nefarious little flirt as she is.

This is the sort of scene that any disembodied spirit (for no one hampered with a body could without a ladder well have got up to the window to look in) might have beheld towards five o'clock, on one of these brief winter days, when the sun hardly got up before he went in his laziness to bed again. A smallish room, with a pleasant odour of tea in it—an odour not very hard to be accounted for, seeing that all the paraphernalia for tea was standing on the round table, with the shabby-coated books, and the work-boxes; no candles or gas, nothing that made one feel any oppressive obligation to do something; nothing but firelight; two or three girl-shapes indistinctly seen looming in different comfortable attitudes about the room; girls with hats in their laps, that showed them to be but strangers, and birds of passage; Maggie standing up by the table, pouring out tea, that steams after its kind fragrantly, standing up with the outline of her slight bending figure neatly cut out against the uncertain blaze; George in his own chair, leaning his head on his hand, gazing with a very contented aspect, first at one of his cousins, then at the other, out of a pair of eyes that had a good deal more brightness and twinkle in them than softness or profundity.

Now for Kate. I always keep her to the last, because it is so sweet to me to talk of her, because I loved her. She never sits decorously on her chair, like other people, when she can possibly help, nor is she doing so now; she is sitting on the rug at George's feet, on a very small stool, a stool suited to a child of tender years, and her hands are clasped under her head, which is resting on the sofa; she looks graceful, restful, comfortable—everything that a woman should look, and that they do not by any means always do. Perhaps Miss Kate was aware, or half aware, of how well this recumbent attitude displayed, how utterly becoming it was to, that lithe waving little figure, with its easy curvings and roundings. What a sin it seemed that that (as man called it) flawless form should ever have to grow skinny and bowed, or shapeless and unwieldy, in unsightly old age! We might have spared our silly apprehensions and regrets on that score. It was never given time to do either. Maggie finishes pouring the tea, casts a reproachful look (unseen in the semi-darkness) at the inattentive hero, who does not offer to help her in handing the beverage sacred to washerwomen; snares the unhappy Tip into supporting himself unsteadily on his woolly hind-quarters; further guiles the accomplished quadruped into walking for about half a second on a pair of tottering hind-legs in a manner feebly imitative of the human gait; listens with interest to some rather dull anecdotes narrated by George of the prowess of various dogs of his acquaintance, and more especially of the "tall doings"[118] of a certain unparalleled bull-terrier owned by Grattan of "ours;" interrupts at last the flow of his eloquence to say: "Blount has made up his mind to exchange into the –th. I forgot to tell you before."

"H'm!" says George patronisingly, "those young fellows are always for chopping and changing. I wonder you let him fix upon the –th, though; it was rather weak of you, was it not?"

"Why?" asks Maggie, her eyes growing round with surprise, and a misty vision of all the very naughty snares, dimly imagined by her to be lying in wait for all her Majesty's servants, as soon as they donned the fatal

118 Tall tales.

red coat, flashing across her ignorant innocent mind.

"O, nothing particular," replies George carelessly, thrusting his hands deep into his coat-pockets, "only they're popularly supposed to be rather a rapid lot,[119] that's all."

"Popularly supposed!" repeats Maggie scornfully; "is that all? I never yet knew anything or anybody to be the least like what it was 'popularly supposed' to be."

"I know one fellow in the –th," pursues George; "and a rattling good fellow he is too! Always getting into hot water about something or other. Hampton is his name; one of the Hamptons of ——shire. Mad as a hatter; always was, his governor had to take him away from Eton[120] for getting into some row or other with a bargee."

"Ah, what a rattling good fellow!" says a mildly ironical voice from beneath him.

"Well, Kate, you may laugh," replies George, who is not fond of irony, not being good at it himself, "but he is a rattling good fellow, for all that. What I was going to say about him now was, that a short time ago his tailor became so unpleasantly unremitting in his attentions, that he had to ask for three months' leave, and go to gaol. Poor old devil, he's in quod now."

"In what?"

"In quod—in gaol, you know. I did not know it till a day or two ago, when I had a letter from him, dated —— Gaol. However, he seems pretty jolly; says he has met a fellow he knows there, and that they manage between them to kill time pretty fairly."

"You speak very coolly of it, as if it was a regular phase of military life. May I ask were you ever in quod, as you call it, yourself?"

"No," said George, pensively gazing into the fire, "but I had a near escape of it once, very near.—I say, Maggie," he continues, "what are the odds against that young hopeful you are so proud of, seeing the inside of one of those mansions where her Majesty entertains her subjects free of expense within the year?"

"O, George, don't say such cruel things," cries Maggie, distressed, and tears filled her simple eyes. "The idea of Blount Chester in prison, like a murderer or a felon!"

Her notions of debtors' prisons are hazy; she imagines each insolvent gentleman solitary in his cell, and his walking exercise confined to the

119 "Rapid" here means "fast," or engaging in improper behavior.
120 Elite boys' school.

dreary promenade of the treadmill.[121]

"What a pair of ravens you are!" calls out Kate lazily, from her lair, running in her head; perhaps she had some recollection of a picture she had once seen of Cleopatra in the posture she had chosen now. Certainly, even the Egyptian queen, "brow-bound with burning gold,"[122] could never, even under the purple canopy of her soft floating barge, lulled by the river breeze blowing freshly from off old Nile, have looked more completely, bewitchingly restful than did this young person I am talking about.

"Maggie dear, never mind what he says. Blount will not go to the dogs any quicker for George's kind prognostications.—George, bring me my tea."

"That I will," says George with alacrity; and he jumps up suddenly, tumbles over Tip, and addresses to that injured animal one short rude word, beginning with the letter D. Tip howls a little, as was expected of him, and is then soothed with bread-and-butter, and gradually calmed. Then George carries over Kate's tea with infinite care and solemnity, carries it over, and stands patiently by while she gazes up at him, too lazy for the slight exertion of taking it, laughing in the firelight from her half-closed drowsy lids.

"Don't be so silly, Kate," says Maggie, rather tartly. "You are getting too old for those infantine airs."

So Kate draws herself slowly into an upright posture, and says, resuming the former topic of conversation:

"Poor old Blount! I hope he'll be a good boy; not too good a boy, though; I don't like very good boys, they're mostly very dull ones. Sowing wild-oats is a disagreeable expression; but I don't think there is generally anything much to be liked in those who never had any to sow. They are mostly negative sort of characters. Don't you think so?"

"I don't know," said George bluntly, looking rather shocked; "but I don't think that's a very nice sentiment for a young woman, Kate."

"Isn't it?" said Kate languidly. "Well, I never was strong at nice sentiments. Wicked men are the pleasantest, you must own," she said, thinking of one wicked man; and so thinking, a tender light came into her eyes, and George thought the tender light was for him, and was more misguided than ever.

---

121 In English prisons convicts were forced to walk treadmills for hours, a draining and spiritually deadening form of hard labor.

122 Inexact, Tennyson, "A Dream of Fair Women" (1832), l. 128.

CHAPTER VII

LIEUTENANT GEORGE CHESTER, of her Majesty's –th Regiment, was, in these aforementioned winter months, something of the same mind as the gentleman in the *Beggar's Opera*, who affirmed, "How happy could I be with either, were t'other dear charmer away!"[123]

"It is '*l'embarras des richesses*,'[124] isn't it, George?" Louisa had said to him that very morning,—"isn't it? It's such a shame that people aren't allowed to have harems in England, don't you think so?"

It is a great mistake making love to two sisters at once. It is difficult at first, and impossible afterwards. The balance will incline to one side or the other, try as one may to keep them even. It did not yet appear whether Maggie's or Kate's side of the scales would go down and win the day. George tried hard to be quite impartial. If he had been unable to resist the temptation of squeezing Maggie's hand, or at least one or two of her fingers when she handed him something, he immediately tried to compensate it by going and sitting very close to Kate, and gazing at her with a longing, despairing gaze, which his well-featured square face could assume at will. Or else, *vice versa*, Kate's hand squeezed, and Maggie gazed at. But it would not do, he felt; and he was beginning to get rather uneasy on the score, to think of taking his departure back to Aldershott. I don't think he got any Κυδος [125] from either of his dear friends for his impartiality; it made them feel rather irritated against him, on the contrary. As for Maggie, she could not help thinking within her own heart, that after the tremendous catastrophe her sister had met with in love , she ought to have done with men for ever—ought to have subsided quietly into the blighted, retired-from-the-world line. Kate did not look at things in the same light at all, as may be imagined. Because she was not a bit happy now, was no reason why should not try and amuse herself a little with the small shreds of amusement that came in her way. When a woman knows within herself that though she is not regularly beautiful, she has got within herself a gift of odd, inexplicable

123 See John Gay, *The Beggar's Opera* (1728), II.13. air 35.

124 Embarrassment of riches (French).

125 Kudos: praise (Greek).

power to draw man to her, she likes to use that gift, to keep it from getting mouldy—to prove to herself, practically, that it is not lessening, or getting damaged. Very commonplace of her, you'll say. Yes, very; but then she was commonplace. I told you so before. She had more faults than I could count on my fingers. She did not care for this man, so I said a page or two ago; but no one would have believed that she did not, she laid herself out so to please him. One day she even went the length of unplaiting with swift warm fingers all the wavy coils of that rippling hair that a painter would have gone wild about,[126] let the ruddy treasure fall heavy round her throat, because he had affected to doubt its being all her own; had asked her, as a favour, to prove her right of possession in it, by this infallible proof. She was heartily ashamed, certainly, the moment she had done it, and twisted it up again pretty quickly into a big, untidy, loose knot; but for all that, she did it, and because he asked her, too. It wounded her vanity that this one dull young man stood out so stiffly against her, hovered so weakly between Maggie and her. He *should* like her best, she vowed internally one day when she felt more reckless and ill-conducted than usual. Yes, he *should*, by fair means or foul; that she was bent on; and then the little villain thought of Dare, and cried, and kissed his battered photograph rather more severely than usual. George knew that Kate had a district; knew in what direction it lay; had been down somewhere there once, a year of two ago, to ferret out a man said to keep a stock of inestimable *pugs* on sale; he knew, also, her usual hour for emerging from the obscurity of her low haunts into the brilliancy and well-flagged glory of the High-street. Kate had told him all this, whether with any ulterior object or no I'll not say. I do not want to make out the child worse than she was; anyhow, whether she intended anything to come of this information or not, something—a not very important something indeed—did come out of it; and on this wise it fell out. Kate was coming back, after her custom, about her usual hour, one heavy-clouded, angry-looking December afternoon, out of the scene of those labours which she had taken upon her as a sort of penance, a sort of safeguard against going utterly to the bad, as she often felt a mad impulse to go in her strong despair and life weariness; was coming back rather sober

126 Broughton refers to the penchant of Pre-Raphaelite artists for painting women's hair, particularly, if it is, like Kate's, "ruddy"; for examples of images where flowing red or auburn hair signifies lush eroticism—and, implicitly, sexual fallenness—see Dante Gabriel Rossetti's "Bocca Baciata" (1859) and "The Blue Bower" (1865).

and solemn. She was tired, too, and cold; her fingers were numb, because, being still haunted by a big basket (a new one, worthy successor of the old), a muff was an impossibility to her. She had rather a good fit upon her now; such came usually about once a fortnight, and lasted for about an hour and a half, or two hours. Rather out of heart, too, and weighed upon by having seen a great many people hungry and sick; and by having very little means or capacity for feeding or healing them. So she passed along rather wearily towards the High-street, where they were just beginning to light the lamps, warming up the cold misty twilight a bit with the yellow glare. But when she emerges into the market-place, and casts a tired indifferent glance around, there comes a gleam of pleasure into the eyes, not a very large gleam, but enough to make her think less about the poor people, less about her numb hands, to mitigate her sufferings generally. It served, too, to make quicker and lighter by a few shades steps that had been very lagging and devoid of energy before. What sight was it then, one feels disposed to ask, that put this sort of galvanic life and movement into Kate's languid limbs? A not uncommon sight certainly: a young man of a thick solid make, the back of whose bullet-head seemed familiar to her eyes, standing with a cigar between his lips, staring at the effigies of the Queen, and the royal family, and Lord Palmerston,[127] and all the other great people, in the window of the bookseller's shop in the corner; a young man, who had been standing there about a quarter of an hour, turning his head round every two seconds to sweep with his gaze the narrow street out of which a figure was expected to emerge. I do not think I need say who the young man was. He turned his head round again now, rather impatiently, saying within himself that he was blowed if he'd stay much longer,—a vulgar expression which I regret to have to record.[128] This time, however, his gaze was a successful one; it took in the object it desired—the woman with the light springy walk. He threw away the end of his cigar, and went straightway to meet her, in an accidental promiscuous way.

"You here, Kate!" says he, with about the most feeble and altogether abortive attempt at surprise that any foolish young man ever assumed. "Who'd have thought of catching you away from the fire on such an unpleasant sort of day? Been doing the good Samaritan, and all that sort of thing, eh?"

His meek little ruse did not in the least deceive clear-sighted Kate—

127 English politician (1784-1865), twice prime minister.
128 "Blowed" is slang for "damned."

not in the least—but somehow she was rather pleased that he should have thought of practising it. She gives him her hand, and looks up in his square British face, dowering him with one of those smiles which those who get them think all the more of, because her face is habitually such a peculiarly sad one; not pensive, but downright sad.

"My dear George," she says, with mild rebuke, "do you know where you'll go to if you tell such shocking stories? Don't I know that you have been looking out for me for the last half hour; straining your eyes down North-street to catch the first glimpse of this gaudy cloak of mine? Now do not deny it, George; it's no good, you know, for you'll not convince anybody, not even yourself."

George is rather put out by this extreme candour. He looks exceedingly confused at this detection; sheepish, too, decidedly.

"Very conceited of her," he reflects, "to say so, even if she thought it;" so he answers, rather on his high horse, pulling at his amber moustache to soothe his feelings.

"You're not shy, Kate, I will say that for you; but do you mean to say you think I have nothing better to do than to be lying in wait at street-corners for you all day? Do you think it is such a great treat for me to walk home ten yards with you?"

"Perhaps not," replies the young deceiver modestly. "I suppose I was judging you by myself." She smiles up at him still, in a coy manner, inwardly tickled at his anger. He cannot resist the influence of that smile, in which sweetness and an admirably simulated shyness are mixed together in such just proportion.

"Let's drop the subject," he says good-humouredly; "perhaps I was waiting for you, perhaps I was not. Anyhow, as I *am* here, I suppose I may be allowed to escort you home? There's no harm in that, I should say."

"Decidedly not," answers Kate gaily; "the road is public property, you know, and if you choose to walk alongside of me, of course I cannot help it—can I?" and she appealed to him with up-turned eyes.

Now, of all Kate's wiles, that glance, innocently wicked and wickedly innocent, was the one that met with her brother Blount's most unqualified disapproval. She never dared practise it when he was by; but he was not by now; so, having shot her Parthian arrow[129] in peace, she and her cavalier toddled amicably along down the hard, slippery *trottoir.*

129 A parting shot; after arrows directed at retreating enemies by troops of the ancient Asian country of Parthia.

"How's your sister? how's Margaret?" inquires George presently; "where is she to-day?"

"How do I know?" replies Kate, pouting; "where she always is, I suppose. Sitting over the fire, with a novel. You had better go and find out for yourself, if you are so anxious to see her."

"But I'm not at all anxious," replies George, delighted; "I cannot manage you both at once—one at a time is enough for me."

"I don't think I am very hard to manage," answers Kate pensively, "at least not by those I love," she adds, turning away her head. "There's a pretty good opening for the old simpleton," she says internally.

"Dear demonstrative little thing," thinks George, meanwhile, "cannot hide her feelings a bit! Those you love?" he repeats sentimentally. "How many come under that fortunate head, Kate, I wonder?"

"O, never mind, it does not matter—not many," she replies incoherently; and George feels his ears growing red hot. He bathed in pleasant confusion—she stifling inward laughter, they walk on in silence.

"What book is that you've got there?" he asks, at length, when the cold air has cooled his feelings a little; "sha'n't I carry it for you?"

"Yes, if you wish particularly, you may," answers his companion, giving it to him. "I cannot say that it is very heavy. It is only a Bible that I have been reading out of to-day to a poor old man, who, I flatter myself, did not understand a syllable of it."

"What an odd mixture you are, Kate!" says George, looking at her as he might have looked at some lovely, uncanny sort of Lurline;[130] admiring her hugely, but not exactly knowing what to make of her, what with her tracts, and "the wicked lightnings of her eyes."[131] "Three parts sinner and one part saint, you are, it seems to me, as far as I can make out."

"Thank you," says Kate, bowing her head ceremoniously to him: "I live in hopes of changing the proportion, and being three parts saint and one part sinner, one of these fine days;" and she shoots out green light of intoxication and mischief from under the shady black hat. The good fit has not lasted an hour and a half to-day; only about twenty minutes.

"If you were my sister," says George, starting a new subject, "I should not allow you to be walking about the town so late as you are now. Indeed, I very much doubt whether I should ever let you go wandering about these back places even in broad daylight. You ought to leave that sort of work to

130 Variation of "Loreley," a legendary siren of the Rhine.
131 Tennyson, "Guenevere," in *Idylls of the King* (1859), l. 521.

old girls in wigs and spectacles, and red noses; you are too young by half—too pretty, too," he adds, rather hesitatingly.

"I daresay you are right," answers Kate, affecting a deference for his opinion which she was far from feeling. "I daresay, if there was anybody who cared sufficiently about me to look after me, that I should be stopped from these prowlings of mine; but, you see, there is not anybody that does care much about me. Blount is too young to exert authority over me; and you see, George, you are not my brother, and—I'm very glad of it," she ends, dropping her eyes demurely.

"So am I," says George, under his breath.

Kate affects to misunderstand his meaning.

"Are you?" she asks naïvely. "Ah, I daresay you think I should not make a pleasant companion for household life. Hot-tempered and *exigeante*,[132] perhaps. Ah, well, you said differently the other night."

"What do you mean?" inquires George eagerly.

"O, nothing. I don't know why I remember such trifles; it is very silly of me; only—I can't help it—only it seems such a few days ago you were beseeching—absolutely beseeching—Maggie and me, that as Providence had not made us your sisters, to constitute ourselves such,—that's all."

"O, that was all nonsense, of course," replies George, dismissing this charge, lightly. "At least—no, it was not, either. I don't think self-dubbed, mock sisters are at all bad sort of things; very superior to the genuine article, in fact. I don't object at all to that degree of relationship. It gives one all the privileges of a brother without any of the drawbacks. A cousin ought, by right, to have one or two of those privileges—don't you think so, Kate?" and he looks hard at her, and has the satisfaction of seeing her blush a little in the gaslight.

"Pretty well," thinks Kate; "he is getting on nicely. Adieu, sentimentality, for the present, or you'll be getting me into a scrape." So she considers it best to drop the subject of cousins' rights, and changes the theme rather abruptly. "I suppose I need not go through the farce of asking you in to tea this afternoon—it would be about as absurd as asking myself. You'll come, and brighten us lonely women up a bit, will not you?"

"Not to-night, thank you, Kate," replies George reluctantly. "I'm afraid I really cannot. I have got an appointment at the billiard-room at five. You see, that young Gresham asked me to have a game with him there to-night;

132 Hard to please (French).

so what could I do but say I would?"

"O, pray make no excuse," answered the girl huffily; "if you're pleased, I am sure so am I;" and to prove how pleased she is, she continues, after a pause, somewhat venomously, "How I hate billiards! Nasty things! I hope to goodness that Blount will never take a fancy to them."

"Nasty they may be," answers George, provoked; "though I don't see why. But all I know is that they have kept me from hanging myself more than once, when I have had a long leave to spend here, and had no earthly thing to do besides."

"Though you call yourselves the superior animals, you men are wretched things, after all," pursues Kate contemptuously, turning up her small white nose. "I begin to look on you as not much superior to the highest class of apes; minds very often closely approximating to the simian type, as they say in books."

"What has put you upon these uncomplimentary reflections with regard to us, now particularly?" asks George, not much relishing the idea of his similitude to a baboon.

"You," replies Kate candidly, gazing straight before her.

George half thinks that "the dear demonstrative little thing" of ten minutes ago is getting unpleasantly rude.

"May I ask," he inquires, rather nettled, "what there is particularly wretched about me? You are the first person to discover it, if there is anything."

"Why, just look at you," replies his cousin, not taking much pains to smooth his ruffled feathers, "how pitiably short of a job you are! So are all ordinary men. So dependent on little trifling outside circumstances; so little self-sufficing. A man with a gun and a brace of pointers, trudging through turnips; or a man pulling up stream in an eight-oar, with seven others, for the bare life; or a man going across country on a good horse—any one of these is fairly happy and fairly respectable; but a creature kicking his heels in a country town, gaping at the silks and satins in the shop-windows—Well, I don't want to be uncivil; but, George, now answer me truly,—do you think there could be a more despicable object?"

George recovers his good-temper. What is the good being angry with this changeable little person, with the—yes, it was loving—with the loving, shy smile, and the odd, deep eyes?

"I do not feel anything particularly despicable," he says, laughing cheerily, "walking along with a pretty girl, who is doing her very best to entertain me."

"Very best?" repeats Kate, melting into *quasi* softness again. "That shows how very little you know of my very best—yet." The last word is hardly audible.

"Well, if it is not your very best, it is your second best," says George philosophically; "and it is quite good enough for me."

"Old booby," says Kate inwardly. "He actually did not perceive that last affectionate hint of mine." She looks up the street, and sighs, "I am afraid—I mean I think that our pleasant *tête-à-tête* is drawing near a close, George. I think those are your sisters that are just coming round the corner now."

"They might just as well have been kind enough to walk in the other direction to-day, and left us in peace—might not they, little one?" asked George condescendingly.

"What an imposing phalanx they make, George! How proud you ought to be of having so many tons' weight of womankind belonging to you!"

"You're not over fond of my womankind, Kate, for some reason or other."

"Yes, I am. They are dear, good, useful girls; but they're not quite my sort. I do not get on with them quite so well as I do with—with—some other people I know of."

"They're not so bright as they might be; I know that. I don't suppose we any of us are," remarks George, with humility; "nothing like you and Maggie; but for all that, they might be worse."

"That is a consolation that may be applied to any calamity," says Kate a little sarcastically. "I don't suppose anything so dreadful ever happened to anybody, that something dreadfuller had not happened to somebody else."

"They are not calamities," says George rather compunctiously. He likes his sisters in a superior condescending way, as Joshua may have liked the Gibeonites when they hewed his wood and drew his water for him with obedient servile docility.[133] "I don't mean to say that if I had had the making of them I should not have made them rather more ornamental; but after all, it is not the ornamental ones that do most work in the world."

"Women are not expected to work," says Kate playfully.

---

133 See Joshua 9: 3-27. After the Gibeonites trick Joshua into making a truce with them, he lets them live but enslaves them as wood cutters and water drawers.

"'Men must work, and women must weep;'[134]

I'm not sure that I quite like the Kingsleyan division of labour."

A chorus of several voices greets George. The two words, "Why, George," repeated in four different keys, all expressive of surprise, "we thought you were going to the billiard-room! You told us you were going when we asked you to take a walk with us. We have just been sending Charley Gresham off there to look for you."

"A little exercise will do the young ruffian no harm," responds George superbly, in answer to the cackle of his womankind. "I did say I was going to the billiard-room, and I am now.—Good-bye, Kitty." And inflicting a rather painful, but well-intentioned, hard pressure on Kitty, and receiving from that artless creature a tolerably eloquent look to sustain him during his absence, he strides off down the street.

"So this is what you call district-visiting, is it, Miss Kate?" remarks one of the quartette, when George has disappeared; "this is going to see the poor, is it?"

"O, Kate," chimes in another roguishly, "the High-street is the scene of your labours, and poor George your one proselyte, is he?"

"Of course it is pleasanter and easier hunting for souls when you hunt in couples," adds a third; and then they all laugh, and their laughter sounds the more unmusical to Kate, because in her guilty soul she knows she has not been behaving in a way that admits of her assuming airs of indignant innocence. She attempts no refutation.

"Good-bye," she says coldly, "the thermometer is too many degrees below zero to make it pleasant standing still." And so she leaves them to their graceful badinage.

CHAPTER VIII

JAMES STANLEY asked for and took a week's holiday in these Christmas days. An unprecedented fact almost; he had not hitherto seemed to have any friend for whom he cared to desert his work, and his worries, and his fat, plausible landlady. And now that he did seem to feel the want of relaxation (none more, anyone would have said to have seen him), where did he go, where did he spend those few days which ought, if he had had his

134 Charles Kingsley, "The Three Fishers" (1851), l. 5.

deserts, to have been all shine, and no shower? Did he go to the sturdy old gray manor-house, with the thick, weather-stained walls, round which the keen Yorkshire winds howled so eerily these December nights; where so many generations of strong-limbed, loyal-hearted Stanleys, good subjects and hard fighters, had been born and bred; where his kinsman, Sir Richard, was now, as the *Morning Post* informed all and sundry whom it might concern, entertaining a select circle of friends? There folks were diverting themselves pretty well, despite the bleak way that the Yorkshire winds had of blowing over the furzy heaths. Lords and Honourables, and a sprinkling of lucky Commoners, thinking they were spending their time well, doing to death on an average about six hundred head of pheasants and hares daily in murderous battue-shooting.[135] Ladies displaying bright-hued petticoats and dainty Balmoral boots,[136] dancing quadrilles[137] on the ice, above the heads of the pike and the tench, in the big frozen mere. No, he did not go there, though, if he had, I am inclined to think that more than one old friend would have welcomed him cheerily, and given him a hearty hand-shake—would have been cordially glad, after Englishmen's calm, undemonstrative fashion, to see him back again amongst them. But neither battue-shooting nor dancing quadrilles on the ice were much in his line. He would have been a fish most grievously out of water in the old house that had been home to him in his boyhood; his aims and pursuits, his thoughts and his ways were different from, opposed to, those of his kinsmen and kinswomen. They were dallying, sporting, fooling in a rose-garden, where the thorns pricked them sometimes—very often, indeed; not regarding how the sun was sloping westward in their life's sky; and he was walking hastily, heedfully forward, picking his steps in a miry, stony lane, towards a gate at the end. His sun was sloping westward, too, but he saw it, noted it well, and it made his heart leap with a solemn joy. However, to return to my subject, if no other cause had deterred him from a stay in Braddon Park, one very insignificant, and yet very sufficient one would, and that was that he had no suitable clothes. Odd, but perfectly true. Apropros of which fact, I remember that Kate Chester, some little time before this, asked him one day, as a great favour, to escort her and her sister up to town to a concert in the Hanover-square Rooms, where some great luminaries in the musical line

135 A form of hunting in which the underbrush is beaten to flush out game.

136 Popularized by Queen Victoria in the 1860s, these heavy lace-up boots were named for her Scottish residence.

137 Dance with four couples.

were to perform. And he, though he was a sort of person that was always ready to go ten miles out of his way to oblige the meanest child in the parish, yet actually on this occasion said, hesitatingly and reluctantly, that "No, he was afraid he really could not."

"Why?" urged Kate, a good deal surprised and vexed; "would not he do even such a small thing as that, to oblige an old friend? Did he think concerts wrong? The Low Church party did, she knew, but he was not Low Church; did he?"[138]

"No," he averred directly, without a moment's deliberation or doubt, "he did not think them a bit wrong. Were not there enough sins in the world already, without manufacturing new ones? It was his belief, on the contrary, that music always raised the soul, and cleared it from low, noxious, earthy vapours."

"All very fine," says Kate impatiently; "but why would not he come then? He liked music, did not he?"

"Yes, loved it, would enjoy going more than anything he knew, almost in a small way; he had to own, being of a truthful turn."

"Why on earth could not he come, then—why, why, why?"

Kate is getting provoked. He hesitates, he stammers in a cowardly manner, he positively blushes, but she keeps him to the point. She urges and drives and badgers the poor little man, till he has to confess that the reason is simply and merely and wholly this, that he has not got a decent dress-coat.

"No dress-coat!" cries Kate, immensely indignant. "How abominable, how unheard of! I can hardly believe my ears. Sir Hugh Stanley's son, a member of one of the greatest of our great old English houses, not able to go to a concert that he wants very much to go to, because he has got no dress-coat! What is the world coming to?"

James laughed, relieved at having made his revelation.

"Put it another way, Kate. Say that the curate of St. Mary's, Queenstown, with a stipend of 80*l.* per annum, finds that he has not any need for dress-clothes, and consequently has not got any; it does not sound anything like so appalling then."

Not in the train to the North then, with the oyster-barrels and the

138 Inflected by the Evangelical movement (see p. 215, n. 100), the Low Church branch of Anglicanism deemphasized ritual while stressing original sin and Biblical fundamentalism.

treasures from Fortnum and Mason,[139] did Mr. Stanley take his departure, nor in any other train that I could find out. One thing I am sure of, and this is, that he did not go a-pleasuring—for he came back, looking thinner, paler, more out of heart, and stooping and careworn than he went. It is my belief that, despite the inclement weather and the unfit time of year, the mistaken little man had indulged himself in the luxury of a walking tour. I think that trudging along for many a weary mile, all alone, he had been doing his very best to bring down the pride and fatness of a too fleshly soul to a proper level. I think he had been inflicting divers mortifications and macerations on his spirit; had been, in fact, tormenting and bullying and maltreating himself after the Ignatius-Loyola type.[140] Anyhow, his boots had to go to the cobbler's when he came home. Wherever he had been, he had picked up a taste for very low company, it seemed. No one had a chance of asking him anything about his unwonted jaunt. Nobody in decent society, nobody in a respectable dwelling and a reputable coat, ever hardly got speech of him now. He was always in and out among the scum, among the publicans and sinners.[141] They had plenty of his society; but I do not believe that they appreciated it half as much as they ought to have done. By the bye, people did see him, too, every Sunday regularly, once always, sometimes twice—for the goodly, well-fed, pleasant-spoken rector was apt to get lazy—saw him and heard him, too; heard all through the big church, with its aisles and arches, every word enunciated by that voice in its distinct, high-bred way. Folks were apt to go away rather grave and pondering from those terse, nervous, quarter-of-an-hour sermons. It was not somehow as if one was reading out of a manuscript book, in a black cover, cold, unconcerned, unconcerning dissertations upon various things that might be true, or might not—that it was the fashion to accept as true nowadays; but rather as if one to whom those same things were strong realities, the strongest realities that existed under the sun, were striving and wrestling and agonising to make them such to the men and women who were listening or pretending to listen to him. Those clear, guileless gray eyes, unbeautiful as to shape and colour, but which were so evidently and unmistakably the windows through which a very broad unmuddled intellect, and a very saintly martyr's sort of soul, shone plain, seemed to be al-

139 London department store with a reputation for high-quality food and picnic baskets.
140 See p. 179, n. 34.
141 Mark 2:16-17.

lowed to see through the gross curtain of the flesh far more distinctly than the luxurious, self-indulgent, comfortable people slumbering and lounging in the red-cushioned pews below him. And yet this high-souled saint had, if his flock could but have known it, a vast deal of the world and the world's interests about him still. Notwithstanding the December walking tour, and the macerations, and the starvations, and all the *ations*, he had not yet succeeded in trampling under foot utterly, in treading the last spark of life out of this robber love that had not knocked at the door of his heart, and asked leave to come in, but had forced its way unmannerly through the windows, close-barred and shuttered to keep it out as they were. Bold robber! It did not seem to be ever weakened, or hand-bound, or got the better of in the least. It never would be got under now in this life, he sometimes said to himself, grievingly, despondingly—never! It would clog and hamper him still, even at the very last, when he should be within sight of the great golden entrance-gates that stand bathed in light that is not sunlight or moonlight or starlight. No man could have defended a house more bravely, more stoutly, than this householder did his—I will do him that justice; but so far his efforts, his fighting, the sweat of his hard encounter, seemed all pretty much thrown away; they did not meet with the success they deserved. What this was owing to, I cannot pretend to say. It certainly could not have been because he did not cut deep enough. He did not weakly satisfy himself with snipping off twigs from this deep-rooted tree of affection. Even lopping off big branches did not satisfy him. He dug up by the root, and spared no clinging fibres—at least, hardly any. And this is the sort of way he went to work with himself—I will tell it for an example to them that shall come after. The thing he prized about the most of anything he had in the world was a photograph of herself that Kate had given him just a few weeks ago. He had not asked for it, she had volunteered to give it him, and that small circumstance had brightened that day and a good many days after. It used to stand in the middle of his ugly black mantel-shelf, in a little carved frame; and his eyes had got into a habit of turning to it, resting on it, being comforted and brightened by it when he was eating his scanty dinner, when he was reading his good books for a rare relaxation, and when—O, worst, naughtiest of all!—when he was writing his short, sharp, pointed discourses. One day it struck him, after he had been staring at it for about five minutes, with his pen idle in his hand—after he had been writing down several suggestive lines and sentences about things of the next world, with his mind brimming over with things of this—an unintentional hypocrite—it struck him, I say, that perhaps he should get on better if this temptation were out of his way. This little picture was one of Satan's smaller gins and snares. Kate herself was the bigger trap to catch a slippery soul in; her effigy was only a lesser trap of the same kind. He had no right wittingly to bend his steps in the direction of such traps. He could not expect to escape being caught by them if he did. So he brooded morbidly, with a mistaken self-anatomising, a too strict analysis of each feeling and germ of feeling; but one does grow morbid, I fancy, living by oneself, being habitually hungry and weary, and having no one to pity one for so being. Something about cutting off a right hand, plucking out the right eye,[142] floated mistily through his mind. One day the resolution came strong upon him to burn the offending photograph. He loved it so much, he thought that a sure sign that there must be danger and soul-poison somewhere about it. So it must go; there was no help for it. Rather different this way of looking at things from Kate's practice of passionate cryings over and kissings of that other woman's pictured husband. So he took it down off the mantelpiece, took it out of its little frame, and, without daring to take one look at it, pitched it into the fire. I suppose his aim was not good, or his hand was unsteady, for it did not go into the hot red heart of the fire; it fell short, and tumbled down among the ashes, and got its low forehead and its *retroussé* nose blacked a good deal. James could not help feeling intensely relieved at its escape; he knelt down on the hearth-rug, and fished it out eagerly, greedily, from among the ashes, singeing his pretty silk brown hair (the one thing commendable about his outward man) against the hot bars in his haste and fear lest the flames should somehow reach his recovered treasure at last. He got it safe into his jealously-guarding hand again, and looked at it, and it was all up with his resolution then as far as incendiary purposes went; even he could not do it; battered and smudged and deformed as it was, it was more precious to him than rubies. He could not stand the idea of seeing it crumble away to a small particle of friable brownness. So he made a compromise with his conscience. He unlocked the drawer in his desk where he kept his valuables. Such valuables! Anyone who could have seen them would have died with laughing at hearing them

142 See Matthew 5:29-30: "And if thy right eye offend thee, pluck it out, and cast it from thee: for it is profitable for thee that one of thy members should perish, and not that thy whole body should be cast into hell. And if thy right hand offend thee, cut if off, and cast it from thee, for it is profitable for thee that one of thy members should perish, and not that thy whole body should be cast into hell ."

so designated. Unlocked it, and laid down his smoky idol very gently amongst them; locked it up in company with a big clumsy old seal that his father, good old Sir Hugh, used to wear at his watch-chain; a seal of the old-fashioned red gold, with the Stanley lion ramping in blood-stone upon it. In company also with a very ancient dilapidated knife, that his long-dead mother had given him to stem the torrent of his tears, when first he went, a puny little chickabiddy of seven summers, to school; a knife with one blade, and that one a good deal notched and hacked with cutting the name of James Stanley on a great many tables and benches and long-suffering walls. And last, but not least, in company with a long twining lock of hair, tied with a bit of black ribbon; a tress of pale yellowish, Norse-looking hair, that he had cut off, not very long ago, from the visionless, restful head of that happy, early-gathered flower, his seventeen-years' sister, as she lay dead in the little sunny chamber, full of mellow evening light, where the sun and he had said their last good-byes to her. The western beams (how well he remembered that!) *would* steal in through the lowered blind—*would* flicker waveringly through the white curtains, bent on giving one last farewell kiss to the pure girl hands, pure as the snowdrops they held, unwitting of them—to the calmly smiling, passionless face; kissed them goldenly, joyfully, telling as plain as anything wordless could tell of that other light which shall enkindle and illume them when the resurrection morning shall dawn in the eastern sky, grandly, with a grandeur that no dimness nor twilight shall ever follow upon.

James never went near the small narrow house standing back from the road, with the laurustinus bushes before it; never set his foot within the narrow room, with the vague sweet smells in it—which always would push itself into his mind, as often as he tried to fix his thoughts on Paradise, with Maggie singing a little low tune to herself at the piano, and Kate pulling blinking Tip's ears lazily, or burying little soft white fingers in his fluffy back. His persistent absence surprised both girls; vexed them in different degrees: hurt Kate bitterly—more bitterly than she ever would own to anyone. She had not so many friends that she could afford to lose one without making a stroke to save him; her very own friend, that she had favoured and been confidential to. After she had learned too to lean her soul restfully on his strong soul—after she had set all her hopes on him, to drag her somehow with him along the road to heaven—it was too provoking that he should turn away and leave her to stumble and struggle along by herself in the dark and the wind; too provoking indeed. One day she met him in the street, on which occasion, I must confess, that he was for taking off his hat and passing quickly on (he to greet her in that way indeed, when they had made mud-pies together near a score of years ago!). But she stopped him, for such a rare opportunity was not to be lost, and asked him, like a child might, what she had done. What had happened to him? Had the devil possessed him with an evil spirit? Seriously, what had made him so fickle and changeable? he who used to be so true and stanch, even when everybody else turned against her. Had he heard any nasty ill-natured, gossiping stories about her? He ought not to believe a word of them, if he had. Did he think her society pernicious, unprofitable? had he got some ridiculous quirk of that kind in his head? Was it some new article of his religious creed, that he must cut himself off, body and bones, from the world as embodied in her person? All these questions, half earnest, half joking, she poured out volubly, breathlessly; questions that would be answered, that refused to be put aside. And he had answered them—answered her coldly, sternly, hastily, as if to be quickly rid of her importunities. Horribly unjust and unfair upon the poor little person, no doubt, for what had she done—at least, that she could avoid doing? But coldness and sternness were, he felt, his only hope now—his very last resource—his sole preventative against falling at her feet, even in the middle of the *trottoir*, at the risk of grazing his knees, calling her his darling Kate, his only treasure, and telling her then and there how utterly and wearily he loved her. And at his short, unkind speech, that certes showed no outward sign of a desire on the part of the utterer to fall prone at her feet, there had come a sudden film of misty tears over the large-pupilled, shadowy eyes (Kate cried at less things now than she had been wont to do), and she had turned away without another word, and gone down the street, wet-cheeked, rebuffed, disconsolate.

But thought is free as air. There is no shackling it, no prisoning it in Chillon dungeons;[143] and imagination, that best gift of the gods, the gift that is as an impassable barrier between us and all the beasts—a more impassable barrier than reason, for some beasts, dogs especially, sometimes seem to make a few steps towards the scaling of that mount, high though it is—imagination, I say, is, if possible, freer still. Despite all James's cuttings and hackings and prunings of himself, there was one vision, one apparition, that no incantations would exorcise; the more its absence was requested,

143 In the sixteenth century the reformist monk François Bonivard was imprisoned in the dungeons of Chillon on Lake Geneva, Switzerland, an episode depicted in Byron's "The Prisoner of Chillon" (1816).

the more it would not go; a vision that lay in wait for him—that pounced on him as often as he came back at night, footsore, down-hearted, faint, to his uncomfortable little sitting-room, with the few black cinders and white ashes on the untended hearth, as the only evidence that there ever had been such a thing as a fire there; with the dingy green-baize-clothed[144] table, with the scattered papers on it, and the old stained bronze inkstand reigning amongst them, the sole attempt at ornamentation anywhere about. He could not help it; it was not his fault, positively—the vision came of itself; but so it was, that with wonderful tantalising distinctness (the weak body reacting on the morbidly excited, overworked brain) he used to see that dingy room undergoing a metamorphosis. He saw it transformed by the agencies of fire and lamplight—genial, warming, spirit-cheering; woman's work littering about with pleasant, ladylike untidiness; on the rug (such a nasty threadbare old rug, too) a small rounded figure, draped in soft gray stuff, of a quakerish hue and simplicity; a small head, with the firelight wandering and rioting over and in amongst the shining hair, that had, assuredly, nothing quakerish about the tone of its deep-hued ruddiness,—a small person altogether; in fact, Kate, with her hands drooping idly in her lap, not covering tracts or doing any other useful thing. James somehow always pictured her as doing nothing. I suppose he considered it a work of supererogation for a person to be at once useful and ornamental, to combine both functions in one, they being in most cases dissevered. And then the vision shifted a bit, and he saw the small person get up quickly off the rug as he came in, and run to greet him with tender joy, as no one ever greeted him now; with that odd smile, coming and going, which was painted so distinctly on his poor, sore heart; only it should come oftener and stay longer now, the vision said, than had been its wont these last two years. And then, perhaps, she would pull an arm-chair close to the fire for him, as she had done on that one ever-to-be-remembered day in Cadogan-place—that day to be marked with the whitest of white stones. The vision stopped there sometimes, sometimes went wandering on through two or three more scenes, each one more highly coloured than the last; but it always ended in leaving him more dispirited and heart-weary than ever, when it sent him back at last to the outer darkness of the reality of the present.

Kate herself—unwitting Kate—inflicted several stabs on him, put several more spokes in the wheel[145] to keep him from recovering from this in-

144 Felt-like fabric used for covering desktops and billiard tables.

145 Gruesome medieval device that tortured condemned prisoners to death.

sanity of his; and this was how she did it. She wrote him, in these days, several little notes. There was no coquetry in this. Coquetry and James Stanley seemed to her two things that could not be mentioned in the same breath; they would no more mix than oil and water; but she was determined that, try as he might, he should not forget her. She would keep herself before his mind's eye; she would keep open a path by which, when this foolish fancy for absenting himself should pass over—as of course it would—he might come back, and, after being well scolded, be forgiven. She had yet another reason, too, for this new taste in letter-writing, and that reason was a sort of desire for self-justification and self-assertion. Though he had deserted her and reneged the situation of spiritual guide and teacher to her, she would show him that she still kept persistently in the laborious path he had chalked out for her; for these destructive little billets hardly came under the head of *billets doux*.[146] They were business notes, asking him to get such a one into the infirmary; to give a soup-ticket to such another one; asking for advice on some knotty point of practical life; dry business notes, just flavoured with a dash of well-measured, delicate sweetness. James groaned in spirit sometimes at the riotous, ungovernable way his heart would leap up when he caught sight of one of these little compositions lying white, three-cornered, on his dingy table, to say, "How do you do?" to him when he came in from his day's work. It would have been a droll sight enough,, if anyone had been by to watch the gingerly way in which he held them between his finger and thumb, as if cholera, typhus, and small-pox lurked in every fold of them; at the white set face, determined not to be pleased at their subtle flattery, with which he perused them; the sort of face with which one might fancy a brave man reading his death-warrant. And then, when they were read and their contents mastered (not a long or a difficult task), he invariably tossed them into the fire (if there was one), and what is more, did not pick them out again; even that delicious one, for whose life his heart interceded so earnestly—that one that for some unaccountable reason ended, "Yours very affectionately," instead of the ordinary cooler "Affectionately." When the greedy flames had eaten them altogether, James would take out some deep, hard old book, in some stranger tongue, resolving to master every word of its dark crabbed old leaves; and all the while there would dance and float up and down, and all over the yellowing pages, a low-browed, dimpled, lily-pale face; a pair of eyes that reminded

146 Love letters (French).

the gazer of the hue of the green water under the wave-worn arches of some lonely shell-floored sea-cave. Hard work! hard work! But still, for his comfort, an inward voice—such a voice as is often sent, I think, to good men hard tried, to bid them be of good cheer—kept whispering to him very softly, telling him over and over again, "Keep up, keep up; it will not be for long."[147]

CHAPTER IX

I SUPPOSE that occupation of any kind was rather slack at the town of Queenstown, in these December days, for her Majesty's servants.

Anyhow, I knew one who had a good deal more time on his hands than he knew what to do with, and spent it very unwisely in burning his fingers—his figurative fingers, I mean—at a fire from which he had much better have wisely kept at a respectful distance. Certainly there was not much to do in the afternoons—too frosty for hunting, too cold for sculling; but still that was no reason why he need be lounging at the corner of the market-place, towards four or half-past four o'clock, so very, very often.

Do I say very often? Well, I may as well be exact: he was there always now, gazing into the bookseller's window at the chalk heads simpering and scowling down upon him. Sometimes he varied his position so far as to transfer his gaze to the pastrycook's next door, where the Christmas cakes and crackers really were rather worth looking at, only they made one's mouth water. Punctual as clockwork he was to be found at his post—he whom his sisters always looked upon as so confirmed a dawdle—he whose persistent, unalterable unpunctuality at breakfast, dinner, and, most

147 Given the apparent influence of *Jane Eyre* on *Not Wisely*, James Stanley invites comparison with the character in that novel on whom he is presumably modelled, St. John Rivers. Like James an ascetic clergyman who contrasts with the Byronic male lead, St. John also resembles James in resisting the charms of a beautiful woman—an attraction he considers a temptation to abandon his duty. While, however, there is some logic to St. John's decision not to marry the heiress Rosamund Oliver—he thinks her unsuited to the missionary work he intends to do in India—James's qualms about romance seem more neurotic than rational (Kate shows at least some interest in James's slum ministry). In this sense Broughton's Ignatius Loyola references seem appropriate: though he is not a Roman Catholic priest and thus not vowed to celibacy, James acts as if he were.

of all, prayers, was wont to excite the ire of his papa. I do not think that the chance of a game of billiards with the best player that ever held a cue would have seduced him now from his station.

Kate was at first rather gratified at this foolish young man's having constituted himself escort in ordinary to her—rather gratified at having shaken his tiresome impartiality. She used to chuckle to herself as she emerged from the narrows of North-street, at first catching sight of the thick-set figure in the pepper-and-salt shooting-jacket—of the white bull-terrier, with the cut over its pugnacious eye.

"I've distanced Maggie; I've won the prize, such as it is," she would say invariably.

"What will you do with him, now you have got him?" conscience began to ask, after a time. But conscience was put off to a more convenient season.

She would go then gaily up to meet the ill-used young man—would call him George, as if she rather liked the name than otherwise, and would beam up wickedly at him from under the hat that he was in the habit of making so many manly comments upon.

And then they would walk off together, in the most natural cousinly way in the world, down the street, past the shops and the carriages, out of the town, past the Roman Catholic chapel, where the vesper-lights were streaming through the stained-glass windows, along the villa-studded road, by the side of the dusk river, that tells no tales of the tragedies that are hidden beneath it, to the little modest white gate, where they must say good-bye. Kate chatters away all the while, tickling his palate with the small rude (not too rude) speeches with which her discourse was always so plentifully salted.

Poor victim! Her little coquetries and honeyed looks were burning him—snaring him with a false delusion. He began quite to forget his sisters' shrewd surmises, their stories about Kate's past—forgot everything which he would have remembered if he had been Solomon,[148] and began to count up his pennies within his silly befooled heart, to see whether he might not manage to afford the dear luxury of having this little woman walking by his side through life, instead of for half an hour a day for a few weeks.

And at the little white gate they used to tarry mostly a few minutes, to

148 Legendarily wise king of the Old Testament.

finish off the ends of their talk neatly—used to conclude with a lingering hand-shake, which verged more and more on the dangerously sentimental.

All very nice, and mildly exciting for the first five or six times—nay, perhaps I may say for the first seven or eight. But all worldly joys pall, say the moralists; I cannot say myself, because I have not tried nearly all.

It is possible to have too much of a good thing, and so Kate found out. The first sign was a discovery on her part of a dearth of subjects to talk about. They seemed to have been too prodigal of their small-chat the first days, and to be pretty nearly run out of that commodity now. It appeared to her (not to him) that they had got into a monotonous mill-round of dialogue, the same questions and answers and remarks every day, with variations so slight as not to relieve the *ennui*[149] of their sameness.

And then George's jokes too! At first she had laughed very heartily at these, though some of them were rather ponderous, and had not stopped to criticise them too closely, or examine whether they fulfilled what Addison says are the functions of wit—to surprise and delight.[150] Now, however, her censuring faculties became keener. She began to tell herself that these *facetiæ*[151] were the poorest and most forced that she had ever had to listen to with unwilling ears.

"Why," she grumbled inwardly, "if people could not make good jokes, might not they leave the province of wit altogether, and stick to the easy thornless path of plain common sense?"

So she gave up the attempt of laughing, looked glum instead, and snubbed him; her keen wit protesting thus against his dulness. Not that he was a particularly stupid young man; only incipient love makes many a fellow look rather a fool, I think.

Kate grew first to dread and then to loathe the sight of the well-known sturdy figure, the smooth-haired, pink-eyed terrier. Then George grew tender—a dreadful grievance that, though one rather to be anticipated; not all at once, but almost imperceptibly at first, manifesting it in small dubious ways that really no one could take hold of; showing the tendency, however, more and more clearly as the days ran by—showing it by a thousand trifling signs of his tongue and the eyes.

---

149 Boredom (French).

150 In *The Spectator* No. 62 (11 May 1711), Joseph Addison famously defined wit as giving "delight and surprise to the reader."

151 Witty sayings (Latin).

Kate did her best to give this new Damon[152] divers hints—some obscure, some broad; but neither the obscure nor the broad would he take. He had been lulled into such a false security by her former rash smiles, that he was past being pervious to any charitably warning hints now.

I have said before, that as men waxed tender to her, Kate waxed sick. The wild, fierce love of one man had been so unutterably much to her, that the weaker, thinner loves of all other men were less than nothing—were abominable to her. Then came the last straw that broke the camel's back, the trifle that exhausted the last drop of the not very deep well of Kate's patience with her mistaken cousin. One of the few people they knew in Queenstown, a gossiping, cackling sort of woman, asked Maggie one day, point blank, whether she might not be allowed to congratulate her sister. And when Maggie, guessing what was meant, vexed and angered (she herself best knew why), inquired with some asperity what was supposed to be the subject of the proposed congratulations, she made answer, humming and hawing, with a meaning smile, that "she was sorry if she had been mistaken, but that people would talk, particularly in a place of this sort; and that everybody in Queenstown was saying that there must be something in it, for that the younger Miss Chester and her cousin were never apart now."

Kate was furious when she heard this narrative; stamped and cried, and invoked the most unchristian and naughtiest of wishes upon the heads of all gossips and newsmongers in general, and upon those of that profession in the town of Queenstown in particular. Well, their blatant mouths should be stopped, and no delay either. She would not have namby-pamby love-stories regarding her hawked about over Queenstown if she could prevent it—so she declared, vehemently, excitedly; and sat and stared into the fire all the rest of the evening, and had not a word to throw to a dog. Next day she tramped off to her district as usual—duties were not to be neglected because silly busybody women trumped up false stories for want of more profitable occupation; and at about the usual hour she made her appearance, after her day's work, in the market-place, scarlet-cloaked and basketed after her wont. One hurried travelling of the eyes to the usual spot; then an ominous clenching of white hands; a most unamiable drawing together of smooth brows. If George could have seen that face then I think that, though not over quick at physiognomy, he must have seen that a storm was brewing against him. "Stupid fellow! Why cannot he leave

152 Traditional name for a male lover in pastoral poetry.

me alone? What a torment he is!" Not another glance in the direction of the offender. A determination not to see that he was coming to meet her; a resolute bending of swift feet down the street home-wards. Of course he would overtake her; for how should he know the cause of this sudden change of demeanour? And how to get rid of him she had not quite made up her mind, though to do it somehow or other she was fully determined; nothing would turn her from that. To have anything more to say to this fellow seemed to her now a sort of profanation of the one prime passion of her life—a sort of faithlessness to her darling, wicked, lost Dare. So she passed along very swiftly, with rather a beating heart, that she might have just a few seconds more to gather herself together; to frame some speech of dismissal to him who was following so hard upon her tracks. Perhaps you do not know Queenstown, or you would understand what a little way she had got when I tell you that, opposite the big chemist's shop, she heard the sharp ring of a man's quick, firm step on the pavement behind her, and a second after the obnoxious wide shoulders, pepper-and-salt clad, were alongside of her; the tanned face that she had got so tired of was looking down upon her with a grin of amusement curving the wide, good-humoured mouth. Poor George! he had no other idea but that this running away from him was nothing else than a little flirting ruse, for the better display of a faultless figure and unapproachable ankles. He believed firmly that this bird only flew away in order to be pursued, and pursue he did accordingly.

"Naughty child," he said, laughing, putting his hand on her arm familiarly; "what spirit of mischief induced you to run away at such a rate to-day? I suppose it was only to make me run after you, as I have done, you see. Ah, Kate, Kate, you forget how old and stiff I am growing."

"No, I don't," answered Kate, rather morose, shaking off his hand sharply, and walking on very quick all the time; "only I did not exactly see what need there was for you to come rushing after me at such a pace; and what's more, I don't now."

"Kate," cried George in great surprise, half-inclined to be amused still, "what are you talking about? Don't I always walk home with you? Is it not the pleasantest half-hour in the day to me by far?" he added sentimentally; and he tried to practise his old friend, the longing despairing gaze; but in this case it was not efficacious, for the excellent reason that he could not get her to look at him and see it.

"That's just what I complain of," she replied very gravely, looking straight before her.

"Complain of!" echoed George in high astonishment, with rather an injured intonation of voice. "Well, my dear girl, if you never have anything worse than that to complain of, you won't be much to be pitied, hanged if you will! I wonder what earthly harm," he pursued, waxing eloquent, getting the steam up, "it can do to you for me to walk along a street parallel to you for a quarter of a mile! Now I come to think of it, you yourself gave me leave to do it. Why, Kate, there's no reckoning on your being the same for ten minutes together; you're a regular weathercock."

"I am a weathercock," owned Kate, contrite and thoughtful, all that was demure and proper in her penitence. "You say that you cannot count on me to be the same for ten minutes together. Why, I cannot count on myself; not a bit. I have no stability."

George was not the sort of man to probe or examine much his own states of mind and conditions of feeling, nor did he understand anyone else doing it. "I don't know about stability," he responded in a downright matter-of-fact sort of way. "You've got plenty to please me. I don't want to have you a bit different from what you have been lately. I think we've been very jolly together these last few days."

"No, we have not," answered Kate candidly, her ingenuousness winning an easy victory over her civility; "at least I have not."

Now candour is an excellent virtue—let no one dispute that axiom; but I think it is hardly regarded in that light sometimes by the objects of it. Lieutenant Chester was now as much mortified and nonplussed as any other luckless youth who, having been flattering himself that he had been tolerably successful in making himself agreeable, found that he had been labouring under a delusion.

"Well," he said, with a sort of *snort* of indignant anger, "anyhow, you counterfeited it better than I ever saw any girl do before in my life. I'd go on the stage, if I were you. You'd make your fortune to a dead certainty." And they walked on in silence for a few paces, George stalking along, gnawing the top of his stick, with his equanimity a good deal shaken.

"Would that do?" Kate pondered. What must she say next? must it come to a regular quarrel between them? That would be a pity. Or might she stop there, and trust he would be sharp enough and wise enough to understand her drift, and accept the portion she destined for him?

She was not left long in uncertainty; for all of a sudden George stopped stock-still in the middle of the street, and again laid his hand on her arm (unforbidden this time) as he turned to her, and said very stiffly,

"Let us understand each other, if you please, Kate; I don't want to go on fumbling in the dark, being made a fool of for your amusement. I know girls generally mean the exact opposite of what they say; and so do you, perhaps, for all I know. But will you be kind enough to tell me, once for all, what is the drift of all these polite remarks you have been making; or is there no drift at all?"

Then Kate looked up straight at him, full in his face, for the first time, without any side glances or oblique arrows of fire, no false glitterings and flashings in her eyes, they shining with steady lustre.

"Don't be cross, George," she said kindly; "there is a drift, of course, and this is it. I'll tell it you without any softening, though it does not sound very civil. It's this—that I want you to promise not to come and meet me any more of a day. There, that's all."

"Why?" asks George, rather blankly; and an unwonted red flush flows into his comely face.

"Because I don't," answered Kate, with an uneasy little laugh, seeing that flush, but charitably looking away. "That's a woman's reason, I know, but I hope you will be satisfied with it."

"No, I sha'n't," he replied, not looking in the least inclined to laugh; "I must have a better one than that."

"But what if I have not got a better to give you?" suggests Kate, rather irritated (very unjustly so) at his pertinacity.

"Then I shall wait till you find one," answers George coldly, looking as if he meant what he said.

"Then I'm afraid you'll have to stay some time," retorts Kate impudently, losing her temper, "and I think I'll wish you good-evening;" and she nods her head to him, and prepares to walk off and leave him.

"Stay, Kate," he exclaims, hastily detaining her; and a very unfeignedly hurt and wrathy look streams into his eyes. "Don't be nonsensical. You're not a child that is not accountable for its actions. Woman though you are, you must have some vestige of a reason for the extraordinary alteration in your conduct."

"I never said I had not," answers Kate, rebelling decidedly against this mode of procedure. "On the contrary, I confess that I have; but I had rather not tell what it is."

"But I'd rather you would, you see," retorts George impatiently; "and you must and you shall," he adds more peremptorily than ever.

Kate would not have stood being addressed in that tone for one second on any other occasion. She was not one of that numerous class of women who enjoy being snubbed and lorded over; but she let it pass now, because she was rather sorry for him, and rather compunctious on the score of her past dealings with him. So she stood silent, with folded hands and lowered eyes, and answered not.

"What is it, Kate?" urges George again, and he gives a little shake to the arm he still holds detainingly.

"Well, since you must know," answers Kate with slow reluctance, at last, bending her head down so low that her face was almost hidden, "it is just this: that the tattlers and scandalmongers with which this fortunate town is so largely peopled have been busy spreading stupid, gossiping tales about you and me, and I will not stand it." Though her face is hid by the brim of her hat, she blushes rosy red, and looks very bashful over this awkward explanation.

"Is that all?" says George, much relieved at this mountain and mouse, and the clouds roll off his countenance as one sees clouds roll away from the sky on some peevish April day. "What harm do the poor creatures do chattering? Let them talk, if it amuses them. Why, Kate, I thought you were too spirited a sort of girl to mind what anybody said about you. Why, I have heard you talk ever so often about despising the world's opinion, and all that sort of thing, before now. But tell me, what is it they have been saying? I suppose it is nothing so dreadful but that I may hear."

Then Kate began to think to herself what they had said, and a horrid idea struck her that he might regard their remarks in quite a different light from what she did. She looks down still, and answers, not very readily—

"O, it's nothing very bad, I suppose; not much harm in it, of course, only they have been busy coupling your and my names together, stupid cockneys! I wonder they cannot be satisfied minding their own business."

That little ebullition relieved her feelings. George is silent for a second or two, and then he says with lowered voice, bending down to catch a glimpse of her shy face in the dusk winter twilight,

"And so that's all! Why should not they, I say again? I wish to heavens they had any good grounds for doing it. Is it so very revolting to you, Kate, to have even your name joined to mine?" and his eyes soften visibly as he looks down at her.

"Yes," answered Kate monosyllabically.

"I was afraid so," pursued George, trying hard that there should be no grain of crossness to mar the resignation of his tone; "but why must it be so, Kate?"

"Because," answered Kate resolutely, "it is unbearable to me to have my name coupled with any man's, whoever he may be. King or tinker, it's all one to me;" and she closed her lips firmly, and a hard look came into their curves, and quite altered them.

"Absurd!" exclaims George, unable to repress the expression of his scorn of so infantine a whim. I am sure if he had ever read Wordsworth's poem about the reason of his son's preference for Kilve,[153] he would have thought of it now; but as he had not, he did not. "I never could have believed that I should have met with such overstrained old-maidish prudery in any human being, much less in you, of all people in the world. It's something in the style of the devil quoting Scripture like a very learned clerk[154]—I declare to goodness it is."

"It is not prudery," cries Kate, nettled.

"Then it is affectation," amends George.

"No, it is not," contradicts Kate flatly.

"What is it then?" asks George, with a grin; "for I'm blessed if I know."

"It is pure, simple, unvarnished truth," answers Kate eagerly, feeling herself humiliated by his ridicule; "and what's more, absurd and highly laughable as this fancy appears in your eyes, I can tell you that it is so firmly planted in my soul, that you will not succeed in rooting it up if you try from now till midsummer."

"I should not think of trying," replies George, with a thin coat of dignity meagrely covering very real vexation. "I could not be so conceited as to flatter myself that I should succeed; but I have small doubt that though I cannot do it, someone else will."

"I do not know what you mean," answers Kate mendaciously, for she knew perfectly well—as well as you or I do.

"You are slow of understanding, then, to-night," replies George, hitting the side of his boot with his stick for something to do. "My meaning is pretty plain. Of course it is not to be supposed that you'll always be hardhearted as you are now; and when you are in love with some fellow or other some time hence, and engaged to him, and all that sort of thing, why, you'll have to get over your aversion to having your name spoken of in the

153 See William Wordsworth, "Anecdote for Fathers" (1798).

154 Aphorism derived from *The Merchant of Venice* (first printed 1623), I.iii.98: "The devil can cite Scripture for his purpose."

same breath as his."

"I shall never be engaged to any man under the sun as long as I live," responded Kate, solemnly emphasising her statement with a little stamp on the pavement. "If I have told you that once, I have told it you a score of times."

"O, I daresay," interjects George, with a world of incredulity infused into that brief speech.

"Of course you do not believe me," exclaims Kate, flashing angry-eyed upon him. "You think, I do not doubt, that I'm to be had for the asking. That's the way men always think about women."

"I wish to goodness you were," grumbles George, only half aloud, under the thick amber fringe of his lips.

"Don't wish for anything so silly. You told me not to be nonsensical five minutes ago, and I return the compliment now. Come, don't be angry with me, O my cousin. Say good-bye prettily, and go and look about for some more profitable occupation for your afternoons." She held out her hand to him, and he took it and held it in both his for just a little minute (but a venial offence, I think), while he said:

"I'll go, Kate; but let me walk with you to the little white gate just this once, for the last time. The gossips cannot say much against that. Come now, can they?" and his brown eyes pleaded very earnestly for this poor little boon. His eyes did not dominate and thrill her like Dare's wicked *blasé* ones in the least; but she was a little bit moved by them.

"O, I suppose you must. It is no use wrangling over a trifle," she said, yielding, half amused and half vexed; "but I warn you that I shall walk as quick as I can to get it over, and it must never, *never* happen again. Mind that." So having made this pact, they walked off side by side; rather silent both of them. Dull company, any looker-on would have said. They had hardly made half-a-dozen remarks to each other altogether, before they reached the parting place—the little gate, shining white in the new-risen moon.

"Well," said George, as they stood together, sheltered by the bushes from the wind, drawing a deep-breathed sigh, "I suppose this is pretty much the last I shall ever see of you, Kate. I suppose I must never come to tea again; at least, I suppose I must never come to see you."

"You may come to see *us*," answers Kate, emphasising the plural pronoun, "as often as ever you like; at least, in moderation," she adds, qualifying the permission.

"Indeed," sighs George melancholily, "I do not think I shall much care to do that. It would only be to listen to my sisters chattering; and I can do that any day at home. We shall never be the same again as we have been," he ends disconsolately; "shall we, Kate?"

"We shall always be cousins and friends," says Kate kindly (she can afford to be kind now). "O dear, O dear, how cold it is! I really cannot stay out here any longer, or I shall be frozen. Good-night, good-night;" and she escapes, passing lightly through the gate, and letting it swing behind her.

After her comes a man's voice, calling, "Kate, Kate!"

"Well," she answers, standing still.

"Come back, Kate," the man's voice sounds again entreatingly. So Kate returns, shivering, and leans her arms on the top of the gate, and demands impatiently:

"What is it? Make haste!"

George comes up quite close to her, and treacherously clasps her in his arms across the gate.

"Let me kiss you just this once; do, darling Kate! What harm is there?" he urges in a whisper; and he bends down his face to hers.

"Never!" she almost screams, struggling in his embrace. "Not for worlds!" and she shudders as the remembrance of Dare's solemn charge flashes over her.

She tears herself out of her cousin's arms, flies up the drive, nor even stops to draw breath till she is safely landed on the top of the white stone steps, and is making the house resound with a vigorous peal on the knocker.

George meanwhile, foiled, wisely takes himself off home, with a rather tail-between-the-legs sensation.

CHAPTER X

WHAT a great institution jaunting is—jaunting in the abstract! What a quantity of insanity it prevents! High pressure on the brain makes a fat madhouse; that is my version of the old proverb.[155] It sounds a paradox; but I am very certain that a day's idleness here and there makes a great deal more honest solid work to be done than any unintermittent labour. What a delicious sugar-plum a day's holiday is amongst the dry bread of one's

---

155 A variant on the proverb "A green Christmas makes a fat churchyard" (meaning that more people die of illness during a mild, damp winter than a frosty one).

ordinary work-days! Only they who toil from "morn to dewy eve"[156] in the sweat of their brow can suck out the full sweetness of the grapes of *doing-nothingness*; but those who get through a fair average amount of work of some kind or other in the course of their lives can give a tolerable guess at its flavour. That must be one of the disadvantages of being a king or a duke, or any other such high mightiness, their lives being, according to popular notions, all holiday-making. The feast of idleness must taste no better to them than our ordinary every-day bread-and-butter does to us. This is going to be a chapter of jaunting; but of jaunting not in the abstract, but the concrete, telling how certain people took a small jaunt, and how some of them enjoyed it.

One fine cold bracing morning, the water in the pipes all over Queenstown was frozen, and parties of disconsolate bricklayers out of work were parading the streets, with the implements of their craft, reduced to a state of temporary mendicity. Likewise, on that morning, you, if you had been there, or anyone else possessed of eyesight, might have seen standing at the railway station, waiting for the 10.12 up-train, a young man, made to look just twice as wide and plump as nature had formed him by a vast, rough greatcoat, comfortable certainly,—beautifying certainly not; a young man in charge of several women, rather overdone and swamped with female accompaniments, a misogynist might have considered, seeing that he had appertaining to him his four ugly-faced sisters and his two rose-and-lily-faced cousins. Perhaps the ugly-faced sisters might have been dispensed with. Anyhow, there they all were, stamping about to warm their feet, chattering and laughing, and making small jokes at the expense of the numerous gentlemen with black bags who shared the platform with them, and their voices rang out clear and sharp on the frosty air. They were not going on a very far journey—only to see Nineveh and Rome and Spain come together, for their behoof, under the brittle glass domes of the eighth wonder of the world.[157] Marvellous pitch of civilisation for us to have attained to, to be

156 John Milton, *Paradise Lost* (1667), I.742.

157 The Crystal Palace, an architectural extravaganza whose iron frame supported 300,000 glass panes, and which originally housed the Great Exhibition of 1851 in Hyde Park. Moved to Sydenham Hill in South London and reopened in 1854, the Palace was a Victorian theme park which showcased not only British technological inventions but such entertaining features as dinosaur models and a series of "courts" displaying the art and architecture of memorable former cultures. Here the reference to "Nineveh and Rome and Spain" alludes, respectively, to the Palace's Assyrian Court, Roman Court, and a replica of the Spanish Alhambra. The

able to do such a thing! we must come soon to the highest pinnacle we are to reach, one thinks sometimes, and then begin to retrograde. Well, it is not much consequence to us personally which we do, advance or retreat; it will not be in our days.

The design of this mild form of excursion had emanated (during one of those afternoon-tea *séances*[158] from which George had been absent of late) from the fertile brain of Margaret, whose soul was always attuned to any manner of diversion whatever, except perhaps going to see a man hanged. Her plan had been received with acclamations by her cousins, and indifferently assented to by Kate—assented to not because she expected to enjoy the little outing, she never enjoyed anything much now, oddly enough—but she was beginning to feel that all work and no play were making Kate a dull girl; that it would be well to see some new objects, and get, perhaps, new ideas from them, and turn thought from running so perpetually in the old, well-worn, deep-hollowed channels. The train came up—puffing and snorting, and making a great fuss about itself as usual—at last, giving one a sensation of surprise at appearing so hot and steaming on such a bitter day; and there was a rush for carriages, a rolling along of luggage, a scramble, and a perfectly unintelligible shouting of something, intended to convey to the minds of the new arrivals that they had reached Queenstown station; and in five minutes the Chesters were whirled away. Whirled away, indeed! Heaven forgive me for telling such a lie! One might as well talk of a snail whirling along in its shell. It would be about as appropriate as applying any such expression to the mode of progression on the line I am speaking of, which (I will do it the justice to say) is bidding fair fast to win from the Eastern Counties the palm of unparalleled slowness.[159]

---

narrator's cynical description of the Palace, however—its glass is "brittle," and only sarcastically can one label the structure a "marvellous pitch of civilization"—undercuts the ostensible celebration of British national supremacy. Nor was such a jaded attitude unknown; as Jeffrey Auerbach claims, "as early as the 1860s . . . the Crystal Palace had, for many writers, come to symbolize not the triumph of progress but its failures" (*The Great Exhibition of 1851: A Nation on Display* [New Haven: Yale University Press, 1999], p. 206). In light of late Victorian anxieties about British imperial decline—a context evoked by the narrator's comment on how cultures can "retrograde"—it is telling that Broughton stages a key scene in Kate's transgressive romance amidst the Palace's memorabilia of decayed civilizations.

158 Sessions (French).

159 J. R. Piggott notes that train travel to the Sydenham Palace (the most common mode of transportation) "was much criticised for long waits, extreme slowness

To how few people a premonition of what is going to happen to them, either of sweet or sour, is vouchsafed! Is it a blessing or a curse? A blessing, I suppose, on the principle of "whatever is, is right"[160]—a blessing even apart from that doctrine, I think. Would the delight of gloating over the coming birth of one's new pleasures overbalance, even compensate, the aching, stinging pain that the forecast shadows of one's many griefs would cause one? I trow[161] not. How is it that some few of us are gifted with a prophetic knowledge of things that will be; live over some bits of their life *twice*, as it were, whilst to other some this endowment of such doubtful advantage is so utterly denied? As well ask why eagles have a clearer vision, why dogs have a stronger power of smell than human beings. Now I come to think of it, this boding instinct is a sort of mental scent; potent to snuff out unsavoury events prematurely ere they rise. Kate's faculty of mental scent was obtuse. Something was going to happen to her to-day; something that would have shaken the very foundations of her being, had she known it, and she was not in the smallest degree prescient of it. It was a Saturday—I remember that—and there was on that day a concert at the Palace, as there always is weekly;[162] what is called, I believe, a popular concert—all big drum, and violin, and violoncello, and piano, in which the voice of man or woman had no part. Very interesting and enjoyable, no doubt, to scientific lovers of music; but, to ignoramuses like myself, wearisome in the highest degree—music of that sort being utterly meaningless; saying just nothing at all to such. This concert commenced at half-past three, and by that time the Chester party were pretty well tired of straying about up and down, of staring at everything that was to be stared at. Their eyes had had almost enough of gazing, and their ankles began to tell them that they were rather heavy to support.

"Well! are you going in or not? Make haste and settle," says George, standing at the opening to the concert-room, and looking vaguely round on his female covey, to try and discover decision on at least one face.

---

and too many stops" (*Palace of the People: The Crystal Palace at Sydenham 1854-1936* [Madison: University of Wisconsin Press, 2004], 60).

160 Alexander Pope, "An Essay on Man" (1733), l. 294.

161 Believe (archaic).

162 According to Jeffrey A. Auerbach, during the latter part of the nineteenth century the Sydenham Crystal Palace was "the most important venue for public music-making in the United Kingdom" (*The Great Exhibition of 1851: A Nation on Display* [New Haven: Yale University Press, 1999], p. 203).

"I must sit down somewhere," grumbles blameless vestal[163] No. 2, rather aggrievedly, having taken it into her head to be delicate of late. "I should not wonder if I should faint else, and I have not got my sal-volatile[164] with me."

Her family are used to threats of swooning, and, as they have always remained only threats, are not much disquieted.

"Tickets are five shillings a piece," gravely remonstrates Jane, who is of an economical turn of mind, and who, subsequently to this history, married a good little ugly parson on 300*l.* per annum, and kept him very trim and tidy on that minute sum.

"What a prodigious outlay!" remarks George contemptuously; for such prudent reflections are not much in his line. And indeed a young man of a saving turn is, to my thinking, a sight more to be wondered at than admired.

"As for the tickets, they are of no consequence whatever," answers Margaret magnificently. "They're my business, of course, as the party is mine."

"Very generous of you, I'm sure. In that case I must say I should like to hear that band again. It does play so magnificently—such time!"

"Yes, dear," adds Fanny, laughing; "and I wish we could introduce a little of the unanimity of the performers into our duets. They would sound better if—"

"Well, if you are coming, come, girls," interrupts Margaret; "I am not going to wait any longer;" and she leads the way down the narrow path, between the rows of chairs, to some vacant seats, her cousins following in single file.

Kate still stands where she was standing before, silent, apparently not in the least concerning herself about accompanying her female associates.

George stands there too, at the entrance, expecting her to precede him. She makes no sign of doing anything of the sort, so he is reduced to saying to her at last,

"Are not you going too, Kate?"

It is the first approach to a *tête-à-tête* they have had since his abortive attempt at kissing, and he feels rather sheepish and ill at ease.

"No, thanks, George," she answers coolly, looking very calmly straight

163 In ancient Rome vestals were virginal priestesses of Vesta, goddess of the hearth.

164 Solution of ammonium carbonate in alcohol, used as a restorative.

into his face. "Don't trouble about me, please. I don't intend to go in."

"Why?" asks George, surprised into brevity.

"For no particular reason," replies Kate composedly, "only that I am very comfortable here, thanks, and that I rather doubt being equally so in the immediate neighbourhood of a big drum."

"Why, Kate," cries George, pointing to the libretto or playbill, or whatever it is called, "don't you see that Arabella Goddard[165] is to play? and it was only the other day you were all anxiety to hear her."

"Was I?" answers Kate, perfectly unmoved; "then my anxiety has quite gone off; not that I remember its having ever existed. *Au revoir*," she adds; and she moves off, after waving her hand to him.

"Stop, Kate," he says quietly; "don't be eccentric, whatever you are. What new freak is this? You cannot go wandering about here by yourself up in the clouds as you do at home. It's impossible; and I will not allow it," he concluded, affecting the protecting elder brother.

"Why mayn't I?" she asked pleadingly. "What harm would happen to me? Don't you see that all these good people are far too busy enjoying their holiday to think of interfering with mine? I assure you I should be as unmolested," she ended, smiling, "as the young lady who made the tour of Ireland in a snow-white wand, and her whole stock of jewelry."[166]

"Very likely you would," George owned, pulling his moustache; "but still it does not look well for a young lady to be wandering about in these public places quite by herself."[167]

"The bump of music is represented on my head by a hollow,"[168] she said, with a persuasive little laugh. "Saint Cecilia has neither part nor lot in

165 Famous pianist (1836-1922).

166 Legend, retold in Thomas Moore's poem "Rare Were the Gems She Wore" (1808), of a beautiful young woman, richly dressed and holding a white wand, who traversed the kingdom of Ireland undisturbed because its citizens were so law-abiding.

167 The growing tendency of late-Victorian young women to explore public spaces unchaperoned sparked considerable social anxiety; see, for example, Deborah Epstein Nord, *Walking the Victorian Streets: Women, Representation, and the City* (Ithaca: Cornell University Press, 1995), and Judith Walkowitz, *City of Dreadful Delight: Narratives of Sexual Danger in Late-Victorian London* (Chicago: University of Chicago Press, 1992). In the *DUM*, Kate's opposition to George's assumption of male authority is even more pronounced; see Appendix B, p. 411-412.

168 See p. 79, n. 86.

me."[169]

"Very well," replied George, with magnificent self-sacrifice; "to tell the truth, I don't care much about these sort of things either. I'll come and take care of you instead, and we'll have another look at that Bohemian glass."

"Not for worlds!" she says earnestly, putting up two little gray-kid hands in a deprecating manner. "I'm not so selfish as to make my amusements hindrances to other people's. Let us each enjoy ourselves in our own way. Surely my taste for solitude is such a very innocent one that I may be allowed to indulge it. It's very kind of you" (with a pretty glance of gratitude) "to take such care of me. I'm sure I'm not worth it. Good-bye for the present;" and to prevent further manifestations of Master Chester's chivalrous nature, she beat a hasty retreat.

END OF VOL. II

169 An early Christian martyr, St. Cecilia was commonly represented as a musician.

VOLUME III

CHAPTER I

THE little pleasant heat consequent on her victory being over, Kate roamed about in her self-chosen, self-soothing solitariness, unremonstrated with, unrebuked by any human being. She was not in the least afraid of being left to her own society and protection: why should she? There were no wolves in grandmothers' guise to lure unsuspecting Red Ridinghoods to their destruction. What harm would these gay-clothed holiday-makers do her? They were far too much occupied in chaffering with the young men and women—gentlemen and ladies, I suppose I should say—at the stalls, in walking about, tightly hooked on to each other in pairs, in courting and eating hot pork-pies, and getting their full pennyworths for their penny, to take the smallest notion of her or appear aware of her existence. The big nave was adorned for Christmas with flags and evergreens and Christmas trees, on which the unlighted lamps hung like glowworms at high noon.

There is no place so lonely as a crowd—everybody knows that; and after five minutes of rejoicing in her delightful independence and freedom of action, Kate began to experience a sensation of soul-barrenness and dreariness; add to which the wind whistled at will through the wide expanse, where attempt at artificial warming is there none. She shivered and actually regretted the warm concert-room, despite the drawbacks of big drum and bassoon.

She had sought this state of loneliness in order to have leisure to think her fill of things past, present, and to come; and now all these swaying, shifting crowds disturbed her.

She would go to the Exotic Court, she resolved: there at least, among the flora of Africa and South America, she could not well be perished with cold nor rendered blue-fingered and red-nosed. One grievance at least would be done away with.

So she passed through the folding-doors into another climate. Ah, that was comfortable, luxurious! So she thought at first, leaning restfully back on a seat over against the bronze mermaids that support the fountain so untiringly on their dark shoulders, watching the tropical plants, big-leaved and spiky, flourishing and greening under the cold glass dome, so utterly forgetful of the blazing sun that saw their birth; at the large feathery ferns, bathing their feet in the still water—very peaceful and quiet and soporific—no sound but the gentle rustling of a few women's dresses, the murmurs of a few voices.[1]

But Kate was hard to please to-day. Thought would not come when she wooed it. It was too quiet and warm and comfortable; perhaps she should fall asleep and be locked in for the night with the bronze mermaids and the ferns and the spiky plants. So she jumped up with a sort of Wandering-Jew restlessness[2] upon her, and sauntered off again. Was the shadow of her destiny falling dark and cold upon her, to make her so discomposed and ill at ease?

Wandering about, doing nothing, and grumbling, take time; and almost half an hour had elapsed when she found herself at last at the entrance to that court where stand together the casts of the greatest marvels of statuary the world ever saw—ever will see, unless it improves very fast on its late efforts—the Venuses and Apollos[3] that try so hard by their dumb influence

1 Kate's perambulations have taken her from the concert hall on the west side of the Palace through the "big nave" of the main hallway, and thence into the Tropical Department, here called the "Exotic Court," at the north end of the building, an area facing the Aboo-Simbel figures (gigantic painted reproductions of Egyptian statues) on one side and the Ninevah Court on the other. Heated by hot-water pipes to recreate a tropical atmosphere of around 85° (Kate enters "another climate"), the Tropical Department showcased plants from such places as Java, India, Tahiti, and South America. The fountain besides which Kate sits, and which features "bronze mermaids" with "dark shoulders," was the work of the Italian sculptor Raffaelle Monti, and depicted four bare-breasted Syrens, each of whom represented a different racial group (Caucasian, Nubian, North American Indian, and Australian native) from the four corners of the globe. Broughton describes the scene as it would have appeared when *Not Wisely* appeared in serial form in 1865-66; by the time the novel was published in volume format in 1867, the Tropical Department and north wing lay in ruins following a fire in December 1866 whose damage was never repaired.

2 In medieval folklore, a bystander who taunted Jesus on his way to crucifixion and was doomed to wander the earth until the second coming.

3 Kate has now arrived at the Greek Court, designed by Owen Jones, and housing over two hundred casts of famous Greek statues, including the Laocoön (see next note) and the Venus de Milo, a semi-nude representation of the goddess of love similar to the Venus de Medici, the statue to which the narrator compares Kate's figure in Vol. 1, chapter 2 (see p. 50, n. 31).

to convince us, contrary to our reason, that the art which expresses form alone is superior to that other sister-art which can express both form and colour. Ah, she would go in and rest there, among those silent petrified demigods. She had not had a good long look at them for ever so long; and it was so much pleasanter and more satisfactory to study them all by oneself than with a whole party of unintelligent men and women, who knew even less about them than she herself did, who could not point out any new excellences in them, nor share her love for the old. She would go in and feast her eyes till they should be sated and saturated with loveliness.

There is a bench running round that rich-dowered room, and on this bench Kate sat down and made herself comfortable, establishing herself in full view of the noblest, most grandly-composed group that ever entered into the heaven-raised imagination of a sculptor to create or his fingers to execute,—the Laocoon.[4] What the Australian aborigines—flat-nosed, dwindle-limbed—are to us, such are we to those colourless, lifeless, motionless wonders. Generation after generation of short-spanned living creatures has ripened and rotted, they looking calmly on, superior in their unwithering amaranthine bloom—generation after generation has gaped open-mouthed, awed by their solemn presence—generation after generation will so gaze and stare until the world is overrun with a new deluge of barbarians from the far West, or till it comes to its final ending. That happy man, to whose deathless glory it was granted to fashion the Laocoon, must have had in his mind to excite the envy and shame of puny, feeble after-ages, long after he and his chisel should be dust together; showing them what manner of men there were in the old time, in blue-skied templed Hellas.[5] But then, again, one feels inclined—perhaps from aversion to acknowledge that we have degenerated—to doubt whether those god-faces and Titan-frames[6] could have been copied from any mere flesh-and-blood creature that, while in life, drudged away on the earth and had material blood flowing in his veins. Could such stainless triumphant beauty and might have been ever found in our world, where perfection in anything is

4 Famous Greek statue representing the scene in the Aeneid in which the Trojan priest Laocöon, who had attempted to warn the Trojans of the danger of the Greeks' wooden horse, is strangled along with his sons by sea snakes at the behest of gods favoring the Greek side.

5 See p. 109, n. 142.

6 The Titans, eventually supplanted by Zeus and the other Olympians, were powerful deities of mythic strength.

proverbially unattainable? Rather must it have been some divine *afflatus*[7] breathed into the fashioner's soul, speaking to him of a flawlessness of outward build such as had never been patent to his bodily eyes. Assuredly the gods must have revealed themselves to him in visions of the night, and even after they vanished have haunted him ceaselessly, driving him to reproduce in the plastic clay those features and limbs of immortal majesty which before had been graven on the tables of his soul. And yet, despite all my reasoning to the contrary, I feel that the father and sons in the Laocoon are men and not gods. In their suffering we recognise their humanity. That is a badge that all the bond-servants of the flesh wear without exception; there is no mistaking it. In the dignity of their eternal agony we recognise their brotherhood to ourselves.

At the end of her reverie Kate fell a despising her fellow-beings, her acquaintances—their *physique* at least. In fancy she compared the men and women who walked and talked around her in her daily life to these Venuses and wrestlers and Diskoboloi.[8] O me, how poor they were, how wretched and slight-framed and sketchy—the men especially—such laths and maypoles! It diverted her in imagination to set plump George Chester by the side of that fighting gladiator with the close-shorn shapely head and the extended arms. Ah, yes! there was only one man she had ever known who could stand a comparison with that deathless athlete. A heavy sigh supervened.

I do not believe in coincidences generally; but I think that was a coincidence, that, as she sighed, two voices burst upon her—two voices talking close to her in the next court, a man's and a woman's; the woman first saying lackadaisically:

"There's no privacy in this horrid place, and nowhere hardly to sit down."

And then the man answering: "Come in here and we shall find both, if I am not mistaken."

At that man's voice Kate started so violently that she almost fell off her seat; her small fingers dug unconsciously into the palms of her hands, and her heart surged and beat so loud that it seemed to shut out all other sounds. Was there only a torturing resemblance in these cathedral-bell

7 Divine inspiration.

8 Greek discus throwers, often represented in statues and on coins; a famous example, reproduced in the Palace's Greek Court, is the nude Discobolus of Myron, the Roman copy of a lost Greek original.

tones; or was it—could it be really the one voice that had ever sounded in the world for her? As she sat there stricken, parted-lipped, wide-eyed, that man and woman came in together. A tall woman, silk-and-velvet clad, with trailing garments, sweeping amply round her; a woman not old nor young; at that dangerous age when a handsome woman has not faded but ripened; when one, whose whole profession in life has been flirting, has, through many years' practice, attained a master's proficiency in that art. That lady was "*somebody*," certainly; so one said to oneself at the first glance, and not a nice "somebody" one added after the second. The purple and the tiara of Livia or Agrippina[9] would have well beseemed that low, lineless brow; a woman with a bold, sensual, snaring face, with a lissom, undulating empress form. And the man? Ay, one with a dark, ugly face; a man, you would infallibly turn to look back at, if you passed him in the street. One which approached more nearly in physical conformation to Achilles or Telamonian Ajax[10] than to most of the men one sees in the present small-boned days. Lean flanked, with shoulders that looked as if, Atlas-like, they could support the burden of the world; and a vast chest that five-and-forty inches could not have compassed. Yes, it was he; there were not many like him, thought the girl, cowering and shaking there on the bench. They came in sauntering; did not see her, they were so much taken up with each other; sat down side by side on the other side of the court, away from her, and began to talk in an intimate, confidential way, or rather continued a conversation which had evidently been begun before.

"It was very good of you to come to-day," said Colonel Stamer, bending familiarly over his companion. "I hardly thought you would have been able to compass it."

"To tell you the truth," she answered, looking up with her bold eyes at him, "no more did I, though I did not say anything about it in my note. He has taken to watching me like a lynx lately. Rather foolish of him, is not it, to do such a useless thing? as if a woman could not outwit a man any day!" she ended, with a careless, scornful laugh.

"I'd back them, indeed," said Dare grimly; "but let's hear how you

---

9 Powerful Roman women: Livia was the wife of the emperor Augustus and Agrippina the mother of Nero.

10 Achilles was the greatest Greek hero of the Trojan War; Ajax, son of Telemon, King of Salamis, was the second. Another mythic strong man, referred to in the next sentence, was Atlas, a former Titan condemned to carry the weight of the world on his shoulders.

managed it this time."

"O," she answered, shrugging her shoulders, "easily enough, as it turned out. He is gone down to that dreary swamp of his in Lincolnshire to-day, and he is going to drag me down there to-morrow, I believe; so I suppose he thought I might be trusted by myself for four-and-twenty hours;" and again she laughed quite heartily at the thought of how cleverly she had circumvented her lord.

Dare laughed too. "Poor thing!" he said, taking her hand carelessly; but, even as he spoke, he smothered a yawn; even this intrigue could not keep at bay the old persecuting sense of *ennui.*

"He threatened to chaperone me to Elise's[11] the other day," continued the fair complainant, pouting at the recollection of her wrongs. "There would have been a nice *esclandre*[12] if he had—would not there? Good gracious!" she added, hastily changing her tone, "we are not alone here. Look at that girl sitting over there listening to us."

Dare put his glass to his eye, and turned round haughtily, intending to *look over* the impertinent intruder who had dared to play eaves-dropper to him; but when his eyes did fall on that intruder, he gave just such another start as Kate had done. "Good God!" he exclaimed, involuntarily, and he paled visibly, even through his bronzed skin; and a flood of light flowed over his face, such as the woman by his side would never have had power to call there.

"What's the matter?" she asked eagerly, in much surprise.

With a great effort he mastered himself sufficiently to answer, almost coolly, "O, nothing; only it's an unpleasant idea being spied upon. Let us come away from here, if you are rested—are you?"

"Yes," she said, and she began leisurely to put on a lace veil she had taken off.

"Come," he urged impatiently, not quite master of himself; and he hurried away, without giving her time to ask any more questions or make any remarks. What became of that virtuous matron, Lady ——, that second Cornelia,[13] after this? I am unable to state whether Colonel Stamer had the good luck to meet with some mutual acquaintance who took her off his hands; whether he hurried her to the railway station, and into the train;

11 Fashionable London dressmaker.

12 Scandal (French).

13 Ironic reference; Cornelia Cornelius, died 100 BCE and known as "Mother of the Gracchi," embodied the Roman matronly ideal.

whether he made some lame excuse for leaving her in the lurch, or whether he made no excuse at all, I cannot pretend to say. Certain it is that, in what seemed about five minutes' time, he found himself again at the entrance to that statued court, ascertained by one swift glance that that girl was still sitting there, huddled up on the bench in the same attitude as he had left her in, and came striding towards her with an eager haste, that formed a strange contrast to his usual proud laziness.

"Is it you, Kate?" he asked rapidly, in a low thick voice; "is it the little Kate Chester I used to know such a long time ago? Let me touch you, that I may see whether it is really you, or whether it is only some phantom that the foul fiend has sent to tantalise me as he has so often done before. Am I mad or drunk, I wonder? I should not be surprised at either. Speak to me quick, Kate, if it is you, and tell me so."

"It is I," answered Kate, almost under her breath, and the room seemed to be going round and round with her, the statues tumbling off their pedestals, and dancing up and down, and a general blackness coming over the face of everything.

"Thank God!" came through the blackness to her ears in the deep soft voice, like the low notes of a rich-toned organ. "Kate, I never thought so before; but I do believe now that there are some higher powers that have a hand in human affairs. To think that you and I should be meeting again after all these weary months and years, as we never thought we should. Did we, child?"

"No," answered Kate faintly; gradually, by a great struggle, getting the better of an inclination to swoon.

Dare stretched out his arms in his triumphant joy, to take her to himself in the old possessive way, despite all that had come and gone; despite that cruel story, which, told and listened to under the solemn stars on that June night, had placed so unspannable a gulf between them. But she shrank away from him, bent on keeping strong and bright before her mind's eye the bare freezing truth that this man was another woman's property; though now that she was in his presence once again, she felt plain enough how entirely futile and gainless had been all her struggles and self-discipline and arguments; how that she loved him far, *far* more intensely and measurelessly than ever. Her capacity and ability for loving had, with all these smotherings and chastenings, only grown broader, and more profound.

"My darling, my darling," went on the rich voice, shaking and quivering, "*how* glad I am to see you again!"

No oath of a dying man could have borne with it more conviction of its entire truthfulness than that simple assertion. He took both her hands in his, and bending down, gazed greedily on the small face almost as pale as the statued Venus above her, on the glorious hair rippling away in its old wealth under the simple bonnet.

"It cannot be chance, Kate, that brought us both here to-day," he urges, speaking low, while the little white hands tremble and thrill in his; "it must be Providence. The Almighty (if there is such a one) has seen that the sacrifice you made was too great for you. He has given it back into your hands. He has brought us together again, never to part any more now, child, never again."

And the voice that had sounded like a brazen trumpet, shouting the word of command to his men through the mists and the fog on Inkerman morning, wavered in uttering those few sweet last words.

"No, it is not God's doing; I know it is not," murmured Kate feebly.

She did not seem to see or hear anything quite right yet; but still dimly perceived and resisted the sophistry of his reasoning.

"It is, it must be," pressed Dare vehemently. "You are ready enough to see the hand of God in very little finger-ache, in every shower of rain, or any such every-day occurrence, and you won't see it now where it is so plain. You say that this God of yours desires His creatures' happiness. Well, He sees that you and I cannot live without one another, so He has given us back to each other. He's omnipotent. What are the wretched rotten straws with which men tie and bind themselves in His eyes?"

"Not live without me!" said Kate, in a distincter, louder tone than she had yet said anything, almost bitterly; for the recollection of that pang of jealousy she had felt roused her, and brought her back to herself. "Then who was that woman whose society you seemed to be enjoying so much just now? She is much more worthy of your love than I, with her beautiful face and her yellow hair. I look hideous and deformed beside her."

"Don't speak of her, darling," said Dare, reddening a little; "she is a bad woman, not fit for you to take her name between your lips, my little pure snowdrop."

"Why do you talk to her and make love to her then, Dare?" asks Kate earnestly, hating to picture her Dare caressing this yellow-haired rival; and the full lips quiver mutely, and just one big tear steals into the corner of each troubled eye.

"Because she amuses me," answers Dare lightly, disliking the subject, and longing to dismiss it; "because she keeps me from thinking," he went on, with a gloomy shadow stealing over his face. "I'm beginning to think, Kate, that thought and madness are synonymous. It is so pleasant sitting down in one's own society, and letting one's fancy run riot amongst the joys that every step of one's life unfolds to one. I wonder you have not found it so."

"Of course I have," answers Kate, a little eased of her jealous fears. "My whole life for the last year and a half has been a hard fight against thought and memory. I have given up fighting against anything now," she added, shaking her head wearily; "I'm so tired of everything. What's the good of kicking against Fate? It's Kismet."[14]

She said no more then, and he was too busy to make her any answer; busy gloating, miser-like, with bold, glad eyes, over his recovered pearl; eyes that she did not blush or wince under, as in the old coy girlish days. She was a woman now, not a girl, past blushing or hiding away from those orbs of fire. In a little while the low man's voice sounded again wooingly through the tenantless room.

"Are not you going to look up at me once, Kate? I want to have one look into the odd big green eyes. Have not you got *one* kind word to say to a poor fellow, after all this dreary time?"

Kate had purposely kept her eyes downcast, their bright lashes sweeping the stainless cheeks. She had not dared to raise them. Dare's had lost none of their old magic. She felt that, throbbing veined. She remembered how, formerly, they had thrilled and maddened her; drawn her with a fascination far exceeding that of the charming serpent; had swayed her as the moon sways the ocean tides. But she could not resist that appeal. Slowly she raised her own and rested them on his, in which the light was flashing and dancing.

"O, Dare, Dare!" she groaned, "why have you come back to torment me, when I was so much better and happier without you?"

"Happier!" echoed Dare, catching at the word, while the pent-house brows drew together thunderously. "I see you have found some one to fill my place much more satisfactorily. Woman's fickleness is a worn-out old proverb," he went on sneeringly. "It's a story nearly as old as Adam. I expect the only reason that Eve was faithful to him was that there was no

14 Turkish word for fate.

one to teach her unfaithfulness. Unstable as water is a weak comparison, I am beginning to think. Unstable as woman would be more to the purpose. So, Kate, you had quite forgotten the old love till his ugly face intruded on you so unseasonably to-day, had you?"

"Forgotten you!" answered Kate, not flinching a bit under the wrathful questioning face, with concentrated passion—not a girl's milk-and-water love—in every eloquent feature. "Forgotten you! I wish to God I could! Every hour of my life I curse the day when I first saw you, standing—O, what a fool I am to remember it so well!—on the shore, in your boating-dress, with your hat off; and you looked down upon me, and smiled away my stupid senses."

"Curse it you may, if it gives you any satisfaction," replied Dare morosely, biting his lips; "but for all that you cannot deny that neither you nor I were ever half so happy before; never shall be again, as long as we live. No, if you must curse any day, Kate, curse that one, when a wretched, prudish quirk, a namby-pamby sentimentalism for that great coarse mass of flesh and blood that I have the happiness to call wife, made you utterly blight and take all savour out of two lives; when you tore yourself—you little cruel, beautiful fool!—out of the arms that would have sheltered you all your life from the smallest gust of ill-luck or harm; tore yourself away and left me standing there so frightfully desolate without you. There has never been a warm night since, Kate, with the south wind blowing coolly over the sea, that I have not lived those tortures over again, thanks to you."

He had grown vehement, rapid as he went on; and now he loosed one of Kate's hands, and with his own freed one pushed off the short twining rings of silky hair impatiently from his forehead, as if with them he could push off the load of sin and suffering that was weighing on that sun-kissed ample brow.

"Poor, poor fellow!" sighed Kate pityingly. That is the best of women; they always feel their friends' pains and aches so much more keenly than their own.

"Ay, Kate," went on Dare, softening a little under the influence of this blandishment, but still looking down very ruefully upon her from his commanding height, with reproach in his anxious, covetous eyes, "you're grown very prudish and cold and correct of late, I'm afraid; but even you would have pitied me, I think, if you could have looked into my soul that night, and seen the utter blackness there. When you took *yourself* away you knew that you took everything, and yet you did it. O, child! how could you be so inhuman? I think, if you could have seen the frightful nothingness and emptiness you caused, you'd have repented, good and strong-minded as you were, and come back to the sinner that loved you better far than all the cold-blooded saints in paradise, or out of it, could ever do. Kate, do you think you would have pitied me? Say you would anyhow."

Kate's heart was torn and rent by the unstudied, unwitting pathos of that broken husky voice, of those world-weary, wicked, miserable eyes.

"O, Dare, stop; do stop," she prayed earnestly, while her white cheeks were watered by streaming tears. "I cannot pity you more than I pitied myself. You were then, you are now, all the world to me. I love your sins better than anyone else's virtues. I think of you all day long, and I dream of your grand eyes all the night. I beg God every hour to let me die and forget you; for that's the only way I ever could; but He won't. Do you suppose it was no trial to me to go away from you, and give you up? Ah, my darling, you don't know how ill I was after that terrible night; they all thought I was going to die; if I had, I should infallibly have gone to hell. I sometimes doubt," she added, with a look of awed reflection, "whether I could have been much more hopelessly unhappy even there."

"Child, don't cry," said Dare harshly; "I cannot bear to see it; you'll drive me to kiss away the tears, and ruin your character for your whole life, I suppose," he added sardonically; "you'd better dry your eyes quick, or you'll run a very good chance of such pollution."

Kate dried her eyes obediently, and he went on:

"Every word you utter only confirms what I said at first. Apart from each other, you and I are like galvanised dead bodies that have a mechanic motion, but no life; we cannot live anything that is worthy the name of life without one another."

"I can live without you, Dare," answered Kate, looking up simply into that long-unseen, haughty face, with eyes mist-obscured still, hard as she was trying to swallow down the fresh torrent of tears that seemed rising in her throat. "I have done it now for a year and a half, and I'm not dead; I'm not even sick or ailing."

"You say you're not sick or ailing," said Dare; and then he led her to a mirror that hung on the wall in a corner of the court. "Look there," he said, "do you see how changed you are? I never saw a person so much altered in the whole course of my life; you were always a pale little lily, but you are almost as white as snow now; and see what dark marks you have got under those great melancholy eyes of yours; you used to be such a cheery, laughing little thing, and now you have got the saddest face I ever saw. You are not sick or ailing, no doubt; but if you do not take care you'll be in your grave soon."

"I'm sorry I've grown such a scarecrow, Dare," says Kate, looking sadly at her own image in the glass, with a very faint poor smile.

"What! you care about your beauty still, do you, Kate?" asked Dare, smiling too—one of his well-remembered curving smiles, half seen under the heavy moustache, quite a pleasant glad smile—"that's more like the wicked, vain, little flirt I used to know in the dear old dead-and-gone days."

"Dare, am I grown very ugly?" inquired Kate, turning to him with a grave face. "Tell me the truth, please. I know I never was very pretty; but am I much gone off?"

"Ugly!"said Dare, laughing, despite all his bitter griefs and mortifications; "God forbid! You may set your mind at rest on that point, Kate, I think. Why, child, have you no eyes? Cannot you see that you are six times as tormentingly bewitching as ever? I could never make out what devilry there was in your little face; do you remember, Kate?" he said excitedly, bending down his lips so close to her that his breath fanned her round white ear, and gently agitated the hair sweeping away behind it. "It puzzles me more than ever now, do you know? I have seen scores of women a thousand times as pretty and as witty as you, and I felt that they might all go to the dogs together, for all I'd do to stop them. You are the one woman in the world for me; do you know that, little one?"

Kate did not answer. "You're changed too, Dare, now I come to look at you," she said, scanning his rough-hewn massive features. "It is not for the better you are changed. You were always a bad man, as I know to my cost; but you are wickeder and more reckless than ever now. I can tell that. How haggard you are too, and hollow-eyed! Poor fellow! poor fellow!"

"Yes, Kate," answered Dare calmly, with a very dreary laugh that the heart denied all partnership in: "that nice pious half-hour's work you did on that night you know of, sent me galloping along the road to hell at an edifying rate. You saved your own soul, I daresay, very comfortably and properly, but you damned mine. O God! how changed you are since that day when you said that even heaven itself would be dull to you without me!"

"I'm not changed in any way!" cried Kate eagerly; "I'm exactly the same as I always was, unluckily for me."

"No, you are not," contradicted Dare, with impassioned mournfulness. "You're not the little girl with the big loving eyes, that sat on that garden-seat beside me in the conservatory at Llyn; whose arms I have felt warm and soft about my neck, incredible as such familiarity seems now."

"Ah, Dare," sighed Kate, interceding for forgiveness, "I did not know then."

"O, of course not," cried Dare, with the bitterness of a soul cut off from friendship and companionship with its equals, "of course, I know that my boyish folly has shut me out for ever from all good women's endearments."

"My darling, my own lost Dare, I *am* unutterably, frightfully glad to see you again. I do not care how wicked it is. I must say so just this once. I should die if I did not."

Dare answered not with words, but he caught her to him and held her as a man might hold the delight of his eyes raised up to him again by a miracle from among the shrouded dead.

At last Dare's voice, sounding unsteady and thick—

"You're mine, Kate. You cannot go back. You'll stay with me always, in life and death. Do you hear, child? I shall hold you here till you say 'yes.'"

His words roused the girl from a happy baleful trance. She struggled a little; she freed herself to a certain extent; that is to say, she raised her chestnut head, and answered him with startled self-condemning eyes, coming back from the gardens of the Hesperides[15] to the world's dusty highway:

"I'd give all the world to be able to say 'yes,' but I dare not." And then this weak girl's good angel, who had been hovering near, heavy-winged, unseen, mourning over her folly—her almost fall—drew near, endowed with holy strength to save, and whispered good words to her heart to say. "O, Dare," she went on, with that blessed impulse driving her forward, "just think what a short wretched span life is. How soon it is over and passed away for ever; and I'm sure, too—I do not know why—but I *am* sure that mine will be even shorter and sooner over than it is the general lot to be. Dare, Dare, I know—I feel certain—that Heaven will be pitiful to us; and not let either you or me drag out weary days to anywhere near threescore-and-ten. But then, Dare, there'd have to come another worse parting at the end—worse, because it would be so utterly hopeless. O love!" she said, with a purer better light replacing the passion glow on her face, "you know what you are to me; you know that I'm like a reed in your hands, to be bent and broken as you will. O, have pity on me! Don't tempt me any longer.

15 Nymphs guarding golden apples that grow in a garden in the western corner of the world.

Let me go away, and try to struggle on a little bit in that good path that I hoped I had made a few steps in, before some devil threw me in your way again to-day."

Dare stroked his great moustache with an impatient angry movement, and answered with fierce irritability:

"You're selfish, Kate; you think of nothing but yourself. It's the old story of your profound affection for me, and your determination to blast my life with your piety. I have no doubt that good books, and good works, and good *men* perhaps" (with a sneer), "would soon compensate you for my loss; but what am I to do, child? tell me that. Do I forget so easily? If you steal yourself away from me again so meanly, so heartlessly, what substitute can I ever find for you?"

"O, my own," she said, with tearful caressingness, "my only love, don't you suppose I was thinking of you too? Have not we both been sinning and suffering in the same way? Won't the same recipe do for us both? Ah, Dare," she went on, "ah, Dare, won't you try and walk in another path too? You will I know, for my sake, for the sake of the poor stupid girl that has loved you better than ever woman loved man before. You'll try to be a better man, darling, won't you? instead of such a dreadfully wicked one; and then, who knows," she added, trying to smile through her tears, "God is very merciful; perhaps He'll let our paths meet at the end. Say you'll try, Dare. O do! for my sake!"

"I'll tell no such lies," exclaimed Dare hastily. "To think of my turning saint, and quoting Scripture at this time of day! I'm rather too old to cry *peccavi.*[16] No, Kate," he went on, clenching his hand, and bringing it down emphatically on his knee, "I warn you that if you rob me now of the one treasure I have got in the world, I'll do to the deuce[17] as hard as I can; and whatever evil deeds I do will lie at your door for this day's work; mind that."

"No, they won't," replied Kate quickly, too spirited not to resist this injustice. "If you go to the bad as you say, it'll break my heart most likely, and not much matter either; but the guilt of your sins will not fall on my head."

Dare left his raving, and his threats—he saw they did no good; his voice fell into the old wooing key, infinitely tender.

"It shall not fall on anyone's head; they shall not be committed at all, if you will but stay with me, Kate. Child, I never asked a favour of human being before, but I implore you now to grant me this one little request; just

16 I have sinned (Latin).
17 Devil.

say 'I will.' Those two short words will marry us so effectually in the sight of God. Say them, Kate, say them."

"No, no, no!" cried Kate, sobbing and gasping in this terrible conflict. "Don't try to blind me with your sophistries. Whilst I'm with you, I lose the distinction between right and wrong; it's all a great black mist to me; but I *must* go, I *must*, I *must!*"

"Go!" repeated Dare, actually laughing in his utter astonishment at and ridicule of this proposal; "go, indeed! when I have hardly seen you for five minutes yet—when you have not told me where you live; nor when you'll meet me again, nor any of the thousand-and-one things that I want you to tell me before we part, if we ever do again."

"We shall never *meet* again, Dare," Kate said solemnly; and by a great exertion of self-command she said it with a steady voice.

"*What*?" asked Dare in a hoarse whisper, and further could he say nothing.

"We shall never meet again, if I can help it," reiterated Kate. "I shall pray God to keep us apart. Never again, dear love, never again;" and she groaned as she uttered those funeral words.

Dare fought with the agony and fear that were gnawing and almost mastering him, and said at last, rapidly, harshly:

"And you can sit there, and tell me so, calmly?"

"Yes, I can," she answered resolutely. "There is nothing harder left for me to do than what I have already done; there is no cup left for me to drink bitterer than that you put to my lips, long ago, on the Pen Dyllas sands."

Dare's swarthy face grew very white—hard even.

"Impossible," he said angrily, "you cannot deny me what hundreds of people, who don't value it, who would as soon see any other face and hear any other voice as yours, enjoy every day—the sight of you, the sound of your voice, the touch of your hand in common greeting. Absurd—quixotic! O, child, forgive me, if I speak roughly to you; but a man does not stick upon forms and ceremonies much, when he is wrestling for the last hope he has in the world, and sees it vanishing away, without power to detain it."

"Dare," she said, enunciating each word slowly and distinctly, "you and I must be either all or nothing to each other; we cannot be the one, so we must be the other."

"Must we?" he said, putting one hand before his face to hide its blank despair; "then God help us!"

His wrath yielded to intense self-pity as he spoke, and the deep voice almost broke down in the utterance of his desolation. She could bear his anger, threats, frowns, but could she bear the bitter plaintiveness of those ringing tones that had whispered away her soul long ago by the summer sea? Her storm-shattered heart wavered. Should she stay with him after all?—for better, for worse—for richer, for poorer—in sickness, and in health, till death should them part? They would be married in the sight of God, he had said. Could it be right?—to send this man back, desperate, hopeless, to his evil companions—to bad men and worse women? Could it be right for the sake of a prejudice of society to damn this soul utterly? But then there rose up before her dazed eyes a pale, thin, holy face—the face of one

"Within whose ears an angel ever sang
Good tidings of great joy."[18]

If she did this thing, if she took this step, she could never look on that pure, kind, saintly face again—could never be worthy to shake him by the hand again as a friend. What a load of sorrow and care she should, by this act of hers, add to the already pressing burden that weighed on the bowed shoulders of that poor good man!

Dare, watching her, lynx-eyed, saw her shaken, hesitating, and seized his opportunity; he had not space to lose many now.

"Kate, a drowning man catches at straws, you know. I saw you waver just now; I know your face so well. After all, you care enough about me to be a little sorry at throwing me away like an old glove that you have no further use for. Kate, it is not too late to repent even at this eleventh hour. I adjure you not to send me back, a ruined undone man, to the society of devils, or to my own, which is worse than any devils'. O child, child, I'm so lonely. Stay with me!"

"Hush," she said wildly, putting her hands to her ears; "I won't listen to you; have not I been like a house divided against itself[19] ever since I knew you? Have not you done me enough harm already, blighting my life with your love that is crueler than any hatred?"

A spasm of pain crossed his face. "Yes," he said, "I have blighted your

18 Owen Meredith, (E. R. Bulwer-Lytton), *Tannhäuser* (1861), ll. 98-99.
19 See Matthew 12:25: "And Jesus knew their thoughts, and said unto them, Every kingdom divided against itself is brought to desolation; and every city or house divided against itself shall not stand[.]"

life; you say truth, and that is the very reason why I want you to stay with me. I *know* I could make you so happy, Kate; I would not ask you if I were not sure of it. O my little one, let me try! Come to me!"

"Never!" she said emphatically, clenching her hands, "the most utter hopeless misery would be better than such happiness."

He made no more effort to move her; he only turned his face to the wall and groaned. "Very well," he said harshly, "you know best, I suppose; go back to your friends and be happy in your own way. I'm not fit company for you, I know that well enough."

She had told him she must go, and he did not seek to keep her; six faltering steps she made towards the door, and then stopped irresolute, and looked towards him. He was sitting bowed together on the bench; his dark face buried in his hands. Some impulse prompted her to pass over and touch him on the sleeve.

"Dare!" she said tremulously. He neither moved nor spoke. "Dare, speak to me!"

He lifted up his head and looked at her. His features were haggard and drawn; rougher hewn and more unbeautiful than ever they looked, and great scorching tears stood in his eyes. "What do you want?" he said roughly. "I told you to go; why aren't you gone? Are you come to mock me in my desolation?"

"To mock you! O no, Dare! I'm come to say good-bye."

"Good-bye, Kate!"

"Have not you got one farewell word to say to me?"

"Kate, the only word I can say to you is, *stay*; if you won't have that, I have none other." He took her two hands in his, and they stood looking at one another silently for what seemed a thousand pulse-beats, her face gradually paling—paling to the whiteness of one that has been a whole day dead.

Then she sighed and drew in her breath. "Yes," she said in a whisper, "I'll stay."

He caught her to him. "My very own at last!" he cried brokenly; "from this day I begin to live!"

"Stop!" she said shuddering, shrinking away from him. "What are you so glad about? Is it matter for rejoicing that you have dragged another soul down to hell with you?"

A few minutes, and then voices are heard; people talking and laughing.

"Dare," said Kate hurriedly, "I hear Margaret's voice; she and my cousins are coming this way. I must go; they must not find me here with you."

"No, that they must not," he said eagerly; "till to-morrow then," with a lingering grudging sigh and gaze; "O why cannot to-day be to-morrow? Why need you go at all? I don't like to let you out of my sight. I mistrust you, Kate!"

"You need not," she said very coldly.

"Are you really speaking truth? are you sure you have not been deceiving me all along?" he asked with passionate earnestness.

"Perfectly sure," she answered stonily. "As sure as that I stand here the most shameful miserable woman upon God's earth."

Then he let her go.[20] Ten minutes afterwards a rather fat young man, four rather fat young women, and one rather thin young one entered the court sauntering, and found it empty, save one big magnificent-looking man, standing with his back to them, attentively studying the Venus Victrix.[21] Margaret started when first her eyes fell on that stalwart form; and she tried by various manœuvres to get a view of his face, in which she was completely unsuccessful.

"No, no!" she said to herself, "it must be my fancy; it cannot be he! What should he be doing here?—Why did not you come with us, Kate? Have you got a headache? you look as if you had; take two grains of aconite[22] when you get home; you don't know what you have missed, does she, George?" cry the female quartette with voluble unanimity, on regaining their truant cousin. "Does not she play superbly? such an exquisite touch! so much improved since last I heard her! I used to think she wanted expression." &c. &c.

---

20 See Appendix B, pp. 412-416, for Broughton's extensive reworking of the version of this scene in the *DUM*. There Kate only agrees to become Dare's mistress when he refuses to let her leave the Greek Court otherwise; hearing Margaret and her cousins approaching, Kate fears exposure should they discover her with Dare and hastily gives in to his demands. In the triple-decker, then, Kate makes more of a conscious, and less of a coerced, decision to live with Dare than she does in the serialization; Dare is also less violent in the volume format than he is in the *DUM*, where he not only pressures Kate into promising to become his mistress, but assures her he will kill her if she does not keep her word.

21 See p. 194, n. 67. The Crystal Palace's statue of the victorious goddess of love was a copy of the sculpture by the Italian artist Canova, who used a semi-nude Pauline Buonaparte as model.

22 Also known as wolfsbane, a poisonous herb used medicinally in small quantities.

CHAPTER II

ALL that night as Kate lay tossing wide-eyed, flushed-cheeked, on a bed from which sleep seemed to have departed thousands of miles, looking every moment towards the window for the first streak of light—wondering, with impatient, feverish unrest, whether a new Egyptian darkness had fallen on the land for a curse,[23] dragging night over the confines of the blessed day,—her good angel and her evil one were fighting and wrestling for her; and towards morning, when first the window-square began to glimmer, faintly seen in the dim, wintry dawn, the evil one got the upper hand. Vanquished utterly, it seemed, the good one fled away, grieved out of heart, almost despairing. She had perjured herself once (Ananias and Sapphira had been struck suddenly dead for lying);[24] she had caused to wither and fade all the fair leaves and flowers of the green tree of his life, had burnt and scorched it into a sapless scathed trunk; but she would not do it again, and it was love, not fear, drove her. She would go by the train he had told her; he should find her there, waiting for him—waiting for a doom that more than one woman had thought worse than death—had courted death to avoid it. She would go up to him, would tell him that she had come to sacrifice herself to him, that she gave herself up to him body and soul; and then he would kiss her as he had done yesterday (ah, that would make up for anything!), would take her away from the ken of all who had known or loved her before. Yes, she should have to turn her back on all the old, life-long known circle—on Margaret, on Blount, on everything virtuous and reputable. Well, he would compensate them all, and far more than compensate. Virtue and respectability, and duty, and plenty of friendly relations, had been unendurable without him; that recipe had nearly killed her; she would try now whether he and shame would make her happier. There would be no one to tell her she was disgraced and vile, or any other of the ugly names that the world heaps on those women whose love is stronger than their prudence, and, consequently, she should forget whether she was or no. Floating about with him on some stormless isle-studded southern sea, guarded in his arms from the least adverse blast, what would

23 One of the plagues visited by God on the Egyptians in Exodus (10: 21-23).
24 See Acts 5:5: Ananias and Sapphira were a couple struck dead as divine punishment for lying about money they withheld from their church.

be to her the odds between honour and dishonour, between evil report and good report? He would not jibe her with all she had lost and thrown away for him; she should never be vile in his eyes, and as for all others, let them look volumes of scorn and prudery at her, she braved them. Then to her ears there came, sounding solemnly, mournfully, through the mist, the distance-muffled, varying tones of an early church bell. That sound might have been her own knell, it sank so like lead into her heart. She locked her burning hands tight together, and flung her head wildly about on the pillow, over which the loosened hair streamed in its glorious waves and tangles. Ah, poor James Stanley! she should never see him again in his shabby old mourning, never hear his simple, strengthening, ennobling words. He had done well to cut himself off from companionship with her; he must have had some prophetic instinct that she was unworthy of his friendship. Why, why had not she died, like that snow-pure sister of his with the golden hair and the tender blue eyes, that this world's light was too garish for, that closed so meekly to open again with immortal joy on "the City of the Saints of God"?[25] She had been pure, too, once, pure as that little dead maiden—pure in thought as in deed, though it seemed many, many years ago now. O, why had he ever come to destroy her? Well, after all, it was just as well that she and James Stanley should not meet again. What could they say to one another if they did? They would have nothing in common henceforth, not a hope, not a thought. He was God's servant, working hard at his post now, and in a very few years would have entered into his rest; while she—Ah! she shuddered at the very name of that she was going to make herself. This train, by which she intended to go to perdition, did not leave Queenstown till between one and two; consequently she should have plenty of time to attend morning-service, and it would excite less suspicion if she did. But it was impossible; she could not. She could not be so awful a hypocrite. God would strike her dead in His house if she polluted it with her presence. She would not expose herself, either, to the listening to James Stanley's earnest interceding voice. It would only make her remorseful, cowardly, unsettled again. No; she would tell Margaret that she felt sick and faint, and preferred staying at home and reading the chapters and psalms to herself. Read the chapters and psalms! Yes, as she and Margaret and Blount used to read them in the long-ago wet Sundays, with the pretty gentle patient mother who had gone from them now. How dared she think

25 See Owen Meredith, (E. R. B. Bulwer-Lytton), *Tannhäuser* (1861), ll. 1894-95.

of that mother now! "O mother, mother!" she cried inwardly, "why did you go away and leave me? If I had had you I could have done without anybody else." She would say she was ill, then. Nobody would accuse her of shamming, she said to herself, with a bitter smile, as she stood before the glass. It looked almost a dying face that she saw there. What could Dare see in those ghastly features to go so wild about?

There had been a sudden change in the weather the night before. All night it had been thawing fast, and the ice sailed in broken jagged masses down the dark Thames to the sea; and now this morning there was nothing but mist and fog and drizzle, blotting out the trees and the farther river-banks. Rain, dimming, blurring all the window-panes, bringing out great discoloured patches of damp on the walls of the fine white-stucco houses, streaming slantwise down the chill empty street, turning the gutters into rapid whirling torrents.

In a back street of Queenstown there stood, stands now, a tidy little mean house, with gingerbread-coloured shutters, and a door with a brass knocker, and the name of Mrs. Lewis legibly inscribed underneath. Inside, in the back-parlour, on this identical wet Sunday morning, sat the lady indicated, with a remarkably complacent self-satisfied expression on her double-chinned countenance, the result of an approving conscience and a modestly flourishing business—sat holding her tea-cup poised in air, in all the glory of her best black-silk dress and bob-curls; while behind her ample back her son and heir, Master Lewis, with a forethought worthy of a riper age, was surreptitiously employed in storing his breeches-pockets with a miscellaneous assortment of marbles, bull's-eyes,[26] and peppermint-lozenges, against the long morning-service which he knew was imminent, having learned by experience that such were effectual weapons with which to contend against the *ennui* attendant on the litany.

Meanwhile Mr. Stanley was sitting in the dingy little front parlour, having finished his apology for a breakfast some time ago, sitting there quite alone; for who should there be to be with him? The little dingy room looked rather more livable and comfortable than was its wont; it always did on Sunday. The owner always tried to furbish it up a little, and make it more passable on that one day that ruled over the other six. The hearth was clean swept, and a bright little fire burned and crackled upon it. The papers that usually straggled so disorderly all over the green-baize[27] cloth were put up

26 Round peppermint-flavored candy.

27 See p. 246, n. 144.

in neat little heaps, and the ink-bottle, for a wonder, had its cover on. James himself sat by the fire in a roomy old brown-leather arm-chair, rather out at elbows, but a snug old chair for all that; and James would not have parted with that old friend for all the newest *fauteuils* and *chaises longues*[28] that could be found in all the upholsterers' shops in the civilised world. It was almost the last of the links that bound him to his childhood, to the days when, gorgeously attired in a black-velvet frock and a big sash, he used to come down from the upper regions with his brothers and sisters; and being the delicate hardly reared pet, used to climb up on Sir Hugh's knee, and ruffle his silk-smooth, faultless hair, nestling his head on that dear kind old shoulder. So it came to pass that he loved the old arm-chair, now that he was no longer any one's pet, nor had ever a loving word spoken to him. At his elbow there stood a little cup with violets in it, at which ever and anon he smelt enjoyingly. Coming, yesterday afternoon, almost dizzy and sick, out of one of his reeking alleys, poisoned by the intolerable stenches that had their home there—that emanated especially from a certain rag-and-bone shop[29] he wot of—he had spied these violets lying blue and fresh in a shop-window, and with reckless extravagance had there and then gone in and expended sixpence in the purchase of them. Violets always reminded him of Kate. To be sure, all sweet odours and fair sights did that more or less, but violets most of all; they were her flowers, *par excellence.* Almost always a little bunch of them might be seen lurking green-leaved in the bosom of the soft gray dress. James was reading over his sermon, a work of some difficulty,—for, like many clever men, he wrote an almost illegible hand, his flow of ideas exceeding his manual power of writing them down,—and, with a pencil between his fingers, was occupied in carefully scoring out anything that appeared like needless repetition or tautology, in lopping off all superfluous ornamentations, in pruning away any small flowers of rhetoric that might chance to have blossomed out. The maximum of matter in the minimum of words appeared to be what he desired. His love, and care, and tendance of his sheep was far too great to run any chance of wearying or sending them to sleep. Nor for worlds would he have exceeded the quarter of an hour or twenty minutes that he allowed himself to address them in, nor would he, on the other hand, pander to vulgar taste, debase his scholarship, pollute the purity of his style, by descending to any of the fa-

28 Types of upholstered chair; a fanteuil had open sides with pads on the arms, while a chaise longue was long enough to lie on.

29 Rag and bone men collected waste material to sell for reuse.

miliarities of expression or grotesqueness of illustration with which many a preacher seasons his discourses for the palate of the unlettered herd. He had so many things yet to say to those people of his, such a vast number of all-important truths to urge, and some voice from a long way off appeared now to be always impelling, goading him on, whispering, "Make haste, make haste, the shadows are lengthening so fast they will soon seize upon and swallow you up, and your work is not half done yet." Sunday was James Stanley's happiest day by far; perhaps that is not saying much for its blissfulness. He seemed to have more rest of mind and body on that day, a pause and breathing space between life's sharp battles; it seemed as if the world, the flesh, and the devil found greater difficulty in climbing over the borders of that holy time. They did get in, certainly, sometimes in the shape of Kate Chester's image, but not in such strength as on other days; their power was comparatively feeble and puny. On Sundays he was able to think more and more undisturbedly of his home, not of his shabby cheap lodgings in Thames-street, but of his real home, where his treasure was laid up;[30] where his kin were standing waiting for him, watching

> "the slow door,
> That opening, letting in, lets out no more."[31]

He had clearer visions of it than on toiling work-days. Walking sometimes to church, rapt in high and serious thoughts, he seemed to see in the fleecy clouds the snow-white palaces, the happy seats, where the spirits of the just made perfect were resting, spending the pleasant brief night between Death and Resurrection. Calmly, satisfiedly, they look down on this troublesome world—for eyes so far above can discern that, despite the chaos and the turmoil and the fret, all is rounding to a perfect whole. And then in church, when God's light was streaming, goldenly, through the highest window, pouring over the heads of His martyrs and apostles and prophets, James, poor and sickly, and earth-stained, felt himself lifted up amongst that glorious company; and, through the prayers going up like incense, seemed to hear the harpers harping faintly, far away in the azure

---

30 See Matthew 6: 19-20: "Lay not up for yourselves treasures upon earth, where moth and rust doth corrupt, and where thieves break through and steal: But lay up for yourselves treasures in heaven, where neither moth nor rust doth corrupt, and where thieves do not break through nor steal[.]"
31 Christina Rossetti, "Echo" (1862), ll. 11-12.

distance. But to-day a certain restlessness and disturbance had destroyed the even balance, the delicate equipoise of his spirits. There seemed to be some agency at work hostile to holy, still meditation, to musing on lofty themes. He was not even attending to what he was doing. He had unconsciously passed leniently over one or two very slovenly sentences, and had even let stand one passage which exhibited a specimen of the most undeniably slip-shod English. What had come to him? Had he left undone any duty? Had he neglected to pour balm on any gaping wounds? Had he neglected to warn and rebuke any sinner, and try and turn him from the error of his ways? In his mind he ran over the little events of the past week. No; miserable as were his shortcomings and general inefficiency, he had no overt act of negligence or laziness to reproach himself with. What was the matter with him, then? He could not make it out at all; it puzzled him all the way to church, as he walked soberly along under his umbrella; and, as soon as he was in the reading-desk, his eyes, involuntarily, naturally turned to a pew near the door, where, under two blue bonnets, two pretty faces—one rosy, one pale—were usually to be seen every Sunday morning, with devout gravity written on them. Only one blue bonnet was to be seen, only one pretty face, the rosy one; where was the other, the pale one? Was it the rain that kept Kate away? Impossible! she who was out in all weathers. Was she ill, then? Heaven forbid! This question would pop up every five minutes, hard as he tried to keep it down. It would come in inopportunely in the prayers he was praying so fervently, in the lessons he was reading so reverently and plainly; and then in his sermon he actually lost his place twice, and bungled atrociously over a passage which he had taken particular pains to polish and work up. He would overtake Margaret after service, he resolved, and ask her what had become of her sister? But after service, as ill-luck would have it, the clerk got hold of him, and inflicted on him some long story, which might just as well have been told any other time as that; by the time he was released Margaret was full half way home, and it would not do for him to be seen rushing down the muddy street, with unclerical haste, in hot pursuit of a pretty young woman. Well, if there were anything wrong, he should hear of it to-morrow; till then, he must wait. It would be a good exercise for his patience to have to do so. It was Mr. Stanley's custom to take a solitary walk every Sunday, after his scant dinner. It was his one recreation, and he enjoyed it. He had no idea of foregoing it to-day on account of the rain. He was not sugar or salt to be melted by a few drops of moisture. But instead of betaking himself as usual, by the shortest cut, to the open country and the fields, some instinct prompted him to-day to wander about the villa-dotted roads that formed the suburbs of Queenstown. As he neared the railway station, which stood at the extremity of these suburbs, James's eye was suddenly caught by a female figure approaching him (an unexpected sight, considering the state of the clouds and the road); a female figure, struggling rather unsuccessfully with a big umbrella, which the wind was doing its best to turn inside out—a female figure with a thick veil down over its face, and a blue bonnet, whose shape and hue seemed very familiar to him, on its head. In fact, in this woman he, with a feeling of consternation ludicrously disproportioned to the occasion, recognised the very Kate Chester, about the state of whose health he had been so needlessly concerned. At the same instant guilty Kate recognised him, with a start of almost as horrified fear as that with which backsliding Balaam first perceived the angel with the drawn sword impeding the progress of his God-forbidden journey.[32] Her first impulse was to turn and flee away like the wind, but in a second common sense made her master this instinct. That course would infallibly excite his suspicions more than any other she could possibly adopt, would cause a hue and cry to be raised after her, before she should be beyond the power of any hue and cry to fetch her back again. So she lowered her unruly umbrella as much as she was able, and, trusting in the disguise of her thick veil, endeavoured to pass him without making any sign of recognition. But to no purpose. He stood right in her path, and with wide-eyed astonishment, uttered the monosyllable "Kate!" She could not well *butt* him with her umbrella, nor yet send him spinning off the pavement into the middle of the sloppy street, as she had done, once, on a previous occasion, so she stopped, perforce too, and answered defiantly, "Well?"

"What are you doing out of doors in all this rain?" asks James, plain-spoken in his extreme surprise, pronouncing each word and syllable slowly and emphatically.

"It's something quite new, your condescending to interest yourself in my goings and comings," says Kate, lifting up her head haughtily, evading the question.

"Where *are* you going, Kate?" repeats James, taking no notice of the sneer with which she had endeavoured to free herself from her dilemma.

"What's that to you?" retorts Kate tartly.

32 See Numbers 22: 22-35: Angering God by journeying to the princes of Moab, Balaam encounters an angel, armed with a sword, who blocks his path.

If she can but succeed in insulting him, in putting him on his mettle, in sending him off wrathy and hurt, and so get rid of him. But he was a man slow to anger; very patient under provocation.

"I know it is no business of mine," he answers very gently. "I know it would be the height of impertinence for me to assume any airs of authority over you; but just think how many years I have known you, just think what old friends we are, and I think you'll forgive me."

"O yes, I'll forgive you, of course," answers Kate, who is on thorns the whole time. "It is too wet to stand still. Good-bye;" and she turns, eel-like, to slip by him. But he does not move. He stands there still close in front of her; but a slight barrier, one would say, to look at him; but able to hinder her for a few seconds from hurrying to her ruin.

"Kate," he says eagerly, forced on by some secret impulse, as if a power within him were uttering the words, without his consent, almost against his will,—"Kate, I feel a conviction that you are out on no good to-day. I beg your pardon a thousand times if I do you an injustice, but—but I'd be very grateful if you'd indulge me so far as to tell me where you are going?"

Thus adjured, and driven into a corner, Kate said hesitatingly, with an uncomfortable, unnatural little laugh, "Where am I going? How inquisitive men, and parsons particularly, are! I'm only going for a—for a walk."

"To-day?" interjects James incredulously, looking at the pea-soup fog and the swimming pavement.

"Yes, to-day," answers Kate sharply; "all weathers are the same to me. If I have learned nothing else in that charming district-visiting of mine, I have learnt that."

"Well, then, if you are really going for a walk," replies James, "I suppose I may come with you. I can hold the umbrella over you at least, and save you that trouble;" and as he utters these words he marvels at his own serpent-like subtlety.

Awkward proposition that for that reckless girl, who is looking forward to the meeting with her dark-eyed lover. But her wits do not desert her. "O dear no," she says, with bitter irony, "I could not think of allowing such a thing for your own sake. You had much better keep to your systematic avoidance of me. You know one cannot touch pitch, and not be defiled.[33] I am not fit company for such as you."

That dart was more poisoned than she that sent it knew of. It went

33 A proverb; pitch is a sticky residue of tar.

straight to the heart and festered there. "O Kate, if you only knew," began James passionately, but then he stopped himself. That she should misjudge him, misconstrue his actions, was part of his discipline, his punishment, and he must bear it meekly, must carry his cross without making a cowardly moan about its weight. After a second or two he mastered himself and his pain completely. Very calmly he spoke: "You are deceiving me—I can see that. What your motive can be I cannot imagine, and I do not know why I think so, but I feel convinced that you are not telling me the truth."

"Yes, I am," answers Kate, with a sort of *pseudo*-frankness, "at least almost the truth. I *am* going for a walk, but it is only up to the post-office to put a letter in, and I did not think it worth while to give you the trouble of escorting me, for just these half-dozen yards."

"It would not be any trouble," answers James, determinately persistent,—provokingly so, Kate begins to think. "I should enjoy it. Kate, I'll give you leave to call me a fool. It is a whim, a fancy, I know, but I own that it would make my mind much easier if you would allow me to see you safe home to-day."

"You should not indulge in such fancies," answers Kate uncivilly; "it is quite contrary to your principles. No," she went on, trying to imagine herself aggrieved, and justly aggrieved, by him, "no, you shall not come with me. You think you can take me up and put me down just as you please, and I want to prove the contrary to you."

Still he would not be angry, would not leave her to herself, despite all her rudeness to him. His heart clave to her still, by reason of the great love he bare her. Only he flushed a little, pale-faced as he was.

"You are unjust and unkind, Kate," he said, "and that is not like you. Why do you try to throw dust in my eyes? Is it worth while to perjure your soul for such a wretched, trifling object? Have I ever been so hard and censorious to your faults and failings, that you must needs cover them from me with a lie?"

"No," answered Kate reluctantly, looking down, "you have not." And the rain dripped from the points of her umbrella, and thence to her shawl, down which it streamed and trickled in manifold little rills, as she stood there, half remorseful, half impatient, speculating on the chance of her being late for the train.

"Well, then," he urged, thinking he had gained a point, "won't you trust in me? Won't you let me know what is weighing on your mind? There is something, I know—something that kept you from church this morning.

Two heads are better than one, you know. How do you know that I may not be able to smooth your difficulties, and make it all plain sailing for you?" So he spoke, persuasively, and utterly ignorant of what her difficulties were.

"I have no weight on my soul," she answers, hating and loathing herself, for all these lies she is driven by his importunity to tell. "I have nothing to confide to you. It's all spun out of your own imagination, because you meet me out walking, without any ostensible object, on a wet day. It's very good of you to be so anxious about me, though your anxiety is quite misplaced. Poor, dear, good James, I'm afraid I have not been very polite to you," she adds, compunctiously, laying a light hand on his wet sleeve.

He begins then, for the first time, to remember himself—to fear for himself—begins to doubt whether he is not drawing out this conversation for his own enjoyment and delectation. This ten minutes will, he knows, entail on him a harder, tougher struggle and wrestle with his own strict-governed heart than ever to-night.

"Perhaps it is my fancy," he says, at last, doubtfully. "I have no reason to suspect you, and no business to torment you with my suspicions, if I have them."

"You do not torment me," she replies kindly; "only living so much by yourself you get hipped.[34] I assure you I have no burden on my soul,—at least," she added, laughing slightly, "except the fear that this letter will not get posted in time;" and she half pulled out an old letter she happened to have in her pocket, skilfully covered the broken seal and post-mark. Women can outwit men. Kate had almost lulled James's suspicions to sleep.

"I'll believe you," he said smiling, as if a great weight were taken off his mind. "I'll not bother you with any more of my inquisitive catechism of questions. I'll not even look which way you go."

And, in pursuance of this resolution, he turned away from her, down another muddy rain-immersed road, and plodded along it soberly, under his umbrella, as he had been doing before this unexpected encounter. For about three minutes he trudged on, lost in thought, and then he heard the sound of small, hurrying feet, pattering through the puddles, behind him; then the quick breathing of some one who had run themselves out of breath. He looked round, and behold, come back to him, of her own accord, after having eluded him with so much ingenuity, Kate Chester!

"You did not bid me good-bye," she said, panting, in explanation of

34 Depressed.

her conduct, "and so—and so—I ran after you. I want you to shake hands with me. Good-bye," she went on, as he put out his hand and took hers, "we part friends, do not we? We have not seen much of one another lately, but we have been great friends, have not we, Jemmy? And after this, whatever terrible tales people tell of me—whatever dreadful things you may hear that I have done, O, for the sake of the old days, do not be too hard upon me—don't turn to hate me—for pity's sake don't!"

For the first time he perceived that she was greatly agitated. Through the masking veil he tried to catch a glimpse of her face.

"Kate," he exclaimed very anxiously, "I'm sure I was right. I'm sure you are on the brink of committing some great sin—that you are going to-day to take some step that you can never untake again. I implore of you to tell me what it is."

"No, no," cried Kate incoherently, afraid she had said too much, "I'm not going to take any step. You misunderstand me. I was only speaking generally. You know one never knows what one may be driven to do when one is utterly, entirely hopeless."

"No one can be quite hopeless," replied James, with gentle, earnest chiding, "so long as they are alive on the earth, and within the bounds of God's infinite mercy."

"His mercy is nothing to me," answered Kate, with impatient anguish in her tone, "I'm outside the pale of it."

"Child," cried James, and a look of almost terror flashed over his face at her words, "what makes you utter such insane blasphemy? Who has been putting such wretched pagan ideas into your head? They used not to be there. O, Kate, Kate! drive them out—do not entertain them for a second."

"Easier said than done," answered Kate, with dreary composure. "Nobody has put them into my head; they come of themselves. But, anyhow, I need not tease you with them. I have said my say, so I may as well go."

"No, no, you must not," answered James vehemently; "I dare not leave you to yourself. How do I know what mad things you may do in your present state of mind? How do I know that you may not go to shipwreck altogether, for want of a helping hand to save you?"

"If I did go to shipwreck, as you call it," said Kate gloomily, "who'd care, I wonder? Whose dinner, whose night's rest would it spoil? Maggie might sigh over it for an hour or two, and Blount for a minute or two. That would be about all."

"If nobody in the world cared for you," answered James very solemnly, with a holy awe in his clear-shining, honest eyes, "don't you suppose that it would grieve the dear Lord, who shed out His precious life to save you from eternal shipwreck? Do you never think of Him, Kate?"

"Never!" replied Kate emphatically, with a shudder. "It's only you, and such as you, that can think of Him; as for me, I dare not. I used to be able to once, I remember, especially of a Sunday evening, but I tell you I dare not now."

"Why *now*, particularly?" inquired James, catching at the stress she laid on the word "now." "Have you been doing anything to make you feel yourself shut out from partnership in all good and holy things? O, Kate! what have you been doing? Whatever it is, do not fear to tell me. I'm so weak myself, that I must needs make full allowance for anyone else's weakness."

"Doing?" repeated Kate impatiently, "I've been doing nothing, except what I'm always doing, grumbling and making a fuss about myself, and wishing I was dead. But what do you go on worrying me with your questions for?" she added, with irritation. "You do not believe the answers when I give them you."

"I believe your voice, not your words," answered James gravely, "and they contradict one another."

She made no response for a minute or two. She stood there longing to go—as if obliged to stay—in an agony of doubt. Then to the ears of them silent came the sharp tinkle of a bell at the railway station, the approach of a train, and immediately after the whistle of an engine, some way down the line. Kate came back out of her reverie, with a great start.

"I must go," she said hurriedly. "I shall be late," she added, forgetting who it was that she was addressing.

"Late!" exclaimed James, excessively puzzled, wondering if she had taken leave of her senses, "what for?" Then a new light dawned on him—a dreadful, lurid light. "I see it all," he said hastily. "I see what you meant, bidding me good-bye in that way. You're going somewhere, going off by this train—going away on some fool's errand."

"How dare you make such unwarrantable accusations?" cried Kate, angry and afraid. "You do not seem to have much of the charity that 'thinketh no evil.'"[35]

"Unwarrantable, is it, Kate?" said James slowly, looking at her keenly. "Then why do I see you glancing towards the station, and perpetually

35 See 1 Corinthians 13:5.

watching that train that is coming up with such anxiety?"

The train was drawing inconveniently near—already it had come full into sight, steaming along the line, with all its many carriages, and this train never stopped more than about three minutes at Queenstown. Stop dawdling there five minutes longer and she should be late. In a second she took her resolution. "James," she said, stamping determinedly on the dirty road, splashing, thereby, a good deal of mud up on his coat and her own dress, "I will not stand being baited in this way; and there's an end of it. I am going by that train. I tell you so, plainly. I do not know why I was so cowardly as to tell a lie about it before. And go I will; so if you are thinking of trying to dissuade me, I advise you to keep your breath for a more profitable occupation." And, avoiding further argument, as she thought, she set off walking fast towards the station, which was not fifty yards distant.

James would not leave her in this imminent soul-peril; he must make a last effort to rescue her. Keeping alongside of her, he asked her, with as much sternness as he could ever say anything with, "Kate, I know as well as if you had told me that you are going to meet that man. Tell me where."

"I shall not tell you; it is nothing to you," answered Kate sullenly.

"Child," pursued James, in low, hurried tones, almost suffocated with his excitement, "this is God's own day; is it a day to do devil's work on? Is it a day to kill your own soul, utterly, for ever? In God's name, I command you to desist from this purpose of yours!"

Every word he spoke seemed to stab her; she could have groaned aloud, but she gave no outward sign. She would be firm—she would not give in. Not even James should stop her from going to comfort her poor, lonely Dare. They reached the station, and Kate went into the booking-office, with a firm step, asked for one single first-class ticket to Clapham, got it, and went out on the platform. James stayed a second behind her and got a ticket too. Then an idea struck him. It would soon be time for afternoon service, and he had not provided a substitute for himself. What a hubbub there would be in Queenstown when he should be found absent without leave! But he must not leave this girl to throw herself over this precipice. His first duty was to drag her back. That path lay clear and plain before him. So he called a porter, gave him a verbal message to the rector (he had not time to give a written one), and sent him off with it. Then his mind felt easier, and he followed Kate out. The train was just alongside; there were not many people to get in or out, for the weather was anything but favourable for travelling. He watched Kate pass along, looking for an unoccupied carriage; and as soon as she found one, got in. Then he followed her. As she turned her face and saw him, an expression of horrified astonishment spread over her features. She had not calculated on this move. Once in the train she had imagined herself safe from him.

"What do you mean by dogging me like this?" she asked, with concentrated resentment in her low tones.

"I mean," answered he solemnly, "by God's help, to save you, if I can, from yourself, and from the devils that have got possession of you."

"Give it up," she answered with bitter gloom; "it's too hard a job, even for you."

James came and sat down beside her, and said with forced composure, "Kate, you may as well tell me where you are going to meet this—this man. I shall infallibly find out if you do not."

"O, I don't mind telling you," said Kate recklessly, "it can be no secret now. Everybody will know soon enough. At the Crystal Palace, in the court where the statues are. Is that exact enough for you? And if you choose to come too, of course no one can prevent you, only I warn you that you'll be rather *de trop*!"[36] she ended, with a laugh that sounded rather hysterical.

James was almost struck dumb at the sight of the abyss that was yawning at the very feet of this wretched woman whom he loved so. "Child, child," he cried, and his voice shook in the intensity of his pleading, "have pity on yourself! Do not you see that Satan is putting a mist on your eyes, that you should not see this lover of yours in his true shape—not as the monster of wickedness luring you to destruction that he is?"

"He is nothing of the kind," retorted Kate fiercely. "Don't dare to abuse him to me. He is the only person in the world that cares about me," she went on, with something like a sob. "You and Margaret and Blount have, perhaps, got a feeble sort of liking for me, but he does love me really. Bless him, poor darling!"

The part of this speech in which she alluded to his feeble liking for her nearly upset poor sore-tried James. He, in comparison of whose pure, deep, utterly unselfish love (a love which, well-hidden, was killing him by inches), Dare's mad, wild-beast passion was as a stinking stagnant pond to a leaping, pellucid mountain brook.

"Love you!" he echoed with a certain just scorn; "would a man that really loved as a good man should love a woman drag down the object of

36 Too much, superfluous (French).

his love to disgrace and shame of everlasting pollution?"

"Yes," cried Kate, flashing, "when he knows that she is most willing—for his sake most thankful—to be dragged down to any depths. What are disgrace and shame and pollution, as you call it, to me in comparison to him, I should like to know? Nothing but bugbears to frighten children with—nothing but empty names that have no meaning in them."

So she spoke, boldly, confidently, but her inmost heart said differently. It said, "A lie, a lie!"

"And then when you come to the reckoning," urged James, with the solemn severity of one of God's ministers—one of His vicegerents, whose business it was to reprove and rebuke sin whenever he should meet with it on the earth,—"when you have to pay the price for this mad surfeit of brief pleasures, how will it be then? How will it be when you come to die? Will that wicked man you are going to be able to help, or comfort, or rescue you then?"

"Don't talk of dying," cried Kate, shivering, "I'm young and strong; why should I die?"

"Is it only the old that die?" inquired James very mournfully. "Ah, no; any paper you take up will tell you differently; but even if you live on in your sin to be an old woman, will even that seem a long while? will not it be but as a watch in the night,[37] in comparison of the countless ages of eternity?"

Kate made no answer; she only covered her face with both hands, and rocked backwards and forwards desolately. The stupendous thought of that eternity (a thought which our weak brains can at their best but hardly support the weight of) almost crushed her, guilty, rudderless as she was, to the dust. Then came the low gentle voice again, not scolding, not upbraiding, trying very hard to be calm, but yet wavering a little in spite of itself.

"Kate, I know this is no time to preach to you in, but let me put it plain and clear before you. Is it wise of you to spend this little space that we call life in sowing the seed of everlasting undying torments for yourself? Of your own choice, too, when you might, in this time that is allotted to you, be laying up for yourself treasures unto life eternal in that heaven that will never fade or vanish away? Kate, our dear Lord is standing at the door *now*, begging you, imploring you to come in. O child, you won't turn away to hell!"

---

37 See Psalm 90:4: "For a thousand years in thy sight are but as yesterday when it is past, and as a watch in the night."

He stopped, he could not go on, he was so moved.

Kate sat there motionless; still the hidden face and a sighing sob every now and then.

"Kate," began James again, almost in a whisper, and tears stood full and bright in his eager eyes—eyes with an angel-light in them,—"what shall I say when I see your dead mother again? What shall I say when she asks for her little daughter, the little daughter that she loved so, that she begged me on her death-bed to look after and be an elder brother to? What shall I say to her? O Kate, Kate, I thank God that in His infinite mercy He took away that poor little woman from the evil to come—from seeing this black day. I thank Him from the bottom of my soul!"

Poor Kate, she could not bear that. The mention of her mother at any time made her tears flow freely; how much more now! She pulled out her pocket-handkerchief, threw herself down in the bottom of the railway carriage, and, burying her face in the cushions, wept unrestrainedly, violently,—would have wept her life away if she could. After a while she raised a disfigured haggard face, and said with great difficulty, interrupted and checked over and over again by fast-recurring ungovernable sobs:

"James, if it was only myself I'd give in this minute. I'd go back with you, even now, to the old dreary life, and try to bear it, and be content with it, for *her* sake" (another passionate burst of tears); "but," she went on, "what would he do, what would become of him? You don't know how he loves me," she said, appealing piteously to him. "He is so sad, so terribly desolate and lonely, and he looks so ill and haggard. O, whatever happens, I must go to him,—I must comfort him, poor, poor, darling Dare!"

Again she flung herself down, and shook and quivered in her mighty emotion.

James left her to herself for a few moments; then he touched her gently on the shoulder. "Do you love this man?" he asked very quietly, looking down pityingly on her.

Kate looked up with dim eyes. "Love him!" she echoed, and she almost laughed in her derision of the absurdity of this question. "Ay, better than you, who do not know what love is, can have any conception of. So well, that the only wish I have left on earth is that he would kill me, so that I might die in his dear arms, and get away from this weary world altogether."

With a sharp pang James let pass uncontradicted that random reflection on his incapacity of loving. "Well, then," he said in a low, firm, impressive voice, "if you do love him, love him truly, love him better than yourself and your own gratification, then, most of all, you'll leave him."

"What!" she gasped.

"If you do love him, I say," went on James emphatically, "if his good, his welfare, are of any moment to you, give him up. Don't you see that you are the bait with which Satan is angling for his soul? As long as you are before him, a stumbling-block in his path, he has not a chance of ever coming back to the light. Your love is the chain with which the foul fiends bind him fastest. O child, child, break the links of that chain, I implore you, and you'll set him free and yourself too."

"No, no," cried Kate, very eagerly, "you mistake; you don't know him. I'm the only hope he has in the world, poor fellow. If he loses me he'll go to the bad altogether. He said he would, and he never breaks his word."

"He said that to frighten you," replied James, with a just indignation at Colonel Stamer's cruel, selfish sophistries. "How could he go more to the bad than living in sin with a woman that is not his wife; with the curse on his soul of having changed a girl once pure, and innocent, and walking in God's faith and fear, into what I daren't name to you, Kate? I hate to talk to you on such a subject," he added, with a shocked, disgusted look, "it seems an insult to do it, and yet I must."

Kate was silent for a few moments; almost torn and rent in twain by the two powers of good and evil that were fighting and hard on the narrow battle-field of her sick soul.

Then she spoke with livid lips. "If it is for his good—O, don't deceive me, and tell me it is, when it is not; don't mislead me from some mistaken idea of doing me good. But if it is for his good—if you put it in that way, I'd do anything—you know I would; I'd do anything in the world for him. O, my love, my love!" Such an exceeding great and bitter cry.

"Then leave him," urged James, with thrilling earnestness, "give him up! Come home with me, and pray and agonise against this wretched, wicked love, that is desolating your life. Lift up your poor heart to that higher, purer, more satisfying love, that is open to us all. O, Kate, give him up, give him up!"

"Even if I do consent to give him up," said Kate, fighting with a storm of tears, —"O God, I cannot, I cannot!"

James would not spare her now. It was the decisive moment, and a second's hesitation might lose her for ever. "You *must*, Kate," he said solemnly, "even if you have the heart to soil and sully the good old name that your poor father tried to keep so clean and bright—even if you have the heart to mar and spoil your brother's and sister's future by your shame—even if you dare to do this great sin against God, by your love to that man I charge you to give him up, and never see his face again. It is the strongest proof of love that will ever be asked of you. Will you shrink from this thing, Kate, hard as it is, or will you do it?"

"Yes, yes," cried Kate, violently excited, almost incoherent, "I'll do it for his sake, as you say. O, poor Dare, poor fellow! But even then," she went on hurriedly, catching at this last straw, "I must see him once again, to tell him so. O, James," she said, appealing to him piteously, with her haggard eyes, "I never said good-bye to him yesterday; just think of that. O, I must see him once again. Don't say no to me; I must hear his voice just once again, that I may have something to live upon afterwards."

"Heaven forbid!" said James quickly, in horror at this mad proposition. "What! thrust your head between the lion's jaws of your own accord? a wise idea, indeed! No, Kate, be a brave girl. Don't palter with this temptation—it is a frightfully strong one, I see. Cast it utterly behind you, and beg of our God (He is very gracious and pitiful) to give you strength to outlive this fiery trial."

Kate struggled up from her crouching attitude in a staggering sort of way, clutched hold of his arm as if for support, and said dazedly, "I—I don't quite understand you. Do you mean to say that I am *never* to see him again—that after all we have been to each other I'm to have nothing more to say to him?"

James took her hand with a brother's tenderness. "Yes," he said very sorrowfully, but resolutely. "Kate, I pity you more than I ever pitied man or woman before, but still I say yes. Poor child," he went on compassionately, "you're blinded and confused now, and are not fit to judge for yourself. Won't you trust in an old friend like me? Won't you believe me when I tell you solemnly that it's the only thing you can do now?"

"Yes, yes," cried Kate with tearful incoherence, "I'd trust you; I'll do whatever you tell me. But, Jemmy, I do so *long* to see him once again, just for five minutes, to tell him how I love him—I was very unkind and rude to him yesterday; I hate myself for it now—to tell him that I'll never forget him as long as I live, and that it's only for his own good that I am keeping away from him. James, you're not a hard-hearted, cruel man I know,—you'll let me do just that much. I shall go mad if you don't."

"No, you won't," said James, trying gently to soothe her; "God will give you strength to endure; I'm confident of that, Kate," he went on with an intensity of earnestness in his tones; "I know of old that you are not one of those feeble, weak-souled women who wince and shrink away from a little pain. Make up your mind to face this ordeal bravely; and you'll come through it yet, safe and pure, for the sake of the poor dead mother who is watching and waiting for you—for the sake of the Lord who laid down His Deity in such unutterable agonies to save you."

The Lord he spoke of gave him strength to conquer. By his words he vanquished and subdued her utterly.

"There," she said hoarsely, "say no more, you may stop; I'll go home with you, and you may do whatever you choose with me. Only do not say anything more to me, just now, please; leave me in peace that I may face my despair."

So he left her in peace. A few minutes more and the train stopped. James almost lifted Kate out, for she was like a log upon his hands, and with some difficulty helped her to a bench. There she sank down, motionless, nerveless, almost senseless. James was frightened out of his wits. In saving her soul had he killed her body? He rushed off to the refreshment-room for a glass of water; came back quickly to her with it, and put it to her pale lips. But she pushed it away feebly. She *would* not faint or go into hysterics. She never had done either in the course of her life, and would not begin now. So by a great effort of the strong will, she got the better of a great inclination to tumble off the bench in a swoon; slowly lifted her eyes, dizzy and swimming to his anxious face, and said with difficulty, "No, thank you, Jemmy, I do not want it."

By the next train Mr. Stanley and Miss Catherine Chester returned to Queenstown. All the way back, Kate sat staring, vacant-eyed, apathetic, out of the window, at the quick-passing landscape, not seeing one inch of it—like a woman on whom a stunning blow had just fallen, numbing her senses, like one whose last hope in this world was extinct.

CHAPTER III

PEOPLE cannot indulge in such frantic emotions as I have tried weakly to portray in the last chapter without paying for them—paying a good price too. Nature will avenge herself on those who maltreat her so uncalculatingly. For the second time in her life, Kate was struck down by a violent brain-fever. Again for weeks and weeks she lay, hovering on the ill-defined borders of life and death, in a sort of debatable land that hardly belonged to either. Again, in delirious frenzies, she raved about her for-ever-lost Dare; imagined that he was in the next room; that they were keeping him from her; flung herself about, and fought violently, wildly, with her attendants to get to him. Again, after a long, weary interval, she struggled back into full consciousness, woke up from her fevered dreams, and saw her

"Set gray life"[38]

in its own dull colours—the colours it would always wear henceforth.

After a person has been as much pulled down as Kate had, it takes some time to build them up again. It was by almost imperceptible degrees that she seemed to creep back to health; but, for all that, creep back she did, surely and safely. The summons had not gone forth for her yet. For many a long hour and day she lay on the green sofa by the fire, wrapped in a white dressing-gown that was hardly whiter than her face, with her great eyes bigger than ever, now full of dreamy, vague speculations. Almost listlessly she thought of Dare, this weary sickness of hers seemed to have interposed such a deep gulf between him and her. Sometimes she thought that she had lost the power of feeling anything; that nothing could any more move her to tears or laughter; that she had used up all her stock of feeling in those two horrible days, that she would gladly have blotted out of her remembrance altogether. Then, too, she used to plan and portion out and plot her future life, making many a resolution which she was as yet too weak to carry out. Sometimes Margaret, or the old servant that had nursed her twenty years ago, would come softly into the still room, would speak gently to her, ask her how she did, and whether she wanted anything, stoop down and kiss her, perhaps, and then go out again as softly, for fear of disturbing her. James came, too, to see her very often, sat by her, and read chapters and bits out of the Bible to her, and sometimes she would listen and say, "Thank you," very gravely, at the end; sometimes her thoughts would wander off, weakly straying away

"To other scenes and other days,"[39]

or she would drop asleep, and only wake to find him going; and to scold herself for her self-indulgence and ingratitude to him.

38 Tennyson, "Love and Duty" (1842), l. 18.
39 Lord Macaulay, "The Marriage of Tirzah and Ahirad" (1827), l. 161.

It was the end of February, and the cuckoo-flowers were beginning to blossom out shyly in the damp green water meadows away down in the country, before she was able to walk about the house in her old, elastic, springy way, before she was restored to full glowing health, before she was quite the same girl that she had been before her seizure. *The same girl*—that is to say, solely as regarded bodily conditions, for as in everything relating to her mental and moral part, it was soon patent to all her friends that she was not by any means the same girl that she had been. There had come upon her a new kind of austerity, a sort of hardness, which, had she been of a different faith, would have made her relish, almost enjoy, the severities and mortifications of such a convent as that of the Perpetual Adoration.[40] She had lost all belief, all confidence in herself. Since that last passage in her history, she believed herself capable of any crime. What security had she that, in some fresh access of insanity, she might not hurl herself upon ruin, when no one should be by to pull her back? No reins, she considered, could be too strait and tight to curb and check so untamed a soul, no manacles too heavy and close to fetter it. In her convalescence, as soon as jealously-guarding nurses allowed her to make any exertion, to be left to herself for ten minutes—with eager haste she had put away out of her sight, without one regretful sigh, those gay garments with which she had been wont to heighten her beauty; those simple little ornaments with which she had decked her fair neck and round arms of yore. She had done for ever with the flowers and jewels of life; the thorns must be her portion now, and she would wear them crownwise, round her brows, and not clamour or complain about the blood they drew. On her past harmless coquetries she looked back as on so many deadly sins, and she could hardly be persuaded to speak civilly to George Chester, because he was connected in her mind with passages of her life, which seemed to her of inexcusable folly and fatuity. It was evident that this exaggerated strictness, sprung from a morbid remorse, could not last. It was only the rebound from her former recklessness. Any one could see that this girl was in a state of transition, though transition to what remained to be proved. Then as to her parish-visiting, and ministering to the sick and needy; formerly, she had gone about this in a very lazy, capricious, dilletante sort of way, tripping about on her errands of mercy, daintily dressed, scattering about, helter-skelter, tracts and

40 Refuge for a time to Jean Valjean and his ward Cosette in Victor Hugo's *Les Miserables* (1862), the Bernardine convent of the Perpetual Adoration is a Gothic horror-show of penitential practices.

religious books, which she had been in the habit of turning into the most complete and thorough ridicule. She had allowed herself, too, to have favourites among her people, partialities and aversions; and had also thought herself at liberty to avoid dens and holes, where churls lurked, and stenches ramped, unreproved. Then, when she got home, she would devise some becoming new headdress, would practise some soft little plaintive song, or prepare one or other of the small traps in which she limed that shy bird, man, so successfully. Oftenest of all she would meet George Chester on her homeward way; would carry on a brisk trade in sentimentalities, as she dawdled along with him, and after leaving, would feel mildly elevated at the thought of having done a little mischief. How different it was now! Heart and soul, with all the energies of her body, and all the faculties of her mind, she went into that work, with which she had formerly trifled and played. Her great object appeared to be, that no second of her life should be without occupation. She could not be too ceaselessly busy to keep thought at bay. It was only the happy and innocent, she used to say, that dare sit down with folded hands and be idle. She took James for her model now; and strove emulously to pull in the same yoke with him. Women are always in extremes; impetuous, passionate women like Kate, more especially so. No earthly power could get her now to go out to any parties, to make any calls, or pay any of the duties people owe to society. She was not fit to go into society, she would answer gloomily, when urged on this point. If people knew the sort of girl she was, they would not receive her into their houses. A system of flagellation, and fasting five days a week, hair-shirt,[41] &c., would have appeared to her distempered imagination much more suited to her case than any meeting of light-hearted, glad friends. She seemed to think that she could not possibly make her present life too different from her past one. "You're going regularly through the stages of a Frenchwoman's life," Margaret said, one day laughing to her, "*coquette, prude, dévotée*,[42] only I think you are running the last two into one." Margaret kept religiously to the first. "How different those two sisters are to be sure! no one would take them for sisters." People made that remark, apropros of the Chesters, very often in those days. Different! I should think they were. As different as summer and winter, as sunrise and sunset, as death and life; as differ-

41 A coarse garment made of animal hair, worn next to the skin for penance.
42 French terms for stereotypical phases of a woman's life: a coquette is a flirt, a prude has the same meaning it does in English, and a dévotée, or devoted one, is a religious fanatic.

ent as any two things most opposed to each other in the world. Margaret had made several acquaintances of late; had found reason to modify her unflattering opinion of Queenstown; after all, it was no worse than other places. Beauty was rather at a premium there this winter, which perhaps accounted for the fact of Margaret being received with such open arms in the drawing-rooms of all the green-blinded stucco villas and lodges and houses. It is a well-known fact that when the moon is not up, the stars shine bright. Now that the moon—to wit, pale Kate—had voluntarily withdrawn herself, that fair star, her sister, had a chance of showing any lustre she might possess. And a fair star she was, shining with a clear, modest, wholesome light, that cheered and illumined, though it did not dazzle. One or two adventurous individuals succeeded in getting up half-a-dozen balls and soirées[43] in these bleak months; and on these occasions Miss Chester made quite a sensation. Numberless gentlemen appertaining to the War Office, the Treasury, &c. &c., never seen in daylight without the encumbrance of disfiguring black bags, at night, freed from these impediments, whispered soft nothings to her under the gaslights. Yes, all was smooth and smiling before her, though it was only little trifles that made it so.

With no great grief cold at her heart, with no evil deed on her soul, with a pleasant face, a fairly quick wit, and a sweet temper, as women's tempers go—what more could a young woman want? But this young woman had her annoyances and grievances too, though she did not kick and scream about them. She was not by any means sure that the romance of her life would end happily, though perhaps nobody might find out that there was anything particularly tragic about it. The hero of it had not as yet behaved in so satisfactory a manner as the heroes of any of the dog-eared novels at the circulating library. The four Chester girls (they always congratulated themselves on being four, because their friends could not call them the Graces)[44] fired many small arrows of good-humoured ridicule at Kate, on her first entering upon her new *rôle*. They thought it only a passing whim that she could be easily laughed out of. But they might as well have aimed their darts at the tough hide of a hippopotamus. So they found out ere long; and, being sensible, good-natured young women, went their own way, and let her go hers unmolested; even helping her now and again with old clothes and broken meats for those poor folk in the tendance of whom she was now so completely wrapped up, to all appearance at least.

43 Evening parties (French).

44 See p. 114, n. 152; the mythic Graces were a threesome.

And James—how did this new phase in Kate's history affect him? What was he doing now? How was he getting on? Doing? He was doing what one told us all to do many, many years ago—what very few of us do—"crucifying the flesh with the affections and lusts."[45] Getting on very surely and bravely with his work; feeling somehow (now particularly after having been permitted to rescue Kate) that it was more than three parts done, though the battle still seemed at is hottest. Getting on so as not to be taken unawares by the Great Reaper, whose harvesting time is all seasons of the year. And did he keep to his old line of conduct, and eschew Kate's society—keep clear of her in her sore need? Not he. That would not have been like him. He saw plain that *now* duty led him towards her; and wherever the pilot star of duty shone, there he would do his best to follow it, even if it led him over quaking morasses and through thorny brakes. Hand in hand, like brother and sister, they went forth to that labour they had set themselves; there would never be any estrangement between them again. Every day they were together, often for hours, and yet no one ventured to mention the name of marriage or love-making in connection with them.

It was twenty times harder now for James to contend against that old enemy, his single-hearted devotion to Kate, than ever before, when, by the aid of his system of absenting himself, he had nothing but memory and imagination to torment and harass him. Now, every day a thousand little trifles—almost invisible, imperceptible, singly, but together an armed host—fed and nourished his deep affection. Kate was not the same girl either that she had been—not the gay, sparkling, witty Kate Chester, who had seemed a being of another sphere. Now she was grave and mournful like himself; far graver and more mournful indeed; for as yet there was no serenity, no restfulness in her melancholy. How he longed often to be able to say something that would comfort her; would bring back the old smile to the set white features! I think her religion did not make her happy. No one ever heard her joking now, or making little witticisms; very seldom she laughed. Perhaps it might have been said, as of another, with truth—

"One face, remembering his, forgot to smile."[46]

Since the service James had rendered her (sometimes even now she

45 See Galatians 5:24: "And they that are Christ's have crucified the flesh with its affections and lusts."

46 Owen Meredith (E. R. Bulwer-Lytton), *Tannhäuser* (1861), l. 327.

caught herself longing that he had not rendered it; longing sickly to have Dare back at any price)—since then, I say, she had trusted in him wholly, had leaned on him, had gone to him in all her difficulties; called him her dear, good, old Jemmy—her one friend; had laid bare her whole heart before him. It was very, very hard for him to keep his great love out of every word and look; but, hard as it was, he did it. Not once, while life and strength gave him power to conceal it, did she guess at its existence.

"'Tis a month before the month of May,
And the spring comes slowly up this way,"—[47]

came up, not borne on the strong winds of loud, blustering, health-giving March winds; not lit by a broad-faced, jocund, spring sun; but creeping in with fog and rotting mist, and low-hanging clouds and ceaseless rain, bearing malaria in its wet bosom.[48]

One afternoon Margaret Chester, returning from an almost diurnal visit to her cousins at Grove House, came hastily up the stairs and into the drawing-room of their own little cottage. Here she found Kate sitting by the table, leaning her head on her hand; for a wonder, doing nothing. She flung herself down into an arm-chair, pulling off her hat, and said impatiently:

"There's no use talking—I cannot bear it much longer."

"What?" asked Kate, looking up, heavy-eyed.

"Why, this fever, to be sure; it's spreading like the plague."

"Ah!" said Kate.

"The Chesters have just been telling me," continued Maggie, "that that wine-merchant's daughter in Queenstown—that pretty girl that George pointed out to us one day—is just dead of it."

"Is she really?" said Kate, with a shocked intonation of voice.

"Yes, indeed," replied Margaret. "She was quite well the day before

47 Samuel Taylor Coleridge, "Christabel" (1816), ll. 21-22.

48 See p. 188, n. 49 on the miasmatic theory that attributed the spread of contagion to noxious vapors, especially those caused by decomposing matter (note the "rotting mist" here). The name of the disease that strikes Queenstown—malaria—in fact means "bad air" in Italian, which suggests that Broughton's choice of this particular ailment may be more symbolic than realistic. Though malaria (traditionally known as "ague") was not unknown in England, the virulence of the Queenstown epidemic is more characteristic of the cholera outbreaks, caused by fecal contamination of water, that periodically struck Victorian cities.

yesterday, walking about on the Parade,[49] and last night she was dead."

"Poor thing!" murmured Kate softly. "It was a sudden message she had sent her."

"It will get into your district next," went on Margaret very discontentedly; "as sure as possible it will; those low, crowded parts so close to the river-side."

"Two cases have broken out there already," remarked Kate quietly; "so I found out to-day. I did not know it before I went there."

Margaret jumped up in a second, and put the length of the room between them.

"And you have actually come back here," she said, with horror, "to bring infection to me! I never heard anything so inhuman."

"I knew you would be in a dreadful fright," answered Kate, almost smiling in her slight scorn; "so I took the precaution of changing all my clothes."

"Of course you'll not go near them again, now you do know," proceeded Margaret, a little reassured by this information. "You could not be so mad."

"I'll take a lodging in Queenstown if you like," replied Kate, pushing her hair wearily off her low, wide brow. "Indeed I think I had better, on account of you and the servants; but I certainly could not be so cowardly as to desert them, poor creatures, now of all times, when they want me so much more than ever."

"I do not know what people mean by throwing away their lives in such a way," grumbled Margaret, angry with the fever, angry with the people who had caught the fever, angry with Kate, angry with everything and everybody. "It would be all very well to be so prodigal if one had two or three lives to spend."

"Two or three lives!" exclaimed Kate involuntarily. "What a frightful idea!"

"Why, I'd have twenty, if I could, or twenty times twenty," said Margaret, with animation.

"And I would never have had half a one if I had had the choice," answered Kate gloomily.

Silence then for a few minutes. Kate leaning her elbow listlessly on the table, still fiddling, white-fingered, with Dare's locket (the one last remnant

49 Public square or promenade.

of him that she could not tear from her heart even yet). Margaret tapping her foot impatiently on the floor, flinging eau-de-Cologne in a wide circle all round her, as a sort of disinfective. Then she spoke again in a fume:

"It is getting nearer every day; why it is not a hundred yards from our own door now!" and she wrung her hands in her panic.

"To every man upon this earth
Death cometh soon or late,"[50]

said Kate, with serious composure.

"Everybody is leaving the place but us; everybody except the doctors and the undertakers," continued poor Margaret.

"O," said Kate.

"The Chesters are going Monday week; they cannot get off sooner, or they would," went on Maggie again; "going down to stay with an aunt of theirs in Kent."

"Are they?" said Kate indifferently.

"I wish to goodness I was going with them," cried Margaret, exasperated at the little impression her pieces of news made.

"It is a great pity that you cannot induce them to ask you," replied Kate drily.

"Ah, but they have," said her sister triumphantly. "They did to-day, all of them—begged me."

"And why on earth did not you say yes?" asked Kate, opening her large eyes in mild surprise.

"O, because I would not settle anything till I had seen you," returned Maggie.

"Seen me?"

"Yes, they want you to come too; they told me to tell you so; and you will, won't you?" Maggie, as she spoke, came over to the table, and put her hand pleadingly on Kate's shoulder.

"No, I shall stay here," answered Kate quietly.

Not much use to try and move her when she spoke in that tone; as well try to lift up one of the old recumbent giant blocks at antiquity-defying Stonehenge[51] with your finger and thumb.

50 Thomas Babington Macaulay, "Horatius" in *Lays of Ancient Rome* (1842), ll. 220-21.

51 Around five thousand years old, Stonehenge, a circle of columnar stones near

"And catch the fever," suggested Miss Chester, aghast.

"Well?" said Kate, shrugging her shoulders in the old devil-may-care fashion.

"And die of it," proceeded Maggie, trying to add blackness to the picture she was painting.

"I do not suppose it is a particularly painful death," said Kate indifferently. "I suppose it is only that you are very hot, and troublesome, and noisy, for two or three days, and then very cold, and very peaceable, and silent for ever."

"Ah, it is all very fine to be so stoical about it now," cried Maggie indignantly; "but let it come close to you, it will be the old fable of the old man carrying the bundle of fagots.[52] You would not be so *nonchalant* then."

"Perhaps not," said Kate calmly; but to her own heart she said that to her death would be "like a friend's voice, from a distant field, calling."[53]

A few more days went by, cheerless, as if a curse had fallen upon those fair fat Thames banks. Fed by the fog, and the river mist, and the warm drizzle, the fever shot up like a tropical plant, from an infant into a full-grown giant. Scorching, livid-faced, it stalked and ramped stealthily among the reeking crowded courts and alleys. In and out of the red-roofed old houses went Death, laying a finger upon such as he chose for himself, as a woodman walks through the forest, marking the trees that must fall beneath his axe. One evening Kate returned very late, past seven o'clock, and came into the room, after a long day's work, languidly, very white-faced, very grave, very tired. Margaret was already dressed for dinner, lounging in an arm-chair by the fire, trying to read, but unable, through the fast-coming thoughts that pressed on her brain.

"Kate, it really is too bad of you," she began fretfully, as her sister entered; then she broke off suddenly, "Good gracious, child, how ill you look!"

"I'm not ill," answered Kate rather faintly, tumbling down on the sofa; "I'm only rather knocked up, and headachy, after being so long in those close stuffy rooms."

"You'll be catching your death in your absurd quixotism, as sure as you sit there," cried Maggie, sitting upright in her chair, with glowing cheeks

---

modern-day Salisbury, is the most famous prehistoric monument in Britain.

52 Fable in which an exhausted old man carrying a heavy load of wood wishes to die, but hastily changes his mind when Death actually appears.

53 Tennyson, "Lancelot and Elaine," in *Idylls of the King* (1859), ll. 999-1000.

and eager eyes.

"Catch a fiddlestick," said Kate rather crossly, from among the cushions, for she had heard something like this once or twice before.

"Well, all I can tell you is that every soul is leaving this pestiferous place," said Maggie warmly. "Only an hour ago I met Mrs. Walton, and she told me they were as busy as possible packing up, to be off to-morrow."

Kate rose up suddenly, and stood by the fire.

"Maggie," she said resolutely, "you shall go too. You are miserable here, and there's nothing to keep you. You shall go."

"What! and leave you?" interjected Maggie.

"Yes; you shall go down into Kent with the Chesters, on Monday. You know you will be as happy as the day is long with them; and the country air will do you no end of good, and—George will be there." So she ended, with a slight, good-natured smile. To herself she appeared now about a hundred years old; felt quite a grandmotherly interest—or rather, perhaps the interest that a disembodied spirit looking down from above might be allowed to feel—in her elder sister's heartaches and love troubles.

"And you?" asked Margaret, with a pleased blush.

"O, I shall do very well," answered Kate lightly.

"If you can do very well here," persisted Margaret, "of course I can too."

"No," said Kate, "that does not follow. I have not got that horror and dread of this complaint that you have, so I'm safer than you, for that predisposes a person to catch it. No, say no more about it, go you shall; I've settled that."

"But," remonstrated Margaret, "suppose you were to be laid up here, all alone, with not a creature near you, how desolate you would be! Just fancy?"

"I shall not be laid up," answered Kate confidently; "at least I do not feel as if I should. Why, I have only just tumbled out of one fever, and it is not very likely I should tumble into another immediately afterwards. However, if I do, I do, and there's an end of it."

The Miss Chesters were not demonstrative in their affection towards one another, but now Margaret came over to her sister and kissed her. "Kate," she said, in a pained voice, "you're so young and so pretty. Why do you care so little about living? It's very sad to see you now, after what I remember you."

"And yet I would not have the old days back if I could," said Kate, shaking her head.

"What! not the old days, when we played with the doll's house, and had bread-and-treacle in the nursery, and planned what we should do when we grew up?"

"No," replied Kate firmly. "Johnson always said that there was not a week in his life that he would have over again,[54] and I agree with him, only I go farther. I say that there is not a day nor an hour in my life that I would have over again."

"What! do you mean to say that you would not have it over again, to be spent exactly as you did spend it; or that you would not have it, even if, with the advantage of your present experience, you might be allowed to spend it differently?"

"O, I don't know about that," said Kate thoughtfully. "It would be a great gift if one could be allowed to put one's remorse and repentance into action. It is its utter futility which is the great sting of remorse; that's its essence indeed. Good heavens! how differently I'd live my life if it were to be given into my hands again!:

"You're not singular in that," said Maggie, sighing; "I expect we all feel that, more or less."

"How different I'd be to mamma," went on Kate, looking very sadly into the fire, "if God would give her back to me—at least I think so now. I daresay if I had her again I should be just as undeserving of her as I was in the old days."

"Kate, Kate, you're getting morbid with the dreadful life you're leading," cried her sister, pained. "You'll send yourself melancholy mad if you feed upon such thoughts."

Kate did not heed her.

"I lie awake so often at night," she said softly, with the tears coming dimly into her eyes, "thinking how I long to see her, if only for a minute, to tell her how sorry I am; to tell her how I miss her."

"She knows, I'm sure," said Margaret earnestly, "without your telling."

"No, she does not," answered Kate despondently. "I am certain she is not permitted to know anything about me. It would mar her perfect beatitude if she were. I'm not the same girl she left me."

"You're a much better girl," said her sister stoutly; "you're too good by half, I think. But what is the use of dwelling on such gloomy themes? 'Let

54 Samuel Johnson (1709-89), essayist, poet, and lexicographer.

the dead past bury its dead.'[55] It is the present we have to do with, and quite enough, too, I think."

"Yes, that's true enough," Kate answered with dejected acquiescence; and she went on gazing into the fire, as though she could read her future history in its little flaming chambers. Then, after an interval, she spoke suddenly, "Maggie, I'm going to make my will."

"What! at two-and-twenty, and outlive all your legatees! Absurd!" said her sister derisively.

"It seems to me that people die full as often at twenty-two as at seventy-two. What is that song I so often hear you singing, about the reaper whose name is Death, that

> 'Reaps the bearded grain at a breath,
> And the flowers that grow between'?[56]

I think the flowers are the easiest mown down of the two."

But Margaret pooh-poohed it.

"It is the exception, not the rule. It is contrary to the course of nature."

"Very likely; but you know we are not a long-lived family. A white-headed Chester is rather an anomaly. And judge for yourself. Do I look a woman likely to last into the *eighties*? I live too quick to live long. Why, even now I'm not unlike a corpse set upright on a chair. I should have done for a *memento mori* at an Egyptian feast."[57]

"Stuff and nonsense!" said her sister indignantly.

"Yes, I should; but that's neither here nor there. What I wanted to say to you is, that I should be very much obliged to you if you would not try any longer to dissuade me from this way of life I have taken to. It'll do no good."

"I cannot help it," said Margaret, "it seems so unnatural."

"I wonder you cannot see that it is the only course of life for me to take to now. I feel that. It is the only thing that keeps me from some great crime. I'm so enormously wicked, that unless I'm bound hand and foot, I'm sure to rush to my ruin, as I have been so near doing twice already."

"But it seems such a throwing away of yourself."

---

55 Henry Wadsworth Longfellow, "A Psalm of Life" (1839), l. 22.

56 Henry Wadsworth Longfellow, "The Reaper and the Flowers" (1839), ll. 3-4.

57 An ancient Egyptian custom of displaying a replica of a mummy at feasts to remind guests of their mortality.

"I'm thrown away already. I've done that for myself. I am done for altogether. But even if I were not, there could be no throwing away of oneself in making it one's prime object to take the kingdom of heaven by violence. It's the only way I shall ever take it, if I do."

"I do not see how you would not have every bit as good a chance of getting to heaven without cutting yourself off from all your relations and old friends and ways of life, without isolating yourself so completely." Thus Margaret spoke with a certain sisterly anger.

"Why, Maggie, even if I did not isolate myself, as you call it, circumstances would soon do it for me."

"How do you mean?"

"Why, before long I shall stand quite alone in the world—rather remarkably so for so young a woman. I shall have a sort of premature old maid's fate come upon me."

"Why?"

"Why, indeed! How can you ask? Just look at Blount. What am I now to him in comparison of what I used to be? Now that he's in the army, and has got new interests, new friends, new views altogether, what is a sister's society to him? I shall see him, I suppose, henceforth for a week at a time occasionally, like any other friend. That will be all. It seems to me that all the ties of my childhood, all the links that bind me to the dear old days when I was so happy, when I used to look forward to such a different future, are falling away from me as fast as they can."

"And, meanwhile, what am I to be doing?"

"O, you'll marry, of course. Ah! you may shake your head; but you will. It's the natural order of things. And you'll have children growing up about you, making you very happy and very miserable; you'll get matronly and staid and careworn, when I have been lying for many a long day in some quiet churchyard (not here, I hope—I hate town churchyards—but somewhere away down in the country), in a green grave, all by myself. And perhaps you'll have a Kate among your children, and will fancy sometimes that her eyes or her hair or her smile are like the sister's that's gone. I feel so weak to-night; I could cry over my own maunder; shed tears of feeble self-pity at my own tomb. Maggie, you will be a happy woman, there's no doubt of that."

"Great doubt, I think."

"You'll marry George Chester; I know that. Not just yet, perhaps, but all in good time. And you'll make him much happier than I could ever have done—I, whose love is a curse, not a blessing; and he deserves to be happy. He is a good, brave, honest gentleman."

"Never, never!"

"And before you do marry and leave me, I want to arrange my few little affairs, make my will, and that sort of thing, so that there may be nothing to hinder me in the execution of a project which I have in my head."

"What is it?"

"O, you'll know soon enough. It would be premature to explain it now."

"I hope it is that you intend to marry someone yourself. You're too bewitching—though I'm not much in the habit of paying you compliments too; formed for sending men wild about you—to be left to 'braid St. Catherine's tresses.'"[58]

"It's nothing about marrying. The word 'marry' might be erased from the dictionary, from existence, for all it will ever have to say to me. No. Don't ask me any more questions. I won't tell you anything about it now."

And so the subject dropped.

On the day but one after, Miss Chester, after many futile entreaties to her sister to go with her, took her departure from Cadogan-place. Went away jubilant with her cousins from the fog, and the fever, and the ever new stories of dying people, and the frequent funerals; off into the breezy country to damson-trees in blossom, and larks singing their hearts out, and all the other delights of showery, feathery April. Kate went with her to the hall-door, bid her good-bye very calmly (Maggie, by the bye, cried a little, the circumstances of this parting being peculiar, and rather impressive), and then went back slowly to the drawing-room, feeling, despite herself, rather lonely and deserted; obliged to acknowledge that, whatever she might say to the contrary, there was yet left in her a capacity for being bored. She drew a chair to the fire, thanked Providence mentally that Tip was not afraid of infection, but still sat there winking gravely as of yore, stroked his white head, and prepared to indulge in a quarter of an hour's musings before she set off on her afternoon's labours. Away she drifted into a sea of thought; but punctually at the end of the quarter of an hour she drew her soul back again from the regions of fancy into the chill land of reality, jumped up without giving herself a moment's law, put on her out-door things, and, laden with her usual supply of beef-tea and jelly and cool drinks, went forth bravely to her unsavoury work. At one of

58 Henry Wadsworth Longfellow, *Evangeline* (1847), II.i.48; the phrase refers to a woman who does not marry (St. Catherine is the patron saint of virginity).

the plague-stricken houses she met James Stanley (these were the sort of scenes that were always throwing them together now), and after a brief conversation, despite all his anxious remonstrances, she resolved on and declared her resolution of staying there all night, watching beside the sick man, so that his poor worn-out wife might get a little respite and refreshment in sleep.

"Why should I spare myself?" she asked, in answer to his objection, looking up with her large sad eyes. "Have not I got youth and strength? What were they given me for but to use? How do I know how long they may be left to me?"

"Youth and strength are great gifts, Kate, not to be lightly thrown away. Don't be extravagant of them. Husband them, that you may not wake up some day to find yourself bankrupt in them."

"They'll last my time, James; but I'm not wasting them. I'm spending them very economically. How often have you told me yourself that one can never waste anything in God's service?"

He could not answer her to that. That speech was so much after his own heart—in his own style. This was the first occasion on which Kate stayed out all night. Hitherto, hard as she had worked, she had always gone home in the evening, her sister's presence had necessitated that; but now that she was gone, there was nothing to prevent Kate wearing herself out as fast as ever she chose. There was no mother or kinswoman to hinder her. So all through the watches of that long night she kept her dreary vigil in a little squalid room, lit by one flaring tallow-candle, alone with a dying man. It was a great ordeal for a delicately-nurtured young girl, and she certainly was very much frightened, particularly at first. Superstitiously she fancied that she heard death-watches ticking;[59] one minute gave a violent start of fright, because her patient moaned or moved uneasily, dreading lest he should become violently delirious, struggle and fight, as she had seen people do in such paroxysms (she a weak woman all alone there to cope with him); the next minute longed for him to stir, to do anything to break the awful stillness, to prove that he was not dead. Then she tried to read the Bible, turned to the most comforting soothing parts (the grand denunciations of the Prophets would have set her mad in her present frame of mind); but the lines danced up and down, swam before her eyes in the dim

59 Associated with death-bed vigils, the ticking sound made at night by the death watch beetle as it chews the wood of old houses was superstitiously taken as a death omen.

light of the one guttering tallow-candle, and the words knocked at the door of her brain in vain, and found no admission. Next she became arithmetical, counted every single thing in the room, multiplied the bedposts by the rungs and legs of the two rickety chairs, and subtracted them all from the drab-and-yellow squares of the tattered paper: that really took some time doing, and was not uninteresting.

Morning came dawdling in at last, and the slipshod rag-wife came back and resumed the care of her lord, and Kate—good, religious, miserable, sleepy Kate—went home by the chill gray river, and did not throw herself in as a present to the fish, though sorely disposed so to do.

CHAPTER IV

SPRING is one of the best things this world has to show us. No doubt of that, I think. We do not need all the poets that have written—from Homer, the morning star of song, downwards generally, nor Thomson in particular[60]—to tell us that. It is a good gift, even when one possesses it only in a dull London square, walled in with tall smoke-blackened houses, with only a few dingy trees in the middle, which the dust turns brown as soon as ever they have attempted to put on their green mantle, and perhaps one or two crippled-looking laburnums that refresh the passer's eye with their

"Dropping wells of fire."[61]

Spring is desirable, joy-bringing, even in the suburban villa. Not even stucco and cockneyism can rob her of all her charms. How much more delicious is she, though, when seen in her true home, where she is born, the blessed country, where one can look up straight to the blue sky and see God's azure vault undimmed by any of the foul smoky clouds of man's own manufacture—can gaze up

"Where, through a sapphire sea, the sun
Sails like a golden galleon!"[62]

My soul sickens with longing when I think of a roomy country-house,

---

60 James Thomson (1700-48), Scottish poet and author of *The Seasons* (1730).

61 Inexact, Tennyson, *In Memoriam* (1850), 83.12.

62 Inexact, Henry Wadsworth Longfellow, "A Day of Sunshine" (1863), ll. 15-16.

with the dignity of a century or two about its stout old walls, clambered round by roses, with fresh lawns, with well-tended myriad-coloured garden squares, with rooks cawing clamorously about it, giving one a loud good-morrow; with broad fields full of lambs cantering clumsily about on their big unwieldy legs; with clucking hens and little round yellow balls of velvet chickens.

Amongst all these delights was Miss Chester now, and revelling in them. She had got a colour like a dairymaid, and was growing *embonpoint*.[63]

If ever it is pardonable, possible, to forget the existence of Death, it is in a gay country-house filled with lively youngish people in the spring-time. There is nothing to remind one of destruction or decay. None of the servants or acolytes of the great king are near to give one a hint of his presence. For a time he is shrouded from mortal sight—not a desirable condition. Better to think of him a little every day—better to look him in the eyes very often; and then, when he does come in all his pomp of terrors, he will wear the aspect, not of a complete stranger, but of an intimate acquaintance—almost a friend.

Some good man—who was it? I forget—advises all men, when they compose themselves to sleep every night, to fancy themselves lying stiff and stark in their coffins.[64] Not unwholesome, I think, nor very revolting, when one accustoms oneself to it.

But to return. In spring everything is full of life and sap and vigour; everything is on the increase, nothing on the decrease. Last year's leaves have vanished, lost shape and substance utterly, and only serve now to deepen the tint of the rich soil, to fertilise the fat meadows. For a few weeks we imagine we can feel the sensations which, in a far higher, more perfect degree, our first parents revelled in their garden between the four eastern rivers.[65]

There was a large company assembled in this month of May in that pleasant Kentish manor-house—people old and young, clever and dull, ugly and pretty, talkative and silent, as in all such mixed gatherings; only somehow it seemed that the preponderance of the young, the pretty, and the witty over the old, the ugly, and the stupid was greater than is ordinarily

63 Plump (French).

64 It is not clear to whom the narrator refers, but the practice was known among ascetics.

65 Genesis 2: 10-14 claims that the Garden of Eden was the source of four rivers of the ancient world: the Tigris, the Euphrates, the Pishon, and the Gihon.

the case. Perhaps it was only that the spring had got into their blood and warmed them up into beauty and animation. What a contrast it was to that life in the little narrow house in Queenstown, with only one face beside the still hearth; Kate's firm white features, that seemed to have lost the power of smiling, marked with so settled a gravity, so unalterable a dejection! What a contrast to the tainted air, the heart-rending tales of families decimated, the few people seen about, and those few so often black-clothed, in sign of some recent bereavement; the church-bells tolling incessantly, and the unavoidable sight of mourners and hearse-plumes and mutes[66] whenever you moved outside your own gates!

Maggie shuddered, looking back upon it, and thanked her stars devoutly that she was out of all those horrors. Her host and hostess were not young people—at least their bodies were not—but they possessed quite as strong faculties of enjoyment, quite as keen a zest for amusement, as when they had run wildly after hoops and found delight in the gyrations of a humming-top, at the age of six years. It was a very easy *laissez-aller*[67] untroubled life that they led in their old stone hall, and that they expected their guests to lead too. A late breakfast, flower-and-fruit garnished, lengthening out deep into the morning; people straggling down one after another, as seemed good to them, not oppressed by any sense of punctuality expected of them, not hurried down from a half-finished hasty toilette by a clamorous bell summoning them.

The squire was a calm-tempered old gentleman, in whom fussiness was not, who liked to get his own breakfast comfortably at the time he had been in the habit of eating it for the last sixty years, and did not much mind when his visitors got theirs, or whether they did not get it at all. A short forenoon, easily got through by the help of dawdling in conservatories, reading newspapers, writing letters, &c. Then luncheon, chiefly a female one, for such as could muster appetite for it, which, it must be allowed, required some *finesse* and management. A long all-golden afternoon—not a bit too long though, thanks to horses and carriages, to balls submitting to be knocked about *ad lib.*,[68] and to mallets, well wielded, knocking them; but, most of all, thanks to rowings on the big pool, where the large-bolled elms dipped their broad leaves continually into their cold bath, where weak-

66 Mutes were employees of Victorian undertakers who accompanied funerals in silence, heavily dressed in black.

67 Indolent, unconstrained (French).

68 See p. 220, n. 105.

armed young girls, tyros in the art, sawed the air with disobedient oars, and caught countless crabs, being ridiculed therefor by strong-armed expert young men. Everybody assembling from the four quarters of that small world to a sociable dinner, at an hour late enough for the chandelier to be lit, for the women to escape the ordeal of having their necks and arms submitted to the hard test of day's piercing eye. But cheeriest of all, the part of those days on which, in after time, those young people looked back with most regret were the evenings. Sometimes they danced in the old hall, and the scutcheons and family-pictures looked down upon them benignantly; while the plainest and most good-natured of the girls—those two attributes very often go together—played waltzes and quadrilles by the hour, and was as often forgotten and done out of her meed of gratitude as not. Sometimes they sang glees and catches and all manner of part-songs—some in time, some out—but all with hearty good-will, and with all the power of their lungs.

Lastly, sometimes they played games suited to the capacity of an infant; games in which bodily agility was more required than any ingenuity of mind; when the furniture was apt to get overset a good deal, and in which the grand object appeared to be to effect a collision between two bodies coming violently together on one chair, or some other end equally recondite and desirable. But most young people have a taste, developed or undeveloped, for romping; and there is not much harm in it. To amuse themselves was people's first waking idea in that house and many like houses, and their grand object through the day; and whether they had amused themselves or not, their last question to themselves at night. Nowhere was Time made to die a sweeter, more painless death. But yet among the flowers, even of that Eden, a serpent lurked for one person, perhaps for many; but it is only with the serpent appointed to sting one particular individual that we have to do. George Chester had not, as had been expected of him, accompanied his sisters and his cousin into the country. He had seen them safely to their journey's end, and had then appeared to think that he had done his duty by them; had left them, and gone off to amuse himself, after his own fashion, in town. His defection was a great disappointment to one of those young ladies, and mortified vanity did not help to sweeten the sourness of it. "There are as good fish in the sea as ever came out of it," says the proverb; and there were plenty better fish, better-looking fish, more valuable fish altogether, than George Chester at this very house; but still silvery salmon, speckled trout, cod, and haddock might all swim finnily by; they could not compare, in her blinded eyes, with the dull carp she was hankering after. When she had been away from home about three weeks, George made his appearance one day; came walking over the grass, in all his pristine beauty and plumpness, as they were playing croquet. It was rather a fortunate moment for Margaret, she was looking so undeniably pretty, flushed, excited, with eyes which, now that they were not seen beside Kate's, might pass for very bright ones. The flush deepened for a second when her glance fell upon the newcomer, then died away utterly. It surprised and almost shocked the girl herself to discover how pale she was getting, how the few words of ordinary greeting seemed to stick in her throat. Absence in her case had certainly and unfortunately made "the heart grow fonder."[69] And then, what made it worse, he was so provokingly cool and unembarrassed, shook hands with her so cordially, said quite loud, with no pretence at whispering or undertones, "Well, Maggie, how are you? Why, you are as white as a sheet!" and then passed on to shake hands with his sisters, in apparently exactly the same way, and stayed talking to them, asking questions about home matters, and answering their inquiries about himself, without another glance towards the place where she stood.

Poor thing! she could have killed herself in her shame for blushing or paling about such a block. As well blush about Cheops or Rhamses,[70] for all the return he made for it. It was too true that Maggie felt, and could not help feeling, an amount of interest, very disproportionate to his deserts, in that uninteresting young man. She had let her heart go out to him. The two feeble strings of prudence and caution, with which she had held it back, snapped off suddenly one fine day, and she could not call it back again now, much as she wished; it had passed beyond her control. Women, nice women especially, do not proportion their love to the worth of the recipient; often the love and the worth are in an inverse ratio. Love is an inmate who creates a great deal of confusion and disorder in the house he tarries in; he does not let his entertainer have much peace or quietness. Love does not make people enjoy their food, or take deep draughts of sleep. Margaret did not in these days draw half the enjoyment she ought to have done out of the rides and the dancing and the love-making; for love-making there

69 Although he apparently borrowed it from elsewhere, the proverb "Absence makes the heart grow fonder" is credited to the poet Thomas Haynes Bayly (1797-1839).

70 Egyptian pharaohs famous for erecting monuments, cited because George Chester is like a stone "block."

was, of course.

I wonder everybody did not make love to everybody else—opportunity and importunity being everything. My marvel was, and always is, in such cases, how all the young men and all the young women avoided falling into hopeless entanglements. The season spoke of nothing but love; and it was the sole thing to do in that lazy time and place. It is not a pleasant thing to get into the habit of studying a fellow-creature's countenance, and putting constructions which torture yourself ingeniously upon each change of expression. Maggie made herself very miserable sometimes if George happened to look grave for two minutes, imagining that he was thinking of Kate; and then again, if he smiled without any apparent cause, of course he was thinking about Kate. Then only the subject had presented itself to him in a different and a brighter light. Often she lay awake at night, pondering over this young man's foolish commonplace speeches; weighing them, one after another, to see what they were worth, and whether they had the ring of true metal about them. It is occupation equally unpleasant and profitless (as many a jealous wife could testify) watching another's actions. All the watching in the world will not avail to keep a person from the most obnoxious courses, if they have a bent for such courses. Such vigilance is either totally inoperative, or else aggravates the evil. But still, it is very hard to abstain from it. For two or three days at a time now, the whole treasure of George's fickle affections seemed diverted to some other of the girls staying in the house. His roving fancy was caught by a fair cheek, a sparkling smile, or a rose-bud mouth. It did not take much to snare him, certainly; but then he always got out of the toils[71] again very, very soon. More than once Margaret caught glimpses of him between the orange-boughs in the conservatory, making such *yeux doux*[72] that she felt morally certain he must be accompanying them with words more than sentimental. Now and again she had overheard him (unintentionally, of course) deep in the gibberish of the language of flowers.[73] And on such occasions she would close her lips very tightly and thinly on one another; would twist her hands together under the table, and make random answers to whoever addressed her.

And then again, Mr. George, more inexcusably perverse than ever, would sometimes get hold of some man friend, and, falling deep into talk

71 See Proverbs 6:5; "toils" are traps set by hunters.

72 Loving glances (French, literally "sweet eyes").

73 Drawing on the traditional symbolism of various blooms, flower arrangements were used in Victorian times to encode messages between lovers.

upon rifles, or pointers, or salmon-flies, or some such manly themes, not come near her all the evening. Every day, and every hour of the day, her reason told her that there was nothing to worship, nothing of the demi-god about this commonplace young officer; not an inch of hero stuff in all his composition. But passion, inveterate in her infatuation, would not hear a word of dispraise of her idol. Sitting brushing her hair at night, after one of these unsatisfactory evenings, she would resolve and vow henceforth to hate and despise him: firstly, for what he was; secondly, for what he did: for being such a noodle as regarded the other half of creation; and for his obtuseness, in neither perceiving nor heeding the good things that Providence put in his way. But the hatred was spurious, and the opposing love was genuine, and it always won the day. Truly, the bed of roses on which she was lying had a good many thorns in the blossoms. Men are so conceited, that I think he saw that she loved him. And what did he think about her? A question of some moment to the unlucky young lady. O, he thought her the jolliest girl he had ever seen except one. That unlucky "except." After all his vagaries he invariably returned to her; but then his vagaries were so very, very frequent, and the intervals between them so brief. For some time he endeavoured to please himself, trying to trace a likeness between Margaret and her absent sister; tried to find out some lurking resemblance in a smile or the tone of a voice; in eyes or other features it would have been evidently absurd to seek for such. But he failed utterly. There was not one grain of similitude between the two. As I have before remarked, hardly any two young women in Europe could have been more unlike. There was not a vestige of that general family likeness which is to be found among most sisters. Afterwards, George got gradually to care for and enjoy those smiles and tones for themselves. He was not a Stoic,[74] nor of a particularly faithful turn of mind, to be utterly indifferent to a rather sweet woman, blushing and trembling at his approach. It made his opinion of himself go up a peg or two higher. I think it was because he felt so secure of her, that he was in no hurry to make assurance doubly sure. And yet, if Kate had been dead now, and he had had a month or so to get accustomed to the idea of her being defunct, he, not being the sort of man to mourn long for a recollection, to widow himself for life for an idea, would have found it in his heart to gift Margaret with royal happiness by condescending to offer her his hand. But Kate was not dead nor dying, nor, as far as appeared, engaged to

74 In classical Greek and Roman philosophy, stoicism encouraged emotional restraint.

anyone else. Consequently, why should not she be engaged to him? After all, she had never refused him. Perhaps that dismissal of him from the office of escort was a little ruse to bring him to the point. And her incivility and extreme coldness since was perhaps to be put down to mortified vanity, and an idea that he had not treated her well. Really it all sounded very plausible to foolish, self-deluded George when he put it before himself. He reasoned it out in a very matter-of-fact, business-like way, on the hypothesis that she would regard it in the same light. True, that Kate was a girl very much admired, and that men had got into the way of making a great fuss about her. But, after all, what were admirers? What good did they do to any woman? often a great deal of harm, fluttering around her. Men of straw almost all of them. In these days a sensible girl would think twice before she said "No" to a good solid offer of marriage. He was his father's eldest son, had no debts to speak of, and was not a particularly bad-looking fellow. Kate could not be so mad as to refuse him. And she had not anyone else that she cared about to stand in his light, at least that he had ever heard of. As for a ridiculous story of his sisters' about a photograph, that was evidently spun out of their own brains.[75] Very likely it was a picture of Blount, or of her dead father; and she was ashamed of being caught indulging in such a manifestation of affection. Nothing likelier. People can get themselves to believe anything almost that they wish by such arguments, I think.

Such was the posture of affairs, and the posture of Lieutenant Chester's mind, when he came to visit his uncle and aunt at Daneham Court, and for several days afterwards. One afternoon everyone all over England, I should think—everyone, at all events, that was not either dying or in an office—was out of doors. Everybody at Daneham was certainly walking and driving and sauntering about, basking in the hot May sun; revelling in the sight of myriad leaves and flowers, bursting through their silken sheaths, the woods spread with their carpets of dim harebells.

"The heavens up-breaking through the earth," as Tennyson (I think it is) says[76] with a liberty, a freedom of fancy, which a lesser poet would not have ventured to indulge in.

The house stood blinking among its drowsy leaves, with all its doors

75 Broughton apparently forgets she cut an episode from ch. 19 (Dec. 1865) of the *DUM* version in which one of George Chester's sisters, teasing Kate for having a "secret grief," claims she spotted her kissing a mysterious photograph (See Appendix B, p. 405).

76 Tennyson, "Guenevere," in *Idylls of the King* (1859), l. 388.

and windows open, so that man or beast might enter if they chose; with Venetian blinds lowered, through which, even though lowered, the smell of the flowers and the hum of bees came faintly into the cool empty rooms—not quite empty, either; in one of them a young lady was cultivating a taste for solitude—Margaret Chester. She had excused herself from going out, in a young lady's invariable plea—headache; and a headache she had, induced by fretting and disquiet of mind. She was not in spirits for the amount of repartee and merriment expected of her, and did not want anybody to notice her depression; and she stayed in-doors, and was now lying on a sofa in a rather dark recess between two windows, smelling vigorously at a vinaigrette,[77] and bemoaning her fate, wishing she had never been born, and occasionally varying the wish by transferring it to Kate. Yes, now, how happy and prosperous she might have been if there had never been such a person as Kate in existence, or if she had been strangled when first her baby-cries made themselves heard in this cold world! How different her lot might have been if it had not been shadowed by the unconscious influence of that odd little sorceress, her sister, who seemed to steal away both hearts that she wished to get possession of, and hearts whose possession rather annoyed her than otherwise, by some species of witchcraft!

But such reflections were utterly useless. There was Kate alive, and not to be put out of life except by killing, or causing her to be killed—for neither of which courses Margaret had the slightest inclination. As she lay there, idle, discontented, in a frame of mind as unlike as possible to that day and the season, the door opened, and the object of her aspirations—an object about as worthy sighing and striving after as those on which we usually waste the blood and sweat of our hard struggles—George Chester walked in. He looked very hot, had his hat on, and a perfect swarm of trout-flies twining round it, and would evidently be rather obliged to anyone who would give him a job to do, suited to his capacity, for he was very short of such. First he rambled objectlessly to the table, took up a book lying thereon, opened it at haphazard, read half-a-dozen words, and tossed it down again. Then he sighed heavily, flung himself into an arm-chair, stayed there two seconds, uttered a brief soliloquy composed of these three words, "Confound the heat!" and then got up again.

All this time he had not perceived the presence of Margaret; he thought he had the room to himself. Sadly he walked to a looking-glass,

77 Small bottle containing vinegar or smelling salts.

gazed at himself steadfastly for some time, considered the sit of his tie, and readjusted the position of his pin, which was of the cheerful pattern of a death's head and cross-bones in ivory.

Margaret began to feel rather uncomfortable; he might not be pleased when he should discover that she had been there all along, spying upon his conceited little manœuvres, watching him make a fool of himself. So she made a slight movement to attract his attention; but he did not hear her, he was so busy dwelling, with a Narcissus-like fondness, on his own image in the mirror.[78] First he looked at himself over his right shoulder, then over his left, with a lurking suspicion that there was something rather baggy about the cut of his coat at the back. He looked so exceedingly droll in this attitude, craning his neck to get a glimpse of his coat-tails, that Margaret burst into a roar of laughter, unrestrained, unrestrainable. At that unexpected sound, George's head came quickly back into its natural position; he started half out of his skin, and reddened with as guilty a flush as any schoolboy caught robbing an orchard.

"Hullo, what's the matter?" he exclaimed, turning sharp round, and then his eyes fell upon Margaret, half hidden in her dark nook. "O, it's you, is it?" said he, very much out of countenance. "I did not know that you were there. I thought there was nobody in the room. I thought everybody was gone out. Why on earth did not you call out before?"

"I'm sure I wish to goodness I had been able to help calling out then," answered Margaret, between paroxysms of unfeeling merriment, forgetting her headache, and her heartache too, completely; "perhaps I might have had some more fun. O, George, you seem so pleased with yourself! Now, on cool reflection, which point of view is best, do you think, tell me?"

These remarks were not calculated to lower George's colour.

"Don't badger a fellow," he said; "of course I was not admiring myself. I was only thinking that this coat had the same fault that Capel's[79] always have, that it bags at the back."

"You really are a very amusing young man—unintentionally, I mean. I wonder now, if I had not laughed, how long you would have stayed there figuring."

"Not two seconds. I should not have come in here at all if I had had

78 In Greek mythology Narcissus starved to death because he could not stop looking at his own reflection in a pond.

79 Presumably a fashionable men's tailor.

anything better to do. I'm not such a carpet knight[80] as you want to make me out."

"Why, I thought you were going to be away all day fishing. You told us at breakfast you were going to have such fine sport."

"So I thought I should, for it was nice and cloudy then—just the day for the May-fly—but no sooner had I got down to the mill-pond, and put my rod together, than the sun came blazing out, just as it is now, hang it! Of course it was all up with it then. They would not bite a bit, the beggars! Any fool could have told one that, with not a breath of wind to ruffle the water, and the pool as smooth as a looking-glass."

"If it was like a looking-glass you might have performed those evolutions there; did you? Ha, ha, ha!"

"Don't tease, Maggie; you have run that joke off its legs. And what are you doing in here in this dark room, where one can hardly see one's hand before one for these blinds? Why are not you out with all the other girls?"

"I've got a bad headache; but, I say, George, it is a pity that you did not come in ten minutes earlier, for that friend of yours, Mr. Erle (is not his name?), was in here looking for you, wanting you to ride over with him to Canterbury."

"I met him as I came in; he asked me himself, but I got out of it."

"Why?"

"I don't think I'll tell you. You do not deserve to hear. You have not been good enough."

"O, do tell me! I'm very sorry I laughed. It was very rude of me. Dear George, I beg your pardon; I'll never do it again. Do tell me."

"Well, then, I thought I'd get you to come out on the lake with me for a bit. I wanted to have a talk with you; but, of course, as you have got a headache I would not think of asking you."

"Never mind the headache! It's gone. I should like nothing better. I'm sorrier than ever that I laughed. I'll go and get my hat this minute."

There certainly did not seem much trace of headache in the alacrity with which she jumped off the sofa; and leaving it and the neglected vinaigrette (now no longer needed), sprang upstairs to prepare herself; and in five minutes more they were walking over the greensward toward the boat-house.

"Will you take an oar?" George asked, as he handed his pretty compan-

80 A knight knighted on the carpet of a throne room rather than a battleground; someone who has led an easy life.

ion in. "You made rather a better attempt last time, and try as you may, you cannot upset this old tub."

"No—it's too hot. I will sit still and enjoy myself, and leave all the trouble to you. Take the boat under those trees over there—it looks so cool and quiet."

So they floated off, cleaving the shining waters. If those two people were not lovers they ought to have been—all the circumstances of time and place were conducive to such a condition. It was a very pleasant scene, as eye need light on: the big mere holding the sun far down in its deep, still breast; the garden, with all its fresh-blossoming flowers sloping down, with its scarlets and azures and goldens, to the water's edge, and the old branchy elms and beeches fringing it shadily; and—best gift of all—far up above the earth and its sorrows, heaven's chorister, the lark, pouring out, in the great cathedral of the sky, some of the unutterable joy that filled him, like a bodiless melody sent from some better country to whisper of peace and gladness to tired human hearts. Out of the sun into the shade—right under the boughs of a wide-spreading horse-chestnut, covered with its pinky-white spikes, and gnarled roots straggling down barely into the pool at its feet; a gentle gust agitating the tall, scented grasses, stirring a bunch of harebells that were bending over the bank to get a peep at their own new-born beauty in the water beneath. George rested on his oars, and perspired a good deal.

"Will that do?" he asked.

"Excellently—could not be better. It was impossible to talk out there in that glare."

"Quite—it frizzled up one's ideas, did not it? Not that I ever had many."

"Don't run down yourself; it is a bad plan. You'll find plenty of people to do it for you. But what was it you wanted to say to me?"

"Was there anything?"

"Yes—you told me you wanted to have a talk with me."

"O, ay; so I did—so I do; but it was not because I had anything particular to say. It was only that I thought we had not had a good talk for a long time."

"No more we have; we have been so busy chattering to other people. I suppose it is because we know we have such loads of opportunities of seeing and speaking to one another when we are at home."

"Yes, have not we? and we made pretty good use of them, too, last winter, over those afternoon tea-parties—did not we? How pleasant they were, to be sure!"

"Tea is always pleasant in an afternoon."

"What a low notion!—as if I was thinking of the Bohea[81] itself. According to my ideas it was the talk and the jokes that we used to have that flavoured the tea."

"O, they were all very well, but I got rather tired of them."

"I did not, then. I hope we shall have them all over again when I come back next winter."

"That I'm sure you won't. One cannot bring things back like that when once they are over. All the spirit is gone out of them. They are like dishes warmed up the second day for dinner."

"I do not see it at all. We shall all be in the same relative position, I hope, as we were last winter; and the circumstances and conditions being the same, I do not see why the results should not be the same."

"Well, you'll see; but what is the good of arguing about such a trifle?"

"Ah, you say that because you are getting the worst of the argument."

"Very likely."

"You're angry now. I rather like getting you into a rage. It makes you look very pretty—not that I'd presume to say you were not always pretty. Girls always are, of course; still it's an improvement."

"Don't be foolish—I hate compliments. Just pull the boat in two lengths farther, in amongst those water-lilies. I want to get some, and I cannot reach them from here."

George obeyed, and then asked, "Are you satisfied now?"

"Perfectly;" and she leaned over the side, and dipping a bare hand in, pulled a number of the great heavy white flowers and their dark broad leaves. Dripping, they lay on the seat beside her, and she took up a green calyxed bud, closed still, and looked at it affectionately.

"Pretty things!" said George condescendingly. "How fond Kate used to be of them!"

"Used she?"

"Yes; do you not recollect last year, when my people gave that picnic sort of entertainment that you and she were at, how she had a lot of them in her hair in the evening?"

"Had she?"

"Yes—I wonder you do not remember. You are rather stupid to-day;

81 Chinese black tea.

you forget everything."

"Now I come to think of it, I have some faint recollection of something about it."

"How well they looked in among the thick plaits of her hair—such a quantity of hair as she has got, too—uncommon well!"

"Did you think so?"

"Yes—did not you?"

"No—I cannot say that I admired them much."

"Poor little Kate!—I wish she was here now!"

Margaret was fond of her sister, but she could not echo that wish.

"Come, Maggie, don't be cross; tell me something about Kate. I have not heard a word about her since I don't know when."

"I have not got anything to tell. She has not time to write to me or anyone else since she turned hospital-nurse."

"Has she done that? I never heard of it before."

"O yes—three weeks ago nearly. The fever-patients increased upon them so quick that they could not take them all in at the regular hospital; so they turned a private house into a temporary one, and Kate is a sort of matron, or head nurse in it. Of course there are plenty of under-nurses, but most of the onus falls upon Kate's and James's shoulders, I fancy."

"James!—what, she keeps to the wizened little parson still!"

"I should rather think so; why, they have been all in all to each other for the last month or two. I do believe they are the two best people in the world. I wish to goodness I was like them!"

"I say, Maggie, do you—do you think she'll marry him, after the fever is over?"

"I wish she could hear you—how indignant she would be!"

"It is not such a very unnatural supposition after all. One does not exactly see what other possible motive, but affection to him, she can have for the life she is leading now—nothing but schools and sick-visiting and district-meetings all day."

"I can understand her motive very well, because I happen to know it. I do not wonder that it is rather an enigma to you."

"She does not confide her secrets to me, certainly—I do not want her to; but I must say, to the uninitiated it does seem rather a throwing away of herself, wasting the best years of her life."

"She would tell you that she is not wasting them; that she is, on the contrary, making the most of them; that it is you and I, and such as us, that are wasting them."

"She is morbid; it is unnatural to hear a young girl preach like that; I wish you could get her out of this fancy."

"It would not be the smallest use if I were to try. I should not succeed; and most assuredly I shall not try. I begin to believe hers is the right view after all."

"For goodness' sake don't you turn Methodist too,[82] Maggie! What on earth would become of me? You'd both be trying to convert me, and I could not stand two female parsons at me at once. I should have to emigrate."

Maggie smiled. "No fear of that," she said. "To admire goodness in other people, and not to like to hear it laughed or sneered at, is the highest pitch of excellence I shall ever attain to, and I am at that pitch now."

"Never mind, you're quite good enough for me. But about Kate now—don't you think that she will get tired of this mode of going on—of this new religious notion? don't you think that when the novelty is worn off, she'll grow very weary of it, and come back to her old way? In fact, tell me candidly your opinion—do you think it will last?"

Maggie was getting impatient of the subject. "How can I tell whether it will last or not? I know no more about it than you do yourself. Dear me! what a nuisance these midges are!"

"They do not bite me a bit; I suppose my skin is too thick for them to get through. Here, I know what will be the best plan; I'll cut you a little bough to drive them away with."

"Thank you."

He stood up in the boat and stretched an arm out to one of the leafy trees bending over them. Then, whilst cutting off a little twig, with his face averted, he began again at the old subject.

"But you must have an opinion one way or another; just say whether you think she'll always live the life she is doing now: if so, she might just as well be a nun."

"Just as well; and so she will be in time, I daresay. I think she is quite capable of it."

"What?"

---

82 Adherents of Methodism, an evangelical sect founded in the 18th century, frowned on dancing and card playing. George's reference to "two female parsons" may allude to the ministerial role that women were able to assume in the denomination's early years.

"I say that I think it is not at all improbable that she will turn nun some of these days. How you do tease about the girl!"

"Do I? Well, I won't make any more inquiries; only let me ask one thing. Don't you think that she will marry anyone?"

"Never; I'd stake all I have in the world (that is not much, to be sure) upon it."

"What a pity! she is so much too pretty and pleasant to be allowed to go to her grave an old maid."

"People cannot marry her against her will, I suppose—at least not in England."

"Who on earth said anything about against her will? I meant *with* her will, of course."

"You did not make it very clear."

"But, Maggie, has she really never seen anybody to care about? I should not have given her credit for being such a stone. Has not she?"

"What's that to you? Cannot you be satisfied with knowing that she has not cared, does not care, and never will care two straws about you?"

George reddened, not with the heat this time. "There's your bough," he said, giving it into her hands, "and I must say for you, you are very rude and disagreeable; and I'm extremely sorry I asked you to come out. I never said that I wanted her to care for me."

Margaret relented. "I am disagreeable," she said, dispersing the midges with vigorous blows of her flail; "but I think that was hardly a fair question you asked."

"O, very well; if you think so, don't answer it on any account. I withdraw it."

"Stay, I don't know what to say; you're not like a stranger, you are a relation of Kate's; I don't know why I should not tell you, only you must not breathe a word of it to your sisters."

"Trust me; do you take me for a born fool? Why, if I did, it would be half over England in less than an hour."

Maggie hesitated still; would it be a dishonourable betrayal of confidence? "I'm not sure that Kate would like it. I don't know that I'm doing right."

"Well, make up your mind one way or another. I won't urge you; though of course, now you have admitted that there is something, I can't help indulging in conjectures."

"You'd never get near the truth. Come, I'll risk it; swear you'll never reveal it to anybody."

"I swear."

"Well, then, she was desperately in love with someone once—is so still, I'm afraid."

"Is so still? Lucky dog! Well, who is it? Anybody I know? Go on, quick."

I do not know whether Miss Chester was justified in what she did; I hardly think so, but I only state a fact. There, in among the water-lilies, with the blue sky laughing overhead, and the blue water beneath, she narrated the whole story of her sister's love and woes and wrongs, to an intent eager listener. At the end George ground his teeth.

"Villain! Blackguard!" he remarked, boiling over with rage. "O, if I could but meet him in the street some day, I'd give him such an infernal licking as he never had before in all his days. I'd pommel the life out of him, the scoundrel! I say, Maggie, describe him to me exactly, that I may be sure to recognise him."

Margaret was rather exasperated at this excessive indignation; what business was it of his?

"I shall do no such thing; you are not her brother; it's no concern whatever of yours; it would only make a disgraceful scene; and moreover, as to licking him, as you call it, I can tell you what—he is an immensely strong big man, and that you'd most likely get the worst of it."

"Well, no matter, I should not care if I did: it would be in a good cause; besides, I'm not quite such a chicken as you think; at all events I know pretty well what to do with my fists."

"Don't be so absurdly bellicose; it is like Bombastes Furioso.[83] You'll make me repent of having told you; and I only did it out of good-nature, to show you how utterly useless and hopeless your dangling after Kate still is."

George sighed heavily.

"I see it myself; I'm very much obliged to you. It was very considerate and kind of you; kinder than you think, perhaps, Maggie. I'll acknowledge to you now, that you have saved me the mortification of a refusal; for like an ass I had fully made up my mind to propose to Kate when I went home."

Margaret bent down her head over her flowers to hide its emotion; after a minute she looked up, and said rather anxiously, "And you will not now?"

83 Burlesque comic opera (1810) by William Barnes Rhodes; the title parodies the title of the famous medieval romance, *Orlando Furioso.*

"Of course not."

Then those two floated back over the bright mere, which did not look quite so bright to one of them as before; rather silent, both wrapped in their own thoughts, giving their tongues a holiday. As she left him at the house-door she turned and said softly, "You're not vexed with me, are you, George?"

"I should think not," he said warmly. "That would be unjust; you're the best girl I know."

He looked half inclined to stoop down and kiss the best girl he knew, but thought better of it, and only squeezed her hand. That evening Margaret came down to dinner with water-lilies in her hair; and George the philosophical began, for the first time, gravely to speculate whether after all gray eyes were not every bit as good as green, and rosy cheeks as pale ones.

"I've made a step to-day," thought Maggie triumphantly, when she went to bed that night; and she slept well upon it.

CHAPTER V

A MAY morning, warm and serene, and brilliant as painter's eye could desire to see it. No barges floating down stream or being tugged up; no shopmen taking down shutters from their windows; no overworked milliners stitching at the ceaseless seam; no toil of any kind going on; for it is Sunday, and the church-bells are striving emulously which can send forth their sounds clearest, most ringing, on the pure air. The fever is abating in Queenstown; it has almost fulfilled its mission, filling many a grave, causing awful gaps and hiatuses by many a hearth—making vacant spaces that can never be filled up any more.

It is nine o'clock A. M., and Kate is standing at the door of the hospital, loitering a minute before she goes in. The fever-patients do not come in with such frightful overwhelming rapidity now; but still it is full, and there is plenty of work to do. Kate has been home to get a few hours' sleep, having been completely knocked up the night before, and compelled to succumb at last. She has arranged her hair fresh, with a neatness befitting the day, and has put on a clean cotton gown and white apron (her hospital-dress). As she goes through the garden she stops for a moment, like Evangeline, to gather a handful of flowers,—lilies-of-the-valley, honeysuckles, and blood-red carnations,—that the dying may enjoy earth's sweetest smells and sights for the last time.[84] As she enters the room, she sees that one or two have died in the night. There they lie, with the rigid outline of their forms solemnly defined against the shrouding sheet, with their dead faces covered up whitely. There they lie,

"Like drifts of snow by the wayside."[85]

She makes her way to the further end of the long chamber, to a bed on which lies the form of a stalwart, fair-haired young man, cut off in the pride of his manhood, and with a figure kneeling beside it. The kneeling figure is James, who, with his head in his hands, is absorbed in silent prayer. As she comes up with her pure pale face, hardly less pale, hardly less fair than the lilies she carries, he raises his head and looks up with a silent greeting. She glances towards the fair-haired young man and says "Dead?" interrogatively, but very calmly, for she and Death knew each other very well by this time. There is no shyness between them now.

"Quite; but I could not say exactly when. He went away so quietly; somewhere between the night and the morning, without any of the struggle I feared; passed away without a sigh or a groan."

"Thank God! Poor fellow! I'm glad of that."

"Kate, that's the way, I hope, I shall pass away before long."

"Don't be cruel, Jemmy; it frightens me the way you have got to talk of late; but how ill and tired you look! No wonder, indeed. Now do go home, there's a dear fellow, and go to bed for an hour or two. You do not know how much good those few hours' sleep have done me. I'm quite a different woman. I feel as fresh as a lark."

"No, thank you, Kate; I'd rather not. I could not sleep if I did; and besides, there'll be plenty of time to sleep by and by."

"You shall not stay here any longer, that I'm determined on. What was the good of my coming, if not to relieve you? As you say to me, don't squander your youth and health. You see I turn your own precepts against you."

---

84 See Henry Wadsworth Longfellow, *Evangeline* (1847), II. v. 71-73. Like Kate, Evangeline nurses the sick during an epidemic: "Sweet on the summer air was the odor of the flowers of the garden;/ And she paused on her way to gather the fairest among them,/ That the dying once more might rejoice in their fragrance and beauty."

85 Longfellow, *Evangeline* (1847), II.v.84.

"Well, I own I should like to go to church. It is Communion Sunday, too;[86] and I own that I should like to kneel at that altar, and taste that feast once again."

"Once again?"

"Yes, Kate; who knows but that next time I may be drinking the new wine in my Father's kingdom."[87]

"Hush, hush! I won't have you talk like that. I'm sure you're quite faint with this long watching. Here, smell these flowers; they'll refresh you, I'm sure. The scent of these lilies would almost bring one back from the dead."

She held them towards him, and he inhaled their fragrance enjoyingly.

"Delicious!" he said, drawing a deep breath. "I wonder will there be flowers in heaven. It is a childish idea; but I cannot help thinking that those we have here are but imperfect, fading copies of immortal types above."

"I daresay; I'm sure I hope so. But go away now," she said, almost pushing him out with a sister's gentle violence. "Go and take a walk before service; go down by the river. You have no conception how heavenly the breeze is there; it put new life into me, and will into you."

"Well, indeed, I almost think I may as well. I'm afraid I could not do much good if I stayed here. My head aches so splittingly that I can hardly see anything."

At those words a sensation of cold came over Kate, the shadow of a great dread falling upon her. Was there more grief yet coming up? Had not she had enough already? So James went, and Kate stayed; stayed all day in those hospital-wards, going through the routine of her usual duties; a routine which had become very familiar to her, and not irksome, by this time. Sometimes she fancied she was becoming unfit for the society of *well* people, she had grown so accustomed to spend all the hours of the day and night tending the sick. And the merry church-bells unwittingly rang one or two more to their homes; and the shadows lengthened, and the sun sloped westward, and the evening tide came. At that blessed season Kate was sitting by an open window, watching the sunset spreading redly over the fields of the sky. She had a hymn-book on her lap, and was saying softly over to herself these words:

---

86 Although the ritualistic Tractarian movement favored communion every Sunday, the custom in mainstream Anglican churches in the nineteenth century was to distribute communion once a quarter or at most once a month.

87 See Matthew 26: 27-29.

"Nearer home, nearer home,–
And nightly pitch my moving tent
A day's march nearer home."[88]

"Ah, that's what he does," she mused; "and he's getting very near home too, I'm afraid; afraid indeed! Yes, afraid for myself; but O, so very glad for him. Poor fellow! what a sad life he has had, to be sure; almost as sad as mine; well matched in that, I think; but when shall I get home too? O, if I could know that! Will it be before twenty years, before ten, before five? O Lord, make no long tarrying."[89] She turned her great soft eyes, brimming with tears, to the serene sky, and that hearty prayer went up like incense. Someone touched her, thus rapt, on the arm, to attract her attention. She turned and found that it was one of the assistant nurses, with a message to the effect that a person of the name of Mrs. Lewis wished to speak to her. Then she knew that what she dreaded had come upon her. For a second she stood with clasped hands, gathering her strength together, and then she walked calmly downstairs. Mrs. Lewis received her with a reverence both respectful and elaborate, and began deliberately,

"If you please, ma'am, I came to tell you about Mr. Stanley."

Though Kate knew it was come, she fought against it still.

"What about him? he has not got the fever? he's not ill? don't say he is."

"Yes, indeed, but he is though, poor gentleman, I'm sorry to say, and more than ill too; he was taken very sudden when he came in from church, and I sent directly for the doctor, and he came, and stayed the best part of an hour with him, giving him brandy and all manner of stimulants to keep him up; but when he came out he told me it was no use, that he could do him no good, and he hardly thought he'd outlive the night; so I thought I'd just come right off and tell you, as I knew you were such a friend of the poor gentleman's."

Kate's face assumed that dead-white, rigid look, which with her always indicated intensest pain kept under, and held in subjection.

"There, that'll do. I'll go to him;" and without giving Mrs. Lewis time

88 Inexact, James Montgomery, "Forever with the Lord" (1835), see ll. 5-8: "Here in the body pent,/ Absent from Him, I roam,/ Yet nightly pitch my moving tent/ A day's march nearer home."

89 See Psalm 70: 5: "But I am poor and needy; make haste unto me, O God: thou art my help and my deliverer; O Lord, make no tarrying."

to say another word (she had intended to say a good many more), she turned away, snatched up her bonnet, and ran hastily out, down the street, not heeding the inquiring surprised glances of the good folks standing, enjoying the quiet Sunday evening, at their doors. What was it to her whether people would laugh or sneer at what she was doing? No such notion ever crossed her mind; the one thought that filled her whole soul, and left no room for any other, was that the man who had saved her from hell, who had been the best friend she had ever had in the world, was dying, and she must see him again to say good-bye.

At the door of Mrs. Lewis's lodgings a little knot of idle boys and men were gathered, and the sound of merry chat and loud laughter fell on the still summer air; but as Kate drew near, the voices fell; silently, civilly the men moved aside and made way for her to pass through. There was that in her face that awed even them. Through James's deserted sitting-room, with its bare, scant furniture; the papers littering over the table as usual; the signs of recent occupation everywhere about; everything the same, and yet so different. She caught her breath quick, as her eye fell on the old worn elbow-chair, that he would never sit in again. The door of the bedroom was ajar. Kate stood there a moment listening; all was silent, and she pushed it gently and went in. A hired nurse was sitting behind the curtains, nodding, but at the slight noise caused by Kate's entrance, she woke up and came towards her.

"You may go," spoke Kate sternly (this stranger should not see her anguish—hear her voice tremble). "I'm come to nurse him; do you hear? Go."

After beginning an ineffectual remonstrance, the woman (only about three-quarters awake yet) obeyed; and then Kate flew forward and threw herself on her knees by the side of the bed, in tearless agony. She would not weep; let her cry her eyes out after he was gone, but she would not harass his last moments with her selfish tears. Truly, to one looking down on that scene there would not have appeared much cause for weeping—rather for triumphant, awful mirth, that another brave soul, having fought the good fight, having kept the faith, was about to be crowned with his victor's wreath. Weep, indeed, for him who lay there—so quiet, so restful, with head thrown back on the pillow, and eyes closed—patiently, with calm expectancy, waiting for the end? There was no cruel struggle between life and death going on here; no battle between those rival powers. The outworks had been carried long ago[90]—hardship and toil and sorrow had done that already. There was only the citadel to storm, and that gave in at the first summons.

Never again would he need the poor threadbare old clothes that he had shivered in through so many a winter day. Ere another morning should dawn he would be clothed in the wedding-garment of the Lamb.[91] The King's messenger, the long-expected, had come at last, and had given His message lovingly.[92] His Father's servant was here, to take him home from the hard schooling of earth to the eternal holiday of heaven. He was willing and ready trustfully to put his hand in His, and launch with Him on the deep broad river that rolled between him and home. Not insensible, or wandering in delirium—as if in a sort of happy, waking trance—his probation over, his work done; already tasting beforehand the rest he was so near entering upon. Perhaps he was thinking softly about the dear gray-haired old father and the little blue-eyed sister he was going to meet again so soon—was picturing to himself how they would greet him, and rejoice at his coming. Perhaps he heard already the first notes of the great burst of music that would clash out harmoniously to welcome him; perhaps all minor joys were swallowed up in the thought of the unspeakable bliss of beholding the dear Lord he had loved so, smiling upon him lovingly, and saying: "Well done, thou good and faithful servant; enter thou into the joy of thy Lord."[93]

As Kate knelt there by the bedside, the heavy eyes unclosed, a smile stole over the wasted dying face—so evidently dying, but yet a death better than any life, and one thin pale hand travelled laboriously to Kate's and clasped it.

"I'm going," he said slowly. "You've come to see the last of me! Poor little Kitty!—you've been a very good little Kitty to me! God bless you for it!"

All very well to resolve not to cry. At these tender words her tears burst forth like rain.

"O Jemmy!" she wailed, "you are not going to leave me? You could not be so cruel! O, what shall I do? I shall be so desolate. O, do take me with

90 Outworks are a minor defensive position located outside a fortified area.

91 See Revelation 19: 8-10: "Blessed are they which are called unto the marriage supper of the lamb"; see also Matthew 12: 22-24.

92 See p. 127, n.170.

93 See Matthew 25: 23.

you!—O, do, do!"

Her excessive grief seemed to disturb him—him who was past all grief. Feebly he stroked the bowed chestnut head.

"There, there," he said with difficulty. "Don't cry; there's nothing to cry about. It makes me sorry to see you cry; and I am so glad. Poor child!—poor child!"

She shook back her hair from her wet eyes; bravely she forced back her tears.

"O, tell me, are you happy? Why do I ask, when I see your face? Jemmy, to-day you'll be with Him in Paradise!"

The holy light came out clearer, stronger, on that dying man's features; vanquished the death damps, the clayey pallor reigned there supreme.

"Yes, Kate; I hope so."

"O, Jemmy, speak to me; say something to me that I may remember after you are gone—that I may keep hold of when I'm left all alone."

James raised himself with difficulty in the bed, and with hands growing disobedient, grasped about darkly (for that dimness that comes but once was obscuring his eyes) in search of something. Then he found what he sought—a little worn old Bible; and lifting it as if it were a great weight to him put it into her hands.

"Kate, take it. I'm going to the place it tells about. I don't need it any longer. It is but a shabby little old book; but you won't mind that. Will you have it?"

"Have it? O, Jemmy!"

If no thanks were conveyed in those broken choking words, James was never thanked for that present till she met him again.

"I'm a very poor man. I have not much to give you worth your taking; but I should like you to take that bit of poor little Mary's hair that is in the drawer over there. I should not like strangers to be handling it. Will you take it, Kate?"

"Yes, James."

At that he seemed content. He lay back, and his eyes sought her face, and dwelt there satisfiedly. Then they wandered away to the open window, through which the sun was to be seen going down, red as blood, behind the trees.

"Kate, I'm like him; I'm going down too; my sun is setting. I shall be gone before he is."

She covered his hand with kisses, and her tears fell hot upon it. She knew that he spake truth. The golden cord was loosed and the pitcher broken at the fountain, and only He who fashioned it could make it whole again.[94] She saw the lamp of his life dying out for lack of oil, and she had no power to re-illumine it. In such moments is it that we feel our awful impotency, that we recognise ourselves as worms. Then the gentle voice, interrupted by slight pantings for the slow-coming breath, came to her ear again.

"It is a beautiful world, whatever they say, and life is a grand mystery; but I'm glad it is over, Kate. I'm very tired."

"Poor fellow! you have had a hard battle; have not you?"

"Yes—rather, Kitty; but it's over now, and the rest is the sweeter."

He closed his eyes, exhausted with the slight exertion, and stillness reigned in that room, broken only by Kate's stifled sobs. James was sinking very fast; he seemed to be floating away into a kind of painless slumber. After a time Kate rose softly from her knees and leaned over him in an agony of fear lest he should be gone—lest she should never hear him speaking to her any more again. His lips stirred, and moved slightly; with her handkerchief she wiped the death-dews tenderly off the wide brow that grief and care had drawn so many lines on—lines now to be effaced for ever, and bent lower to listen. These words, murmured indistinctly, with pauses between each, she caught:

"For—ever—with—the Lord,
Amen.—So let—it—be."[95]

On her thus hanging tearfully over him the dim eyes unclosed once more; unselfish to the last, in the very jaws of death, he tried to smile upon her. With a last effort he put his arms about her neck, and whispered, in a voice nearly extinguished by the strength of the Great Victor, but loving and tender in its utter weakness still:

"Kate, it will not be quite heaven till you're there too. I shall stand and watch the door for you. You'll come, won't you?"

"Yes, dear; yes, if I can. O, God, help me!"

"Kate, it's getting very dark; are you here still? You have been more

94 See Ecclesiastes 12:6 , although here the cord is silver instead of gold: "Or ever the silver cord be loosed, or the golden bowl be broken, or the pitcher be broken at the fountain, or the wheel broken at the cistern."

95 James Montgomery, "Forever with the Lord" (1835), ll. 1-2.

than a sister to me. Good-bye, darling! Kiss me this once."

"Good-bye, Jemmy! O, dear, dear old fellow!" and as she spoke she laid her pale lips on his for the first and last time.

Then the weary arms loosened their clasp languidly; a slight shiver passed over the toil-worn, patient body, and James fell back gently on his pillow—dead. Never hungry, nor lonely, nor sick, nor sorry again—at rest, for ever, in the bosom of God.

CHAPTER VI

NOT a day, not an hour, not a minute can anyone pass over of their real lives without living through, tasting its good and its evil; but of the fictitious life of a book one may overleap centuries if one chooses; that is to say, if one is not shackled by a Frenchman's slavish subjection to the unities.[96] I will avail myself but moderately of this privilege—a privilege I might use so largely—and will content myself with skipping a month. It is June then, the trees have put on a fuller deeper green, the birds are growing less vocal than they were a few weeks ago, and the fever is over and gone—one of the things of the past; but still people know that it has been, by the long rows of new graves in the cemetery outside the town, by the preponderance of black over all other hues in the dress of people in the streets. There was a new face to be seen in the pulpit of Queenstown church every Sunday now—a new voice exhorting to repentance, and faith, and charity; a fresh lodger in Mrs. Lewis's apartments; the new curate, in fact, who, having bought James's furniture at a valuation, was sitting in the old leathern elbow-chair, and thinking seriously that he must get the shabby old thing new-covered. It is somewhere about five o'clock, P. M., and Kate Chester is sitting alone in the drawing-room at No. 1 Cadogan-place, in a plain black dress with a bunch of white roses in the front. A white rose herself, and a very fair one. The look of hardness and austerity is gone out of her face; it could not find a permanent home in those soft features; it had never come back since the day when it had been washed away with scalding tears by the bedside of dying James Stanley. Very grave and serious she looked indeed, the causeless gaiety and light-heartedness of youth and animal spirits were banished, never to return; but there was no hope-

96 In French classical drama, the rules of unity derived from Aristotle's *Poetics*—unity of action, unity of place, and unity of time—were more scrupulously observed than in England.

less sadness as there used to be. At last she had learned experimentally that the time is short, that before long it will be that "those that weep shall be as though they wept not."[97] After toiling like a galley-slave for so long, she thinks she is entitled to a little rest; so she sits there luxuriously, on a low chair by the open window, smelling her roses and reading her Shakespeare. She does not get on very fast with her play, for every minute her eyes are lifted up from her book to glance down the road; she is expecting her sister home this afternoon, and is looking out anxiously for the first sign of her approach. At last her listening is rewarded. Off in the distance is heard the rumble of a carriage, five minutes more and it turns in at the white gate. A peal on the knocker, voices in the hall—not only women's trebles but a man's sonorous bass (not the cabby's either). Steps on the stairs—two steps, a woman's light one and also a man's heavy one. Kate is quite alone, but at these sounds she smiles to herself. Then the door bursts open and Maggie rushes in, blooming as any damask rose, all blushes and smiles and pink ribbons. A fire of kisses ensues.

"Well, Kitty, how are you? it seems quite funny seeing you again."

Kate returns the kisses with interest. She has so few to love now that she clings the more to those that are left.

"I thought you were never coming," she said, and her green eyes shone with a quiet gladness. "I am so glad to have you back again."

"Kate, here's George; he has taken the trouble to escort me all this long way up; is not it good of him?"

At this introductory remark, the said young man, who had been hitherto standing by as a spectator, grinning pleasedly, came forward and greeted his cousin.

"O," cried Kate, with amusement in her tone. "I begin to see.—How are you, George?"

"I suppose you guess, don't you?" Maggie asked, with a rather embarrassed laugh.

"Of course she does," said George, putting a hand on each of Maggie's shoulders, as if to proclaim himself owner thereof. Kate smiled softly upon them both.

"Perhaps I do a little."

"I suppose you found it all out from my letter this morning, did not you?"

---

97 See 1 Corinthians 7:30.

"No, I cannot say that I positively found anything out; I had my suspicions. I'm not surprised, but I'm very, very pleased."

"That's all right; I was sure you would be—was not I, George?"

"I congratulate you both most heartily. People always say that, as a matter of course, I know; but I do mean it really. You believe me, don't you?" and she put out a hand frankly to each; both to the sister who had been jealous of her, and to the man who would fain have married her.

"Yes," they both said, as unanimously as if it had been a response written down for them.

"I shall have two brothers instead of one now; but come, are not you very tired, and hot, and dusty after all that railway? You'll have some tea, won't you? I told them to bring some in."

Then George spoke up. With great discernment and amiability of feeling he perceived that at this conjecture his room would be better than his company. Those two sisters had a great deal to say to one another, which, though it was all about him, and because it was all about him, could not be said before him, so he said:

"Not for me, thank you, Kate. I must be going down to our place to look up the old people. Good-bye."

As soon as he was fairly gone, Kate kissed her sister again, and looked her full in the face.

"Well, who was right—you or I?" she asked.

"O, you; but I did not think you would have been."

"You see it has all come right, as I said it would."

"Yes, so it has; but I thought it then too good luck to be true."

"Well, I won't ask how it all came right, for I suppose that would not be a fair question; but I may ask how long it has been settled?"

"Only the day before yesterday."

"The same day that you wrote to me?"

"Yes, the morning of that day."

"Well, I suppose you are in a state of the most complete beatitude now—a sort of seventh heaven?"

"O, yes, now I am, but I can tell you I was anything but that three days ago. I began to think it was never coming—began to be afraid that he was hankering after you still."

"After me? Absurd! You should not get such notions into your stupid old head."

"Ah, but I did though. I could not help; it was no great wonder, considering what he had told me. But then that morning he asked me to come out walking with him, and it was all smooth after that; but I can tell you I was pretty miserable before."

"I suppose he is going to tell his father and mother now?"

"Yes. O, there'll be no difficulty there. Louisa told me they had all been longing for him to marry one of us ever since we came. He has been very unsettled of late, and they think that getting a wife will be the best thing that can happen to him."

"I think so too. Dear me, how odd it all seems!"

"Yes, does not it? But, come, let's have a look at you. Well, really, you do look uncommonly well, considering."

"I never was better in my life."

"I am so glad to see you again alive, after all this dreadful fever. At one time I hardly thought I should."

"It did seem doubtful."

"I wonder how you ever managed to live through it."

"I wonder so myself sometimes. I don't think I could go through it again if it were to come back directly, without giving me a little breathing-time."

"Heaven forbid! I should take to my heels pretty quick again if it did."

"O, no fear of that; it has done its work."

She shuddered a little, and sighed as she thought of what had been a part of that work.

"And so *he's* gone, Kate, too?"

"Yes, he's gone."

"Poor fellow! I *am* so sorry. I don't know when I've been so shocked as when I opened your letter that morning. It was so very sudden, too."

"Yes."

"And you were with him at the last?"

"Yes. Maggie, please, we won't talk about that any more; I cannot manage it quite yet."

"Poor thing! I'm sorry; it was stupid of me. I see that we must try and cheer you up a bit."

"I don't think I need cheering, Maggie; I feel very cheerful."

"You must come and live with us when we are married."

How pleasant that "we" and "us" are to young people before their novelty is worn off!

"Must I? There'll be plenty of time to talk of that by and by."

"Which means that you intend to shirk us. Ah, I know you so well."

"It means that I think young married people are much better left to themselves, without the encumbrance of a permanently spinster sister attached to their establishment."

"I don't see it at all. It would be the pleasantest arrangement possible; and I'm sure George would say the same if he were here."

"George is very good-natured, and would say anything to please you just at present; but have you settled where you are to live?"

"O no; it is early days to talk about that; but wherever it is, there'll be always room for you. I wish you would make up your mind to that."

"Thank you, Maggie; I have made up my mind; but I'll tell you all about that by and by."

CHAPTER VII

IN these days it did seem that Kate's words concerning herself were coming true. She was becoming isolated, as she had prophesied of herself long before. The ties that bound her to the world seemed to be snapping off one by one; there were very few left now. Well, perhaps it is better that they should break before life breaks too. The thread of life by itself is a slight one, broken off without difficulty or pain; it is the strong cords of love and interest that make the fracture so complicated, so agonising in the execution. Maggie, the sister with whom she had waked and slept, had quarrelled and made up again, and been one in interest with for so many years, going to be married, and enter into another sphere altogether; Blount away soldiering eleven months out of the twelve, and thinking more of his new red coat than of her; James dead, and Dare lost to her for ever;—what more had she to live for? Whom would her dying grieve much? Whom did her life profit much? she sometimes asked herself. With nobody was she first or even second. Yes, still she was first, and always would be, with poor wicked Dare. Though she prayed to God nightly, often with burning tears, that she might never see his face again in this world, she could not help being glad of that. How things were changed since four short years ago she had been the gayest of high-spirited young girls, the pet and darling of a happy home, whom the breath of care and trouble was not allowed to come near! Now she was a woman, and a very lonely woman, who had gone through a furnace of affliction, and did not seem to have much to hope or to fear in the world any longer now. Before her she saw spreading the path of her future life. Down a barren slope it led; no flowers grew by the wayside, no green grass upsprang thereon; and at the bottom of that drear slope sat "the shadow feared of man."[98] To reach him, to be taken into the folds of his mantle of night, was all she had to look forward to now. After her return home, Maggie Chester's time was very fully occupied buying wedding-clothes, receiving wedding-presents, attending to the exigencies of a sufficiently importunate lover, and lastly, making preparations for a ball to be given on the eve of her wedding at a hotel in the town, on account of the smallness of their own house. Consequently all thought about her sister's future was crowded out of her head. If any idea concerning her ever crossed her busy happy brain, she dismissed it lightly, saying to herself, "O, of course she'll get over her scruples; of course she'll come and live with us; what else is there for her to do?"

One afternoon, about a week before the day fixed for the marriage, Maggie and Kate were both together in the store-room, on their knees, surrounded by a sea of cotton-wool, hay, and silver-paper, packing up a quantity of glass and china which appertained to Mrs. George Chester elect. For some time they were too busy to say much; but as the white sea of cotton-wool diminished, and they began to foresee an end to their labours, Margaret lifted up her head, pushed off the straggling hair from her flushed face, and said:

"By the bye, Kate, let me ask you before I forget it again,—I was thinking of it only this morning,—what are you going to do with yourself whilst we are off on our wedding-tour? Of course, when we come back and set up housekeeping, you'll join us directly; but what do you intend doing till then?"

No answer. Kate buries her head in a deep box; only some red-brown plaits are seen emerging.

"Kate, do you hear? Why don't you answer? I want to know what you'll do with yourself while George and I are off honeymooning? Will you stay here, all by yourself, or will you go to the Chesters? They want very much to have you."

"Well, I don't think I shall do either."

"Not do either! Then what will you do? Perhaps you intend to come and chaperone us."

"No, I don't; but I shall leave Queenstown the day after the wedding."

"Where are you going to?"

98 See Tennyson, *In Memoriam* (1850), 22.12.

"To Manchester."

"Where?"

"To Manchester."[99]

"And who on earth do you know there? It must be some new acquaintance that you have made while I have been away."

"I don't know anybody there yet."

"Kate, you are very enigmatic to-day. What do you mean? I wish you would be a little more explicit."

"Well, the truth is I am in no hurry to tell you, because I am going to do a thing that I know you'll look upon as utterly absurd and quixotic and young-ladyish."

"Well, out with it. I must know, of course, whether you tell me or not. How slow you are!"

"I have decided to turn Sister of Mercy."

"Nonsense!"

"I was afraid you would take it in that way."

"Turn Sister of Mercy—*nun*!"

"Not nun, certainly. I'm not going to turn Roman Catholic, don't think that. I don't feel inclined to change my faith for the sake of wearing a rosary. It is a Protestant Sister of Mercy I'm going to be."[100]

"Is that the plan you darkly hinted at some time ago? No wonder you did not dare to explain it fully. I would have worked heaven and earth to stop it."

"Yes; that's the plan."

"And why, in the name of goodness, if you must do such an insane thing, did you fix upon Manchester of all places in the world—such a horrible smoky hole, and such an immense way off?"

"Well, I'll tell you how it came about. I got upon this subject one day

---

99 A northern industrial city whose dire poverty was detailed in Friedrich Engels's *The Condition of the Working Class in England in 1844* (1845).

100 In the wake of the Oxford Movement, Anglican women formed monastic communities analogous to those of Roman Catholic nuns. By 1900, over 90 Anglican sisterhoods existed, many devoted to serving the poor. As Margaret's response to Kate's announcement reveals, the establishment of Anglican convents was highly controversial. While to some extent this controversy reflected a long tradition of English anti-Catholic sentiment, Anglican sisterhoods were also criticized for siphoning women's energies away from traditional domesticity to work outside the home. See Susan Mumm, *Stolen Daughters, Virgin Mothers: Anglican Sisterhoods in Victorian Britain* (London: Leicester University Press, 1999).

with Miss Nugent, and she told me about this establishment, and that she had a sister who belonged to it, and that it is about the best conducted and managed altogether in England, and does an infinity of good; and she also told me that through her sister she could get any information about it for me, and, indeed, get me to be made a member if I chose, without any difficulty; so I thought such a good opportunity was not to be lost, do you see?"

"I see in the sense of understanding; but in the sense of approving I do not see by any means."

"I'm sorry for that; but it cannot be helped."

"May I ask how long this has been settled?"

"Not much more than a week, finally. I have had an idea of this kind of thing for months past—ever since I saw prophetically that you and George would make a match of it; but up to the time of James's death I always pictured to myself going to one of those places in London, or somewhere near here; but now that he has gone away and left me, it does not matter how far I go—the farther the better. Indeed, I would much sooner be at a great distance from you and everybody I know; for you would only be tempting me away from my work out of kindness and good-nature."

"And you coolly adopted this plan, and made all these arrangements, without asking anyone's advice, without consulting any human being under the sun,—a young inexperienced thing like you."

"Inexperienced do you call me? I think I have gone through as much in the last three years as many people do in eighty; but the reason why I told nobody about this was that I knew they would only 'pooh-pooh' it—think it a silly whim, born of an idea that 'Sister of Mercy' sounds nice and interesting and romantic; and I knew, too, that I was old enough to judge for myself, and knew my own soul much better than anyone else could possibly do. I don't think it was any conceit or obstinacy that made me do it. O Maggie, you'll get reconciled to the notion in time, I assure you."

"I'm sure I shall not, if you'll excuse me for saying so. I think that with your face and figure and gifts generally it is the act of an idiot. O Kitty, Kitty, do think better of it. Give it up."

Kate shook her head. "No, Maggie, I cannot indeed. I have been so unsettled and tossed about in mind for ever so long, that I look forward to this sort of life, in which one learns to forget self, and act as if self were not, as a kind of haven of rest."

"You are too young to talk in that strain. All very well for a battered old woman of sixty to talk of longing for a haven. Why, Kate, if you come and live quietly with George and me, you can be as independent as possible, and as much your own mistress as you chose; you will be able to do every bit as much good, without making such an utter sacrifice of yourself and all your prospects."

"No, I could not; one can do six times as much working in concert as alone. If I lived with you, I should have a thousand pleasant little distractions; besides, how often you have told me that I am too young to visit all these low parts of Queenstown, and that I was very much talked about and blamed for doing it. Now, with the protection of the name and dress I shall have,[101] I may go anywhere unmolested; that is an undisputed fact."

"I should have thought you would have had enough of that sort of thing the last month or two."

"No, I have not, Maggie. I have tried pleasing myself, and hoping for things in this world, for one-and-twenty years, and every hope I had in the world is shipwrecked; you know that; I don't often talk about it, but that does not make me feel it less. Now it is my only wish to do some little good before I die, to grow a little like poor dearest Jemmy. O, Maggie, I do miss him so—and then, perhaps, God will let me die like he did."

"Die, die, die! don't be always harping upon dying! it is not lively talk for a person who is on the verge of matrimony."

"I'm rather a kill-joy, I think. I used not to be, used I?"

"No indeed, you were not, and you shall not be for long either; old Piggy and Blount are coming here to-morrow, you know; well, as soon as ever they arrive, I shall set them both upon you; you shall have no peace till you promise to abandon this plan altogether. There!"

"Old Piggy as much as ever you like; but please do not set Blount upon me. I could not bear him deriding me, and thinking me a fool."

"I want him to think you a fool; I want him to make you think yourself one."

"Ah, even he could not do that; I am so persuaded, far down in the bottom of my heart, that I am in the right; but I don't intend to tell him anything about it while I am here, not until I am in Manchester, and fairly

---

101 The distinctive habits worn by Anglican sisters—one of their more obviously "Papist" practices—provided, as Susan Mumm puts it, "a passport into the worst and most lawless slums, allowing the wearer to go with impunity anywhere, alone, at any hour of the day or night" (*Stolen Daughters, Virgin Mothers: Anglican Sisterhoods in Victorian Britain* [London: Leicester University Press, 1999], 78). Contrast Kate's earlier fear of assault when she visits the slums wearing a fashionable crinoline.

settled at my new work, and it's all done and irrevocable; then, and not sooner, I shall write and break the news to him."

"He will be in a great rage, I expect."

"Very likely."

"I should not be surprised if he were to get two doctors to prove you of unsound mind (it is very easily done nowadays), and put you into a madhouse."

"Hardly, I think; but, Maggie, you will not say anything to him about it, will you? I know exactly in what light it would appear to a young fellow just entering life, with everything before him, a young fellow who could have no more conception of how tired of everything I feel, how stranded and finished off altogether, as concerns this world, than I have of the sensations of that cow out there. You'll oblige me very much if you'll grant me this little thing; promise me this, Maggie; promise me."

"O, I'll promise anything you like, though I don't see the object of it; promises are like pie-crusts, you know, made to be broken."

"No, it must not be that kind of promise. Ah, Maggie, don't bully me this last week."

"Kate, I always hated those sisterhoods; they have been a curse to numberless families, I am certain; a number of women huddled together, cut off from their lives, and their friends, and all their prospects in life. Why cannot women keep to their right functions of marrying and being happy?"

"Be happy if they can, by all means; people's ideas about happiness differ, you know. We had better not get upon a definition of happiness; and marry also, by all means, if they can have your luck, and get the man they are in love with, otherwise marriage would be a punishment hardly inferior to being tied to a dead body."

"Well, I remember once reading in some book that a bad husband was better than no husband at all; and, though I was ashamed to give out that sentiment myself, yet I always agreed with it cordially. Hush! yes, it *is* him—there's George outside, I hear his voice."

Out of her head went all thoughts of Sisters of Mercy, and their abominable practices; away went all recollections of Kate's existence. Up she sprang, and ran out into the passage to meet her lover. The door was left ajar, and Kate could hear the sound of murmured words and kisses.

Her hands lay idle on her lap, and her eyes turned to a patch of blue sky seen through the window. "How happy they are!" she said to herself.

"Ah, so was I once, but that is over and gone. O, that day among the flowers with you, my poor, wicked old fellow! Well,

'I have lived and loved, but that was to-day;
Make ready my grave-clothes to-morrow.'"[102]

CHAPTER VIII

KATE was rather superstitious—excitable women, warm-blooded, imaginative, mostly are. Let it not be supposed that this remark is a prelude to some dismal tale of how Kate saw the ghost of her dead father, or her mother, or an uncle, or an aunt, or of any individual whom she had never beheld before. No such thing. Kate Chester was never visited by any apparition during the whole course of her short life, and in this I consider her rather exceptionally fortunate. But that night she had a dream. This in itself was rather an event to her; very seldom did she dream; mostly she lay lapped in the deep untroubled slumbers of youth and health. But this night she dreamt that she was standing before the altar of the old village church where her father lay buried, with Dare, being married to him. Oddly enough, the altar was draped with black. The parson was reading out of a big book to them, and this parson was James Stanley; at least he had his face, but the voice was the droning voice of the new curate of Queenstown. And she herself was robed in bridal white, and had a chaplet of flowers about her brow; but somehow the flowers did not seem like roses and myrtles—they were more like rosemary.[103] And it was not the marriage service the parson was reading; distinctly she heard these words, "Earth to earth, ashes to ashes, dust to dust."[104] Then the ceremony appeared to be ended, and she and Dare stood there with their hands clasped in each other; and she, with a throb of intensest ecstasy, looked up in his face and said, "There, Dare, it has all come right as I said." The dream was so vivid that at first she doubted whether that were vision and this reality, or that reality and this vision; then full recollection came back, and boding fears

102 Inexact, from Samuel Taylor Coleridge translation (1800) of Friedrich Schiller's play *Wallenstein* (1799), II.vi. 32-33.

103 Symbolic of fidelity and remembrance, rosemary was used both in funeral wreaths and wedding bouquets. Conflating both uses, Kate's dream equates love with death.

104 Lines from the burial service in the Anglican Book of Common Prayer.

crowded thickly about her. "Dreams go by opposites," she said to herself. "If you dream of a marriage, it foretells a death, that never fails. I remember Maggie dreamed of a marriage just a week before mama died. O, nonsense! How weak I am! Of course it is that I have been thinking so much of Maggie's wedding, that it has put such ideas into my head." But still that dream made her thoughtful all through the day. In the afternoon Blount Chester arrived; in the evening, Mr. and Mrs. Piggott. The whole former Pen Dyllas party were assembled now. Blount, I have said, arrived in the afternoon. Leisurely he strolled into the drawing-room, and nodded to his sisters. To show emotion of any kind or degree was not permissible to a Greek philosopher or a Red Indian—is not permissible to an Englishman. He stooped his comely young head, and submitted patiently, while they flung glad arms about his neck, and gave him a hearty kiss. Then he calmly repaired the damage their impetuosity had done to his toilette.

"There, girls; that'll do. Baking hot it is, and you are not making me cooler."

"I suppose you walked up from the station?"

"Yes, of course I did. Did you expect me to drive up in a fly? Has not old Fleecy come yet?"

So he designated his reverend uncle.

"No; we don't expect them till the evening."

"Of course he'll come by cattle-train, in a pen with a lot of other baa-lambs."

Maggie laid a beseeching hand on his shoulder.

"Blount, I entreat you, don't make fun of him after he comes when I am in the room; it will infallibly set me off laughing, and then there'll be no stopping me."

"I have no intention of making fun of the wretched old beggar. I wonder does his addled old pate ache as much as it used to do."

"It's to be hoped not, for aunt Harriet's sake. If I had been her, I should have been tempted to make it ache still worse, or stop aching altogether, many years ago."

"Good hearing for George, Maggie; that's the way you'll be serving him some day."

"By the bye, Blount, do you think he'll kiss George? You know he'll be his nephew now."

"Hardly, if he is wise. George's bristles would draw blood."

Maggie looked rather foolish; she began to look upon those bristles as her own particular property, and to resent insults to them as such.

Life is full of disappointments. Very seldom the good things on which we count, to which we look forward, come to pass; generally they elude our grasp. But that evening, by the train, and at the time expected of him, Daddy Piggott made his appearance, and also that attendant spirit, Mammy Piggott—only, somehow, one never thought of her existence, she was so swallowed up and merged in her lord's brightness. Down ran a brace of dutiful nieces to greet him as his big meek black body emerged slowly on the white stone steps.

"Well, Maggie, my love; well, Kate, my love, I hope you are pretty well."

How is it possible, with what single letters, or combination of letters, to write down a kiss?—for at this period each of the girls performed a chirping little salute on the fair large surface of their uncle's extended cheek, flabby as of yore.

"Yes, thank you, dear loves; I'm pretty well, only that this dreadful railway always shakes me so terribly. But I really am better than I thought I should be—ain't I, my love?"

"Will not you come in and sit down, Mr. Piggott? and aunt Harriet or one of us can settle with the cabman."

"Well, indeed, my dear loves, I think that perhaps I had better.—By the bye, dear Ma, will you be so very kind as to see that they take my medicine-chest up into my room? I think I had better take my draught as usual before dinner—had not I, dear love?"

"Yes, love."

"I don't want to give you any trouble, dear Ma, but I think perhaps it would be wiser not to let the servants carry it upstairs, as they might let it fall and break it; and you know, dear love, that would never do."

"Very well, love; I'll take it up myself."

"And now, my dear girls, I think I'm quite ready.—Kate, my little maid, I'm afraid I must trouble you to give me an arm, for, after all, I'm afraid I'm a little giddy—a little slower, please, dear love."

"Would you like to go to bed, Mr. Piggott?"

"No, thank you, my love. I shall be all right presently, I hope. I think, dear Ma, that I had better, perhaps, go straight to my room and take a little nap before dinner, and then I trust I shall be pretty well all the evening."

By these fragments of conversation it may be seen that Mr. Piggott was unchanged; exactly the same as when at Pen Dyllas he had baaed and bleated to ears that did not hear him, they were so full of the echo of another's deep tones.

Next night, as the two Chesters were going to bed, Maggie stopped suddenly, with brush suspended in mid air.

"Kate," she said, "I heard you stammering and stuttering this evening, when old Piggy asked you something about the ball; you don't mean to say that you are intending not to go to it?"

"Well, I was rather thinking of staying away," Kate owns from under a torrent of warm curls.

"What absurdity! of course you must go. I shall take it as an insult to myself if you don't. Who ever heard of the bride's sister not being present on such an occasion?"

"But, Maggie, I have no dress."

"What does that matter? Leave all to me, and I'll turn you out better dressed than ever you were in your life before."

"But I could not go in black to this ball, and I should not like to go in colours."

"Kate, that is overstrained, false sentiment."

"No, it is not. I don't want to put off the outward signs of mourning for poor James, even though I know that I shall carry the inward mourning with me to my grave."

"Kate, I am going to say a disagreeable thing, but I must. The way you are going on people will be sure to say that you were in love with James Stanley; that you are making a great fool of yourself about him, and perhaps—it is not at all improbable—it may come round to Colonel Stamer's ears—you would not like that, would you?"

The torrent of hair droops lower and lower—not an inch of face to be seen.

"Maggie, don't be cruel," says a stifled voice; but she winces and succumbs.

CHAPTER IX

IT is the night of the ball—a ball that so many a little heart has been beating expectantly for through the last lagging fortnight; that many a little seventeen-year-old has been counting the days to.

"There was a sound of revelry by night."[105]

105 Lord Byron, "Childe Harold's Pilgrimage" (1812-18), III.21.8.

The noise of carriages rolling along the streets of Queenstown is continuous—almost ceaseless; a long row standing before the door of a large hotel, whose hospitable portals stand open in the summer night, welcoming all comers. Every minute some vehicle, having discharged its load of tulle and tarletane,[106] is being driven away, and its occupants swell the crowd within. And within there was a pleasant sight to be seen, whatever anyone, with jaundiced eyes and a misanthropic turn of mind, might say to the contrary. A big room, festooned and decorated—wreaths of laurel and ivy, with roses and asters laughing out between, lit up with branching chandeliers, almost into the brightness of day. Nothing but flowers and music, pretty faces and low voices—the bright side of the picture of life. Nothing to remind one that there is a dark side. Chaperones and matrons reposing on the benches, scarlet-cloth-covered in all the dignity of feathers and brocades; each one apparently absorbed in hearing and retailing gossip, but in reality keeping a keen eye on her own particular lamb among the gauzy flock, watching unconsciously to see if there seemed any chance of business being brisk this evening; or whether, on the other hand, the said lamb were laying up for herself any matter for rebuke when they should have returned home, and have laid aside the brocade and the remnants of gauzy rags. A knot of men—officers, principally importations from Windsor and Hampton Court, lounged abut the doors, knowing nobody as yet; amusing themselves criticising the girls as they passed, and perfectly conscious of being in return the object of a good deal of interested notice.

"The harp, violin, bassoon,"[107] were clashing out loud and clear, and nobody could hear their own voices hardly. If people wanted to make love they must not whisper it, according to approved ideas, but roar it. Round and round went the mad whirl of men and girls—faster and madder it grew, every minute as the music surged and swelled out, and then sank, and died away in luxurious cadences. Men clasping vigorously slender waists; little maidens leaning confiding heads almost down on their lovers' shoulders—soft cheeks swept by manly whiskers; as they floated and swam round in utter enjoyment. Maggie stood at the door as hostess, receiving everybody; longing for the end of the arrivals, that she, too, might go and join the dance, with feet that seemed barely able to help keeping time to the music. Every now and then she looked piteously at George, who stood dutifully near her, as the entrance of some new party again deferred the

106 Light-weight fabrics suitable for evening wear.
107 Inexact, Tennyson, *Maud* (1855), I.XXII.14.

period of her felicity. And where was Kate meanwhile? Not being hostess, nor having any duties on her white shoulders, she might be dancing all the breath out of her body if she chose. But such is the contrariety of human nature, what people can do, without anyone attempting to prevent them, they often do not care to do. Kate was not dancing at all; she was sitting alone at an open window, leaning one white elbow on the sill, and the roses and jasmines were straggling in to greet her; telling her, with their cool, sweet odours, how pleasant and still the July night was outside. At her entrance into this house to-night she had been assailed by a variety of exclamations and ejaculations from all her female acquaintances.

"You here, Kate! Well, wonders will never cease. Why, I thought you had turned so religious that you thought dancing one of the seven deadly sins. Never mind what they say, Kate, I'm very glad to see you back among us. You are a very wise girl, I think."

Kate did not think it worth while to explain—they would all know soon enough. As she moved up the room on Blount's arm, not being deaf, she could not be unconscious of the murmurs that buzzed around her.

"What a lovely girl! Who on earth is she? What a figure! I say, just look at Kate Chester! How brilliant she looks! She is six times prettier than ever!"

Hitherto Blount Chester had not admired Kate much more than it is the wont of brothers to admire their sisters; now, however, he did feel proud of being seen with her, of having her in his charge.

"I say, Kitty, I flatter myself we are creating quite a sensation," he said, looking down on her, and his jolly, good-looking young face dilated into a gratified grin.

Kate laughed too. She did not pretend not to have heard these commendations of her.

"I think we are," she answered; and though she was going to turn Sister of Mercy to-morrow—to wear an unbecoming poke bonnet[108] and a black serge dress for evermore, yet her heart beat and swelled a little under the influence of that pleasant incense.

Blount was besieged with requests for introductions, but Kate was obstinate—would not dance, did not dance; only intended to look on. Blount lost his temper at last, told her she was a fool for her pains; that anyhow he would not be bothered with her any longer; shook off her hand from his

108 See p. 217, n.103.

sleeve, and left her sitting by herself, to amuse herself as best she might. There were many women at the ball that night with far more regular features than Kate's, with noses that had no tendency to the forbidden upward curve, that went down, as noses should—not up, as hers did; with cheeks twice as rosy, figures twice as tall and imposing;—but for all that, singular to relate, there was hardly a dissentient voice among the men, when someone suggested that the little thing in green, with the lot of bright hair, was the belle of the night. The women, indeed, tried to set up a rival beauty, but they had her all to themselves. Many an eye-glass, and many an eye without a glass, was continually turning to the corner where Kate sat, an obstinate little wallflower. If this refusal to dance had been a design of the most deep-laid coquetry, it could not have tantalised her admirers more.

At last Maggie's duties were ended, and she had leisure to think of something else beside bowing and saying:

"How do you do? So glad to see you!"

After looking round for her sister, and discovering the posture of affairs, she turned to George and said, in rather a vexed tone:

"Just look at Kate! What a goose she looks huddled up in that corner over there, as if she were performing some penance! Just go over to her and tell her from me that it's all nonsense—she *must* dance; she is making herself so remarkable sitting there, with everybody staring at her: people will be sure to put it down to conceit. Go, there's a good fellow."

"I don't expect she'll mind me much."

"O, yes, she must, and—stay, take somebody with you to introduce to her, that she may have no excuses."

"Who shall I take?"

"Let me see—I'm sure there's plenty of choice. O, one of those men that are standing over there—those officers, they don't know a soul. I'm sure it would be a charity to get them partners."

"I know who I'll get—Tankerville. I did not see him before; he's in the 3d Buffs;[109] such a good fellow, and a capital dancer."

Off he went, and attacked the unconscious Tankerville.

"I say, old fellow, do you want a partner? I can get you one if you do."

"O, I don't know; I don't seem to care much about it," responded Captain Tankerville languidly.

Perhaps it occurred to him that the 3d did not dance.

109 3rd East Kent Regiment of Foot, called Buffs after the color of their coats.

"Nonsense! don't be lazy."

"Well, to oblige you, then; only I'll have a look at her first. Mind, I won't have anything to say to her if she is ugly, or if she squints."

"She is the prettiest girl in the room, and it is very doubtful if she'll have anything to say to you."

Kate was getting rather tired of talking to nobody, so perhaps she was glad when she perceived George skirting the dancers to come to her, with a large young man with a blonde moustache and no whiskers following in his wake. George stooped down to whisper to her:

"Kate, Maggie has sent me to you to tell you that you must dance; that you are making yourself so remarkable, sitting here with everybody staring at you; and I have brought a friend of mine who is dying to be introduced to you."

"But, George, I have refused so many, I could not possibly dance now."

She lifted up her little piquant face, and her great pensive eyes to his, and Captain Tankerville peeped at her over George's shoulder, and an evil intention he had been nourishing of bestowing a quadrille upon her vanished like morning dew.

"Fiddle-de-dee!" said George. "You must say you made a mistake.—Here, Tankerville.—Kate, will you allow me to introduce Captain Tankerville to you?—My cousin, Miss Chester."

Ten minutes after, Kate, the non-dancing recluse, was flying round in the arms of a large young man whom she had never beheld before. He was a capital dancer, as George had said, and, for the matter of that, so was Kate. Light as a feather, and as springy as—a fit comparison fails me—those round, soft white women often are. Ten minutes of spinning round, swiftly and smoothly, with complete agreement in their supple movements; then they stop to take breath. Kate pants a little, and fans herself. Captain Tankerville pulls out his pocket-handkerchief, wipes his forehead and says, "Thank you; that is a treat." It is exciting, certainly, Kate says to herself. She does not repent of her determination, but she feels the seduction of the hour. Formerly she had been passionately fond of dancing; was always of a nature singularly susceptible to outward influences; to anything that spoke to the senses. Her love for dancing seemed to have come back; her blood went through her veins with a quicker rush; everything around had a temporary spell for her—the hot atmosphere, scent-laden, the blaze of the hundred wax-lights, the happy, animated faces, the voluptuous music pealing still in its harmonious madness, the handsome man standing beside her, looking down with undisguised admiration on her downcast face. I think the members of Kate's new sisterhood would have been surprised to see their proselyte to-night. I think they would have stared, if their meek eyes could have lit on this girl, with the waves and seas of tulle, pale sea green and virgin white, floating crisply round her, with that one big heavy garden lily, shining star-like among the twisted wealth of such hair as seemed borrowed from one of Guido's Magdalenes;[110] this girl, with polished shoulders gleaming bare, and flashing eyes. There was no use denying it, Kate was enjoying herself, and looked as if she was. Meanwhile Maggie and her lover were standing together, resting likewise, in a pause of the surging, whirling waltz. Maggie looks up in his face, with her head rose-crowned, like some guest at a Roman banquet, and says with a sigh:

"Ah, George, this is the last day that you and I will ever be able to dance together."

"Why so?"

"O, married people cannot go valsing about together; it is so undignified; nobody ever does it."

"We will set the fashion then, Maggie, and show them what a good plan it is."

"Ah, it won't be the same."

"I don't see why it should not."

"George, I'm glad that cluster of men at the door is dispersed at last; they did look so disconsolate."

"Yes, they have all got partners somehow; Kate and Tankerville seem getting on like a house on fire, don't they?"

"Yes, is it not amusing?"

In another part of the room, one of Blount's partners, one of the most promising of the seventeen-year-olds, is saying to him:

"You must take me back to mamma, please, now; she does not like me to stay away long."

"Nonsense," says Blount, protectingly; "I could not think of such a thing; it's so much jollier walking about like everybody else."

"Ah, but mamma will not be pleased, she is so particular."

"She's not looking this way at all; she is talking to that old woman on the other side; she'll forget all about you if you don't remind her. Come and have an ice."

110 See p. 93, n. 122.

"O, very well, but you must not be long, please, because I'm engaged for the next dance."

And then she shows him her card, and he writes his own name repeatedly down the length of it, and they flutter off together, two remarkably happy young butterflies. So the night wears on; and the flowers and garlands on the walls swing and vibrate with the motion of the dancers dancing in tune; and the music sounds on, now clashing and blaring out, now sighing and whispering; and pretty faces get flushed, and little feet fly faster than ever, and dresses get torn and dishevelled. Maggie has retired into a corner with George, and sits demure, and thinks of the morrow. Blount is dragging along a portly fat woman, piloting her with infinite skill among the shoals and quicksands of the crowded room; and Kate, a white-armed siren, is swimming lightly and buoyantly round in the embrace of a heavy dragoon. Then supper comes, and champagne flows like water, and laughter bubbles up from jocund hearts,

> "And all went merry as a marriage-bell."[111]

As Kate mounts the stairs from the supper-room to the dancing-hall on the arm of the master of the house, a sound comes to her ears, very incongruous with the sounds she has been hearing—the luxurious music, and the soft words that

> "Seemed a part of the music,"[112]

—the sound of a solemn bell tolling mournfully.

"What's that?" she says breathlessly, and she looks up, trembling with affright, in her companion's face. "What's the bell tolling for? is there anybody dead?"

He laughs.

"It's not tolling," he said; "it's only the old church clock striking midnight: you know how it is close at the back of this house, so we hear it so plain."

She smiles palely.

"I don't know what's come to me to-night," she says; "I'm so absurdly nervous. I feel as if I could scream with fright at my own shadow. I wonder

111 Byron, *Childe Harold's Pilgrimage* (1812-18), III.21.8.

112 Longfellow, *Evangeline* (1847), I.i.94.

what's going to happen."

"Nothing," he answers, "except that you are going to give me the next dance, I hope; a good galop[113] will soon shake the terrors out of you."

Kate is reassured a little, but the impression made upon her by that grave heavy sound booming out upon the summer night cannot be quite shaken off. Reason tells her that it was but a clock striking, but still it seems to her to have been sent as a warning;—but warning of what? Again she dances; sliding down the long room in the bounding galop they go; and men straggle up from supper, and commend again the sinuous form and the brilliant face. Suddenly something drops from Kate's arm with a ring on the floor; her partner stoops to pick it up, and gives it back into her hands. It is a gold bracelet with dark blue enamel, and "Gott schütze dich" (God protect thee) in gold letters upon it. The enamel is cracked across, the letters split and riven. Kate turns pale again.

"What a bad omen!" she says hastily, "I have dropped that bracelet often and often, and it never broke before; O, I'm certain that something is going to happen."

"You don't believe in omens, surely?" asks her partner incredulously.

"Yes, indeed I do; and besides I feel such an extraordinary oppression, such a dull weight on my soul to-night, that I am certain, perfectly certain, that something dreadful is hanging over me. I'm afraid you'll think me a great fool," she added, trying to laugh.

"No, indeed, I don't, but I think you're very needlessly alarmed."

Kate would not dance a step more; all the springy lightness was gone out of her feet. Those two trifling circumstances had completely broken the spell—destroyed the brief enchantment of the hour. She longed for the ball to be over—longed to get that haunting music out of her ears, those blazing lights out of her eyes—longed to be home again, and able to close her lids in the dark, and shut out the images of fear that came crowding before them. Try as she would, she could not get free from the entanglement of those groundless fears, those childish shudderings. Ever in the midst of the gay crowded room there seemed to be a blackness rising up round her. I called the room crowded, but the truth was that at this time of the evening it was still rather empty, rather thin; champagne and cold chicken held their own completely against music and dancing. People were slowly dribbling back, by twos and threes, indeed, but the majority were

113 A lively dance step inspired by a horse's gallop.

feasting still. Kate looked round with searching gaze. Neither Maggie nor George nor Blount to be seen anywhere. Then her eyes fell on Mr. Piggott reposing on a bench in a corner, after a light repast of calf's-foot jelly and sherry-and-water. This had been a very happy evening for him, for he had had the good luck to make acquaintance with an old lady, whose symptoms, as regarded shooting pains, derangement of the system, &c., strongly resembled his own. He was now sitting beside her, amicably comparing notes with her on the subject of their mutual disorders. Kate made her way across to him. "Mr. Piggott," she said, "will you tell Margaret, when you see her, that if she wants me, I am to be found in the conservatory? I really am so hot and tired that I cannot dance any more."

"Very well, my dear love. I'll tell her, if you wish," replied he blandly; "but, my little maid, don't you think that it is a little bit imprudent of you to be going straight out of this heated room into the cold air?" (it was a sultry July night)—"and besides, I am sure I have heard many doctors say that the smell of flowers at night is very injurious. Do try and be a little careful of yourself, my love, I beg."

"O, I'm not afraid; they'll do me no harm," Kate said. She moved away to the door, and then sauntered slowly down the long conservatory to a seat there was at the end, half hidden in green orange-boughs. There she sank down and rested, *perdue.*[114] Down the long vista of waving leaves, and glowing flowers, and Chinese lanterns, she saw the brilliant ball-room at the end, and figures passing to and fro. Hither the music came with a subdued mellowness of sound. Here it was quiet and fragrant and very cool. "How I wish the night was over!" she kept saying to herself over and over again. "How I wish it was morning! I should feel safer then; one never feels such vague terrors of a morning. Why was it that I felt such a sudden consternation come over me when I heard that simple common sound? It is perfectly inexplicable."

Then her dream flashed back, vivid as reality, upon her. Dreams do that often in the evening; even if forgotten and blotted out of memory during the daylight hours, at evening-tide back they come again, fresh as when first written on the waxen tablets of the brain. Where they go or whence they return, we know not, but so it is. That dream did not come for nothing, Kate felt very sure; it meant something. It was a shadow cast before by some substance not yet come up, coming up, though, surely, si-

114 Lost (French); in this context, unnoticed by others.

lently, against her. Dreams went by opposites; if you dreamt of a marriage there would ensue a death. But who was going to die? Was it herself? The bravest of us shriek and quail when we picture ourselves in the embrace of the great king. We cannot look the sun in the face, he is too bright; we cannot look death in the face, he is too dark. Gloomy thoughts these for a marriage feast!

Suddenly[115] the solitude she had sought with such eagerness became oppressive, irksome to her; as no one attempted to disturb it, it lost its value. It struck her, too, with surprise that the music had entirely ceased: there was a much longer interval than that usually allowed between the last valse and the cotillon[116] that was to follow it. Curiosity prompted her to rise and reënter the dancing-room. It was almost deserted; here and there half-a-dozen people were grouped, near the door principally; but the musicians were gone; the dancers' feet were still. Two men she knew were standing, talking together quickly, earnestly, and their faces looked pale in the gas-light; but gas-light does impart a ghastly look to even the rosiest.

"Is everybody gone?" she said with her charming smile. "What a hurry you are all in to leave us! Is it Cinderella over again on a large scale? When the clock struck twelve did everybody turn into kitchenmaids, and their coaches into pumpkins?"

"Is it possible you have not heard?" exclaimed the younger of the two men. "Good heavens! where can you have been?"

"Heard what?" she said, her smile fading into a surprised gravity.

"Well, you see," began the other man, to whom nature had originally given a long face, and who thought it necessary to lengthen it artificially on the present occasion,—"well, you see, there has been an accident, a very serious accident; a man driving down from town to the ball here, thrown out of his dog-cart[117] at the very door—actually at the very door," he repeated emphatically; as if the fact of its having occurred at the door instead of the window formed the gist of the catastrophe.

"How terrible!" exclaimed Kate in a shocked voice. "Poor man! how did it happen?" and the divinest light of pity streamed into her eyes.

"Coming round that sharp corner, don't you know, by the stables, the horse shied at something—a heap of stones, or a wheel-barrow, or something—everybody was talking at the same time, and I did not exactly make

115 The original ending continues from this point; see Appendix B, pp. 418-428.
116 Also cotillion; like the quadrille, a square dance with four couples.
117 See p. 93, n. 121.

out what—threw the groom out one side, and Stamer the other, and the wheels went over him."

The inquiring pitying look changed into a frozen, stony stare of horror and fear.

"*Who*?" she said, clutching the narrator's arm.

"Stamer—Colonel Stamer; he is in the Guards. You don't know him, do you?"

"Is he *dead*?" she said in a hissing whisper, and her breath came quick and short, like one that has run a weary way with a deadly foe behind him, and her face looked pinched and drawn.

"No-o-o, not yet; but I'm afraid it must come to that: crushed internally I think; *may* last till morning. Dear me, Miss Chester, you are not going to faint, are you? Let me get you a glass of water. It was very thoughtless of me telling you so suddenly!" he ejaculates with flurried compunction.

Twice she tried to speak; twice the disobedient voice refused to pass the portals of the parched white lips; at last with a tremendous effort of the will, she succeeded in articulating hoarsely the one word "Where?"

"Where is he, you mean?" said the younger man catching her meaning; "as I came upstairs they were just carrying him in, and laying him on a sofa. O, let me get you a chair; you look terribly ill, and I'll go and see how he is."

She put her hand to her head dizzily.

"No, no!" she said in a harsh whisper, "I don't want you; I'm going myself."

They watched her with a dumb astonishment, as she passed with a step that did not falter out of the room, and down the stairs.

"I had not a notion she knew him," says one to the other with a dismayed intimation, "poor little girl, she looks as like death as he does; one of his many victims, I suppose?"

"De mortuis nil nisi bonum!"[118] says the other gravely; "and if poor Stamer does not come under that head yet, he is not far off it, unless I'm very much mistaken."

The hall and the vestibule of the hotel are full of people, and there is a dull confused noise of voices and footsteps: girls in opera-cloaks with pale scared faces, hurrying to their carriages—hurrying away from the place where they came to meet Love and Pleasure, and where instead the officious "spectre with the bony head"[119] has thrust his grisly presence

118 Of the dead speak nothing but good (Latin).

119 See p. 207, n. 88.

upon them. A crowd of men, gentlemen, waiters, boots,[120] and servants are pressing round a man in a groom's livery, who, with torn coat and battered hat, is telling over and over again, to an ever-fresh audience, the tale of his own escape and his master's destruction. Chambermaids in smart caps and white aprons are huddling together, sobbing vociferously (the tears of the uneducated are proverbially near their eyes); emulously vying with each other in the race to hysterics. The fact of a man having been killed at his door has imparted a prestige to his establishment, of which the landlord is, with modest pride, aware. Strange, is not it, that the rabid love for horrors should be an instinct, and deeply planted in the vulgar mind, that it requires the education of a lifetime to outroot our love for "raw-head and bloody-bones"?[121] A murder, of course, is the source whence the keenest enjoyment is to be derived—a wife-murder with a good deal of poker, and of hair torn out; but still there is a fair amount of pleasant excitement to be extracted from a good accident, always presupposing plenty of mangling and broken bones.

At the foot of the stairs Kate comes upon George. An habitually jovial laughing face looks so exceedingly odd when compelled by circumstances to assume a sad and solemn air: George did not look like George.

"Where are you going, Kate? This is no place for you; go back, dear," he says authoritatively, but very kindly.

"Don't stop me," she replies in hard metallic tones, from which all emotion is entirely absent, "let me pass, please."

"No, indeed, you must not," he says, seizing her hand with eager compassionate remonstrance; "you cannot do him any good; poor fellow, it is all up with him."

She makes no answer; she only endeavours unsuccessfully to slip past him. Maggie standing by, shawled and clothed for departure, her face looking out pallid from a little cherry-coloured hood, interposes:

"You must not, indeed, Kate; just think what you are doing. George, she does not mind a word I say; *do* stop her. What *will* people say? it will be all over the town, to-morrow."

To-morrow! What was to-morrow to her? What are all the endless to-morrows that the world will open its tired eyes on? What does she care if every vulgar soul in Queenstown follow her with hootings and hissings,

120 Hotel servants who polished boots.

121 According to Irish legend, Rawhead and Bloody Bones were bogeymen who drowned children.

and shameful names to-morrow? She wrenches her hand out of George's grasp; she would leave it there torn off, if that were the only way of freeing herself. A door ajar—one or two people hovering about it with attentive eyes and ears, a sort of audible silence within—tell her whither to direct her steps. She neither knocks nor hesitates. Whose leave should she ask? Who has so good a right to be near him as she? She finds herself in a large, bright sitting-room; Utrecht velvet,[122] walnut-wood, a great chandelier;—it looks a room to live in, not one to die in. They carried him in here, because it was the nearest place—because he was a dead-weight on their hands and in bitter, bitter pain.

Well, he had always said long ago that he hoped he should not waste away tediously by inches on a sick bed; and his wish will be gratified. A man in a black coat, who might be a doctor, might be an undertaker (and are they not brothers-in-arms?), and two or three women, are standing round, whispering loudly, disturbingly about him. He is still "*he*;" not yet "*it*." They have partly undressed him, and laid him on the sofa, and there he lies, his dying head—the short rings of silky hair damp with the death-dews—thrown back, his broad shoulders indenting the cushion, and his strong right hand hanging nerveless towards the floor. There he lies, like a fallen Colossus,[123] weak as a two-years' child,—Samson robbed of his strength; only the Dalilah who has shorn this Samson's locks to-night is Death.[124] There he lies, open-eyed, full-conscious as in the heyday of his youth and strength, while a voice keeps dinning into his ears, "Thou must die, thou must die!" and his soul answers unflinching, "I know it; hold ye your peace!"[125]

Kate pushes aside the attendants unceremoniously, rudely. In moments of profound mastering emotion we shake ourselves free from the artificial restraints of society and education, as some strong runner, ere setting forth on a long hard race, casts away the heavy garments that would hinder his flight, and returns to the instinct and impulses of Nature. They look at her open-mouthed, in inquisitive astonishment; but something in her face prevents them from asking what brings her here, what business calls her to this dying stranger's side.

122 Mohair plush, once produced exclusively at Utrecht in the Netherlands.

123 A colossus is a particularly large statue, like the Colossus of Rhodes, considered one of the Seven Wonders of the World and which collapsed in 226 BCE.

124 See p. 66,. n. 60.

125 2 Kings 2:5.

"One of the Miss Chesters," says the landlady, in a loud explanatory aside to the doctor, "the younger one. I'm sure, sir, I cannot imagine what brings her here—no relative,—nor how her sister can let her; if she were *my* daughter—"

Dare turns his head restlessly on the pillow.

"What are you all whispering about?" says the deep voice, with irritation. "For God's sake speak out loud, if you must speak at all." He raises himself a little to have a better view of his surroundings, and his eyes fall upon Kate. He does not seem at all surprised at seeing her. He might have been expecting her, from the little astonishment he expresses. To the dying nothing is a surprise. The one immeasurable, unimaginable, supreme surprise on whose closest marge they stand takes away and utterly annihilates the force of all lesser ones. I think that, were the very dead to come back and hold speech with the dying it would seem to them no strange thing.

In his eyes was no astonishment, only a great, quiet, satisfied joy, triumphant over pain. In that look passion was dead, and love reigned immortal among the ruins of mortality. He said, "Send them away, Kate."

She turned with composure to the doctor, "You hear what he says; will you go, please? We should like to be left alone."

So they went. Then he held out his arms,—the arms that two hours ago were an athlete's, that now were feeble as any sucking child's,—and she fled to them. Anyone listening at that door might have thought Death come already, so utter was the silence of that supreme embrace. At length Stamer spoke.

"At last!" he said, with a long-drawn sigh, and a faint tender smile. "Kate, you are not afraid of me now, are you? I shall never be able to do you harm any more; the lion has had his teeth and claws drawn."

At James Stanley's deathbed Kate had wept and wailed; the lesser grief unlocked the floodgates of her tears, the greater sealed them in their hidden founts. She rocked herself backwards and forwards.

"Is this the end? is this the end?" she said, in her great despair.

"The *very* end," Dare answered, speaking slowly. It was rather a labour to him to talk; one is not fluent when one is dying. "O, child, child, to-night I'm going *somewhere*, or—" (with a pause) "who knows?—*nowhere*!"

A spasm of agony crossed her face.

"Don't talk that way," she said, with a gesture of despair; "it kills me to hear you. O, my poor dear fellow, you *are* going somewhere indeed! O, I wonder is it anywhere good?"

"It's not much worth while wondering," he answers calmly; "before morning I shall *know*."

She threw herself on her knees, and laid her soft burning cheek on the cushion beside him.

"My darling," she whispered, "let me say one little prayer for you! let me, O let me! O, love, love, you are going to God! Won't you ask Him to have pity on you?"

Dare shook his head.

"Little woman," he said, speaking with difficulty, and stroking her face very tenderly with his hand, "it's no good; it's—too late—too late!"

"It's *never* too late," she said with passionate earnestness; "O, don't think that! God's goodness is infinite; greater and fuller than we can imagine or conceive. The gate of mercy stands always open! O Dare, Dare, at this last moment try to enter there; no one ever yet found it shut."

Her voice broke down, choked with overwhelming emotion; her whole soul went out in that passionate pleading. But she spake to inattentive ears.

"Child!" he said, after a while, and his voice was hollow and weak, "give me your hand; sit where I can see you!"

So they sat, the dying and the living, hand-in-hand, through the short hot summer night. Few words exchanged they: he could not think of much beside his grievous pain; it was only with a mighty wrench that the reluctant soul tore itself away from the strong young form that cased it. The stars sink softly into their Western graves: a rosy smile begins to play about the cold lips of the East; then the sun comes up laughing above the garden wall and the climbing roses, and shoots a whole sheaf of his arrows into the dim shadowy room.

The bright shafts strike up along the ceiling, and play in little flames about the pendants of the chandelier, and paint with their own delicate crimson the clammy brow, the drawn sharpened features, and the damp sunken features of the dying man; paint, as if in mockery, the lips and cheeks that the quick human blood will redden never more. Then she knew that his hour was come. He had been lying passive in a sort of heavy slumber, that yet was not slumber, a sort of intermediate state between sleep and death; and when the light smote sharply on his heavy eyelids, they raised themselves once more, and one languid hand lifted itself very feebly towards his breast, as though seeking something.

"Love, what is it?" she said, stooping over him, and trying to interpret with the agonised keenness that only the watcher beside a deathbed knows the last doubtful difficult signs of consciousness, the last waving of hands, and syllabling of adieux of him who is already half way over the black ferry of Death. She laid her face close to his lips, and heard him whisper between struggling gasps for the slow-coming breath, "Pen Dyllas,—long ago!" Then she knew that what he sought was the withered poppy she had given him in the Pen Dyllas corn-field years ago, when their love was young. He saw that she understood him—"Buried with me!" he said in a husky whisper; and, babbling the words over and over again purposelessly, as the dying do babble words from which the meaning has fled, he fell into a stupor, and so passed.

CHAPTER X

AND so Dare Stamer, like the Israelitish king of old, departed without being desired,[126] save by one infatuated woman whose life his love had laid waste. And indifferent hired women came and made his sad toilet for the grave, and then closed the shutters—as if the light could hurt his quiet eyes *now*—and left him. And guests came and went about the house on errands of business or curiosity, and talked and drank, and heard with careless interest of how he had died, and how much he had suffered, while he lay there in the dark alone. And when five days were come and gone there rose a stir in the house, and the neighbours put their heads out of window, and gaped and stared at the black array of mourning coaches, at the crape-scarfed mourners, at the long dark hearse, with its nidding-nodding plumes that seemed endowed with a sort of ghastly life, and at all the silly paraphernalia with which we try to clothe in childish terrors not his own our already sufficiently terrible victor. So they took Dare Stamer away, and carried him down to far-off Pen Dyllas, and laid him with his fathers in the Stamer vault in the cemetery by the sea. There the waves come twice a day and sing his requiem; there the flowers blossom out freely under the rain and the shine; and the night winds come and go at will above his dreamless head.[127]

---

126 See the account of Jehoram in 2 Chronicles 20-21: "Thirty and two years old was he when he began to reign, and he reigned in Jerusalem eight years, and departed without being desired."

127 Broughton alluded to this quotation from Tennyson's *In Memoriam* (2.3) earlier; see p. 171, n. 24; she also used it in the *DUM* version to describe Kate's grave in the last paragraph of the serialization (see Appendix B, p. 428).

About a month after Dare's death there was a wedding in Queenstown—a very quiet wedding, *sans*[128] cake, *sans* cards, *sans* breakfast, *sans* speechifying, *sans* everything almost, save the unavoidable parson and the indissoluble vows. And after the wedding and a short honeymoon, the wedded pair established themselves in a charming little cottage in the country, all roses and myrtles and earwigs, and the bride's sister went with them. They had said to her very kindly, "Come with us;" and her heart being sore and thirsting for the balm of the love of any human thing, she had gone with them. She had put on no mourning for him; they would not let her; and, indeed, what right had she? To have worn black would but have been an insult to his memory; would but have brought back the remembrance of his evil deeds. So she went about in her coloured clothes, and fought day and night with the grief that was a sin.

George Chester has sold out;[129] he's turned his sword into a ploughshare, has invested in a broad-brimmed straw-hat, has abandoned the struggle with his increasing *embonpoint*, leans over his pigsty-wall on a Sunday afternoon, and walks about with a spud. I think that prosperity is mostly intolerant of adversity; it's very, very difficult figuratively to get inside another person; regulate your pulse-beats by theirs; quicken or slacken the pulsation of your heart in harmony with theirs. Human power of sympathy is limited. I confess myself totally unable to estimate the sensations of the man who fancied himself a tea-pot;[130] it is a very admirable divinely compassionate maxim that bids us rejoice with them that rejoice, and weep with them that weep; but, O, it is often most difficult of execution. When one feels that tears are miles away from one's jubilant eyes—jubilant over some pleasant green meadow in one's own life; when the corners of one's mouth insist upon turning jocundly up, instead of lachrymosely down, the sight of reddened eyelids, puckered brow, and swollen nose, excite in one rather a sense of infuriation and aggrievedness against the owner of those pleasant pieces of property, than of pity or sympathy with them. One does not like such ugly pieces of furniture, does one, amongst one's ormolu

128 Without (French).

129 In this period army officers purchased their commissions and sold them when they wished to retire.

130 Nineteenth-century medical texts and journals often refer to this particular delusion in discussions of insanity. It is not clear if any one example brought such fantasies to people's attention.

writing-cases and buhl clocks and rosewood tables;[131] at all events Maggie Chester did not. Her very sisterly love and pride put weapons in her hand against Kate. "Is *that* Mrs. Chester's pretty sister?" she had heard somebody saying to somebody else, one hot Sunday afternoon, as somebody and everybody and nobody came drifting together out of church, feeling very cross at having had five minutes more brimstone and sulphur than usual inflicted on them by the Low Church curate. Yes, that strange woman might well ask. Kate will never be Mrs. Chester's pretty sister any more at all. She laid down her beauty with the green-and-white filmy garments in which she had knelt in dishevelled despair by dying Dare, and prayed in an agony for his reckless, prayerless parting soul. If Kate had been a widow, an interesting young widow, with crape up to her chin, clear lawn sleeves, and a Marie-Stuart cap coming down in a peak on her forehead,[132] and sweeping away in crisp freshness behind her little round ears,—a widow accomplishing the days of mourning lugubriously yet becomingly for a lawful husband who had been fitly and properly ushered into the next world with bell, book, and candle, it would have been very well; but to go about in pink muslin, sunken-cheeked, hollow-eyed, for a remarkably wicked and (odder still) a remarkably ugly married man was more than could enter into Mrs. Chester's philosophy.

"What she ever could see in him!" she says one morning, in impatient ejaculation to her husband, as she goes about the garden in gardening-gloves and a pair of big scissors, snipping off defunct scarlet geraniums. "There certainly was plenty of him. Well, poor man, I suppose one ought not to speak evil of him now he is gone—though, indeed, if one talks about him at all I don't see what else one can speak—and O, George, what an ugly shape his nose was!"

"Well, poor fellow, he did not make it himself," says George with magnanimity, passing his finger at the same time complacently down the ridge of his own straight blunt feature. "He was the best shot I ever saw at a rabbit," he adds pensively, on the principle of (however irrelevantly to the subject in hand) giving the devil his due.[133]

---

131 Rosewood was used to make high-end furniture, and buhl and ormolu—respectively, a type of marquetry and finely ground gold—to decorate it.

132 In paintings representing her in later life, Mary Stuart, Queen of Scots, wore a peaked white widow's cap, a style adapted by Queen Victoria following the death of Prince Albert.

133 In revising the ending Broughton seems to forget that she had earlier implied

"How Kate," continues Margaret, viciously pinching off a dead Trentham rose, "with her ideas of religion and goodness, *can* reconcile it to her conscience to go about wearing the willow for another person's property I can't imagine; and such an unbecoming vegetable as the willow is to wear too!"

That same afternoon the two women were sitting together in the little cottage drawing-room. The furniture was almost exactly the same as it used to be in the Queenstown drawing-room; there were the same faint unmistakably amateur water-colours on the walls, the same Broadwood in the corner.[134] The women were the same too; the same, and yet—O, not the same; Maggie is already getting the staid prosaic matronly look of one who has fulfilled her vocation, of one who has no longer on her brow the weight of a destiny to accomplish, but who, having fulfilled that destiny, may sit down and grow fat and comfortable over it.

As for Kate, poor stranded Kate, she is like the wreck of some fair brave ship that once, not long ago, breasted the billows gallantly, and cut the green water with strong sharp prow; whose friends the loud winds were, and whose stout timbers defied the waves' rough play; but now, dismasted, shattered, can but pray for some little gentle breeze to waft her softly to a kindly port.

"Kate, I wish you would go out for a walk of a day; you look so pale," Maggie says, after a lengthened survey of her sister's countenance.

"I always was pale," Kate answers, without looking up.

"Yes, I know that; but it was quite a different sort of pale," with a discontented intonation.

Kate raises her eyes with a rather sorrowful smile in them. "You mean that it used to be a pretty pale, and that now it is an ugly one. Do you think I need anyone to tell me I have grown ugly? I don't even require a looking-glass to give me that information. I can see it in the faces of the people I meet."

"It's uncommonly uncivil of them, if you can," Maggie says with indignation. She sees plainly enough herself the wreck of her sister's beauty, but she is exceedingly enraged that anyone else should see it too.

Silence for ten minutes or so; then Kate rises suddenly, comes over to her sister, and kneels down beside her knees like any simple docile child.

"Maggie," she says earnestly, "do you know this won't do?"

---

that George, unlike Blount, did not know Dare; see p. 333.

134 Piano, after a noted manufacturer.

"What won't do?"

"Why, I have tried your plan of life. I have taken your advice; I have not been obstinate, have I? I have given it a fair trial, and it's driving me mad as fast as it can."

Margaret seizes her sister's two hands in hers. "Why can't you forget that man?" she says impulsively. "I wish to God you had never seen him. I do believe he was the very wickedest man that ever lived."

Kate snatches away one small cold hand, and covers her eyes with it.

"Can't you see," she says very passionately, "that it's his very wickedness that puts the sharpest sting in my grief? If he had been a good man that I could think of in some good happy place, don't you think I could wait patiently enough through the little space that would elapse till I should go and meet him again, if I were good too? But now—now what can I pray for? what can I hope about him? Too late! too late!" she cries, wringing her hands wildly; "they were his own words, and they keep dinning in my ears like some dreadful ghastly knell."

Maggie is silent. On such a subject what consolation can she give?

"Maggie," continues Kate excitedly, "I must go and find some work in the world to do. Don't try to hinder me; while I sit here idle, with hands folded in my lap, I feel the solid earth slipping away from under my feet. Hope went away from me long ago, and now faith is going too. I begin to feel growing on me an incapacity for believing anything. O Maggie, Maggie! let me go away and try to pray and work and *tire* myself into belief and peace again."[135]

So they strove no more against her; they perceived that some voice, such as spoke to Christian, bidding him flee from the City of Destruction,[136] had spoken to her too, and they could not counsel her to disallow it; so with tears and kisses and blessings they sent her forth, and she returned to them no more. She joined that band of holy devoted women whom Evangelical clergyman condemn as acolytes and hand-maidens of the Scarlet

---

135 That a Victorian woman struggling with religious doubt would become an Anglican nun was not as implausible as it may seem; Susan Mumm claims that "it seems that sisterhoods actively encouraged women with 'doubts' to enter" (*Stolen Daughters, Virgin Mothers: Anglican Sisterhoods in Victorian Britain* [London: Leicester University Press, 1999], 15).

136 At the beginning of John Bunyan's *The Pilgrim's Progress* (1678), the character Evangelist instructs Christian, the protagonist, to flee his home town, the City of Destruction (the world), and seek the Celestial City (Heaven).

Woman,[137] whom lazy loiterers in the gardens and vineyards of life "damn with faint praise."[138] With these she went in and out, trembling at first, shrinking at first, yet brave and constant always, among the smoky reeking alleys and courts of filthy, suffering, heart-rending London. Truly she wrought, striving ever, as the days went by, to set her faint stumbling feet firmer and surer in the footprints of that greater One than John the Baptist, who eighteen hundred summers back healed the sick, raised the dead, cast out devils beside Genesareth's[139] still lake and Jordan's blue river. Early and late she toiled, giving her days and her nights, her feeble strength, and all her tender woman's heart, to the abating by but a few drops the great ocean of human anguish; and, for meed of her labours, won much weariness of body, oftentimes discouragement of soul, and small cold praise. Sometimes the mists came down about her thick and black, and demon voices whispered in her ears, demon faces grinned before her eyes; but she held on boldly, and would none of them. Sometimes a faint shaft of light reached her from the great distant fountain-head towards which we have all been struggling, making small progress, as it seems, through six thousand dragging years.[140] And when many days had come and gone, when youth was just beginning to merge into gray beautiless middle age, he who is always reading over the long muster-roll of human names came to the name of Kate Chester; and she, hearing, rose up—yea, rose up very gladly; and having ended, whether well or ill, her day's work, passed as we, knowing not, yet hope,

"To where, beyond these voices, there is peace."[141]

THE END

137 British anti-Catholic discourse traditionally associated the so-called Scarlet Woman in Revelation 17 (the "great whore" dressed in purple and scarlet) with the papacy.

138 The phrase originates in Pope, "Epistle to Dr. Arbuthnot" (1735), l. 201.

139 Also called the Sea of Galilee in the gospels (the Lake of Tiberias in Luke).

140 The span of the world's history according to the Bible.

141 Tennyson, "Guenevere," in *Idylls of the King* (1859), l. 692. Like Kate, the adulterous Guenevere becomes a nun.

APPENDIX A

Correspondence from the Bentley Archives Relating to *Not Wisely, but Too Well*

This appendix reproduces, in chronological order, the most important correspondence related to *Not Wisely, but Too Well* in the archives of the publisher Richard Bentley and Son.[1] The documents are organized as follows:

1) Letters 1-4: J. S. Le Fanu to Richard Bentley recommending publication of the novel.

2) Letters 5-6: Geraldine Jewsbury's report on the novel and a follow-up note in which she urges Richard Bentley to break the contract he had already signed with Broughton.

3) Letters 7-8: Le Fanu to Richard Bentley after being informed of Jewsbury's report.

4) Letters 9-10: The conclusion of two letters by Broughton to Richard Bentley about the manuscript of *Cometh Up as a Flower*, in which she makes barbed allusions to Jewsbury's report and the withdrawal of *Not Wisely* from publication.

---

1 This material is available on microfilm: *The Archives of Richard Bentley and Son, 1829-1898* (Cambridge: Chadwyck-Healey; Teaneck, NJ: Somerset House, 1976). Geraldine Jewsbury's readers reports, the originals of which are at the British Library, are on Part I, Vol. 99, Reel 47 of the microfilmed *Archives*. J. S. Le Fanu's correspondence—the originals of which are, like Broughton's, housed at the University of Illinois, Urbana-Champaign—may be found on Pt. II, Reel 39, while the correspondence from Broughton that I include here is on Pt. II, Reel 22. The numbers that I give the letters in this appendix should not be confused with the numbers pencilled on the originals to organize them in the *Archives*. In transcribing this correspondence as accurately as possible, I have to the best of my ability deciphered handwriting and punctuation (or lack thereof).

5) Letters 11-14: Broughton's correspondence with Richard Bentley regarding the revision of *Not Wisely.*

6) Letter 15: Broughton's letter to Richard Bentley's son George[2] about her decision to publish the revised *Not Wisely* with Tinsley instead of Bentley.

7) Letters 16-17: Le Fanu's correspondence with George Bentley about Broughton's publishing *Not Wisely* with Tinsley.

8) Letters 18-23: Broughton to George Bentley expressing dissatisfaction with the revised, triple-decker form of *Not Wisely.* In Letters 18-23 she hopes that Bentley will buy back the rights to the novel from Tinsley and proposes completely rewriting it, using the same or a "nearly similar" plot with "entirely different characters"; in Letter 23 she expresses her preference for the original ending in the *Dublin University Magazine* over the triple-decker one.

Letter 1: J. S. Le Fanu to Richard Bentley, 2 August, 1865

... Will you look at the tale called "Not Wisely but Too Well"—it is a first one & I think of so great promise and power as to induce me to believe the young authoress will be ultimately a great success. It commences with the No. of the D. University Mag. just out ...

Letter 2: J. S. Le Fanu to Richard Bentley, 17 August, 1865

Miss Broughton—who is my niece by marriage—(the authoress of "Not Wisely but too Well"—) is at present making a short visit to us here. She agrees to your proposition—she being guaranteed against all expense or loss—& if you will forward the papers here she will execute the agreement & return it. The work extends to 34 chapters—I think it will be ample as you will see on looking to the average of the first & second Nos—to form two Vols—but not more—You could have the copy I fancy revised for printing early in December next—I think if she continues to write she is sure to succeed—& you will I am sure recognize the same evidences of talent as you read the forthcoming No. It strikes me as a story that might

2 Both Broughton and Le Fanu's letters to the publisher are directed to George after summer 1867, as he took over the running of the firm following his father's injury in a train accident (the elder Bentley died in 1871).

quite possibly make a hit. Her wish is that her name should not be divulged.

Letter 3: J. S. Le Fanu to Richard Bentley, 21 April, 1866

… I have a very high opinion of "Not Wisely but Too Well"—I have written to the author to revise it—which it greatly wants—Its success very much depends on it—but that done—I have great confidence in it—I think it could be in your hands early in June. Say when you wd publish it—If in June I will hurry the author—& give you the copy next month—

Letter 4: J. S. Le Fanu to Richard Bentley, 13 June, 1866

… By this post I send the copy of "Not Wisely"—carefully revised—I think it is nearly certain to do well—it is very clever. Will you kindly let me know by return when you mean to bring it out. If you have proofs to send within a week from this date send them here …

Letter 5: Geraldine Jewsbury to Richard Bentley, 2 July, 1866

"Not Wisely but too Well" is returned PDe[3]—

There is undoubtedly a certain force of strong epithets in it & as a picture of strong unregulated sensual passion it is life like enough—but the story—it is nothing but a series of love scenes (if love it can be called) & the point of interest turns upon the man being a "big Titan" with "brawny athlete arms" "superb broad shoulders" & "cavernous gleaming eyes"—a thorough blackguard contrasting with the heroine who is "little" "round" "soft with [']soft white shoulders' "soft white arms" "seagreen eyes" a witching power & face—who the aforesaid "Titan" "crushes" & "kisses" & "devours" & "holds in [his] iron grasp"; & with the little girl herself it is a case of animal magnetism. It is the most thoroughly sensual tale I have read in English for a long time—artless imitation & exaggeration of Guy Livingstone only without the talent & I am sorry it is going to be published at all—the interest is of highly coloured & hot blooded passion & the influence is pretended to be quenched by a few drops of luke warm rose water sentimentality & I entirely disapprove of the tale—It is not a well put together story [it] is absolute and unredeemed nonsense and the interest

3 This is apparently an abbreviation for "payment on delivery."

is of a kind that I shd carefully keep it out of the hands of all the young people of my acquaintance[.] I am sorry you have accepted it[.] I shd have recommended you to decline it (for as a tale it is perfect nonsense)[.] If you have agreed to take it I am sorry that is all I can say—It is a bad style of book altogether & not fit to be published.

Letter 6: Geraldine Jewsbury to Richard Bentley, 3 July, 1866

This is a PS to my letter of last night.—"Not Wisely &c" is a bad story please have nothing to do with it—It will not do you any credit—indeed people will wonder at a house like yours bringing out a work so ill calculated for the reading of decent people. The story is vulgar & the force that is in it, is merely that of high coloured epithets & sensual appeals to the feelings—sentiment there is none—It is just an improper book as bad as any French novel—I entreat you if you have made any bargain to break it[.]

Letter 7: J. S. Le Fanu to Richard Bentley, 6 July, 1866

Many thanks for your frank letter. I am not authorized to act for the writer—but have communicated—I am of course very sorry that the critical examination should have resulted so unfortunately. But my impression respecting the cleverness & power of the writing is very strong—Your critic's decided feeling against the tone & subject of the tale has I hope told upon the general estimate he makes & which includes other points—I was intending to write to you today advising your sending back to the author the last scene—for remodelling and careful revision—as on reading it, I am satisfied it wd not do—

Could you recommend any publishers likely to take the work up in the event of the author's agreeing to withdraw it—

I ought to say that the writer's boldness of style & description (objected to—) arises from an unfortunate ignorance of the actual force of some of what is set down & of the way in which the world—wiser in the knowledge of evil—might read it—Pray do not mention that any difficulty has arisen—So soon as I have heard anything—you shall hear from me …
P.S. a line as soon as you can respecting other Publishers

Letter 8: J. S. Le Fanu to Richard Bentley, 28 July, 1866

I have communicated with the author of "Not Wisely" & strongly urged the expediency of withdrawing the book seeing the very strong view which your critic had taken respecting its tone—a view not unlikely to be that of many of the reviewers. She will consent to substitute a story which she has written & [which is] now coming out in the University Magazine entitled "Cometh Up as a Flower[.]" You will see that it is perfectly free from the particular objection urged against the other—I do not think when finished that it will make more than 1 Vol. but you could in the agreement say "one or two vols"—Our friend Fitzgerald[4] talked with me twice lately about it—I merely said that I had advised the author to postpone it—at which he expressed strong regret & his conviction that the work wd be a success—& might be a great one—I merely mention this as a counter-poise to adverse criticism. But looking on your critic's opinion as a foreshadowing of what some of the reviews might say—& considering how peculiarly painful such a view of the work wd be—I thought it right to advise her distinctly to withdraw it.

Pray do not mention to any one respecting its postponement than that your advisor thought it's [sic] tone bolder than might generally suit family reading—and that having referred the doubt to the author the book was withdrawn ... When returning the agreement for Not Wisely,—will you kindly write across it "This agreement is cancelled by mutual consent—" adding your signature—

Letter 9: Rhoda Broughton to Richard Bentley, 3 December, 1866

... I shall hope to be able to send you the whole tale [*Cometh Up as a Flower*] early in February if not sooner, & should be much obliged if you could send me a line to tell me how soon after, it will be in print, as I hope there will be no miscarriage of this work ...

---

4 Percy Hetherington Fitzgerald (1834-1925), Irish barrister, author, and artist. Like Broughton, he published work in *The Dublin University Magazine*. Broughton used to tell a story of how, before Le Fanu accepted *Not Wisely* for his journal, she read it aloud to him and another gentleman who appears to have been Fitzgerald (see Ethel Arnold, "Rhoda Broughton As I Knew Her," *Fortnightly Review* [Aug. 1920], 275).

Letter 10: Rhoda Broughton to Richard Bentley, 30 December, 1866

By today's post I am forwarding my tale "Cometh Up as a Flower" to you … Hoping that this tale may avoid offending your Reader's delicate sense of propriety[.]

Letter 11: Rhoda Broughton to Richard Bentley, Summer of 1867

… I am anxious to know whether you could ever be induced to bring out "Not Wisely" if modified to a very considerable extent. I could if you gave me any encouragement to attempt such a thing with ease omit all the slang and coarseness of expression, and soften the violence of the situations and rewrite altogether the end, which is melodramatic and savours of a Surrey theatre.[5]

My friends agree in telling me that tho' an improper book, it is cleverer far than "Cometh Up" & I myself confess to thinking that there is infinitely more verve and strength in it.

I should be much obliged if you would look it over and give this plan a thought. I am almost sure it would be read which after all is the great thing, dullness being the one unpardonable fault in a writer. If you decline this proposition I must defer the hope of appearing again before the public for some little time, as I never can write except when the fit is on me. Would you kindly send me a line in answer …

Letter 12: Rhoda Broughton to Richard Bentley, [summer of 1867]

Thanks for the willingness you express to give "Not Wisely" further consideration if remodelled. I have been looking over it again, and quite agree with you as to its unfitness for publication in its present state. I will do my best to expunge it of coarseness & slanginess, & to rewrite those passages which cannot be toned down.

If I fail in altering it sufficiently to meet with your approbation you can but refuse it again …

---

5 In the mid-Victorian period the Surrey Theatre in London was known for highly melodramatic productions.

Letter 13: Rhoda Broughton to Richard Bentley, 22 August, 1867

I have been & am very busy altering and rewriting parts of "Not Wisely" & it will be quite ready to appear in your autumn lists as you appear to think that advisable. But before finally coming to an arrangement, I should wish to know what sum you would be willing to give me for the M.S. as I confess to being somewhat disappointed as to the probable commercial success of "Cometh Up" as stated by you in our last interview.

I care too little about publishing "Not Wisely" at all to think it worth my while to bring it out unless for some certain & sufficient remuneration. If we can come to an agreement on this head however, I will send you the story as soon as you wish.

Letter 14: Rhoda Broughton to Richard Bentley, 25 August, 1867

I am not by any means inclined to let "Not Wisely" go for the very small sum you mention; add to which I have not the slightest interest of spoiling the story by padding it out to three volumes.

We will therefore if you please say no more on the subject[.]

Letter 15: Rhoda Broughton to George Bentley, 20 September, 1867

I am sorry to say that your father and I have been utterly unable to come to an agreement about "Not Wisely." He offered me £250 for it & insisted on my padding it out to a three vol novel. The price tho' very small I should probably have accepted as everybody tells me that the sale of my two books is materially injured by the fact of their having appeared before hand in the Dublin Mag. As I could not make up my mind completely to spoil my tale for the sake of a little additional profit to your father I have consequently been compelled to make an agreement with Mr Tinsley for it.

If Mr Bentley is inclined to give me a good price for some future work, perhaps we may be able to come to terms. I am glad that you derived any pleasure from reading "Cometh Up." What you say about Scriptural associations is very fine, & I have often been struck with it myself.

Regretting that your father and I have been unable to come to terms about "Not Wisely" …

Letter 16: J. S. Le Fanu to George Bentley, 23 September, 1867

Miss Broughton seems to [think] that my advice is simply impertinent & I have got my "head in my hand" accordingly—Mr. Russell, the "Times" correspondent she tells me introduced her to Mr Tinsley—& that she has concluded an arrangement (<u>what</u> she does not say) for "Not Wisely" with him—Her note reached me this morning—& I have written acknowledging it & [am] quite resolved to trouble her with no more advice on literary matters. I could not have anticipated such an answer as I have had …

Letter 17: J. S. Le Fanu to George Bentley, 10 October, 1867

… I wrote at great length to Miss Broughton—<u>twice</u>—on the subject of "Not Wisely"—and after considerable delay, received a short & rude letter, which seemed to imply by its tone & temper, that she considered my interference impertinent—which considering the persevering trouble I had taken about her writings—I had not expected—I thought your offer to her, a spirited one, & that she ran a risk in declining it, & was much pained at the result of my interposition …

Letter 18: Rhoda Broughton to George Bentley, 6 February, 1870

… I have the greatest desire by & by to rewrite in a condensed & modified form "Not Wisely." Would you reread it? I <u>hate</u> it as it stands & so does every body else. I remember your saying once that you should like to get it from Tinsley that I might do something of the kind …

Letter 19: Rhoda Broughton to George Bentley, 13 February, 1870

… As to "Not Wisely," if I write on the same plot a story with entirely different characters & situations etc would it be necessary to get the old "Not Wisely" from Tinsley? Might not we start quite fresh with the new version. I should be careful to avoid anything in the treatment of the story that could give offence & should leave out all the minor characters the wishy washy good parson the idiotic old uncle, who tho' drawn from life was a failure, etc. It makes me uncomfortable to think of the present "Not Wisely." It is not worthy of me …

Letter 20: Rhoda Broughton to George Bentley, [Feb or March 1870]

… I rather long to begin whitewashing "Not Wisely" …

Letter 21: Rhoda Broughton to George Bentley, 21 May, 1871

I am delighted to say that "Goodbye Sweetheart" is quite finished … I still think that it will not be a great favourite with the public, tho' certainly quite as well written as "Cometh Up" & "Red as a Rose" & a great deal better than that vile "Not Wisely." That really is a thorn in the flesh to me & I should be too grateful if you could get it back …

Letter 22: Rhoda Broughton to George Bentley, [late December?] 1871

… I am still very anxious to do what I spoke to you some time ago about & that before I embark on a new story of which I have the haziest possible outline running in my head. i.e. to rework Not Wisely as it at present stands I simply detest it, & am unwilling that anyone should know I wrote it: it is crude vulgar & in parts *canting*, all in the highest degree. I think the plot is the best I ever had—my plots are generally deplorable: there is absolutely none in "Goodbye Sweetheart". I am very anxious to write a different story with different characters with less violence, diffuseness & vulgarity, on the same or a nearly similar plot. I wish you would help me, as I have it very much at heart, & not put me off as you did before with the difficulty of interfering with Mr Tinsley's rights …

Letter 23: Broughton to George Bentley, 25 August, 1876

Have you any idea where I could get the back numbers of the Dublin University Magazine in which "Not Wisely" first appeared. I have just found in this house the end of the story as originally written & am struck with its much greater power than the later published version.

It ends in July 1866. I do wish I could get the numbers. I should like you if it is not too much trouble to read the old ending as tho' crude & coarse it seems to me rather fine.

Oh! I have bought my increased refinement of a great wealth of power.

APPENDIX B - TEXTUAL VARIANTS

This appendix lists variants between the novel's serial version in the *Dublin University Magazine* (*DUM*) and the three-volume first edition, published by Tinsley in 1867, which forms the basis for this edition. (For the publication schedule of the *DUM* version see "Note on the Text.") Below, to the right of the page number and bracketed text from this edition, is the text from the *DUM* that the triple-decker rewrites or cuts; passages in the triple-decker not in the *DUM* version are also noted. I have not included changes in paragraphing, punctuation, or italicization except as they appear in passages whose wording is different between the two versions. I have also silently corrected obvious errors in both the *DUM* and triple-decker versions.

Vol. I

43 pundits] bigwigs
45 small white tablet] small new white tablet
49 deeply put in;] deeply put in; almost too much the exact reverse of bulgy;
49 Laughing … one long pleasant jest.] Unkissed, as yet, those lips, but some day they would kiss the very heart out of some one lucky man, and *but* one; which is more than could be predicated of all such woman lips.
51 princess like her?] princess like her? I declare I would not put anything past me.
51 dangerous drunkenness] dangerous drunkenness (as a parchment-skinned old parson would tell one)
51 misguided] brute of a
51 breathing] sniffing up
51 is not unlike a gentleman] might be worse.
51-52 They are bride and bridegroom… ivory back.] My dear creature, I would not poke my lord in the ribs with my parasol, if I were you, however painfully inclined I might be.
52 What absurdly false pictures … one great imposture] What loads of

twaddle novels do cram down one's throat about love; all bosh, and kisses, and false sentiment. I declare it is enough to give one a sickener for the whole concern. I do believe it is all one great sham, one huge humbug,

52 *Juste ciel!* What an exhibition of] My goodness!—what an exhibition of legs! I do not think I would be so prodigal of a display of such thick ones, particularly if they were cased in

52 'Oh, wad some power … than there are at present.] Not in *DUM*

52 sense.] sense, by a good bit.

52 keep to truth] stick to truth

52 how silly!] what an ass I am!

52 makes one.] makes one. Good gracious!

52 get a homily] catch it

54-55 She was rather haggard and mahogany-coloured now … let it be clearly understood that he was] She had rather gone out in the haggard and mahogany line now, a good deal run off her legs by the requirements of her exacting old *bell-wether*, who, however, although his best friends could not deny that he *nagged* a great deal, was yet

55 people] folks

55 not ungraceful] anything but ungraceful

55 The Americans … dairy-maid type.] Not in *DUM*

55 If that be the case … more refined still.] Not in *DUM*

55 passable nose, … clear unmixed complexion,] good nose, and a rather clear, unmixed-looking colour

55 After all … young.] Not in *DUM*

55 loose-jointed,] Not in *DUM*

56 tradespeople] tradespeople here

56 for some little time his slow plump hands] for some little time he, with those plump dumpling hands of his

56 all, indeed, pappy."] all Pappy, indeed."

56 "It was not ten minutes," said Maggie … been to bathe to-day, Blount?" she continued,] "Been to bathe?" asked Margaret

56 great presence] much presence

56 her brother,] Blount,

56 "I should think so," said he] "Rather," said Blount,

56 "My good girl … dabbling them away in the water?] Not in *DUM*

56 and I kicked up] so I kicked up

56 "Promising, amiable youth!" … or for what remarkable virtues] "You're an amiable boy, I don't think," said Maggie, with a loving smile. (I do not

know why

56-57 "but you might have saved yourself the trouble . . . that's the sensiblest speech I've heard you make for many a day.] "But I did not once think of you as it happened."/ "Did not you? What a sell!

57 idiots] *blokes*

57 one of them. What's] one of them. By-the-by, what's become

57 By the bye … it was Jessie."] Not in *DUM*

57 "I don't know,"] "Don't know,"

57 never called one another "dear," and only kissed … returning from a journey] Not in *DUM*

57 harm."] grief."

57 eloped] hooked it

57 the sad sea waves … deplore her infatuation."] dining off cold tallow it is her look-out, not mine."

57 "Early dinner … mixture of metaphors."] "Oh, come, shut up!" replied his dutiful niece, in a stage whisper; and aloud, she remarked to the clock, shaking a small fist at it as she passed to her seat. "Bother you, you old ticker; you are always getting me into scrapes. I wish I had a sundial, or was one, and then, I suppose, I should feel what's o'clock. Oh, no more of that mutton stuff, please, for goodness sake; it will only stick in my throat."

57-58 Well he knew that it was … so prematurely spread.] Not in *DUM*

58 you two] you

58 garment] rag

58 "Well, there are degrees … prodigy of good luck."] They both wanted to go *horribly*, and yet Kate was accustomed to vow that she loathed dinner parties. Oh, women, young women especially, what odd birds ye are!

58-59 "I'll tell you what you shall do, my children," suggested Blount … you cannot suspect him."] "I'll tell you what you shall do girls," suggested Blount, "draw lots, and I'll hold them for you. I'll hold them quite fair. I'll take my oath I will. You know I do not care two pence which of you comes."

59 dangerous] ticklish

59 And yet dinner parties generally were a decided *gêne* to her.] and besides she was always unlucky with lots.

59 yield to her] give up to her

59 fast-cooling] fast tallowing

59 to-night in these close dull lodgings, with nothing to do] to-night, *a la Cinderella*, in these nasty, stuffy lodgings

59 broad hand] broad, sinewy hand
59 to get rid of] to let off
59-60 Certainly it is possible to love … crooked nose.] Not in *DUM*
60 Maggie jumped up … has not it?"] "May your shadow never be less," said Maggie, with a pretence at speaking *sotto voce*; not caring very much whether she was heard or not.
60 dear boy, because we can both go … But for all that, she] old boy, because we can both go, though, indeed," she added, when a recollection of how Kate generally behaved to her, came over her, "I'm sure I do not know why I congratulate myself upon that, because the chances are a thousand to one, that, as usual, no one will take the slightest notice of me. I suppose I shall do gooseberry[1] all evening to you, Kate, according to custom. Bah! How sick I am of it!" and she made a face as of one who had just taken a jorum of cough mixture./ "Bosh!" said Kate briefly, but for all that Miss Kate
60 Colonel Stamer] the Colonel
61 "Probably," said Maggie …mimicking of his uncle's voice,] Not in *DUM*
61 that your little brother would give a great deal] "I'd give something
61 iron," he ended rapturously, turning to his sisters.] nails. If you could but see the muscle on his back," he said, rapturously, turning to his sisters./ "Not very likely," laughed Maggie./ "Well, I hope not, I'm sure, but it really is tremendous. Now I call that something like."
61 "What is the use of physical strength nowadays? … even if you don't mean to try."] Not in *DUM*
61 "Hem!" answered Blount, "neither one thing nor the other, I should say.] "Middling for that," answered Blount,
61-62 "and besides, what does a man's *face* matter? … he called Margaret's attention to] I suppose he will be there, won't he?" and then, as if a new thought had dawned on him, the unfeeling young person went on, with much delight. "Why, of course I know now what you wanted to go there so desperately for, Kitty. What a fool I am! I could not imagine what you were in such a state about it for." And then he nudged Margaret secretly (saying nothing), to observe
62 this most foolish of foolish virgins] this little she-donkey
62 in spite of all defects] in spite of cocknose and all other defects
63 pack] cram

1 To "do gooseberry" is to act as chaperon or unwanted third person in the company of two lovers.

63 mock towers] mock Brummagem towers
64 deceptive exterior] nasty, humbugging exterior
64 Jane of the dirty fingers!] Jane of the dirty fingers, whose stays, at the least exertion on the part of their wearer, *creaked* so distressingly.
65 comfortless] hugger-mugger
65 different from Kate's] different to Kate's
66 fervour of passion] fervour of earthly passion
66-67 with a big powerful figure ... Children thought him hideous.] and with the form of one of the fabled sons of earth and heaven; one of that iron-handed, mighty-limbed family of rebels, the Titans;[2] an ugly, magnificent-looking man. Those are the words that exactly describe him. Arms hard and firm, and tough as bent leather; with the muscle well developed in many a boxing match, on many a cricket field, rising in sinewy cords; such arms as one could imagine those were with which Samson embraced the pillars in a giant gripe, when he bowed himself to the accomplishment of his last great task; a chest which, by its depth and vastness, always excited the astonishment and admiration of his tailor every time he made a suit of clothes for him; and a great columner throat, guarded like the trunk of an oak.
67 no light reflected] the light reflected
69 and him only.] and him only. He had caught himself before now reflecting what a singularly delightful sensation it would be to have those warm white arms flung round his neck.
69 well lost for love.] love, would, if put to it, do anything desperate, nor count the cost.
70 how unbecoming it is to her to laugh, she would look grave immediately.] how unbecoming it is to laugh so wide as that; ear to ear, positively.
70 would have thought but meanly of her understanding] would have thought her a precious fool
72 it looked underbred] it had a *missish* look
74 his wife's example] his lady wife's example
74 rather damaged rose-bud] rather *frouzy*, damaged rose-bud
75-76 *rétroussé* nose] turn-up nose
76 dear little nose] little cock nose
76 depreciating] running down
76 "except that she is extremely pretty ... Lady Stamer and her eldest

2 See p. 267, n. 6.

daughter as] "and do stop bothering, Augusta; there's no end of it when you begin *nagging*," and
76 "How peculiarly unfortunate … What an idiot] "How spiteful old girls do get," he mused (he alluded to his dear sisters), "and what a deuced idiot
77 That is something new.] That is something new—conscience be hanged!
77 getting in love with] getting *spoony* about
78 kindness] *sneaking regard*
78 neglected] *humped up*"
78 "Ahem!"] "Hookey Walker!"[3]
78 "Ahem!" again] "Hookey Walker!" again
78 "Margaretta, Margaretta, … anyone else in the room,"] "Do not pretend you do not know, you old humbug,"
78-79 "don't you know that it is wicked … should not you, Kate?"] "You know as well as I do. I should think he would be sure to come and call on you to-day," he added, descending from the general to the particular. "Should not you, Kate?"
79 "And bring a gift … quarrel with their bread-and-butter."] "What a shame it was, the way you cut out Kate last night," pursued Blount, the young inquisitor. "I thought the Colonel was her property. If I were you, Kitty, I would not speak to her again. I would not indeed," and he patted Kitty's shoulder in a benevolent, brotherly sort of way./ She pulled her shoulder away sharply from his hand, but could not say a word, good or bad.
80 smooth] rub
80 straw] rush
80 manœvre.] manœvre./ If people could but annihilate distance, and see through stone walls! For instance, if Dare now could have seen his little Kate *mopping* the heavy-lidded eyes, that he had been dreaming of all for his sake, the hot blood would have rushed hotter and quicker still through his veins, and she would have finished out her fit of crying upon his broad breast—would have had the last drops of that bitter shower dried up by the warmth of another shower of burning kisses unfelt before. But as not even a guardsman can annihilate space, or see through stone walls, nobody thought of interfering with the functions of Kate's poor little damp pockethandkerchief; and Dare read the *Times* sulkily meanwhile, and knew nothing about it.

3 Colloquialism conveying disbelief.

80 weeping] howling, as her sister would have expressed it,
83 It was not the sense of her own mortality … incapable of eating her breakfast.] Not in *DUM*
83-84 Since this time yesterday she had made … What a digression!] Since this time, yesterday, she had changed from the cheeriest of cheery little damsels into a woman, on whom love had come like a burning fire, and had wrapped her suddenly round in its fierce flames. She made no effort to cast off that cloak of flame, though it began to pain her terribly in the wearing. She folded it, like a maniac, across her soft breast. On some women love steals slowly, by imperceptible degrees, wearing affection's cool garb; on some (passionate, southern sort of natures, these), it springs like a tiger, *at once*, without delay or warning. It may seem a ridiculous exaggeration to speak thus of a power, whose existence some wise folks would deny if they could, but it literally is a fact, that to Kate's distorted eyes there did seem to-day to be nothing but darkness that might be felt, within, without, and all around her.
85 "Kate, you might infuse a little more courtesy … civility costs nothing."] "Well, then, don't," answered Margaret, nettled. "You stupid little thing, who cares?"
85 Tip's most frantically excited] Tip's utmost, most frantically excited
86 "All right! I'm very sorry … what won't!"] "I'm awfully sorry, but I'm blowed if I knew it would damage your head."
87 her feet upon] her feet up upon
87 small quarrels,] small squabbles out,
88 Blount, laughing] Blount, roaring laughing
89 O, Dare, I'd do anything wicked,] Oh, Dare, if I had you, what should I care for heaven, or hell either? I would defy heaven to make me more utterly happy; I would defy hell to make me miserable. I'd do anything wicked,
90 that I might be everything to him,] that I might put my head on his breast, and look up into his eyes, and feel his arms round me—to be everything to him,
90 kill me] finish me off
90 fortunate little ethereal creatures] lucky little threadpaper things
90 Ugly great fat thing,"] Nasty, great fat thing!"
90 soul. One thing] soul–the ravings of a woman who, according as things fell out, might, either for the sake of love or urged on by jealousy, commit one of those startling crimes—startling through their blackness—which

have made some women's names a beacon to all ages; or might possibly, by a course of bitter discipline, find peace at the last. One thing

91 a rage] a fine rage

92 good luck] deuced good luck

92 tiresome] bothering

93 how fortunate] how awfully fortunate

93 sauntering] mooning

93 he added, with] he added, devouring her face with eyes, greedy for the prey, and with

93 how stupid] what a donkey

93 incoherence.] muddle-headedness.

93 flirting] spooning

95 your neck."/ Kate's heart] your little neck," and then he fell a-wondering within himself, whether there could possibly be any Southern blood in Kate's blue veins; there was a something (he could not describe what) about her mouth, which did not tell of the cold North./ Kate's heart

95 "Mr. Piggott be— … revered uncle,"] "Bother Mr. Piggott,"

96 snared;] *limed*,

96 deliberate intentness,] deliberate intentness—a bold, fervent steadiness,

96 cheerful,] jolly,

97 "What were you crying about? … little protest.] Not in *DUM*

97 "they should never shed a tear again, if I could help it."] "I wish I could have kissed away the tears from them."

99 caught her hand … And his eyes] caught her arm, and held it unreproved, with a familiar unhallowed fondness which would have made her brother's blood, or her father's, if she had had one, boil with an intense desire to "*floor*" him. And his eyes

99 glittered on her] glittered on her evilly

99 a story-telling,] fibbing,

99 telling stories,"] fibbing,"

99 a straw] twopence

100 your head.] your naughty little head.

100 anywhere else] anywhere

101 a little one)] a shabby little box)

101 pinned] tacked

101 where for this new] where of this new

102 enfolding Mrs. Price … nothing less."] and she hugged Mrs. Price violently, by way of exciting her sympathy, "*I* am in such a fright, if you

like. Just think what a scolding I shall get. I shall never hear the last of it."
102 turn informer, will you … Mrs. Price's shoulders.] tell upon me—will you, you old duck?" and she gave hug number two.
102 nonsense,"] bother,"
104 hopeless, boundless] hopeless, lawless, boundless
105 the dishevelled locks,] the creaking stays,
105 dreadful thing away!" cried Margaret] dreadful thing away; it's all bloody!" cried Margaret
105 "You idiot!"] "You great fool!"
106 rushing about … a burden to me.] cutting about before dinner, pitching into me.
107 pretending.] *bamming.*
107 indescribable feeling,"] *all-overishness,*"
107 malicious smile,] queer sort of smile,
107 wandering about] mooning about
107 encouraged by an approving look from Blount.] egged on by an encouraging wink from Blount.
107 ugly sea-gulls, instead of staying and teasing here."] nasty seagulls, instead of staying bothering here."
109 mortal eyes)] mortal's eyes)
111 stories.] fibs.
111 "Stop you, my good child!] "Stop you! Lor'child!
111 ever so much.] ever so?
111 no business of mine.] no earthly business of mine.
111 steal off to meet your admirers] slink off to meet your lovers
111 *roué*,"] rip of a man,"
112 bad man] nasty man
113 bad—] nasty—
113 your uncle] your old muff of an uncle
114 nonsense] balderdash
115-16 "Was it the scolding … some of the passion of his.] Not in *DUM*
116 And then she rose up] And she rose up
116 Then some girlish caprice prompted her to put] Her next move was to stick
116 bunch of poppies] bunch, poppies
116-17 the plaits of her hair./ "Are not they lovely?" … "because if not—"] the plaits of her hair; to look up in Dare's face, smiling, and ask him whether they were not lovely? That smile was like the smile with which

foam-born Aphrodite dowered him who "came up from reedy Simois, all alone;"[4] that smile which, in one moment, gained her the palm of fairer far than white-armed Hērē, fairer far than gray-eyed Athene; that smile which made forsaken Œnone shudder on the heights of "many fountained Ida."[5] At that moment Dare's blood surged through its channels like the waters of a great river in flood-time. He felt almost dizzy with passion. Never had anything like such a tempest burst on his dark soul before. He felt, blindly, that this girl, this little sorceress, must be made utterly his own, somehow; it did not matter what price he would have to pay for so sweet a gratification. He seemed to be enduring the punishment of Tantalus,[6] alone with her, in such close proximity that he almost felt her warm breath fanning his cheek, fanning it as a wind fans fire, and yet to be compelled to observe towards her the cold, decorous formalities of ordinary society. / "Give me one of those things," he said, hoarsely./ Unsafe to disobey him now; and again Kate shrank away, with a tremor that was half real fright, under those reckless caverned eyes, that had such devil's fire in them.

117 "Give it me," he said again, almost in a whisper … one of the very ones you have got in your hair;] "Not one of those others," he went on, almost in a whisper—a rather alarming whisper; "one of the very ones you have got in your hair. Give it me, Kate—

117 put forth his hand and] put forth a bold hand, and, hardly master of himself,

117 kissed it madly, passionately—a piece of sentimentality … any other man.] rained mad kisses upon its innocent petals, which withered under the hot shower.

117 raised./ "You need not have taken it," she said … and as they sat, a light sound] raised; a little awed by those eyes; but she would have done anything self-destroying on earth he told her, joyfully; at least she thought so then, and did not even wish to check him, or stem the lava torrent of his fierce love, if love is the right name for it./ Dare stopped kissing the poor little poppy at last. It is dull work kissing by proxy; not likely to satisfy a man of Dare's stamp, most assuredly. It only whetted his strong longing for kisses of another sort. Montaigne's definition of love, which shows

4 Inexact, Tennyson, "Œnone" (1833), l. 52.

5 Tennyson, "Œnone" (1833), l. 23.

6 In Greek mythology Tantalus, a son of Zeus, offended the gods and was punished for eternity by being placed, hungry and thirsty, next to luscious fruits and water that vanished when he tried to eat and drink.

him totally ignorant of it in its higher aspect, affecting the soul, exactly described the sort of love Dare was capable of—/— "not a joy where soul with soul unites/ Only a wondrous animal delight."[7]/ His eyes turned now; thirsty, eager, and drunk deep of the fountain-head of intoxicating witchery contained for him at present in Kate's face, so eloquent sometimes; so poetic, some folks said; but I don't think they could have described what they meant by a poetic face, in that luxuriant form of hers, rich in a sort of full southern development. He was quite close to her now, quite. He *must* do it. The future be hanged! so he threw honour to one wind, prudence to a second, and all other objections to the two others, and stretched out rash arms to take her to himself, to possess her utterly, to strain her to his heart, as he had never strained woman so passionately before, that she should be his, and no other man's, for one five minutes at least, one five minutes that they could never, either of them, forget again. And when, years hence, little Kate should throw herself away on some confounded country boor or other, she should think of this five minutes, and loathe her lord. Selfish great animal! It was nothing to him what her tortures would be, living with this loathed lord, loving *him*, Dare, still with all the oneness and intensity of a resolute soul. Meanwhile, unconscious, Kate sat still where she was, on the grass, and said nought against Dare's approaches. He loved her then, and would marry her, and she should be always with him! How willing she was to sink away into his arms, and lie on his great, broad breast, and look up into his face, and be his for life and death, as she had dreamed in her vision of joy in the dark wood, when that dream had seemed so impossible of fulfilment. It was on the point of fulfilment now. His arms were closing round her, tighter, tighter, when, at this very opportune or inopportune moment, a light sound

118 visions … guilty little soul.] Not in *DUM*.

118 By no means pleased … I thought it was uncle Piggott!"] Balked he was of his prey for a while, and in bitter wrath and vexation, in consequence.

118 "What on earth] "What the deuce

118 consideration.] money.

118 Kate involuntarily held up her head … and having so said,] Not in *DUM*

118 she was not slow in obeying his injunctions.] Kate was not slow in

7 Inexact, ll. 105-06 of "The Clergyman's First Tale" in Arthur Hugh Clough's "Mari Magno" (1861). This section comments on Michel de Montaigne's essay "On Friendship" (1580).

obeying his injunctions.
118 “Good-bye,” she said, smiling, and nodding … and was out of sight in a moment.] “Good-bye,” she said, and nodded her little head at him, and was out of sight in a minute.
119 charmingly girlish,] awfully girlish and jolly,
120 rush off] cut off
120 extremely hot] awful hot
121 spoke the truth] spoke truth
121 “Only three days,” said Kate] Only three days. “Cheer up, Sam,” said Kate
121 much like one with a headache] much like a headache
121 O no, no,] Oh no, oh no,
121 said she, giving a glad little nod] said she, popping down into her place, and giving a glad little nod
122 “Holy Saint Bridget;] “O, good gracious,
123 “Make haste and tell us … if you know what that means.”] “Let’s have it. I bet something it’s some rotten thing I shan’t care twopence about.”
123 “Hallelujah! Hallelujee!”] “Best of all,”
123 Let’s leave] Let’s cut
123 “How provoking!”] “What a bother!”
123 pleasant] jolly
123 not particularly lively] uncommonly poor fun
123-24 my poor child,”] you, poor thing
124 useless.] no go.
124 smile upon her again … to see this day!”] come round again. My eyes, what a bloke!”
124 some such violent form of dissipation,”] some such humbugging thing,”
124 mild entertainment.] mild form of dissipation.
124 hate my sisters—] hate my sisters like poison,
124 in fact, I’m not at all certain that I don’t agree with you;] Not in *DUM*
127 a resolution, and was in such an amiable humour] a resolution, and had had his hair cut, and was in such an amiable humour
128 nonsensical] humbugging
128 will you not,] will not you,
129 untimely mirth.] untimeous mirth.
129 prince of shams!] prince of Brummagem shams
130 you’ll bring them to acknowledge, in time.] you’ll see satiation set in,

in time.
130 uncomfortably soon after tea as it was,] uncomfortably full as they were,
130 fifty squeaky little voices,] fifty stuffed-up, squeaky little voices
131 fairy bust!] ravishing bust.
132 Kate did not accompany them … I don't know which *came first.*] Kate did not "come tumbling after," after the example of Gill.
133 your hat, won't you?] your hat, child,
133 black as a coal."] the colour of your hat!"
133 negro] nigger
133 pushed away] kicked away
133 "I do believe … "lose the lark in heaven."] "You'll make me put it on myself, and tie it under your obstinate little chin."/ But this awful threat he did not put in execution, and Kate, hatless, won the day.
134 emaciated] threadpaper
134 smelling first one, and then another.] poking her little nose, first into one, then into another.
134 gardener here.] gardener here" (sniff, sniff).
134 character. O, O!"] character (sniff, sniff). Oh, Oh!"
134 adept at] tiger for
134 worshipped at the shrine of one more gardenia,] took two more sniffs,
134 comfortable] snug
135 valuable dog of yours] valuable door-mat of a dog of yours
136 furzy] fuzzy
136 stroll about] moon about
137 tighter, tighter, and] tighter, tighter, till they were as fetters of iron binding her; and the strain that fulfilled the wild longing, the burning dreams of weeks, was quite painful; and
138 to himself.] to himself; never could be sated with kissing her.
140 young women in] young women of vast circumference, in
140 panting,] perspiring,
143 freshly] freshly now
144 there were stillness] there was stillness
144 out of the sight of the little cottage by the railway] out of sight of the sauntering families—out of sight of the little cottage by the railway
145 arms again. It] arms again. What! after having gone thus far—after those kisses yesterday among the flowers, those kisses which had made his blood rush and surge so madly, that it seemed as if it never could

flow quiet and sluggish again—should he, by his own act and deed, refrain henceforth, for evermore, from any repetition of that most intoxicating draught; just taste it, and then pour away the rest. That would not be much after Dare Stamer's fashion, assuredly. He knew as much about self-denial as I know about Sanscrit. Why, he positively thirsted for this girl—a parching, burning thirst, which could never be slaked till he had her utterly to himself, body and soul, for ever and ever. It

145 aren't I,] aint I.

146 rattled away] jawed away

146 if you were."] if you were." He liked to feel her little heart beat against him; it was such an odd sensation.

147 fuss] hullabaloo

147 did not care about me!"] did not care twopence about me!"

147 he said, "but what] he said, and the great prisoning arm tightened round her waist; "but what

147 awhile. I could not spare you now,"] awhile. You need not begin to bother about going there, till you are an ugly wrinkled old hag. I'll give you up then, willingly enough, but I could not spare you now,"

147 Wicked Kate … ten days ago.] ("Oh, Kate, how fast you've run down the hill this last week; you'd have shuddered to say that ten days ago.")

147-48 Let no one think … to return.] Not in *DUM*

149-50 returned the soft voice, resolute still … O, Kate, Kate, if I]returned the soft voice resolute still; resolute to follow wherever he should lead on. He was going to ask some great sacrifice of herself at her hands; something that would ruin and slay her in the world's eyes for ever; well, she would do it thankfully; he was her world. As for his asking anything that would injure or wound anyone besides their two selves it never occurred to her that her Dare could by any possibility do that. She patted his silky locks with little soothing tender fingers. "And then, after all, I may

150 great tender firmness.] gentle, tender firmness.

150-51 arms about his neck. She] arms, which she had always considered so unpleasantly unbecomingly fat and massive, as a close soft sort of comforter round his great knitted throat; she

151 hypocrisy] humbug

151 hardly a bit.] hardly a bit; the Dare for whom I'd stick at nothing./ He kissed her passionately when she said that, over and over again; it seemed as if he could not stop.

151 you must keep] you must stick

152 the prudish world?] the humbugging, prudish world;
152 the fire she had been wont to shrink under …but since you will have it, I swear] She had grown worse of late, bolder; she did not shrink now; she fronted those eyes, undaunted, reckless./ "Yes," she said, "of course I will;" and she looked up to Heaven to bear her witness. "I swear," she said.
152 "There!" she said … soul in your hand."] I swear to refuse nothing that he asks of me to-night."/ Did not it seem as if she must be lost, past redemption; as if she was putting the sign and the seal to her own black doom? Could infatuation go to a more frightful point?
152 intensely relieved./ "Brave little child!"] relieved at the manner in which the victim went to the altar; no need for ropes to drag her there; she ran there, jubilant.
153 a sigh,] a little satisfied sigh,

Vol II

154 my father.] the governor.
154 I'll punish them some day.] I'll be even with them some day.
154 quarrel] row
154 and no wonder;] small blame to me;
154 seen of him."] seen of the old boy."
154 "How cruel of him!"] "Bother the old gentleman!"
154 "Why are people's fathers so often their worst enemies … if he had lived.] Not in *DUM*
155 two old men will lay their wise heads together,] two old asses will lay their addled heads together,
155 two old men] two old asses
155 your old uncle?] your twaddling old uncle?
156 This, then, was the sacrifice … I choose you!"] One great shuddering, sobbing sigh she gave, and then her resolution came back again, firm as ever. Well, she'd do it. Why count the cost? No looking back now—no shrinking. She had gone over the river, and the bridge was cut away behind her. What was self-respect to her in comparison of him now?/ "Yes," she said, "I'll do it. I'm past praying for now, I think," she added, with a reckless, dreary sort of smile. "It's very horrible of me to leave them all so easily when they have been so kind to me for these many, *many* years, at your beck, too, whom six weeks ago I'd never seen. But I cannot help it."
156 though great, sobbing sighs] through another of those great sobbing

sighs
156 Still the thought would recur, the puzzling unanswerable doubt … Then Dare spoke:] One thought, passing bitter, would come across her love and her joy; the thought of what Blount would think of her; dear, jolly old Blount, who was always saying funny, rude things to her, with whom she had been sparring and joking for the best part of the last seventeen years. Dare spoke at last.
157 Margaret and Blount's grieved surprise at her want of sisterly confidence in them.] Blount's quick-coming suspicion and scorn.
157 dreadfully tired."] dreadfully knocked up."
157 you going?] we going?
157 worries] bores
157 my little coward] you little coward
157 as this usually is,] like this usually is,
157 my old father] my old governor
157 said Kate, almost inaudibly.] said Kate again, almost inaudibly.
157 that quarrel with my father] that row with the governor
157 composed] concocted
157 a good pace] a rattling good pace
158 (strong young man] (stalwart young man
158 a great knife were running into his heart.] a big knife were sticking right into his heart.
158 sort of place] sort of hole
158 just to kill time, in fact,] being very short of a job,
158 skipper,] skipper sort of fellow,
158 Forever accursed be the day when I first saw her] Curse her! curse the day I ever set eyes on her great
159 wander about] moon about
159 she with her great meaningless black eyes drawing me] she goggling with her great black eyes at me, drawing me
159 in love with] spooney about
159 I have made a full confession now, haven't I?"] I've done it with a vengeance now, haven't I?"
159 unpleasantly fond,] unpleasantly so,
159 my usual ill-luck,] my usual deuced ill luck,
159 heard some false, trumped-up stories] got wind of some trumped-up, lying stories
159 the most lamentable effusions] the most maundering, mawkish

effusions
159 and agony—all that sort of absurdity—] and agony—curse her!—all that sort of bosh;
159 kills me] makes me sick
159-60 I really believe … always threatening to do.] I do believe she'd have thrown herself over Waterloo-bridge, as she was always threatening doing.
160 I should have died laughing if I had been spectator instead of sufferer … She would make ten of you.] I could have split laughing if I had not felt so inclined to be sick. I thought she'd never have done slobbering over me; and I can tell you, Kate, it is a serious thing to have a great female of six feet six hanging all her weight round your neck. Such a strapper she is, Kitty! She'd make six of you.
160 in sheer] out of sheer
160 laid his iron hand on her arm,] griped her arm, and no tiger could have griped his victim more fast and surely,
160-61 She turned and faced him in the moon-light, all the youth gone out of her face… . Dare sprang to his feet.] "I'm not in the humour for joking, I can tell you. Take care, Kate, take care. I warn you before it is too late. People do not trifle with me with impunity. Loathe me as you may, you must be mine; so you had better make up your mind to it."/ "Loathe you, indeed!" said Kate; and her hard-kept firmness would relax a little bit. "You're talking like a fool, a maniac; loathe you! Why, don't you know that, heartless brute and devil as I see you are now, I'd be thankful to lay my head down and die this minute."/ "You don't mean that, Kate; you'd shudder and tremble like other women if death was to come near you. You know you would. But, take care," he went on, menacingly, ruled and dominated by the passion which was rending him," or I may take you at your word. You *may* die there to-night, perhaps, in reality, if you don't look out;" and he looked like a person whose love might, as it does sometimes in these days, take the form of murder./ "I'm sure I wish to goodness you *would* kill me, if that's what you're threatening," said Kate, in her perfect hopelessness. "You need not think to frighten me with that bug-bear. Good heavens! it would be the best thing that could happen to me now, God knows!" and she wrung her hands. That cup was unbearably bitter to drink.
161 "Where is your vow, Kate?" he asked hoarsely, great drops of perspiration standing on his brow;] asked Dare hoarsely; and the iron manacles tightened round her white wrists;
161 braving him. She was quite past fear now.] braving him; for she was

quite past fear now.

161 made to your wife, and how have you kept them?"] that unfortunate wife of yours? and how beautifully you've kept them."

161 You shall see that I *can* keep an oath … stand here.] You shall see, to your cost, that I *can* keep an oath; and that oath will be fulfilled as soon as I stand here."

161 "No, it won't,"] "No, it shan't,"

161-62 "It is too late to go back now," said Dare… she ended with concentrated bitterness.] "Take care, Kate," said Dare, with a great effort, mastering himself enough to speak tolerably collectedly. "What a little fool you are to brave me as you are doing. Just think now what hinders me from lifting you up and carrying you off this minute. Much good it would be your struggling with me, would not it? And you might scream your little heart out; not a soul would hear you here./ This dialogue resembled rather a single combat between a small soft sort of dove and a sharp-beaked hawk; though, indeed, Kate was a woman too strong-willed, of too stern a stuff to be well compared to a dove. There was nothing of the insipid, cooing sweetness of the dove about her. She spoke up boldly again despite his warning, nor abated one jot of the scorn in her tone./ "Of course, if you intend to employ that bodily strength you're so proud of in bullying one small weak woman, there is no doubt that you can do that. It would be a feat worthy of your prowess; but, if you think a moment, you'll see that you'd be ill paid for your everlasting disgrace. You'd only have gained a log, that's all; indeed something worse than a log, for a log can't hate, and I should hate and abhor you!"/ He could answer nothing, dumb-founded by that calmness of hers that feared nothing.

162 feared nothing. Then she changed her tone.] He only held her tight still. Then she changed her tune.

163 touch them again as long as you live.] touch them—come near them again as long you live.

164 vanishes] vanished

164 two astonished old gentlemen.] two flabbergasted old gentlemen.

166 so safe and secure] nestling and *snuggling* so safe and secure

166 line into the water.] line, flop into the water.

167 a multitude] ever such a lot

167 all to be covered] all going to be covered

167 furzy] fuzzy

167 skeleton,] scrag,

168 one-sided] *lobsided*
168 "Little torments,"] "Bother you all,"
168 everyone,] every man Jack of them;
169 Such nonsense] Such bosh
169 morsel;] ha'porth;
169 come to the end.] come to the end; so here goes.
169 I've got no needle now!] I've got no needle now! What a bother.
170 Pen-Dyllas Jane),] then Pen Dyllas' Jane of the creaking stays),
171 just in time,"] in the nick of time,"
172 Such a fit of the blues!"] Such doldrums!"
172 "Blues!"] "Doldrums!"
172 he went on, to make her mind easy,] he went on fibbing, to make her mind easy
172 jumping] jumping up
172 old things—] old frumps;
172 when they tell me all their unpleasant ailments,] when they show me their nasty bad old legs,
173 telling their ailments] showing their bad legs
173 talking about] showing
175 He was cheated] He was humbugged, and got round, and taken in
175 simplicity.] *gullability.*
176 incurable] bad
176 pull in] lug in
177 utterly freed] utterly free
178 cheerful;] jolly,
178 those members.] those members as dead as mutton, as herrings, as a door nail, or as anything else more intensely defunct than these three objects.
179 like a fairy tale, in that warm scented room.] like a fairy tale, in there, in that warm scented room,
180 plenty] a lot
180 six times as large] six times as big,
181 male creature] *he* creature
182 ugly fingers] *stubby* fingers
184 mischievous wretch.] mischievous donkey.
184 snub for your poor sisters."] slap at your poor sisters."
184 a snub?"] a slap?"
184 vanquished by Kate] knocked over by Kate

184 "you always are … I conquered."] "she's a dreadful man-slayer."
184 "a little white-faced thing."] "A little, cock-nosed, white-faced thing.
184 turn-up noses."] cock noses."
185 two hours.] the last two hours.
185 Never saw it before.] Never saw that before.
185 turn-up-nosed Kate,] cock-nosed Kate,
186 a straw] twopence
186 joke in Hebrew."] cut jokes in Hebrew."
187 teasing] boring
188 I'll come instantly] I'll come straight off
188 walking about,] traipsing about,
188 those back streets all alone."] those blind alleys and back slums all alone."
188 an umbrella] gamp umbrella
188 harm] grief
188 charitable philanthropic plan] charitable philanthropic dodge
189-94 "It would be quite a different matter if you were a clergyman's daughter … Kate would flirt with the undertaker who came to measure her for her coffin.] "I believe," begins Jane, quasi roguishly, a bright thought dawning on her, "that you do all these pious labours for the love of that little wizened, half starved parson we saw at your house the other day."/ "Indeed," says Kate, I almost believe I do; at least I don't think I should ever have taken it up but for him."/ She spoke very openly and ingenuously; she would as soon have thought of denying her affection for Blount as for James Stanley, it was so nearly the same in mind, though not in degree./ "It is such a comfort to be able to give him any gratification, he has so few pleasures, poor dear little fellow!" she says softly, thinking of the thin white face, and the grave solemn spirit-lit eyes./ "I always suspected how your Platonic would end," remarks Jane. "I always said it would terminate in a neat walking wedding to Queenstown church, and I'm sure of it now."/ "I wish you had hit upon a more respectable sized individual, Kate," suggests Fanny; "it is difficult to see him without a magnifying glass. I don't think I'll own him as a cousin." A harmless, pointless, stingless piece of wit, one would say, much in the Miss Chesters' usual style. But Kate did not look at it in that light at all. *She* marry any one? *she* give herself into any man's possession, with Dare Stamer's rugged, strong marked features, his deep sunk eyes, full of dark woe, always before her mental sight whether asleep or awake, pursuing her still with as cruel a persecution as ever they

had done. *She* marry James Stanley! Detestable, revolting idea! She almost loathed him as she thought of it; almost resolved never to speak to the poor unoffending little man again as long as she lived. Her voice sounded quite harsh when she spoke at last, vehemently, rudely, and the colour came rippling hot and fast into her cheeks, and fire shot out arrowy from under level fronting eyelids./ "Marry, marry, marry," she says with utter scorn; "you are always talking of marrying, you girls are; I believe it's the one idea that possesses you all four by day and by night. Take my advice now," she goes on, smiling rather sardonically round upon them, "and leave such jokes to the maid-servants and the foot-men; or if you must make them, let them be about yourselves; don't make them about me, please, at all events, for strange to say, I don't appreciate them; they make me feel rather sick."/ "Goodness, Kate, exclaims Jane, when this climax was reached, "don't bite my nose off! What a little fury you are to be sure."/ "Once for all," says Kate, very firmly, cooling down a little, and instinctively clasping Dare's locket in her small fingers as she speaks, "I request you not to make any more of your nice little plans for me. Will you be kind enough to believe me, once for all, when I tell you that I shall never marry any one as long as I live, not if I drag out my life to a hundred!"/ "Of course not," says Emily, joining in the conversation, for the first time, "we all know that; we all know that. Kate's got a secret grief."/ "Secret grief!" exclaims Fanny, with animation; "has she? Well, I never knew that before. Oh, Kate, you slyboots, you never told us about that 'worm in the bud,' and that sort of thing, of course. What awful fun!"/ "Secret grief!" call out George's manly tones; he, having from the other side of the room, caught the sound of the twice repeated words. "Who on earth has got a secret grief? I'm sure I wish to goodness I had, it is such a delightful, jolly, interesting sort of thing to have."/ "Kate has," answers his sister, raising her voice. "Ah, yes. Miss Kate, I'll tell of you now to punish you for giving us such a scolding all round just now. Well, then," she said, turning to the other three, "you must know, girls, that the last time I went to see these girls, I did not find anybody in the drawing-room, and I ran upstairs to Kate's room. She had her back to me, and did not hear me come in; and what do you think she was doing now? I saw her in the glass. Why, gazing at a photograph she had in her hand, and kissing it—oh, over and over again. I could not quite see who it was, I'm sorry to say, but I did find out that it was a man. There, that's the young lady that's never going to marry, if she lives to be a hundred! What do you say to that?"/ "If there was no truth in that accusation, why, oh Kate, did you blush up, so furiously, such a deep distressful red, that it seemed as if you could never pale again? Why did you clench your hands into a hard, round, white ball? Why did you feel so completely disposed to murder the funny narrator of this romantic incident? Alas, there was a great deal of truth in it; alas, it was every bit true. Poor Kate."/ How weak she was. She had not been able quite to divorce herself from this clinging sin; she hugged a little relic of it. That other woman's husband could not be nothing to her, even yet. Night and morning, and as often in the day as she felt particularly desolate and empty-hearted, craved more especially for that scant sustenance that was left her; she would go and take out that effigy of Dare leaning on a broken pillar, scowling, in a great coat, with a Liliputian umbrella in his hand; would look at it till, somehow, it grew misty and dim before her, and then would kiss it again and again, with trembling passionate lips. She always slept with it under her pillow, and it was getting quite a defaced, battered look, through those numberless fevered kisses that were rained upon it; through the chance tears that sometimes would fall hotly on the indifferent, sinister-looking picture face. Right or wrong, it seemed to Kate that she only lived on those long gazes, those foolish, profitless kisses. Twice or thrice she essayed to speak, but it would not do; she felt choking, and unable to bear the six pair of eyes upon her, covered her face with both hands, and rushed out of the room. They were all silent from astonishment, while the clock ticked audibly for a few seconds; then Emily spoke rather aghast./ "What an unfortunately good hit I made. But who was it, I wonder?" and she looked toward Maggie for light on the matter, for the satisfaction of their spirit of inquisitiveness. But Maggie did not feel particularly inclined to gratify them. She looked rather grave and rather disgusted, while she said within herself that really those girls were hopelessly vulgar in themselves./ "So she's fond of some one," thinks George; "it is lucky I don't feel inclined to go in for her;" and he feels a little vexed, unaccountable as it is that the knowledge of this two-hour-known cousin having a lover, should have power to annoy him. That unpleasant incident succeeded in raising Kate on a pinnacle high above Maggie, in George's estimation, for the time. The knowledge that some other fellow covets the object of his affection, makes her go up ever so many degrees in the estimation of any ordinary man. It is only one of a very high, self-contained soul, who can prize the woman he loves for just what she is, independent of other men's verdict concerning her./"Who could it be?" thinks George; and his curiosity beat his sisters' altogether, though he is a man, and a warrior, and they are only girls. He runs over all the eligibles of Queenstown in thought, and rejects them one after another; not one will do. Kate comes back, after a time, and gives little, sedate, matter-of-fact answers to George when he resumes his station at the back of her chair; does not glance up at him once, talks to him as she might talk to her grandmother, were that venerable old lady alive. All her coquettishness has taken to itself wings./ "Who can it be?" thinks puzzled George; "who can it be?"

194 Jane went up] Jane goes up
194 asked smiling:] asks, smiling—
194 Venus Victrix,] a manslayer
194 "Don't be absurd,"] "Nonsense,"
194 hastily shaking her off … bread-and-butter element in her.] crossly, shaking her off. "What bosh you talk!" and that is all the answer he makes.
195 open pages. Vary the recipe] open pages; vary the receipt
195 build many of] build a good many of
196 swallowed] bolted
197 pushing them back] poking them back
197 "What a figure] "What a Guy[8]
197 dragging] hauling
198 undesirable] undescribable
203 "Stupid old thing!"] "Stupid old fool!"
203 bones. What an imposition] What humbug—what bosh—what an imposition
204 to the census.] In *DUM* this chapter is split in two installments, the first ending here and the second picking up in the Jan '66 issue.
205 straw] halfpenny
206 never seen] never set eyes on
206 they did not care] they did not much care
206 somehow more sociable] somehow snugger, more sociable
210 she pushes] she pokes
212 her appearance] her cut
212 enveloping scarlet cloak and] enveloping scarlet cloak, full short petticoat, that would sway so as she walked, and
212 gets opposite the] gets opposite to the

8 A grotesquely dressed person; after the effigies of Guy Fawkes, the seventeenth-century conspirator who tried to blow up the House of Lords, that are traditionally paraded and burned on Guy Fawkes Day (November 5).

213 knock him down; but] knock him down, floor him; but
214 this bogie,] this *bug-a-boo*;
214 such a noise] such a flop
214 died laughing,] split laughing,
216 now by bursting out laughing in his face.] now, by opening her mouth and bursting out laughing in his face.
217 flirting and silly] flirting, and donkeyish
217 why we should stand here,] why we should stand stockstill here,
217 would like intensely] would like hugely
218-19 a great brutal butcher] a great hulking butcher
219 unsavoury puddle] stinking puddle
220 delicate] ticklish
220 boldly for each behind] boldly, each behind
220 –to quarrel a little] –to squabble a little
220 listen a little,] listen a bit,
220 "Ma teases so about] "Ma bothers so much about
220 lectures] bother
221 hundreds of things] oceans of things
221 is it not, girls?"] is not it, girls?"
221 thoroughly tired] mortally tired
222 rustling his newspaper,] rustling his paper,
222 a victim to her, poor little fellow."] rather *gone* in that quarter, poor little beggar."
222 twenty-two."] twenty-two."/ "About that man whose photograph you caught her kissing, no doubt; whoever he was. Silly little cat! Fancy saluting a photograph! Poorish fun, eh, girls? Got a nasty taste from those dirty chemicals, I should say. I wish to goodness I could find out who it was. I should die happy then."
222 stagnant.] deadly lively.
226 He is such a flirt] He is such a slippery fish
226 two small strings] the small strings
226 a straw] twopence
226 nor a quarter of a straw;] nor a quarter twopence;
226 big dark person] big dark blackguard
226 the big person,] the big blackguard,
227 she is sitting … they do not by any means always do.] all along on the rug she is lying, at George's feet, with her hands under her head, which head is resting on a cushion that she has tugged down off the sofa, with a

view to making herself as comfortable as circumstances will permit. A very free-and-easy sort of way to be reposing in, no doubt; but then George was nothing but a cousin, so what did it matter?
228 fairly.] tidily.
228 near escape of it] near squeak for it
229 upright posture] sitting posture
230 morning,—] morning, laughing,
230 to think of taking his departure] to think of "hooking it," as he phrased it,
230 in love,] in the love line,
230 Because she was not a bit happy now,] Because she had been more unfortunate than any woman ever had been since Ariadne;[9] because she was not a bit happy now
231 rippling hair] fuzzy hair
231 hovered so weakly] shilly-shallied and livered so weakly
231 by fair means or foul;] by hook or by crook;
231 his battered photograph] the battered photograph
232 not a very large gleam] not a very big gleam
232 unpleasant sort] ungodly sort
233 British face,] British phiz,
233 such shocking stories?] such shocking fibs?
233 "Very conceited] "Monstrous conceited
234 Sitting over] Poking over
234 old simpleton,"] old blockhead,"
234 cooled his feelings] cooled his ears
234 "Three parts sinner] "Three parts devil
234 one part sinner,] one part devil,
234 wandering about] poking about
235 nonsense,] bosh,
235 into a scrape.] into a hobble.
236 no earthly thing] no mortal thing
237-38 but for all that, they might be worse." … Kingsleyan division of labour."] but for all that, they might be worse—though their legs could not well," he concludes, with some chagrin./ "Their legs, George?"/ "Yes, to be sure. I could tell Loo all over Queenstown by those unlucky pins of

9 In Greek mythology Ariadne, daughter of the Cretan king, helped Theseus, with whom she fell in love, defeat the Minotaur; in many versions of the story Theseus later abandons her.

hers."/ "Poor Loo! 'If ignorance is bliss,' &c.[10] How conceitedly she comes stumping along, happily unaware of your ridicule."/ "It is not ridicule. I don't want to ridicule the old girl. It is a fact. Loo's warmest admirer could not deny that her supporters are columner."/ "Hush!" she'll hear you. Well, girls."
238 "we thought you were going] "we thought you were gone
238 "Good-bye … badinage.] "Adieu, young ladies," she says coldly; "if you are going to be witty, I'm off."
243 died with laughing] split with laughing
244 pure girl] pure girl's
244 unwitting of them] unwittingly in them
251 "Stupid fellow!] "Bother the fellow!
252 torment] ass
252 little flirting ruse,] little flirting dodge,
252 run away] cut away
252 run] cut
252 rushing after me at such a pace;] posting after me at such a mailcoach rate;
253 an injured intonation] a hoity-toity intonation
253 along a street parallel] along the street parallel
253 That would be a pity.] (That would be a pity.)
254 drift] upshot
254 drift] upshot
254 George,"] old fellow,"
254 drift,] upshot,
254 softening,] mincing or hashing,
254 stay some time,"] stay some time, cooling your heels,"
254 vestige] rag
255 tattlers and scandalmongers] dolts and boobies
255 too spirited a sort of girl] too spirited, plucky a sort of girl
255 ever so often] ever so big
256 closed her lips firmly,] closed her lips firm,
256 in love with] spoony about
257 O my cousin.] my dear boy.
258 my sisters chattering;] my sisters jawing;
258 What a quantity] What a deal

10 Reference to ll. 99-100 of Thomas Gray's "Ode on a Distant Prospect of Eton College" (1742): "if ignorance is bliss/ 'Tis folly to be wise."

259 ugly-faced] putty-faced
259 ugly-faced] putty-faced
262 blameless vestal] putty-face
262 sal-volatile] salts
262 "What a prodigious outlay," remarks George contemptuously;] "You screw; you old skinflint!" remarks George, becoming objurgatory,
262 Very generous] Very handsome
262 "Are not you going too, Kate?"] "Go along, Kate."
262 attempt at kissing,] *kissatory* attempt;
262 "No, thanks,] "No, thank you,]
263 "Don't trouble … go in."] "Very much obliged to you—all the same; but I have no intention whatever of going in there, whatever any one else may do."
263 thanks, … big drum."] thank you; and have no particular desire to sit for two mortal hours and be banged, and squeaked, and thundered at."
263 see that Arabella] see here, Arabella
263 wandering about] mooning about
263-64 "Why mayn't I … beat a hasty retreat.] Kate blazed out on him at this assumption of authority. It was only very mighty love that could make her submissive to any man born of woman. Soft and kittenish and playful, no doubt, but proud as Lucifer.[11] "Allow me," she said, with anger in her voice. "I should just like, for curiosity's sake, to see how you would prevent me. If I were to choose to walk on my head from here to the organ, it would be a very foolish thing of me to do, but you would have no possible right to interfere." / George waxed angry too, at this snubbing; and, consequently, obstinate in his unreasonable intentions. "Right or no right," he answered, doggedly, getting rather red in the face; "one thing is certain, and that is, that if you do not go into that concert, neither will I. I shall stay with you, much as you may dislike my society; I cannot have you seen sauntering about at public places, quite by yourself. It's all nonsense; I won't have it, and there's an end of it."/ Kate turned the corners of her mouth down, after a peculiarly infuriating fashion she had, smiled witheringly, and drew herself up till she looked at least an inch taller than nature had made her. "Won't you?" she asked, scornfully; and then she went on, with a pale, flickering smile, "You were always a bit of a blusterer, George; but you are not quite a fool, though you seem like one now; you know you'll do

11 Traditionally, the name Satan bore before his prideful rebellion against God caused him to be exiled from heaven.

nothing of the sort; you'll go into that room, and take care of your sisters and Margaret; and you'll not be so exceedingly silly as to follow me; if you do, I warn you, I'll never speak to you again, as long as I live, and you know I can keep my word at a pinch. Good-by for the present;" and she walked away slowly (unmolested now), in a quasi-dignified manner./ George stood and looked after her crestfallen, and said within himself that he was always worsted in these passages of arms with his cousin.
264 a hasty retreat.] In *DUM* there is no chapter break here, and the chapter is run together with what would become the first chapter of Vol. III in the triple-decker.

Vol. III

270 much surprise] great surprise
270 put on a lace veil] put on again a little lace veil
271 more profound.] She experienced, in bitter strength, the old temptation, to pitch away shame, and conscience, and religion, and nestle her head once again on the broad breast, that might never pillow it more, guiltlessly.
272 gazed greedily] gazed greedily, devouringly,
273 bold, glad eyes,] bold, unfettered eyes
273 flashing and dancing.] flashing and dancing a wild hell-dance.
274 more to the purpose.] more to the purpose. And then his hands tightened their grasp of her slender wrists; and the eyes, late so tender, glared tiger-like upon her, as he whispered,
274 had you?] had you? Well, I warn you that your Damon will do wisest to keep out of my way to-day, or he may chance not to go home with a whole skin."
274 more keenly than their own.] Kate lost sight of consistency, decorum, and the usages of society, bent down her little head and laid a light warm kiss on the iron hand that, cased in lavender kid, still held hers in a willing bondage.
275 sick or ailing"] "You're crying again," exclaimed Dare, angrily. "What's come to you, child? you used not to be such a puling, weak-spirited thing. I hate tears, I tell you; are you bent on making me kiss you? I swear I will soon, whether you like it or not. No, don't be afraid," he added, proudly, seeing her draw herself away a little, "I do not force my caresses on any one."/ "I'm not afraid," said Kate, "I never was afraid of you yet; I never was a cowardly woman either."

276 as tormentingly bewitching as ever?] as tormentingly bewitching as ever? A fellow might well go wild with longing for one kiss from those rare soft lips of yours. I'm doing it myself as fast as I can."/ "No, no; you must not," whispers Kate, hurriedly./ Dare, even before, when they did not meet under such moving circumstances, after so long a parting, could never keep very cool in Kate's presence. He was anything but cool now, Heaven knows! He sat down on the bench, and pulled Kate down beside him (poor little girl! she resisted feebly, ridiculously feebly); drew her close to his side without much ceremony, or consulting of her wishes, and kept her fast prisoned there by an iron arm binding her.
276 damned mine.] damned mine. You do not mind plain speaking, I hope; at least you used not to."/ "I am not squeamish any more than I used to be," answered Kate, taking no notice of his wild assertions;
276 "O God! … dull to you without me!"] Not in *DUM*
277 what a short, wretched span] what a little, short, wretched span
278 your piety.] your confounded piety.
278 same recipe] same receipt
278 Ah, Dare," she went on,] Ah, Dare," she went on, softly laying her head down on his shoulder (she had released herself from his embrace at last, and was sitting beside him on the bench again)
278 such lies,"] such preposterous lies,"
278 exclaimed Dare hastily.] exclaimed Dare, savagely shaking her off, "D——d if I do.
278 cry *peccavi*.] cry *peccavi* and slobber over my sins, thank you."
278 clenching his hand,] clenching a great sledgehammer fist
278 I can;] I can drive;
279 in this terrible conflict … "Go!" repeated Dare,] in this terrible conflict, but held up still by an unseen arm, and kept from succumbing utterly, "I will not listen to you," she said, stopping her ears, "nor look at you," and she covered her face with her hands./ "You *shall* look at me then," answered Dare, pulling down the poor little guarding hands roughly. "You *shall!*" and he glared upon her with frantic, wild-beast eyes—frantic at the thought of his prey slipping out of his grasp this second time./ "Let me go, let me go," moans Kate, incoherently. "What's the good of making me stay any longer? Give me one last kiss, darling, to comfort me afterwards, and let me go away—let me go!"/ "Let you go!" repeated Dare,
279 utter astonishment at] utter scorn
279 "go, indeed!] "Let you go indeed; a likely joke,

279 And you can sit there, and tell me so, calmly… on the Pen Dyllas sands."] "Don't be theatrical! Do you think to come over me with your upturned eyes, and your 'never agains,'" (mimicking her tones as he spoke). "You had better find out your mistake before it is too late, and give a plain answer to a plain question. Tell me," he said, seizing both her hands again, "once for all, where is it you are living at now? Answer me, I say."/ "I must not, I cannot, I *won't!*" said Kate, and at the last word, boldly spoken, she turned and faced him, braved him and his wrath, through that new strength that was given her in her need.

279 Dare's swarthy face grew very white—hard even … forgive me, if I speak roughly to you;] Dare's swarthy face turned very white, livid, even; but he governed his outward demeanour still, and only replied ironically—/ "Civil and explicit. But perhaps you'll be so kind as to tell me then at what place it would be most convenient for you to meet me to-morrow, or the day after? You see I leave you a wide choice."/ "I'll meet you nowhere, Dare," answered Kate, low-voiced from intense excitement, but firm as a rock./ Dare set his strong white teeth hard, and his clean-cut nostrils dilated; then he forced himself to say, coldly, sternly—/ "You *must* meet me somewhere, I tell you child. It is only a question of where. Will you be here to-morrow if I come down by the 12:30 train from town to meet you? "You see," he added sardonically, "your feminine fancy of mystery as to your place of residence prevents my deciding on a more desirable *rendezvous* for you. Do you hear? Will you meet me here or not?"/ "No, I will not," answered Kate, enunciating each word slowly and distinctly. "I told you so before," she went on, goaded to indignation by his pertinacity. "What do you mean by tormenting me so? It is not gentlemanlike of you to persecute any woman so."/ Dare's eyes flamed with fury at this taunt; but a man, and a big man especially, must not slay a little woman, or even knock her down, however impertinent she may be; so he only bit his lip hard, and answered her with a pale, fierce smile./ "Ungentlemanlike, I am, very likely; I do not deny your charge, Kate,

279 "Dare," she said … "then God help us!"] Not in *DUM*

280 threats, frowns,] threats, his pent-house-browed frowns,

280 wavered.] wavered still.

280 in the sight of God, he had said.] They would lead together a life chaster than many whom a parson binds together in a kindred-filled church, amongst flowers and music.

280 a prejudice of society] a miserable prejudice of society

280-81 "Hush," she said wildly, putting her hands to her ears … "Dare," said Kate hurriedly,] The cold perspiration stood on Kate's satin-smooth brow; the sweat of that hard fight. Such a half hour as she had been living through, takes ten years off man's or woman's life, I think./ "God have mercy upon me," she groaned, "what have I done to deserve such a horrible trial?"/ "Don't call on God!" said Dare, with rash blasphemy. "Even he cannot save you out of my hands now. I have been very enduring to you. I have borne long enough with your womanish caprices. I have tried persuasion and soft words. Thanks to your cursed obstinacy, I must try harder means now. You *must* stay with me, I say. I'll kill you if you don't."/ "You threatened me that once before," answered the girl with a dreary smile, "and I believe you'll do it, too, some day."/ "No, no , I shan't," muttered Dare, growing quickly remorseful. "I shan't kill you, Kate, whatever you do. I could not have the heart to stop that sweet breath, nor close those dear, big, cruel eyes, for ever; but, Kate, darling, I'm not over-patient; you know I never was a very patient fellow; you must not thwart me much longer. I cannot bear such persistent opposition. Just say you'll not cut a poor beggar, because he made a fool of himself, when he was a boy; just say you'll stay with me; only those few words; such simple easy words, too; 'I will stay Dare.'"/ But Kate only murmured the old tune, "Let me go, let me go," and tried with little trembling fingers to pluck off and thrust away the great arm, that, like a close pressing iron girdle, almost hindered respiration./ "You shall go this minute, Kate," said Dare, breathing quick and short, "if you will only promise to meet me here to-morrow at the time I mentioned. We shall both be less stupid and muddle-headed then, perhaps. To-morrow, mind; can anything be fairer or plainer than that?"/ "No, no," cried Kate, turning restless, tortured eyes around, seeking the help that was not forthcoming. And then another fear got hold of her, and she said, in a quick, terrified tone, "Oh, Dare,

282 I must go; they must not find me here with you." … one rather thin young one] Oh, what shall I do? I *must* go. If they find me here with you, I shall be done for, for ever!"/ "D—n Margaret and your cousins," said Dare, savagely, "let them come if they choose. I have no character to lose, and I wish to heavens you could get rid of yours, for then we should be on a par."/ Again the voices; Margaret's clear treble alarmingly distinct and near./ "Let me go, let me go," cried Kate, struggling frantically. "You villain! How dare you?"/ "Tiger cat!" said Dare, pale to the lips with rage, and balked passion, while two-edged swords of flame came forth from his

devil-lit eyes. "Stop fighting and struggling. Just listen a minute. If you'll say the monosyllable 'yes,' you shall go this minute; if not, *never*."/ Light laughter heard. George's manly tones apparently close to the entrance. Kate was driven to desperation. "They'll be in, in a second," she whispered, horror-struck. "Oh, I'll say anything! Yes, yes, I'll come. Let me go now, I say. You said you would."/ Dare bent down his haggard face to the level of hers, and, as if he could not help it, snatched one last, wild, fierce kiss from her trembling lips, while he said very hoarsely, "Kate, if you foil me, if you deceive me a second time, I'll be the death of you. There, be off now." Then he took off the iron manacles, and she stood a free woman before him. Not a second did she wait. With one lightning-swift, parting glance, in which all the pent-up love of her poor, rent heart, found vent, at last, she fled away like a hunted hare, unable to face those gay, laughing, questioning girls, with her tear-stained face, and her battered, dishevelled *tout ensemble.* In two minutes they

282 various manœuvres] various clever dodgings

282 –Why did not you come with us, Kate … &c. &c.] "What have you been doing to your bonnet, Kate? Why, it's all manner of shapes. Have you been sitting upon it?" enquired one of her cousins, as they stood under the flaring gas, on the railway platform, waiting for the down train, and that was all the result, to all appearance, of her unlucky rencounter with Colonel Stamer.

283 again, and it was love, not fear,] again. It was not because of his solemn vow to kill her if she disobeyed him. Very likely he meant it, but many fates would be worse than that. No, it was love, not fear,

286 sixpence in] sixpence on

290 looking forward to the meeting with her dark-eyed lover.] looking thirstily forward to the meeting with her dark-eyed lover, to the hiding her sorrow, and her guilt, and her shame, on his pillowing breast.

292 eluded him] dodged him

293 tease you] bother you

300 I must hear his voice just once again,] I must hear his grand voice, and kiss him just once again,

300 outlive] overlive

304 &c.,] &c.,&c.,

306 –what very few of us do—] –what very few of us *do* do—

306 towards her; and whenever the pilot star of duty shone,] towards her, instead of, as formerly, away from her; and, wherever the Pilot Star of Duty

shone,
316 poor worn-out wife] poor worn-out rag of a wife
321 dull carp] dull twopenny-halfpenny carp
323 noodle] nincompoop
324 Tennyson] Wordsworth
327 Never mind the headache!] Bother the headache!
329 "Don't be foolish—] "Don't be a fool—
330 keeps to the wizened] sticks to the wizened
331 religious notion?] religious dodge;
331 intent eager] attent, eager
333 "Villain!] "Snob!
333 I'd pommel the life out of him, the scoundrel!] I'd pommel the life out of him. I'd ornament his figure-head, so that his own mother should not recognise him, the scoundrel.
341 re-illumine it.] re-illume it.
345 smooth after that;] plain sailing after that;
346 had quarrelled and made up again,] had squabbled and made up again,
346 pet and darling of a happy home,] pet and darling of a snug home,
347 smallness of their own house.] smallness of their own.
348 fix upon Manchester] pitch upon Manchester,
349 obstinacy] pig-headedness
350 harping upon dying!] bothering about dying;
351 great rage,] awful rage,
351 put you into a madhouse."] clap you into a madhouse."
351 those sisterhoods;] those humbugging sisterhoods;
351 keep to their right functions] stick to
353 a hearty kiss.] a hearty hug.
354 all the evening."] all evening."
355 better dressed] better got-up
356 large hotel,] large house,
357 jasmines] jessamines
358 capital dancer."] clipping dancer."
359 capital dancer,] clipping dancer,
360 valsing about] hopping about
360 disconsolate."] disconsolate, kicking their heels."
360 is it not amusing?"] is not it a joke?"
362 alarmed."] alarmed."/ That man remembered his words subsequently, and altered his mind. It was a subject he was not overfond of talking of in

after days.
363 Kate said.] Kate said, and those were the last words that Mr. Piggott ever heard his niece, Kate Chester, utter.
364-75 Suddenly . . . there is peace."] Suddenly the figure of a tall man, whose shoulder she had before dimly seen, leaning lazy, against the entrance to her retreat, standing out black against the light, filled up the doorway, obscuring her vision into the bright interior. Then the figure came slowly sauntering down the path in her direction. "How provoking," she said to herself. "Why cannot people keep away? Of course lots more will be coming now." Resolutely she turned away her eyes. If it was any one of her acquaintance she would pretend not to see him; perhaps, by great good luck, might remain unseen herself behind her orange tree. On and on came the measured steps, not hurrying, not pausing, till they stopped close beside her. She looked up, angry and surprised; looked up, and beheld the figure of Dare Stamer. At that sight, the most unlooked for, the most petrifying the earth could show her, a scream rose to her lips, rose, but died there. For a moment she thought it must be his ghost, but a second glance convinced her that those thews and sinews were made of flesh and blood, not of air and vapour. This, then, was what her dream, what those chill tremors, those premonitions of evil pointed to. This was the form in which her doom had come, for that her doom had come, she did not doubt for one single instant./"You seem very glad to see me," he said, sardonically, looking down grimly upon her./ She essayed to speak, but the disobedient voice would find no passage through the hot, parched throat./ "I knew we should meet again," he went on with a sinister calm, in his steady tones./ "Oh, what have you come for? Where have you come from?" she got out at last, gaspingly./ "Not from hell, as you seem to think, by your scared face. I'm not there *yet*, anyhow."/ "Heaven forbid!"/ "What is it to you where I am come from? Is not it enough for you that I am here?"/ "Enough! Oh, more than enough, God knows."/ He stood like a pillar of night between her and life and light and mirth. Then to her ear came again the ironical cutting voice./ "You forgot to bid me any good-bye the last time I had the pleasure of meeting you, and you have given me no greeting this evening. What has become of your manners?"/ She put out a little hand, shaking like a leaf, to him, and said, in a trembling voice, "Dear Dare, I'm very sorry; I could not help it."/ He did not take her hand; left it there neglected, wooing his. With folded arms, he stood erect, motionless./ "Don't give me your hand," he said, disdainfully. "I don't want it; it is the hand of a false, lying woman.

What good could it do any man to take such?"/ She looked up in his face piteously, imploring mercy; as well seek it from a Libyan lion, or a panther in act to spring. There was no mercy there; not a grain to be found in those bronzed features, white now, deadly white to the lips, set in such cruel iron lines; the strong jaw squarer, more resolute than ever—resolute for something; the eyes that she would not look into, because she knew that a fiercer passion had replaced and quenched the old love that used to blaze there. Dare was not wild, or excited, or threatening to-night; very calm and cool, but yet her heart died within her when she looked up in that face, bending down there above her. Dare was perfectly sober, as sober as a judge; hard-headed to a proverb, it would take a vast deal to make his strong brain reel, but he had been drinking, drinking hard, for he had a job to do to-night that required nerve, and nerve he had got./ Kate gathered courage from her misery, and his injustice, and spoke firmly. "There are some promises that it is a virtue and a duty to forget."/ "Very likely, very likely; I don't pretend to know much about virtue or duty either. I used to have some absurd notions once about such trifles as honour and truth, but that was when I was a boy. Of course they are long gone now. No doubt you are a far better authority on such subjects than I am."/ He turned away, walked to a glass door that led down into the garden, opened it, and for a few minutes stood looking out into the serene night. Then he came back to Kate, and said with a laugh:/ "Kate, it's ridiculous, after all, to be going into heroics, because a woman has chosen to cut you; such an every-day occurrence. Come, I'm not vindictive. I'll forgive you. We may as well be friends; may not we? Give me your hand."/ "Yes, friends—always friends," she answered, breathing freer, and she put out her hand a second time./ This time he took it, grasped it for a second, and then dropped it hastily, as if he feared the touch of those warm, soft fingers might unman him./ "Kate—it's very hot in here; don't you think so? Come just outside into the garden with me, will you? I should like, now we are at peace again, to have just a few last words with you before I go, for I am going on a long journey to-night."/ "Where are you going, Dare?"/ "I don't know, just yet; there are two directions, in either of which I may go. I want to ask your advice about it; that is why I came here to-night, indeed."/ "*My* advice?"/ "Yes, yours; is there anything very odd in that? my *friend*, you know."/ "But cannot I give my advice in here just as well?"/ "No, no; it is so public here. There are such heaps of people moving backwards and forwards, and that dinning music stuns one; now, out there, we should be as snug and private as possible. You are not afraid of the night dews, are you?"/"Not in the least."/ "Look, the moonlight is as bright as day; you used to be fond of moonlight *once*."/ "Ah, Dare, so I was, long ago; those happy days! I like it still, but it is getting so late, they'll be looking for me to go home, and not be able to find me."/ "Never fear; I'll take care that you go home to-night."/ The words were simple, but they curdled her blood; there seemed to be some second meaning in them./ "Dare, if you don't mind—I think I'd rather—I think, perhaps, it would be better not."/ "Of course I do mind; of course it is a disappointment not to have a chat with you, after coming here on purpose; of course, one likes to talk to one's friend."/"If you please, dear Dare—I think—I'd rather not."/ The dark eyes flash scornful./ "What is the objection, Kate? let us hear it; a summer night is generally considered a pleasant thing enough. Are you afraid of going? Are you afraid of me? Do you think I should cut your little white throat among the roses?"/ "Dare, don't be angry with me, please; it is very stupid of me, I know, but—I am rather frightened at you to-night; there is something in your eyes and your voice that scares me, I don't know why. Oh, what has come to you?"/ "Come to me!—nothing, of course. Well, you have grown a timid fawn to be terrified out of your wits because a man asks you to take a turn in a garden with him. I wonder you did not shriek and cry murder when Tankerville asked you whether you would have some tea just now; it was full as alarming."/ His ridicule startled her; perhaps it was all her fancy, after all./ "If I say I'll go with you, will you swear not to do me any harm, Dare?"/ Eagerly she scanned that marble mask, waiting for her answer./"Do any harm to you!—what do you mean? Do the men of your acquaintance generally do their friends harm when they take an evening stroll with them? The worst injury a man would inflict in such a case, I should say, would be a kiss, and you need not fear; I have not the smallest inclination to kiss you."/ "It was very rude of me, and insulting, I know, but I am nervous and foolish to-night; forgive me, will you? Dare, I'll come out this minute with you, if you'll swear not to hurt me in any way; if you'll swear to let me go home unmolested to-night."/ "I'll swear, of course."/"What'll you swear by?"/"By everything I hold most sacred. A person would hardly dare break such an oath as that, would they?"/"I'll come then. Dare, let me look in your face; are you speaking truth? Will you really leave me in peace, and not torment me?"/ "I will leave you in peace, perfect peace, certainly."/"Is there a double meaning in your words? Are you sure you are not deceiving me?"/ "You judge by yourself; when did I ever deceive you?"/"Never, poor fellow! no more you did; it is a shame of me to doubt you. I don't doubt you any more—I'm coming now."/"Nobody will ever hear you say you are sorry—that I'm certain of; take care, mind the steps, or you'll fall."/ Out into the serene night that man and that woman went, and in came they never again./ CHAPTER XXXV./ OUT they went down the gravel walk, that shone so bright between the rows of folded flowers asleep. From the windows of the house streamed lines of rosy light athwart the moon-lit grass, and music, softened and sweetened, travelled out on the summer air. Dare had taken Kate's hand to help her down the steps, but he did not let it go again. He held it tight grasped in his, as he hurried her along. Well, surely there was nothing to be frightened at in that. They did not stop just outside, somehow; on and on they went to the bottom of the long garden. There, there was a little plot of old sward, tree-shaded, dotted with rose bushes—in that little plot, under those trees, they stayed their steps./ "It is nice and quiet, and private here," Dare said in that voice that did not seem the same voice that had told her he loved her long ago. "We may do pretty much what we like here, I fancy. I don't think that anybody will dare to disturb us, will they?"/"No, I should think not," she faltered./ "And now that we are here," he went on (and he stood back further in the tree-shadow that she might not see his face), "there's a question I want to ask you, Kate."/ "What is it?"/Low, like the roar of distant thunder, came the slow words, sinking into her heart:/"Kate, how *dared* you disobey me? How *dared* you fail me a second time?"/ No verbal answer, only a catching of the breath—a heaving of the white bosom./"I must have an answer; I must have this cleared up. Was it accident that kept you from me, or did you know you were lying when you stood there with me, and promised so solemnly to come back to me?"/ He waited for an answer; she must speak, hard as it was./ "I did not think I was telling lies; I fully intended to come back to you, but I was stopped."/ "Stopped! Who stopped you?" he asked, and some of the old, eager passion burst through the constraint of his hard voice. "You were kept from me by force? You would have come if you could—that was it, was not it? Oh, little darling, say it was so, and it may come all right even yet."/ "I was going to bear shame, and ruin, and death here and hereafter for you. I loved you so wickedly, that I thought you would make up to me for it all; but God saved me."/ "Stuff! Let's have no cant here, Kate; such twaddle may do very well for children and old women, but you know, and I know, that God does not lay a finger on men's affairs now-a-days, whatever he used to do."/ "I know nothing of the kind," said

Kate, and indignation lent clearness to the poor young voice. "Have I come out here to hear you talk weak, silly blasphemy? Don't dare to say such things to me. God is my only hope in this world or the next."/ "Poor thing! I pity you then."/ "I had given up everything for you; I had said good-bye to home and friends and good name; I was hurrying to you, but I was turned back, thank Heaven for it."/ "Spare me your pious ejaculations, please, and be a little quicker. Who turned you back?"/"Oh, my darling, you ought to rejoice with me, that I was saved from such a fate; you ought to be glad. I had set off, I was half way on the road to destruction, when a good man turned me back—not by force, I don't mean, but he over persuaded me, and I went back with him."/ Dare had great power of self-command, that had been proved already to-night; but now there was a pause, several pulse-beats before he could drill his voice into the former cutting, icy tones./ "Kate, would you mind telling me where that good man lives?"/ "Ah, his home is a long way from here."/ "Never mind. I should not care about the distance in comparison of the pleasure of making the acquaintance of so excellent a person."/ "Ah, he is beyond your reach; he is in heaven. How I wish I was there too."/ "Perhaps, by this time to-morrow, you may be—who knows?"/ "Why do you think so, Dare? What do you mean?"/ Hurried and quick came the breathless words. She strained her eyes to get a glimpse of that purposely-shadowed face, and failed./ "Mean? Oh, I mean nothing, of course; I was only talking at random. But, you know, odd things do happen; people die more suddenly than they expect sometimes—that is all."/ "Dare, you did mean something; I'm sure you did, by your voice. Oh, why do you stand so far back in the shade? Come out into the light, and let me look into your face. What is it you mean—tell me?"/ "You shall know by-and-bye—quite soon enough, I fancy. By-the-bye, Kate, do you happen to remember a warning I gave you last time we parted. You were in such a hurry to get away, that perhaps you did not hear it."/ She made no answer. What answer could she make?/ "Do you hear, Kate? Do you remember that slight circumstance? It is such a trifle that I dare say you have forgotten it."/ How that measured calm, that frosty voice, chilled the marrow of her bones. Reluctantly, timidly, she made answer—/ "No, no, I don't forget—at least I think I remember something about it. But you were angry, Dare; you did not mean what you said. Oh, don't think that I bear any malice to you for it; I've quite forgotten it—indeed I have."/ Poor Kate! She did not ever see how she was contradicting herself./ "Forgotten it, have you? Well, I have not; I don't easily forget those kind of things. Kate, did you ever know me to break my word?"/ A light came into the green eyes; she looked up quick at him./ "Yes, you are breaking your word now. Did not you vow and swear that if I came out with you, you would not hurt me in any way, would not torment me, would leave me quite unmolested? Are not you tormenting me now?"/ "Did I vow not to—? My memory is not very good."/ "You cannot have forgotten; it was not ten minutes ago. Oh, Dare, I am so frightened. I wish I had not come. May I go back? Oh, dear old fellow, do let me."/ "Be quiet, please, for a minute, and listen to me, Kate. Do you remember a night like this, some two years ago? Do you remember lying with your head on my breast, and swearing solemnly that you would stick to me through thick and thin, in life and in death—that nothing and nobody should come between us? How long afterwards was it that you broke that oath or forgot it?"/ "Oh, Dare, don't speak in that voice. What have I done? You are not the dear old Dare to-night, the dear old Dare that I loved so, that said he loved me long ago. Oh, darling, you forgave me for that, did not you? You said you would."/ "Forgave you! Oh, of course; there was nothing to forgive; women have had licence to lie and torture men with their white faces and their black hearts, ever since the world was. Only it is as well to pay off old debts. To-night you and I shall be quits, Kate. You have not kept your oath, and I don't intend to keep mine."/ She was losing her self-control in her terror; that man was capable of anything to-night. And through it all still surged up the wild joy in being there alone with him under the moonlight./ "You won't *kill* me?" she asked, in a whisper, indistinct with horror, and she clasped both her little soft white hands on his arm./ He shook her off; he could not stand that light touch; it made his brain reel./ "Are you so afraid of death, child? You used to say you would not mind it."/ "Oh yes, I *am* afraid of it; I thought I should not be, but I *am*, horribly afraid, oh Dare! I should be dreadfully frightened if it were to come near."/ "It *is* near, Kate, very near; there is only one way you can escape it."/ Hard words those for one unprepared to bear; one of whose ears had but now been full of the strains of voluptuous music; of words of sweet flattery and incense. She turned deadly white, poor lily, that the Great Reaper was putting out his hand to gather into his fairest nosegay, and drops of cold sweat stood on the smooth young brow./ "You're only joking, I know, Dare," she said, trying pitiably to laugh, "but it frightens me; it's a terrible joke, oh darling, I'm silly to be afraid of you, but just say that it *is* a joke."/ "Kate, do I look like a man in a joking humour, to-night?"/ She looked up at him; his countenance was the book she must read her fate on. And at that moment, through the interstices of the thick trees, an arrow of moonlight shot slantwise, and fell on a dark, evil face, inexorable in its utter haggardness, lit up eyes hopeless, pitiless, haughty as those of the Arch-Fiend, writhing, with his proud beauty marred and faded, among his compeers, in the burning gulf.[12] Even then, in the midst of her own imminent danger, standing on the brink of two worlds, she had leisure to pity him; if her death could have brought him comfort or hope, she would have fought against her woman's shrinking, would have tried to have faced it bravely./ "Ah, poor fellow! I won't look at you; it's not your own face you have got on now; oh, why are you so angry with me, my darling? Dare, if you were really not joking just now, what was the way of escape you spoke of? Oh, death is so dreadful! anything would be better than that. I'd do anything almost to avoid it. What must I do? oh tell me! tell me!"/ "Death is dreadful, child; more dreadful than you can conceive. Kate, I know that I am a brute and a blackguard, but you used to love me in spite of that; do you love me still?"/ Perfect love casteth out fear;[13] at those words she laid aside her terrors, she forgot them, complete in her devotion, she bent down and kissed the coward hand that was threatening death to her. "Love you, oh yes, darling, of course I do, as well as, better than I ever did before. I shall always love you, whatever you do to me; whatever it is, it cannot make any difference to me, my love for you is part of myself; I could not get rid of it, even if I would."/ "And is it pleasant to you to be with me? impossible! It cannot be pleasant to you to be with a man who is always bullying and scaring you."/ "Yes, it is pleasant, pleasanter than anything; it is the only pleasant thing for me in the world now."/ "Kate, I give you one last chance; you have deceived me, lied to me twice, you have made me a ruined man, a man so vile and reckless that no good woman ought to speak to him, and yet I forgive you, forgive you freely, if you will but undo the mischief you have done. Kate, will you come away with me, to-night, *for ever*? will you come and be the light of my eyes, my one treasure, my own, my wife!"/ She hid her face on his shoulder, and a light gust came out of the chambers of the night, and rocked the sleepy roses, and swayed the big fading lily in her hair. The lily was fading, and she was in the flower and freshness of her ripe bloom, yet which would be dead first? In that slight

12 At the beginning of Milton's *Paradise Lost* (1667), Satan, cast out of heaven for his rebellion against God, lies in hell in a "fiery Gulf" (I.210).

13 See I John 4:18.

warm wind she shivered. "I cannot," she whispered, with difficulty, "anything but that; oh, darling, I cannot do that, even for you; oh, ask me anything else, I cannot ruin my soul, even for you!"/ A sword seemed to go through his riven heart, but there was no change in the cruel immovable voice. "Very well; then you don't go out of this garden alive."/ She was getting faint in her great horror; feebly she clung to him, and, in her faintness, said "God have mercy upon me!"/ And that weak prayer went up, and scaled high Heaven, and found acceptance there. That man was not quite stone or marble, not altogether butcher, desperate ruffian as he was. As she leaned upon him, his veins throbbed with the old wild ecstacy, a flood of frantic, tender passion, rushed over him; he caught her in his great athlete arms, and kissed her, over and over again, fiercely, eyes, and lips, and neck. "Whether I kill you or not," he whispered hoarsely, "I must kiss you, you are so beautiful; I should like to die kissing you! What a white skin you have, and what lips? do you suppose I could ever bear to think of any other man kissing those lips? as I told you long ago, I'd cut your throat sooner!"/ "Oh, Dare, have mercy upon me! you would not do any harm to a wretched weak woman, would you? a brave, strong man, like you; darling; I swear that no other man shall ever kiss me, again, as long as I live; won't that content you?"/ "Do you suppose I believe you?" he asked with a laugh, which sounded hollow and malignant like a fiend's, on the still night air; "it is not half an hour ago since I saw that fellow Tankerville clasping you to his heart, as tight as I am clasping you now, and you at your old flirting tricks, laughing up in his eyes. How do you suppose I felt then?"/ "Oh Dare, I did not want to dance with him, indeed I did not; I was a fool to do it, but I was made to; but indeed, *indeed*, if you'll believe me, after to-morrow, I shall most probably never see the face of man again. I'm going away a long way off, to be a Sister of Mercy. You did not know that, did you?"/"Kate, you'll never be a Sister of Mercy; before twenty-four hours are over, you'll either be mine, so irrecoverably and completely, that I shall dare any other man to put in a claim for you; or else, you will be put beyond any man's reach, a thing that men will no longer feel any violent desire for. Take your choice, which?"/ She fell at his feet; she grovelled in the warm, green grass, interceding for her life./ "Oh, neither, neither! what a frightful alternative! Oh, darling! please don't kill me! I'm so young to die! and I have not done anything to deserve it either; oh! it's so awful to die so suddenly, without any warning, with all one's sins upon one's head! Oh Dare, have pity upon me! Oh, please, please!"/ She clung about his knees; she embraced them pitifully; it was her very last chance. It is hard work killing a woman; but the brandy and the fiends kept him up to it. He stooped and lifted her in his arms, bent down his stern lips quivering now, to her ear, and said harshly—/ "Will you come then? Life is very sweet at two and twenty; and a sudden, violent death is a tremendous prospect at any time."/ She felt that she was wavering. The flesh is weak, and woman's white flesh especially, shrinks from the torture of imminent dissolution./ "O Lord, look upon me! give me strength!" she groaned, and the good Lord knew that His poor servant was weak, and He sent her strength—such strength as He gave to martyred Faithful, in the midst of Vanity Fair[14]—sent her a happy vision of shining streets and jasper walls, and blessed serene faces, smiling down across the fiery gulf of death upon her, stretching out familiar arms to greet her, and help her up the steep path. In that might, not her own, she defied him. Brave in all her womanish tremblings, she spoke—/ "No, darling, I cannot."/ Then the devils got hold of that man altogether. Despair and rage mastered him./ "Very well," he whispered, hoarsely; "then it must be," and as he spoke, he took a pistol out of his breast pocket, and cocked it with a hand that did not shake. She flung her white arms around his great gnarled throat; in mortal terror; she buried her face on his breast./ "Oh, for God's sake, don't shoot me! It would hurt so dreadfully! oh, leave me in peace, if not for my sake, at least for your own! Just think, Dare, what dreadful remorse you'll have! just think how my face will haunt you, day and night."/ Her voice failed; she seemed almost swooning./ "You need not concern yourself about me, Kate. I shall not be long after you; you may be sure of that."/ "Oh Dare, please give me one half-hour—just a little half-hour to put up one prayer, to make myself a little ready. Oh, I'm not ready to die—not to-night; oh, just five minutes, my darling. Oh, do, *do*."/"Not one minute, Kate."[15]/ "O love, love, you're cruel. Think of murdering your own Kate! Well, if it must be, oh, for pity's sake do it quick, and put me out of my pain. Will it hurt much, do you think?"/ "I don't know; it'll soon be over?"/ "O God have mercy upon me! it's awful work!"/ He wrapped her in his arms once again; once again

---

14 In book 7 of Part I of Bunyan's *Pilgrim's Progress* (1678), Faithful is tortured and burned at the stake by the inhabitants of Vanity Fair, but his soul ascends to the Celestial City, or Heaven.

15 Compare the scene in *Othello* (first printed 1622) in which Desdemona pleads with Othello for more time before he murders her—"But half an hour … But while I say one prayer" – and he replies "It is too late" (V.ii.82, 84-85).

he devoured her face with his deepset murderous eyes, wells of burning hell-fire; once again he kissed the poor, pale, willing lips, as if he never could kiss them enough./ "I shall kiss you again, Kate, when you're dead, but this is the last time I shall ever kiss you alive. O God, it's a sin to kill you, you're so beautiful; but I must, I *must.* Good-bye, my pretty one; I'm sorry for it, but it must be. One kiss more.[16] Good-bye."/ "Good-bye, Dare darling. God forgive you for this. I do."/ He put the muzzle to the little fluttering heart, pulled the trigger with a resolute hand—nerves turned to iron—and fired. One low groan of bitter pain; then the head fell back, and the splendid hair, moon-bathed, flowed like a mantle over his shoulder. Oh, the ages of hell crowded into that moment! The unspeakable, unimaginable remorse! He laid the calm, white face, on his breast, and kissed the damp brow./ "O darling!" he moaned, brokenly; "come back to me. You are not dead and gone from me? O come back to me; don't you know my voice? speak to me once again. O Kate, my little white lily. O Kate, Kate!"/ He might call, and wring his hands, and beat his breast now; he could not bring one jot of terror or love, or sorrow, into that fair dead face, smiling up at the sailing moon. There were the dark stains of his little Kate's warm life-blood crimsoning his hands, like a butcher's at a shambles, and hell was in his heart. Her spirit was gone beyond our ken, beyond even *his* call; gone somewhere; whither we can but conjecture, only we trust, humbly, we shall see her again, some day, with the others, whose places are empty here, sitting upon the Hills of God. That rare form of hers lay motionless, sleeping its last sleep, on the midnight grass among the roses; to be wept and lamented over, for a few days, by soon-comforted friends, and then to be hid away for ever from sight and remembrance, consigned to the charnel house, and the pasturing worms./ That pistol-shot which startled so much the ears of the gay merry-making throng inside, was quickly followed by another; hardly five minutes elapsed between them. Then the music ceased, and girls clung together, terrified, aghast, knowing that some awful deed had been done, under the starry midnight, and men rushed out hastily to find out the cause, the origin of those strange ominous sounds. They had not far to go; on that little plot of velvet sward the cause stared them in the face. At their feet lay Kate Chester, among the sleeping roses, asleep too; smiling up, with calm, tender gravity, at the dusk summer sky overhead. People who die by gun-shot wounds mostly wear that

16 See Othello's final kisses of Desdemona before killing her: "One more, one more ... One more, and that's the last" (V.ii.17, 19).

strange, quiet smile—perhaps it is a sweet death. There she lay, stone dead, the soft white limbs fast growing cold and rigid; and at ten paces from her, like a fallen Colossus, among the grass, stretched the magnificent Titan form, the massive shoulders that so many had envied to-night. Nobody envied them now; they were but carrion. He had hasted, as he said he would, to follow after the woman he had loved; but follow her as he may, I think that he'll never overtake her again through all the ages of eternity. Death had not been sweet to him; he had died hard, with a mighty wrench, the reluctant, shrinking soul had torn itself away from the grand form that cased it, and the horror of that parting was still visible in the clenched hands, that no human power could unlock again—in the writhen, stiffening features, staring up, with a world of despair in the ghastly wide open eyes, at the solemn stars.// Oh, my pretty Kate! my lost one! how dark the world has grown since that July night! It is twelve months to-day since they lifted you up reverently, a dead weight, off that crimsoned sward—since, weepingly, for pure love, they cut off lengths of your silky hair, that would never need braiding or plaiting more, and laid jessamine, and lilies, and sweet white buds, like yourself, in your whiter hands, to say a last good-by to you. In but a few days it will be twelve months since that white-haired, good man, whose voice shook and wavered, so called you "our dear sister here departed," since they laid you down in your narrow green bed—not in the Chester's charnel vault, where crowded relics of mortality jostle each other, for they knew that you would not rest there, but out in the breezy north-country churchyard, where the flowers might blossom out freely under the rain and the shine, and the night winds come and go at will above your dreamless head.[17]

17 See p. 171, n. 24.

APPENDIX C

Contemporary Reviews and Responses

1. Unsigned review, *The Athenaeum*, 2 November, 1867: 569.[1]

We suspect that this book is written by the author of "Guy Livingstone,"[2] from its peculiar heroes and very peculiar morality. In fact, Guy Livingstone himself, under the name of Col. Stamer, is here again introduced to the public with his old characteristics—his gigantic strength and form, fascinating manners and delightful wickedness; so that if this book is not written by the novelist we have mentioned, we can only say that the author is guilty of very decided plagiarism, and has allowed his admiration of the model to mislead him into imitating his master "not wisely, but too well."

We sincerely hope our original suspicion is correct, for we should be very sorry to see two writers of ability pandering to the gross tastes of the day by writing such books as "Guy Livingstone" and "Not Wisely, but Too Well." The great object of books like these is apparently to teach immorality by representing it in an interesting and seductive form, and by making good people, who live according to the ordinary laws of decency, appear tame, stupid and despicable. At any rate, if this is not their object, we can assure their authors that it must inevitably be their effect. This has been pointed out time after time, but still we find these books being written and published, and the almost unanimous voice of rebuke and morality despised and neglected. It is time, then, for critics to speak out boldly, and to declare in plain language what they think of the tendencies of these books, and see by so doing whether they cannot put a stop to their production. Now this may seem to some very strong language, but it is not stronger than the occasion requires. If any one doubts this, let him take the book we are now reviewing and read it coolly and critically, and ask himself at the end what is its tendency, and what impression on

1 The online *Athenaeum Index of Reviews and Reviewers, 1830-1870* identifies the author of this review as Sir Robert Romer.

2 See p. 66, n. 60.

the mind of an ordinary reader it is calculated to produce. We distinctly affirm that in this novel all the personages who do not continually break the commonest laws of society are made to appear uninteresting and foolish, as if the only reason for a man not being a profligate was a want of spirit or an absence of ability. While all the art of the writer is lavished on the hero—Col. Stamer—whose wickedness we are frankly told cannot be exceeded, and in making this man obtain the morbid sympathy of the reader, as he obtains the passionate love of the heroine.

A short sketch of the tale will do more, perhaps, to reveal the nature of this book than all our animadversions. The hero, Colonel Dare Stamer, loves and is equally beloved by Miss Kate Chester, the heroine, an extraordinarily beautiful and clever girl, and before the Colonel knew her a very ladylike and modest one. This Colonel is but Guy Livingstone again. We take his description from the very words of the book:—

[reviewer quotes the description of Dare in vol. I, ch. 4, pp. 66-67 here, from "This is he" to "he sometimes subjoined."]

And so on. This colonel, after a few interviews with Kate, asks her to run away with him. She replies she will do anything for him, but naturally inquires why not be quietly married at home in the ordinary way. Whereupon Dare mentions, as a small objection, his being married already, his wife being, as he confesses, very good and loving; but then he is tired of her and loves Kate much more. It can certainly be said as his only excuse that he was tired of his wife; but Kate reluctantly feels she ought not to run away from home with him for that only, and tries to make him understand her sentiments on this point. Then ensues a desperate scene; embraces, kisses, &c., and the Colonel nearly succeeds in seducing her, when she saves herself at the last moment by appealing to him thus:—

[reviewer quotes Vol. II, ch. 1, p. 162 here, from "'Oh, Dare'" to "'let me go, let me go!'"]

At this highly pathetic appeal he gives way, and she is saved, for the time; the whole moral of the scene being, what a monstrous shame it is that two loving hearts like these cannot be happy merely because of the paltry prejudice against a man marrying two wives! This takes us up to the beginning of the second volume, and the remainder is occupied with Kate's despair, and the imbecility of the good people of the novel. After eighteen months' separation, Kate, still unmarried and only about nineteen years of age, meets her beloved Dare once more in a quiet nook of the Crystal Palace.

Scene number two, similar to the first, only worse. More kisses, more embraces, he "busy gloating, miser-like, with bold, glad eyes, over his recovered pearl; eyes that she did not blush or wince under, as in the old coy, girlish days. She was a woman now, not a girl, past blushing or hiding away from those orbs of fire." After a lot of disgustingly immodest and unnatural ravings, she consents to be his mistress, and to meet him the following day. And all this though at the time she first met him in the Crystal Palace he had another lady with him, who he frankly confesses is one of his numerous victims, a married lady of rank, whom he had seduced merely to keep him from thinking of Kate; but this seems rather to make Kate pity him than otherwise, and she is certainly not at all shocked by it. To conclude this miserable tale, as Kate is coming the following day to meet her lover, she is persuaded not to go, after a severe struggle, by an attenuated parson. Dare is pitched out of a dog-cart some short time after, and dying from the fall, has a farewell interview with Kate, in which he expresses no penitence for his past life, but only a half kind of dread for the future. After his death she becomes a Protestant Sister of Mercy, and is wretched ever after.

Comment on this story is needless. We may observe, though, that the dressing and details of the novel are worthy of the tale. To justify us in saying this we could quote hundreds of passages but they are too bad for us; so we only give this one as an example. It is part of a speech made by Kate at a time when she was uncertain as to the Colonel's love, and when she had only seen him two or three times. It must be remembered, too, that Kate is supposed to have been educated in a good English family and to know nothing of the world:—[reviewer quotes passage in Vol. I, ch. 7, pp. 89-90 here, where Kate laments "'O, why will not God let us have what we like'" to "'what grand eyes you have! How they seem to scorch and shrivel up my soul, looking always, always, through it.'"]

And so on, with the sickening blasphemy with which we must no more pollute these pages. Nothing but a sense of duty compels us to quote even so much as we have done. This is the kind of speech the author of this book imagines innocent young ladies make when apostrophizing their loves, and gives a fair specimen of the tone and thought of the work. Worse than even the immorality of the whole novel are the stupid, misplaced attempts at sermonizing throughout. They might be very well in another work, but being where they are, they simply disgust. We need say no more.

2. Unsigned review, *The Times*, 25 December, 1867: 4.

It is not long since we reviewed *Cometh Up as a Flower*,[3] which was apparently the authoress's maiden essay in the field of fictitious literature, and now she comes again before us with a fresh story. We are not disposed, however, to blame her very severely for this rapidity of production. When a first novel achieves a success, both publishers and readers are eager in their demands for another work from the same hand; and, as the arguments used by the former in favour of this course are weighty and convincing, very few writers are able to resist the temptation. Besides, in these high-pressure days, a first effort, however successful, runs the risk of being forgotten, unless it be speedily followed by a second. Some works, too, are best struck off at a white heat, and we are not at all sure that any amount of elaboration would enable the authoress to put forth a better novel than that which we are about to examine. These several considerations have, no doubt, induced her to set her pen to work again as soon as possible.

As a general rule we object to that species of criticism whose chief strength lies in comparing an author with himself, which remarks in stereotyped phraseology that "Mr. X. is scarcely up to his usual level," or that "Mrs. Z. fully maintains her brilliant reputation;" but there is such a peculiar quaintness and originality about the authoress of *Cometh Up as a Flower*, her merits and her defects are so especially her own, that we cannot avoid referring to her former work as a standard of comparison. The two books bear a strong resemblance to each other; they both tell the story of a passionate yet barren and blighted love, their leading personages are closely allied in form and character, the catastrophe of each is sombre and tragical. A morose critic might assert, especially after a cursory survey of the two books, that the authoress, being in a great hurry to compose a second novel, had not time to construct a fresh plot, and so furbished up her old scenery, dresses, and decorations. But a careful perusal of *Not Wisely but Too Well* does not justify so injurious a supposition. The incidents and characters bear a strong family likeness to those of her first novel, but they are not mere copies from it. We should rather infer that the writer, feeling that her chief power lies in these stormy, passionate creations, determined to give us a fresh version of them under different moral aspects. Kate Chester

3 *The Times*, 6 June, 1867: 9. This reviewer of *Not Wisely* is obviously unaware that it was in fact written before *Cometh Up*.

superficially resembles Nelly Lestrange, but Kate's love is of a darker and more ungovernable type … Still there remains, it must be confessed, a substantial similarity between the two books, and, as a third series of these vehement but abortive love-makings might weary the novel-reading world, we recommend the authoress for the future to exercise her undoubted talent in a different field. Of the moral tendency of such books as these we propose to speak presently, after a brief survey of the plot.

The scene opens on a hot June day at Pen-Dyllas, a small watering-place in North Wales. Kate Chester is seated on the beach, in a contemplative attitude, with a dog at her side. We at once discover that she is in love, for she is reading a novel, and proceeds to compare the hero of it with a certain Colonel Stamer. When we read that "this young woman was not a beauty, and that she would cut but a sorry figure among a set of straight-featured lily and rose fair ones," we know what to expect. Though not a beauty, she contrives to secure a great deal of masculine attention. Several pages are devoted to an enumeration of her charms. She has a great quantity of bright brown hair (raven-tressed heroines are still apparently at a discount), a low forehead, great green eyes, deeply set, a small turn-up nose, pale cheeks "not very apt at blushing prettily," a wide, full-lipped, smiling mouth, and a small, plump, round figure. Our inventory sounds tame and passport-like, but then we have been obliged to make it very brief. The authoress takes a good deal of pains over her personal descriptions, and achieves the rare merit of conveying some notion of what her *dramatis personæ* are really like. Let us return to our story. Kate Chester is an orphan, and, together with her elder sister Maggie and her brother Blount, is staying in the same seaside lodgings with her uncle and aunt, Mr. and Mrs. Piggott. Mr. Piggott is an invalid clergyman, perpetually bewailing his aches and pains, and as in outward appearance he resembles a sheep, whenever he opens his mouth he is referred to as "baaing." Mr. Piggott is not ill drawn, but the frequent reference to his sheep-like characteristics becomes gradually rather tiresome. The authoress is careful to inform us that the Chesters are not dependent on their uncle and aunt for support, as they have a small independence of their own. This condition of things supposedly absolves the young people from any necessity to pay them any deference, or even to treat them with common politeness. Blount invariably speaks of Mr. Piggott in the rudest language, although confessing he has no dislike to the "old beggar," and when, at the opening of the story, Kate comes in late for the 1 o'clock dinner, and Mr. Piggott offers the mildest possible remonstrances, the young lady, without making the slightest apology, begins a series of ill-natured sneers at the barbarism of dining at such an hour. We dwell on this apparently trifling point, because in the third volume Kate develops into a saint-like creature, full of heroism and self-sacrifice, and the writer evidently regards her throughout the book as a very lovable little woman. But in all the ordinary affairs of life she is utterly selfish, and never allows any other person's will and pleasure, if she can help it, to interfere with her own. A kind speech now and then towards poor valetudinarian Uncle Piggott would have weighed more with us than all her grand doings as a Sister of Mercy in the last volume.

[The reviewer describes the dinner-party at Llyn Castle, compares Dare, as do Jewsbury in her reader's report and other reviewers in this appendix, to the protagonist of *Guy Livingstone*, and quotes several passages from Vol. I, including the description of Dare in Vol. I, ch. 4, p. 66, Kate's soliloquy in the wood in Vol. I, ch. 7, p. 89, Dare's conversation with Kate in the conservatory in Vol. I, ch. 14, p. 133, and the scene, spanning the end of Vol. I and the beginning of Vol. II, in which Dare reveals why he and Kate cannot marry.] The secret is that he is married already to a poor woman of inferior rank, concerning whom he speaks to Kate in the most brutal, heartless manner. Miss Chester is shocked, her young voice becoming like that of an old man. True to her selfish nature, however, she has not a word of reproof for the scoundrel when he coolly expresses a wish that his first wife would commit suicide … The whole of this scene is described with great power and vividness, but for all that it is, to our thinking, both unreal and repulsive … As for Kate, we dislike her so thoroughly that we can scarcely say a civil word about her. We dislike her all the more when, after all her tall talk about "an eternity of torment for a month with Dare," she is staggered by such a trivial obstacle as his marriage. Prudence in such a character becomes detestable.

After this the story for the greater part of a volume becomes rather uninteresting. Dare disappears from the scene, while Kate and her sister take a small house at a place called Queenstown, the geography of which is of the vaguest sort, for all one moment it seems a great London suburb, at another a large country town. During this period Kate does nothing to lessen our aversion to her; on the contrary, in spite of her secret worship of Dare, which is as strong as ever, she flirts prodigiously with her cousin, George Chester, and then, as soon as she hears that people are beginning to ask if they are engaged, remorselessly throws him overboard. She inspires James Stanley, a self-denying little High Church curate, with an ardent affection for her, which he is always trying to stifle, when one day at the Crystal Palace, having deserted the rest of her party, she comes across Dare Stamer. At the sight of this evil-disposed gentleman our flagging interest revives. The colonel is amusing himself at the Crystal Palace with somebody else's wife, and Kate overhears their conversation. A recognition takes place, and Dare gets rid of his lady in some mysteriously convenient fashion, which the authoress does not explain. He could scarcely be so discourteous as to pack her off alone by the train to Victoria; perhaps he left her in company with a particularly delicious strawberry ice; at any rate, he returns to Kate, and another of those stormy, passionate interviews ensues. The end is that Kate succumbs to his entreaties; she will violate all the proprieties for his sake; she will come and be his companion for life. The following Sunday is selected as the day of the fatal journey. James Stanley misses her face in church; is surprised afterwards to discover her struggling in the rain towards the railway station; begins to disbelieve her excuses; and at length extracts the truth from her. He jumps into the train with her, and brings her back before the irrevocable step was taken.

We could select many powerful and eloquent passages from this book, but we will leave our readers to find them out for themselves. The novel is decidedly clever, and belongs to a much higher category than the mass of tame, colourless nonentities which every season sends forth. It will, doubtless, find many admiring readers, especially among the young and ardent, to whom Love, in all his phases, is naturally such an attractive deity. But we would beg our youthful readers not to bow down and worship the Love-God whose image the authoress of *Not Wisely but Too Well* has set up. His name is not *Amor*, but *Cupido*;[4] he is not the fairfaced boy, whose wings are dipped in heavenly radiance, the type of the true and elevated affection which is ready to sacrifice its own pleasure for the sake of benefiting its object; he is a grovelling, little earth-bound monster, in spite of all his fine phrases, and on his brazen arrows the word "Self" is indelibly engraved.

The next time we meet the writer of this book in print, we hope to find that she has devoted her powers, which are undeniably much above the fiction-writing average, to some pleasanter and wholesomer topic than this fierce, lurid, overpowering Love which hurries madly over every obstacle,

4 Amor ("love" in Latin) is the Roman god of love, counterpart to the Greek god Eros. The reviewer makes a distinction between the embodiment of the god as Amor, or love, and his embodiment as Cupido, or Cupid, who represents desire.

and even crushes its own heart for the sake of attaining its object.

3. Unsigned Review, *The Spectator*, 19 October, 1867: 1172-74.[5]

[Though focused on *Not Wisely*, this review, like the one from the *Times* above, also compares the novel with *Cometh Up as a Flower*. All three reviews of *Not Wisely* reproduced in this appendix quote from Kate's speech in the woods in Vol. I, ch. 7 (see p. 89), though the *Spectator*'s is by far the most sympathetic interpretation of the passage.]

"O why will not God let us have what we like, and be happy in this world in our own way? she groaned, instead of making us always be lifting up our eyes strainingly to a country we cannot see, and which we shall most likely never get to at last?" So moans the heroine, in a love that seems for the moment hopeless, and in that sentence is the key-note to both *Not Wisely, but Too Well* and *Cometh Up as a Flower*. The dominant thought of the authoress,—the writer, of whom we know absolutely nothing, cannot be a man, though she may have learnt much from some man's mind,[6]—is a kind of despair which yet knows that despair is a mistake, a distrust which yet in some dim way desires to trust, a contempt for life as it is lived, which yet has at bottom a respect, and cannot develop into scorn. She is the novelist of revolt, and it is in this revolt, scarcely indicated in words, but penetrating and flavouring every sentence, that the curious charm, the nuttiness, the vanilla flavour of her tales consists. She expresses through fiction an emotion, a doubt, a sentiment—call it what you will—which has rarely been expressed except in poetry, but which surges up now and again in the mind of every human being with a mind at all, beaten back by the pious, indulged by the pleasure-loving,—a feeling not only that all is Vanity, but that all ought not to be, that there is some mistake, some misarrangement,

5 Unfortunately it is difficult to trace the identity of the author of this sensitive review, as the information on contributors to the *Spectator* during this period seems to be lost.

6 Here the reviewer may be responding to the theory bruited by Geraldine Jewsbury in her *Athenaeum* review of *Cometh Up as a Flower* (like *Not Wisely*, an anonymously published work): "That the author is not a young woman, but a man, who, in the present story, shows himself destitute of refinement of thought or feeling, and ignorant of all that women either are or ought to be, is evident on every page" (*Athenaeum* 2060 [April 1867], in *A Serious Occupation: Literary Criticism by Victorian Women Writers*, ed. Solveig C. Robinson [Peterborough: Broadview, 2003], 140).

some failure in the grand scheme. Her heroines say what Clough sang.[7] Arthur Helps, we remember, expresses a similar idea somewhere in his *Essays*, in a lament over the want of foresight in humanity.[8] To be happy, he says, men ought to have been enabled to see one inch further forward, though he does not, as we understand him, assume that happiness is the noblest end for which the world can have been designed. Neither does this author, rather assuming, at least in her present work, that there is a higher object towards which all ought to strive, but harshly questioning the reason why the right road is made so full of toil and boulders. In each story the central figure is the same—a girl of a full and noble nature, round as to her lines mental and bodily, with full bust and an exuberant mental life, despising conventionality and contemning the usual cut-and-dry formulas for living, ensnared, but not stained, by a burning passion for a man who cannot, or does not, become her husband,—by a real love, a sovereign entrancing hunger such as few feel in real life, and all civilized men believe at heart that they might feel ... The love in [*Not Wisely* and *Cometh Up*] is as an emotion marvellously described, though for some readers it will have perhaps too much realism; there is too clear an intrusion of the sensuous—we do not mean the improper—too much of clingingness and disposition to embrace. We never see precisely either what it is in the hero that the heroine loves, except a vague idea of manliness and force, and a strong love for herself; and Kate in her revolt against circumstances brings out the idea that she *prefers* bad men rather too strongly, even for a nature which probably would express its contempt of the merely respectable in that way. What she really loves is power, not the application of power either for good or evil, and the failure to indicate that sometimes produces an unpleasant effect; but apart from this, and from the vagueness of heroes whom the author has scarcely cared to sketch, the love-making is wonderfully vivid ... In *Not Wisely, but Too Well*, for example, Kate indulges in this extraordinary tirade:—[the reviewer quotes from "O, why will not God let us have what we like and be happy in our own way" until "But God will not let us make such bargains, I know. If He did, life would be starved and death-glutted within six weeks."] She did not want any bargain of the kind, and when her prayer was granted, rejected it, and went out into the cold rather than

7 Arthur Hugh Clough (1819-61), Victorian poet known for satiric social commentary and poems about religious doubt.

8 Arthur Helps (1813-75), dean of the Privy Council, and author of books and essays on various topics, including commerce and politics.

accept her own ideal of joy at the price of degradation, and she only says it because the author can think of no milder language in which to represent a delirium of passion, a love fever, such as hitherto only poets have ventured to depict. There is weakness in such violence, all the more because it is unreal, English girls like Kate Chester being no more likely to express mental revolt in blasphemy, than to swear like bargemen to relieve wrath. It is in spite of that weakness, and not in consequence of it, that the portraiture is strong; but it is strong, nevertheless, and one sees Kate Chester with her love fit on as one sees Francesca of Rimini, and in her, and in her mental state, is the sole but the great charm of the tale. Everything else in *Not Wisely, but Too Well*, except the writing, which is clear and cutting to savagery, is poor … the other figures are poor, Maggie being scarcely outlined, Mr. Piggott a coarse and feeble caricature, and Dare Stamer the regular bad Colonel of *Guy Livingstone*, and Ouida,[9] and writers of that kind, a variety of the species of whom even the novel-reading world must be heartily tired. Colonel Stamer does not do anything, that we see, except look cruel usually and smile occasionally, and curse his wife, an invisible person, who is, it appears, too fat for him, and beseech a girl whom he really loves to be, in the teeth of her own convictions, his mistress. He may be real, no doubt, fierce selfishness is common, but we see nothing in fierce selfishness, though displayed by a man six feet high and stalwart in proportion, which should utterly enthral a girl like Kate Chester. She is high-spirited and she has little belief in conventionalities, and both her spirit and her love of realism would, we conceive, have revolted against the selfishness of her lover, would, once she had discovered it, have enabled her to beat down and keep down her love fever by the vivid recollection of what its object really was.

When *Cometh Up as a Flower* first appeared, there was great dispute in quiet households as to its morality. It fluttered women as *Jane Eyre* did, and almost for the same reason, but we should no more pronounce it immoral than *Jane Eyre*. The author indulges, as we have said, in certain audacities of expression, sometimes witty to an enjoyable degree, sometimes profane, sometimes feebly flippant, and some of these audacities reveal, like some passages in *Villette*, in the *Mill on the Floss*, in many another work of female genius, a consciousness of sex which in its persistency is not either healthy

9 For *Guy Livingstone*, see p. 66, n. 60 above. "Ouida" was the pen-name of Marie Louise de la Ramée (1839-1908), author of sensational romances such as *Under Two Flags* (1867).

or realistic.[10] But we cannot admit that the general drift of these two books is in any degree immoral. Each has for subject a love which might have ended in adultery, but in each case the love is so treated as to create a horror of that consummation ... In *Not Wisely, but Too Well*—oh for sensible names to novels!—the very depth of Kate's love, her passion and *abandon*, serve to set off the strength of the principle which, for one brief moment, enables her to resist an almost irresistible temptation. The reader is made, too, with really wonderful art, to sympathize wholly with that resistance, to feel that Kate Chester, tempted in the highest degree on the best as well as the worst side of her nature, must, if she is to keep his sympathy, win the struggle which, as he early foresees, will cost her life. There is no sermon on the Seventh Commandment,[11] but adultery is represented as at once a degr[illegible]ation and a treachery which not even a passion like Kate Chester's can [illegible]tenuate, and if the subject is to be treated at all, we know of no mor[illegible]rcible way in which the true lesson of all such temptations could b[illegible]lcated. We must add, too, that the audacities of the first story are a[illegible] wanting in the second, the main, we might say the only, defect of [illegible]h is an utter slovenliness of workmanship when the subject is not [illegible] Chester. How anybody who could write this little description could [illegible]en the offensive nonsense intended to depict Mr. Piggott we are unable to conceive:—[reviewer quotes the passage beginning "But Mr. Piggott was revelling in the vision of his own many and great ailments" through "What a deplorable thing a wet day at the sea-side is, to be sure!" (see p. 122 here)] Surely the writer of that passage must have humour and observation too sufficient to see that Mr. Piggott is not a portrait, but a daub, a bit of work of which she ought, as artist, to be most heartily ashamed.

4. From [Alfred Austin], "The Novels of Miss Broughton," *Temple Bar*, 1874: 196-209.

[Austin (1835-1913), who became Poet Laureate in 1896, was an outspoken critic of sensationalism and the "'improper' feminine," as he called the

10 The reviewer compares Broughton's fiction with two other works by women featuring unconventional, passionate, and discontented heroines, Charlotte Brontë's *Villette* (1855) and George Eliot's *The Mill on the Floss* (1861).

11 The seventh commandment is "Thou shalt not commit adultery" (Exodus 20:14).

literary representation of transgressive femininity.[12] Yet, although he linked Broughton to the sensation genre in his 1870 essay "The Sensational School,"[13] he nonetheless liked her work and went on to write two admiring assessments of it in 1874 and 1887 in *Temple Bar*, the journal which had published his earlier attacks on sensationalism, and which also serialized a number of Broughton's novels. Despite defending Broughton against her more hostile critics, however, Austin had mixed feelings about her depiction of female sexuality and unconventional young women, an ambivalence evident in the two excerpts below from the 1874 essay. The first excerpt discusses *Not Wisely, but Too Well*, and the second describes in more general terms how Broughton's heroines reflect changing gender roles.]

… her [Broughton's] human beings are mainly and almost wholly engaged in the pursuit of that passion which is usually called tender, but which Miss Broughton understands is also, not uncommonly, fierce, and which has never been so tersely or so truly expressed as by the poet of the "Divine Comedy":

> "Questi, che mai da me no fia diviso,
> La bocca mi baciò tutto tremente."[14]

This is the central thought and pivot of Miss Broughton's novels, and the consequence has been that no small offence has come of them in certain quarters. We have no wish to dictate to any one, and least of all to any set of people, what is the true definition of love, and within what limits precisely love, as understood in the foregoing simple but penetrating

---

12 See Austin's essays "Mr. Swinburne" (*Temple Bar* 26 [1869]: 457-74) and "Our Novels: The Sensational School" (*Temple Bar* 29 [1870]: 410-24).

13 Austin uses Broughton's *Cometh Up as a Flower* as an example of the difficulty of classifying sensation fiction, admitting the novel's resemblance to other sensation novels but claiming it is still "brilliantly distinguished" from them (see "Our Novels: The Sensational School," rpt. In Andrew Maunder, ed., *Sensationalism and the Sensation Debate*, Vol. I of *Varieties of Women's Sensation Fiction: 1855-90* [London: Pickering and Chatto, 2004], 248).

14 From Canto V of Dante's *Inferno*: "This one, who never from me shall be divided,/ Kissed my mouth trembling" (Italian). This description of the first illicit embraces of Francesca da Rimini and her lover is, in Byron's translation "Francesca da Rimini," one of Kate Chester's favorite pieces after she falls in love with Dare; see Vol. I, ch. 8, p. 104.

couplet, is a proper theme for the novelist. Every novelist who handles it handles it at his peril; for assuredly he is playing with fire. But the greatest masters of human passion have shown that it may be handled fearlessly yet without offence; though it must be owned that they have done so rather in verse than prose, and that poetry, from its superior nobility of character, shakes from its wings the dust that too often clings to the feet of prose. Nevertheless, as we have said, *solvitur ambulando.*[15] The walking novelist may venture, if it pleases him, and he will be judged by the result.

Judging Miss Broughton by the result, we should say that men and women of the world—and after all, books are not written for Puritans who live comfortably in semi-detached villas, any more than they are for "narrowing nunnery walls"[16]—will not be inclined to assert that the fire she undoubtedly plays with has burnt her fingers more than once. The occasion we refer to is in "Not Wisely but Too Well," and we believe the authoress is herself of that opinion. She was neither untruthful nor exaggerated on the occasion; but she had better have "left it alone." There is a limit in describing the tumults of deep and disappointed or despairing love; and it was transgressed in that scene. [p. 203]

She has been accused of "vulgarity," and if we really thought she had fallen into that exceedingly common fault of our time, we should not hesitate to say so. But we do not think so; indeed, we are sure that the epithet is flung at her with all that sweeping haste of which critics nowadays are so lamentably guilty. They mean something else; but they have neither time nor sufficient habitual accuracy of thought to say what it is they mean. They mean that Miss Broughton paints characters that are unruly, rebellious, "fast," and at times even what is called "slangy,"[17]

---

15 It must be solved by walking (Latin); one can only solve a problem through experimentation.

16 Tennyson, "Guenevere," in *Idylls of the King* (1859), l. 665.

17 This description of the typical Broughton heroine tallies with the popular (and hostile) stereotype of the modern young woman, "the Girl of the Period," created by the antifeminist writer Eliza Lynn Linton in an article for the *Saturday Review* in 1868, the year following the publication of Broughton's first two novels. The "slangy" nature of the Girl of the Period's speech—Linton accused her of "talking slang as glibly as a man"—signified both lack of modesty and infringement of male territory (Eliza Lynn Linton, "The Girl of the Period," in *Criminals, Idiots, Women, and Minors: Victorian Writing by Women on Women*, ed. Susan Hamilton [Peterborough: Broadview, 1995], 175). "Coarseness and slanginess" were among the elements Broughton sought to remove in her revision of the *DUM* version of *Not*

and that there is, from a certain and not unreasonable point of view, a very decided element of the ungentle, the ill-bred, and even the vulgar, in such characters ... She certainly does portray very outrageous young ladies indeed; young ladies we would rather not have for our sisters, sweethearts, wives, or sisters-in-law, but with whom, nevertheless, we could imagine ourselves spending a not unpleasant quarter of an hour; and we do not think we could enjoy spending a quarter of an hour with a vulgar person... . The truth is, that Miss Broughton's typical heroine is of a sort neither common nor uncommon, but, we suspect, growing more common every day, in this forcing-house of an age in which we live. It is an age of women's rights and the emancipation of a sex supposed to have been long-enthralled; and freedom in one direction, entailing freedom in another, is pretty certain to encourage it most of all in the direction most desired and most easily taken. We mean, of course, the direction of love and sentiment. If women are to do pretty much as men do, it follows that they are to do pretty much what they please, instead of, as heretofore, doing pretty much what other people please. We are not going to discuss the propriety and desirableness of the change; but we are compelled to indicate and record it, and to show what must necessarily be one of the first consequences. Doubtless a select minority of women will avail themselves of their new liberty to deliver lectures, to study medicine, to follow an honourable trade, and to sit on school boards. But the vast majority will employ their time in listening to the whispers and promptings of love with an indulgence never before permitted them, whilst a certain number will not be too particular in drawing the line between being made love to and making it. In a word, they will take their hearts and lives into their own hands, instead of leaving them, in their maidenly years, as a precious deposit in the hands of their parents and guardians ... It is not Miss Broughton's fault that [such young women] are on the increase, but her merit to have observed or felt—for there is an intuition in such matters—that they are so much on the increase that they have become interesting. And uncommonly interesting she makes them.

Do not let us be misunderstood. Such girls are still exceptional. The world would be a pandemonium if they ever become a clear majority[.] [pp. 204-05]

Wisely (see Appendix A, p. 381).

Victorian Secrets

Victorian Secrets is an independent publisher dedicated to producing high-quality books from and about the nineteenth century, including critical editions of neglected novels.

FICTION

All Sorts and Conditions of Men by Walter Besant
The Angel of the Revolution by George Chetwynd Griffith
The Autobiography of Christopher Kirkland by Eliza Lynn Linton
The Blood of the Vampire by Florence Marryat
The Dead Man's Message by Florence Marryat
Demos by George Gissing
East of Suez by Alice Perrin
Henry Dunbar by Mary Elizabeth Braddon
Her Father's Name by Florence Marryat
The Light that Failed by Rudyard Kipling
A Mummer's Wife by George Moore
Twilight Stories by Rhoda Broughton
Vice Versâ by F. Anstey
Weeds by Jerome K. Jerome
Weird Stories by Charlotte Riddell
Workers in the Dawn by George Gissing

BIOGRAPHY

The Perfect Man: The Muscular Life and Times of Eugen Sandow, Victorian Strongman by David Waller
Below the Fairy City: A Life of Jerome K. Jerome by Carolyn W. de la L. Oulton
Hope and Glory: A Life of Dame Clara Butt by Maurice Leonard
The First Adman: Thomas Bish and the Birth of Modern Advertising by Gary Hicks

For more information on any of our titles, please visit:

www.victoriansecrets.co.uk

CPSIA information can be obtained
at www.ICGtesting.com
Printed in the USA
FSOW02n0627270717
36927FS

9 781906 469450